THE FLAMES OF SILVER-HAWK
SERIES/BOOK I

FIREBRAND

Created and Written by
Melonye Wolf

Printed by KDP, An Amazon.com Company
Available from Amazon.com, KDP and other retail outlets. Available on
Kindle and other online stores.

From the Author:

I want to say thank you to my family, my brother, Barry and the special friends who encouraged me to keep pressing forward with my dreams. This book, and the editions to follow are only some dreams I want to accomplish. Thank you to my husband and my devoted and feisty, little mother who put up with me during those days in which doubt tried to get the best of me. And, I want to say a special thank you to Becki Hamel (Rebecca Brady) for all your help. I hope and pray, by His grace, the best days are yet to come.

A wise friend and brother once told me, "It would be difficult for a reader to understand mercy and redemption without revealing the sin". Please consider the content of this story is of a real nature in relation to the daily choices between good and evil.

The Flames of Silver-Hawk Series/Book I, **Firebrand**

The small town of Westville, Texas is a proud, God fearing community and its citizens, devoted patriots. The Liberty River snakes through the heart of Liberty County, some say the red water of the Liberty is the pulse of life for the land and the people who live there. Benjamin Hawk and Jacob Silver were trusted friends and spiritual brothers who loved their family and the land. Their heritage is rich with the history of Liberty County, and the friendship between their sons is as deep as the river. Since boyhood, Coleman Silver and Rueben Hawk have shared a vision of building a productive farm and ranch, and their fathers helped them unite their lands to accomplish this dream.

These men believe the quest for happiness in life and love is not a secret, because the guidelines to obtain these things can be found in the 'Good Book'. They learned at an early age that consideration and respect for the Maker, and the life He creates, must be the foundation on which everything else is built, yet the instructions on living an easy and fair life cannot be found among the Bible's sacred pages.

The families at the Silver-Hawk ranch regard nature and the circle of life. They are passionate about protecting their world and each other. They work hard and are good at growing a diversity of things; still, good seeds sometimes bear bad fruit. Come and share the lives of Coleman Silver and Rueben Hawk as they discover that esteem and consideration for others can sometimes go hand in hand with harmful secrets. And, there are some secrets which are accompanied by consequences which can lead to disaster.

BREAUX FAMILY TREE (America 1851)

VINCENT LEFLORE BREAUX (born 1820 – died 1898)
Married 1850 - Paulina Danielle Beufontaine Breaux (1829 - 1850)
Married 1854 - Little Star (Native American/Cherokee) (1830 - 1933)

ZANE LEFLORE BREAUX (1854 - 1931)
Married 1874 - Hanna Camille Sterling (1852 - 1930)

PRESTON RENEE BREAUX (1875 - 1940)
Married 1894 - Ophelia Marlene Lamoure (1873 - 1934)

STAR LEFLORE BREAUX (adopted/1894 - 1900)
LEE RENEE BREAUX (1894 - 1938)
Married 1916 - Carol Ann Braxton (1895 - 1938)

CAROLINE JANEE BREAUX (1918/1948)
Married 1939 - Dane Stewart Reid (1916 - 1967)   Emmett Gabriel Cotton (1917)

PRESTON GABRIEL BREAUX REID (born 1942)
Married 1958 - Jaden Michelle Sullivan (1935 - 1958)

HAWK FAMILY TREE (1870)

TYSON ELIJAH SWIFT-HAWK (1870)
Married 1890 - **Nina Tala (Strong Wolf)**

BENJAMIN ELIJAH HAWK (1895 - 1958)
Married 1913 - **Mary Dawn Berch**

ETHAN BERCH HAWK (1913 - 1957)   **RUEBEN BENJAMIN HAWK** (1924)
 Married 1956 - **Aspen Tall-Tree**   Married 1949 - **Celia Ann Sutton**

                                         ELIJAH BENJAMIN HAWK (1946)
                                         SCHERRY DAWN HAWK (1950)

SILVER FAMILY TREE (1822)

TRUMAN GRAHAM SILVER (1822-1901)
Married 1845 - Brook Lynn Heart (1826-1847)
Married 1854 - Eden Michelle Tate (1828-1885)

MICHELLE TATE SILVER	**JACOB COLEMAN SILVER**	**GRAHAM TRUMAN SILVER**
Married 1873 — Tucker Davis Messer	Married 1878 — Leslie Faye LaRue	Married 1881 - Annabelle Rose Messer
TRAVIS GRAHAM MESSER	**TRUMAN TATE SILVER**	**ANNA ROSE SILVER**
Married — Letty Aileen Coats	Married 1892 — Eliza Hope Gentry	Married — Logan Marcus Mather
		RANSOM DAVIS SILVER
		Married - Rachel Ann Nash

ELIZA BETH SILVER (1892-1893)
JACOB GRAHAM SILVER (1894-1955)
Married 1918 - Sarah Evette Kemp

COLEMAN GRAHAM SILVER (1923)
Married 1946 - Lana Elane Saucier

TRAVIS JACOB SILVER (1948)
MOLLIE ELANE SILVER (1952)

CHAPTER 1

Rueben pushed his hat back from off his face and rubbed his sleepy eyes. He knew Cole was awake without looking in the backseat because he had felt the truck move after Owen had gotten out. They were parked in front of a diner. The neon coffee cup in the window blinked on and off to entice the weary motorist passing by to stop for a jolt of hot caffeine.

Rueben closed his eyes and scrubbed his face with his palms trying to stimulate his brain. His voice was somewhat rasped when he spoke.

"I hate to admit it, but I'm getting too old for a 400-mile, weekend hop around the state, Cole."

"I hear ya," breathed Cole from the darkness of the backseat. "We should have brought the boys. At least..." his words were interrupted by a weary yawn, "... they would have kept us awake."

"Yeah, we would have wanted to put them in the trailer with the stock about three hours ago," commented Rueben. He chuckled quietly, then reminded his friend of the last time the boys had attended a horse show with them. Their excitement had spurred a string of non-stop questions during the drive, and they didn't catch so much as a wink of sleep.

Owen snatched the door open with a robust energy that his employers and friends didn't share. The smell of strong, fresh coffee stirred their senses. He had thoughtfully retrieved it for them after checking the stock trailer.

Rueben picked up the cup from the cardboard holder, and a large, outstretched palm appeared next to his shoulder from the darkness behind him. He sat the cup in it and reached for another. He heard Cole yawn again.

The night sky was a velvety, dark blue heaven, even though a slight glow from downtown Corpus Christi tinted the bottom of the starry picture. Seven hours had passed since they left home, and each of them had put in a full day of work starting at 4:00 a.m. But the breeder show was worth the trouble, due to the quality of the stock that was on display for sale or trade. They were looking for five, three-year-old mares to breed with Owen's Appaloosa stallion. The stallion was a fine animal with a smooth and sturdy gait, a spirited heart and yet, diligent in what was asked of him. Cole and Rueben did not have a specific breed in mind but were certain Owen would have five solid suggestions once they walked through the stalling area to see what was available this year.

Owen's lively voice seemed to bounce around the sleepy cab of the truck.

"I feel bad because the boys didn't get to come… seeing how I'm picking up Charlie. It doesn't seem fair."

Rueben shook his head as he reassured Owen.

"You shouldn't. They chose to join the baseball team knowing there would be some conflicts. They have to learn to be good at their word, being trustworthy is the backbone of a good man."

Owen agreed with his friend, then closed the door of the truck, and walked to the pay phone. The night wind smelled like the ocean and mingled with a mellow tune on the truck radio. Rueben and Cole sipped the hot coffee and absorbed the pleasant temperature of the April night while they waited for Owen to contact his mother.

Owen had told her he would call when they got into town to see if it was possible to come by and pick up his little brother, Charlie, for the weekend. Owen's kid brother had a way with horses. He had witnessed the boy's charismatic, but firm manner toward the animals with his own eyes. The youngster had gone with them twice before without their step-father knowing; however, his mother was wary concerning Charlie doing so this time. Owen suspected her husband, L.B. Thomas, had found out about Charlie spending time with him, and now their mother was too intimidated to make decisions without consulting the man she had married. Owen remembered the last time he saw his brother. Charlie had a black eye and a cut in his left brow. When questioned, Charlie had blamed the injuries on a new bully at school. Owen didn't believe him because Charlie had avoided looking him in the eye when he answered.

Owen's mother, Patti Lynn Thomas and his little brother, Charlie lived on the highway along the beach front. Owen's father had bought the craftsman style house some 25 years ago. His parents had been surprised but blessed with another child in their later years. He was 18 when Charlie was born.

His little brother was an infant when their father, Mason Kagel had died from a fatal accident in the stockyard. He had worked for the Imperial Stock Auctions as their livestock foreman and gave Owen his first job as a cowhand. They were pushing the work day into the night, loading a large sale of cattle into the railroad cars that would take them to California. The lot had been sold under the conditions of next day shipment, and they were loading the last car when the accident took place. The engineer didn't know that Mason Kagel's arm had been pinned by the railcar door when they were closing it, or that his conductor had dropped his radio while attempting to help free him. The engineer blew the horn a couple of times to signal the conductor and it spooked the animals. The conductor and his father were crushed to death when the stock bolted, and the unsecured, wooden door splintered under their shifting weight. His mother received financial compensation from both companies, which was more than enough to meet their needs. Still, money couldn't compensate for the empty heartache Owen and his mother felt. He had worked and moved stock next to his father at the stockyard half his life, and the job was a daily reminder of his loss. He felt he was in a stranglehold between grief and guilt, and even though it was a sound job, he could not spend his life there trapped in the memories of that tragic day. He had to find a new life for himself.

In the few months that followed, Owen realized God had blessed his mother with the infant to consume her days and fill her heart with new joy. The infant needed her and gave purpose to her life. He was glad, especially since his own restlessness seemed to be growing. He had never known another home until he joined the armed service. Owen left his small family, and the stockyard at 21 years of age, to contribute his skills and find his own way in the world.

Owen returned home after four years of service to find his mother newly married to a tall, solid man that was of French-Cajun and native descent. It was a hellacious mixture of blood, especially when mixed with alcohol and no spiritual conscience. He supposedly owned his own shrimp company, and the boats which brought in the profits. He offered Owen a job on the pretense that he could always use a good hand. Owen refused the job to find something more to his liking and with no ties to the man. He could tell that L.B. Thomas didn't like him or his exercising free will.

Owen was reunited with his family only two days when he realized his mother had made a life-altering and dangerous mistake in marrying L.B. Thomas. He despised his mother's husband for his drinking, and his ill treatment of them. She confided in him with a saddened and heavy heart. The man she lived with was not the same man who brought her roses, mended the house, and went to church with her and Charlie every Sunday for eight months prior to her marrying him.

Owen had stayed with his family for only a month; it was long enough for him and Charlie to bond in a way that made their next separation painful. The little boy needed a man in his life, and he fell into hero worship of Owen in only a matter of days which rubbed L.B. Thomas the wrong way.

Despite the constant conflict between himself and the obstinate, mean man his mother had married, Owen felt he needed to be there to protect them. He broke his drunk, step-father's nose on a Thursday afternoon. That was the day he came home after work to find L.B. Thomas with his mother backed into the corner of the kitchen. She was gasping for air due to his step-father's angry hand squeezing her throat while the other groped her body beneath her skirt. Owen heard her pleading for him to take her to the bedroom, so Charlie couldn't see his lustful behavior. His six-year-old little brother, who didn't understand what was happening, was trying to wedge himself between them to protect her. Owen saw red, it didn't subside until red soaked the front of L.B. Thomas' shirt.

At first, Owen didn't understand when she asked him to leave. He felt that she was choosing a monster over her sons, especially Charlie. But she saw the hurt in his eyes and was unable to keep a stiff chin. When she broke down emotionally, Owen realized she was scared for them. She begged him to take Charlie and leave before one of them was hurt by the unpredictable and hateful man. Owen was shocked when she shoved a roll of bills secured with a rubber band into his hand. She told him that every dime he had sent home from the service was there then she explained her train of thought. He listened, realizing his mother's ardent reason made practical sense. Owen agreed to take his little brother and the sum of $14,000, under the conditions that he would find and set up a household for them then he would come for her. Charlie was only a little boy, but he refused to leave without his mother. Owen left as his mother requested, determined to make a safe life for them some place away from this man. He left her enough money, so she could escape in case of an emergency.

Owen found work in Amarillo. He rented a comfortable house and in only a couple of weeks he had everything ready for his family. He called his mother and told her of the good schools and stable, safe life which awaited them. Her excitement could not be disguised. They agreed that she would withdraw Charlie from school and leave on Friday. Owen had two bus tickets waiting for her on the 10:00 a.m. to Midland and he would meet them there.

Patti Lynn and Charlie settled into a peaceful life in Amarillo with Owen and were happy and content for eight months. It was the last Friday in May when Owen came home to a broken-down front door and an empty house. Owen, nor his mother had realized until that day that L.B. Thomas was not a man who would tolerate being abandoned.

A different kind of concern took root in Owen's heart that day, and he began a campaign to get the man out of his mother's life. After a year of suspicions and flaring tempers, his mother ended up in the hospital from an "accidental" fall. Charlie was too scared to say anything about what had happened. The law couldn't help unless the child would make a sworn statement that he witnessed his step-father intentionally and maliciously hurt his mother. Owen was told that even then, the man would be jailed for only 30 days, if found guilty. Owen managed to talk to his mother and again, she begged him to take Charlie and leave her. She told him she was tired, and she couldn't keep trying to out-guess her husband's reaction to his efforts of trying to rescue them. She told him that she had offered to sign over the house to the brutish man she had married in exchange for her and Charlie's freedom, but L.B. was making a twisted game out of keeping them prisoners. Owen began to understand that he was making things worse for them. He spoke to Charlie about their mother's wishes and again, his brother refused to leave her side. Owen hugged him and shoved an envelope in his pocket telling him to hide it and guard it for the moment when they may need to escape from the man.

Owen found good money in the rodeo circuit. He was restless with worry and drifted around a few months as a trainer. When the feeling of helplessness became more than he could stand, Owen threw his hat in the competitive arena and rode the wild mustangs against other reckless cowboys. He was competing in the Texas Panhandle Rodeo and Horse Show when he ran into a service buddy that had a large spread in northeast Texas. Rueben Hawk was tickled to see Owen, and he introduced him to Coleman Silver, his childhood friend and business partner in the ranch. The men spent three days together getting reacquainted and talking about the aspirations Rueben and Cole shared in building their home into a strong, and financially successful working ranch. When Rueben and Cole began preparations for the trip home, they asked Owen Kagel if he would work with them.

Owen Kagel had been the Silver-Hawk's ranch foreman for the last four years.

Charlie could tell his mother was sad again by the music she was playing. He had done his outside chores, and even a few that were not his responsibility, in hopes that his step-father would allow him to go to the horse show with his brother. Charlie eased into the kitchen by way of the back door. His mother was ironing. Her back was to him, but he could hear her crying as she worked at the ironing board. He was 11 years old and had lived in a house full of strife and conflict for so long that he had almost forgotten what it was like to wake up feeling a contentment in his heart. His young heart would not allow him to forget those eight happy months they had spent with Owen in Amarillo; it was the last time he had heard his mama sing when she worked. Instinct cautioned him as he stepped up beside her, and when he spoke his tone of voice conveyed pure devotion.

"Mama, are you okay?"

She kept ironing as she cried, but she wouldn't look at him. A few moments passed, then she put the iron on its stand and hung up the crisp shirt she had finished pressing. She swiped at her cheeks a few times then released an exhausted sigh as she turned to face him. Her right eye was a shiny purple and puffed out to the point she could barely see through it.

Charlie started towards her as he spoke.

"Mama! No!"

Patti Lynn wrapped her arms around her son and squeezed him tight. She needed his strength to help her do what she had to do.

"It's all gone, Charlie," she squeaked. She pushed him away, so they could look at each other while she explained. "The money Owen left for you... he found it on the top shelf in your closet. I tried to stop him. I told him it was your money for college... that your brother had given it to you." She shook her head as tears spilled down her cheeks. "I'm so sorry I've done this to you, Honey." She sniffed. "I want you to do something for me, okay? No questions... no arguing with me."

"Yes, Ma'am, what is it?" responded her young son respectfully.

She took his blue Sunday shirt off the hanger and handed it to him. This was the first time she had ever told Charlie that she wanted him to go with Owen.

"He's at a poker game tonight... he's already gone. I have your suitcase packed and ready. I want you to change into something nice then gather the rest of your things, which are important to you, in the duffle bag I laid on your bed. Hide them in the tall saw-grass in the side yard just in case... then I want you to go wait across the street under the boardwalk. When Owen calls, I'll tell him where to find you. Do this for me, Charlie. Owen will take good care of you. It's time for you to be free of this mess I've made of our lives."

Charlie stared at her in disbelief. He knew that a whipping was in store for him because his step-father believed he had deceitfully hidden the money from him. The boy's eyes stung with hot tears as he shook his head.

"No, Mama. Please… you come too! You can pack and wait with me!" pleaded Charlie. "He won't find us under the boardwalk, please!"

She looked at him. There was a faint glimmer of hope in her expression.

"Who will tell Owen where we are if we are both hiding across the street?"

Charlie thought about this. He had spent six years staying out of L.B. Thomas' way.

"Pack your things and I'll put them with mine. When Owen comes to get me, he'll have Mr. Hawk and Mr. Silver with him. If he comes home, L.B. won't stand a chance against the three of them. He'll let you go!" Charlie smiled suddenly at the thought of strength in numbers. "You'll see, Mama." He took her hand and tugged on it. "Come on."

Charlie hid his things amidst the tall grass that bordered the yard then started back to the house to retrieve his mother's bag. He recognized the squeal of the brakes as they ignored the stop sign and rounded the corner. Charlie ducked in the shadows and raced around the edge of the house to the back door to alert his mother. He saw her through the small window of the back door as she froze in the hallway between the kitchen and living room. She recognized the sound of his brakes as well.

She hurried into the kitchen dragging the bag. Charlie was about to open the door to help her when the front door bounced off the wall with a jarring thud. Charlie froze. His mother dropped the bag and spun around to face the man she had blindly married. The boy watched through the window as his mother got out of his step-father's path.

"Is that little bastard home yet?" L.B. stumbled to the ice box and took out a long neck bottle then slammed the door. He twisted the cap and threw it in the direction of the waste can then guzzled half of the content as he watched her. "What's this shit?" He kicked the duffle bag.

"It's some ironing I've been putting off," she answered. "My son is not a bastard… please don't insult me by calling him one." She picked up the bag and walked over to the ironing board which stood in the corner where she worked.

"Answer me dammit! Is he home?"

"No. He's not home." Patti Lynn answered calmly. "Did you lose every dime of it already? Is that why you're home so early?"

"Where the hell is he? He can't shit unless you wipe his ass for him!" declared L.B. Thomas.

Charlie held his breath as he watched and waited for his mother's response.

"He's gone. He's not coming back."

"What the hell does that mean?!" growled the angry and drunk, devil-of-a-man.

Patti Lynn tried to remain calm as she spoke, but her emotions made it difficult.

"I sent him away to live with Owen. He's my son. It's what's best for him. Besides, you've already taken everything material he has; I won't let you take what self-esteem he has left."

Charlie moved to the larger window where he could watch over his mother; however, L.B. moved on her so fast Charlie was stunned.

"You did what? What did you say to me?"

Charlie witnessed the man grab a fist full of his mother's beautiful honey colored hair. She cried out in pain, and still he twisted it until her knees buckled under the force of his furious assault.

L.B. snatched her up next to him and bellowed in her ear.

"YOU DO NOT MAKE ANY OF THE DECISIONS IN THIS HOUSE!"

Patti Lynn struggled against the man's violent treatment of her.

"He's my son! I will protect him from you! I may have to tolerate you, but he's not going to anymore! He's free of you!"

Charlie watched his mother claw at the man's arms as she screamed at him again.

"HE'S FREE OF YOU!"

Every muscle in Charlie's young body jerked when the man slammed his mother's head into the concrete floor then grabbed her throat with both hands. He began to shake her. Her body flailed about like a rag-doll in the hands of a spoiled child that was having a temper tantrum. The boy's jaws clamped together. He wanted to help his mother, but he didn't know how to over-come such a perilous threat as his step-father. When his mother's head drooped, and her arms fell limp at her sides, Charlie panicked.

The boy burst through the back door like a locomotive. The youngster was steaming with years of pent up fear, anger, and disdain. He lunged at the man armed with a baseball bat which had been leaning against the house. He cocked it and hit L.B. Thomas in the shoulder with all his might. The blow caught his step-father off guard and hurt him.

The man called him every degrading vulgarity Charlie had ever heard in his young life, and then some. Charlie swung again, yet for a split second, his eyes went to his mother's battered body. It was a crucial mistake to take his eyes off his enemy.

The horrible man caught the bat in mid-air and twisted it out of Charlie's hands with an enraged snatch.

"You spoiled, little bastard. You're gonna wish you had never been born!"

Charlie turned and dove under the kitchen table as the bat sent the metal chairs flying in all directions. He crawled on his hands and knees toward the living room as the wooden bowl of fruit shattered the picture window in the kitchen.

He didn't know what to do. He couldn't leave his mother. Charlie ran down the hall feeling the man close behind him. He was not allowed in their room, but it had a connecting door to the bathroom which was as far as he could think in the way of a plan.

L.B. Thomas struck everything in his path with the bat. Charlie pushed the bathroom door open in the hallway as he ran by it and then rounded the door facing into their bedroom. It was off limits to him, but it was the only room in the back of the house with two means of escape. He clipped the chest of drawers with his shoulder as he turned into the bathroom. It tore his shirt and cut into his arm, but he couldn't feel it due to the potent adrenalin that sped through his system.

Charlie stopped and crouched down where he had a clear view of both doorways. He couldn't tell where his step-father was at this point. He heard something. He had heard the sound before, but he couldn't place it. Charlie's little body was shaking all over. 'What was it,' he asked himself. He peeked around the edge of the chest of drawers and saw L.B. Thomas squatting in the floor on the far side of the bed. Suddenly, the metallic click jogged Charlie's memory. It was the pistol L.B. kept under their mattress. He had seen his step-father clean it a couple of times, and L.B. had flashed it around one night when his buddies came over for poker. That was the night they all got drunk, and one of them was bold enough to accuse L.B. of cheating.

Charlie made a mad dash for the hallway, attempting to reach his mother. He was almost there when the gun discharged. A bullet zinged passed Charlie's ear then splintered the door facing next to him. The boy ducked his head and kept running. He was terrified. He knew he was going to die, and he wanted to touch his mother's face one more time. Charlie dropped to his hands and knees and crawled over to her. His arms went around her as he pressed his forehead to her cheek.

"Mama, I love you. I love you," he sobbed.

A large, unbending hand snatched him from her still body. Charlie heard his shoulder crack before he felt the pain. The heartless tyrant held the boy in a fisted grip, dangling him like he had made the catch of the day. L.B. shoved the pistol into the waist-band of his pants as a wicked grin distorted his hateful brow. Charlie gritted his teeth and balanced himself on the toes of his shoes, determined to endure his step-fathers bent punishment.

20

The despicable man slapped the boy's face over and over, but he quickly tired of it and slammed a brutal fist against his nose.

Stars burst in front of Charlie's eyes and a hot liquid drained down the back of his throat, then the cold floor rose abruptly to meet him. He laid there a moment, but the need for air sent him rolling to his hands and knees in search of air. The blood from his nose pooled in dark, red clumps on the tile. He blinked impulsively as his eyes watered with overwhelming sorrow and pain.

A pair of expensive, scaly boots stopped next to him. Charlie couldn't process the danger that loomed above him, not until the sharp toe of the left boot struck him in the side. Charlie gasped at the pain that ripped through his gut and around into his spine. He saw the polished silver pistol flash in the overhead light as he rolled to his back. The twisting seizure of pain crippled his entire body. Charlie's spirit cried out to the Maker for help. He thought he heard his mother call his name, and he opened his eyes just in time to raise his arms as a shield from the heel of his step-father's boot. Charlie's chest caved beneath the sadistic blow and his world went black...

Charlie awoke to the bright light that surrounded him. He thought that he was in Heaven... he wanted to be in Heaven. If this were true, then his mother was here somewhere, and his real father. Charlie had studied his father's face from the picture hidden in his closet; it was the same kind face of his older brother. He was going to look for them as soon as he could get up. A few moments passed, and the ceiling fan turning slowly above him gained definition. Consciousness brought pain to his little body and tears back to his eyes.

He thought he heard his mother crying again, but realized it was his own emotion. He turned his head and pressed his hand to his aching chest. He saw his mother lying on the kitchen floor a few feet away; her arms were lifeless at her sides. Her legs were bare and pale beneath his step-father's large, salacious hand. L.B. Thomas was on top of her, his assault on her body was punishing and his grunts were depraved.

The pistol hopped across the floor as the man's boot unintentionally kicked it during the lustful attack on his mother. Charlie's mind shifted into a forbidden realm of thought at the sight of it. He was not six years old any longer; he knew what was happening to her, and he also knew he didn't stand a chance of seeing tomorrow's light. It was the hate and scathing contempt that welled up inside the young boy which gave him the strength and determination he needed to ignore the pain in his body and get up.

Charlie reached for the gun as he willfully pushed himself to his feet. He approached their captor and pointed it. It was his mother's watery gray eyes that jolted his reason and made his heart skip a beat. He had feared she was dead. She turned her head slightly to look at him then nodded in silence as she stared at him through puffy, swollen eyes which were full of hopelessness.

Charlie's blood went cold. Had she silently given him permission to shoot? He didn't know what to do. If he shot the man at that moment, would he kill his mother as well? He stood in a smothering, indecisive fog of doubt and trepidation.

Suddenly, the telephone squealed out into the room. L.B. Thomas ignored it through his insatiable groaning; his pants were gathered around his knees and his naked backside bucked wildly between his mother's legs.

It was the ringing of the phone that caused Charlie to remember how the evening was supposed to have gone and that Owen was going to call. He turned and tried to hurry to the phone cabinet in the hallway. Charlie snatched it from the receiver while at the same time crying out for help.

"Owen! Help me!" screamed Charlie; his limited breath echoed with the terror in which he was trapped.

"Charlie? What's wrong?! Buddy, what's going on?!"

Owen heard his mother cry out for Charlie to run.

Charlie turned to see L.B. Thomas fastening his pants as he came down the hall towards him.

Chills ran down Owen's spine at the frightful wail that was his little brother's voice.

"He's gonna kill us!"

L.B. Thomas' words were as threatening as a lion's roar from the unknown shadows of a jungle.

"You got that right, you tuff-nuts, little son-of-a-bitch. I'm gonna break your damn neck this time... you little pussy, bastard! COME HERE TO ME!" yelled L.B. Thomas in a menacing fury.

Charlie threw the receiver at him and tried to run, but he was not as fast this time. He was captured at the back of his shirt and drug into the living room. Still, he managed to conceal the pistol in the front of his jeans. His step-father's breath was retched with the smell of beer and cigarettes as he cursed Charlie for being born. The wicked man yanked his belt off and began striking him. The thin strip of leather struck at the boy's body like a viperous snake.

Owen's hair was already standing straight up, but when he heard the tortured screams of his little brother pleading for mercy, his heart turned cold with hatred. He slammed the phone down on the receiver and ran to the truck as all sorts of dreadful things began to terrorize his mind.

Rueben pulled the hot coffee away from his mouth as it sloshed out onto his shirt from Owen's abrupt arrival.

"He's beating them! Right now!" declared Owen angrily. "I'm going to kill that man with my bare hands! I swear I am!"

They were five blocks away if they took the Old Bridge Road. Cole tossed his coffee out the window as they circled the parking lot then pulled out on to the road in front of a semi. He questioned Owen about the conversation. Owen relived it for them as they sped in and out of traffic towing a trailer and 8,000 pounds of horse flesh. They crossed the boulevard to avoid a traffic light and cut in front of a half a dozen vehicles that were more than willing to give them the right of way. They went up a one-way street to gain a few extra minutes of precious time. In less than ten minutes, they arrived in front of the house. Owen shut off the motor, and they rolled to a stop.

Cole was the size of a bear, but nimble on his feet and was out of the truck before it came to a complete stop. They were almost to the house when a gun shot rang out. Owen broke into a run.

He flung the door open and froze at the destruction in the room, and the condition of his family. Charlie was standing between their mother and her mean-spirited husband pointing a shaking gun. L.B. was swearing and holding his arm. When he took another angry step towards them, Charlie fired two more times, one of the bullets struck the man in the gut. L.B. Thomas finally changed his mind and backed away from the boy. He was bleeding profusely and covered the wound with his hand as his heavy body clumsily folded into the chair in the corner.

Clearly, Owen was in a state of bewilderment at what he had just witnessed, so Rueben nudged his friend forward to see about his mother leaving Cole to attend to Charlie. Cole knelt in front of the battered little boy and turned his horrified face away from the deed he had just committed. The boy's young body was suffering from uncontrollable jerks. Cole pulled Charlie against him and wrapped his large, protective arms around him. It was an overwhelming trust offered to him as the boy laid his head on Cole's shoulder. He sensed the child was on the verge of collapse.

Cole had consoled him for only a few seconds when Charlie's little body turned rigid and Rueben called out in warning. Cole turned to see L.B. Thomas coming towards them with a large butcher knife. There was no time to think... no time to do anything other than react. Cole's arm went up in defense as L.B. Thomas lunged at them. A shot rang out as Thomas shanked the knife into Cole's arm with a crazed sneer. Cole flinched at the pain as he saw the long blade rip through the bottom of his shirt sleeve.

L.B. Thomas stared at Cole with cold, vengeful eyes. The front of the man's shirt turned crimson, and he began to sway, then he stumbled backwards a few steps. Cole's right arm held the young boy steadfast against his enormous chest while the other held a sharp, bloody knife. They watched in silence as L.B. Thomas' knees buckled, and he fell backwards to the floor with a bullet next to his heart. The clicking sound drew Cole's attention from the fatal truth. Cole looked back to find Charlie still holding the pistol pointed and ready; his thumb and index finger reacted to the mechanics of it, like a needle skipping at the end of a record. An eerie calm consumed the room.

Rueben appeared next to his friend.

"Hold on there, Cole. We need to think smart." Rueben squatted next to the man to check for any sign of life. He shook his head as he spoke. "He's done." His voice was reverent, out of respect to the Maker, and the life this man had wasted on wickedness.

Charlie's breathing faltered.

Cole was touched beyond words at what had just happened, and the fact that this child had just saved his life. The little boy's outstretched arm and hand, fixed with the weapon, began to tremble. Cole turned the boy's face to him and away from the lifeless man lying on the floor. The youngster's eyes seemed rather vacant. He took Charlie's wrist in a tender grip and eased the pistol from his hand, then laid it on the floor. Cole wiped the boy's bloody nose and cheeks on his shirt sleeve. He cuddled Charlie close as though it were his own son who he held, then pressed his lips to the child's forehead in thankfulness.

"You're safe now little-man," promised Cole. He ignored the knife in his arm and fixed his concern on Charlie's frame of mind and his injuries. The boy's behavior and his breathing were troubling, and Cole knew something was terribly wrong. He tried to give the boy something to think on other than the horror of tonight.

"Listen to me, Charles; I need you to promise me something. I want you and your mama to come live with us. There's nothing to keep you here anymore. Owen needs you, and we need you too. We'll take you to a place with rolling green hills and horses grazing among clouds. The smell of grass is so sweet you'll get dizzy... the birds will sing your name once they meet you. There's blue sky as far as you can see. We even have a lake that mirrors Heaven. A new life is waiting for you, little man. It's a safe life and a peaceful life. Promise me you'll come.

Charlie stared at this brave, fearless man and noticed that his eyes were the color of the sky. He wanted this to be true. He was afraid to believe in anything anymore, especially a place so wonderful. He didn't believe it. His throat was tight with emotion and he was finding it hard to catch his breath, but he managed to speak.

"Honest... Mr. Silver?" he squeaked.

Cole smiled and wiped the boy's cheeks with his fingertips this time.

"I give you my word, Charles," answered Cole.

This man smiled at him; there was kindness and assurance in his voice. There was also gentleness and comfort in his touch, like that of his mother's. Charlie looked at Owen, whose attention traded off between him and their mother.

"It's true, Charlie. There is such a place. I live there, Buddy. Remember the picture I gave you of the horses standing in the lake? It's real. Come with us, Charlie. We'll take mama too."

Charlie nodded his head.

"Okay. But... I don't... feel so good." He collapsed in Cole's arms.

Cole cradled Charlie and sat down in the floor.

Owen got nervous; he didn't trust the law in town from his previous experiences of trying to help his mother and brother. Although in self-defense, he was fearful of what could happen to Charlie after shooting a man.

Cole pointed out an alternative; after all, the proof to back up the facts was in his arm.

26

The next eight minutes was all the time needed for these three men to conspire on their version of the facts. Acting on behalf of a battered and terrorized child, they agreed that: Upon entering the house they saw Charlie standing between his mother and L.B. Thomas, only Thomas had the gun pointed at the boy. Cole interceded, and they struggled. Cole's size got the upper hand, and he took the pistol away from Thomas. Thomas backed off because there were three of them and sat down in the corner, but due to the shambled possessions scattered about, none of them noticed the knife on the floor next to him. When their attentions went to Charlie and his mother, L.B. Thomas' hatred surfaced, and he came at Cole with the knife. Rueben yelled out. Cole turned and was forced to pull the trigger in self-defense. L.B. Thomas still managed to stab Cole before he fell.

The sound of sirens grew close. The three of them looked at each other as the conspiracy was accepted and became a part of the rest of their lives.

The blue and red lights lit up the night around the house. Law enforcement photographed the crime scene while the ambulance personnel prepared Owen's mother and Charlie to be transported to the emergency room. Cole answered the questions asked by the investigative officer while sitting out of the way on the fireplace hearth. Police Detective Manny Runnels had already spoken to Owen and Rueben. Cole was trying hard to answer the man's questions as truthfully as possible based on the agreement he had made with his friends.

Cole's attention traded off between the boy, Owen's mother, and Rueben, who was on the phone in the hallway talking to his father. Benjamin Hawk had a diplomatic way about him that could defuse a situation in a matter of minutes, and they needed his wisdom tonight. He didn't understand why, but the old saying that tragedy comes in three was true. The tragedy of death had come to the ranch in a mighty way these last few years, taking his father (Jacob Silver) and Rueben's mother (Mary Dawn Hawk). The final blow was Cole's beautiful wife, Lana Elane Silver. The entire family and community missed each of them, but tonight he felt overwhelmed by lonesomeness. He realized how easily things could have gone in another direction, and his motherless children at home would be orphans if Charlie had not acted on his behalf.

"Mr. Silver?" Detective Runnels' voice had gotten lost amid all the confusion and Cole's personal thoughts. He saw Rueben hang up the phone and start in his direction. He finally looked up at the officer.

"I'm sorry. What did you ask?"

A paramedic interrupted them and encouraged the Detective to expedite the statement at the hospital, so he could take Mr. Silver to get the knife removed from his arm.

The Detective shook his head.

"That won't be necessary. I only have one more question, Mr. Silver... for your own peace of mind. Could you have done anything else other than kill this man?"

"You've got to be kidding!"

The Detective turned to face another verbal intrusion by Cole's friend.

"No! He couldn't!" exclaimed Rueben in an aggravated disbelief. "There was no time. He would have been stabbed in the back... and if that maniac had gotten his hand on the gun again, you all would be rolling out five bodies instead of one. That's the truth of it."

The Detective gazed at Rueben a few seconds, and then silently dismissed him and his opinion by focusing his attention back to Cole.

"Detective Runnels... when we arrived, we heard gunshots from outside. I can't give details of what happened before the fact. Christ Almighty man look around you! There were no options... no reasoning with this man. We... I... tried. He could have sat there and let us leave; instead, he picked up the knife. That child and that poor woman have had the shit kicked out of them. God knows what state of mind they're in. No, I've never met the man before tonight. It's like I said, I was protecting the boy. I wrestled with Mr. Thomas a couple of minutes and took the gun away from him. He backed off and sat down in that chair over there. I went to Charles... Owen and Rueben went to Ms. Thomas. I knelt down in front of the boy and the next thing I know; Thomas is almost on me with this." Cole moved his arm slightly. "I raised the pistol and pulled the trigger. I don't really know how many times." Cole's mind calculated the details, so he could give a sound answer. "I would say three times."

"Are you right or left-handed?" asked Detective Runnels.

Cole exhaled as he shook his head at the man's antagonizing question.

"Both... but, I'm more accurate with the right."

The officer closed his note pad and thanked them. He stepped back out of the way and the medic helped Cole stand up; they started walking toward the door.

Detective Runnels touched Rueben's arm when he began to follow his friend.

"Mr. Hawk, wait."

Rueben turned to the man.

"It's not my intention to be difficult. It's just... we've had suspicions about this man for a while now. He came down here from Louisiana, Gaidon... to be specific. He has buried two wives there and left a lot of trouble. It seems he left a 16-year-old boy of his own behind in prison, serving time for first degree murder. Yeah, this man was associated with some bad ones, outlaws... running wild in those bayous over there. I can't say he broke ties with them. We've had a criminal element move in the last several years. The Coast Guard has seized floaters full of drugs and illegals; they even confiscated one of his shrimp boats full of explosives. The crew was arrested, but they wouldn't roll over on him. He claimed they had been out of the dock for over a week and he knew nothing about it. We've had him under surveillance the last six months."

The Detective didn't know that Cole had stopped to listen to him while he spoke. He turned abruptly when Cole's hand clutched his shoulder and spun him around.

"And what? We've screwed up your investigation? Is that all you can see in this?" Cole took another step closer to the Detective's face. "You mean after all of Mr. Kagel's ignored attempts to help and protect his family, you can stand here and tell us that you've been watching this man for six months and no one even cared enough to believe, or notice that this woman and her boy were living in hell? What the hell good is your surveillance? Better yet, what damn good are you as a peace officer? You've looked the other way and allowed them to suffer... for what, just so you can build a case?" Cole's jaws stiffened, and his eyes glowed with contempt at Detective Runnels' silence. He shook his head. "You and your department are as useless as tits on boar hog. You make me sick." Cole turned hastily and left the officer standing there.

Rueben drove Cole to the hospital following the ambulance. Owen went with his family.

"Rueb, I want you to do something for me," mumbled Cole in the darkness of the truck.

"Name it," exclaimed his friend.

"I need you to call Morris Raynard for me. That Detective and his questions feel like quicksand to me. You'll have to tell him what's happened, and if he can't come and represent me, ask if he can send someone trustworthy."

"I've got it covered already... he's sending Sawyer," exclaimed Rueben.

"When did you do that?"

Rueben could feel his friend's attention come to him in the darkness.

"When I called home," he replied. "I was antsy. We've never killed a man before."

"We?" mumbled Cole.

Rueben glanced over to him as they turned into the emergency entrance.

"That's how I see it. Besides, if the gun had been in my hand, I would have shot him myself!" stated Rueben passionately. "That man was a savage brute! My daddy is right. A man of his sort is a 'firebrand'. L.B. Thomas marked his life by provoking trouble then reveling in the aftermath of chaos. Death would have come to him sooner or later... by the hand of vengeance or righteousness. He pushed righteousness one time too many, and tonight it pushed back!" Rueben's soulful words echoed with righteous truth.

"Yeah, I know you're right, so why don't I feel any better?"

Rueben came to a stop.

"Because you live by and answer to the law of God." He got out and came around to help his friend. "He was there Cole, watching and protecting... even after we arrived. It's a miracle they were still alive. Don't feel bad about protecting the boy. And you're right, there is something about that Detective that stinks."

Cole looked at him before he got out.

"Which story did you give Morris?"

"The truth we all agreed upon. That is how it has to be from now on?" Rueben's tone turned the statement into a question. He had to hear for himself one more time that Cole was committed to this strategy.

"Yes. It's the only way to protect Charles. He needs to leave here as soon as possible."

They found Owen standing in the hallway of the emergency room. Charlie and his mother were in x-ray. The staff pushed Cole into a wheelchair and rolled him down the hall as well.

Owen was beside himself with worry.

Rueben caught his shoulder in a firm grip as he spoke.

"Keep it together, Owen. Don't overlook the most important fact... they're free now."

"Rueben?" The deep masculine voice spun him around. Morris Raynard and his oldest son, Sawyer were standing a few feet away. "How's Ms. Thomas and the boy?" questioned the rugged looking older man.

Rueben was relieved to see them.

"We don't know yet." He introduced Owen to them again. They had all had supper together after a show in San Antonio a few months ago.

They talked a half hour about the facts, and what they wanted to do about Charlie should his mother not make it. Sawyer Raynard left his father at the hospital with their clients while he went to work. He needed to make some phone calls, and it was crucial that he make his presence known to the Detective.

Patti Thomas was in a coma and the doctors expected a paralysis on the right side of her body, when and if, she regained consciousness.

It was three weeks before Charlie was well enough to leave the hospital. He had four surgeries: one on his shoulder, one to mend a punctured lung, another to correct the damage to the bones in his chest. Then, the doctors had to do emergency surgery and remove his spleen that had ruptured due to swelling. He was a broken little boy in spirit and body. They had not given him details about his mother yet, but he knew something was wrong.

Detective Runnels questioned Charlie about that night, but the boy was afraid of him. He told the Detective that he couldn't remember. Sawyer Raynard made sure that Charlie had been left alone after being questioned.

Cole was not the only one who noticed how Charlie seemed to cling to him every time he came to visit. Owen assured him he was not offended. He told Cole that in talking with his little brother during the last week at the hospital, he believed the facts were jumbled in Charlie's mind and he truly couldn't sort through them at this point.

The press did not let it go unnoticed that a prominent and upstanding citizen such as Coleman Silver had shot and killed a man. There were some in the media that were supportive, giving statistics on domestic violence and calling for new laws to protect the innocent. Others sensationalized the story for the sake of circulation.

The Detective was hung up on the fact that three bullets were found in the walls of the home, and Coleman Silver was only able to account for firing the three that were the demise of L.B. Thomas. He had been quoted by a news publication that, 'It doesn't make sense for Mr. Silver to try to hide something when he's already admitted to fatally shooting Mr. Thomas. Sawyer Raynard countered the man's statement by pointing out that they understood that the Detective needed an explanation for all the bullets found, but sadly, his explanation needed to come from the man who had created the conflict, and that wasn't possible.

The case on the death of L.B. Thomas was documented and reviewed by the District Attorney and found to be a matter of self-defense in a domestic disturbance encounter. It was closed even though the three bullets were still in question by the police department. The media lost interest after the District Attorney declared his position on the matter.

Sawyer Raynard had convinced the Chancellor to put Charlie in Owen's custody. Owen Kagel placed his mother in Whispering Oaks, a residential care facility in Liberty County that was close to the ranch. Cole and Rueben brought Charlie home with them, so he could get the care and nurturing he desperately needed.

Life began again.

CHAPTER 2

Celia Hawk was growing weary of listening to her seven-year-old daughter squeal.

"Eli, stop! I'm gonna tell mama. Stop it right now! Ma! Eli won't quit pulling the bandages off my frogs!"

Celia sighed then called out through the screen door one more time before she made an unwanted appearance.

"Eli, for God's sake and mine, leave Scherry alone. If I have to come out there... neither of you will find it a pleasant experience."

"But Ma, she's stickin' tape all over a bunch of poor, helpless frogs. They'll be dead by nightfall if she doesn't turn 'em loose."

"They will not! They're sick, and this is my frog hospital. They need me." The little, dirty-faced girl slapped the top onto the brown shoe box then stuck her nose up in the air; it was quickly joined by a jab of her tongue.

"She was playing quiet 'til you started aggravating her... go on 'bout your own business and leave your sister alone. If you wake Mollie, you're gonna have to tend to her 'cause Estelle and I are canning tomatoes. If you can't find

35

something to do, I'm sure I can find it for you. Why don't you go fishing?"

"My pole's in the truck... and they ain't back yet," informed Eli. His voice revealed a clip of anger.

Celia Hawk understood her son's restlessness. He would be 12 years old in four months, but he reacted to life like a grown man sometimes, especially when it came to his heart. He had deliberately made himself unavailable earlier that morning when the others left for the stockyard. During the last three years, Eli, Travis, and Charlie had cared for and nursed the little fillies that went to market today. It was hard to sell something that you love, and even worse, to sell something that loves you back. Celia knew her son was mad at himself for not going, and for not saying goodbye.

"Aren't back yet," corrected his mother.

"Aren't back yet," interjected Eli with a heavy sigh.

"I'm sure they'll be along any minute now," claimed his mother. Her confidence was something that always made him feel good. He wondered sometimes if it would be that way when he got older.

Celia Hawk was a thin, average size woman with a glowing smile and honey blonde hair that, at 29 years old was already showing traces of gray. A distinctive part adorned her left brow due to the determined growth away from her face; the weight of her thick curls swept it delicately to one side. She was good in nature when someone called attention to it but was self-conscious about the graying at her temples. She worked hard to keep every hair groomed to perfection, even on a scorching day like today while her elbows were deep in tomatoes. Her square face and high cheekbones gave her a look of distinction. Her skin was smooth, always protected from the sun. Celia Hawk's blue eyes were dreamy like the evening sky. They held an unmistakable glow of patience in them, and they twinkled when she laughed or was up to something. It was impossible for her to stay mad at her loved ones, especially her son.

The stretching squeak of the screen door announced his mother's concern.

"You wish you had gone after all, don't you?"

"Yes 'em, I guess so." A moment of silence hung between them as Eli unconsciously dug at a loose rock in the concrete patio with the toe of his boot. "It's just that... it's so hard to watch 'em be sold. They don't mean nothin' to those other folks... not like they do to me. They didn't raise 'em... I did!" exclaimed Eli boldly. His heart felt like it was stuck in his throat.

Celia did understand. But her son was overlooking a very important aspect about life.

"How do you know the people that buy them haven't been looking for just the right one? They could have a child at home who needs a friend to love and care for... just like you did."

Celia watched her son's expression change several times as he looked at her. She sat down on the back steps and Eli willingly sat down next to her.

"I ain't... I mean, I haven't thought of that," he said quietly. "You think there's a boy out there like me that is waiting for his daddy to come home with Larx?" Eli said the horse's name; there was an edge of finality in his voice.

"It's very possible. Perhaps, there was a boy like you that has given up one of the horses that your father has brought home in the past... maybe even today. We don't mistreat any of the stock. Do we?"

Eli shook his head as the truth in his mother's words gained understanding in his heart.

"No Ma'am... we don't, but everybody ain't us."

"Well, Son, all I can say is, you knew Larx was a market breed. If you can't separate your feelings concerning the work and purpose of the breeding stock, then maybe it would be best for you not to..."

Eli leaped to his feet.

"No! I'll do better, Mama. I love training the horses with Owen. Please don't make me quit. Please Mama."

"Honey, I understand that it's not easy letting go of something that you raised from just a little thing, but I think you will be pleased with your father and Uncle Cole's reason for doing it. She's not the only one they took, you know."

Their conversation was interrupted by a faint squeal echoing beyond the inside of the house. The shrill page was unique and meant for Eli's ears. It was carried by the afternoon wind in search of a response.

"Well, I guess little Prissy is up from her nap," exclaimed his mother.

Eli rose hastily and started up the back steps before his mother could even stand.

"I'll get her, Mama."

"I know you will, Honey. Thank you all the same."

She caught her son's hand before he was out of reach from her, and when he looked back, Celia tapped her cheek with her finger. The corners of Eli's mouth curled up, and he leaned over and smeared a kiss on his mother face.

Eli climbed the outside staircase to the balcony and then turned right towards Mollie's room. He stopped in the open doorway of the French doors and watched the tiny wisp of a girl in silence. The array of storybooks strewn across the bed and floor was evidence of her boredom. She knew she was not allowed to get off the bed until the radio on the nightstand cut on to signify the end of her designated nap time. It wasn't that the child needed a nap so much as his mother needed a rest from the lively toddler.

Eli smiled as she dangled upside down off the edge of the big bed. Her foot was hooked between the spindles of the headboard while she tried to fish a specific book out from underneath it. Her crazy, beautiful pile of curls swept at the floor, and he could hear her grunt as she tried to stretch her little arm another inch to reach what she wanted. The little girl attempted to read every book which was in her path.

The terrible twos had not become part of Mollie's disposition as they had his little sister's. It seemed Scherry still suffered from them even though she had completed first grade and was bound for the second grade in a few weeks. Never the less, Mollie possessed a stubborn streak that was as steadfast as any mule on the ranch. She took direction without conflict, but she would not give up on anything that presented her difficulty. Clearly, she embraced this life, and she wasn't going to miss one second of it. Eli found her determination and enthusiasm fascinating. He also liked the fact that she trusted him like she did, and that she could keep up with him on her pony when they rode. She didn't back up from trying to saddle the animal, or attend to its daily need, even though she required assistance. He liked the way she engaged in the world around her from the moment her eyes opened in the morning, and he never grew weary of her inquisitive nature, or her energy. His mother compared her to a worker-ant. It was accurate and one of the things that he liked most. He enjoyed tending the horses with her because she liked it too. She caused him to challenge his own reason sometimes, with her questions about why things were. There were times when she got so excited, her words were strung together so that they made no sense to the family; however, Eli seemed to be able to understand her. He guessed it was so because he had always taken the time to observe and listen. He felt overly protective of her, and like everyone else in the family, his heart went out to her. He liked to think that he possessed a powerful charm over her that no one else had, but he knew that it was much simpler than that. He and Mollie shared a private understanding; he saw things her way. Eli had a grasp on the bigger picture of Mollie's life, and his place in it. He and her pony were treasured, and her books were like rare gems to the child, but her daddy was the center of her world. She no longer had a mother; this was the way her life should be.

Lana Silver, Mollie's mother, had nurtured Eli for the first seven years of his life. She had been a gentle and loving woman who possessed a magical way with the horses. Her aura was complete peace, and the animals felt it, just like every person who knew her. Even in her death, she conveyed an all-knowing serenity. Eli had loved her; he knew no one that didn't. Still, she had left two motherless children - his best friend, Travis, and this innocent, vulnerable, living thing who was almost doll-like in her physical features. She was the tiniest baby he had ever seen take a first step. Her smile was like a ray of sunshine, and her large green, pony-like eyes got to him in a major way. She was a living and breathing reflection of her mother. Eli enjoyed her, unlike his squealing, always-into-something-she-shouldn't-be younger sister.

Scherry Hawk was another matter. It only took one look in the girl's direction to send her into a whining spasm of aggravation. Eli wondered if the day would come when he would ever really like her. He knew it was biblical, but Eli believed Noah would have jumped off the ark, if Scherry had been on board. Until she stopped whining, or he went deaf, he was steering clear of her.

"Eeeee!" Mollie's cry of joy widened his grin. It was her name for him and always had been. The family thought it was funny. They even made jokes about Elvis suing them over the infringement. Eli laughed with them, but he considered it an honorable title given by his own little Pricilla.

Eli scooped her up along with the book she struggled to reach and tossed them onto her bed. She bubbled over with giggles as she bounced back to her feet. The little girl jumped over to him, then clutched his shirt sleeves in her little fists and began to climb on to his shoulders where she rode at some point every day.

"Do it again, 'E'!" she pleaded.

"You're rotten, Ollie. Do you know that?" He scooped her up and tossed her again.

Her blonde ringlets bounced loosely as the little girl added a couple of spurred jumps of her own for an extra thrill.

"Do you need to go to the potty?" Eli had learned the hard way that sometimes she got too engrossed in her interests and ignored her bladder until it was too late. His mother insisted that she and Scherry conduct themselves like a lady even though they were surrounded by men. He found it easier to remind her periodically rather than see her get scolded for soiling her clothing.

She gasped suddenly and covered her mouth with her little hand. He picked her up in haste and put her down; she trotted off to the bathroom with her knees together.

Eli grinned at her when she came back with her dress tail stuck inside the waistline of her drawers.

"Here, let's put on some horsy clothes."

"We can go ride?" cried the little girl. She scampered over to her dresser and began matching strength with the bottom drawer.

He told her what was on his mind as he went to help her.

"You know; one day you could ride your horse in the rodeo. But you'll prob'ly be wantin' to do all that girl stuff. You know... like baby dolls and tea parties... junk like that," he exclaimed with an exaggerated frown.

"I like my horsy, Coco! When can me ride in the roheo... just me?" she asked him.

"R-o-d-e-o," stated Eli slowly. She repeated it after him while he pulled out her overalls and held them steady for her. Mollie skillfully worked her feet into the pant legs. She grabbed his shoulders and Eli took hold of the sides and picked her up, so she would slide into them. He whisked the dress over her head then wrestled her over anxious hands through the tee shirt's arm holes. He stood her up and began to fasten the shoulder straps because they were difficult for her. She insisted on doing it herself, so he tactfully engaged her in conversation about the rodeo as a diversion, while he helped her.

Mollie released a fizz of giggles as he caught the straps in the back and playfully swung her back and forth letting her dangle in mid-air. Eli tossed her back to the mattress of the big bed, so he could harness her busy little feet with her boots. She liked to do that on her own too, but because she wanted to go outside more, she didn't interfere while he wiggled a sock on each foot. He noticed that she studied him with such concentration. Eli wondered what revelation was going through her mind.

"Ready! Go!" She sang out suddenly then leaped off the bed; her feet were in a run when she hit the floor.

Eli bursts into laughter. He caught up to her near the top of the stairs and scooped her up into his long, elbow-clad arms. The tiny girl released a convulsive shriek and held her arms out in complete trust as he flew her over his head while descending the stairs.

Eli's head snapped up and his attention was redirected as he recognized the lonesome sounding horn from outside. He responded immediately. His steps were quick and nimble as he maneuvered the stairs with Mollie in his arms. At the back door, he tossed her up onto his shoulders and headed for the stables. His enthusiastic pace relayed the excitement at hand, and Mollie began to jabber about the truck, her daddy, and Travis. His little sister stayed true to form as he passed her and ignored her attempt to run down the back steps and not spill her box of hospitalized creatures.

"Eli... Eli, they're back... they're back!" cried Scherry.

Celia and Estelle abandoned the tomatoes and were behind Eli on the back steps.

The entire mechanics of the ranch could be seen from the back patio of the main house. The low ground clearance of the horse trailer was an easy give-a-way that new arrivals had come home to the Silver-Hawk.

It seemed all the ranch hands had gathered as Eli waited patiently for them to back the trailer up to the corral gate. The truck came to a stop, and the doors on the old truck popped open. Rueben Hawk got out and stood idle for a second. He reached above his head with both arms then leaned to the right side in a stretching motion. Eli knew this was his father's way of waking up after a nap. He said nothing and went straight to Travis, who had managed to squeeze out from the cab into the gathering of men.

Eli could hardly wait to know what was in the trailer. It seemed everyone was just as excited as he was.

"What'd y'all get, Travis?"

His friend's voice conveyed an excitement that was contagious.

"Eli, we seen the biggest horse ever. It was white and had a head as big as me! He used to work in the circus but this man, Mr. Tanner, bought 'em and is tryin' to raise more of 'em... kinda like savin' 'em from being hurt... and used... and stuff. He was somethin' to see; he was so quick. He moved like a deer, but he was HUGE! His name was Zeus. The man said I could ride 'em if I wanted... but daddy wouldn't let me. Man, Eli! I wish you would 'a come with us. I wish you could 'a seen 'em."

Eli's heart began to sink as he visualized Travis' words.

Coleman Silver appeared at the gate of the trailer. A delighted smile graced his face as he extended his arms towards Eli. He had nearly forgotten about his passenger until Mollie tried to use his ear for leverage in the process of relocating to her father's arms.

The trailer door swung open and Eli's eyes widened as Travis' grin stretched from one ear to the other. The onlookers backed up to give Owen Kagel enough room to back the patchy, gray and brown Appaloosa stallion off the ramp. A thrill was spiraling inside the young boys' chests. When Charlie came out with the mare, Eli's questions began to burn his tongue.

"They're ours, Eli!" exclaimed Travis proudly. "We bought 'em from the sale of the Quarters. We're gonna breed 'em!" announced the scruffy, curly headed boy rather boldly. He stopped short and cut his eyes back to his father and Rueben. His face reddened with embarrassment from the reality of what he had just declared. The two men standing there smiled and gave a nod of approval. It was the assurance Travis needed to feel confident in his excitement.

Rueben Hawk spoke up.

"That's right. You two will be completely responsible for them... just like Charlie, when he bought Ransom last year and brought him home to train. Owen will teach you everything you need to know, and I imagine Charlie will be helping you too. Boys, this isn't something that you only do when you're in the mood. This is a commitment. Owen's one of the best horse-men in Texas. His time is valuable."

Eli's eyes widened even further. Owen was his mentor. He knew everything about horses, specifically, the way they think. People were always calling him to come and see about their stock and seeking his opinion concerning a problem they were having with an unruly horse. Owen Kagel had been the ranch foreman for seven years. Eli really couldn't remember when he wasn't a working part of the ranch.

Charlie had lived here with Owen for the last three years. He had stayed in the big house with them for a while. Preceding Charlie's arrival, the children were told the truth; he had been injured while protecting his mother from an outlaw. They were told that it wasn't necessary to ask about everything that brings speculation to one's mind. They were cautioned about asking questions because of the horrible things that had happened to Charlie, and his mother.

Eli remembered the first time he saw Charlie.

The older boy looked so frightful Eli forgot to breathe. His face was marred and bruised, and one of his eyes was hideously bloodshot. His upper body was in a cast, and so was his arm. They had been curious about him, but they didn't dare ask.

After several weeks, Charlie got his cast off and began accompanying them around the ranch. It seemed the normal thing for him to do. They introduced him to the horses and other animals, the people at church, and their neighbors. They showed him the lake, the old cabin, the caverns along the river with Owen and their fathers. They shared everything with him, including their favorite play spots and fishing holes on the two hundred acres surrounding the house. It wasn't long, Charlie moved into the mobile home next to the hay barn with Owen. That was when Charlie started to become his own person.

Eli had come to admire Charlie just as much as he did Owen. Charlie was only three years older than Eli, but no one treated him like a kid. He was a part-time hand at the ranch and got paid just like the others. He allowed Eli to sit with him on the school bus rather than the older boys his age. It made Eli feel like he mattered. He also knew that Charlie took school very seriously, almost as serious as his job on the Silver-Hawk. There were several older boys at school that were cruel to newcomers, and sometimes to the awkward, wiry boy that was Rueben Hawk's son. Their ridicule made Eli angry, but Charlie just ignored them and encouraged him to do the same. Eli didn't understand this; after all, Charlie was a protector of the weak and a crusader in his eyes. Eli told his father about the bully on the bus and that Charlie just read his book and ignored them. Rueben had helped Eli realize that Charlie valued the fact he had his older brother's reputation and his life at the ranch to stand with him. He told Eli that Charlie had stood alone in the battle to protect his mother, and he wasn't alone anymore. He made Eli see that a wise man picked his battles, and for Charlie, fighting with a boy who called him names was not worth jeopardizing Owen's faith in him, or the harmony he had found living at the ranch. It was the first time since Charlie's arrival that his father had brought up the conflict which had brought Charlie to them. Eli wondered about Charlie sometimes and the details of what had happened to him, but no matter what they were, Charlie had become one of them and it was good enough for Eli.

The boys were alike in their admiration for Owen. But most of all, Eli liked the way Charlie talked to folks so friendly like, even the ones that weren't so nice to him. Charlie didn't begrudge his inquisitive nature either. Obviously, he didn't see Eli as a spoiled little rich boy like some other boys treated him. Eli thought his friendship with Charlie made life easier. He had always thought it would be neat to have an older brother; he and Travis had decided that Charlie was the closest thing to one they would ever have. The three of them had secured this bond on a hot, rainy July afternoon in the hay loft. Charlie had pulled out his pocket knife, and they all poked their thumb then mashed them together while declaring they were blood brothers forever.

Eli looked forward to the day when he would be a ranch hand instead of the eldest son. He knew it was silly, but he wished sometimes that he was Charlie and that Charlie wore his boots, because being the oldest child of the Silver-Hawk was often difficult.

"I wouldn't go so far as to say that," commented Owen, a tad embarrassed at Rueben's verbal endorsement of his skills. "But I sure do like an animal that can run so fast and smooth that it makes me feel like a gust of wind." Owen stepped up beside Eli and patted his shoulder. "We got some work to do fellas." A big grin stretched across the man's face.

Eli tilted his head back and squinted to block the blinding sun out of his eyes, so he could get a better look at the man who could talk to horses.

Owen handed the reins to Eli and Travis.

"Okay men, let's get back to work." The gathering of cowhands began to disperse. "You two lead these animals to the corral, and then you need to feed them and brush them down really good. We'll stable them on the north end next to each other."

The boys leaped to obedience at Owen's instructions.

Cole tossed Mollie up into the air; she burst into a seizure of laughter. It caught Charlie's attention. He hid behind her father and peeked around at her playfully. She thrust herself from side to side trying to grab his hat. It was a game he and Owen sometimes played with her.

Owen instructed Charlie to move the truck and trailer to its usual spot in the shed, and the young man wasted no time in doing so.

Cole disappeared into the barn with Mollie and Scherry's tongues fluttering faster than the wings of a hummingbird.

Rueben noticed his wife as she stared after the large, quiet man. He knew Celia was sensitive to Cole. He too, worried about Cole's frame of mind since Lana's death. His friend only seemed content when he was in the middle of the children or his little girl was in his arms.

He and Celia had exhausted the subject of Cole getting out and dating. He simply would not hear of it. He was still in love; there was no substitute for that. He was hurting, and he missed Lana desperately. They all did, even her Uncle Lucien couldn't seem to shake it.

Dr. Lucien Saucier was Hoyt Saucier's younger brother. Hoyt had taken him in at the age of 13 after their parents died in a tornado. When he was 17, Lucien moved to Liberty County to go to the University. The institution had a wonderful veterinary medicine program, and Lucien went to work as an assistant for Dr. Buford Zachary, in his veterinarian practice. He and the stubborn old doctor got along so well that he sold Lucien the practice for a meager sum after his graduation. The doctor had no living relatives, and he had enjoyed his final years with the out-going and blunt young man who reminded him of himself. Lucien had been to the Hawk farm and the Silver's ranch many times before the sons purchased the 800-acre tract of land that lay between them and created the Silver-Hawk Ranch. When Lana called him and told him she had met and fallen in love with Coleman Silver, he was happy. Lana was like his little sister, and he doted on her. He knew how narrow-minded and unbending his brother could be. Lucien had always been driven by his work. It was the underlying cause for his own marriage falling apart, but since Lana's death, he was worse.

Life seemed to be waiting for something, some reason… closure to her death. Sometimes, when the day was slowing down, and the house was quiet, it was like she was there. Rueben and Celia had experienced several strange events around the house, like the day Celia brought an armload of clean clothes inside from the line. She heard the children arguing in the living room, so she tossed the clothes onto the kitchen table as she went to see what was wrong. When she returned some half hour later, the clothes where all folded nice and neat, stacked and sorted just as they should be. Celia glanced out the back door and saw Estelle (the woman that lived in and helped her) down in the garden, where she had been most of the morning. She assumed Estelle had done it during a cooling off spell and was appreciative. Several days later, Rueben called up to the house from the stable office and asked Celia who was visiting. She replied, 'no one'. The phone went dead and in a matter of minutes, Rueben came through the back door, his face was pale and his eyes large. Celia curiously followed her husband up the back stairs to the east balcony, not finding anything for him to be upset about, she questioned his behavior. His explanation was that he had watched a woman with long blond hair and a blue dress, rock for almost 20 minutes. She had sat in the same chair which Lana had claimed each afternoon as she rocked Travis for his nap. The event motivated Celia to ask Estelle about the folded clothes. Estelle had denied the chore, for she had been planting fall peas that afternoon and was covered in dirt. That day, Rueben and Celia agreed not to mention either event to Cole.

They were stunned once again when Cole came in telling the most incredible story about Lana's horse. Everyone on the ranch knew that Lana's horse, once gentle and trustworthy, had turned into an unmanageable devil since her passing. The animal had always had an unruly coat and Lana had spent a great deal of time grooming him. He wanted to care for the animal as Lana would expect; however, the animal had bitten three of the hands and kicked out two stall gates. His appearance was to the point of hideous. The stallion had not allowed one soul near him until that day when Mollie toddled into the stall. Cole elaborated on how he had almost had a stroke when he realized how far the child wandered in only a matter of minutes from turning his back. Charlie had heard him call out for the toddler and responded due to the fear he heard in her father's voice. The young man found her first and motioned to him. They stood side by side in the open gateway of the animal's stall, watching while the baby stood underneath the wild gelding patting and hugging its leg. The horse stood quiet and calm as he nuzzled the child. Mollie giggled as she reached out and touched the horse's nose with her tiny hand. Cole was too frightened to say anything, so Charlie squatted down and called to her. Mollie smiled and started toddling back to him. When she was clear of the gate, Cole interceded and picked her up practically in tears while Charlie closed the stall gate. But how it had been opened, no one seemed to know. The event reinforced Rueben and Celia's decision to remain quiet. They loved Cole, and they feared he would never release his heart, if he knew what had happened to them.

Charlie flourished on the ranch, and as he grew up, he became confident and proficient in his place there. He was not one that required a lot of direction concerning chores around the ranch or his job responsibilities. He unhitched and stored away the horse trailer to its rightful place in the shed just as Owen had asked him to do. Charlie went to the duty wall outside the office to retrieve his clip board where his chores were listed. He changed the oil in both tractors and the flatbed work truck before mucking out all the stalls. He deposited the last wheel barrow of manure to the pile beyond the hay barn. He washed the tools he had used and put them away in the shed. The sun was near setting, so he decided to take a closer look at the new additions to the ranch. He set out for the north corral.

Charlie had just turned 14 years old the day after Independence Day, and he was growing into a tall, muscular young man. He had come to appreciate the feel of sore muscles. A year after his surgeries, Owen took Charlie for a final check-up. The physicians were pleased with the young man's progress and assured him and Owen that his bones had healed perfectly and were growing as they should. Their test determined that Charlie had excellent bone density and good muscle tone, finding no reason why Charlie could not achieve whatever path he chose in life. That had been two years ago. It was the same afternoon that Owen hired Charlie as a ranch hand. The young man was determined to work as hard as any grown man on the payroll, to reinforce his brother's trust in giving him a job.

Charlie rounded the corner of the barn and his stomach moaned out loud. The sweet scent of apple pie hung thick on the evening breeze, along with the mouth-watering smell of onions. The work yard smelled of something delicious every night, due to the abilities of Cookie, who lived in and supervised the bunkhouse. Ms. Hawk and Estelle worked together daily to create some enticing delicacies in the kitchen of the big house on the hill.

Charlie swallowed the excess saliva and poked his stomach a couple of times to make it be quiet. The last church social was over a month ago. He and Owen fancied eating, as much as a hog did the slop trough, but their cooking skills lacked a seasoned flare. Charlie glanced toward the two-story clapboard house over-looking the west pasture and remembered how comfortable and homey it was inside. The house was not off limits to him, it was just that he preferred going there by invitation, and the last supper invite they had enjoyed was two weeks ago. His mother had taught him manners, and Owen had taught him about respect. He may be the ranch foreman's brother, but he still was a hired hand.

Mr. Silver had been right; he had found true peace in this place. It was a kind of peace he never knew existed. In these years since Charlie had come to live with his brother, Owen had made it a point to build a strong relationship with him. They had become exactly that - brothers. Charlie believed Owen was the best brother in the world. He made Charlie feel like he was in this world to accomplish anything he wanted. He encouraged, challenged and believed in him unconditionally. Owen had told him that he did not know how to be a father to him. The problem had worked itself out naturally. Mr. Silver shared a bond with Charlie that Owen respected. How could they not after all they had been through together? Charlie had come to understand that it was a hard thing for a God-fearing man to accept knowing he had taken another life, even a fruitless and reckless one like L.B. Thomas'. He thought it even more difficult to bear the responsibility for that loss of life when you had not been the one who committed the transgression. Charlie wondered sometimes if, knowing he had not committed such a horrible deed made the burden of blame easier for Mr. Silver to bear.

Charlie knew they were concerned about what had happened, and whether it would have an adverse effect on him one day. He understood their concern. When it came to boyhood interest, there was a big difference between him, and the youngsters who had become his friends and his blood brothers here on the ranch. He enjoyed the activities they shared; however, his buddies lived in the moment while he looked at life for its possibilities. Owen teased him by calling him, 'old man'. He wasn't offended because his spirit felt old. He had grown up that day; he had been forced to, for the sake of others.

Charlie recalled the first time Owen had taken him to the nursing home to see their mother. *The visit had secured his hope and trust in the new people in his life. Owen had warned him about her paralysis. The head injury she sustained that day had stolen the motor function in her left arm as well as pertinent memories of her life. It had proven to be a blessing because the sadness in her eyes was gone and a contented expression claimed her face. The Lord had given her peace in an unexpected way. Still, he was sad and bothered by her handicap. But when she cuddled next to him, he realized she was alive, and he could wrap his good arms around her. Sadness left him as he held his mother close.*

During the drive home that afternoon, Charlie confessed to Owen that he had believed their mother was dead. He admitted to doubting the story of her being in the nursing home, believing it had been created to protect him until he was stronger and could deal with her death. He apologized to his brother for thinking him a liar.

Charlie's honesty had given Owen the opportunity to ask about that night and the things he remembered. Charlie admitted to Owen that he had found the newspaper articles in his desk drawer a few weeks earlier and read them. He wanted to know why none of them mentioned what he had done to his step-father.

Owen was honest with Charlie and explained the many obstacles he had faced in trying to protect his family. He expressed his fear concerning how very weak Charlie was after being mistreated. His brother's voice shook as he spoke of being terrified to face life alone, should he lose his family. Owen was unable to disguise the resentment he felt while summarizing the failed attempts he experienced in convincing law enforcement to help him protect them against L.B. Thomas. His brother's candor gave a clear account of his apprehension. Owen was not willing to jeopardize Charlie's well-being by trusting the proven indifference of the local authorities. Charlie was also enlightened to the risk involved concerning the media. Owen was determined that his (already) battered family was not going to be scrutinized by an opinionated spotlight which would subject them to ridicule and biased judgment.

Their discussion gave clarity and brought an order to the details of that dreadful night. Charlie was convinced of miracles. The presence of Owen and his friends, the night L.B. Thomas lost control of his humanity, had been anointed by the Almighty. Because of these men, and this family, Charlie understood the full meaning of friendship and compassion. Thanks to Mr. Silver, he had learned firsthand about sacrifice. Coleman Silver had voluntarily assumed the blame and responsibility for L.B. Thomas' death; after all, the knife in his arm would ultimately prove and justify an act of self-defense. The villainous temper of L.B. Thomas had been the cause of his demise, and none of them could change this fact. Likewise, the agreement made between his brother and these men had established a path parallel to the truth. This path was documented and was a matter of public record. The consequences of that night had become a part of their futures.

Charlie had wondered many times since then, about the man who had risked something as valuable as his personal freedom for a boy who was a stranger. He had been confused about this kind of caring between people that weren't kin. But with time, he had stopped wondering, because he was not confused about the gratefulness inside of him. That feeling of gratefulness was one of the reasons why he would not speak about the truth of that night. His subjective upbringing had shaped an insightful and clever youngster. Charlie realized his silence would protect Mr. Silver's reputation, and at the same time, honor the sacrifice the man had made on his behalf.

Life here at the Silver-Hawk ranch had clarified a lot of things for Charlie. The concept of 'love thy neighbor as thyself' was practiced every day by this family. This truth, as well as, the other nine, was the spiritual covenant he would embrace through-out his life.

Charlie had been taught by their mother: God had made each person and had a plan for that person, even when things are bad from the struggle between good and evil. He was learning what she meant by watching this hardworking and loving family live.

He knew this life was the kind of future he wanted to build for himself. He wanted a little piece of land, a nice barn for his horse, and a little house. He understood a good education was the key to supporting himself and making his dreams a reality. He wanted part of his reality to include caring for and providing for his mother. Her jumbled memories had not improved, but her body was stronger, and she was learning alternative ways to deal with her immobility. She seemed content at Whispering Pines, and she was happy knowing that her boys were together and safe.

Charlie would never be able to repay these people for what they had done for him. They loved him and Owen like family, and the only thing he could do in return, was love them back. He found it was an easy thing to do. His mama had always said, "The Lord was in control". He knew this was true, because L. B. Thomas no longer needed poker, money, alcohol, a slave of a wife to abuse and belittle, or a small boy to punch and kick around.

Charlie found the entire family gathered around the fence. Eli's and Travis' enthusiasm was amusing. Owen had introduced the Appaloosa breed of horse to the ranch when he bought his stallion, Salvador, five years ago. Since then, they had bred over 30 mares with the stallion. They had produced some beautiful and strong colts, and customers were on a waiting list to buy them. It was one of the reasons why Cole and Rueben had decided to invest in the pair.

Charlie considered himself very fortunate to have been given the horse with which he worked, and even more fortunate, to be given the job in which he earned the money to buy the red quarter horse. His stallion, Ransom had approached him at the horse sale one day as he stood by the fence looking at another with Owen. Charlie was surprised when the stallion snagged the hat from his head and walked off with it. He laughed as he followed the animal along the fence then asked him if he was going to have to pay a ransom to get his hat back. He produced a carrot from his coat pocket and held it through the fence. The stallion turned abruptly and trotted over to him. He put the hat back on Charlie's head and then snagged the carrot. Owen had witnessed it too, or Charlie would have never believed it had happened as it did. He bought the horse that day and called him Ransom befitting their first meeting. In Charlie's way of thinking, the Appaloosas were strong, fast, and resilient. He would like to own one someday, but it would be a working relationship. He shared a friendship with Ransom that went beyond understanding. They were pals, and nothing could compete with that.

Charlie climbed up on the fence next to Eli.

"Ain't they somethin', Charlie?"

Charlie smiled and pushed his hat back on his brow a fraction.

"Yeah, 'E'... they're great!"

Eli's excitement could not be contained.

"I think they're the most beautiful horses I've ever seen! She's so gentle too." The mare nudged Eli for another piece of apple. Charlie watched Eli's hand go out to her with the treat then slide over her nose to her ear. The younger boy was in love with these majestic animals. The ghostly stallion that was Ms. Silver's was the only horse on the ranch which didn't respond to him; still, Eli had patience with him and tried every day to gain his trust.

Owen spoke up.

"That's their way. They have a lot of endurance, and they're also cunning, so you better watch your back. Remember, they aren't broke yet."

Celia Hawk spoke up because the sun was going down, and she had several tasks to complete in the preparation of supper.

"Well, they are beautiful, but I'm hungry!" She leaned over and stood Scherry up out of the dirt then brushed off her clothes. "Owen, Charlie is looking a bit puny these days. Why don't y'all come on up to the house in about half an hour and have supper with us? Estelle has roasted a turkey and made some of her cream cheese deviled eggs. We have fried squash, butter beans, bacon-cheese potatoes, and hambone turnip greens to go with the jalapeno cornbread. I sliced some tomatoes from the garden and washed a mess of green onions, and there is a cinnamon-apple cobbler ready to go in the oven. We're gonna turn a freezer of ice cream too."

Owen's eyes met Estelle's and held for a moment as unspoken feeling exchanged between them.

Charlie had already figured out that Owen was sweet on Estelle. They would meet in the evenings and walk down to the big oak in the east pasture. He and Travis had built and hung swings in several of the trees surrounding the house. Owen had told him the oak was Estelle's favorite because of the wisteria vine that wound through its branches, especially in April, when it bloomed. A magical thing happened when the oak turned into a purple tree.

Charlie wasn't about to let this opportunity pass him by while his brother just stood there and daydreamed about Ms. Estelle; so, he took matters into his own hands.

"Lord, thank you for your mercy... for Ms. Celia... and her takin' pity on a starvin' man." To every one's surprise, the usually-too-serious young man did a theatrical roll from the top fence rail to the ground and fell still; his leg kicked a couple of times to give the scene a humorous ending.

A lazy, but amused smile stretched across Cole's face. He waited for his partner, and the biggest prankster he knew, to comment.

"Sakes alive!" protested Rueben. He yanked his hat off and started fanning Charlie's body. "Eli, go get daddy the shovel. We got to throw dirt on 'em before he starts stinkin'. We can't let the flies and buzzards get supper before we do."

Owen was embarrassed at his little brother's shenanigans.

"Charlie, get up from there!" he commanded. The flabbergasted expression on Owen's face was even funnier than Charlie's desperate plea for food.

Celia glanced over at Estelle, who was trying to suppress her laughter for the sake of Owen's pride.

Celia spoke to the young man in keeping with the rules of her table.

"Supper's in half an hour, Charlie. You had best crawl over to the water pump to wash up. Dirty hands don't eat at my table... even if they are bony and starving." Celia noticed her daughter tuck the box of frogs under her arm as she called out to Travis. The youngster was already on his way to the house; still, he stopped and waited for her. He grabbed her hand when she caught up to him, then they started for the back steps as she chattered about the horses. Celia shook her head at the way Travis appeased her daughter. It was then that she noticed Rueben was waiting on her as well. She took a step to join him, and he held his hand out to her and smiled.

CHAPTER 3

Rueben came in through the back door with a bag of ice he had retrieved from the huge freezer in the storage shed. He could hear Cole and the children playing in the living room. His friend made play time an evening ritual, to keep the kids busy so the ladies could get supper on the table without them under foot. Rueben slipped up behind his wife and wrapped his arms around her. She paused from slicing the cornbread as his lips gently nibbled at her neck.

"Mmm, I'm hungry," he mumbled.

"Supper will be ready in a few minutes," replied Celia. She rested her arms over his and gave them a loving pat.

Estelle looked over in time to see him whisper in Celia's ear.

"Oh Rueben!" Celia affectionately kissed his lips while she pushed his hands away.

"Guess we'll talk about it later," he goaded then gave her rump a playful little buff with his palm. "So, what can I do to help?"

"Well, after you apologize to Estelle for being so brazen in front of her, you can get those plates off the second shelf and set the table... be sure the utensils match so that nobody has to eat with a spreading knife."

Estelle waved off Rueben's playful apology. She had grown use to his flirting with his wife and Celia pretending to be embarrassed. It was part of why she loved this family so much.

They had only known her as the old maid from the church. A woman who had already seen her 30th birthday and had no life other than caring for an invalid mother who had long since lost all reason due to her illness. Estelle had never been permitted away from her mother's side for very long, even less had she the chance to court. It was two years ago that lightning had struck their old house. Estelle was outside trying to get the livestock secured in the barn from the storm when it hit with a boom. She struggled against the wind to make it back to the house, but the small, dilapidated dwelling had become completely engulfed with flames. She tried at the risk of her own safety, but there was no way to reach her mother. When Celia was contacted and told of the tragedy, she wasted no time in consulting with Rueben and Cole. That night, Estelle left the emergency room with her hands bandaged and moved to the ranch where she was given her own room. When her burns were healed, a job was waiting, if she wanted it.

Estelle was a shapely woman of average height, and she had smooth ivory skin and strawberry colored curls that she kept in a neat bun. Her blue eyes glistened with life and her smile was gentle and almost shy. After the initial shock and pain of her mother's death had subsided, Estelle began to heal. Her hands had been the easy part, but her heart was another story. She suffered unfair guilt because she could not save her mother.

But in God's plan, she and Owen were thrust together one afternoon; he had taken it upon himself to disc the garden spot for her. They began to talk over a glass of lemonade in the shade. He shared that he had brought his mother and brother here to live and start over. She was receptive to his honesty and understanding of her broken heart. She began to heal emotionally, and she seemed to flourish with them. She had acquired a huge new family and from the moment Owen laid eyes on her, an admirer.

The energy and life at the Silver-Hawk had nursed her back to the gentle, yet strong woman she was meant to be. She was as graceful as a cloud, and seemingly, could grow anything in the dirt with only her breath as sustenance. She had helped Celia nurture the rose garden into a showcase of trellising blooms.

Everyone at the ranch knew that Owen had eyes for her. They rode to church together on Sunday and sometimes, they took long walks along the north ridge where the view of the land was spectacular.

She had even gathered the courage and gone to the nursing home with Owen and Charlie while they visited their mother. The older woman was attempting to brush her long hair when they arrived; it was obvious she was trying to get ready for their visit. Owen introduced them while Charlie checked her plants for water.

Patti's delicate fingers touched the jagged, pink line over her right eye, followed by her smooth cheek. Clearly, this side of her face did not respond like the other. Owen had wanted them to like each other, but Estelle could see that his mother was uncomfortable concerning her appearance. Estelle's gentle and subtle way drew close to Owen's mother as she offered her a gift for her birthday. She helped her open the box that held a book of water-colored landscapes. Each painting was accompanied by a scripture, which was articulately chosen to be spiritually uplifting for a woman. They looked at it together for a moment before Estelle told her she was proud when Owen asked her to come with them and share her birthday. Estelle confessed that she missed her own mother very much. Her honesty had broken the ice.

Charlie climbed on to the bed next to his mother and offered his gift. Estelle tucked pillows behind Ms. Thomas, so she could get a better look at her son's accomplishments. It was a scrapbook. Estelle had helped him make it so that it included: all sorts of pictures and assignments from his school work, his report card for the year, his and Ransom's first place ribbon for calf roping at the rodeo, and a couple of poems he had written for her. Charlie told her about almost everything in the book. Estelle acquired the brush from Patti's hand, seemingly without her knowing, while she listened to her son.

When Charlie commented on how pretty she was, her hand went up to her temple. Her hair was in a beautiful, Victorian bun; the front swept over the side of her brow to cover the nasty scar on her forehead. Patti looked in the mirror that Estelle held up for her and half her face lit up with satisfaction. Her fingers traced the front sweep of hair that covered the place which bothered her.

She smiled as she gripped Estelle's hand in a loving and appreciative way. Estelle's heart was lost to the older woman and she could not help but love her. It was an inborn sense that women share. She knew this woman appreciated the fact that she cared for her sons. Estelle could think of nothing more she would rather do.

WHAMMMM! The backdoor slammed so loud the lid on the pot of greens shifted. Celia spun around to see a little, brown ponytail bobbing up and down on the other side of the counter. Rueben stepped into the doorway from the dining room; his expression was stern.

"Just a minute young lady," his tone of his voice was in keeping with the frown on his face.

The little girl stopped and looked up at her father and then blinked several times.

"Sir?"

Rueben walked over to the child and squatted down in front of her.

"What ya got there under your shirt?"

The child hesitated a moment; her eyes revealed the consideration of a fictional answer.

"Well?" encouraged her father.

She blinked at him again, but her father seemed unmoved. Finally, she answered in a small voice.

"Frogs."

Rueben bit the inside of his bottom lip in an attempt not to smile. He leaned over towards her.

"Let's see."

Scherry pulled out the box of bandaged frogs from under her shirt.

Rueben covered his mouth with his hand and coughed to hide his amusement. He was careful of his expression as he slid his hand underneath the box and gave it a gentle shake. The frogs didn't move.

"I don't think they will live in this box, Honey. They need to live outside in the grass to be happy. It's nature's way."

"Oh." Her little voice was barely audible.

Rueben felt sorry for her, but not as much as he did for the poor animals in the shoebox.

"You go put them outside and close the door like you know you're supposed to."

The little girl stood there with her head down. She hoped against hope that he would change his mind.

"Go on now," urged her father.

They watched as Scherry dragged over to the back door and disappeared through it without a sound.

Rueben stood and turned to his wife.

"She's just like you," commented Celia softly.

The family gathered, wearing fresh shirts, clean hands and combed hair. Cole sat at one end of the table and Rueben at the other. They joined hands and bowed their heads as thanks went up to the Maker.

The food was passed around the table and everyone began to eat; however, Scherry seemed to be distracted from her plate. She sat across from Owen and studied him intensely until her curiosity got the best of her.

"Gee, Uncle Owen, you smell like you're goin' to church! How come? It ain't Sunday!"

"Scherry Nicole!" scolded her mother. "That's none of your business young lady." Celia shook her head. "You children need to work on your manners."

But Owen only found humor in the little girl's honesty and he obliged her with an answer.

"Well Scherry, I've been working in the barn this afternoon and I didn't smell too pleasant. I thought since I was gonna share some supper with you all, the least I could do was take a bath and look a bit more presentable."

"Oh," replied Scherry. "Is that why you cut your chin whiskers off too?"

Surprise seemed to be the mood of the evening. Eli spoke up after seeing Travis cut his eyes to him in a side gesture of encouragement.

"Dad, when can we saddle the Appaloosas?" Eli's tone was cautious, not from fear, but from the timing in which his courage prodded him to spit out the question. Eli reasoned the three men who would be making that decision were all present, so it was practical timing. What better circumstances could a man want before deciding, than to have a fork and a plate full of Estelle's squash dressing setting in front of you, while you were thinking?

Rueben looked to the other end of the table where Cole was enjoying another helping of greens, and then his attention went to Owen. It was clear neither man was going to come to his rescue.

"Well, they have to be broke first," stated Rueben. "You know that."

Travis jumped into the conversation.

"Yes Sir! Me and Eli thought we could do that. I mean..." Travis hesitated when he saw his father put down his fork.

"Go on," encouraged Cole. He listened as he added the cut pieces of his turkey to his little girl's plate. She sat on a stool next to him; the food that was put in front of her usually disappeared without her making a sound. He smiled and handed her some of his roll; she stuck the piece half way in her mouth, tilted her head back and grinned at him. He caressed her cheek with his knuckle.

Travis finished his proposal by pointing out the most important fact of all.

"Well, you said they would be our responsibility, and seems to me that gettin' them saddle ready is part of it. Don't you think so, Daddy?"

Charlie chimed in with a reminder.

"I saddle broke Ransom... myself, Sir."

The boy had a point. It was a dangerous aspect that still should be considered. Owen was the one who took care in meeting the needs of the stock.

Cole took a sip of his tea.

"You boys think you're up to a rowdy task like that?"

"Yes Sir!" Eli echoed Travis' commitment.

Cole glanced to Owen who had conveniently kept a full mouth since the beginning of this conversation. Clearly, the boys would need his guidance in this venture.

Owen sensed Cole's uncertainty and reached for his glass. He assured them.

"That would be fine with me boys, as long as both your fathers agree."

Eli's eyes darted back to his father.

"Please Daddy, we can do it. We won't quit 'til the job is finished."

Rueben speared another piece of turkey with his fork and wondered why his wife had not voiced an opinion concerning the matter. A few seconds passed then he smiled and nodded in agreement. He was proud that the boys showed the initiative to take this new venture so seriously.

"I think this is a lot for you boys to bite off and even more to chew... but, I reckon you got to start somewhere," stated Rueben. "The only stipulations are that you boys follow Owen's instructions, and don't take it upon yourself to do anything other than what he tells you to do. It'll be wisdom he's sharing with you, and I expect both of you to take it to heart."

Cole pointed out from the other end of the table.

"We've got several irons in the fire with the orchards being ready and the extra help arriving tomorrow. It will be a couple of weeks before you can get started. Can you agree to that?"

Both boys agreed instantly to the conditions.

Eli stood up.

"Can we be excused, Mama? We want to get back to the barn and check on Lottie and Hobo."

"Surely, take your plates into the kitchen," answered Celia. She gave the boys a gentle smile.

"Thanks... we enjoyed it!" The children's manners echoed from the kitchen just before the back door slammed.

Rueben sighed.

"I've got to do something about that door."

A gentle summer breeze blew against them as they settled on the patio to enjoy the dessert. The smell of fresh cut grass and roses blended with the warm aroma of apple pie, and there was a slight scent of rain coming in from the south. The sounds of the evening were comforting; the crickets chirped, and the bawl of the cattle echoed up from the south pasture. The evening sky was aglow with brilliant, glistening stars. The soft, grinding of the ice cream churn mixed with the songs of a mockingbird which had joined the festivities.

Celia's patio was adorned with planters filled with blooming flowers. The backyard tapered down into three elevations and was landscaped to where one could stroll through the garden and visit all the benches throughout. The scent of earth was so intoxicating in the heat of the August night that one would have to stop and rest just to get their breath. The entire garden was designed with a woman's touch and was nothing but romantic.

Cole busied himself turning a freezer of cream. Mollie sat on his knee and Scherry got tremendous joy in situating herself on top of the freezer to steady it.

Rueben and Celia took advantage of a few moments together in the swing while Owen led Estelle into the gardens where they could find some privacy.

"I wonder when that man is going to get enough grit to ask her to marry him?" queried Celia.

Rueben smiled at her.

"What makes you think he wants to marry her?"

"Well, look at him! He can't keep his eyes off her. He stutters when she's within ten feet of him, and as our daughter so gracefully put it... he smells like Sunday. I think he's in love, don't you?"

A sly grin took over Rueben's face.

Celia glanced up at her husband when he didn't answer and found his eyes a glow with mischief.

"Rueben, you know something don't you?" She sat up and turned to him. "What's going on?"

Rueben shrugged his shoulders.

"I'm not sure. He asked me and Cole the other day if we had any plans for Paw Silver's old house place. He said he wanted to rent it and make it livable, so he would have something to offer Estelle."

"Oh my! It's been empty for two years and it has some foundation problems. Can it be fixed? It wouldn't be right to rent him something that needs to be rebuilt. I bet with some hot water and soap, and a few coats of paint, some wallpaper and curtains... we could make her a show place again." Celia's enthusiasm bubbled as usual and her husband jumped in when she took a breath.

"A few days before daddy died... he told me and Cole that we did a good thing... joining the ranch and the farm. He said that he would be watching us from heaven. We had no idea that it would flourish like it has; it's a dream come true. Cole and I discussed it last night, Honey. We feel like Owen had something to do with the success. He did sign on with us with nothing more than our dreams to take to the bank. We're thinking about deeding the house and the corner acreage it's sitting on to him as a wedding gift."

When tears swelled in Celia's eyes Rueben became alarmed; he reached for her chin.

"Celia?"

She caught his wrist and smiled.

"I'm fine," she whispered. Her eyes drifted over his shoulder to where Cole sat discussing life with their daughters. "I love you Rueben, but it sounds like one of Cole's ideas."

Rueben brushed a tear from her cheek.

"You know him well, Honey."

Celia's concerned eyes clung to their friend as she spoke.

"He's been so lost and inside of himself since Lana passed. He seems to be sustaining himself through the children. What will he do when they're gone?"

"Well, that's still a way off," stated Rueben.

"I know, but what if he never allows himself to love again. It could happen. I mean... Mollie's almost five years old, it'll be four years Lana's been gone, come October. Other than the church, he's not been in the company of another woman, other than Estelle or me, the entire time."

Rueben understood what his wife was saying and in truth, he too was concerned about his friend's heart. But he also knew that if the situation were reversed and it were him living without Celia, well... yesterday would be a lot more meaningful to him than any tomorrow.

"It's been a while since we've had anything this joyous to celebrate." She smiled as Rueben's arms pulled her closer; her eyes never left the gentle man holding his little girl. A sad sense of irony overwhelmed her reason as she spoke the things that came to her mind.

"My father used to say that love is as dangerous as a sharp blade. It's forged by the Master and it bears so much strength. It offers a sense of safety, even a comfortable peacefulness. But how do you protect yourself from it? If you're careless, or you disrespect it, a person can be fatally injured. If it's stolen from you... a person can lose their sense of peace, and they become vulnerable." Celia's thoughts lingered there a moment. "There is no substitute for inner peace." She paused briefly in her thoughts then pushed the unwelcome memories of her youth out of her mind as she agreed with her husband. "I think the house is a wonderful idea, Rueben. What can I do to help?" She snuggled next to him offering an appreciative hug.

"Well, you can start by getting me a scoop of that cream and some pie before those boys get a good nose full and treat it like it's their last meal." He glanced down to her; the twinkle in his eye was familiar. Celia knew they would be sharing a lot more before the night was over.

"I can do that." Celia stood up and began serving the pie while her husband's attention went to the work yard below the house. His loud, sharp whistle told everyone that the sweets would not last long.

They were cleaning up the supper dishes, and Celia couldn't help but notice the absent and dreamy frame of mind Estelle was displaying. Celia had already caught herself re-washing several dishes that were supposed to have gone in the cabinet after Estelle had dried them. Finally, her curiosity got the best of her.

"Estelle, how are things with you and Owen these days?" The question was like Celia turned on a faucet. Estelle's eyes pooled with huge tears.

"He asked me to marry him tonight," she blurted out.

"What?" Celia's face was full of surprise. "All ready?" Celia turned to her friend. "My goodness... when Owen Kagel makes up his mind to do something, he certainly doesn't waste any time with his efforts."

Estelle smiled suddenly and pressed her hand to her chest.

"Estelle, this is wonderful news! But, why are you crying? Did you tell him no?" That was an option that Celia had never considered.

"Oh... no, I said yes. I don't really know why I'm crying. I just can't seem to help myself. I suppose I just never thought I would have this blessing in my life. I'm 31 years old Celia, and..." she looked up to see tears in Celia's eyes as well. They burst in to laughter.

"Looks like we've got a wedding to plan," announced Celia happily. She embraced the woman and friend on whom she had come to depend.

CHAPTER 4

The next few weeks passed quickly. Owen spent all his spare time fixing up the old house place. He didn't know of the plans Cole and Rueben had in store for him and Estelle concerning the deed of the property.

The family worked diligently to restore the house inside and out to an updated tribute of yesteryear. The weak foundation was strengthened and leveled with sturdy, new blocks, while at the same time; framing new walls gave a fresh and practical function to tired spaces. The house needed modern conveniences to make it more comfortable and efficient. Owen and Estelle were limited when it came to household possessions, so one Saturday was spent shopping for housewares, appliances and furniture for themselves, as well as Charlie's room. Estelle had become a true sister to the boy, and she made it perfectly clear that no family decisions would be made without Charlie's opinion. Owen was so proud of her love and consideration for his family that he would have tried to change the location of the moon for her if she asked.

The huge, magnificent house was no longer rundown and sad looking, but reborn. The new tin roof, freshly painted porch planks, and decorative wooden accents on the outside of the old place were restored right down to the roof over the well in the backyard. Love and hope had breathed new life into the old house. The only thing missing was a pair of lovers to give it a heart.

They had chosen the first Friday night in September for the ceremony and the wedding day was fast approaching. Things around the ranch were busier than ever as Owen and Charlie were preparing to move within the next couple of days.

The house was enormous. Owen and Estelle grinned at each other the day they stepped into the massive dogtrot hallway that went all the way through the house to the French doors. The elaborate doorway presented the formal dining area and a sitting parlor on the left. It housed an old piano and joined the dining room. Cole had told them after supper Pa Silver would clean up the dishes in exchange for his mother playing the piano for him. Estelle loved the idea of the guests being able to retire to the music room after a meal. She kept their use as it was but gave both rooms a fresh coat of paint and some wallpaper.

The massive kitchen was on the right of the dining room and had a separate entrance from the hallway as well. A smaller set of French doors off the kitchen led to the back hallway where there was a sewing room, a canning pantry, a walk-in closet for storage and a door that led to the attic staircase. The barren attic was renovated into a comfortable and fashionable sleeping loft for guests; the space boasted a full bathroom and a generous walk-in closet. The huge pantry and storage room spanned the width of the kitchen. Owen left a substantial size pantry but took some space on the opposite side to make Estelle a separate washroom. This space housed the washing machine, a stainless utility sink, and a chest freezer. The washroom was connected to the kitchen by a wide hall which incorporated the doorway to the side porch, making it the entrance into the new mudroom. This space held a settler's bench, closet storage, and a designated rack for coats and shoes.

The front porch started at the double entry doors and wrapped all the way around the right side of the house to the mud room. The dogtrot separated the front of the house, offering three doors on either side. The rooms were versatile and could be customized for the family's changing needs. Each room had a working fireplace and was connected to the next by an inside doorway. The first door on the left was Charlie's private space. Estelle had wanted him to have the large room on the front of the house which was once the main parlor. It had a separate entrance onto the front porch and was connected to a smaller bedroom, which was styled into two walk-in closets and a private bathroom. Its size was as impressive as the rest of the large old house. She told Owen that as Charlie got older, he would appreciate the privacy factor of the space seeming more like an apartment than just a bedroom in the family house. When the time came that he didn't care to live with them anymore, she was sure they would find another use for it.

Estelle left the front room on the right as a guest room for Mama Kagel, the next was a large sitting parlor for her and Owen to relax and entertain company and the third was their bedroom. It was almost as large as the front parlor that had been converted for Charlie, and it had a private hallway that led to the original water closet and the kitchen. Owen staked claim to it the first time they walked into the room. He told her they needed to be as far away from Charlie as possible when they were together privately. She smiled at him and said nothing to discourage his way of thinking concerning the matter.

Estelle planned to move most of her things in the Thursday before the wedding, and she would join him as his wife on Friday evening as soon as their vows were sanctified.

Charlie asked if he and his school friend, Preston could spend the weekend in the bunkhouse with Cook and the other hands. They were going to help run fencing along the East Ridge on Saturday morning, and then fish and swim the rest of the Labor Day weekend before school started on Tuesday.

Preston's father, Colonel Dane Reid was retired from the army. He also had been a war consultant to Dwight D. Eisenhower in his glory years. He had married a local girl; it was a few months later that he was summoned by Eisenhower because of the changing security needs during his Presidency. The Colonel's job took over his life, and he came and went in their marriage at his convenience. She gave birth to Preston on her own, and she did so with pride. The Colonel came and went a few times after Preston was born. Preston was a toddler when the Colonel sold the house out from under them; after that, he didn't see his father for a long time. Preston and his mother moved into the old Willow Bend boarding house across the river in Denton County. His mother worked teaching piano lessons, and she opened a small gallery so local artists could display and sell their work. She took care of him alone until he was seven years old; she was immobilized by a brain tumor and died a few weeks later, leaving the youngster to be cared for by the older woman who owned the boarding house. That was until his father came back some four months later, to assume responsibility for him.

It was the second time in Preston's young life that Colonel Reid had up-rooted him from his home and familiar surroundings. The first time he was motivated by spite, but the second time was out of guilt.

The community knew Dane Reid in his younger years to be a quiet wanderer who lived with an older sister and stayed to himself. He worked at the Swift Gas Station every afternoon, and on Saturdays. He never really got into trouble, but he never seemed too far away from it either. He walked everywhere he went, and his cautious nature caused people to react to him in a negative way which only reinforced his harsh perspective of life. He enlisted in the service at 18 years old and learned how to apply his energy in constructive ways. He became a soldier who served his country before all else; his rebellious spirit was found to be useful for many duties, particularly the ones that were dangerous. He maintained a residence in town during his career in the service.

Dane Reid's civilian life was controlled by alcohol. He was known as a difficult and angry man. There were times when his son's face wore his temper. When Preston got older, Dane would leave the teenager for days at a time while fishing and binge drinking at a camp he owned on the river. No one in the community knew of anything Dane Reid did with his life other than fish, drink, and chase women.

Owen could see that Charlie was super sensitive to his friend. When Preston was around them, the boy's manners were that of an enlisted man in the presence of a superior officer. Owen would not allow Charlie to go to Preston's house to visit, but he and Estelle made it clear that Preston was always welcome in their home.

Everyone's attention had been captured by the joy and festivities which surrounded the wedding and the Appaloosas had been forgotten by everyone but Eli and Travis. Charlie was taking in the excitement and happiness of it all. He had never seen a wedding before and he was thrilled the legality in the ceremony would make Estelle his sister-in-law.

With only finishing touches to go, Owen left Eli and Travis to complete painting the backside of the house with the last coat, while he went to town to pick up the new plumbing fixtures they had ordered.

"I wonder when we're gonna get to mount 'em?" snapped Travis. He carelessly slapped at the side of the house with the paint brush.

Eli dipped his brush again and studied the lap board in front of him as he pulled the brush evenly over the surface.

"There ain't nothin' we can do about it Travis, not 'til Owen and Ms. 'Stele get married. Uncle Owen ain't got his mind on nothin' else right now. Daddy said we better mind our chores first and the day will come 'fore we know it that we can ride. 'Sides, it ain't like Lottie and Hobo are goin' anywhere. They belong to us. We just got to wait our turn. Remember? We promised. Daddy says, 'A man that can wait on the Lord, will have riches stored up in heaven'." Eli's attempt to appease his younger friend was genuine. He wanted to ride the horses too; however, they had made a deal, and he wasn't going to break it. Besides, he liked the grooming and feeding almost as much as he did the riding. He knew the animals did too.

"Well, the Lord ain't tha one waitin' to ride 'em... and He ain't tha one doin' all these chores neither," growled Travis. He looked up at the sun and shaded his eyes. "I'm hungry. Let's go get some lunch."

Travis haphazardly dropped his brush in the bucket of paint causing chunks of the white liquid to splash up the front of his overalls. The boy was as serious about chores as Tom Sawyer.

Eli watched Travis disappear around the corner of the big house they were painting. He wiped his brow on the shoulder of his tee shirt then swallowed the sticky salvia in his mouth. His stomach growled at the thought of a bacon and tomato sandwich, and a glass of his mama's sweet tea. Eli suddenly realized just how hot and thirsty he was, and that his stomach wanted to gnaw on a sandwich too. He looked back at the mess his friend had made, and his attention drifted some 25 feet to the end of the house that still needed a second coat of paint. He shook his head and released an exasperated sigh. He reasoned that they had at least another couple of hours of painting before they would be finished. He leaned over and smoothed the sloppy clumps of paint neatly over the surface of the board, the way it was supposed to be done. Once Eli was satisfied with the job, he put the lid on the paint bucket, placed the brushes in the paint thinner jar, and broke into a run towards home. His long strides passed Travis on the steps of the back porch.

The boys gobbled down their lunch as they had done for the last three weeks then headed for the barn to check on the Appaloosas. A fresh bucket of water and an apple were on the menu. When the animals saw them coming, they trotted to the fence to greet them.

Travis climbed up on the top rail and held out his hand. The apple was plucked from his palm by the soft snout of the mare. These animals were something that Travis had concentrated on since the day they had brought them home. He thought of little else when he was awake, and in sleep they galloped through his dreams. The deterrence of the wedding was on the verge of being aggravating, especially since the Appaloosas had been purchased before Owen proposed to Estelle. He thought nothing could be more important than these wonderful creatures. Even when he tried not to think about them, he could not stop it. He saw himself on the back of the animal, the wind in his face and nothing but green, rolling hills in front of him and the sky to keep them company. He even imagined the horses with wings like the picture he had seen in Mollie's storybook.

"Why can't we break'em, just us?" spouted Travis bitterly.

Eli looked over at his friend and reminded him again.

"It's harder than you think; besides... we promised. Remember? We gave our word that we would wait 'til Owen could oversee us, that's why!" Eli snapped at Travis just as Estelle called out to him from the patio. He jumped down from the fence and started toward the house. He was used to Travis' stubborn notions. Eli looked back over his shoulder in warning. "I'll be along in a minute, Travis. Those paint brushes ain't gonna move by themselves."

Eli helped Estelle push the last piece of living room furniture into place then stood there anxiously waiting for her to dismiss him. She gave him a sweet and appreciative smile as she patted his face, then she turned him abruptly and gave him a little push towards freedom. Eli was a sucker about helping his mother, or Ms. Estelle. Sometimes they needed someone strong. His father and Uncle Cole were not always available on this working ranch. Eli was told the day would come when he would be unavailable as well. It was something his mother pointed out to him occasionally; however, he couldn't imagine not being there when his mother needed him.

The back door slammed, and Eli leaped from the porch to the patio below. He steered his big feet toward the back walkway, careful to avoid the heavy blooms of his mother's roses. He inhaled their drugging scent as he ascended the back steps when suddenly an excited whinny drew his attention. He looked up just in time to see the stallion's back hoofs kick the top rail on the fence.

Eli screamed to the top of his lungs in warning.

"Travis! No!"

It was too late. He witnessed Travis sail through the air where he met an abrupt and horrifying smack against the side of the stable. Eli saw his friend fall to the ground like a squirrel that had been shot out of a tree.

Eli began running toward the corral as though there was a trail of fire chasing him. He reached Travis only to find his lifelong buddy lying motionless while blood soiled the dirt beneath his head.

"Travis, why couldn't you wait? Why?" Eli sobbed like the scared child he was.

Estelle had heard Eli cry out, and she knew that something terrible had happened. She reached him in a matter of seconds; Mollie and Scherry were on her heels. Estelle bent down to assess the situation. When she saw Travis lying in the pool of blood, an icy fear surged through her veins to cripple her reason.

It was Charlie that appeared by her side and acted quickly to the emergency at hand.

"Estelle, help me." Charlie folded Travis' arms over his chest and began scooping him up into their arms. They stood together holding him carefully. He shifted his little blood-brother against his chest as he spoke. "I'll get the truck. Eli, go get Mr. Silver. He's in the orchard with your parents. Hurry, 'E'... there's no time to waste. Tell 'em we're on our way to the hospital."

Before Estelle could say anything further, Eli jumped the saddled Appaloosa, and with a swift kick was over the corral fence and on his way. Eli did not even realize he was on the stallion until he was halfway to the orchard. The animal's gait was smooth and gentle. He was as responsive as any horse Eli had ever ridden. Together they soared faster than he knew was possible.

Rueben noticed the oncoming rider, and with his sight fixed on him he commented.

"Would you look at that?"

The pride in his son had no time to swell for Eli's warning cry rang in their ears.

"Daddy, Momma, where's Uncle Cole? Travis has been hurt bad! He ain't movin', Daddy. I couldn't get him to move!" Eli's dirty face was marked with streaks from his tears.

"What happened?" asked Rueben.

"He got throwed, Daddy! He hit the barn." Eli shook his head. "He's bleedin' bad. Ms. 'Stelle's takin' him to the hospital."

Rueben looked at Celia. They knew it had to be bad because Estelle did not know how to drive amidst traffic, especially with an injured child and two little girls in tow. Rueben went to the flat bed and began honking the horn to get Cole's attention.

Rueben gave Eli a task to accomplish while they retrieved Cole.

"Son ride that horse back to the stable. We'll get Cole and meet you there."

When they reached the house, Cookie informed them Charlie was the one to take charge of the situation and drove the injured boy and 'Stele to the emergency room. They didn't waste time by asking questions.

The trip into town was torture. Fear of the unknown gripped the adults' hearts and squeezed until no one could move, much less breathe. Eli relived the afternoon for them as they drove. Their imaginations played the horror over and over in their minds. Celia glanced down at the grip Cole had on her hand; her knuckles were white, and the circulation was gone. She knew what he was thinking, but no one dared voice it. She honestly didn't know if the man could deal with the loss of his son too.

The electric doors to the emergency room flew open, and the first thing they saw was Charlie sitting in the waiting area with his arm wrapped around little Mollie. She was plastered against his chest, one hand gripping the sleeve of his shirt and the other idly twisting her hair around her fingers. The look on her face was fearful. Scherry sat sideways in the chair next to them, Charlie's hat hung crooked on her head where he had tried to comfort her. Her hand was inside of his and an unnatural calm surrounded the three of them.

Cole went to the nurse's desk to see what he could find out. Eli held his arms out to Mollie and she went to him. The little girl rubbed her face into his shirt. She knew Travis was hurt, and she was scared. Eli patted her back as he held her tight.

"Mr. Silver, Travis is in room four," informed the nurse. "Dr. Jordan said for you to come on back." She pointed. "Go through those doors and take a right. It'll be the fourth door on the left."

Cole took a step toward the double doors but stopped. He looked back at Rueben and Celia. His throat constricted. Celia had to fight her emotions.

"Would you come with me?" His voice was shallow because fear had a tight grip on his wind.

Celia looked up at her husband as she slid her hand into Cole's. She attempted to hold it tighter than his fear could hold his heart.

Upon entering the small room, they were met by a friendly, yet unfamiliar face. A distinguished, young doctor stood and turned to offer his hand.

"Mr. Silver? I'm Dr. Joseph Jordan."

Cole nodded, but his eyes were fused on his son. Travis lay motionless on the table; a tight bandage capped his head. He was pale and too still for comfort. Estelle appeared by his side.

Dr. Jordan had conversed with Miss Fletcher about the child and the accident which had brought them to the emergency room. He discovered these people were his neighbors, and Travis was the friend his son, Joel, talked about all the time. The youngsters had met at church during the summer after he and Joel moved to the community. Dr. Jordan was relieved he had found a friend in another fourth-grade boy, so he would know someone at school this fall. Because of his son's kindred friendship with this boy, Joe Jordan was aware that Travis' mother had passed away three years ago. He had also learned that: Travis had turned nine years old two weeks ago, he could dig for worms faster than any dog could bury a bone, and his little sister had the exact same birthday as Joel. Dr. Jordan had not met this family yet because of his busy work schedule. He had attended church services several times but had arrived late because of his obligations to the hospital. Joe Jordan was the new trauma specialist on staff in the emergency room at Westville Memorial and for now, he was on call more than usual. He had hired a live-in housekeeper for them, but Joel had assured him he could safely ride his bike back and forth to church.

Dr. Jordan sensed Cole was on the edge of madness and he offered his compassion.

"Mr. Silver come sit down by your son. He's a fine boy."

Cole still said nothing.

Dr. Jordan looked at Celia; they exchanged silent concern.

"He's resting, Mr. Silver. Really, he's going to be all right." Dr. Jordan laid his hand on Travis' chest for a moment then patted him, so his father would not think him so fragile.

Tears welled up in Cole's eyes and his bottom lip quivered; still, he didn't make a sound.

Joe Jordan pulled off his glasses and retrieved a stool. He pulled it up next to the bed and sat down. His words offered genuine understanding.

"He's a strong boy, but he did take a good whack on the head. The impact was behind his ear. I put in ten stitches. He's got a concussion, and he's going to have a doozy of a headache for about a week, along with some dizziness. There was some bleeding from his eardrum. I can't be sure yet, Mr. Silver... it's possible that his hearing will be affected. We can't know that for a few days when the swelling goes down. He needs to stay overnight so we can keep an eye on him. It's precautionary. If there are no unexpected problems, then you can take him home tomorrow." Joe watched the large man for a moment. "Do you have any questions?"

"He looks so pale?" mumbled Cole.

"Yes. He bled a good bit. It's the trauma." He continued to observe the boy's father. "All children make bad decisions; it is part of growing up. I know those lessons were the hardest learned and they're the ones I remember most."

Dr. Jordan reached across the small bed and touched Cole's shoulder. Their eyes met for the first time.

"I live out your way, Mr. Silver. I bought the old Worsham place. If it's all right, I'll drop by to see Travis and keep a check on him. I have a boy his age. Joel talks about Travis all the time. I believe he was one of the 20 or so Royal Rangers campers you hosted a few weeks ago. I understand they're already great friends. Joel tells me he and your little girl have the same birthday."

Cole offered his hand to the doctor again in a more congenial manner.

"You're Joel's father?"

Dr. Jordan smiled and nodded his head.

"Please, call me Joe. You remember him out of so many! Hmm, should I be worried?" The doctor's words were playful as he accepted the gesture of friendship.

Cole's eyes went back to his son as he spoke.

"He's easy to remember because Travis has laughed more since he met Joel. That weekend they caught a catfish that took them nearly ten minutes to pull out of the pond. After all that effort... they put him back because they said he was so old he had an extra set of whiskers." Cole chuckled. "I have a picture of the three of them I bet you would like to have."

"As a matter of fact, I would." This momentous event had enabled them to connect as neighbors.

The bright, white uniforms the nurses wore complemented the subtle odor of disinfectant which lingered in the atmosphere. Cole went back to the waiting area while they prepared Travis to be moved to a room. He found the family anxiously awaiting news of Travis' condition, and Cole relayed the details with a confidence he had not possessed half an hour earlier. He thanked Estelle for taking control of the situation. She smiled but shook her head as she informed him that Charlie had been the one with a level head. Thanks to Charlie's quick thinking and driving skills, they had managed to get Travis to medical assistance within minutes of the accident.

Estelle hooked her arm around Charlie's elbow and kissed him square on the cheek.

"I don't know what I would have done without you, Charlie. I'm real proud to know that you're gonna be my brother." She hugged him because it was comforting to know that this young man was as solid as his brother.

This was the first time Charlie understood what it would be like to have this woman as his kin. It occurred to him that she was gentle and loving like his mother. He realized that it must be why Owen loved her like he did. A warm, contented feeling spread throughout Charlie's chest. When Estelle let go of him, Cole was waiting. The large man's mighty arms squeezed Charlie tight while he thanked him for helping the Lord save Travis. He felt respect and the vindication of trust in this man's embrace. The gesture reminded Charlie of how much they were a part of each other's lives, and an immense feeling of pride accompanied his contentment. Charlie could not help but respond, and he hugged Cole back. He swore to himself that he would never be so complacent that he would not thank God, every day for Owen and his friends who had come to rescue him that day.

Rueben took it upon himself to make plans for the next 24 hours. Since it was getting late, he and Celia would take the children home for their bath and pajama's. He handed Charlie a few bills and asked that he take the truck home, stopping at the drive-in along the way for enough hamburgers to feed the entire brood. Rueben told Cole he would return later with an overnight bag and something for him to eat.

When the nurse came to get Cole, the rest of the family began to make their way to the door. That was when Owen came running in with panic etched across his face.

Estelle hurried to meet him and explained what had happened.

"He's gonna be all right, Owen," she assured him lovingly.

Owen pulled her up next to him. Estelle's arms slid around his waist.

"Cole, I'm so sorry! I should have attended to those horse's weeks ago!" apologized Owen. Guilt haunted his voice and his expression.

"Owen, I don't see this matter as anyone's fault other than the impatient, hard-headed boy that chose to disobey. However, I'm thankful that the Lord saw fit to give it to him because it saved his life. Which horse was it anyway?" surveyed Cole.

"The stallion," answered Eli.

"The stallion? That's the horse you rode to the orchard," barked his father in surprise.

"Yes Sir." Eli shifted Mollie to the other arm. She had drifted off to sleep due to exhaustion from all the confusion.

"If the horse wasn't broke… and it threw Travis, how did you ride him to the orchard?" His father sounded confused.

Eli shrugged his shoulders.

"He just responded to me," he exclaimed.

Cole reached for Mollie's little hand, caressing it tenderly between his rugged fingers.

Celia offered to stay with Travis, but Cole wouldn't hear of it.

"I need to spend some time with him by myself. Don't worry," he assured her. "We'll be fine."

The house was still and quiet as Eli lay in his bed. The day's events kept his mind busy. His thoughts stayed on the stallion and the gentleness in his response. He shivered with excitement from the memory of the surge of power he felt pounding the earth beneath him. They had looted the wind with a swiftness like a force of nature. He wondered when he would get another chance to ride the magnificent animal. He envisioned the stallion as a magical creature, his hooves throwing sparks as they pounded the earth and then they galloped over the surface of Cloud Lake. A smile crept over the boy's face. This horse was truly amazing and special, and he hoped to form a lifelong friendship with him.

The next morning, Travis opened his eyes to full consciousness. He found his father stretched out in the chair, his ankles crossed in front of him and his hands clasped behind his head.

"Good morning," greeted Cole quietly. He leaned forward to touch his son. "You're at the hospital. You got jolted off the stallion. Do you remember?"

Travis frowned at his father and Cole remembered Travis' hearing was in question.

"Can you hear me, Travis?"

The boy nodded his head.

"I... I have a headache." His voice was weak and shaky.

"The doctor said you would probably be dizzy too. You've got stitches behind your ear, and some inner damage that may result in a permanent loss of hearing," explained Cole. When he finished, he sat and waited for his son to reply.

Travis could feel his father's eyes on him and he understood the nagging discomfort that was swelling up inside him. His chest hurt. It wasn't from his injuries, but from disappointment in himself and the shame he felt from not keeping his word. He looked at his father; the pain in his body seemed unimportant for he knew he had undermined the trust his father had placed in him. Trust was the foundation on which their lives were built. It was what made their family work.

"Daddy," Travis' voice was louder this time when he spoke, and it was full of sincerity. "I didn't keep my word to you and Uncle Rueben about the horses. I'm sorry, I know I deserve to be punished. I'll do whatever you say, and I'll understand. I don't deserve to claim one of them anymore. If you can't trust your own son... then... I... I..."

Cole studied his son's eyes as he confessed to disobedience; he realized that Travis would become a fine man one day. It made him very proud.

"The first step to becoming a good man is to realize a mistake, admit it, and then you correct it. I think you've just done two of them. I love you, Travis, and I'm very proud of you."

The boy searched his father's face as hot tears burned his cheeks.

"I love you too, Daddy."

For Cole, the moment was priceless. Like himself, Travis had been deeply hurt and misplaced by his mother's death. These were the first tears Cole had seen from his son since the day of the funeral. Cole stood and pressed a kiss to his son's forehead while he held Travis' little hand tenderly inside his large one. He was truly thankful that the Almighty had protected his son and made a lesson of his pain in the process.

"I guess I better go see about getting you moving this morning. I'll tell the nurse that you're ready for some breakfast." He started for the door then stopped and glanced back to the boy. "Travis, I'll decide your punishment when you get to feeling better. That ought to take care of the correcting it."

Travis looked at his father with an understanding smile and nodded his head.

The wedding day was upon them. The front of the church was simple but beautifully decorated with two candle-stands sporting nine tapers in each. They were accompanied by three, column-like pedestals adorned with ferns which stood behind Pastor Storey. Estelle was lovely and glowing with happiness.

She had made her own dress out of antique silk. The sleeves were full and gathered at the elbow by a small cuff. The midriff was a solid silk and styled with a drop waist in the front and back; it was enhanced by the elegant full skirt which fell to the floor in soft tufts of silk lined lace and tapered into a dramatic six-foot train. Estelle had added her own special touch of small teardrop pearls sewn to the midriff at every other inch and pearl buttons on the cuffs. It added the personal finesse that was Estelle's overall personality. The silk lined, lace collar stood high around her long neck while the same unlined lace plunged into a daring bodice that demurely hinted at her feminine body. Celia had encouraged her to buy the pattern when they found it in the fabric store. After careful thought, Estelle decided she would like to do something elegant and yet, daring for a change. Owen was the man she was about to marry, and she wanted him to desire her.

Estelle wanted to respect tradition, so she wore an antique Cameo that Celia had given her as a special thank you for all that she did to make the woman's life easier. She pinned it to the base of her collar to represent something old. She held a linen handkerchief trimmed with a blue ribbon that was borrowed from Owen's mother. Estelle's wedding ensemble was completed by the new husband on her arm, and the new life they would build together. Estelle had asked Celia to stand up with her as did Charlie for his brother. The ceremony was traditional and beautiful.

The reception was a glorious celebration underneath a constellation of diamond-like stars. Celia had decorated the patio with fresh flowers, paper streamers and bells, and oil lanterns. She had white tables and chairs distributed throughout the garden, and a reception table full of goodies which made a person's mouth water and your stomach growl. The festive table was loaded with: spicy meatballs and little sausages, hot cheese dip, spinach quiche, fresh vegetables and fruit with creamy dips, peppered crackers, and smoked brisket with hot sourdough rolls and sweet mustard. The centerpiece of the buffet was the round table which held a five-layer wedding cake. It glistened with sugary white roses and candy pearl swags, and the scent of sweet French vanilla was drugging. Owen's laughter filled the evening air when he saw the groom's table. The guests gathered around to watch and chuckle at the unusual groom's cake. The comical mountain of chocolate fudge was shaped like a tractor and iced with the traditional green and yellow colors. It was stuck in a pond of chocolate pudding with a candy figure, which bore an uncanny likeness to Owen, sitting at the steering wheel while a crew of farm animals attempted to push him out of the bog. The newlyweds ended up with fudge on both their faces, and a happy smile in the middle of it as they posed for the photographer.

Estelle had included Owen's mother in as much of the wedding planning as the older woman could stand. During the process, Estelle had begun to refer to her as Mama Kagel. Owen had suggested she take her name back since that horrible season of her life was over. It had made Patti very happy to share the same name as her boys again, and to gain a daughter. The day of the wedding, Patti Kagel's sons checked her out of the nursing home so their mother could participate in this special day. She cried at the ceremony and clapped her hands with joy. She celebrated this happy occasion with her sons and absorbed all the happiness a mother could feel. The older woman giggled like a girl as Lucien danced her around the patio while she stood on the toes of his boots. Estelle even encouraged Preston to the dance floor while Pastor Storey and Charlie played the guitars and sang some traditional western tunes. The guests ate until they were stuffed. It was a party like none other they had ever had at the ranch.

No one noticed as Travis piled a second piece of vanilla cake on top of the plated one in his hand. He nosed around the table of food, selectively adding a few other things he knew she liked. He walked away from the celebration with the intension of finding, Scherry, who had disappeared shortly after arriving home from the church. He found her across the street, sitting in her favorite tree, on the massive limb that loomed out over the pond. She was still wearing the long and frilly, white flower-girl dress, matching satin slippers, and the flower wreath was still in her dark, curly hair. He thought she was pretty on a normal day, but today she was dressed like a princess and she glowed in the moonlight. He hoped nobody had noticed, but he had stared at her most of the day. He was curious about the way a girl could look so different depending on what she wore and how she fixed her hair.

He called to her; she smiled down at him and dared him to come up. He stepped up into the first elbow of the low limb and then handed her the plate to hold while he climbed the rest of the way. She scooted over as usual and he settled in next to her. The plate got jilted in the movement and the fork fell into the pond, so they ate with their fingers as they talked about the day.

She asked him if he still had a headache.

He was honest with her and confessed that he had made a mistake in disobeying his father, and he deserved the headache. She smiled at him and her eyes seemed to reflect the stars above them. He told her he had never seen her with flowers in her hair and he liked it.

The subject naturally changed to the wedding. They had never participated in one before today and it had fascinated them. Scherry asked him what made Owen and Estelle different now after the wedding.

Travis told her that they got to live with each other like her parents.

Scherry thought about that a moment and pointed out that they lived together, and they were not married, then she asked for specifics.

Travis told her they would sleep in the same bed, laugh and giggle at night. They would go to the grocery store together and she would take care of Owen's house, his cooking and dirty clothes. He told her they could kiss and hold each other whenever they took a notion to and that Estelle could have a baby now, like his mama gave his daddy, Mollie.

His answers brought silence to her for a moment.

Travis couldn't stop staring at her. She looked so different in girl clothes and with the flowers in her hair. He liked it very much. When she asked him why he kept looking at her, he told her the truth; she was even prettier than Ms. Estelle, in that dress.

She told him she had seen Owen and Estelle kiss in the garden one night in the moonlight. She asked him if kissing was just for grown-ups.

He told her he didn't think so because he had seen Preston kiss a girl at the carnival back in the summer.

She held her sugary fingers up to his mouth to offer him the last bite of cake. Travis opened his mouth, and she sat it on his tongue. She asked him if he might want to kiss her one day.

Travis smiled as he chewed the cake and thought about this proposal. He nodded his head as he swallowed the pastry. He asked her if she wanted him to do so now while there was no one around to see them.

She agreed.

Travis took her hand then leaned over and pressed his lips to hers and closed his eyes like he had seen Preston do. He held them against hers a moment thinking something specific was supposed to happen. The sweet aroma of the vanilla mixed with their warm breaths did stir his senses. Her lips were also warm, sweet and soft. He pulled away and looked at her.

Scherry asked him why he closed his eyes if she was so pretty.

Travis shrugged his shoulders. He told her they were supposed to feel a kiss, not stare at one.

She asked him to kiss her again, so she could feel it.

Travis kissed her again.

When they opened their eyes, Scherry smiled and nodded her head as though she understood. She asked him if he was planning on kissing a lot of girls as he got older.

Travis shook his head and told her that he was happy just kissing her.

She smiled and tilted her head to one side as she looked at him. She asked him if he thought they could get married one day; she said she would like to sleep next to him.

Travis thought on this a moment and reasoned that it was one of the private times that was restricted between them. He also considered that they had never been told they couldn't marry each other. Suddenly, Scherry's mother's voice echoed through the darkness in summons of her.

Travis turned toward the house and saw that cars were leaving; he told her that they better go. He started the climb down first then waited to make sure she didn't get tangled up in the dress and fall out of the tree into the pond. He reached up and caught her hand to help her with the final jump. They held hands until they got to the house.

The reception was winding down and Lucien had offered to take Owen's mother back to Whispering Oaks. The wedding had seemed to energize the entire community. It was a day that everyone would remember, and some would cherish for years to come.

As the night closed in on them, the look of yearning grew in Owen's eyes. Rueben called for all the family and guests who had lingered to gather around the happy couple. They were handed a roll of paper fastened with a satin ribbon.

"What's this?" exclaimed Owen. Estelle shook her head and stepped closer as he unrolled the scroll. He held it up to the light of one of the gas lanterns, so they could read it. Owen's eyes grew large with surprise, and Estelle's filled with tears.

Rueben spoke up.

"Owen, we want you and Estelle to have your own home and land, and well, we want it to be with us. You've been our right arm. Your belief in our dreams never faltered, even when we were weary... you believed. We think of the three of you as a family, and well... we love all of you. We hope you'll accept the house place. We hope y'all will stay... build and share your lives with us."

Owen's voice was humble as he told them there was no other place he and Estelle would rather be. His wife nodded her head in agreement because she was too emotional to speak. It was with great joy that Owen, Estelle and Charlie reaffirmed their commitment to be a part of this family.

CHAPTER 5

The fall brought gusts of crisp, cool wind and colorful foliage that was breathtaking. A wintery cold snap had swept across the northern part of Texas, dumping some unexpected weather on the ranch. Owen, Estelle and Charlie had settled into the large, comfortable house. There was excitement in the air because Thanksgiving was only days away, and Estelle was baking and decorating for the holidays. Charlie considered himself rich beyond measure. He loved his life, and his sister-in-law's cooking. He also treasured his own personal space and the possessions he had been encouraged to choose which added an extra measure of comfort to his daily routine. He never dreamed he would be so blessed.

Charlie had favored the pull-out sofa that Owen already owned; it was where he had slept when he moved in. Since the room was so large, he asked if he could keep it. He checked out a book from the library then studied the practical, how-to instructions before removing the worn fabric from the sofa. Charlie recovered it with dark brown suede and placed it in his room along with the refinished sofa table. It turned out so good that Estelle made him some thistle-blue throw pillows that had a small tan horseshoe on each. The second-hand store called about a claw-footed tub they had located for her. When she went to look at it, she noticed two squatty, but over-sized chairs. They had heavy walnut-knob feet, and the arms were supported by a hand carved, galloping stallion. The worn and crinkled leather that covered them was a perfect effect to the overall design. She thought they were a perfect addition to the large Indian print rug in front of the sofa which boasted a beautiful array of earth and sky colors. She knew Charlie would love them, so she bought them, and the tub for his bathroom.

She and Charlie arranged the pieces in a private sitting space which complemented the fireplace. He even had his own radio and stereo. He was happy. But they told him he still needed some other things in a room so large, and surprised him with the heavy walnut dresser, a matching chest of drawers and the queen bed with large square posts. The black wrought iron bars designed into the footboard and headboard gave it a masculine edge. A trundle mattress beneath it could be pulled out for company. Estelle had asked his opinion about the pieces a few weeks earlier when they were looking for some other furniture items to go in the house. He had never seen anything so fine, and he told her so, but had assumed he was representing his brother's opinion concerning the pieces. He had never dreamed they were for him. His family wanted him to feel free to have company over on a regular basis. He felt as though he had his own little apartment, with his own front door that opened onto the front porch. He treated his space like he had the privilege of living in the White House. He kept everything in a certain order and cleanliness was a must.

The November night bordered on frigid. The northern wind danced in the trees outside his window while pings of ice struck the metal roof. The sky and the radio had been threatening snow all day. He had never seen snow before, at least not in any accumulation; he thought of it as something magical. Charlie had not been long turning out his light from studying his history for the next day's test, when he was awakened from a warm, sound sleep. The spring on the front screen door stretched and a soft knock followed it. It was Preston's knock.

Charlie tossed his cover back and hurried to the door that opened to the front porch. He did not turn the light on because he did not want to alarm or disturb his family. He had glanced at the clock and he knew it was after midnight. Charlie opened the door to his friend and found him standing there in a white short-sleeve undershirt, jeans and barefooted. Because Preston just stood there a few moments, Charlie knew something bad had happened to his best friend. He began to worry that maybe Preston couldn't speak. Finally, he heard his friend sniffling.

"Charlie, I'm sorry man. I got nowhere else to go." Preston's voice had changed during the last year, along with his physique.

"Preston... man, come in here! It's freezing," insisted Charlie softly.

Preston's head was down, but he did as Charlie said. Charlie closed the door and locked it then he pushed his friend over to the sofa in front of the fireplace. He saw that Preston's feet were almost purple and his undershirt was stained with blood.

He went to his closet and took out a woolen quilt and an extra pillow. Charlie stopped at the dresser for a thick pair of his hunting socks, a pair of boxers, a thermal shirt and some flannel pajama bottoms. He placed the clothing on the sofa next to Preston then fanned out the wool quilt and draped it around his shoulders. He tossed the pillow on the arm of the sofa as he sat down in the chair across from his friend to assess the situation.

"You should get a hot bath, Preston. You know where everything is... so help yourself to the closet and whatever else you need. Have you eaten anything today?"

Preston shook his head.

"I'm hungry too... roast beef and Swiss on wheat, okay?"

"Yeah, that sounds great," breathed Preston.

Charlie stood and headed toward the bedroom door when Preston mumbled his name. He looked back at his friend.

Preston looked up at him; he could barely see out of his right eye. His jaw and chin were raw and swollen, his nose was bleeding and his bottom lip was split open. Charlie noticed Preston's shaky hands; his knuckles were bloody too. He had started fighting back a few months ago, and he wondered what Dane looked like. That was what Preston called his father; he refused to call him Colonel anymore because he was a disgrace to the soldier he used to be.

"I hate to ask, but... I think you need to wake Mr. Owen. I think the sheriff is going to come for me this time. I had to hit him hard to get him to let go... then I just ran. He's never taken a fall from one of my punches before... he didn't come after me. I'm scared, Charlie. He's a drunk, mean bastard, but... he's still my father."

"Get out of those wet things... put on some socks and get warm, Preston. I'll be back in a minute."

Charlie cracked the door to Owen and Estelle's bedroom and peeked inside; they were resting and had not been disturbed. He hated to do it, but his buddy needed them. Charlie stepped over to the bed and touched his brother's shoulder. Owen's eyes popped open instantly. He looked at Estelle first before noticing him standing there in the darkness. He sat up. Charlie didn't say anything as he turned and exited the room back to the kitchen. Owen was only a few seconds behind him.

"What's wrong, Charlie?"

Charlie didn't waste any time in telling his brother what was happening as he mechanically took out the things needed to make a sandwich.

"He's pretty bad, Owen. He asked me to wake you. He said you would need to call the sheriff to come get him this time. He's scared he hurt his father when he tried to get away from him. I'm scared for him, Owen. He's never been beat up this bad."

Owen could see the ominous fear in his little brother's eyes. It had been a while since he had seen it, but it was still familiar. Some things can be rooted so deeply by life that they never leave you.

"Hey, are you two hungry again?" Estelle's sleepy voice turned their heads. She tied her robe then pushed her flowing red locks back from her face as she snuggled beneath her husband's arm.

Owen's embrace welcomed her with a squeeze as he pressed his lips to her forehead.

She pulled away slightly when she saw Charlie's worried eyes and her husband's stiff jaw.

"What is it?" She knew her husband was all right, so she instinctively went to Charlie and touched his forehead to see if he were ailing.

He thoughtfully clasped her hand inside of his when he spoke.

"Preston's here, Sis," stated Charlie.

Estelle was on her way up the hall before either of them had the chance to warn her. She knocked but opened the door to Charlie's room without waiting. She stopped short when she saw the young man wrapped in a blanket and huddled on the couch in front of the fire. He stood respectfully at the sight of her. She flipped on the light.

"Preston!" Her voice was strangled by her concern. She went to him and lifted his chin, so she could inspect his face in the light.

"I'm sorry, Ms. 'Stelle... I..."

"Hush, Preston," she told him softly. "Are you hurt anywhere else?" She pushed the blanket back like a mother and quickly inspected the blue hand marks on his neck then his bottom lip. This was the third time this had happened since she and Owen were married. She fought back the tears as she shook her head. Estelle could not help herself, and she wrapped her arms around him and hugged him for a long moment. She forced herself to swallow her emotions, so she could focus on his immediate needs.

"Sit down before you fall down, Preston," commanded Estelle with a voice as gentle as an angel. "Are any bones broken, Sweetie?" She knelt in front of him.

Owen hung up the phone and followed them to Charlie's room. He had seen another side of his wife emerge when she saw Preston the first time. He had not shared with her the details of that horrible night his family's life changed forever. He thought it was probably a good thing they weren't a couple then, if it meant protecting Charlie, or she would have tried to spar with L.B. Thomas all by herself. She had vowed she would file charges against the Colonel if this happened again.

Owen stepped up behind her.

"I called Sheriff Cotton, Preston. He's going to go by your father's place first." Owen inspected the young man in front of him. He had become a familiar face in the last few years. Owen had been truly glad when Charlie found a friend his age. He had never had the chance to do that because L.B. Thomas had never allowed outsiders to come into the house. Preston was a year older than Charlie, but they had become the best of friends. The boys had things in common that Owen was only now beginning to understand. Preston wasn't quite as tall as Charlie, but he was strong and carved with lean, powerful muscles. The conflict of late was Preston could defend himself now and his drunken father had not figured it out yet. If Preston gave as good as he got tonight, then Owen was a bit apprehensive about the Colonel's condition as well.

"Why? I don't understand how he can hurt you like this?" mumbled Estelle.

Preston defended him.

"He's an alcoholic, Ms. 'Stelle. He's been trained to not feel, but he's out of practice. When reality closes in on him and makes him feel the things that hurt, he drinks it away. I think he tries to drown the guilt he feels over my mother dying while he was gone tending to someone else's needs other than his own. I remind him of her; it causes him pain to look at me. He loses control when he reaches a certain point... most times I can stay out of his way, but tonight wasn't that night." Preston shook his head. "I hate him so much... but I love him just as much."

Estelle's soft, warm hand touched his cheek. The glow of the fireplace made her long red curls glisten as they fell over her shoulder, her skin was pale and smooth, and her blue eyes were the color of wild clover that covered the ground in the west pasture beneath the sad oak. He thought Mr. Owen was the luckiest man in the world, for other than his mother, Estelle was the gentlest and most beautiful woman he had ever known. He had wondered more than once if this God they spoke of so often had made another like her. If so, he surely wasn't good enough to hope for her.

"You are a good son, Preston... no matter what you think... no matter what is forced upon you. I do know what it's like to be made to feel like you're a disappointment by someone who is supposed to love you. But don't dwell on it... and don't believe it, Honey, because it's not true. You're special, Preston. God has a special plan for you. You have leadership qualities like your father. But you are blessed with a heart for people and you have as much courage, if not more, than most grown men. These qualities in you will be used when the time is right. Trust me, Preston... you have all the qualities of a good man." She smiled at him as she caressed his jaw, then she stood and took a step back while she tugged on his hand. "Charlie will eat your sandwich and mine too if we don't stop him. I have some loaded potato soup to go with that sandwich. Come on."

They nibbled while Preston ate. Estelle had nursed his hands and cleaned his face up somewhat. He assured them he didn't need a doctor.

Sheriff Emmett Cotton drove into the gravel driveway at the Kagel residence at 2:00 a.m. He called dispatch with his location before he got out and went to the back door where the light was on inside the house. He started to knock, but Owen opened the door before he got a chance. They greeted each other with a friendly hand shake. Ned Ingram, the Sheriff's second in command, followed him and was welcomed in the same manner.

Estelle greeted them respectfully as she poured each of them a cup of coffee; it was accompanied by a small plate which held a wedge of Vanilla-Buttermilk pie. They sat down at the kitchen table as though they were neighbors visiting. The sheriff picked up the cup and took several swallows before he addressed the reason he was there.

Preston was scared. He had known this man to hold one authoritative position or another in Liberty County his entire life. He knew Emmett Cotton to be a fair and just man. It wasn't the sheriff he was afraid of but, in his case, the rule of law that he represented and would have to enforce. He looked the man in the eye as he spoke to him and truthfully answered his questions about the relationship between himself and his father. Sheriff Cotton told him his father was all right other than being passed out in a stupor. The sheriff told him that they put his father on the couch on his stomach, so he could sleep it off. Preston was surprised when Sheriff Cotton told him he was worried about him. He tilted the boy's face up to the light. The man sitting across from him seemed larger than life, yet kind and respectful of other people and their problems. He assured Preston that he would file charges, on his behalf, against his father. He explained it was the only way he knew to get the Colonel's attention and make him understand; he could not keep treating Preston this way.

"I appreciate it, Sir... but... it won't get his attention. Besides, he's all I got in the world. If you file charges, you'll have to arrest him. That means the welfare people get involved because I'm a minor, and I go to a state home." Preston shook his head. "I'll stay out of his way until I turn 18. I swear Sheriff... I won't be a bother to you anymore. Please, I don't want to go to one of those places."

Sheriff Cotton studied the young man for a moment and as always that lonesome ache moved over his chest every time, he saw the boy. The young man looked like his beautiful mother, Caroline Janee Breaux, and he too was victimized by the arrogant and hateful man she married.

Sheriff Cotton had gone to school with Preston's mother when they were kids. She was two years younger than him and, at the time, insignificant to his active agenda named Vicki Rushing. Caroline was a pretty girl but reserved and shy which made it difficult to get to know her. He remembered how mysterious she seemed when they were children and because of it, a lot of the kids were mean to her. They called her a mouse-girl, and some talked about her elusive family and her river pirate grandfather stealing their fortune from other boats on the river. Other than the teachers, she never looked anyone in the eye, and she always ate lunch by herself with her head in a book. That was the way he had remembered her as a girl, the woman in his memory was something completely different. *He recalled the day he turned the corner in the hallway at school and slammed into her. Even though the tardy bell was ringing he stopped and picked her up out of the floor then gathered her books as he apologized. He knew who she was, and that she lived just beyond the edge of town in the large two-story mansion that everybody thought was haunted. He was intrigued by it and the rumors he had grown up hearing about an old ghost that roamed the property. His father had taken him there one Halloween to prove there was no ghost. Since then, he rode past it every chance he got in hope that the spirit was real, and he would catch a glimpse of him.*

That day, he forgot about the ghost, because he had met a living breathing part of Whisper Bluff. He was surprised when she met his attention with large, penetrating eyes that were so blue they were almost purple. He thought she was appreciative because of the courtesy he had shown to her. She smiled a thank you, and he realized that it was a beautiful thing. He would never forget the perfect, plump shape of her lips. When her eyes relocated to his arm, she reached out and touched the scratch he had acquired during their mishap. He remembered, even now, the physical charisma given off by the tips of her fingers; it was a warm charge that had stimulated his skin as a boy and electrified his body as a man.

That was the day he discovered that there was indeed a mystery about her. He handed her the small stack of books that she had held then told her he would see her around and walked away. He had physically bound himself to Vicki Rushing, and she was pregnant with his child. But he had thought of the dark-haired gypsy with bluish-violet eyes, knowing that she could cast a spell with only a glance, and speak through the tips of her fingers. He had not understood it then, but she had taken a piece of him that day when she touched him and gave a piece of herself in return.

When they collided again in their adult years, it was like fate had given them another chance, only this time it was Caroline that was bound in a relationship. He was still lost in that living fantasy. His time with this young man's mother had trapped his heart in a parallel reality that caused his mind to contemplate yesterday more than it did today. Those days with her had left him with so many unanswered questions. She had cast the spell of a memory over him and left it to grow wild, and its roots deep inside of his soul. God help him, he had found that to be the truth. It was one of those momentous things that happen in life which you wish you could go back and relive to change in your favor.

Emmett studied the young man for a moment; he had always felt a bond with the boy that he had tried to resist. Today, he asked himself why? It was his job to protect this young man. He had not been able to protect his mother from the man's tyrannical temper, but he was going to protect her son if it killed him. He owed it to her, and to what they once were to each other.

"Sheriff?" Estelle's soft voice stirred him from his thoughts. "Can I warm your cup?" She smiled and held the coffee pot up as he made eye contact with her.

Cotton thanked her and slid his cup towards her with a smile. His attention went to Preston again as he concentrated on the immediate problem.

"I realize that it probably doesn't take much to set him off, but I have to do something, Preston. My conscience won't allow me to ignore this. I understand that you don't want me to press charges, but son... I need you to understand that the law requires me to contact him. What kind of lawman would I be if I didn't? He needs to understand I know he has a problem. He needs to stop hurting you, Preston. You don't deserve to live this way." Cotton paused as he saw the boy's mother in his mind with her arms stretched out and spinning around in place. The gesture was something her grandmother taught her to do as a girl to change her mood; she did it as an adult to make fun of herself when she got too serious. A new perspective moved in his spirit. He had always tried to be respectful of the man Caroline had chosen, but not anymore. He had made up his mind. He was going to establish a connection with this young man because he had cared so deeply for his mother.

"I grew up with your mother, Preston; we were good friends. She would be very disappointed in me if I didn't try to change this situation. I owe it to her, and I owe it to you as a resident of this county.

There's a fine line between love and hate. Things can happen so fast when violence gets the upper hand. I don't want to get called out about you and be too late to change the consequences. Do you understand?"

Preston swallowed the emotion that was rising in his throat. He was to the point that he couldn't speak, so he nodded his head that he understood.

Cotton picked up the mug that Estelle had refilled with hot coffee while he tried to figure the boy's age.

"You've just turned... what... 16, Preston?" surveyed Cotton.

"Yes Sir... on October 9," answered the young man.

Cotton's head rose suddenly, and his attention met the boys gaze again. Preston's eyes were every bit as blue and deep with feeling as his mother's. He studied the young man's features and saw nothing of Dane Reid in them. Finally, Cotton took hold of his wandering mind and secured a plan for the boy.

"Owen, can you and Estelle find room for him a couple of days?"

"Absolutely, Sheriff... Preston knows he's always welcome here."

Sheriff Cotton became absorbed in the details of Preston's face again. There was something in this boy's eyes that weighed heavy on his mind and heart. The young man had never been in trouble, and he always stopped and spoke to him with courtesy and manners which would make his mother proud. He was not a delinquent even though his father treated him like one. When his mind ventured to the day, he had discovered she was pregnant, Cotton caught himself. He refocused his mind before his preoccupation with the young man became obvious. It was then that he noticed the dark stains around the young man's fingernails, and it gave him inspiration.

"Have you got a driver's license yet, Preston?" asked the sheriff.

"No Sir. That's not likely," responded the young man.

"Do you know anything about engine mechanics?"

Preston nodded his head as he spoke.

"Yes Sir, I rebuilt the motor in my mother's old '32 coupe. Dane sold it before I could drive 'er."

Cotton remembered that car. It had left Caroline stranded more than once. He thought of Dane Reid and construed that he wasn't any more dependable than the car. Cotton wasn't surprised that he had sold it.

"How are your grades at school?"

Charlie spoke up on behalf of his friend.

"He's on honor roll, but he won't tell you that."

Preston glanced to his friend. He knew Charlie was in his corner even if he had promised to keep that to himself.

"Can you handle school... and a part-time job, Preston?"

Preston studied the sheriff's eyes; there was something in them that stirred a huge amount of respect in him. This man was trying to help an impossible situation.

"Yes Sir, but Dane..." he stopped mid-sentence when Cotton's hand went up.

"I need a man to help out at the county barn. We must maintain all our county vehicles and that includes all the patrol cruisers as well. You will have to take instruction from Floyd Cox, the head mechanic. Are you interested?"

"Yes Sir!" Preston tried to smile. His buddy, Charlie, had worked a paying job for almost two years and Preston liked the idea of being a working man. He had not had the opportunity since Dane Reid was not well thought of in the county; it was hard to be the Colonel's son without his reputation having a negative effect on Preston's life daily.

Sheriff Cotton stood then without thinking about it, he ran his large palm over Preston's short hair.

"I'll be by to get you tomorrow afternoon at 3:30, Preston. There are a couple of things we need to do before you can start. Will that be all right with you?"

"Yes, Sir, I'll be ready," answered Preston.

"All right then... I'll see you tomorrow." He smiled at the young man then shook his hand. "Try to get some sleep."

Owen walked Cotton and Ned out to the porch. He assured Cotton that Preston was safe with them and welcome in their home.

Preston felt better after the meal. He swallowed the aspirins Estelle gave him then took a hot shower. He lay down on the bed his friend had made him on the pull-out in front of the fire and released a weary breath. Tomorrow was Friday and his father would be at the roadhouse over in Denton as usual on the weekends. He wished that he could have a quiet life like Charlie, living with people who cared about you and loved you no matter what. He thought about the older man that sat with him tonight like a gentleman; he had treated him as 'Preston' rather than Dane Reid's boy. Preston admired him and fell asleep while picturing himself in a uniform like the sheriff's.

The following morning, Preston got up and got ready for school with Charlie. Owen pointed out that it was Friday and tried to convince the young man to take the day and the weekend to heal a little before subjecting himself to a lot of questions. Preston told him he had two mid-terms he couldn't miss.

Owen loaned Preston a pair of jeans, a shirt and a worn pair of lace up boots, because his was a better fit than Charlie's clothes. Estelle insisted he wear a jacket too because of the temperature. When they got off the bus that afternoon, Estelle had his jeans and tee shirt clean and free of blood. He and Charlie had a glass of milk and a slice of hot banana-nut bread before Charlie went to work. Preston sat on the porch and waited for the sheriff. The sun had liquefied all signs of the previous night's ice.

Sheriff Cotton pulled into Owen's driveway at 3:30 p.m. just as he said he would. Preston got in the vehicle and Sheriff Cotton handed him a driver's manual as he spoke.

"Are you familiar with that at all, Preston?"

Preston looked at it and smiled. It was getting easier to do when he was around this man.

"That grin tells me you are." Sheriff Cotton told Preston that he had spent an hour with his father that afternoon and the Colonel had agreed to let him work for the county.

"How did you manage that, Sir?"

Sheriff Cotton smiled.

"I told him I needed a smart young man who was mechanically inclined, and that you had been recommended. He thinks it will be good for you and give you direction in life."

Preston was quiet.

Cotton stopped at the flashing light on Highway 5.

"He told me that you were the boy I was looking for. I didn't tell him you were studious, Preston; he should know that already. Anyway, I asked him about his black eye. He was up front and told me that you gave it to him, but that he had asked for it. He didn't tell me anymore than that. I reminded him that he could borrow trouble from the law with that kind of behavior. He said he was a hard man... too hard sometimes. I told him I would pick you up this afternoon and show you the ropes at the garage. He assumed you were at school."

Cotton turned and headed to Westville while he talked to Preston like a man.

"It doesn't matter what his misguided reason tells him, Preston... it's a small price to pay for peace of mind. Don't you think?"

"Yes Sir. I appreciate what you're trying to do for me, Sheriff."

They pulled into the local state highway patrol office next door to the county jail. There was an old relic of an Army Jeep parked in front which had a fresh primer job on it and new tires. Sheriff Cotton held up a set of keys.

"Do you understand the concept of a standard H shifter?"

"Yes Sir. I drove the hay truck in the west pasture for Owen last week, it was pretty simple."

Cotton nodded his head.

"What about the driver's manual? Could you pass a written test?"

Preston handed the driver's license to the sheriff with a proud smile. It was an unexpected opportunity that had been given to him and he had accomplished it because this man had given him a chance to prove himself.

Cotton looked at the state issued license and read it out loud.

"Let's see... Preston G. Breaux Reid, Texas Department of Motor Vehicles." Cotton smiled at the young man not realizing that he would feel so much satisfaction in his accomplishment. "That's fine, Preston. I understand you scored a hundred percent on written and driving." Cotton looked back at the small document once more. "That's as good as it gets! Congratulations, Preston." He shook Preston's hand as he gave the official card back to him. "What's the G. stand for?" asked Cotton with a pleased smile.

"Gabriel," answered Preston. "My mother told me it was the most important part of my name and to never leave it off anything. They didn't have enough room for all of it... so the officer suggested that I use the initial for legalities."

Emmett's smile slipped from his mouth and his eyes clung to this young man while his mind went back to the day Preston's very pregnant mother walked out of his life.

Preston slid the driver's license into his billfold then shook the trooper's hand who had given him the road test.

Sheriff Cotton re-directed his mind to the present and cuffed Preston on the shoulder as he told him that the Jeep was his to take care of, use for work and to get about town. He told Preston that the motor needed a little work and that he would keep the insurance and tag current for him. He said they would consider it a county issue and that his father would accept that.

Preston got in the Jeep and followed the sheriff to the county barn where he met Mr. Cox. He was a small man, and grungy. Preston thought it understandable with the kind of work he did and this late in the day. He showed Preston his locker and gave him four pair of coveralls with the county identified in stitching on the front breast pocket. Preston agreed to see him at 3:00 p.m. every afternoon after school, starting on Monday.

Preston waved at the sheriff as the civil servant turned right onto the highway. Preston respected the man, and he admired Sheriff Cotton, too. He found himself wanting to be like him; he wanted to help others that couldn't help themselves. He wanted to go tell Charlie what had happened but knew the longer he put off seeing his father, the worse it would be.

He turned into the yard next to the houseboat and parked heading out. He found his father sitting on the deck with a hook in the water and a beer in his hand.

His father spoke to him first.

"Well... how did it go? Did you get the job?"

"Yes Sir, I start Monday at 3:00 p.m. They had me get my license, so I could legally move the vehicles around the yard. And they issued that Jeep to me to run errands and such; it needs some work."

His father took a long swallow from the brown bottle then looked up at him. He surprised Preston when he spoke.

"I know I'm a real asshole to you... it's not your fault, Preston. I never meant to become this person, and I don't like him."

Preston leaned against the rail and crossed his arms. He saw the cork bobbing up and down. He pointed, and his father stood and pulled up a huge catfish. Dane was the only person Preston had ever seen that could catch a stringer of fish in January.

His father said no more on the subject and took the fish to the cleaning table. Preston knew that was all he was going to get in the way of an apology. Cotton's words came back to him. 'It's a small price to pay for peace.' He could live with that. Preston started for the stairs that led to the small room up top that was his.

"Hey."

Preston turned back to his father.

"That's a great opportunity for a guy your age, Preston. You do right by Sheriff Cotton," stated Dane.

"Yes Sir, I will."

CHAPTER 6

Estelle pulled the door closed on the truck and sat there a moment. They had not been protected from a pregnancy since they got married. Owen was not consumed with the idea, but Estelle knew he liked the idea of having children. During the ten months since they married, he had kept up with her cycle better than she did. They saw life as it was, and neither of them was getting any younger.

"February," she whispered. "What a great Valentine." She smiled as her hand went to her belly. Owen took great care in exploring her intimate needs; still, she was surprised. It was the third day of July, and they had let the idea of a baby rest and were enjoying what they could do to each other in bed and several other places, when Charlie was not expected.

She had not known it was possible to be needful of her husband's body like she was, or that he would want her to be. But Owen loved for her to touch him whenever and wherever she pleased. She was cautious and used discretion, but he treasured the fact that she desired him and in turn, he thanked her for her devotion in the most

111

exciting of ways. There were days when they would come home at lunch under the pretense of an unfinished task, and they would spend the entire hour naked with her legs wrapped around him. His large, tough hands and his full lips cast a passionate spell over her while his kingly body and confidence would push her into an obsessive and compulsive realm where she worshiped the feel of him. She had learned the more desperate she felt, the more he wanted to give. 'He had given something to her that was for sure,' she giggled out loud at the thought.

Estelle rolled the window down and cranked the truck. She made a stop at the grocery for staples and several special things she needed to make Charlie's birthday cake. There was a convenience in Charlie's birthday being the day after the Fourth of July. Charlie insisted that Owen combine the two, but his brother always did something special for him on his birthday. This year, they had all weekend to celebrate.

Estelle stopped at the cleaners to pick up their winter coats she had cleaned for next year, and then she stopped by Franklin's music store. She had ordered some sheet music and Charlie a birthday present.

Thomas Franklin waved when she entered. He was always asking her to come and work for him giving piano lessons and sell demonstrations. She thought it would be a pleasurable job, but she wanted to be Owen's wife more.

Mr. Franklin was speaking to a young, distinguished looking gentleman when she entered. Estelle could feel his eyes study her as she stopped in front of the rack of sheet music to see what was new. She heard Mr. Franklin as he spoke to the man.

"I can explain about tone, but this lovely lady can show you." Mr. Franklin called to her, then motioned her over and pulled out the square stool to the large, grand piano. He hoped she would not be able to resist touching the keys in front of her.

Estelle played the piano for the stranger. She answered a few questions about key action and responsibility of owning such an expensive instrument when there were so many more economical options. She pointed out that she thought it to be an investment into the world of music and fine, collectible furniture.

He asked her to play something classical. Estelle chose, 'The Moonlight Sonata'. His eyes flashed with appreciation for her skill. He introduced himself as James Breland, a new attorney in town. He asked her if she would like to go to dinner with him that evening. Estelle's cheeks turned red, and she shook her head as she declined.

He smiled at her and thanked her for the private concert. He checked his watch. She noticed that Mr. Franklin was with another customer. She witnessed the handsome gentleman pull out his checkbook and make out a draft for $6000. He tore the check out, handing it and his calling card to her.

"Tell Mr. Franklin that amount is as much as I'm willing to go on it. He can call me at this number if it's acceptable. If so, my address is on the card. He can deliver it at his convenience." Mr. Breland shook her hand with a charismatic smile and then left the store.

Estelle instinctively stuck her hand behind her back like a child that was hiding something. She stood there a moment as she rubbed the back of her hand on her skirt to dispose of the strange feeling his touch had left behind on her skin. She closed the piano, put the stool back in place and waited at the counter for Mr. Franklin.

The bell on the door jingled as the other customer left. Mr. Franklin took a few moments to put away the violin which was his specialty, before he joined her.

"We lost the big fish, huh?" He chuckled as he retrieved a large brown envelope from under the counter and handed it to her.

"No, actually... you didn't." She handed him the check and the card as she relayed the gentleman's message.

Mr. Franklin's face was stunned for a moment.

"My goodness, Estelle, how did you manage this?"

She shrugged her shoulder as she thought about the sharp looking man's confident demeanor.

"The Moonlight Sonata," she answered plainly. A huge smile claimed her face as she changed the subject. "Did it come in yet, Mr. Franklin?"

He put the draft in his pocket and turned his attention to the fact that she was there as a patron.

"Yes. Let me get it for you, Estelle." In a moment, Mr. Franklin returned from the stock room with a guitar case. He opened it and turned it to where she could see it. He watched her expression develop a question.

"Mr. Franklin... it's very beautiful... but this isn't the one I ordered. I can't afford this one," she confessed softly.

Mr. Franklin closed the case and handed it to her.

"This is the one I want you to take, Estelle. It's your commission... for the 'Big Fish' you caught for me." He smiled at her.

"Oh, I... shouldn't."

"Yes, you should. I insist. You should teach Charlie how to make it live, Estelle. Do it for those of us who are getting old... do it for the sake of the music."

Preston pulled in behind Estelle as she shut off the engine. She glanced back to make sure he was alone. He appeared at the passenger door and seeing the paper bags, he opened it and gathered the groceries for her. He grinned when he saw her grab the guitar case.

Preston had become a fixture at the ranch now that he had transportation. A few weeks after Cotton intervened for Preston with the job, Dane had tied on another hard drunk in Jasper County. He slugged one of the arresting deputies, sending him to the emergency room, and then to the dentist. The circuit judge locked him down in Jasper County for 30 days. Sheriff Cotton intervened again and spoke to Judge Adler, who allowed Dane to make a care plan for his son. Preston was naturally absorbed into the Silver-Hawk family because he had become a part of them and they cared for him and had grown to love him very much. He took up residence with Charlie during the holidays because Estelle and Owen insisted, he was not going to be alone during that festive time of year. They didn't understand that Preston saw Dane's incarceration as a gift of freedom and peace; they didn't understand that being alone was not something that frightened him. Preston had celebrated Christmas with the family and Sheriff Cotton came over for dinner like he always did. The sheriff gave him a set of new seats covers to go with the title of the old Jeep. Rueben and Celia gave him a new pair of boots and a brown suede Stetson to go with the new jeans and shirts that Estelle and Owen had picked out for him. Charlie gave him a bridle and a saddle that he made in 4-H. Cole had him pick a horse for his own.

They knew the responsibility of a horse was a lot to put on Preston with his life like it was, but they wanted him to feel welcome and at home when he was at the ranch. The men had consulted with Charlie about offering Preston his own mount; he assured them he would see to the needs of the animal and Preston without fail. Preston had chosen the buckskin they had purchased at the sale a few weeks earlier. He was saddle broke and spirited, and they seemed to take to each other from the beginning. He named him, Ritter. Preston felt comfortable at the ranch. He was a hard worker and embraced any task that was the objective for the day. Owen always had a chore that could use his willingness.

Preston pushed the truck door closed with his boot as he spoke.

"I'm glad it came in time for his birthday!" He followed Estelle up the back steps.

"Me too," agreed Estelle with excitement in her voice. "It's not like the one you showed me in the catalog... that's the one I ordered. But this one was made available to me, so I took it. Do you think he will mind that it's different, Preston?" There was apprehension in her voice.

Preston sat the bags on the kitchen counter. He turned to see true worry in Estelle's eyes. She cared so much about making Owen and Charlie happy. He knew that she even fretted over him too.

"I don't think so. Let's see it, Ms. 'Stelle.

She opened the case and held up the dark, exotic wood grain guitar with the silver accents.

Preston's eyes grew huge and his smile stretched across his face.

"Good golly!" he exclaimed in surprise. "That's nothin' but fine. He's gonna love it! Honest Ms. 'Stelle... I can't wait to see his face." Preston's finger lightly plucked the top string. A mellow twang came from it. He nodded his head. "I want to get something to go with it. Umm, have you got a suggestion?"

"Well, a black leather strap came with it." Estelle pondered over his question a moment. "I didn't think to get him any picks! He'll need some, Preston."

"Is that all?" he questioned. "What about a polishing cloth to keep in the case with it?"

Estelle nodded.

"That's a great idea. But are you going back to town in the next hour?"

"No Ma'am, I'll go in the morning," answered Preston. He could tell by her expression that there was a problem. "Why?"

"He closes early on Friday and tomorrow he'll be closed for the holiday. I know... we'll call Mr. Franklin and tell him what you need. He can bring it home with him and you can go by and pick it up. Will that work?" Estelle had walked to the phone and picked up the receiver as she spoke.

Preston smiled and nodded his head.

Estelle dialed the number and handed him the phone. She began putting the groceries away while Preston made the arrangements with Mr. Franklin.

Preston hung up just as the familiar voice echoed up to them from beneath the kitchen window. Estelle jumped to put the guitar away while Preston hurried to the back door to head off his friend.

Preston started talking before he was out of the back door completely. He saw that Charlie was accompanied by the oldest boy from across the road.

116

"Hey, Cuz." Preston turned his attention to the boy. "Hey Eli, I heard you're competing against Chuck here… in the calf roping this year." He shut the screen door easy like then ignored the stairs and jumped the four feet difference from the edge of the porch into the yard. Preston drew up his fist at Charlie like a boxer and danced around playfully. Charlie's tall, lanky body had begun to answer the call of manhood as well; he responded impulsively and punched his buddy fast and hard in the arm with his knuckles. Preston's face grimaced as his hand covered the spot and began to rub the kink out of it.

"I registered," laughed Eli; he enjoyed watching the older boys' foolishness.

Preston made eye contact with the tall and wiry, blond headed boy; Eli shoved his nervous hands into his pockets. He liked Preston. He was nice to him considering he was four years older, and he was always doing something funny and wacky to Charlie. The girls seemed to be drawn to them wherever they went. Eli thought Preston was cool, but he was Charlie's buddy and Eli didn't really know Preston like he did Charlie.

"I've been practicing. My roping is spot-on, but it's harder than Charlie makes it look. My legs aren't long enough to help me get a good time."

"Well, just think of yourself as a skinny, little spring that's wound up tight and ready to jump," suggested Preston. He took another unannounced swing at Charlie like he was Joe Frasier.

Charlie dodged him playfully a few times, and then he finally pulled up his fist to air-spar with his buddy.

"What are you doing here on a work day?" questioned Charlie with a satisfied grin. He punched Preston's palm with a crossover jab.

Preston bobbed back and forth a few seconds then punched Charlie in the arm while accompanying it with sound effects.

"They closed the garage at noon for the holiday since the Fourth falls on a Saturday this year. I came out to groom and spend some time with Ritter. I thought when I got through, we might go set some jug lines. My father's down river this weekend on the houseboat... new girlfriend. I'm at the camp house. It would be great if I could just live there and Dane would stay on the boat." He shrugged his shoulders. "What ya think, mosquitoes and catfish sound good to you?"

"No foolin'? What ya got for bait?" surveyed Charlie.

"Catawba... Mr. Floyd brought them to me from his trees." Preston grinned.

Charlie laughed at his friend. It was a fact that Sheriff Cotton's intercession had made a huge difference in Preston's life. His father had not really changed. He liked alcohol and women more than he did Preston; at least, his actions made Preston feel that way. But he took it seriously that his son worked for local government and he had not interfered. The fact that Preston had a means of quick escape had also helped the problem. He still showed up late at night sometimes, but not in a bloody mess. The key to the front door in Charlie's room had not been found during the renovations, so Owen had installed a dead bolt. Preston had been given his own key to Charlie's room. He knocked when he needed to use it, out of respect to his buddy.

Charlie looked at Eli standing there next to him.

"I'm done for the day. Me and 'E' were going to walk up to Newsom's Store and get a soda and some sparklers for the girls to burn tomorrow. That'll take an hour. I'd like to go with you... but, I'll have to ask Owen."

Preston could tell he had interrupted a promise that Charlie had made to the younger boy who was like his little brother. He was not one to mind sharing a friend. He didn't have enough of them to risk on foolishness.

"Well come on... let's drive down to the barn. Eli can show me those horses of his again. We'll ask Mr. Hawk if we can take him with us. I haven't seen Ritter since Tuesday. He probably thinks I'm a bum."

Eli couldn't believe his father was going to allow him to ride to the store with Preston in his Jeep, or that he was going to set the trot line with them. He couldn't believe they had included him. His father had felt badly because Travis got to fly to Oklahoma City with Lucien and Cole two days ago for a tractor show. He had made a commitment by registering for the rodeo. Preliminaries for the calf roping competition had been Wednesday morning. Eli figured this was something nice his father was trying to do because he had accepted the disappointment without comment.

Preston assured Eli's father once more that he would be careful driving; they would wear life jackets and be back before 10:30 p.m. They turned on to another dirt road that Eli had never been on before, each one got narrower as they drove. He could see that his companions were talking to each other and he could hear the hum of their voices; however, clarification was impossible due to the wind and the sound of the motor. A couple of times they looked back at him while he sat in the spot his father had designated and smiled with satisfaction.

They had made, so many turns Eli didn't have an idea where he was, and considering he was with Charlie and Preston, he didn't care. Finally, the road emptied into a clearing and Eli's jaw dropped open at the cabin that was on stilts and almost as tall as the surrounding trees. They stopped beneath it next to the ladder. Charlie motioned for him to get out with a toss of his head. Preston had climbed halfway up the ladder and Charlie told Eli to follow him.

The room was sparsely furnished with a sofa, a table and chairs, a set of bunk beds and a makeshift kitchen with a real sink that was piped out to the ground. The wall that faced the porch area was a glass sliding door; he figured it was the only way to get the furniture in the small dwelling since the back door was in the floor.

Eli turned when he heard Preston swear softly. He witnessed the older guy smack the end of the cabinet so that it shifted and dropped forward. He watched as Preston removed a pistol, a box of ammo and a holster from a secret compartment. It was then that Eli's attention was snagged by the picture of the naked woman on the calendar next to the bunks; he instinctively took a step closer.

Her upper body was enlightening to his ignorance of the female anatomy. He was nearing his 13th birthday, but he had never seen anything like her. He had been taught respect for a woman by example. The only naked picture he had ever seen of a female was in his science book at school and it didn't look anything like this. He wasn't aware their breasts were so defined by two shades of pink, or that they were so round, pointed, and fascinating. He took in the whole of her body; the waist was small beneath her ribs, her belly flat and her hips square, yet curvy. Her leg was propped up to conceal anything else, leaving his imagination on its own. His eyes followed the line of her hip, the round bottom and her long legs then went back to her breasts again. He felt the private part of his body stiffen and press against his jeans and his cheeks turned red because of it. He noticed the calendar was out of date and concluded it was still hanging there because of her.

"Umm-umm," Preston cleared his throat.

Eli turned around to face him.

His older friend smiled mischievously as he spoke to him.

"Do you want to go with us, or would you rather stay here with Miss July?"

Eli's face felt warm; he hung his head as he started towards them.

Charlie shoved him playfully.

"That's the Colonel's. I wouldn't mention it to anyone if I were you."

Eli nodded his head. He understood that Charlie was giving him good advice. Eli wouldn't tell anyone; it was too personal. He wondered what kind of woman would bare herself like that? The image of her was fixed in his mind; he could see her whether his eyes were closed or not.

He and Charlie gathered wood while watching for snakes. Preston got the boat ready and retrieved the bait. Eli was quite aware of the pistol that Preston had taken from his father's things in the shack and had strapped around his waist. He had watched Preston load it, just in case they had an emergency with an aggressive and unwanted critter. Charlie handed him a bandana and told him to tie it around his face like a television bandit. They worked together to build a fire in the fire ring. Eli put on his life jacket as he promised; they all did.

They trolled around the murky water and avoided the lurking creatures that lived there while pulling up one jug after another; they baited it then put it back in the swamp. The sun was melting behind the treetops and casting an orange glow over the earth. The frogs and crickets were singing so loud it was like a solid ringing in his ears.

Charlie had handed him a can of bug spray to use when they first got there; it was a good thing, especially when they were on the water. The smaller insects moved over the water in swarms; the bandana kept them out of his nose, so he could breathe. It was so hot and muggy that when the insects landed on their sweaty and treated skin, they just stuck.

When all the jugs were baited and floating, they headed for the bank. Charlie got out and pulled the boat far enough on to land that they wouldn't lose it to the slough. Eli knew now why they had started a campfire in July and welcomed it; the smoke kept the insects at bay.

They washed their hands with a piece of soap and a jug of water from the Jeep. They gathered around the fire to cook hotdogs on a stick. They warmed the buns on a rack that Preston got from the cabin and put on a spit next to the fire. They sat around the fire talking and laughing while sharing a feast of hotdogs, corn chips, sweet pickles, some slices of cheddar cheese and a bag of chocolate chip cookies they had bought at the store.

Preston started laughing at the goofy way Eli could make his entire scalp shift to move his hair, and in turn, they got tickled at Preston when grape soda came out his nose when he tried to swallow.

At 8:30 p.m. they went to check the jugs. This time, they took a lantern, a spotlight and a foam ice-chest with them. Eli dipped water into the chest with an old coffee can as they quietly and steadily cut through the water.

They pulled in one large, chubby catfish after another. The older boys pulled the hooks out with pliers and handed them to him. Eli ignored the way their gills pleaded for mercy and dropped each one in the chest. He watched Preston cut the heads off two snapping turtles that would die a slow death anyway from the hook in their mouth. They didn't reset the jugs because of the time.

Preston cranked the Jeep and turned on the headlights, so they could see what they were doing. He cleaned and gathered the things they had used and then climbed the ladder to the cabin to replace the equipment and secure the pistol in its hiding place while his buddies loaded. He kept the lantern and the spotlight, so he could see when he returned. They put the fire out with water from the slough and then were on their way.

The hot night air was stimulating. The energy from his first taste of manly freedom pumped in Eli's veins; it was going straight to his head. He thought about all they had done that day, what he had learned, and Miss July.

Owen caressed the plump tip of Estelle's breast with a kiss as he felt her body sing to him a silent song of ecstasy. He inhaled deeply and slid his palm beneath her smooth, round bottom then lunged forward.

Estelle's lips touched his ear with words of adoration as her legs impulsively tightened around his backside and pulled him into her body. She pushed with him for several moments then stopped; her lips took another kiss as she opened herself to him again.

He knew the feel of her and what her body craved because she had become part of him. Still, he was always amazed in the magical essence that enthralled them every time they took each other into the realm of physical pleasure.

"Oh... Honey, that feels good." Her voice was raspy with passion.

Owen's inspired body changed rhythm naturally. The hunger in her hands and her kiss tonight was somehow different and caused a frisson of extreme sensitivity to attack the nerves throughout his body. The private depth of her seemed fevered and charged with excitement.

The moments were suspended in over-indulgence of one another; it was their right and their purpose to satisfy the other.

She panted his name and worshipful words of love as she fervently moved in harmony with him. Her fingers dug into the flesh of his back; the way her hips pressed into him drove him temporarily insane. There was no one around to hear them when the sting of physical gratification rushed their bodies. When she began to quake deep within; his body responded and poured his devotion into her.

The ceiling fans stirred the warm night air around them and the evening echoed in through the open windows, filling the room with the sounds of crickets and a soft breeze swishing in the trees. The outside world was finally absorbed by their awareness. Owen rolled to his side, and she turned with him, so she could stay in his embrace. His kiss covered her mouth tenderly, needing and wanting the taste of her again; he wasn't sure why, but tonight was special for them. The sultry aggressiveness she had shared was as addicting to him as the thrust of her hips.

She nibbled at his bottom lip as her sigh conveyed heart-felt bliss. That was when she really rocked his understanding.

"Owen, I got your valentine today while I was in town. I'm so excited; I can hardly wait to give it to you. Trust me; it's the best thing I've ever given you. You're gonna love it."

He considered her sparkling eyes and smiled.

"My valentine?" he chuckled. "You are my valentine 'Stele, and you can't top what you just gave me, Honey." He kissed her softly.

"Yes, I can," she whispered against his lips.

He pulled back slightly so he could study her excitement. She wasn't a devout shopper like he had heard some women could be. He couldn't imagine what she had found that could have made her so inspired.

"You were just the little shopper today, weren't you?" He went to kiss her again but stopped in curiosity at the silly grin that inched across her mouth. "You want to give it to me now, don't you?"

"Oh Honey, I wish I could... but you're going to have to wait seven and a half more months, or 33 weeks, or until there are 15 more pounds between us, or..."

"Wait, 'Stelle!" He pulled back, so he could see her clearly in the moonlight. "You're kidding me?" He sat up and pressed his hand to her middle and his expression changed several times as he spoke. "Baby, you're kidding me! You better not be kidding me! Are you kidding me?"

Her face told him he was right.

"Say it for me, Honey."

"No, I'm not kidding you. Yes, you got us pregnant. You're going to be a daddy."

Owen's hands slid over her body with adoring and possessive strokes. He stretched out beside her and pulled her close. Their arms and legs intertwined as they kissed over and over. He tugged the sheet up when he felt her shiver. They talked for an hour about new dreams. They were wise enough to treasure this special moment in time and the blessing which had been bestowed on them.

The phone rang and stirred them from their joyful rest. Owen held her close as he reached over and answered it. The conversation was short; he hung up the receiver then snuggled back down in the sheets with her. He knew she would wonder, so he told her.

"Charlie is at the barn cleaning catfish with Preston, Eli and Rueben. 'If we want to come see 'em... they're beauts'."

Estelle chuckled at the way Owen mimicked his little brother. She knew he had conveyed the information just as his little brother had said it.

"How many did they get?"

"I don't know," mumbled Owen against her forehead.

"You know, those things can be a bugger to skin," she pointed out.

"Yep, that's what I hear."

"We haven't had a fish fry since last year," she stated factually.

"Yep, it's been a while," he agreed in a lazy hum while his lips went to her shoulder.

"If we go help, we could see for ourselves whether there's enough to cook tomorrow. We could fry some new potatoes and some hush puppies with green onion. I've been craving some sweet coleslaw for a couple of weeks. And, we may as well cook a pot of fresh turnip greens and some corn on the cob too." She nuzzled his chin. "When we get finished... we could come back and get in the shower together... and make love again."

"Throw in a platter of Mexican okra and you got a deal," bartered Owen.

"Mmm, that sounds good too! Okay, you twisted my arm."

Estelle's laugh sounded as warm and dreamy as her body felt. Owen climbed over on top of her and pressed his lips to hers; his kiss trailed down the front of her body to her belly.

"Your mama is wacky sometimes, little one. I love her very much! She keeps your daddy on his toes, just like you will." He hastily tossed the cover off his naked body and leaped out of the bed. He held his hand out and Estelle slid her fingers into his palm.

"Come on Darlin', let's go." He started for the door.

Estelle started giggling as she crawled out of the bed on her knees.

"Who's the wacky one of the two of us?" she questioned playfully.

Owen pulled her next to him and danced her around a few seconds as he hummed.

"You are, because you love me."

She looked at him and shook her head.

"No... it's more than that. I adore you, Sweetheart."

CHAPTER 7

The sound of a boat motor awakened Preston Saturday morning. It wasn't unusual; however, this one had stopped. He heard it choke. Preston figured someone was fishing the slough.

He had dozed in and out of sleep for the last hour. It was to be a full weekend with Charlie and his family, celebrating the Fourth and Charlie's birthday. He had to go to Mr. Franklin's house and pick up the guitar picks for his pal's birthday.

Preston looked out the window and saw a bass boat floating 50 yards out in the cove; the man sitting in the front seat was casting. He had the same thought that he did every time he spent the night out here. He wished his father had installed a catch tank, so a body could wash the sticky off before they dressed.

Preston brushed his teeth and rinsed his mouth with a warm soda. He glanced out the doorway when the motor of the fishing boat fired up; it turned towards the gap where the river's current ran steady and then zoomed toward open water. A few seconds passed, and it was gone. He took advantage of the isolation and quickly gathered the few things he needed to clean up. He stepped out on to the porch and stripped off his dirty clothes. Preston poured a generous portion of water over a clean cloth then scrubbed it with the bar of soap to make some dignified foam. He was quick with the bath, but thorough. He poured the last jug of fresh water over his head and body to wash away the soap and used his pillow case to dry himself. The grungy feeling on his skin had eased, so he pulled on clean jeans while thinking about the hot shower on the houseboat. He yanked on his boots and stuck his arms in the button-down shirt he had worn the previous morning. He rolled his soiled clothing up in the dirty sheets from his bunk, blew out the citronella bucket on the table, and then gathered his wallet and his keys.

Preston sat on Mr. Franklin's porch with a glass of sweet tea and looked over the selections the man had been kind enough to bring home. The cleaning cloth was an easy choice. The thin lambskin came in a small pouch, and he could choose white or yellow. He remembered the lining of the guitar case was yellow, so he chose the lambskin to match. The picks were different. He had told Mr. Franklin what he needed the day before and asked if he had something special. The man had assured him he did.

Preston looked at the half dozen small cases of custom guitar picks; they were in all shapes and colors. Mr. Franklin told him that different ones gave a different feel to the musician and the sound he was trying to achieve. Mr. Franklin must have picked up on his uncertainty. He took a leather pouch out of his brief case which looked like a thin wallet. Preston didn't think too much about it until Mr. Franklin handed the pouch to him. Preston's fascination was challenged by the collection of eight shiny silver picks, each one was individual in size and shape, and each was etched with a design.

Mr. Franklin explained his reasons for showing him this unique piece of merchandise.

"These were issued by the company in the leather wallet as a collector's set, Preston. They are solid stainless steel, and each one is engraved with a symbol true to the state of Texas. You can see the rose and the star... there's the letter T, a horseshoe, a boot, a cactus, a skull and a mustang. I brought them home because their beautiful... and because the company that makes them is Chapel-King. Look on the back of one of them."

Preston pulled one out of its velvet lined perch and turned it over; a smile crawled across his teeth. The initials C. K. was in a fancy Spanish lace design. They looked expensive; however, they were perfect for his friend, so he asked Mr. Franklin about the cost.

"How much, Mr. Franklin?"

"They are $12, Preston. I know you want to get something special for Charlie... turning 15 and driving a car is a rite of passage into manhood for a hard-working guy. I'll be happy to work with you on them, if you think it's what you're looking for."

Preston shook his head.

"I really appreciate that Mr. Franklin, but it won't be necessary. I'll take them, and the lambskin." He stood and pulled out his billfold.

Preston held the old cowboy hat on his head as he crossed the trestle bridge. The updraft from the river bend had the capability to swipe many a dependable hat if a person wasn't careful. Habit caused him to look down river to the secluded nitch within the willows where his father's boat dock was located. He did a double take when he saw the red and white stripped flag blowing over the roof of his top story room. He realized that the houseboat was tied up to the dock which meant his father was back. He stopped at the crossroad and then turned left.

Preston pulled into his usual spot under the trees and cut off the motor. The blue and white convertible Impala that was sitting under the Cottonwood in the side yard assured him that his father still had company. He debated on whether he would be interrupting, but it was a large boat and his room was only accessible from the outside staircase. He reasoned he could board and take care of his needs without making himself known. A quick shower and a change of clothes, and he'd be on his way to the ranch for the rest of the holiday weekend.

His father had left a note on the gate the day before, so he had not cleaned up since Thursday night. He closed the gate quietly then boarded the large boat. Preston passed the door to the main cabin then turned left to undertake the stairs to his room. He stopped suddenly and turned his ear towards the cabin, a few seconds passed before the sound came to him again. His father's irate voice was nothing new, but a woman sobbing was out of the ordinary, and troublesome. She shouted at him to get out of her way. Her demanding temper surprised Preston that anyone would be brave enough to speak to Dane Reid in that manner. He reasoned that it had to be the new girlfriend. Preston thought she must be new in town as well, to not be aware of his father's reputation. He started up the stairs and was halfway up when her fearful scream made the hair on his arms stand up. She cried out pleading for him to stop, just before something hit the wall on the other side of where Preston stood.

Preston backed up and looked through the slight crack in the blinds and saw that the new coffee table was smashed. He jumped suddenly when a floundering hand hit the blinds then began to grasp for help as she cried for him to stop. He knew in his gut that this was not his old man just giving-it-to one of his bar-hopping girlfriends. The short, well-groomed nails and the dainty, gold class ring on her hand told him it was a young woman, and she had taken on more than she could handle with his father.

He hesitated to open the door, but he felt he had no choice. His father had his hand around the young woman's throat and the other held her arm behind her back. Her feet were thrashing about attempting to kick him while her free hand now tried to push him away. Her face was red from the lack of oxygen, and the fear in her blue eyes made them look like ice. Her long, auburn-red hair had come loose from the fastener that held it, and her nose was bleeding. She saw him; her mouth formed the word 'help' because she couldn't breathe.

Preston thought of someone treating Estelle this way. The emotional tie and urgency in the situation pumped raw, youthful adrenaline into Preston's blood stream. He couldn't help but feel he had a responsibility toward this stranger. She didn't know the man she had consented to spend time with like he did.

"Dane! Stop! You're hurting her!" Preston hurried to them and wedged himself between his father and the woman. He struck his father's forearms with his fist and broke the hold he had on her then forcefully pushed him away. He was even stronger now since he worked a manual labor job. He heard the woman fall into the floor in a seizure of strangled, sputtering coughs.

Preston's hands went out in front of him to keep his father at bay while he chanced a look back at the woman.

"You need to get out of here while you can," he encouraged.

She looked up at him; her eyes were wide with fear. She cried out a warning.

Preston turned just as his father's fist caught him in the nose and the other in the temple. His neck twisted under the brute force while it sounded like a canon had gone off in his head. Dane's attention was focused on him now; his eyes were glazed and red with fury. He grabbed Preston around the neck in a chokehold, but Preston had been wrestling around with one of the mechanics at the garage who enjoyed playing gags on him. Preston stepped to the right and shifted his weight like the guy had shown him; he tossed his father over his head and to the floor.

This time, the struggle was in defense of someone else. Preston had been around decency enough to know he could choose not to be like his father. Dane was a mean, selfish bastard that recklessly drowned his sorrow with alcohol, not caring that the elixir calls up his inner demons that were bent on destroying anyone who gets too close to him.

Preston went to the woman and picked her up off the floor. He realized that she was a little thing amid her spunk; still, she was shaking all over. He started toward the door with her, but Dane got up and cut them off. He had the leg of the coffee table in his hand and cocked his arm back. Preston shoved the woman out of the way as his father swung it and caught him in the ribs. Preston felt them crack. He swore out loud as the pain in his body and in his heart, stole his reason and tainted what decency he had tried to claim as his own. Dane swung again and nicked Preston's forehead; a jagged edge sliced open his flesh. But Preston's arm turned into the canon this time and his fist struck his father center of his forehead; a lifetime of disdain and frustration delivered it with tremendous force. Dane's eyes lost their fire as he collapsed to his knees then sprawled face down on the floor.

Preston bent over and blinked several times as the blood dripped to the floor; he stumbled backwards a few steps as dizziness came over him. He didn't know if it was the blow to the head or the lack of oxygen that had him spinning. He tried to catch his breath while blood splattered to the floor from his nose and the open gash in his head. The pain in his side was excruciating. He closed his eyes and shook his head to clarify his understanding. All he could think of was being sent to some group home away from the people he cared about, and away from the contentment he had managed to find these last eight months. He spit a mouthful of blood on the floor with contempt because he had swallowed enough of his father's maltreatment of him.

A cool, damp cloth gently touched his face and bathed away the sweat and blood from his eyes and nose while a warm concerned hand held the back of his neck. He could smell the sweet, thriving scent of her. Her tender way caressed his chin as she squatted down next to him to get a better look. She handed him his old hat appreciatively.

"Hey there cowboy, can you hear me? Take short breaths; don't try to pull in too much all at once."

His ears were ringing, but he could hear her voice in it. Preston looked at her; there was genuine concern in her crystal blue eyes.

"Can you straighten up?"

Preston nodded.

She put her arm around him and they rose slowly; it was like he could feel every section of his spine re-align as he did so, and it hurt like hell.

"My name is Jaden... Jaden Sullivan. How did you come to be here just when I needed you?"

Preston caught her small wrist in his hand and took the cloth away from her. He turned and slowly went to the refrigerator where he took out a soda. He pressed it to the side of his forehead for a moment then he opened it and gulped down half of it.

"I live here," he mumbled. Preston studied his father's still body. "You should go now... while you can."

She looked at Dane laying there in the floor and shook her head.

"I can't. I should call the sheriff. He would have killed me if you hadn't come..." She hesitated as her thoughts changed perspective. "Why did we take the boat upriver last night if you live on it? What's your name, anyway?"

"Preston," he growled. "He did it because he's a self-centered asshole, who was more interested in making-it with you than to consider anything that his son might need."

Her expression tensed at his rudeness, but he didn't really care.

"Go ahead call him. You'll have to go to the store up on the highway to find a phone."

He watched her expression change several times as she rubbed her throat. Preston could tell that she was trying to let all of this catch up to her, so she could think smart. He'd been there more times than he could count. He had hoped this part of it was over; he guessed it would be now after the sheriff found out.

The young woman pulled out a chair at the kitchen table and sat down. Her short cotton skirt revealed shapely legs, and the green matching blouse defined a small waist and a full, womanly body hidden beneath it. She was a classier female than those which Dane usually kept company, and younger. He watched her prop both elbows on the table and rub her temples. She was stressed; he knew how that felt too. The longer Preston looked at her, the more he thought she looked like a girl, hardly older than him.

"The two of you have fought like this before now, Preston?" she asked him in a soft tone of voice.

He answered her because she needed to leave.

"Self-preservation until tonight... until..." he paused, feeling awkward about his life being revealed in such a way to a stranger. He changed his answer to encompass the seriousness of the moment. "You should go, Jaden Sullivan. Go make your call... tell dispatch Dane Reid's at it again. They'll know where you are. You can tell them Preston's waiting for the sheriff. They'll ask you to come to the station, so they can take your statement. That'll give me time to pack."

"Where are you going, Preston?" she asked as she looked at him.

"I've been on borrowed time with him. Sheriff Cotton told me he would take him to jail the next time this happened. It'll stick with your assault charges in the mix. I can run or go to a group home." He was silent for a moment. "I can't run. Sheriff Cotton has stuck his neck out for me, and I owe him my respect. I'll just have to take whatever comes."

Dane's breathing evolved into a deep, sound snore.

Her attention went to the man in disbelief, and she shook her head as she asked Preston another question.

"So that jerk is all you got in the world?"

"He's my only kin. There are a few people who care, but I can't take this to their doorstep, not again. They worry as it is." Preston rubbed his side. "Please, Ms. Sullivan, go make the call. I really need to get this over with."

She could tell the young man was beginning to feel lousy. She stood up and walked over to him then brazenly pulled out the tail of his shirt and lifted his arm. She frowned at the deep purple bruise that was swelling. Her warm hand covered it in a practical survey as though she knew exactly what she was doing. Preston flinched, and his breath trembled from the pain, but he said nothing.

She would have to be blind to not notice the fine, muscular cut of him. She looked up into his handsome chiseled features. His eye was swelling as well, and the cut on his forehead was clotting on the side of his face.

"Those ribs are broken... looks to me to be the fifth and sixth. I'm sure you've got a bitch of a headache too." She dropped his shirt.

Preston knew after this short interaction with her that she was not a girl.

"Okay... here's the way I see it. I owe you, Preston. I'm not a stupid woman... just a lonely one." His father shifted positions; she turned in a defensive start and her hand reflexively went back to the red marks on her throat. A few seconds passed before she accepted that Dane was down for the count. She exhaled then continued what she was saying, "And just for the record... I didn't 'make-it' with him."

Preston watched as she let go of a weary and frustrated breath then smacked herself in the side of the head with her palm. It was as though she was temporarily insane, and the sudden jolt caused the smarter side of her personality to emerge. He heard her mumble to herself.

"You're smarter than this Jaden! What in the hell were you thinking?"

Preston was curious. Her behavior was like watching River Pete, the old vagrant that wandered along the boardwalk and talked to himself.

A few more moments passed then she put her hands on her hips and her spine straightened as she made her decision. She proceeded to tell him what was on her mind.

"He was charming last week when I met him, and persistent. He said he was retired from a consultant position for President Roosevelt. He was older, handsome, smooth, and yet direct; I thought he would be safe. I like a man that doesn't beat around the bush, but I like one that doesn't beat me much more. He was tight when I got here yesterday. My gut told me not to go... that it would get worse, but he was such an overwhelming presence and I couldn't find a way to get off the boat before it was too late. I paid attention to what he did as we went down river, and he drank. It was a good thing. He passed out on the deck a little after midnight, and I brought us back.

"I sort of bumped the dock trying to come alongside; it woke him up. I hurried down here to get my things. He stopped me on my way out. That's when you came in. Truthfully Preston, I'm a good person. I work hard, and I practice treating others with respect and hope it will be returned. But I have a lousy record with men. I have a knack for picking jerks." She turned back to confront him. "I'm really sorry. It hurts me to know that I'm the cause of you being forced to disrespect your father. I can see that you still care for him. I understand how, in the eyes of a son, you may assume I'm a whore. I can accept that, but more than that... I'm also a nurse. I work in Dallas. I have a friend; she's a doctor. She's trying to build a free clinic... taking notice to the problems in our society that fall through the cracks. I work with her on weekends when I'm not on shift at the hospital... or I have a brain-fart and go out with another asshole." Jaden bit down on her bottom lip to stop herself from saying anything negative to this young man about the jerk lying in the floor a few feet away from them. She sucked in a calming breath as she continued. "Anyway, she has a 'no questions asked' policy. You need those ribs x-rayed and wrapped, and we need to make sure you're not bleeding internally. You're going to need some stitches in that cut next to your brow too.

"I'll pass on the phone call, against my better judgment I might add, and you come with me for treatment." She smiled slightly as she picked up her bag and her purse. "You do need to get away from him, Preston. He's a disaster waiting to happen. You sure don't deserve it to happen to you. What will he do when he wakes up? Does he always remember what he did?"

"No. I don't know." Preston shook his head as he stared as his father a moment. "If he does, he never says so," he exclaimed.

"In other words, he never apologizes," she interpreted in a compassionate voice.

Preston shrugged his shoulders as though it didn't matter; still, he was aware that this woman knew better.

"So... what's it gonna be?"

Preston stared at the petite and incredibly interesting woman in the tiny dress that stood only feet in front of him. He sensed that she was sincere. She was as much a refugee of his father's dysfunctional approach to life as he was. He reasoned that taking the time to clean up, which was his original reason of coming on board in the first place, was no longer a good idea. He didn't feel like battling Dane again should he be prodded into consciousness by one of his demons. And there was no way he was going to show up at the ranch celebration in his present condition; it would put a damper on Charlie's birthday and the weekend festivities. He knew Cotton would find out, but he needed to get a grip on himself and prepare for the worst. He could tell by his short breaths that his injuries were more than superficial this time.

"Does Dane know where you live?" asked Preston.

"No. I'm not in the phone book either," she replied.

Preston nodded his head.

"Okay. I'll follow you."

Jaden Sullivan and the beautiful, cinnamon-skinned Spanish woman studied the film of Preston's ribs while he studied them. He had never really known professional women, other than his teachers at school and Ms. Bagley, the principal. He sensed both these women were their own person and did not depend on a man to tell them what she could and could not do. At least, he knew that to be a fact about Jaden Sullivan. He admired them, and he respected them. He recalled that Jaden had said she was lonely. He figured most men didn't take to her ability to think for herself; however, he was confused about these things. He respected Celia and Estelle even more, knowing they worked as hard as any man on the ranch.

He thought about Ms. Estelle being pregnant. It brought warmth to his heart as he remembered the excitement, she and Owen shared the night before, and the way they couldn't keep their hands off each other even though they had fish guts up to their elbows. He looked at the clock; it was almost 1:00 p.m. He realized they were probably cooking by now and wondering where he was. Preston left his thoughts there when Dr. Enriquez touched his shoulder.

"Mr. Reid, the film has revealed three cracked ribs. Jaden was smart to bring you to me. The best thing we can do for them is to bind you, so they won't shift until they bond. You're a young, strong man... the bone will regenerate very quickly. A week to ten days and the ache will disappear. You'll be tender for a few weeks." She looked at his head. "We'll suture that cut. I'll send an antibiotic with you and a couple days of pain medication to take the edge off. I'm glad you were nearby when Jaden got attacked. It makes me feel good to know there are some willing knights left in this selfish world, who were born with the soul to serve something greater than one's self. Thank you for helping her young man; she's very important to me." Dr. Enriquez patted his face.

Preston leaned his heavy head back against the seat of Jaden's car and closed his eyes. The medication the doctor had stabbed into his hip was pulsating wildly through his blood stream. The hot July wind swirling around his body and through his hair seduced him into a feeling of contentment.

He had left the Jeep at her place and she took him into the city to the clinic. He thought of the little house of hers he had seen. It was tucked under some large oaks on a wooded lot with no close neighbors. It needed painting, but still looked comfortable from the outside. The small porch had a rocker in the corner, a birdhouse and a fern hung from the trim. When they came to a stop, he opened his eyes and saw the exact picture that had been in his mind's eye.

Jaden touched Preston's hand, and he turned his head and looked at her. His pupils were huge, and his eyelids were heavy due to the narcotic in his system.

"Preston, you're in no shape to drive while you're under the influence of that pain medicine," assessed Jaden plainly. She gazed at him for a few moments while silently deciding what to do about the situation. She had been so concerned about the young man's injuries and feeling responsible for them, she had not thought this far ahead. Whether she liked it or not, she was invested in Preston's well-being and could do nothing other than care for him until he could function with a clear head. She pulled the keys out of the ignition then looked at him again. "Are you scared to stay with me... here... tonight? I have a phone if you need to call someone."

"No," he answered. Preston turned his hand over to expose his palm.

Jaden looked down at it and was moved by the trusting gesture. She responded without thinking and slid her slim fingers into his hand. His strong, warm grip folded around her small hand as he spoke.

"There's no one to call. Thank you, Jaden, for giving me a chance to control what happens to me."

She nodded her head.

"I owe you, Preston. Come on... you can take that shower you want so badly while I fix some lunch... then we'll tape you." Jaden gathered her wits and acted on her words. She retrieved her things then got out of the car, leaving Preston to follow. She heard the passenger door to her car close as she clumsily poked her key at the lock. The small porch gave under his weight and she could feel his presence behind her. The lock gave, and Jaden pushed the door open wide then stepped to one side, so he could enter her small home.

Preston glanced around the room as he entered; it was orderly and furnished with a collection of old, but tasteful basics. The pale green color of the walls and the dark pine flooring, combined with the refreshing clean smell, made it feel homey and welcoming. The accents in the room revealed her love of the ocean. The simplicity of it, along with her confident manner, made him feel comfortable.

He took in the smooth and gentle way she moved while following her down the short hallway. She stopped at the large doorway on the left and flipped on the light for him. Preston stood in the doorway of the black and white bathroom while she conveyed the information he should know about this aspect of her home.

"Towels and whatever else you may need are in the closet... shampoo and other stuff is on the window sill. You should be careful that was a pretty stout narcotic Ava gave you." She walked towards him and somehow, they traded places. Her hand caught the doorknob, and she smiled slightly before she backed out into the hallway to give him privacy. She suddenly pushed the door back open with a second thought. "If you don't mind, leave the door unlocked... just in case you have a problem and need help. Okay, Preston?"

Preston made visual contact with her then nodded his head in response. The bright light over the sink enhanced the vibrant blue rings around his dilated pupils. There was something about the way he looked at her; it was penetrating to the loneliness which dwelled deep within her soul. Jaden sensed Preston was kindred to this feeling, basing her reason on the unfair treatment and living conditions he endured from the drunken bastard that was his father.

"Drop your things into the hallway and I'll throw them in the washer."

Jaden pulled the door closed and stood there a moment. 'He was too gorgeous,' she thought. Dane Reid's furious eyes popped into her mind's eye and she shivered all over. She took a deep breath and slowly released it. Jaden started up the hallway when the bathroom door opened, and the young man's clothing fell in a heap on the floor. She went back to pick them up, and she heard the water cut on and the hooks on the shower curtain slide over the rod.

Jaden turned down the burner beneath the pot of left-over vegetable-beef soup and took the skillet of fresh cornbread out of the oven. She looked at the clock again. She could still hear the water running. She was passed the point of being worried.

She knocked on the door; it cracked open upon making contact.

"Preston?" He didn't answer, so she opened the door a little further and spoke his name louder this time.

Jaden forgot about niceties and invaded the privacy of the room out of concern. She peeked around the shower curtain to check on him. He leaned against the wall with his hands supporting him. Her eyes were drawn to the massive span of his shoulders, and then his muscular backside. The sound of the water splattering against his skin and channeling over his muscles to the thin, dark patch of hair at the base of his spine was hypnotic.

She dared to reveal her intrusion and spoke to him again.

"Preston, are you, all right?"

He lifted his head; the water hit him in the face. His scruffy dark hair curled with moisture.

"I'm afraid to let go of the wall. The room started spinning about the time I got in... I haven't even touched the soap yet."

Jaden asked him.

"Can I help? Do you mind?"

His voice sounded rather weak.

"I don't... if you don't."

Jaden looked down at her dress. She had spent a shameful amount of her earnings on it with the hope that Dane Reid would be her path to lasting companionship. She was wondering now if there were forces at work greater than her own hopes. She had talked herself into dating an older man and now, here she was in a compromising situation with the younger one. She released the zipper on the skirt and stepped out of it then unbuttoned the matching blouse and hung both on the door hook. She stepped into the shower in her underwear.

The cool water felt wonderful on this hot July afternoon. She picked up the cloth from between his feet and slid beneath his outstretched arm. She retrieved the soap and scrubbed it against the wash cloth. She began to rub his shoulders and neck and then reached around him to take in the span of his back. He flinched when she touched his side; he flinched when she touched him in several places.

The tips of her breasts swelled into hard, painful nubs as she brushed against him in accomplishing the task at hand. She worked her way down his body to his legs. She deliberately skipped the masculine part of him because it seemed to be an invasion of his person. He was very much a man in that aspect. She stood with her attention focused on the dark, fur coverage and the impressive erection this young man possessed. She wasn't sure how to proceed in the name of helping him.

"Gosh, Preston... what do you want me to do?"

"It would be disrespectful to you for me to answer that," he mumbled.

She looked up into his face, certain that the vulnerability she felt inside glowed in her eyes.

"I think we had to redefine the meaning of respect a few hours ago... so answer me."

"I want you to finish what you started," he admitted in a voice that was almost a whisper. He stared at her with those eyes again. His attention went to her breasts; the way they pushed against the thin saturated fabric of her bra left nothing to his imagination. She didn't know if he was flirting with her, or if he was just being honest. She knew she shouldn't encourage his attention. It was hard to do when he stood so vulnerable and masculine in front of her like this.

"Be careful... you can't look at a woman like that and not touch her."

His piercing eyes came to her mouth.

Jaden tried to ignore them and took the shampoo down from the window sill. She filled her hand with the silky, thick balm then scrubbed her palms together. She stood on her tip-toes and raked her fingers through his hair.

It caught her off guard when he shifted his weight to one arm then took her inside the other and pressed her next to him. His attention went to her throat as she arched her back to gain balance.

"He left a wicked bruise on your throat," mumbled Preston in a husky voice. "Does it hurt?"

His thoughtfulness was real; she could feel it and she was deeply moved. She gazed into his eyes.

"It's okay," she breathed.

He nuzzled her brow with the short growth of stubble above his lip. It was such a simple gesture, but the nerves in her body responded to the sensuous nature of his presence.

"You're so beautiful, Jaden. You deserve a damn sight better than my old man."

She massaged his scalp with trembling fingers. His chin caressed her ear, and Jaden tilted her head back a little, so he would not break the contact with her. He inhaled her into his lungs as he tenderly rubbed the side of his face against hers. His mouth touched her ear, and she lost her train of thought as the energy inside her body swelled at the intimate and gentle contact with this young man. She pressed her lips to the side of his mouth without giving thought to the reasons why she shouldn't.

He parted his lips and kissed her several times. She got swept up by the loneliness between them and she dared to experience the taste of him for a couple of minutes.

It began as a timid and sweet exchange, but somewhere in that few minutes, the adrenaline of physical desire escaped into their blood streams. Her soapy hands went to his private body. She bathed him as she stretched him. Their kiss became more demanding as his hand went to the small of her back and pressed her body against him.

"Preston... how old are you?"

His lips lingered against hers for a moment; their breaths were laced with passion, and so much more. He looked into her eyes and was sensitive to the reality that if anyone knew they were here together, she could be in trouble. But there was so much in the world that was wrong, and everyone just ignored it. This woman was a breath of tenderness, a soft caress of hope in his calloused life. He wanted to be here with her. He wanted to know this part of life with someone who knew his painful shadows and still thought of him as worthy.

She shook her head when she saw rejection wilt his handsome features. She wanted to hold him all night. She needed his company, and she knew he needed hers.

"Never mind... it doesn't matter."

Preston shared his true self with her, anyway.

"Yes, it does. You have a right, like you needed to tell me why you were with Dane earlier. I..." he paused knowing he should be as open as he could. "If I had aged a year for every lesson, he attempted to teach me with his intimidations, his belt and his fist; I'd be older than Dorian Gray." He rested his forehead against hers and brushed his lips over hers so lightly that it felt like a whisper. "I'll be 17 in three months, Jaden. I will protect you before myself," he pledged in earnest.

He was right; he had an old soul. She wrapped her arms around his neck and offered him the sweetest smile.

"I already know that, Preston."

Jaden's soft lips covered his mouth. His strength caught her off guard as he continued to balance himself with one hand holding the wall while his other arm tightened and slid her body upwards.

'His lips were so kissable', thought Jaden.

"Preston, this is so dangerous," she whispered.

He nibbled at her bottom lip as he looked at her.

"We've already survived dangerous for today," he mumbled. "I'm not sure if I know about all the things a woman needs. You can teach me. Show me what you need to feel, Jaden. I'm a fast learner."

She was set back by his words. He was green. She suddenly felt self-conscious.

"Oh Preston, you deserve better than me your first time. Sweetie, I've been used... a lot."

He shook his head as he pointed out his negatives as he saw them.

"I'm not the lover you hoped you would find this weekend... or the man."

Their attention held as they continued to nibble at each other's lips.

His arm relaxed, and he slid her down his body to stand on her own. His hand slid over her bottom between her wet panties and her skin. There was a hunger in his grip. It didn't belong to a boy.

Jaden allowed loneliness to decide for her. She released her bra then pushed her briefs down, and he helped her. She stepped out of them then took the bath cloth and began to bathe herself. Preston's hand slid over her slick wet skin as she encouraged him to touch her anywhere, he desired. He pressed his chest next to her back and slid his hand over the soft fur between her thighs. His palm, and the hunger in it, explored the intimate and private part of her body. Her hands found the wall beneath his. Preston's fingers teased her a moment, inflicting a yearning ache she could not ignore. Jaden clutched his wrist and held it as she pushed into his touch. It was only a few minutes before she sucked in a deep breath and the jerking tension in the pit of her stomach let go of her. She leaned her head back against him in weakness.

"I'm sorry... it's been so long since a man has touched me with tenderness.

His arm tightened around her waist and he kissed her below her ear then down her shoulder without saying a word.

She cut the water off and squeezed out her hair. She helped him steady himself as they left the tub. Jaden opened the adjoining door to her bedroom as he leaned against the door facing. She twisted her hair in a towel then she dried him. He watched as she dried herself taking the time to scrub the water from her long tresses.

Jaden tossed the cover back then went to his arms. She kissed him as she walked him backwards towards the bed. He lay down, and she crawled up his body and sat down, and then she pulled a pillow under his head for comfort. They couldn't stop touching each other. When it came to physical contact between a man and a woman, Jaden recognized the burn of lust, the sting of betrayal, the cold grip of contempt, and she knew the empty caress of a one-night stand. There was a gentleness in Preston. She sensed it was his innocence. It was real and so alive. He had been hurt by someone he should be able to trust. He was brave and yet, still willing to trust. She was drawn to the goodness in him; she couldn't help it. His essence was that of a man, and it was overwhelming to her as a woman.

She studied his handsome face and wondered if she were corrupting him... if she were misleading him.

Her first experience with sex and trust invaded her private thoughts. *It was with the older college son of her ninth foster family. She was crazy about him and he knew it. He had encouraged her infatuation by teaching her how to kiss one afternoon when she was in the basement doing the family's laundry. She was barely 13 at the time and knew nothing of a man's body, or her own for that matter.*

A couple of weeks later, he came home to do his laundry, and he dared to touch her again. The rest of the family was out, and she was attending to her chores when he arrived. That afternoon they kissed, and he took her deeper into the world of physical contact. He explored her body with his touch and discovered she was innocent. He told her he loved her, but that no one would understand. His mother had placed a sofa downstairs and relocated her bed and other possessions there as well, so it would be more convenient for her to complete her chores and her school work without being underfoot. He laid her down on the sofa and looked at her body, taking the time to touch her before he kissed her. It had been an embarrassing thing at first, but the pulsating, electrical thrill he made her feel that afternoon was addictive. She pleasured him in the same way because he wanted her to. That afternoon marked the beginning of their personal and intimate encounters.

The next morning, he left going back to school and his parents were off to the country to visit the grandparents. She was washing the breakfast dishes when he opened the back door. She was smothered by his attention and accompanied him downstairs. He undressed them, and they became intimately familiar with each other's body. They repeated the afternoon before, only this time he held her against the wall and rubbed himself against her.

In the weeks that followed, her surrender became an obsession for him. He made a game out of tempting her until she pleaded for him to tell her what he wanted her to do. She grew more enslaved by his affection, and bold in her willingness to have someone love her. It was to the point that he had manipulated her young body into feeling and craving the things of a woman with only a glance from him.

Christmas Eve night things between them changed again. He was daring and came to her bed while his parents were asleep upstairs. He locked the door then stripped her of her night gown. He put a towel beneath her bottom. She had learned that his objective was that they touch each other to the point that his body released a slick fluid. They touched and kissed as usual, and then he pleasured her young body with his kiss. He left the pit of her belly trembling with a revelation of feeling and then rose above her to teach her something new. She was more than willing to surrender to his direction and did not object when he pressed her legs far apart and covered her with his large muscular torso. His biceps pushed against the back of her thighs, parting her legs so that the bend of his arms held her behind her knees, all the while, his hands squeezed her small arms above her elbows. He held her firm in this awkward position while he pressed himself between her legs. Her innocence was finally stripped away as she learned the purpose in the design of their bodies. He had entered her with a fraction of restraint, slowly pushing his long, engorged body into her minor one. He became fearfully aggressive stabbing her trust and her inexperienced body in a seizure of manic, steel-like thrust of his erection. She cried out, and he silenced her with his kiss. She was helpless beneath his strong, athletic torso where he rocked their conjoined bodies until she was almost delirious with pain and confusion. He got his fill of her, seemingly with no regard for her tears until he was satisfied. She was jerking in spasms of emotional shock as she felt his body release the hot liquid into her. He held her a moment; his breath heaved with gratification before his grip subsided. He spoke to her in the gentle voice; it was all she had known from him until this night. He told her it was supposed to hurt the first time, and that was why he had waited so long to share this with her. He kissed her until she stopped crying then he told her she was bleeding, but it would stop and that she should take care of it like her period. He smiled and told her he loved her and that what they were doing was making love. He gave her a necklace for her Christmas present. It was his Varsity necklace from football. He reminded her that no one would understand their love for each other until she got older and he instructed her to wear the necklace inside her clothes. He promised her again that they would be together forever.

The entire next week during his holiday visit at home, he had come to her every time they were left alone during the day and every night. He acted as though he was *consumed with her love and proclaimed how special she was to him. She learned that she could relax and move with him until her belly burst with that exalted feeling of excitement. She began to look forward to their love making, and she became very good at celebrating what they could do to each other.*

He went back to school for the new semester. It had been over a month since she last saw him. The weekend of Valentines, he brought a friend home with him. His parents went on a long weekend to the coast and left him to see to her and a younger brother. She was anxious for him to come to her. But he and his friend helped themselves to the liquor cabinet and insisted she participate. She went to bed that night with her head spinning and her senses disoriented under the influence of the alcohol. She opened her eyes and recognized her lover's body as he coupled with her. His glassy eyes gazed down at her as he shared his kiss, but then he stopped and spoke to someone. He withdrew from her arms and her body then turned her over where he entered her again holding her on her knees. His friend appeared in front of her holding himself and waiting for her to cooperate. She didn't understand what was happening and resisted against his presence. He grabbed her by the throat in a menacing grip and shoved his hard, stumpy penis into her mouth. His threatening fingers dug into the flesh of her neck forcing her to service his lust while her lover took his feel from her private body at the same time. It was the beginning of a night of betrayal and drunken cruelty she would never forget. They had even held her down for the little brother who hadn't yet reached puberty and goaded him into violating her body and his own innocence as well.

As Jaden sat on Preston's lap; she felt his erection between her legs pressing against her super sensitive body. She looked down at it protruding out between them. She did not want to hurt him in any way. He was not naïve or a stupid boy, and he was not intoxicated either; however, he was under the influence of medication. She studied his face while wondering how to explain all of this to him, and would he remember her words in sobriety?

"Talk to me, Jaden," he mumbled. Preston sat up and nuzzled the side of her mouth until she met his gaze.

"I want you to understand how much I want to feel you hold me and touch me." She touched his cheek with her palm. "You're medicated, Preston. Try to understand... if you share this with me, I need to know you chose to do so when you were thinking straight. I need you to know what you're doing without being in a daze. You should be aware and know what is happening to you and your body. Can you understand that?"

"You look tired too, Jaden. I'm in your bed." He put his arms around her tenderly and put his head on her chest as he hugged her.

She smiled softly at his way. She kissed his brow and his lips yet pulled her body away from his lap and his arms. She retrieved a slip of a gown from the back of a tall chair in the corner of the room. Preston watched as she tossed it over her head, and the slinky fabric slid into place over her delicate body.

"Come on... stretch out for me and rest. Do you want to eat something?"

"No. I'm all right, Baby," he mumbled. He caught her hand and looked at her. "You are so beautiful, Jaden. Is there any way you could fall for a guy like me?"

She felt her heart grow warm at his words. She smiled and leaned over where she kissed his swollen nose.

"I'm afraid... I'm already on my way, Preston. You're not going to break my heart, are you?"

"There's no chance of that, beautiful. No chance..." He whispered as he closed his eyes.

Jaden dried her hair, and then she poured the soup into a deep casserole bowl and slid it in the oven with the cornbread to keep it warm. She finished two loads of laundry and listened to the radio as she pressed her uniforms for the coming week of work. She was pulling the early shift this entire month except for tomorrow. She had offered to work this Sunday to cover for a co-worker that had a new grandchild they had not seen.

She hung up the last petite white dress, put her iron and board away then went and peeked in on her patient. She checked the front door again to make sure it was locked then curled up on the small couch and spread the small comforter over her legs. She left the radio on for company and closed her eyes. She listened to the soft hum of the country song as her thoughts drifted to the cowboy that occupied her bed.

CHAPTER 8

Jaden awoke to the sound of the toilet flushing. She glanced at the clock to see that it was 8:35 p.m., then determined that Preston had slept for six hours and was stirring. She tossed the cover from her legs and stretched as she uncurled from the small sofa. She poured a glass of cold lemonade and went to check on her patient.

Preston was lying across the bed with the sheet haphazardly covering his private body; one foot was on the floor while the other leg rested on the edge of the mattress. She eased over to him and touched his cheek with the back of her fingers. His eyes popped open, and he gazed up at her. She smiled.

"Hey, do you remember where you are?"

He nodded his head and caught her hand in his.

"I brought you something to drink. You must be thirsty."

He sat up slowly then took the glass. His hand released hers and found the back of her knee; he urged her to come closer to him as he drank. He handed her the glass then his cold, damp hand went to the back of her other leg as he cuddled his head next to her bosoms. She smiled as she looked down at him.

"Are you flirting with me, Cowboy?"

"Yes Ma'am," he answered, his voice was a deep masculine hum.

She sat the glass down on the dresser and he urged her to come to his lap as she had been earlier. She ran her fingers through his hair and witnessed him turn his head into her touch as though he was starved for the contact.

"You are the most gorgeous man I believe I've ever seen, Preston. You must look like your mother?" she told him as her eyes moved over his features.

His mouth kissed the bruises on her neck as he whispered against her skin.

"I'm sorry I didn't get there before he did this to you."

"I'm sorry you got hurt rescuing my dumb butt." She told him as she tilted her head, so his lips could venture further beneath her chin. His hands had begun to massage their way over her thighs and beneath the gown. She exhaled at the incredible warmth he inflicted on her body. She kissed him, and he kissed her back.

"Preston, I want to tell you something that I've never told another soul on earth. I have to... as you put it earlier, you deserve to know." She shared with him what her childhood years had consisted of, her first experience with sex, and how she had come to be where she was now. His attention became enthralled by her honesty.

He asked her some questions about her real parents, and why she was in the system. She was honest and told him her mother abandoned her at a church in Dallas when she was five years old and she never knew anything about her father.

"What happened to the foster-creep, Jamieson Hargrove?" asked Preston.

"You mean after that weekend?"

Preston nodded his head as the story she told him took shape in his mind.

"His little brother went to school and told all his friends what happened... who told their teacher... thus the principal. Their parents got into trouble for leaving me in his care in the first place. The social worker put me in a shelter because she didn't have another foster family that would take a sexually active teenage girl. I stayed there a few months until I was raped by the weekend house parent."

Preston opened his mouth to ask. She filled in the blanks, so he wouldn't have to.

"I was in bed sick with the flu. His wife took the other six girls to the movies. He was in college and he stayed behind to work on his dissertation for school and oversee me. I woke up with his hand over my mouth and his pulling my pajama bottoms off. He was into me so fast and so hard, there was no way to stop him. I bled for three days afterwards. He told me that if I told, no one would believe me to be anything but a liar. He said I'd be labeled a nymphomaniac and my next placement would be a psychiatric hospital. I didn't know what a 'nympho' was at the time, but I knew what a psychiatric hospital was... so... I ran.

"I guess you could say I lived on the streets the next year. When winter came, I met this older Hispanic woman at the laundry matt. I would go there a lot because it was always warm from the dryers. I would offer to help her fold or iron... since I had an abundance of experience it was easy work. I thought she worked there, but I found out later that she and her husband owned the place. She let me help her and was pleased with the job I had done, so she asked me to come back. She let me have some of her customers... people who didn't have time to do their own or want to. I could have made a lot more money on my back but, I just couldn't do that. I was tired of being used and I wanted so much more for myself. After a few weeks, she figured out I was sleeping in an old shed in an ally a few blocks down from the laundry. She didn't push herself into my life, but rather she placed a cot in the storage room and suggested that I use it and the bathroom facilities to take better care of myself. There was a small shower, and she brought me the leftovers from where she prepared breakfast for her family. I began to realize that she prepared enough for me too. I didn't want to go back to foster care, and I didn't want to get her into trouble, so I made a purposeful effort to stay out of the way of any law enforcement. After a year, we both realized nobody gave a shit. I turned 18 while living there. In the first year, I met her daughter, Ava Enriquez. She was in her first year of residency and she helped me with the educational things I needed to know by loaning me some of her old school books. I took the high school equivalency test and passed it, and then I enrolled in nursing school at a local hospital in Dallas. I bought the basics but saved most of my money for my text books. I went from 3:00 p.m. until 10:00 p.m. every weeknight and worked my laundry job during the day and on weekends."

Jaden caressed the backs of Preston's hands as they wandered up and down the front of her legs.

"I've had a few men in my life that I thought loved me enough to deal with my being honest about who I was and who I've become, and a few who tried to smack me around." She smiled at him then shrugged her shoulders. "I was wrong. I seem to be wrong a lot when it comes to trusting men." She kissed him lightly. "I don't want you in one of those places, Preston. I just couldn't be responsible in any way for doing that to you. I don't want to take advantage of you either, Cowboy. Have I made you feel that way?" she asked softly.

"No, Jaden! No!" Preston shook his head. "You could feel the same way." His hands continued their gentle scrub on the fronts of her thighs; his palms had become electric. "Do you? Do you think I followed you here, so I could get a piece of what my old man wanted?"

She gazed into his eyes. His hands relocated to her shoulders and his fingertips trailed down her arms to her hands where he threaded his fingers through hers. It was such an innocent and simple gesture. It was the gesture of a young man who had no expectations of what awaited him except the hope of discovery, and some tenderness.

"No. I don't think that at all." She brushed her lips over his soft ones as she told him. "God help me Preston, but you make me want you so bad. I'm afraid I may put a bad hurtin' on you."

He found that funny.

She looked at him and realized that considering how their day had started, he didn't believe there was anything she could do to accomplish such a thing. He didn't understand the kind of hurt she was talking about.

She leaned over, and he parted his lips to meet her in a sultry kiss. She could feel his manly body taunt and ready to be taken seriously. Jaden followed the craving force pounding in her blood stream. She shared his lips as she skillfully teased him with the slick portent that had seeped from her body due to his nearness. His breath was erratic. She aligned her private self with him and as she deepened her kiss; she came down on him burying him deep inside of her. He gasped and gripped her bottom beneath the slip of a gown; he became a moth, and she was the flame.

She began an easy, piston-like grind on him; he met her blue eyes with his dreamy, honest ones. She watched the light of understanding grow bright until the shadow of innocence was gone. There wasn't time for her to be sad, for the way he kissed her went straight to her heart.

"Oh Baby... that's incredible," he admitted with a faltering breath. His passionate kiss licked at her throat; it was erotic. "I want to push with you."

The way he said it sounded like a question. She told him.

"Not this time, Honey... just let yourself feel."

He kissed her lips in a yearning trust then closed his eyes and went back to his elbows.

She held his shoulders and watched him absorb the solace that a physical partner could give. This time of coupling brought Jaden a new wisdom of her own. There was such a thing as blind trust left in the world; she also realized her heart was not dead to love. Was she in trouble on that aspect? She pushed the thought away from her mind as a heightening awareness began to tighten the inside her body. She reminded herself that it was his first time; she fought the urge to press him for more.

Preston's head went back as he inhaled a slow breath. She saw his hands grip the bedding beneath them as the inner muscles of her body held on to him in a covetous grip. She heard him moan as the surge of tingling energy began to churn and grow in her belly attempting to lure her attention away from him. It was an even bigger rush when Preston's hands clutched her behind her knees and he sat up spreading her legs further and pulling her closer. The gesture sent him deeper and filled her with physical delight, but also with an emotional charge that was alien to her in the dimension of intimate physical contact.

He fastened his arms around her waist and held her firm as his body began to respond to the call of something wild and primitive.

"Jaden... I have to... please. I can't help it," he breathed in a raspy voice.

The expression was an act of a desperate man and it made her feel important to him; she knew he was important to her. She pressed her cheek next to his forehead; a shuddering breath escaped from her lungs at the spine-tingling thrill he was inflicting upon her body.

"Oh Preston, that's what I need, Sweetie." She kissed him deeply with a growing urgency to feel everything he could do to her. "Take us there... you were born knowing how."

Her arms tightened around his shoulders and he rolled her to her back; she intertwined her legs with his. Her mental state was elevated to a plane of awareness that could comprehend nothing but this tender man that held her while he sent a rhythmic chaos through her body in the most tender of ways. She had not known how powerful the closeness and the essence of two people sharing could be until this moment; she had always felt the rush during the practice of taking. She had been guilty of such since she had grown up. But she had known the moment she put her hand into his that afternoon, he wasn't a selfish person. It was in everything he did. This was the first time she had felt as much a part of her partner as she did herself. His way was like an artist who had a painting inside of himself and yet, possessed only a brush and the talent; her body and her heart offered the paint and a canvas in which he created something beautiful.

Preston lay there feeling completely numb; it was like his entire body was made of concrete and he couldn't move if the bed were on fire. He suddenly realized that the bed had been on fire, so was he and Jaden. He understood now what it was like for Owen; he had a cozy place to live, a work that he enjoyed, a beautiful woman he loved and that loved him back. He and Estelle shared life together every day knowing someone trustworthy was by their side to confront whatever life brought to them. They had someone that was ready and willing to exchange this wonderful physical bond... someone that craved and trusted them as a life partner. Preston knew that was the kind of life he wanted. He told himself that Owen had probably never been guilty of doing what he had done today. Preston couldn't find it inside himself to feel bad about it. Jaden was that something special that happens to a person and yet, you can't manage to believe it's real.

He felt the bed move and in a moment her voice drifted through his mind.

"I forgot I still have the stove on... I'll be back in a few minutes."

He felt her legs straddle him again. He smiled at the gesture. It was his favorite place to be now. He opened his eyes to her smiling face.

"Are you hungry? I have some soup made."

"Not really... I had a hurtin' put on me a little while ago. I can't seem to move."

She laughed softly.

"You're a keeper, Preston." She kissed him then climbed off the bed. He watched her disappear through the open doorway.

Preston closed his eyes. He couldn't feel the pain in his side tormenting him anymore; all his feeling seemed to have relocated to his groin.

He heard the water cut on in his subconscious and her singing. She appeared next to him with a glass of cola and some medication. It was the antibiotic. He took it, and then she bathed his body with a warm bath cloth. The interaction gave him another erection; she commented that he should rest for a while.

The next time his eyes opened, was when he felt something tickle his stomach. It was her hair brushing over his skin as she touched his cheek.

"I'm sorry to wake you. It's been several hours, Sweetie. I was just checking on you."

He sucked in a deep breath and was reminded of the pain in his side.

"You're overdue for a pain pill, do you want it?" she asked him. There was a tenderness in her voice and compassion in her fingertips. Preston had found out there was a passionate fire deep within her body and he craved to feel her burn him again. He reached up to her.

"No. I want you to lay down with me."

This time she tossed the slip of a gown over her head and pulled the sheet away from his nude body. She sat down next to him. Her warm, soft hand caressed his chest then his stomach. Preston gazed at her beneath heavy lids; his fingers discovered the shallow valley of her spine. He felt her skin explode with tiny, pin-like bumps and the tips of her breasts tightened. It was a magical thing to watch a woman's body respond to him. She was radiant and her body flawless. Her breasts were round, slightly weighted and elegant; the pointed tips dared him to suckle. His hand urged her closer to his face as he went to his elbow for support. She smiled at him, tossed her hair over her shoulder, and then turned and offered herself to him.

Preston felt her delicate fingers slide into his hair behind his ear while her other hand gripped his masculine body. The feel of his hard, throbbing shaft in her velvety hand brought him an indulgent feeling of power. She kissed his brow as his tongue circled the excited flesh of her breast.

He began to push into her hand.

She spoke to him in a loving voice.

"Try not to let-go, Sweetie. Do you know how to stop yourself?"

His hand slid beneath hers to manipulate his body while his lips moved to her other breast.

She enjoyed the feel of his suckling a few more minutes, but then she denied him her body and relocated her kiss with the purpose of casting a mind-altering spell over him. She kissed and thrilled his body until he had to take charge and clamp down on himself with a more assertive grip. Preston's legs felt as though lava pumped through his veins. He pushed into her kiss because he couldn't seem to help it.

She kissed her way up his body to his lips. He was hungry for her. He was very thorough with his kiss, sometimes sharing a feather-light brush of his lips and sometimes taking a deep, passionate drink. He was attentive to every touch, every whisper, and every breath that exchanged between them. She had never experienced any man that touched her with his soul like Preston. Jaden realized that was the key. He cared about her and he needed her to connect with him on a level that had never been expected of her. This was the first time she had ever felt needed for something more than physical.

Scherry and Mollie ran down the back steps with sparklers sizzling in each hand to greet Sheriff Cotton. He got out of his car, and the little girls handed him a sparkler for each hand. He squatted so they could light another from them then they twirled them together. Cotton chuckled while the little girls giggled non-stop.

He had accepted an invitation for fresh catfish and all the trimmings. Cotton stepped onto the patio and greeted Celia with a smile as he thanked her for the invitation. He accepted the large glass of sweet tea and an empty plate to fill, which he did very well. He sat down at the table with the men and began to enjoy his food. He commented on the flavor, and Rueben told him about the boys catching them at the river the previous night.

Cotton wiped his mouth on his napkin and stuck his thumb up in the air when he saw Charlie and Eli come up the back steps. Charlie went straight to him and shook his hand. Eli did likewise. Charlie asked him if he had heard from Preston.

The sheriff frowned and shook his head.

"You all are expecting him?" questioned Cotton. He shoved a hush-puppy in his mouth as he listened to Charlie tell him that the Colonel had taken the houseboat up river the day before and left Preston to make do at the camp. Cotton didn't say anything, but his instincts told him something was wrong. It was the way his hair on his arms stiffened. He guessed it was silly, but he trusted it. The built-in warning had gotten him out of many a close call.

Cotton finished his meal and visited another half an hour, so he wouldn't be conspicuous in his worry. He radioed in that he was back on duty then he patted his belly and thanked his hostesses for the wonderful meal. The girls held his hands and chattered while they walked him down the back steps to his patrol car.

Cotton went by the camp house first because of what Charlie had told him; however, he found the houseboat docked in its normal spot. Preston's Jeep had not been at the camp house and it wasn't here. Cotton rang the bell at the gate; the only response was a deafening silence. He found it eerie. He turned to leave when his eyes noticed dark spots on the board walk. He opened the gate and squatted down for a closer look. He touched it with his finger tip and found it to be red and sticky. Cotton knew it was blood, and it shook him to his core. He ventured further onto the property and found more.

He knocked, but no one answered. He found a side window going up the outside staircase and looked through the wayward blinds to discover Dane Reid lying in the floor. He went back and forced the door open with a push from his shoulder and the toe of his boot. He could hear him breathing deeply and contented as he lay in the middle of a room in shambles. Cotton noticed the leg from the table still in his hand. There was blood on it, and there was a puddle next to it that had run from a larger, more concentrated spot in the kitchen. A closer inspection assured him that the only injuries the Colonel had were the knot on his forehead and his skinned knuckles.

Cotton called for back-up on the radio. He began a careful inspection of the houseboat and was careful not to disturb anything while doing so. He called for the forensic specialist on duty to assist him at the address. Cotton found blood in several small dried and coagulated puddles on the floor between the door and the bathroom sink, drops on the counter, a smear on the refrigerator, and a beaded necklace broken and scattered. He also noticed two partial bloody boot prints formed in the drips of blood that marred the kitchen floor, and the hint of a smaller one that looked very dainty. Cotton knew Preston had been there. He checked Preston's room upstairs and found no sign of him.

Cotton had enough. He pulled his cuffs out of his belt and fastened Dane Reid's hands behind him. He left him lying there as assistance notified him, they were pulling into the yard.

There was still no sign of Preston. Cotton recalled the boy telling him months back that he wouldn't bother him again concerning the conflict between him and the Colonel. The sinking feeling in Cotton's gut was getting deeper with every dead end. It was evident the boy had escaped once again... but to where? How badly was he hurt? Was there someone else injured as well? Had they left in Preston's Jeep? Was Preston able to leave on his own? The questions kept popping into his mind and he had no answers to them. He tried to organize his thoughts as to where he should start to look for the young man. He decided on the obvious, but none of the surrounding emergency rooms had treated him. Cotton was frustrated, and he had no idea where else to look. He had already been to the three places Preston would find shelter.

Deputies Hunt Abernathy and Boudreaux Sonnier' called to him as they cautiously pushed the door open. Cotton met them outside on the boat deck. His deputies listened closely as the sheriff told them of his suspicions and what he had found at the residence. His men were fond of Preston. He serviced their vehicles and came to the jail every Thursday to wash them. They also knew the sheriff had taken to him, and the boy's father was a son-of-a-bitch.

Hunt asked if he had thought to look at the garage, suggesting that maybe Preston had gone to the break room for the first aid kit. He offered to go by and check. The sheriff told them to arrange for emergency medical personnel to transport Colonel Reid to the emergency room for treatment and when he regained consciousness, they were to read him his rights. Cotton left them to follow through with the Colonel while the forensic specialist worked the crime scene at the houseboat. Cotton headed to the county barn to see if Preston was there.

The sheriff found the garage barn locked tight, but he went in and called to Preston just in case. He was frustrated when he found no trace of the young man. He used the phone while he was there to call the ranch. Cotton told Owen what he had found at the boat. Cotton could tell that Owen was as worried as he was, and he tried to help by suggesting several places for him to look. Cotton told him he had tried them already. Owen told him he didn't know where else they could search; however, he suggested that Sheriff Cotton talk to Charlie considering the boys were best friends. The idea spurred new hope in Cotton.

Sheriff Cotton entered the emergency room to find Deputy Abernathy waiting to escort him through the busy corridor to the exam room where Colonel Reid was being treated. Cotton asked Hunt if they had read the Colonel his rights. Hunt responded in the negative and respectfully reminded his boss of the Colonel's lack of consciousness. Deputy Abernathy's radio sounded off and Deputy Sonnier informed him that the prisoner was conscious and, on his way, back from x-ray.

They turned the corner and stopped in the hallway as hospital staff and Deputy Sonnier came towards them with the Colonel laying on the gurney. Cotton had been aware of the anger inside this man for as long as he had known him. Colonel Reid's military training enabled Dane, the civilian, to keep the anger caged like a dangerous animal. Still, when alcohol was involved, the beast had been known to gain control over its jailer, and Preston was usually its prey. Cotton didn't like the fact, but he understood this man. He too wrestled with his own inner beasts, especially when it came to this man. He wanted to respect the Colonel as a patriot and a veteran, but the man's on-going behavior made it very difficult. Because of Preston, his perspective had changed drastically in these last few months. Cotton's concern for Preston far outweighed any respect Colonel Reid's service record demanded.

The Colonel was rubbing the knot on his forehead with his free hand while the wrist of his other hand was securely fastened to the frame of the small portable bed on which he laid. His red and swollen eyes connected with the sheriff's. Cotton tapped into his own professional training to reign in the contempt he felt for this man. He followed them into the exam room.

Colonel Reid was used to having his way and exercised this authoritative demeanor while expecting people to respond to him in an obedient manner. He did not hesitate to question Cotton about his confinement.

"What happened? Why am I here? And why in the hell am I being restrained to this goddamn bed?" The Colonel's voice was scratchy and the large, protruding lump between his eyes would insinuate he possessed an enormous headache, and yet his arrogance seemed to suck the air out of the room.

"I have an employee that's missing," answered Cotton plainly. "No one has seen or heard from Preston in almost 24 hours. He was expected at Charlie's birthday dinner and never arrived. That's not like Preston. Charlie is important to him. When I went to check on him, I found you... passed out... a broken table leg in your hand with blood on it. There is blood everywhere... from the kitchen to the outside gate. It's not your blood, Colonel," specified Cotton for the sake of clarity.

"Dammit man, that boy deserves a hell of a lot better than you for a father. You're a disgrace to humanity like this... not to mention your country, and you're dangerous. I'm tired of it!" shouted Cotton as his emotions gained the upper hand. He paused a few seconds to calm himself then started again. "I need to know what happened. I need to know where Preston is, Colonel. The boat is in shambles. The evidence at the scene leads me to draw only one conclusion; he's got to be badly injured. I demand to know what happened! What did you do to him? Is he even ali-" Cotton clamped his jaw teeth together when he realized what he was about to say. He sucked in a frustrated breath and rubbed the knot in the back of his neck.

The Colonel's explanation only added to his stress.

"He left for school." There was an uncertainty in the man's voice as he frowned at the ceiling; obviously, his memory was as vague as his answer. "I haven't seen him since."

Cotton wasn't going to allow this man to ignore the seriousness of the situation just because he was suffering from a memory lapse, which was alcohol induced.

"That's it? That's all you've got to say? He left for school, and you haven't seen him since," parroted Cotton. "Since when? What day was it? Wednesday? Thursday? Friday? I need to know. You're supposed to be his father... so you should be able to tell me!" exclaimed Cotton in a condescending tone of voice.

The man looked at him through murderous eyes.

"Don't talk down to me, Emmett," snarled the Colonel. He snatched on the hand cuffs with a bit of temper as he attempted to sit up, but all he managed to do was puke in the floor. Dane Reid shook his head as he wiped his mouth on his sleeve.

The deputies took a step back from the repulsive and drunken excuse of a man, but Cotton stood firm in his disgust.

"Tell me what happened!" he demanded again in a voice that exercised his authority over the retired Colonel.

"I DON'T KNOW!" yelled the man in response. The Colonel grabbed his head as though it was about to crack open then fell back on the uncomfortable, makeshift bed.

Cotton's experience assured him this man couldn't remember the last 24 hours. He thought of the young man's loving and beautiful mother and his heart skipped a beat. He silently prayed that she was watching over her son, because the man responsible for Preston had no clue of his well-being, and even less knowledge of where he could be found.

Cotton's mind and spirit were finally in one accord concerning this man. The former glory Colonel Reid had earned while a patriot in service to his country had been degraded by his own lack of self-control, and his arrogance. Cotton felt he owed him nothing in the way of respect. The professional way he addressed Dane Reid conveyed the esteem he felt for the trusted office to which he had been elected.

"We've talked about your treatment of that young man, Mr. Reid. I gave you a choice... and unfortunately; your behavior has left me with none.

Dane Reid, it's my duty as sheriff of Liberty County to inform you that you're under arrest for assault, child abuse and neglect, and child endangerment. You will be informed of any additional charges should they come to light. When the doctor is finished with your treatment, these men will inform you of your rights under law, and then escort you to the county jail for processing." He waited for Dane to object, but he didn't.

"Dane, I'm fed up with your treatment of that young man, and I'm not going to rest until life changes in his favor," declared the sheriff with conviction. "But first, I've got to find him!"

Dane Reid glared at the ceiling in a questionable and awkward silence. Anyone could see he was worried, and he truly didn't have a clear thought in his head. Cotton shook his head as he studied the man.

"My God man... you need help."

Boo's steady voice came from over Cotton's shoulder to re-direct his thoughts. His deputy's Cajun tongue was something Cotton had become accustomed to years ago.

"Mon cher, we din't look in de riva 'round da boat earlier dis afernoon... ya know it be gettin' dark soon."

Boo's after-thought sent chills down Cotton's spine, and the hair on his arms was yet to relax.

"The Jeep was gone, Boo, I can't think like that." He turned to his deputy. The man was wise and river smart. He was part of the huge family tree that had migrated from Gator Creek just south of Lafayette. Cotton knew he couldn't take the chance of not looking.

"I need you here... can you get your brother to do it from the water?"

Boo nodded his head.

"I'll cawl, Tug." Deputy Sonnier left the room to make the arrangements.

Cotton turned back to Dane just as the man puked in the floor again.

The radio in the kitchen echoed through the small house like a dream lingering on the edge of consciousness. Jaden lay still next to Preston listening to him breathe while studying his magnificent, strong face in the moonlight. She had already studied every inch of his body, and as articulate as Preston was about the sensitive places on her body, she was certain he had memorized them. He had asked her about every little scar and told her the funniest stories about him and his best friend, Charlie. She knew he liked carrot cake, his favorite color was green and that it bothered him when a day passed without thinking of his deceased mother. She knew where to find him at work, which school he attended, and that he wanted to join the police academy if he didn't get detoured by the service first. He was hilariously funny, an honor roll student, a good mechanic, a good listener and he could play the radio in tune. He obviously wasn't squeamish at the sight of blood, and he was a good fisherman and hunter. She knew he could break down, clean and put back together over 30 different firearms in all makes and models that she didn't understand. He was handy with tools and fixing things, and he had a horse named, Ritter. He had bedroom eyes that made her knees weak, and strong, sure hands to match his heart. He was, without a doubt, the best lover she had ever experienced. She knew in this one afternoon that he had stolen her heart. She wanted to keep him in her life more than anything she had ever wanted. He was a man if ever she had known one. She didn't want to close her eyes because if she did, morning would be upon them sooner and their time would be over.

She thought about his appetite when they had eaten a bowl of soup together. He had bragged on it. It made her happy to know he enjoyed it. Afterwards, they had soaked in a hot bath by candle light. He used her toothbrush and her deodorant with no hang up about its sweet smell.

Preston sighed with contentment. A few seconds passed, and his hand went to his head where the cut had been mended. His eyes fluttered open. She didn't speak because she was so full of emotion, she didn't think she could hide it.

He turned his head to her then he rolled over. He smiled as his hand ran over her bare shoulder and then her hip. He pulled the cover away from her body then pulled her knee up and scooted closer, so their legs could become entangled. He kissed her over and over; his hand eased between her legs and caressed her. She pushed into his touch and was rewarded with his willing, craving fingers to please her. It had been a long time since she had felt this trusting with her heart, and excited to hope that someone trusted her. She knew Preston was someone special and he would become someone that others looked up to in his life. She felt it in her soul. She knew that he would live in her heart for the rest of her life.

He rolled to his back and took her with him; his stamina was uncontested. His hands held her waist, and Jaden noticed the discoloration on his side next to her inner thigh. She voiced her concern.

"Sweetie, this is looking really bad. It's got to hurt. I shouldn't be sitting on you like this."

His palms glided over the planes of her hips and thighs.

"I like for you to sit on me." He sat up slowly; their arms enthralled each other. "I like everything about my baby."

She felt tears burn her eyes at the way he addressed her again. The first couple of times she thought of it as an endearment and it touched her, but this time he said it in a possessive way.

He held her easy-like as he rolled to his good side and laid her down. She turned and pressed her back against his chest.

He held her and touched her as though she belonged to him. It was like he gave himself to her as if he loved her.

She reached out and took hold of the headboard and pulled her knees upward hoping he would share himself with her again. The rush of his hot body branded her deep within; it was on a level of intimate fusion that went all the way to her heart. She held on tight knowing that emotionally she was sliding into the most unexplored and hazardous place she had ever been in her life. It was wonderful. It was forbidden. It was so unfair. A swell of emotion made her breathless for a moment. She had sworn to herself never to give her heart away again, but she didn't know what to do when someone just took it from her. She couldn't restrain the strangled sound in her throat as she tried to breathe.

Preston stopped suddenly. His lips and breath touched her shoulder.

"Jaden... Baby, am I hurting you?"

She shook her head.

He was tuned in to her on a level of closeness and consideration that led him to just hold her in his arms and heed inner caution until he was sure she was all right. But she continued her efforts to raise his awareness and prime his body; she was in complete surrender to this powerful force that she had awakened in him. Preston was encouraged by her passionate motivation and after a few moments, he re-joined her efforts.

In the minutes that followed, Preston realized something. He came to understand this craving; the force inside of him impacted him more than any drug the doctor had given him. He could no longer feel any pain in his body, only the pounding force of his heartbeat as it pulsed in harmony with hers; it was even in his fingertips. He found himself, once again, at that place where instinct took over and shoved reason from between them. Desire impulsively drove him to his knees, and he took her with him then reached past her for support. She shifted her bottom so that his exploration could realize another dimension of compatibility with her.

The moon bathed the entire room with a soft blue hue. Their breaths panted softly while sharing the excitement in this union. Their bones and flesh moved together as practiced lovers, but their essence was like two carefree spirits celebrating flight. This venture soon changed as the dangerous winds of ecstasy blew them into an emotional and physical storm. It was like they were a shooting star together... both on fire and neither of them cared if they got burned.

Preston learned for himself, the kind of hurt she had spoken of earlier. They climaxed together; his erotic tortured allegiance to her resounded throughout the small dwelling.

Preston went back on his haunches; his strong arms held them on this side of sanity. They were welded together by an inferno of passion. His head rested against her shoulder and her smooth back clung to his chest while his hands coveted the feel of her breasts and his virile, adamant body throbbed in the secret depth of hers. He loved the way she breathed his name, and the way her chest rose and fell beneath his palms. He memorized the way their bodies shook together, and he cherished the way they clung to each other until they felt like nothing more than a sated heap of embers crumbling together.

She cried softly, but this time Preston was not alarmed. He just held her because understanding had come upon them. They willingly shared a disabling vulnerability that stripped them of the callousness a person's soul develops in this unfair world. There was joy and hope in it; a celebration of acceptance for the true person that was left. She looked back at him as he brushed her cheeks with his fingertips. He nuzzled her brow. Their lips met and sealed the wordless covenant their bodies had made.

CHAPTER 9

Preston's thoughts were consumed with Jaden as he drove back to Westville. The memories of what they had done together floated through his mind as the hot July wind whipped around the Jeep. He could still feel her arms and the way she had clung to him, and the taste of her goodbye was on his tongue. It had hurt when they opened the door and stepped out onto the small porch because they knew the bond between them would not be accepted in either of their worlds.

Tears came to her eyes as she looked up at him. She confessed that she was worried about him going back to the boat and warned him to watch out for his self. She told him he was the best thing that had ever happened to her, and then she kissed him like she would never see him again. She shoved an envelope in his pocket and hastily walked away. Preston watched her car disappear around the curve in the road on her way to work. He pulled out the envelope and found a small slip of paper with her phone number and address, and an extra key to the front door. The paper had a simple note artfully scrolled across the top. It said, 'Don't forget me... with love, Jaden'. It made his heart pound to just touch it in his pocket. How could he ever forget the emotional storm he experienced with her?

The longer he drove, the more he dreaded seeing his father. He craved independence. It was a restless ache that Dane reinforced every time they got into a conflict; only now, he wanted it for different reasons.

He turned on to River Road and after a few minutes and two more turns; he drove into the yard at the houseboat. He did a double-take when he saw the yellow tape across the gate. He knew Sheriff Cotton had found out. Preston felt a panicky feeling attack his resolve.

He thought of Jaden encouraging him to be honest about going to Ava for treatment and staying at her place. She had not acted as though their making love with each other was a mistake. But if she had, it would have tainted the cherished feelings that were all jumbled up in it for him. He was not seasoned at understanding a woman, but he sensed she felt the same way. He believed he had impacted her life as much as she had his. Preston knew he would protect her no matter what and, to do that, he had to be the boy he was yesterday, even though that person no longer cowered inside of him. He was different now, there were specific things he wanted for his life. A good woman was one of them. He wished he was old enough to offer Jaden a good life, but he had nothing to offer her at this point.

She had told him she was used to disappointment, and she had learned to embrace it because it was the only thing in life that had always been there for her. He wasn't sure he understood how a woman as beautiful, smart and gentle as Jaden could have this perspective. He reminded himself, his father had been one of her disappointments. He swore to himself, if he got the chance to establish a viable relationship with her, he would not be one of them.

He looked at the yellow tape and wondered what his next move should be. Obviously, his father wasn't here, or the tape wouldn't be there. 'Where was Dane?' thought Preston. His gut told him he wasn't going to like the answer to that question. There was only one source of information that he could count on and trust without feeling obligated because of it. He needed to talk to Charlie. He knew his friend well, and at 10:30 a.m. on a Sunday morning, there was only one place to find him.

Preston was lucky the Jenson kid was horsing around outside instead of going into service. He gave the kid a quarter to deliver his note. He waited in the shade of the cottonwood trees next to the cemetery.

It was only a few minutes until Charlie emerged from the back door of the sanctuary. The organ echoed through the swaying limbs above Preston's head as he watched his buddy approach. It was a fact that the loyalty and alliance he shared with Charlie, clashed with the need to protect Jaden. He wanted to tell Charlie everything; there wasn't much they didn't know about each other. He thought about this as he watched Charlie get closer; his friend's worried expression assured Preston things were bad. He was true of heart. Preston realized that, when it came to Jaden, it wouldn't be fair to involve his buddy.

Charlie broke into a trot as he passed the parking lot and saw Preston waiting.

"Hey!" His friend called out as he neared; however, he stopped abruptly when he saw Preston's bruised and swollen face, and the line of stitches over his eye. Charlie's strong brows shifted towards the straight line of his nose as anger distorted his handsome features. "Dammit, Preston!" He thrust himself sideways into the passenger seat and turned to get a closer look at his buddy.

Charlie's reaction surprised Preston. They were real around each other. He had heard Charlie say a colorful word a couple of times during their friendship; however, this was Sunday, and they were at the church of all places. It was sinful, but somehow funny.

Preston smiled.

Charlie huffed.

"It ain't funny, dammit!" He spat out the words as though they tasted bitter. "I was scared as hell he had killed you this time... so is Cotton! He's been looking everywhere for you! Dane's in jail; he couldn't tell the sheriff anything. I heard Owen tell Rueben and Mr. Silver that Sheriff Cotton even had Tuggle Sonnier lookin' over the river for a body... just in case. What happened? Where've you been?"

Worry pushed the smile from Preston's face.

"Shit," breathed the weary young man. He closed his eyes and laid his head back against the seat for a moment, knowing it was time for him to face the reality that would eventually find him. He figured by night fall, he would be in a shelter with a bunch of scared kids. The only thing they would have in common was two artificial parents and an officer of the state deciding what was best for them.

"What are they holding him on? Do you know?" questioned Preston.

"No. But I know that the sheriff was really pissed at him. You should call him, Preston. We can go to my house. You can call from there. Let me tell Owen I'm leaving with you." He started to get out of the Jeep when Preston caught his arm.

"Wait... Charlie."

"What?" Charlie sat back in the seat as he turned his attention back to his friend.

"This is probably the last time we'll get to be..." Preston paused, "... just us. You know... pals. I'll probably be in one of those shitty group homes by nightfall. Anyway," he reached over to the small compartment in the dash and pulled out the white paper bag and handed it to him. "Happy Birthday Buddy!"

Charlie took the bag and pulled out the small leather case. A slight smile cracked his worried expression as he stared at the collection of fine silver guitar picks.

"Preston, these are so cool. This must have cost you a wad."

"They're stainless steel. Silver bends too easy... each one has a symbol for Texas etched on it. Turn one over," he encouraged his friend.

Charlie grinned at the beautiful initials on the back of the pick. He didn't know what to say. He would value them the rest of his life as much as the things Owen and Estelle had given him.

Charlie felt his throat trying to close due to the turmoil of feelings churning inside of him. He needed Preston in his life.

"Dang it, Preston... I just don't understand life sometimes!" Charlie was speechless for a moment. He didn't want to lose his best friend. It was all so unfair. He felt sick at the thought of Preston with people who didn't know him and who wouldn't see his worth as a friend, or how brave he is. "I swear Buddy; I'll have them in my pocket the day they lay me to rest." He sighed. "I know we seem like know-nothin' kids to a lot of people, but... you and me... we know different. We have plans for our lives. You're going to the police academy. I'm gonna have my own land management company and raise horses." Charlie fell silent for a moment as he tried to put all of this in perspective. "It ain't right, Preston. This is your home. I'm not giving up on the chance that things will work out in your favor, and I don't want you to either. Something good could happen. You won't be this age forever. It won't be long until you can go where you please. You hear me, Preston... no matter what... you will always have a place to crash where ever I am. I swear!"

Preston knew Charlie meant every word, and it made him feel good despite his troubles. Preston's mind went to Jaden. He wanted Charlie to know about her. He wanted Charlie to understand the hopefulness they had exchanged with each other. He opened his mouth to tell him but stopped suddenly. He did not want to get Charlie into trouble and due to the circumstances surrounding him and Jaden, Preston fought the urge to tell Charlie about her.

Charlie's words butted into Preston's thoughts.

"I'll be back in a minute. Thanks for the lambskin and the picks, Preston. I know they'll make that raggedy ole box I've been plucking on sound better."

Preston nodded at him.

"Well... they'll make you look like a hot shot anyway," he joked then forced a smile.

Preston stared at the brass house key that Jaden had given him a couple of hours ago. He wished he could pack his things and go back to her, but he knew that was an impossible dream.

Preston sat lost in thought as the music had stopped and the pastor's faint, teaching words could be heard every few seconds. The birds sang cheerfully, and the wind blew through the trees above him to make the leaves sway gently back and forth. He was a wayward soul, but he was not so wicked that he did not notice how the earth stilled on this Sunday morning. The surrounding peacefulness was completely opposite of what was going on inside of him.

The hum of distant tires coming down the country road could be heard before the vehicle came in to sight. When it topped the hill, Preston instinctively looked up. A huge knot tightened in his gut as Sheriff Cotton impulsively hit the brakes to slow down, and then he steered his patrol car in to the shaded spot in front of the Jeep.

Preston pulled his keys out of the ignition and slowly got out of the Jeep. The taped binding Jaden had put on him that morning would not allow him to bend in any direction above his waist. Preston saw the sheriff speak into the radio while his trained eyes inspected him. He could not read the expression on the older man's face. He thought it was fear, but that didn't make sense because Sheriff Cotton was the bravest man he knew. He stopped at the front fender of the patrol car and waited.

Cotton got out and left the door standing open. He stopped just in front of Preston. Cotton's hand touched his chin and then turned his head for a closer look at his face. He was surprised when the man pulled him into his arms and held him. They were strong arms, full of caring and thankfulness; he could feel it. Preston had never experienced acceptance on this level, not even Owen had ever hugged him. He responded without thought and wrapped his arms around Sheriff Cotton. The older man didn't make light of it either by pushing him away in a couple of seconds. It seemed the most natural thing in the world for them, like Cotton was the one responsible for him. He had been so good to him. This man obviously cared more for him than his own father.

"God knows I'm glad to see you boy. I'm thankful that you're all right." Cotton gripped the back of Preston's neck as he looked him in the eye for a moment. Preston saw the sincerity in the sheriff's face. The man pushed him backwards a little further and then lifted the tail of his shirt because he felt the teenager's immobility. Cotton's jaws went stiff.

"Tell me what happened, Preston. I need to know, Son."

Charlie came back. He remained quiet as he listened to his buddy tell about the clash with his father and how the woman Dane had invited there had been caught in one of his father's drunken rages. He told Cotton that he had no choice but to intervene. He told them he insisted she leave while she could, but because he was injured, she felt responsible. She wanted to call the law, but he talked her out of it. Cotton and Charlie knew why he had done so.

"She took me to the clinic in East mid-town. She's a nurse... and volunteers there sometimes. I followed her in the Jeep. The doctor put stitches in my head and took x-rays... three of them are cracked. She gave me a shot, ten days of antibiotics and some other stuff for pain. I haven't taken any of those, I... I didn't realize the shot would make me so loopy." Preston paused a second. "She suggested that I not drive until I was clear headed... so I crashed at Ms. Sullivan's house last night. I didn't know that anyone other than Charlie would miss me." Preston's eyes met those of his friend. "I wasn't in any shape to call you, 'C'. I can see now that was a mistake, but... I wasn't sure what to do. Truth is... I'd rather take a beatin' from him every day than go to some pretend parents and have a stranger decide what's best for me. I guess that's been my path all along, and I've just been too stubborn to accept it."

Cotton spoke his mind; it was the crutch of his job.

"She's an adult, Preston. She should have called someone. Your father couldn't remember a blasted thing. We've been in a tizzy trying to figure out what had happened... where you were, and if you were alive."

Preston's defensiveness came out before he thought better of it.

"She was almost strangled to death by the mean bastard, Sheriff! I asked her not to report it, so I wouldn't end up in some shelter and she still felt like she owed me something! She got me treatment and tried to help me the best she could... because I helped her! Who was she supposed to have called?"

Preston's senses were on edge. He couldn't fight the helplessness that was suddenly all too real, and the truth of how his life really was. He was scared to let himself want or need anyone. The people who seemed to drift through it were like gusts of wind blowing him around then dropping him somewhere on their way to somewhere else. He was grateful for the time they cared, but it still hurt to know there wasn't someone he could turn to no matter what. The few hours he was with Jaden, confiding in her and listening to her pain, being inside of her, absorbing her heartbeat with every pore of his body was the most needed and loved he had felt in his entire life.

He turned away from them as his eyes began to sting with anger and frustration; the hot, uncontrollable tears rolled down his face despite his trying to control them with his will. He shook his head as understanding choked him with sorrow. Preston's hand went to his hip as he buried his pain in the sleeve at his elbow. He called upon the memory of Jaden's arms around him that morning, and the bond he felt with her calmed him somewhat.

Charlie watched his friend in this private moment of suffering, and old memories gave him insight to know some of how Preston felt. The only difference was, Sheriff Cotton gave a damn about Preston, about people in general, and tried to help when the system did not. Still, Charlie knew Preston better than anyone and there was something more going on inside of him. It was why he had turned away; Preston knew he could read the truth in his face. They had always been able to sense things about each other because of the kindred nature of their friendship. It was impossible for them to keep anything from one another.

A few minutes passed then Preston turned back to them.

"I'm sorry things are so damn screwed up, Sheriff. But Charlie's my friend... not my keeper, and I told you I wouldn't bother you with this again." He sighed. "Don't you understand? I know how to fight Dane Reid, but... I don't know how to fight the system." He shook his head as he looked at Cotton. "I'm tired of fighting... so let's just get it over with."

Preston turned to Charlie; he took four long strides towards him with his hand stuck out. Charlie grabbed it in a firm, yet desperate grip. Preston bumped his shoulder against that of his best and only friend in a rash and hasty goodbye then shoved the keys to the Jeep into Charlie's hand. Preston avoided looking at either of them as he walked over to the passenger side of the sheriff's cruiser, got in and closed the door.

Cotton was set back by the systematic savvy of this young man. He knew exactly where he stood within the guidelines of the law and his situation. It would be his guess that Dane had threatened him with it to keep him in line as a boy. Cotton already knew Preston was intellectually sharp and wise for his age, but for the first time, he saw a broken spirit in this young man. It almost killed him to watch him relinquish it in such a way and surrender to his fate.

Cotton looked back at Charlie then impulsively started towards him, but didn't stop until he reached Owen, who was standing a short distance away from them. The concerned expression on his older brother's face assured Charlie that he had heard everything.

"We'll take him, Cotton, if Judge Adler will allow it," exclaimed Owen.

"I'm willing to do so myself; he already knows that. But the way I work, it may not be what's best for him. The judge told me the boy's father will have to make a responsible care plan for him, and this time, it's mandatory that he go to the hospital to dry out and get some help. His doing so would keep it out of the courts for now. We could talk to Colonel Reid together. What do you think?"

Owen nodded his head in agreement.

"We love Preston, Emmett. I'm willing to try anything that will keep him safe and enable him to be happy. He's a good man... despite the faults of his father."

The sheriff only asked Preston two questions on the way to his office: Could he tell him how to get in contact with Jaden Sullivan, and would he mind staying with him and Owen until they can get his father some help?

Preston had been surprised and asked how that was possible? He listened, while at the same time wondered, if he should tell Sheriff Cotton how to reach Jaden. He had memorized her number and address the first time he read it. He decided not giving him something about her would be too obvious. He did not want to be dishonest. He thought about the people that had hurt her in her young life. He could remember his mother's suffering through the illness and the relief in her face as death found her. Somehow, he had understood there was mercy in it. But there was only one person who seemed bent on hurting him. He thought about Jaden and all the wrong which she had endured at the hands of others. He realized just how blessed, as Ms. Estelle always said, he had been even with Dane as his father.

"She lives in Satartia off Highway 540. I remember seeing the county sign... the house is on Sparks Road. Her name tag on her uniform said East Dallas Memorial."

Sheriff Cotton called dispatch and asked Lennis if he would see if he could contact her and let her know he needed to talk to her about Colonel Reid's assault. Preston believed the sheriff was concerned about what had happened to her as well.

They entered the station and several of the staff expressed their affection for him with a handshake or a pat on the shoulder. Sheriff Cotton needed to make some call-backs, so he sent Preston to the kitchen to eat some lunch.

June Lee Pickett, the large woman who ran the jail's kitchen was also a prisoner. She was funny and nice to everyone. Preston liked her very much. The details of why and how she had shot her husband in the chest six years ago, was a matter of public record. Cotton was always encouraging him to ask questions and study the procedure of county government if he was serious about making law enforcement a career. Preston was curious as to how a woman as gentle and caring as June Lee could commit murder. She was open about her life, but he felt compelled to ask her permission before reading the facts of her case.

He stopped in the doorway of the kitchen because he had never heard her sing. He stepped out of the way of foot traffic to the corner to listen because it was a beautiful thing. Thanks to Dane, Charlie and June Lee, Preston's mind and heart were full of the reality of life. The hardships in their lives were similar. He had thought about this a lot because of his relationship with Dane and had begun to feel like he wore a target. But after meeting and getting to know Charlie, he could see things from a different perspective. He understood that alcohol was the ammunition, and Dane became the weapon. He was close to Charlie because they had the scars of this realism in common, and he had discovered the same connection with June Lee Pickett. Suddenly, the image of Jaden's beautiful face popped into his head, and shadows of the ill-treatment she had endured came with it. Her burdens were of a different nature; still, his eyes had been opened to anomalous truth. There are people in this world who are beleaguered with unjust cruelty which, more times than not, is inflicted by those who are supposed to care about them. He could not explain, nor did he understand the force behind this principle of nature; still, he believed it was so.

The older woman's joyful song of grace was uplifting, and the devotion in which she sang captivated Preston. A smile claimed his face, even during his current trials. Her peaceful essence had the power to calm his spirit and nurture hopefulness to grow inside of him.

June Lee was serving a 15-year sentence handed down by the judge. She had admitted to killing her husband in cold blood even though she denied that it was premeditated. The facts of June Lee's life tugged at Preston's heart. He realized, though the law may be written in black and white; the gray areas of life were many and seldom as simple. He thought of the things he had come to know about her and a deeper respect stirred in his chest.

The documentation on her case was plenty. Moby Pickett, June Lee's husband and the father of their eight children, was an alcoholic. There were dozens of reports in the file made by June Lee, as well as her oldest daughter, Leigh Ann Pickett-Newsom. She had married the year before and was visiting at the time. No arrest could be made because charges were never filed. There were many reasons why, but Preston could see that money and fear were the main issues. Apparently, Mr. Pickett had a habit of threatening his wife with an old pistol he kept on his person. There were three documented occasions when Moby threatened his wife while holding a pistol to her head. The deputy that worked the case had documented the man's words as exact, 'just one bullet is all it would take to end his misery'.

The oldest daughter testified in court on behalf of her mother. She stated that she had come to visit a few days to share the good news of making them grandparents. Ms. Newsom stated her father had been intoxicated the entire duration of her visit, which was three days. She told law enforcement the dispute had begun because Moby accused her mother of putting eggs in the cornbread, which he did not like. When her mother denied it, Moby punched her in the face for talking back to him, breaking her nose and dislocating her two front teeth. The daughter stated, when she verbally defended her mother, Moby pointed his pistol at her. Her mother reacted and pushed him over a chair because she was carrying her first child. Her father fell to the floor, and the pistol went off during the fall. The bullet struck and killed the old hound dog June Lee had loved and considered her friend for the better part of 17 years. Moby ordered the daughter to bury the dog. She took her siblings to help her at the insistence of her mother.

June Lee's testimony placed Moby in his chair with a labeled bottle of spirits. The hateful man scolded June Lee for her tears and blamed her for the animal's death. He told her she was going to have to put meat on the table since he no longer had a hunting dog to tree a squirrel. According to June Lee, she cleaned up the mess made by the animal's death, and then went outside to help see to the grave. When she and the children came back to the house, she found the cornbread and the stew she was going to feed her family dumped on the ground by the back gate. She admitted her anger and disgust for her husband and was given the chance to explain by her attorney. She told the judge that Moby was wrong to accuse her of putting eggs in the cornbread because she didn't have any eggs. The fool she married had spent all their grocery money on liquor and she was forced to boil their last laying hen to make the stew that day. She stated, seeing the bread and the stew on the ground hurt worse than the punch to her face because she did not have anything else to feed her children. She told the court room that she picked up the cornbread and salvaged as much of it as she could. After wrapping it in a cloth, she gave it to the oldest daughter and instructed her to take the younger one's home with her and she would come for them as soon as Moby was done with the bottle. The record showed that she contemplated packing their things and leaving for good, and since Moby had drank his self to sleep, she saw the opportunity. She admitted taking the pistol off the side table where he had laid it. Reason and self-

preservation motivated her to do so in case he awoke and caught her before she could leave. She was making her last trip to the truck when he stood up out of his chair and yelled at her. She was startled and dropped the suitcase in her hand. Moby had a fist full of her hair before she could get down the front porch steps. She heard the roots being ripped from her scalp and thought of the pistol. She had put it in her pocket because she was going to throw it in the river when she crossed over the bridge. He spun her around by her hair and cocked his fist to punish her. June Lee stated that she panicked and shoved her hand in her coat pocket and then pulled the trigger. Her final statement in the record was short and to the point. 'Come to find out, one bullet didn't end his misery, it took two'.

Preston learned from the case file that Sheriff Cotton had gone beyond the call of protector and written a letter to the judge requesting June Lee serve her time here at the county facility in exchange for her culinary skills. June Lee always wore a smile, and he had not noticed that her front teeth were false until he read her case file. She was happy because her children were here, and they were in and out to see her all the time. It was hard for some people to understand, but not for him. She was incarcerated, and yet she was freer than she had ever been in her life. The sheriff had stuck his neck out for June Lee and now he was doing the same thing for him.

"Preston!" June Lee's song stopped as she called out his name in surprise. Her cheeks plumped because of her smile. She grabbed a plate from the stack on the shelf above the huge stove and scooped up a helping of tomatoes, onions and okra. The woman added several planks of fried squash to the medley, a scoop of mashed potatoes, and two plump pieces of fried chicken on the side. She bathed the potatoes with a spoon of gravy then placed a slice of corn bread on top before she handed it to him.

Preston grinned as he took the plate from her.

"Thank you, Ms. June."

She took a motherly look at his face. He saw old pain come to her eyes; there was an unspoken understanding in them.

"Is Sheriff in his office?" she surveyed.

Preston had come to understand that a lot of his friends and staff called Emmett Cotton, 'Sheriff' as a proper name and a show of respect. He had been with the Sheriff's Department for 21 years, and 13 of those were as the elected man-in-charge.

"Yes Ma'am," answered Preston. He took the glass of tea she poured.

"He was worried sick about you, Preston," she told him.

"Yes Ma'am... I know." Preston couldn't stop looking at her. She was a fine woman, and he felt kindred to her on so many levels.

"Hon are you alright?" questioned June Lee softly.

Preston smiled and nodded his head. He changed the subject, so he could stay in control of his feelings.

"I'll take this one to him, Ms. June."

Her smile widened, and she nodded her head as she reached for another plate and began the process again.

Cotton looked up from the notes he was scratching down as Preston eased in with the plate of food and a glass of tea. He was on the phone with Judge Adler and nodded a thank you as the young man sat it down then left as quietly as he had entered. Cotton pulled the plate over and picked up the fork.

Preston ate his lunch then settled in the small office the county nurse used on Tuesday and Thursday, to write out his statement for the sheriff's formal report. The afternoon had become long and tedious with waiting. Preston sat with his elbows resting on his knees and his head in his hands, his body was aching, and his fate teetered on the decisiveness of his alcoholic father. The door opened, and Charlie's voice gave him an escape from his oppressive thoughts.

"Hey, can I come in and wait with you?"

"Yeah, please do. I'm going nuts in here... just waiting for the other shoe to drop." Preston turned in his chair as Charlie sat down at the table across from him. His friend tossed an open package of a cinnamon gum on the table then sat a bottle of grape soda down in front of him. Charlie turned up the bottle in his other hand and took a long swig before he spoke.

"You knew I was getting the guitar, didn't you?"

Preston smiled and shrugged his shoulders. He opened a piece of gum and stuck it in his mouth.

"You figured it out after I gave them to you." Preston took a moment to observe his friend while he chewed the spicy gum.

Charlie pulled off his worn hat and placed it on his knee as he tossed his head slightly to shift his hair off his brow. His curls were thick and heavy at this length, so much so that it parted naturally down the middle, and the sun had toasted its chestnut color into a glimmering gold. He had let his mustache fill in over the summer and gained three inches in height since Christmas. He always wore a braided, leather band around his left wrist, and today he wore one on the other too. The girls were intrigued by the personal flare in his appearance and his reserved distance, but Charlie didn't take it seriously. Preston was amused that Charlie had begun to express such a free spirit, and he respected Owen and Estelle even more for giving him the liberty to be himself. Preston recalled the day he had heard a couple of the girls at school talk about how the new boy's silver eyes seemed magical. Preston had teased them with an elaborate tale that the new kid lived with a horse which had wings. He realized today that metaphorically, his buddy really did because Charlie lived with people who loved and supported him.

"You're looking like an outlaw, Cuz," Preston's smile reflected the one his friend wore. "You're enjoying every minute of it too, aren't ya?"

One side of Charlie's mouth stretched a little further towards his jaw as mischievousness claimed his expression. His finger absently traced the ring of moisture the soda bottle had made on the table.

"We've always been on the same page, Preston... you know that."

Preston turned up the soda for a drink while his buddy's bluish-gray gaze studied him. It caused Preston to swallow more air than he did soda, and it went down hard as he sat the bottle down. He searched his heart knowing Charlie was giving him an opportunity to be truthful with him. He didn't know what to say.

"Charlie, I want to tell you all of it, but... I wouldn't be the only one who would depend on your trust and your silence. If I tell you what's happened to me, it could compromise your relationship with Owen at some point. I respect you and him, and I don't want to damage that."

Charlie shook his head.

"Nothing will compromise my relationship with Owen or you, Preston. I'm here for you, whether you need me to listen or just sit here and keep you company. You are my best friend... we're pals, but I don't have to know every time you fart."

"Well, that takes a load off my mind, Chuck." Preston knew Charlie hated that nickname; he thought he might get a colorful growl out of him again for amusement's sake. Instead, Charlie stunned him.

"I can see she's really special to you." He picked up his drink again and changed the subject.

"I've got the rodeo coming up this week. We'll be pulling the tack trailer in on Tuesday night with the stock. Owen and Rueben will come and go, but I'll be there until late Saturday... maybe even Sunday afternoon, if we place. You can go back and forth to work from there... showers are available and there's a laundromat across the street. I thought you might stay with me. You know, one day I'm going to enter in El Paso. I hear it's unbelievable at the events and stuff they cram into ten days."

Preston knew the fairgrounds had a small security staff during large events like the Northeast Texas Sizzler. Customarily, each ranch entry accepted the responsibility of having a representative available to the event staff should a problem arise with the stock or anything else they felt was important. Preston knew this year was about more than winning to his friend; it was his first time to be the designated delegate for the Silver-Hawk Ranch. It was an awesome responsibility and a huge honor to be trusted with such an important task.

The tack trailer had private quarters built into it, with two tight-fitted bunks, a small kitchenette and a hanging space for clothing. It was all a cowboy needed. But Preston was listening, between the lines.

"You're assuming I'll walk out of here with the opportunity to get on with the life and the responsibilities I had Friday," commented Preston.

"It's as much a possibility as not," stated Charlie. He polished off the grape soda, stood, and then pointed to Preston's. His buddy downed the rest of his and handed him the empty bottle. Charlie left the door standing ajar as he walked across the hallway to the vending area.

Preston heard Charlie talking to someone; the voice was familiar. He stood abruptly when Charlie pushed the door open and stepped back politely so Jaden could enter. He followed her, closed the door and leaned back against it as he crossed his arms.

Preston's attention went back and forth between them a couple of times. Jaden stopped at the foot of the table and looked at him. Her curly locks of hair were pulled up in a pony tail and she still wore her nurse's uniform from that morning. It didn't make her look any older.

"Preston, are you, all right? They called me at work and asked me to come when I got off." She stepped a fraction closer while her eyes looked him over for anything alarming.

"I'm okay, Jaden. Dane's in jail." He told her a quick version of the situation he had found upon his return then his attention shifted to his buddy. "This is Charlie, Jaden."

190

She stuck her hand out and spoke to him with a pleasant, but worried smile. Charlie politely returned the gesture then she turned back to Preston.

"Is this room... monitored?" she asked him in almost a whisper.

Preston shook his head.

Charlie witnessed the truth unfold before his eyes as this small female, who looked younger than either of them, leaped into his best friend's arms and he caught her. Charlie tried not to stare, but it was almost impossible because of the way they held each other. He could feel the intimate bond between them, and he knew it was a serious thing.

Preston absorbed her; he held her as close as he had that morning. Her breath warmed his ear. He leaned over closer and tightened his hold on her. Her fingers sank into the hairline at the back of his neck as he picked her up in his arms and squeezed her.

"I've been crazy with worry!" she admitted. When she pushed away to look at him, her hands came to rest on both sides of his face.

Preston reacted as if he had been given the key to her heart. He shared his lips with her in a seizure of soft, short, meaningful kisses. She returned them with great feeling; they gave in and tasted each other in a moment of helplessness. When she felt herself begin to mold against him, she took a deep breath and severed the kiss, but her arms still held him for a few seconds.

"What's going to happen to you?" She pushed away from him and Preston put her to her feet.

Preston slid the chair Charlie had occupied around to the end of the table for her. She sat down and so did he. Charlie remained in front of the door where he would be bumped with prior notice that someone was entering.

"I'm not sure... the judge has given Dane the option to make a care plan with the sheriff and, Charlie's brother, Owen. The judge says he's got to go get help. They are talking to him now. I told Sheriff that I asked you not to report it for obvious reasons... that I agreed to accept your help and see Dr. Enriquez, and I stayed with you because of the medication. He was bent out of shape because no one called to say I was okay." He told her the rest, and she listened closely.

"I should have called Charlie," stated Jaden. She glanced to him for a second then back to Preston. She reached over and wiped the shiny lip gloss from the edge of his mouth with her thumb. Preston clutched her wrist and pressed his lips into her palm.

Charlie cleared his throat in such a way that Jaden pulled her hand back in haste and crossed her arms over her chest. The tall boy shifted his weight to the other foot and caught the door knob then stepped back as Owen and Sheriff Cotton joined them. Their pleased expressions revealed that they had successfully convinced the Colonel to help all of them by seeing things their way.

Preston stood and introduced Jaden Sullivan to them. She shook their hands.

"Sheriff Cotton, I was contacted by your dispatcher and told that you needed to speak to me about Colonel Reid?"

"Yes Ma'am." His eyes went to her throat where the bruises were obvious. "I understand that Preston got you out of a bad situation with the Colonel? Those are some nasty bruises."

Jaden's hand went to her throat as she nodded her head. She elaborated.

"He saved my life. I told him, and I'll tell you as well… my first impression of Dane Reid was nothing like the man whom I was confronted with on the boat."

In the minutes that followed, she respectfully answered the sheriff's questions. She told him she chose not to press charges, not only because Preston asked, but for a personal reason as well. Then he pushed her by asking what that might be. She told him she had grown up in the foster care system and she didn't consider any of the ten fosters in which she had been placed to be a haven, much less a home. She told him, in her opinion; they fostered a paycheck for the lazy and licensed numerous perverts who felt validated when they mistreated someone that was already vulnerable.

She apologized for not making contact, but pointed out the obvious, which was the only legal guardian Preston has is his biggest threat. She stated that Preston impressed her as practical minded and she respected that about him. She understood his reasons for wanting to keep trying to manage his place in his father's twisted and dysfunctional life.

Cotton's expression was controlled as he studied this small woman. He had not expected her to be so young and smart, or attractive. It disturbed him to think that Preston had stayed with her the previous night.

She asked him if there was anything else, she could do for him. He shook her hand and thanked her for her time, and for helping Preston.

Jaden stood with a slight smile and smoothed her clothing. She told Owen and Charlie it was nice to meet them, and then she turned to Preston and stuck out her hand. He took it but was surprised when she stepped up awkwardly and hugged him. She told him thank you and to take care of himself. He couldn't look at her when she stepped away from him and out of the room; he feared it was out of his life.

Preston was asked if he wanted to see his father. He asked if that was Dane's idea and then declined until his father wanted to see him.

Preston pulled out on the boulevard after the log truck turned in front of them. He and Charlie were to pick up burgers from the *Taters & Mugs Drive In* while Owen went to the church to pick up Estelle. It had been agreed that Preston would stay with Owen. The Colonel would not allow his son to be the responsibility of Sheriff Cotton. The animosity between them had grown thick, and with good reason. Cotton felt contempt emanate from the Colonel. Dane Reid's point of view was narrow-minded; his life had been turned upside down because of the sheriff. He was sitting in jail and the only way that was going to change was to agree to undergo rehabilitation from alcoholism.

They drove into the restaurant parking lot, Preston cut the motor and they rolled to a stop. Charlie got out and went inside to place the order. He returned with two large orders of fried potatoes with cheese and chili on top of them and two huge cups of root beer. He sat down and handed Preston his food. They munched a few of the fries in a comfortable silence then Preston acknowledged what his friend had done for him.

"Hey Charlie, what you did for me... for us... at the station earlier; it wasn't a small thing to me. I just want you to know that."

Charlie stuck another fry in his mouth and chewed on it a few seconds then washed it down with a swallow of root beer.

"She's real pretty, Cuz. Is it a good feeling? I mean... to have someone kiss you and touch you like you're the center of her life?"

Preston glanced at his buddy who studied the tray of fries in his hand and kept eating while he waited for an answer. He thought it was a sensitive and very personal question for his guarded friend to have asked, and that he had to muster the courage to do so. Preston's surmised that in their world of reason, Charlie had earned the right to an answer.

"Good doesn't even come close to how she made me feel, or what! I didn't know a person could have such power over another with only a brush of their fingertips, or a breath on your skin." Preston felt chills on his arms at the mention of it. He didn't think Charlie, or anyone else, could understand until they had experienced it for themselves.

His friend surprised him again.

"Do you love her, Preston? Is that what's happening to you?" Charlie shoved the last fry in his mouth then wadded up the empty paper tray and tossed it at the outside trash can by the door to score a fictional two points.

"I'm not sure. I don't know what love feels like exactly. I thought of your brother a couple of times during the night. I began to understand the way he treats Estelle, and the way he looks at her... like she's what makes his heart beat. I want that, Charlie. I want a home, work I enjoy, and a partner to share my life. I want somebody that wants to share their life with me and wants all those things for the same reasons I do."

"Do you want it to be Jaden?" surveyed Charlie.

Preston thought about that, and the answer was easy.

"I couldn't do any better. You're right, Charlie; she's special."

Charlie voiced his opinion on the matter.

"She looks at you like Estelle looks at Owen." He finally looked at Preston when he sensed a hesitation in his friend. "It's true. I know what I saw."

Preston smiled, but still didn't comment.

"So, when will you see her again?" asked Charlie.

He shook his head as he sighed.

"I'm not sure I can."

"I don't understand. Why not?"

Preston turned to him slightly.

"Umm, I have to respect your brother and what he's doing for me. I don't think he would allow it, do you?"

"I wasn't saying that you should ask permission. Your heart didn't ask you if you wanted to feel this way, did it? You want to see her again, right?"

"Yes. But I don't know how that is gonna happen. I can't go against Owen, Charlie, and I'm surprised you think I should."

"I didn't say that either, Preston. It's just... Owen doesn't plan on keeping you in his hip pocket. There's no reason why the two of you can't know the course of each other's day... your paths could cross again without anyone saying they can."

Preston's palm absently traced the curve of the steering wheel as he thought about what Charlie said. His attention was snagged by the lady at the counter waving at them.

"The order is ready; I'll get it. Will you drive? My side's throbbing like a toothache." He got out and Charlie slid over into the driver's seat.

Charlie watched his friend and recalled the way the small, attractive woman had kissed him. He thought about the way she had drawn close to him, like she was a wild rose bush wrapped around a sturdy oak. He understood the need for secrecy because she was older than Preston. But he had never seen Preston respond emotionally to anything but pain, and even that was guarded and controlled. Charlie knew Preston wanted Jaden Sullivan in his life, and even more, he needed her to be. This was the first time in the four years they had known each other that he had heard Preston say he wanted anything more than peace with his father, and to go to the police academy one day.

Sheriff Cotton leaned back in his chair and closed his eyes a moment. He felt a tremendous relief come over him; there was comfort in knowing Preston was safe with Owen Kagel, and the family on the ranch. He had allowed himself to love that boy, he couldn't help it. He realized it would have been a conflict of interest for Preston to live with him; after all, he held the key to his father's freedom, not to mention he had come to despise the man.

Cotton's thoughts went to Jaden Sullivan. She didn't look as old as Preston or Charlie. There was something about her; she was educated, but street smart. She had an edge about her. She was like a stray dog which would take the food you gave it as long as you laid it on the ground, still she watched as she ate in case you tried to hurt her. He wondered why she had agreed to see Dane Reid; she was not the normal sort of women the Colonel used. Jaden Sullivan was a beautiful, young woman and obviously, self-sufficient and smart. The only explanations he could come up with were: she was duped into thinking he was respectable and a sound benefactor, or she was promiscuous by nature. It didn't matter, really; he couldn't trust her. He had not liked the way Preston had defended her so passionately.

Cotton picked up the phone.

"Lennis, I need you to use your law school researching skills for me when you have time. I need you to find out all you can about Jaden Sullivan. And, I need you to keep it under your hat too."

CHAPTER 10

The Silver-Hawk's show stock was re-located to the fairgrounds on Tuesday afternoon. The heifers, quarter horses, and donkeys that were for sale were registered and stalled in the huge industrial barn. The bull that brought the ranch handsome stud fees was secured in the adjacent barn with the appropriate contact information hanging outside the stall. Charlie and Eli filed their paperwork for the calf roping competition and then settled in the mounts they would be riding. Charlie was going to be busy seeing to the stock and handling interested customers. The event staff urged all the ranches to acquire their own handheld radios so that they could be reached in one area in the event they were needed in another.

Preston went by the houseboat and cleaned up after work because it was closer than going all the way to the ranch. He arrived at the fairgrounds just before sundown to help Charlie with whatever was needed. The animals were restless in their temporary surroundings and it was after midnight before Charlie and Preston could stretch out on the bunks in the small living compartment of the stock trailer. They turned on the small roof mount air conditioner and slept like rocks until the clock cut on at 6:00 a.m. on

Wednesday morning. They shared a carton of chocolate milk, pouring it over some cornflakes, and joked about how good it tasted.

The whole family had brought the children on Wednesday night after church. Preston had worked late due to one of the patrol cars having a wreck in a high-speed chase. He had helped Mr. Cox hook it up and wench it out of the gully then tow it to the garage. He pulled in at the fairgrounds after dark hungry, sore, tired, and covered with filth. He had spoken to Jaden at lunch from a pay phone in town and she was excited to hear from him. They talked for the entire hour. Because of the time, he skipped eating and went straight back to work.

Preston teased Scherry by trying to get her to pull off his nasty boots. He had not seen her in a dress since the wedding, and she was adorable. She informed him, the only way her mama would let her come was if she promised to be a lady. Preston told her she was pretty in a dress, and she was very much a lady just like her mother. She told him that's what Travis had told her too.

Preston gathered clean clothes and the things he needed to visit the men's facility. He traded Rueben a quarter for two dimes because a hot shower was ten cents. Rueben told him as nasty as he was; he had better buy a dollar's worth of water and take the jug of saddle soap and the grooming brush with him. Preston wasn't offended; he enjoyed Rueben's goofy sense of humor.

The family walked around the fairgrounds together; it was a special treat allowing the children to choose their personal preference for supper from the aromatic selections on the midway. The girls rode the Merry-Go-Round while the boys drove the bumper cars. They watched the pig races and munched on a syrup biscuit, and then they visited the canning exhibits where Estelle and Celia had won first place for their watermelon jelly and cinnamon pickles. At 11:00 p.m. the family started the walk to the truck through the labyrinth of vehicles. The boys were quiet and Scherry was already asleep in her father's arms, but Mollie rode on Cole's shoulders chattering about everything she saw.

Sheriff Cotton and Ned had stopped by the fairgrounds to visit with Charlie and Preston. They shared a box of taffy and talked a few minutes while sitting around the metal drum that had been cut in half and legs added for a campfire. The night was too hot for a social campfire, but useful to keep the biting pests at bay. Cotton and Ned didn't stay long because they got a call to go to Dry Creek on the other side of the county on a domestic call that involved a house fire.

The rides were still running, and an occasional scream could be heard in the distance. A radio played somewhere beyond where Preston and Charlie sat visiting around the makeshift fire pit. Preston's attention was distracted by a shadow that moved over the side of one of the ranch's trailers. He was surprised when Jaden stepped out of the darkness into the firelight. Her magical auburn hair and her smooth fair skin made her look like a living flame which had escaped onto the grass. She wore a pair of worn jeans that hugged her hips defining them with feminine distinction, and a deep green vest that buttoned down the front and stopped a few inches above the silver buckle of her belt. It was a beautiful garment that stirred a man's imagination.

Preston stood anxiously, and his hands reached out for her as she neared him; however, their lips met first.

She told him she had gone home after her shift that afternoon but couldn't stop thinking about him. She took a chance and came over to wander around in the hope of seeing him. She made the comment that for a Texas girl, this was the closest she had ever been to livestock. The guys grinned at her in disbelief, and Charlie teased her about being a Yankee.

They visited a little while, and then Charlie asked if they wanted to go look around before it got too late. She looked up at Preston. He squeezed her close and told her it was up to her. She nodded her head with excitement.

Charlie went to the tack trailer and came back with a brown cowboy hat he had used when he first arrived at the ranch. It was too little for him now, but fit Jaden perfectly. She smiled and expressed her appreciation over the simple gesture. They took in some exhibits that were close to the barn area then walked to the livestock area to check on the stock for the last time that evening.

Charlie showed her the wild mustang which the South-Wind Ranch had brought to sell. Jaden had commented that the mare's feet and coat were patched with the color of rich earth, but her mane and her nose were like moonlight. The animal allowed Jaden to stroke her nose a few times.

On the way back to the trailer, a man they knew from one of the local rotary clubs called to them; he insisted they take two pizzas rather than his tossing them into the trash.

They retrieved a soda from the cooler Charlie had brought from the ranch then sat down together and shared the pizza. The three of them talked about everything. Charlie discovered he was very comfortable around Jaden, and he liked her very much. It was obvious she was truly smitten with Preston, and his friend felt the same way.

She sat between Preston's knees and leaned back against his chest on the opposite side of his injured ribs. They laughed and told funny stories about each other. Charlie noticed that Preston was free to touch her whenever he pleased. He noticed she even craved it and sometimes in the middle of a conversation or enjoying the quiet of the campfire, she would lean her head back to caress his jaw line with her cheek. Preston's arms tightened instinctively, and they would get lost in each other's kiss for a few moments.

Charlie found himself content sitting on a bale of hay next to the trailer watching them slow dance in each other's arms until the fire was a pile of cinders. The carnival sounds had quieted, and the moonlight caressed them as a distant, soft tune from someone's radio echoed over the fairground like a surreal dream you would barely remember come morning.

He considered how perfect they matched each other. Their wit was original and playful like they had known each other their entire lives. The consideration exchanged between them was genuine and from the heart. Charlie had learned to recognize love when he saw it by living with Owen and Estelle. He knew that Preston did too. Jaden was in love with Preston, Charlie was sure of it. They were not guarded around him, and because Jaden trusted Preston, she had shared some things about of her life with him. Charlie understood the magic that was happening between them. The trust they exchanged in front of him was reason enough for him to accept her as a friend, and to protect her as he would Preston. He felt they deserved to be happy.

Charlie surfaced from his private thoughts to notice that they had stopped dancing. Preston's hands caressed her bottom, and she clung to him as they kissed deeply. Charlie decided to leave them alone for a while and he mumbled to them that he was going for a walk and he would be back in an hour or so.

He checked the stock again then visited the mustang that belonged to the South-Wind. He wanted to buy her. He had seen the boy with his arm in a cast earlier that week; he was still competing in several events. The boy saw him with the mustang again and introduced himself as Shane South. Charlie told him who he was then inquired about the filly. He found out that Shane was Eli's age, six months older to be exact. He told Charlie that the filly had thrown him and broken his arm. He admitted to Charlie the wild hearted mare had thrown most of the hands on the ranch, and his father was determined to get rid of her. He wanted $200 for her. Charlie was excited; he had enough saved that he could buy her, but he didn't know if Owen would see that he needed a wild horse on the ranch. Shane told him a rancher in Santa Fe was looking at her for his daughter. He told Charlie his father had warned them about the animal's unpredictable temperament, but the woman was convinced that she could rein her in.

Charlie started back to camp while wondering if he could break the animal of her nasty behavior. If she could not become useful, a working ranch was not the place for her, no matter how much he wanted her. He thought of the moody stallion which had belonged to Mr. Silver's wife. The animal was unruly and basically useless for anything other than stud; however, he was mean and tended to bite which made him a danger to the other stock.

Charlie passed the car that was Jaden's and was suddenly convicted of just how much he had been given for which he should be thankful. He had a safe, comfortable home and provisions, and a family that loved him no matter what. He had Ransom, a job, and friends which were like brothers. He admitted to himself the ranch in Santa Fe could give the mustang a good home, and he should be happy with things as they were.

He smiled as he remembered; his best friend was in love with someone who loved him back. He didn't have to question where they were; he had purposely left, so they could be alone. He went back to the hay he had relaxed on earlier and shifted a few of the bales. He spread a blanket over them then lounged back and propped up his feet. He folded his hands behind his head and gazed up at the glistening stars above him. The small windows of the private quarters were open, and he listened to the soft voices and satisfied sighs of Preston and Jaden making love to each other. It was like they played beautiful, sensuous music together. It was nothing like the so-called affection that his step-father had forced upon his mother.

He thought about these things in relation to what the scriptures taught. He couldn't judge them, especially since his mother had stayed within spiritual guidelines and was still deceived and brutalized. She had lived in constant fear of L.B. Thomas in the name of spiritual and legal obedience. He was older now and he could see it had been a scam for the man to trap his mother in a marriage to look respectable while at the same time have the benefits of a domestic slave and a concubine at his disposal. Charlie could see he was the string that was attached to his mother, and L.B. Thomas had detested him.

Living in this place and being loved by these people had given him a sound perspective on life and enlightened him to the spiritual presence which lived inside of him. Since coming here, he had asked God every day to forgive him for not being sorry the man was dead and for committing such a deed. Charlie felt his face grow hot, so he pushed that part of his life out of his mind. He redirected his thoughts to the wild mustang. She was spirited and wanted to be in an open field where she could run free.

Charlie gazed at one star that seemed determined to out-shine all the others. He heard Jaden quietly sing Preston's name a couple of times and tell him she loved him; her breath was full of faith and promise.

Charlie smiled big and crossed his feet. He wondered if there was a special girl somewhere out there that would need him next to breathing. He wanted to be loved by a girl who was as spirited and wild about belonging to him as the mustang was about belonging to the freedom of the range.

It may have been silly, but it was as though the star beckoned to him and he wished on it for her. He told the Maker about his dreams, and how much he wanted a girl who would be his soul mate in every way. He expressed in silent prayer how he needed her to love horses as much as he did, and he confessed that he hoped her eyes would shine like the stars above and her hair would glow like the color of the moon. He told the Almighty he wanted her to love him to the point of being wild and free like a runaway mustang then Charlie promised he would love her just as much. He admitted to the Maker that in feeling a love so wonderful, he would live with enough zeal to make up for the sad existence of his mother's life. He thanked Him for the family which had made him a part of their life. He finally closed his eyes to rest, but the image of the star remained in his mind. Charlie fell into a contented sleep in this world he had come to love so much.

Preston woke him before he walked Jaden to her car. Charlie sat up feeling a bit disoriented. His eyes focused on Jaden's smiling face just as she reached out and patted his jaw then scuffed his hair. It was her way of telling him thank you without speaking.

Thursday night was ushered in by an afternoon shower to cool off the hot day. Charlie and Eli would be competing against each other for the first time in the calf roping event. The competition had over 60 entries. And, by the end of the night their scores were good enough to move them into the top 20 which would compete on Friday night. The family ate supper at Crazy K's barbecue tent then departed for home.

Preston had no plans to see Jaden because he needed to go to the laundry and wash his clothes and uniforms for work. Charlie asked if Jaden had a washer and dryer. He pointed out the opportunity to see her would not always be available to him. Preston grinned at him and shook his head. He gathered his things, and Charlie's, aware that being a delegate meant seeing to your own needs. Charlie chuckled as he sat the box of washing powder on top of the pile of soiled laundry.

The next morning, Charlie awakened to the sound of Preston's Jeep pulling in next to the tack trailer. Preston knocked softly. Charlie rolled out of his bunk then looked at his watch; it was almost 7:00 a.m. Charlie shivered as he pulled on the light string. He flipped the inside lock on the door then shut off the roof air.

Preston dropped the stack of clean clothes on the empty bottom bunk and then sat a bundle of foil on the small counter with two quarts of chocolate milk.

"Mornin' sunshine!" exclaimed Preston with an annoying energy that his buddy did not share. "You got to wiz... or are you glad to see me?"

Charlie shoved him out of his way with his elbow and grabbed his jeans off the foot of his bunk. He tugged them on and stepped outside. In a moment, he came back and helped himself to a clean shirt. Preston ripped off the metal lid on one of the containers of milk, took the foil bundle and relocated to the reserved seating outside. Charlie joined him with his hair groomed, boots on his feet, the carton of milk in one hand and his hat in the other. He settled on a bale of hay that was covered with a blanket, sat the milk on the ground next to his foot then rubbed his face with his palms as he sucked in the smells of the morning.

Preston held the warm, tin-wrapped bundle in front of Charlie's nose, and witnessed his buddy's eyes pop open.

"Good Lord, that smells good! Did Jaden make those?"

Preston smiled with happiness.

"Yep, this half has egg and cheese... the rest are just sausage. The woman might be a little thing, but she likes to eat, and she can cook," he boasted.

Charlie smiled at his friend then took one of each. He began to eat like it was his last meal. He gobbled the first biscuit in exactly three bites.

"How's my girl this morning?" Charlie spoke through a full mouth as a sparkle claimed his eyes. He swallowed then took a long swig of milk.

Preston watched him examine the second biscuit as if trying to make up his mind where to bite it.

"This is brain food," stated Charlie factually. "She made these for me you know, so I can stay sharp today. She's just enjoying you for a wild and crazy roll in the hay." He sank his teeth into it then his jaws began to move like an oil well siphoning crude. He grinned the entire time waiting for Preston to get riled.

Preston started to chuckle as he kicked the bottom of Charlie's boot with the heel of his own.

"You need some brain food dip-shit." Preston thought of the competition he had witnessed the night before and asked Charlie if he was going to do his best to beat Eli that night.

Charlie looked at him in surprise.

"Why, don't you think I'll do my best?"

Preston shrugged his shoulders as he spoke.

"You got off Ransom twice last night like there was molasses on your saddle. I know you love him like a little brother, but he should win because he gives his best. You should push him to beat you because you care about him... not because you want him to be proud of winning. He has enough pride."

Charlie made a blowing sound.

"I can't believe you noticed that one second delay in my dismount." He shoved the rest of his breakfast in his mouth.

Preston laughed.

"Yeah, well... I've watched you practice enough. Besides... he's more competitive than you are, Charlie. He'll come back next year after his legs are three inches longer, and he won't be so kind to you."

Charlie stared at Preston knowing he was right. Eli's competitive nature was strong. It was a fact that his friend had moved the manure pile a time or two with only a shovel and a wheel-barrow because Rueben thought his son's humility needed some tweaking.

The sounds of the Sheriff's Department were busy on the other side of Cotton's door. He was on the phone with one of the citizens who elected him. This was the fourth time the south gate to their pasture had been vandalized, the lock cut, and the chain gone each time. They had not had any stock taken, but they wanted something done about the invasion on their land. It was suspicious, and Cotton promised to investigate.

Lennis knocked on the sheriff's door then stuck his head in holding up a cream-colored folder. Cotton motioned him forward. Lennis closed the door and sat down. When the sheriff hung up the phone, Lennis handed him the file.

"This is the information you asked me to find, Sheriff. You should know it took some doing. Jaden Sullivan's juvenile history is extensive and disturbing, as you can see, she dropped off the face of the earth when she was 14 years old.

"I went through one of the social workers in Human Services to help me. It cost you dinner and a ride on the river boat; I put them on your credit card," teased Lennis.

Cotton cut his eyes up to Lennis from the open folder. He had been told by the Chancellor's secretary that Oscar Lovett had requested another social worker be assigned to the county. She was to start on the 15th of the month. He had not met her; however, he could only assume that Lennis had, because the other social worker on staff would rather chew her arm off than bend a rule and help the Sheriff's Department. He thought he would take a jab at Lennis just for fun.

"If that's what it took to get 'Old Iron Stove' to give up something, then it was my pleasure. You earned it. Umm, this is all she gave up, isn't it?" he asked with a stone's-like expression.

The stogy Ms. Stovall was a prudish, old-maid who had the answers to everyone's family crises. She had never had a husband, children, or siblings with which to interact. It was easy for her to look at the world through social blinders and render solutions and judgments that were not practical in the real world. She was devoted to solving other people's problems based on a policy manual; she invested no emotions and was left with no consequences that were not outlined in a signed case plan, or a court order.

Lennis Sutton's expression was priceless. Cotton had never seen him speechless. His cocky, lawyerly arrogance bugged Cotton sometimes, but Lennis was a brilliant student, a faithful employee and he was going to be an excellent litigator. Cotton liked him for his straightforward outlook on society and his dedication; so, he didn't hold the man's abundance of self-esteem against him. Still, he deserved to be flustered; it may help him remember the essence of humility when he needs it most. Besides, Lennis had been smart enough to fall for one of the most precious little ladies in these parts. They doted on each other, and Cotton wanted it to stay that way.

"Sheriff, you're kidding me... right? You don't really think that I took Ms. Stovall out, do you?"

Sheriff Cotton read while Lennis' juvenile groveling lingered in the corners of his mind. A few minutes passed while he became engrossed in the shameful truth of why he didn't trust Jaden Sullivan. It was obvious that she didn't encourage it because she did not want to trust anyone in return.

"My word, Lennis... that's enough!" stated Cotton in an abrupt tone of voice. "I concede for Christ's sake! All attorneys are just alike... you'd argue with a brick wall. Besides, Wren would make both of us regret it if you did anything you shouldn't have." Cotton leaned forward in his chair as he saw that Miss Sullivan had disappeared as a runaway in March 1948.

"So, what happened in 1948, I wonder? She ran away from the Dillard Village Group Home and that's it?"

Lennis had become an advocate for this girl without even realizing it.

"Well, that's what I thought, so I did some more checking. I checked out the house parents that managed that home. Their names are listed in the back. I got a hit on Professor Walter Griffin. His history is attached.

"He's been arrested for numerous sexual offenses since then. He's presently in lock-down over in Shreveport for exposing himself to a group of kids on the playground in the park. The man's a creep. I bet you anything he raped her, Sheriff. I mean, think about it. What would it take for a girl not even 15 years old with no money... no family... no friends, to leave a warm bed, three meals a day and a roof over her head? He even wrote the report. He determined that she displayed all the classic signs of being fixated on the human body. Yeah, right... he's in jail for being an exhibitionist, and has a prior on voyeurism. He's a sick and dangerous fucker, and I use that word because it fits. There's no telling how many children he's molested. So... why did I research this for you, Sheriff? May I ask?"

"I think Preston has gotten involved with her. I just wanted to know what I was up against," he commented.

"Really?" surveyed Lennis. He waited for his boss to respond, but he was in deep thought. "Sheriff, Preston's different from the other guys his age. You do know that, don't you?" questioned Lennis delicately.

Cotton looked up from the file as he spoke.

"That depends. What do you mean... different?"

Lennis pulled his ankle up to rest on his knee.

"My daddy calls it, Leo's Pride." Lennis could tell by the way the sheriff looked at him, he had never heard the expression, so he elaborated. "He was born to a dominant male that has slapped him down his entire life... a Leo. He may be younger and obedient, but he's still a lion. He watches and waits; his skills are getting sharper, and he's growing wiser. The day will come for him to take control. He'll have his own pride one day... even at the cost of overpowering the teacher. If Preston has gotten involved with this young woman..." Lennis shook his head as he looked at the sheriff, "... he's not just passing time. He'll be possessive... he'll defend her. Good God, if anyone has ever needed to be protected, it's this girl."

"You don't think she's taken advantage of him, Lennis? Preston is underage."

Lennis shook his head.

"Sheriff, Preston's lived with a predator the span of his life. Don't you think he recognizes one? Besides, I remember my first intimate contact with a female... let's just say she wasn't a kid, and neither was I by the time she was finished with me."

Cotton leaned back in his chair and fastened his hands behind his head. Lennis's point of view was food for thought. He had no proof she was using Preston. What could he offer her anyway, other than sex? It caused him to think of his own impetuous youth and how the world of female companionship was exposed to them by his buddy's older sister and her friend.

The girls had been 17 and 18 years old in comparison to their 16 years; it was a rainy summer afternoon when they got into a game of spin the bottle on a dare. Jimmy had a major crush on his sister's best friend, Jill. After the first two spins landed on brother and sister, Jimmy's sister, Vicki, tossed the bottle then asked him to come to her room if he wanted to learn how to kiss. Jill stayed with Jimmy to teach him a few things as well.

He never told Jim the details of that hour in time. It was the deal he and Vicki had made with each other when things got heated between them and they traded more than spit that day.

Vicki was an outgoing and pretty girl with silky, wheat-colored hair that brushed her waist when she walked, and her full, pouty lips were perfect for kissing. He was younger, but taller than she was and like Preston, he was strong and muscular.

She had been chewing a piece of sour-apple gum; her kiss was like savoring a taste of hot apple pie. He touched her breasts during the kissing because she took the liberty to feel the front of his jeans. She unbuttoned her blouse and unfastened the strapless bra. She told him he could touch her. She kissed him again then guided his mouth to her body. Her breasts were fascinatingly beautiful; their plump tips were like candy in his mouth. The way she kept rubbing the front of him was making him brave. She asked him if he wanted her to touch him and he unfastened his jeans for her. She used both hands to set his body free of the confines of his shorts.

His eyes traded off between her ample, pointed breasts and the small bottle she retrieved off the shelf next to them. It was sweet oil she used as an agent to create friction between their skin to pleasure him. In only a few moments her hand nurtured his body into that of a craving man while he suckled at her breasts.

He had been a fast learner and his hands wanted to explore her body as well. He clutched at the curve of her bottom; she gazed into his eyes as he boldly slid his hands beneath her panties. They were bothersome; she said nothing when he pushed them away from her body. She stepped out of them and pulled him back into her arms. He led her hand back to his elongated body. He touched her hand where she had primed him and rubbed some oil onto *his fingers. His touch eased into her narrow, hot body; she gasped with feeling and her hand began to pump him faster. Their eyes met, and he stabbed her with his finger every time she pulled on him. They knew they were playing with fire, but it was thrilling, and they had not been burned yet. His mouth covered the tip of her breast again as they made each other feel like thermometers in the August sun. When she whispered, 'Come on Em, give it to me', that was all he needed to hear. He was already braving the unknown and doing a good job at it. Instinct took over, and she pushed his jeans down over his bottom. He displayed his strength and held her against the wall in the way he had overheard some older varsity guys talk about in the locker room at school. He would never forget that moment when he pulled her skirt up and watched as she parted her knees for him. His palm was full of her light silky hair, and her nipples were swollen from his kiss. His virile in-experienced body felt like hot lead.*

She folded her smooth legs around his bare bottom and teased him at the entrance of her private body for a few seconds; then, she eased her tongue into his mouth at the same time his hard body penetrated her. She didn't have to tell him to start pumping; the feel of her body gripping him with a hot fist of desire turned him into a working piston. She felt so fine. It was a mystery to him as to how he lived through something that inflicted such physical chaos, and the only cure was to explode inside that which gave the pleasure.

He realized after the fact, she had known how to kiss from experience and had been touched enough in the process to know there was a lot more to explore. Carnal nature had taken over, and they both surrendered their innocence to it. He had all of her that day, and in doing so he discovered how vulnerable she was, and how vulnerable a woman's body was designed. He couldn't help it; he left that day feeling she was marked as his.

They continued to meet and marked each other, at some point, every day for the rest of the summer. The last day of August, she came to meet him in the woods. The tree house that was once a boy's fantastic adventure was now a

213

secret haven for two stupid kids, who had discovered thunder in each other's body and were addicted to it.

He remembered it had begun to rain hard, and he wondered if she was going to meet him. She did. They had become brazen enough to grasp the added thrill of getting completely naked with each other. He studied her wet body as her clothing clung to it. She was so sensuous. He pulled his shirt off and reached for her; she began to cry as she wrapped her arms around him. She was trembling. He was scared to admit to her that he loved her, but not so scared that he suppressed his concern. He kissed her into a calmer state.

She told him she had been stupid, and so caught up in loving him, she hadn't recognized that she had gone over six weeks without bleeding. During this time together, he had been curious about a lot of things concerning a woman and she told him what he wanted to know, but she didn't have an answer for this.

Amid so many fears, and the summer thunder shaking the earth and all that was beneath them, he undressed her and laid her down on the cushion of blankets. He made love to her as a man would to the woman he loved.

"Sheriff?" Lennis' voice drew Cotton's mind back to the present.

Cotton put the memories of his ex-wife and their intimate life out of his mind. He stood abruptly.

"You did a fine job, Lennis. You're going to be a kick-ass attorney!" He came around his desk and shook the dispatcher's hand. "I get what you're saying. I should respect Preston and mind my own business."

Lennis shook his head as he smiled at the sheriff.

"You said that, Sir. I didn't."

CHAPTER 11

Jaden had agreed to pull a double shift on Friday and didn't get to see Preston. She was disappointed but couldn't say no to the overtime. Instead of dwelling on the fact, Preston focused on the next time they could see each other, and they made plans to meet at the rodeo Saturday night. Preston hung up thinking about ways he could practice living as an independent adult. He understood and respected Jaden's struggle to make her way alone in the world, but it gnawed at him. He surmised that an extra shift from her point of view could be a lot of things: the phone bill, groceries, gas for the car, or an emergency fund for the unexpected things life could put in her path. In that frame of mind, he thought about the money he was earning while working full time this summer. The savings account he had opened upon his employment was growing. He decided he would use this week's paycheck to become a distinct and useful part of Jaden's reality.

Jaden pulled into the yard and noticed the blooming pot plants lining the steps. She smiled because she knew Preston had been there. The vase of daisies on the table was proof that he listened to her when she talked to him.

He had asked about her favorite flower just before they drifted off to sleep in the wee hours of Sunday morning.

She dropped her purse and keys on the table and went to the refrigerator to get a glass of lemonade. She stared at the refrigerator full of fresh vegetables and other foods then she opened the freezer and found it full as well. The pantry had been replenished with staples and all sorts of things that she liked but could not afford. There were several things she knew Preston had bought for himself too. She smiled, because it meant he planned on being a part of her life.

Jaden giggled at the immense joy that lived inside of her now. She took out a stem bulging with green grapes and rinsed them, cut a few slices of cheddar and opened the buttery crackers she found on the second shelf in the cupboard. She turned on the radio that sat atop the refrigerator, sat down and ate her snack. After she finished, she rinsed her plate and left it in the drain rack then took her drink to the bedroom where she kicked out of her shoes. She sat the glass on the dresser and took off her name tag. She unbuttoned her uniform and tossed it over her head then stripped down to her underwear in preparation for a hot bath and a nap. She turned to the bathroom door, and her eyes touched the cowboy hat Charlie had given her. It sat in the middle of her bed full of daisies, along with a bar of handmade, lavender scented soap which she had admired while in the exhibit building the other night. The large candle that completed the set was next to it. There was a small bag in which she found a necklace. It was made of three, thin braided leather strips and decorated with silver and green beads in various sizes. They were fastened together in an artistic design and a silver 'P' dangled from the center of it. The small card which accompanied it read, 'Made for us by someone who cares. I love you, Baby. Your Cowboy.'

Jaden shook her head in disbelief. No man had ever done anything like this for her.

Jaden climbed up the stairs into the stands at the equestrian center then walked over to the railing where she had a broader view of the activities. The building was like a large anthill and she tried to scan it with her sunglasses on while it was still daylight.

She touched the necklace that lay against her smooth skin. She had been undecided about what to wear and had taken a couple of things with her to the salon. She wanted to dress to please Preston and yet, did not want to call attention to herself. She wore a pair of jeans and a black camisole then added a brown, cotton-gauze shirt that was embroidered with turquoise and black horseshoes. She left the blouse partially unbuttoned and added a black leather belt for flare. It was a relaxed look and yet, still had a touch of sex appeal. Her makeup looked good even if she did say so herself. Her hair had been trimmed into healthy, curly layers then swept to one side and bangs snipped. She had gone to a small shop a co-worker's sister owned. They had taken her on short notice and allowed her to finish dressing in their bathroom.

Jaden's mind went back to the ladies at the shop. She had held up her choices of tops and three out of the four ladies put their stamp of approval on the gauze top with the bronze camisole, but the sister of her friend told her she should wear the halter top. She told Jaden she needed to enjoy being young, beautiful and in love, and there wasn't a man breathing that wouldn't appreciate being seen with her in that sexy little number.

The halter top was a deep chocolate color with tiny embroidered wildflowers in the fabric. It tied around her neck and fastened between her breasts with a sturdy hook that was hidden behind a bow. It had short tailored panels that came to the top of her jeans to conceal her middle and was very feminine and sexy. Jaden wished she and Preston were an acceptable couple, so she could dress for him without being so cautious.

The ladies at the shop teased her about the man she would be meeting hoping she would tell them the details of her heart. She smiled and put a five-dollar bill on the counter. She felt guilty splurging on herself after Preston had spent his money on groceries and flowers for her. She told herself that this was for him as much as the flowers were for her.

She didn't see a soul she knew in the crowd below except for the man that gave them the pizza the other night. He waved, and Jaden turned to look behind her. There was no one there. She turned back, and he pointed to her. She held her hand up and smiled. She was suddenly nervous. She had come here thinking nobody would notice her. No one ever had; still, she wondered if this was a mistake. She had been so swept away in Preston, thinking of him, loving him and being with him every moment they could manage. They had shared each other's company without an audience because she didn't consider Charlie as such, but tonight was different.

Jaden decided to make her way back down to the main floor where she could walk around and look for Preston. At the bottom of the stairs, she got trapped by a parade of sheep being led along by a group of younger boys and girls. The children wore 4-H banners and numbers across the back of their shirts; the animals wore the same identification. She waited and admired the children whose families had encouraged them in such ventures. The concept was so innocent and so were the children.

Suddenly, a forceful pair of hands took a hold of Jaden's waist, sending her nerves into a state of alarm. She spun around and pushed away from the intrusion to find herself looking up into the face of Russell Butler, an old boyfriend. His eyes were red because he had already started drinking; she could smell it on his breath as he stood over her.

He was a roughneck for a major oil company. They had two months of casual dating when she finally gave in, due to her own loneliness, and let him take her to bed. His laid-back demeanor changed with that stupid decision. He became rough and hurtful in his lust to dominate her body, and she ended up with a fractured collar bone and two broken fingers. She left before he woke and went straight to Ava for help. She couldn't afford to miss any work.

When he called, she told him that she didn't appreciate the broken bones, and the pain he had inflicted on her was clearly a sign that they did not need to continue seeing each other. She told him to leave her alone. After that, she avoided him and the friends through which they had met. He left her alone until six weeks later when they ran into each other at the gas station one afternoon. She had just got off work and was in her uniform. When he attempted an apology, and asked her to dinner, she thought fast, and told him she was on her way to work. That was when he surprised her the second time and dropped by late, loaded and unannounced at her old apartment in Dallas. She ignored him even though the television was playing, and the lights were on. She was tired of trusting only to be used in the most selfish and hurtful of ways.

"Hey Gorgeous... you're looking fine. I went by to see you a couple of months ago. An old lady with no teeth answered the door. She said she had been in the place almost three months. Where did you move to?"

"Russell... hey." Jaden pushed her hair over her shoulder and then shoved her nervous hands in the back pockets of her jeans. She looked down at the ground between them while thinking about turning and walking away, but she knew Russell better than that. It would make him angry even though he was standing there playing this asinine game with her about the level of their relationship. She was beginning to wish that she had not ventured out this evening.

"Jaden... cat got your tongue?" His words held a mocking and arrogant tone; he knew he had gotten to her by just speaking to her.

"No. I was just wondering how you found your way up here to a small-town rodeo."

He smiled at her.

"A buddy I work with rides the bulls. This is one of the titles he wants under his belt before he goes to State...

then Nationals. You should come and party with us later. It'll be fun. He said there's a wild-ass saloon over here somewhere called, The Wild Boar."

She shook her head.

"No thank you, I don't do bars any more. Listen Russell, someone is waiting on me. I've got to go. I'm glad you're doing well. Bye." Jaden turned to leave, and Russell's hand caught her elbow.

"Wait Jaden... don't leave. I know I hurt your feelings... and I'm sorry. Damn! What does a guy have to do to get forgiveness from you? Come on... let me make it up to you. I swear... we'll have a blast!" Russell's hand kept a vice-like grip on her arm as he spoke.

Jaden concluded by his words and actions that she needed to just tell him flat-out how it was for her in a way he would understand. She looked up at him and pushed her sun glasses back, so she could make eye contact with him.

"You hurt more than my feelings!" she pointed out factually. "I'm not mad at you, Russell. Why can't you understand that it's a matter of respect for me? Just because we met at a party, doesn't mean I want a life with alcohol and raising hell. I never have... it's not me. But you wouldn't know that because you never really bothered to get to know me. I shouldn't have kept going out with you, and I shouldn't have slept with you. I was lonely, and I apologize to you for that. Surely, there's someone special in your life... there's someone in mine. I'm with someone who really cares about me, and I'm very happy. I have a different life now. I'm done with being stupid and... we were stupid."

Russell's jaws stiffened as he stared down at her.

"You were someone special to me, Jaden." He pointed out in a voice that was pinched with anger. His fingers dug even deeper into her flesh as she attempted to pull away from him. "I see you still have a tongue like a razor, and you will always be a whore. My prick still has scars on it from your last blow job."

Russell stood before her the same self-centered drunk he had been eight months ago. He was deliberately being nasty; obviously, she had hit a nerve. She looked him square in the eye wondering why she thought he would listen to reason. When she spoke, her voice was suppressed due to the surrounding people, but just as condescending as he had been.

"No, you're mistaken about that. I never gave you a blow job, you thick-headed jerk. That must have been one you got while you were at work."

Jaden snatched her elbow free and turned to make a hasty exit. She didn't get more than half a dozen steps when Russell clamped down on both her elbows this time and began pushing her through the crowd of people until they were outdoors. She tried to pry herself free, but his height gave him undeniable leverage in manipulating her feet. He turned abruptly and released one of her arms as he headed into the maze of vehicles and parked horse trailers while forcefully dragging her alongside of him. Jaden tried to pry her arm free, but his hold was menacing. His legs were long, and he was walking so fast that his stride had become interminable. She stumbled several times because her feet were having trouble keeping up with him. Her heart was pounding, and she was so frightened she couldn't think straight.

"Russell, stop! I have a right to decide not to see you!"

The toe of her boot caught on a sturdy clump of grass and she tripped. Russell Butler snatched her up like she was a child in need of discipline, and they were going to the switching closet. He made a right turn at her verbal objection to avoid the people that were approaching from the opposite direction. It was so abrupt her small body raked against the parked trailer. Her right breast and arm met the chain-pin on the gate; it tore the thin soft fabric of her blouse while delivering a stabbing pain to her tender flesh.

"STOP! YOU'RE HURTING ME!" She screamed at him impulsively.

Russell saw a couple of cowboys turn suddenly in response to her verbal resistance. The velocity of hostility and frustration in her voice shocked him. He released her as though she had stuck a branding iron on his hand, but it was too late. The sound of hooves coming up behind him made Russell defensive and even more aggressive, and he shoved her out of his way as he tried to flee. Jaden hit the ground so hard it jarred her bones.

Preston came out of the late evening sun and knocked the tall, thin man off his balance. Russell was blinded by the glowing orange horizon. He became a clear target as Preston slugged him in the diaphragm with all his might. It forced the air and the alcohol from Russell Butler's body at the same time; he dropped to his knees as he threw up the contents of his gut in a swearing, sputtering weakness. He called Jaden a whoring-bitch between coughs. Preston's other fist rattled his jaw and his teeth, and his ability to think. Butler dropped to the ground and rolled around in a daze.

Jaden fearfully scrambled to her feet, turned and began to run back to the small, safe world she had managed to find in the country. She needed to stay there and ignore the need to be loved. It was dangerous for her to want or need such a thing, and it was becoming too dangerous for the young man that she wanted so much.

She made several frantic turns in search of her car, attempting to scan the maze of vehicles through watery eyes. She was full of disconcert and unable to get her bearings.

That was when Preston caught up to her. He didn't snatch at her; instead, he stepped up next to her and swept her small body up in the tender cradle of his arms. He pressed his face to her ear as he ventured even deeper into the maze of trailers for privacy.

"Baby, shhh... I got you. Shhh, don't cry. Baby, please don't cry."

She hadn't realized she was crying. Her eyes were closed, and she didn't want to open them out of fear of seeing an accusing look on his face. Men always blamed the woman for conflicts with other men. She was an emotional mess when she spoke.

"Preston put me down. I shouldn't have come here. I don't belong. I love you, but I don't belong."

Preston looked at Charlie. He had been the one to first see her from the door of the stalling area because of the view he had from being mounted on Ransom. When the man started man-handling her, he knew something was wrong. He urged the horse over to where Preston was buffing his boots with one of the grooming brushes. By the time they got a visual on her through the crowd, the man was shoving her out of the building. Charlie held his hand down and Preston swung himself up behind the saddle. They had been able to cover more ground, get through the spectators and have a better view on horseback.

"Yes, you do, Baby. You belong in mine and I belong in yours, Jaden. That's just the way it is... and the world may as well get used to it." He kissed her lightly.

She opened her eyes and looked at him. Ransom's head appeared over Preston's shoulder as though he were seconding the motion. He nuzzled her neck and nibbled at her blouse. Her hand went to the animal's velvety nose. She didn't understand why, but it was a calming thing to her.

Charlie asked him to back up from them then he dismounted and came to stand next to them.

Jaden was honest.

"I'm so sorry. I feel like I'm nothing but trouble, Preston."

Preston shook his head.

"I don't feel that way, Honey. So, who's the asshole?" Preston walked over to a flatbed trailer and sat her down. He knelt in front of her and smoothed her wet cheeks with his fingertips.

Charlie sat down next to her and produced a bandana for her.

She told them about Russell Butler and what had happened as she primped her face.

Charlie started laughing when she told them what she had said that made him so mad.

Jaden looked at the lanky fellow next to her, who had shoulders like a brick wall and a wacky sense of humor; he was true of heart like Preston. She thought about what she had said and realized it was offensive to a man like Russell, which was exactly why she had said it.

Preston shook his head as he looked at her.

"God knows... I love a spunky woman." He laughed softly then leaned over and kissed her square on the mouth.

Jaden really looked at him. There was something so masculine about him now. She had shaved him Sunday morning before they made love. He had let his mustache grow this week like she had trimmed it, only he had let it grow down to frame his chin. He looked even older because of it; still, it was more than his outward appearance. She was very familiar with the manly body beneath the clothing he wore, and was certain that was part of it, but there was something about him that was different. He had appeared out of the sunset and delivered a blow of justice while putting himself in harm's way a second time on her behalf and then offered compassionate and tender words of comfort. He was possessive of her. She liked that and felt the same way. She studied him a moment, seeing him in a different light, as understanding came to her. He was a man of self-sacrifice; she knew him as a protector and a warrior. Jaden realized this was his true personality, his calling, and his dream for his life. He was meant to be a man of justice. The irony was that in all the unjust things that had happened to her in life, this young man, whom she shouldn't love by the standards of society claimed her as his and was proud to do so. She felt like the luckiest woman in the world. She had nothing to offer him but herself, and her heart.

His fingers touched her torn shirt.

She explained.

"I got all spiffed up for you." She blew her nose in Charlie's crisp, clean handkerchief real big, adding a little extra noise for special effects then shoved it in her new friend's front shirt pocket.

Preston flashed a handsome and mischievous smile at her as his friend's face distorted in surprise that she had done such a thing.

Charlie pulled the handkerchief out by two fingers and handed it back to her.

"I can't accept it, Miss, really... you keep it; you may need it." His head went up suddenly as the electric voice in the arena, announced the category in which he was competing. Charlie stood abruptly and touched his horse's nose before he swung his leg over the animal's back. "Gotta ride... I'll catch you two later!" Ransom reared up in excitement. Charlie nodded at them then commanded the animal forward.

Preston talked about several things as he and Jaden walked around and attempted to locate her car. The sun had disappeared, and the moon was unusually low in the sky. She was calmer now and remembered parking her car next to a row of black and red trailers. Preston had seen the trailers earlier in the week and knew they belonged to the South-Wind Ranch. He knew they were parked on the last row past the stalling pavilion. This was what Preston needed to hear to know which direction to go to find her car.

When they stopped next to the blue and white Impala, Jaden smiled up at him. Preston had the ability to always change her outlook and make her day better. She opened the trunk of the car and retrieved a small case and then did the best she could to straighten her smeared makeup in the moonlight. When satisfied, she stripped off the black shirt and discovered the strap on her camisole was torn as well. She reached in the small clothes basket which she had taken with her to the beauty shop earlier that afternoon and took out her only alternative. She turned it for easy access then handed it to Preston. He watched as she looked around the darkness then quickly thrust the torn shirt over her head and released the skimpy black lace bra that held her full breasts. He was waiting and swiftly covered her body with the garment he held. He smiled down at her and touched the necklace that lay against her skin as she began to tie the straps around her neck. Preston's hand ventured beneath the blouse to caress the full soft flesh he had come to worship.

She flinched slightly.

He looked down at her as his hand covered her flesh.

"He ran me into one of the trailers and I got caught on a chain-pin. It's what tore my clothes." She told him in a hushed voice. She guided his warm hand to the touchy spot on the side of her breast, so he could feel the whelp. It was swollen and hot. Jaden wished they were at home in bed. She wound her arms around his neck and pressed her cheek against his chest, so she could hear his heartbeat.

His touch possessed a healing ability for her. His thumb teased the tip of her breast as his fingers messaged the whelp. When he leaned down and kissed her brow, she lifted her face to him. He bent his knees and kissed her deeply as his loving arms encompassed her body.

"I should go kick his butt again just for good measure," he mumbled against her lips.

She exhaled and fought the urge to touch him intimately.

"Let's go watch Charlie win or we're going to have to go find a place where we can make love." She kissed him this time. He pressed her belly against the front of his jeans. It assured her that he was just as susceptible to her feminine nature as she was to his masculinity.

"All right," he breathed against her ear. But neither of them made a move to do so. His magnetism drew her to look at him. His eyes were on fire with desire. When he spoke again chills attacked her entire body. "I still hope to get into you later, Baby. I need to feel you wrapped around me... some-kind-a bad."

She drew closer to share her lips with him and Preston expressed his intentions in a torrid, consuming kiss. It was more than crippling to the weakness she harbored for him.

"Will we be able to get away? Your family is here," she whispered.

Preston's scalding touch was making her nerves surface.

"I hope so," he answered truthfully. "But I can't be deceitful, Honey. We're bigger than that."

She knew what he meant. It was one thing to be discreet, and something completely different to be dishonest.

"What number is Charlie?" she mumbled as their tongues began to dance together at the erratic pounding of their hearts.

"He and Eli are #19 and #20," he answered. He looked down at her. "We've got a little while."

Preston was so weak now he could barely pull himself out of the backseat of her car. He shut the door, and she slid her arms around him. Her small arms held him tight, and steadied his tall, muscular statue. He pressed his lips to her forehead then leaned against the side of the car for a minute.

"Dang, Baby... that was a rush," breathed Preston.

Jaden looked up at him and found his eyes were a smoldering blue in the moonlight.

"I'm crazy about you, Preston." She pressed a soft kiss lightly against his lips. "Thank you for the thoughtful things you did last night. The plants... the flowers and the groceries, they were a wonderful surprise! And thank you for the special things... the soap and the candle. I'm saving them until you can enjoy them with me. And, thank you for taking up for me earlier... for the necklace... for everything! You make me so happy, Preston!"

His mystified expression changed to one of satisfaction, and he smiled at her.

"You make me happy too, Jaden. Did you notice my necklace?" he asked weakly.

She nodded her head as her hand slid inside the open collar of Preston's shirt. She turned slightly so the moonlight could give a definition to the ornament hanging around his neck. It was an identical version of what she wore only it was a bit bulkier and it had a 'J' hanging from it. She caressed it with her fingertips.

"Preston, what does this mean to you?"

He gazed down at her. His voice was as serious as she had ever heard it.

"I know we've been like a brush fire, Jaden, and that I'm young. I'm just a simple man. You know what my plans are. I don't think either of us have had an abundance of happiness, but we both know what it feels like. I won't put words in your mouth but, you're my happiness, Baby. I just want you to know that. This bond between us is a serious thing to me. I've thought about how long I should wait to trust my heart, but I trust it now. Should I wait until a problem threatens us to tell you that I love you?" He shook his head; there was a conviction in his eyes. "It means that I love you. That's all, Baby. I love you, Jaden."

The tips of her fingers caressed his lips. He had convinced her with his words, his actions and his eyes that she had secured her place in his heart.

"I'll wear mine for the same reason... because I love you too, Preston. I swear on my life that I'll never hurt you."

"A man can't ask for more than that!" Preston's arms held her close against his body as his mouth covered hers.

CHAPTER 12

Dane sat in silence and watched as the dark thunderhead swept over the enormous span of concrete and civilization. It was the 60th day in a row he had come to this sunroom, at this same time and sat in this rocking chair, while incarcerated in this place that was considered a hospital. He had sobered physically, but he had sobered in wisdom as well since coming here. The State Veteran's Hospital in Dallas was the most depressing place he had ever been, and patriotism for most of these men depended on how they felt when they awoke each morning. This dreadful experience had been enlightening and made him realize just how useless he had become, and it bothered the hell out of him.

He could hold a cup of coffee now without spilling it on himself from shaking hands, and he had an appetite to taste food again. The lack of nicotine had been twice as hard to cope with as the alcohol. He missed both. It was the hardest 60 days he had ever lived through in his life, other than when he realized his wife decided he was a failure as a husband and replaced him with another lover. He had no real proof of her infidelity, yet vengeance consumed him, and he struck back by taking away the thing she loved most. He knew he had committed the worst sin of his life the moment he signed the deed to Whisper Bluff over to the new owner. But there were so many wrongful deeds chaining his soul to hell, he didn't care about adding one more link to its length. The day he found out she had died still haunted him. He had not known her illness was terminal; clearly, she despised him so much she had chosen to die alone. He would never be free of the guilt and misery that imprisoned his heart concerning her.

Dane re-directed his thoughts, but due to his circumstances his mind went to Emmett Cotton. It still made him angry to think this sobriety had been forced upon him by that wise-ass sheriff and the legal system. He was a miserable excuse of a human being, but he was no fool; if he wanted out of here, he had to play the game. He was good at games, especially the kind that had to be won from a perspective of strategic battle. This place, and looking in the mirror every morning, had been as important a battle as any he had ever fought. This battle was one in which he had a personal gain even though he hated to admit it.

He had gone over that weekend a thousand times in his mind. The little red-head was a knockout. She had been a weakness, he should have left alone. He remembered the surprise he felt when she agreed to go fishing with him. He could remember her sitting up top with him as he navigated the boat up river. She was half his age, and he was nervous of all things. That afternoon, he had opened the bottle of Kentucky that the Commander had given him upon his retirement. It calmed him enough to acknowledge just how bad he wanted to have her. She was special; she had spunk. He liked that about her. He remembered how the wind blew her hair out behind her and her blue eyes shown like sapphires. He remembered telling her she was beautiful, and that she made him feel like he was 25 again. He remembered the shape of her lips and the feel of her delicate throat beneath his fingertips, but he couldn't remember kissing her, or laying her down. Instead, he remembered how smooth the iced-down bourbon tasted, and how it seemed like he had swallowed hot coals when it hit his stomach. He remembered looking at her and thinking how young she was, and how her accusing blue eyes lingered in his awareness as he continued to drink. Her eyes were the trigger that sent his mind into a realm of truth as he recalled all the women he had enjoyed while his young and beautiful wife waited for him at home. One after another flashed through his mind and he remembered thinking the Kentucky was kicking his ass. That was the last thought he had until he came to in the hospital, throwing up the embers of his guts.

If what Sheriff Cotton told him was true, then he would have to apologize to the girl. There wouldn't be a snowball's chance in hell that she would give him another chance. Besides, the administrator had told him earlier that the sheriff was coming by this afternoon. He was in no mood to be reminded that he had become a complete shit, but he wanted out of here.

His mind went to Preston. A warm feeling that he found extremely painful stirred in his chest. His eyes were full of compassion just like Caroline's. He was the son every man dreamed of, except he wasn't the boy's father. There was no way he could be given he had been diagnosed sterile the year before they married, due to the fever he contracted in the crude tropical land where he served his country. Even in the realm of a miracle, and he had a sperm left that was healthy, the time factor of when he was with Caroline and the boy's birth was flawed. He had calculated it at least a couple of times a day ever since the boy's birth. The doctors had said the baby was strong and healthy to be born a month early. He knew it was a lie; he could feel it in his gut. He was in Washington at the time the boy was conceived. His mind went back to the day he had returned to her.

Dane had tried to hold his wife upon his return home, but he remembered the distance in her all too well. They had fought about his just dropping in without letting her know. He pointed out that he lived there. She told him that was a joke; he came home when he couldn't find anyone else to screw. Her newfound spunk was like waving a red flag in front of his face and suspicion was born. He was curious to see her response, so he accused her of having a lover. He went so far as to threaten to kill the man when he found him. It was the first time he had ever struck her, or any woman, and it was the first time he had taken her body in anger. He remembered the feel of Caroline's creamy warm flesh and how desperate he was to possess her. He also remembered that she did not touch him even once. He remembered because it was the thing, he had craved the most - the way she touched him with the hands of an artist. He was ashamed he had been so cruel to her and convinced himself that her distance was because he had been gone so long. He needed to believe that she was picking a fight with him and pouting for being left alone for almost a year. But she didn't get over it this time and after weeks of cohabiting with her, she told him that she thought she was pregnant. He finally admitted to himself, there was someone else in her heart, and obviously, it was the same person who had been in her body and left her with a child. He had no idea who it was, short of accusing the entire town. If he did that, he would have looked like the damn fool he was. He left her for a while, but he was curious if maybe he had been able to father the child. After the baby was born, he saw only her in the child and the way she loved and doted on it, as though he was of no concern to either of them. He reasoned his suspicions must be true, and it began to eat away at him.

He remembered how she would hum and sway as she walked about the house with the infant at her breast, smiling and talking to it as though it were the most precious thing on earth. He knew that distant look that came to her eyes. It assured him she had made love to the child's father in that house, and she relived the intricate details of them in her mind daily. He turned bitter because of it. They began to argue, and he began to drink.

The alcohol had a vicious grip on him one night and disconcert swelled inside of him until he exploded in a jealous rage. He hurt her that night. She was hysterical when he collapsed beside her in a drunken and satisfied *level of consciousness. The child was screaming because of the commotion he had caused, and she pushed him off her then sprung to her feet and scooped the child from his crib. He sat up and yelled for her to come back; he wasn't through with her. He followed her and witnessed her bare body, with the robe hanging from her elbows, as she fled upstairs. He had followed her, but she and the child had vanished. He had looked everywhere for her. He remembered how furious he had become when he couldn't find her. He remembered threatening her with burning the house down with her and the child inside of it. It was then that something grabbed his arm with an enraged grip and spun him around to face nothing but empty space. He remembered the icy chill that stiffened the hair on the back of his neck just before his world went . black. He had awakened lying in the floor of the vestibule in a pool of gooey blood with a lump the size of an egg between two black eyes, his nose three times its normal size, and a headache that was close to a jack-hammer pounding in his ears. He had felt a strange energy on more than a few occasions while there with Caroline, but that night the hostility was so thick he couldn't breathe. He couldn't explain it, but he knew something in that house had warned him about his treatment of his wife.*

After that tormented night, he decided to sell the bluff top house. He did it for spite against whatever had lashed out at him and because he knew she loved it; he knew she could survive without him if she had it. Taking it away from her was the thing he regretted most.

The money still sat in a bank at Worthy and Massena. He wondered if he should give it to her son. The boy had not been the one to blame for his mother's deceitful act of adultery. He had wondered so many times why the man had never surfaced to claim Preston as his son.

He had been out of line with his treatment of the boy. He never deliberately intended to hurt him. It seemed when he got smashed and looked at him, all he could see was Caroline's pale, cold body lying on that cold slab in the

233

morgue. The tumor in her brain had caused her beautiful body to waste away to skin and bones after she got sick. She had needed specialized treatment, and he had alienated her to the point she would not ask him for help even though she was legally his wife and was provided for on his health insurance. The memory was a reminder that he had put her there; it turned the guilt he felt over her death into bile. He remembered the last argument they had was when he got drunk enough to question her about Preston's real father. She had looked him in the eye and told him to look in the mirror. It made him so angry because he could see no deceit in her. That was the night she told him to go back to Washington and all his whores and don't come back. She told him she would find a way to take care of herself and Preston without him. She swore she would never ask him for anything else. She cut him deep that night and selling the house was the only way he could hurt her as much as she had hurt him.

Dane's bitter heart asked his clear mind if vengeance could be a murder weapon. He knew it was so. He knew he had killed her with his vengeance just as much as if he had strangled her with his bare hands. The man whom kept flowers on her grave probably knew it too.

His mind embraced the gesture of giving the estate money to her son. Dane looked at his watch; it was after business hours. He had no idea how much interest it had accumulated by now; he had stopped reading the statements years ago. He thought if he did leave the money to Preston; he needed to be old enough to put it to good use.

The sound of the squeaking door was insignificant to him. He had no one that would come here to see him, and the judge had told him he was not to contact Preston until he was released from this shit hole. It was then he remembered the sheriff was coming.

The echoing sound of sure, distinctive steps turned Dane's head. He thought his eyes were mistaken as the young officer stopped in front of his chair.

"Colonel Reid?"

The seriousness and respect in the voice that spoke to him was on a level he understood, and it was greater than the actual words spoken. Dane's blood surged through his veins with a familiar energy as he stood in response to his address and faced the sharp soldier; the young officer saluted him. It felt good to be treated like someone again.

"What can I do for you Captain?"

The distinguished officer handed him a brown envelope then saluted him again.

Dane knew this wasn't good news, not when it's delivered this way. He slid the document out of the sleeve and began to read. The report gave a basic outline of the communications which had been intercepted. He turned the page and his heartbeat quickened as he read the hypothesis of this information and how his strategic skills were needed to protect his country. He scanned the document again in search of specifics as to when this incident took place but did not see any. Dane looked at the Captain as he spoke.

"When did this happen?"

The young officer responded factually but did not look the Colonel in the eye out of respect.

"Sunday... 0900 hours, Sir. Colonel Reid, if you are willing... I am to notify the Secretary, and you are to be reinstated immediately. I am to escort you to Washington, as soon as possible, Sir."

"This is a hell of a time to be sober!" he rumbled out loud as he stared at the letter from the Secretary of Defense. Dane sucked in a deep stabilizing breath then commented.

"I have a son, Captain. I will need to make arrangements for him, and as you can see... I'm being rehabilitated."

"Yes Sir, Sheriff Cotton is the one who informed the Secretary of where you could be located. He has taken action on this matter as the Secretary has requested," stated the officer.

The door to the sunroom opened, and the Captain turned as Sheriff Cotton entered and approached them.

"Captain Able, I took the Administrator the release order from Judge Sandifer as you requested." Cotton looked at the Colonel thinking not everyone gets a chance to redeem themselves. "You're free to go, Colonel." Cotton faced the man, noticing Dane's eyes were clear, and he looked younger. It was the first time he felt intimidated by the Colonel. Cotton was surprised when Dane stuck his hand out. He looked at it and was compelled to accept the man's gesture, even though he wasn't sure why. The Colonel's grip was like a vice when he clamped down on Cotton's hand.

"You pissed me off, Sheriff... by forcing this on me."

Sheriff Cotton's instincts were fine tuned. His hand tightened around the Colonel's as he mentally prepared for a confrontation. Emmett's jaw teeth clamped together as he made a visual connection with the mean-spirited man he loathed as a human being.

"I'm not proud of my actions, Sheriff Cotton. Despite what you and everyone else may think of me, I'm not a complete fool. These weeks of 'rehabilitation' has made me take a long hard look at myself... at my life. I've discovered that I still have a strong mind, and a spine. It's time for me to be useful again." The Colonel released his hand and his stature straightened accordingly in response to his words, and the man's title. "I can see that you had motive... that you were trying to help Preston, and me. Thank you, Sheriff."

Preston saw Jaden's car was at the house when he topped the hill; a fraction of relief stirred in his chest. He pulled into the yard and cut the ignition.

He had spoken to her from the pay phone on campus that morning. The high school held registration from 8:00 until 10:00; afterward, he was scheduled to work. He could tell during their conversation that she was upset about something. She had said she was all right when he questioned her, but she quickly changed the subject and asked him how his day was going and if he had registered. She had encouraged him again to apply himself and forget about everything else while he was there. It was important for him to get his diploma, so he could follow his dream. He had hung up knowing she was crying due to the short gaps of silence in their conversation. He had gone through the morning like a robot doing what he had to do, all the while, he wanted to go see if she was all right.

Mr. Cox had met him at the door when he arrived at the garage and suggested that he take the shift off as personal. He told Preston the sheriff had called and told him his father had been released from the hospital that morning. Preston was sure Jaden didn't know this because he had found out only a couple of hours after they had talked.

He stuck his key in the front door of the small house knowing it was locked due to her inner precaution of living alone. Preston pushed the door open and found her lying on the couch with the small television on and her eyes closed. He closed the door quietly and shoved his keys in his pocket.

She still heard him. Jaden sat up and held her arms out to him as she began to cry again.

Preston went to her.

"Baby, what's wrong?" He sat down and pulled her over into his lap.

"Preston... you're going to be upset with me. I've made a mess of things. Please don't leave me. Please."

He became fearful because of what she said and her apprehensive frame of mind.

"Jaden, tell me what's happened? We can fix it... I promise."

She started crying harder.

"I don't want to fix it. I... I just don't want you to leave me!" Her blue eyes were burdened by something very serious.

Preston didn't know what else to do but kiss her in hope that the level of personal closeness they shared would calm her. She kissed him back just as he had hoped.

"Talk to me, Baby."

She rested her forehead against his and sighed.

"I'm pregnant, Preston."

He pulled back and looked at her.

"What?"

"I'm pregnant." She shook her head as her small hand gripped his shirt. "Please... don't be mad... don't leave me."

He was stunned, but she said it again, so he had heard her right and the crease didn't appear over her eye like it did when she was teasing him.

"Are you serious?"

She nodded her head as huge diamond-like tears rolled down her cheeks.

He sat there a moment while processing this unexpected information. He had thought about them having a child together one day, but with things as they were, that day seemed a long way off. He had done his homework on the legal ramifications of his and Jaden's relationship. He knew they needed to continue to keep a low profile until his next birthday which was five weeks away, at which time he didn't care who knew about them. He had already decided on a plan of action. He could take his equivalency test and keep his job at the garage. When he turned 21, he would enter the police academy. The only drawback was that he didn't want her going through this alone and he wasn't sure what he could do to change that. He couldn't legally sign a marriage license until he was 18 years old.

Her uncertain voice interrupted his train of thought.

"Preston, are you planning an escape?"

A smile cracked his stunned expression.

"We made a baby together? You're sure, Honey? How long? I mean..."

"Two months... I'm due April 5. I'm as shocked as you are. Ava told me two years ago that I would have to work hard to get pregnant due to the old scar tissue. I've never missed a period... ever."

Preston gazed at her; his eyes were dancing with excitement. She needed clarification. This was fixing to change her life and her body; if he was going to turn into someone else, she wanted to know now.

"You aren't worried, scared, or feeling trapped?" she surveyed quietly.

Preston had developed a keen sense of this woman and her moods. She was, in her own way, asking him to be honest with himself first so he could be open with her.

"Of course, I'm scared. I want to be a great father and I can't say that I know exactly how to do that. I'll worry until the baby's here and I see for myself that both of you are all right. I'll feel even better when we come home and get the hang of parenthood. I'm surprised... and I'm excited." He pecked a kiss to her lips. "You couldn't run me off with a shotgun, Baby. We have a little one growing in here." His hand went to her belly as a huge, toothy grin claimed his face. "You know what... Dr. Ava was right. We have been working hard at loving each other." He pressed his warm, soft lips against Jaden's several times, and a feeling of harmony washed over her body. Preston stood up with her in his arms and started down the hall.

"Are we going back to work?" She whispered in between kisses.

"Yep," breathed Preston.

Preston felt the icy-hot chills slide through his veins like she had given him an injection of desire. He looked up at her bare body sitting atop him and admired her pale, full breasts. Her appetite for him grew bolder, and he rose to his elbows. She took hold of the headboard and shifted her hips, the tips of her breasts danced seductively in front of him. His kiss greeted her tightened flesh with loving tenderness. She sighed passionately because it was the inspiration she needed and wanted to feel at that moment.

They had learned how to please each other and took care in doing so every time they touched. It was the essence of being in love with that one special person.

The universe of this bed and this room where they glorified each other physically and reverenced the hope each of them gave to the other, was his life now; it was his purpose. He lived to love her. Taking care of her and their baby was all that mattered.

The icy chills in his veins began to melt under the salacious yearning she was so capable of inflicting upon his body. It was like sweltering waves of feeling, stimulating every muscle and every nerve. The bottoms of his feet tingled in response to the millions of cells that were celebrating his adoration and devotion to this woman. He pulled his knees up slightly dragging his feet across the sheets as the urge to push into her became more than he could bear.

She kissed his forehead as her hips encouraged him to join her rhythm. When she pressed her breasts against his chest and folded her arms around him, Preston knew she wanted him to take them the rest of the way. He rolled her over and impressed his possessive nature upon her in the most pleasurable of ways. The sigh that eased past her lips assured him she was getting what she needed. When her body began to tremble with ecstasy, he slid his arms beneath her and drew even closer. He needed reassurance she would stay grounded in his arms while the gift of physical bliss emanated through them.

They lay still and sated once again. Suddenly, he thought of the baby inside of her. He shifted his weight to the space beside her and then wrapped his arms around his little family. He sucked in a deep, contented breath and let go of it slowly. She tilted her head up and looked at him, and Preston smiled as he pressed his lips against hers.

They became lost in sharing their dreams for the future.

Preston called Owen from Jaden's making sure he knew that his father was being released today. They talked a few minutes. He told Preston to be prepared because Cotton told him the military had been the ones to get him released. They wanted him to come to Washington because of something that was brewing. He couldn't say what. Preston was surprised when Owen told him he was proud of him. When Preston asked why, Owen told him that forgiving his father and wanting to keep their relationship despite the hurt and disappointments was the foundation of a godly man. He told Preston everyone grows during their life, and it's the Lord's intention that we grow closer to Him. Owen told Preston that he was doing a good job in his journey of life.

Preston hung up feeling overwhelmed by Owen's faith in him and the unknown truth in his words. He had managed to guard his and Jaden's relationship from them without being deceitful. He believed he and Jaden had been put in each other's path of life. They needed each other so desperately; still, a part of his heart told him that it had not been intended for them to be so physically consumed with each other. Preston knew they needed Owen's and Charlie's God to be in their lives. He was bothered by the fact that as a man who loved her, he should be more than a physical lover to her. She deserved so much more. He began to contemplate the possibilities.

"Sweetie, are you okay?" Her arms slid around his waist from behind and she hugged him.

He caressed her arms with his palms.

"Yeah, I'm great. Jaden, do you believe in God?" He sighed as he turned to face her. He knew she did from some things she had said, but like him she had questions. "What I mean is... do you think God cares about people like us?" He gazed into her eyes as he explained. "Owen is so wise, and he treats Estelle like a queen. I want to do that for you. I want to give you everything, Honey. I want us to be able to give this baby the love and guidance you and I didn't have. I can't help but feel that... somehow... He should be included. Owen says that God is at the center of everything... like the way we treat each other, and the way we react to the world around us... even when it's unfair and cruel. What do you think?"

Jaden nodded her head as she gave him her opinion on the matter.

"I know what you mean, Preston, I feel the same way," she professed. She tilted her head as she searched his face for a few seconds then she stretched up to kiss his lips. "I have to be honest with you... the concept of Almighty God overwhelms my understanding. Maybe we can talk to Charlie about it. I think he knows both sides... rather, he knows a lot more about it than you and me. I believe he can help us."

Her suggestion seemed genuine because he knew she trusted Charlie. Preston squeezed her hand as he kissed her back several times.

"So, for the sake of asking... will you have me as a husband?"

She gave him one of her beautiful, adoring smiles.

"Absolutely! It'll happen, Sweetie. We may have the cart before the horse... so to speak, but we can help push it for a while. I love you, and I love my life with you. I feel like the luckiest girl on earth! I couldn't ask for more."

There was a joyful glow in her eyes, and Preston knew she meant every word. He picked her up and shared a fierce kiss with her.

"I've got to run. Dane's probably already at the house and wondering where I am. I'll call you in a little while and let you know how it went." He put her to her feet then turned and took a step toward the door. Ever since the day their lives had slammed into one another, Preston had discovered that leaving her was a hard thing for him to manage. He had always felt like he was leaving a part of his heart with her, but today he was leaving a living piece of himself inside of her. He opened the door but hesitated as he looked back at the woman he loved. His eyes drifted to her middle then he reached out and pressed his hand to her tummy. Jaden smoothed her warm palm over the back of his hand as the smile on her face widened.

"I love both my babies," he mumbled as he pressed one more kiss to her lips.

Jaden waved as Preston backed out of the yard. It was love that caused her to watch his tail lights disappear over the asphalt hill. She stepped back over the threshold and closed the door. Habit made her secure the dead bolt.

Dane had seen the photographs Cotton had taken of the inside of his disheveled houseboat. They were in the case file Sheriff Cotton had built against him and were documented evidence of his failure as a father. They proved he was a miserable human being. He had come home believing he had a mess to clean up; however, the boat was spotless, and everything was in order, minus another coffee table. Dane realized the cleaning up that had to be done was the relationship he had with the boy.

He was waiting for the coffee pot to finish perking when he heard the humming tail pipe of the Jeep pull into the drive. He grabbed a mug from the hook above the sink and poured a cup, willing to accept whatever degree of caffeine it could give at this point.

The door opened, and Preston stepped through it without hesitation. Dane was surprised; he was prepared to grovel to get the young man to talk to him. He picked up his cup then turned to face Preston. He was tall and had shoulders like the mast of a ship. The young man was cut with rock hard muscles, and thanks to the daily influence of a hard-ass drunk, the boy possessed a keen sense of survival and sound common sense to go with it. His crystal blue eyes and dark walnut colored hair was Caroline's, but Dane believed his square jaw line, the flat plain on the bridge of his nose and dimpled cheeks belonged to a stranger. It was insignificant to Preston because he believed him to be his father, and for 17 years the young man had respected him as such. Dane felt shame and regret over the fact because he had not earned it.

Preston stopped several feet away from him as their eyes met and held. Dane thought he had to have been out of his mind to tangle with this youthful example of a man. It hit him suddenly that Preston was not a boy anymore. This was a man standing in front of him, and if the country went to war, he would not be spared the conflict.

Preston had only seen his father with a crew cut once and it had been years ago. Because he had important things in his life that needed to be taken care of, he spoke first.

"How are you, Dad? You look really good."

Dane put the mug in his other hand then held the one that was hot out to Preston. The young man didn't hesitate to grab it in a strong confident grip. It was that moment when Dane realized that the law and everyone else in this world believed and accepted him to be Preston's father, and he sure as hell didn't deserve him.

"I'm sober, Preston," stated Dane. "Let's see... the last time you saw me in this shape was..." he paused a moment then shook his head, "Never... I suppose." He pointed to the cup. "You want some coffee?"

Preston nodded and took a step to retrieve a mug. He liked sugar in it, but he left it black, so he could be reminded to keep his edge and do what he had to do.

Dane sat down at the table. Preston remembered it was the same spot Jaden had sat the first day they met. He pulled out the adjacent chair and joined his father.

"I need to talk to you, Preston, but I need to tell you something first, it's personal... and important to me."

"Yes Sir," he answered respectfully then waited and watched as Dane seemed to search for the right words, or maybe even the courage, to tell him what was on his mind.

"First, I want to apologize for being a mean bastard to you, Preston. The only excuse I have is that alcohol makes a mean bastard... an even meaner bastard. You sure as hell deserved better. I... I am very proud of you... as a person, and the man you've become. It's not any of my doing that's for sure." Dane sat there staring into his coffee cup for a moment. When he spoke, the tone of his voice matched the seriousness of his words and Preston became enthralled by the personal nature of his father's candor.

"I worshiped your mother... honestly, I did. She was the most beautiful and incredible woman I have ever seen or known... she still is. But, as you already know, I'm very good at allowing other things to get in the way of taking care of the people I love. I was just as shitty a husband as I am a father. I let other things get in the way of taking care of her like I should have.

"I told myself if I took her to Washington with me, she would be bored when I was working, but I was lying to myself, and her. Truth was... I was jealous as hell and if she was there, I would be distracted from what I had to do. She was a weakness for me. When we were together, I couldn't get enough of her."

Preston watched Dane sit in a still silence. There was pain in his expression and he sensed the man across from him was lost in another time and place that had tormented him every day of his life since his Caroline had passed away. Dane's next admission echoed with remorse.

"I was gone almost a year back in '42... the war was unfolding. When I came home on furlough, I sensed a distance in her. When I drew close to her, she wasn't with me... if you know what I mean. I was convinced that I felt the presence of another man in her. I accused her of being involved with someone else. The way she looked at me was so odd; I remember thinking that her eyes were accusing me. It angered me that she could make me feel as though I was betraying her by thinking such a thing. She was my wife, but I didn't believe her. I was furious, and I didn't know what to do with the rage. I shouldn't have touched her until I cooled off." He shook his head. "I convinced myself that I bore no fault in it. All I could see was that I had been gone in service and when I came home, she made me feel like I didn't belong in my own bed anymore... much less inside of my wife. I told her when I found out who he was that I would kill him, and no one would ever find his body after the swamp got through with him. She had even painted our portrait to hang in the gallery with all her family; she depicted me as an evil shadow lurking at her shoulder. It infuriated me too, and I snatched it off the wall and slammed it over the back of a chair destroying it. I think about it now and I don't know why it offended me so much; after all, I was domineering and controlling, and I treated her like a possession." Dane sighed and shook his head as the memory came back to his mind in living color, and sorrow came with it. "I used physical force and fear to try to make her turn back to me Preston. I... I hurt her. It was the first time I had ever touched her in anger. I knew it was wrong, but I couldn't manage touching her without thinking and wondering about the stranger that was in her heart. I look back now... and I realize that I was the stranger. Anyway, it was six weeks later she found out she was pregnant with you. I was convinced she had someone else in her heart and I started looking for any signs that would prove it.

"I found a key in her jewelry box from Worthy and Massena; it was on a small gold chain. I remembered seeing it around her neck after I got home, but I didn't realize a key was on it. It made me suspicious. I went to the bank because I knew it went to a safe deposit box. I found the old deed to the house and a new one that had separated the bulk of the property from the house. The new property deed had been filed with her name alone, but the new deed to the house added me as a tenant in common with joint rights of survivorship. There were no signatures on it. I found divorce papers too. She had signed them already, but she hadn't told me about them. It started me to thinking that maybe she had changed her mind because she didn't want to take her child away from his real father. I was hopeful I had not lost her. I took the house deed and the divorce papers with me. I used her signature on the divorce papers to forge hers on the new house deed then I got a friend who owed me a favor to notarize it for me. I filed the deed at the courthouse, and then I burnt the divorce papers.

"I was able to come and go more often for a while... until I received orders sending me out of the country two weeks before you were born. I didn't want to leave her, especially at a time like that. I spoke to my superiors, and they agreed to allow me a later departure date. When I told her, what was in the works, she said my motives were based on jealousy rather than concern for her and the baby. I remember, she shook her head and told me that it didn't bother her to be alone and I may as well go. It was so frustrating. I was trying to be her husband, but my jealousy had become more than she could take. Her disregard for me had continued to grow, and it hurt, so I left.

"She had you at home with a midwife two days later. I came home half a dozen times in the next year. But it didn't matter, she loved you so much and you had become the center of her life. It was spellbinding to watch her with you, Preston. The way she carried you in her arms... the way she smiled at you and sang to you was full of devotion. I found myself wondering if it were you, or the fact that you were a part of someone else that she loved. When she looked at me, I felt like a pane of glass and she was looking straight through me. I convinced myself, if I were your father, she wouldn't have been able to dismiss me so easily.

"One night I got tight... and I was standing in the doorway of the bathroom watching her bathe. She had you in her lap and had rinsed the soap from you and herself; she started to get out, so I reached for you to help. She slapped my hand away then shifted you to her other arm. It was at that moment I realized that I had never held you; it bothered me even more that she didn't want me to either. I asked her who your father really was, and she told me to look in the mirror. I couldn't help it... my temper flared at the way she would say one thing, yet her behavior would suggest another. She wasn't expecting it when I plucked you out of her arms and took you into the bedroom. She followed me demanding that I give her back her baby. When I stopped to lay you down on the bed, she slapped me and told me to go back to Washington and never come back. Her contempt kicked me in the gut. She despised me; I saw it in her eyes. That was the night I realized I had lost her. I was an arrogant and spiteful man, and I wanted to make her pay for the way she just wrote me and our marriage off. I was so angry that... I hurt her again. It was the last time I ever touched her while she was alive. Damn it! I've regretted it every day of my life since it happened.

"I left the next day and a couple of months later, I sold the house. I did it because she loved it so much... because it sustained her when I couldn't... because the ghosts of her family were there in every corner to comfort her. I sold it... because I thought it would force her to turn to me for her livelihood. She was proud and determined to be through with me, and she refused. It was another terrible mistake I made concerning her. She couldn't forgive me for what I did. She couldn't forgive me for selling her heritage. The week she was notified I had sold the house, I got a registered letter in the mail. It was her wedding rings. It couldn't have hurt more if she had stabbed me in the heart with a knife. That feeling... it made me realize how she had felt in losing her home. We were never legally divorced, and I wanted a chance to change. I wanted her forgiveness, and to try again to be what she needed. I wrote to her dozens of times and told her how sorry I was... how much I loved her. I asked her to forgive me... I asked her for another chance. I promised I would retire and be with her, and we could raise you together. I even tried to buy the house back, but it was too late. I sent you a card and a gift on your first birthday, but she sent it back to me with a note. She told me that she was doing well, her son was perfect, and that she was happy with the way things were. She said you didn't need a man like me in your life, and neither did she.

"I had to hire someone to keep up with her and let me know that the two of you were all right. It wasn't until you were six years old that the detective contacted me and told me she was sick. I didn't know it was a brain tumor and that it was terminal until it was too late. The day he called and told me that an ambulance had taken her to the hospital, I was out of pocket... as always goddammit. I dropped everything. I had to... I had to see her. I was about to board the plane to Dallas when I received word she had died, and you were with a friend. I swear, the news... it almost killed me. I stood in the head for over an hour during the flight and bawled like a baby. It was the only place I could go where I could shut the world out.

"I only thought I was miserable... when I saw her lying on that cold table in the morgue; it put a rusty knife in my gut that has poisoned me every day since. I deserve to live in torment... she was an earthly angel if ever there was one. I... I didn't know how to manage the way she made me feel, or the devotion she offered to me. I had never been exposed to anything as innocent as your mother, Preston."

Preston witnessed the Colonel wipe his cheek on the shoulder of his coat as he turned up the coffee cup and took a big gulp. He sat there and waited out of respect while he thought about the things his father had told him.

"I never had a father... my mother had no idea who he was," stated Dane plainly. "Still, when I saw you... I knew I had to try to be a father to you. I wanted to try to do right by you, Preston... because I loved her so much and I had foolishly thrown us away. I'm truly sorry for being such a bastard all these years. I know you would have been better off without me, but... in these last two months, I've come to realize that I wouldn't have been better off without knowing you."

Preston felt like a strong fist had suddenly grabbed his heart and was squeezing it.

"I need to know something." Dane's honesty was out of character for the man Preston knew, so much so that it was almost eerie, and it gave Preston chills. "Do you put white roses on your mother's grave?"

Preston shook his head.

"No Sir, I've always thought you did."

Dane shook his head.

"No, it wasn't me."

Preston could tell what his father was thinking; he still believed his wife had been unfaithful. Preston thought about that in relation to the things he remembered about his mother. She was gentle, loving and incredibly beautiful, but there was a sadness about her. She did not speak badly of Dane, but she never tried to assure him that his father was a good man either. And she had never given him the impression that Dane was not his father.

"I'm sorry you got stuck with a bitter, drunken son-of-a-bitch to raise you. I'm sorry that I've taught you hate, and that I've hurt you. I'm not proud of it." Dane gazed at him and Preston could see remorse in his eyes. "You look so much like her, Preston." He pulled his wallet out and removed a photograph then handed it to Preston.

Preston took it then smiled at the image of the beautiful woman that was in his memory. He had never seen this photo, and it made him realize just how much he did favor her. He handed it back to Dane, but the older man shoved it back.

"Keep it... I want you to have it. There are possessions of hers... and the Breaux family that I stored away for you, and I have some things that I want you to have as well."

Preston put the photograph in his wallet as he listened. It sounded like his father was getting his affairs in order. His feelings were jumbled and confused where Dane was concerned, and even though he had pretty much raised himself, the thought of never seeing him again was disturbing.

"Dad, I already know the service has contacted you again. I take it that you're going?"

Dane sat there a moment then he nodded his head.

"I've been a lousy parent. It's time for me to be useful again, Preston. I was hoping you would help me figure out how we're going to do this. What I mean is... it's time for you to have a say in your future. You've grown into a smart and self-reliant young man; still, the law considers you a minor." He took a sip of his coffee. "By the way, I'm sorry I put you in the middle of myself and the little redhead too. According to the Sheriff, I should thank you. Your intercession saved her from my alcoholic rage... but you saved me too. I understand that I owe her one hell of an apology."

Preston saw the opportunity and he took it.

"Her name is Jaden... and I should thank you."

Dane's eyes targeted Preston's.

"Dad, we've been seeing each other for the last two months."

Dane didn't explode as Preston expected, but he was straightforward as he re-visited the only personal fact, he could remember about her.

"Do you know she's 23 years old? She's too old to be dating you, Preston."

"Well, that's a classic statement considering you are almost twice her age, and it didn't stop you." Preston leaned back in his chair and scrubbed his face with his palms. He looked across the table to where Dane sat studying him. "I'm sorry, that was disrespectful. No Sir, she's not too old for me. We have so much in common when it comes to life and what we want from it. I've found someone to love and care about, and she feels the same way about me. That's what she had hoped to find in you. It's ironic that she found it in your son. Besides, we don't question the way we met, we're just thankful that we did." Preston paused to organize the rest of his thoughts into a factual agenda.

"Dad, the years won't mean anything to anyone in a matter of weeks... you know that. The truth is... we're passed dating. I'm not asking for your understanding, or approval. I'm telling you, she's my happiness and my future. I've got to respect the fact that she's scared of you, so I won't even hope that the two of you could come to a mutual understanding. It's like you said, I've raised myself, and I've made plans. I have a good job to meet our needs. I want to enroll in the law enforcement academy when I'm old enough to get accepted... until then I'll take my high school equivalence test in October and go to work full time. Jaden has her job at the hospital and an affordable place to live that has everything we need. We'll be fine.

"I've never asked you for anything, but I'm asking you for this. I need you to do this for me. It's the solution that serves all of us. You can get on with your usefulness without being burdened with me, and you can leave knowing I'm truly happy. I love her, Dad."

Dane frowned at him then shook his head as he spoke.

"I don't understand. What are you asking me to do, Preston?"

"I want you to sign for me to get married. It will make me a legal adult... and her husband." Preston could see that his father was surprised.

"Dad, you said that you were a lousy parent. I need you to do this for me. I don't want to enter parenthood being an absent father. I don't want my child born without my name. I don't want his mother going through this without me lying next to her... next to them every night. I want to feel him and experience the miracle of watching him grow in her... and after he's born. Please Dad, do this for me. It's not only the answer for all of us... it's what I want."

Preston could tell by the glimmer in his father's eyes that he had made his point.

CHAPTER 13

Jaden was shaking in her shoes when the soft knock came to the front door. It was Preston's way of letting her know that his key was in the door lock. She smoothed her dress over her thighs and stepped to the center of the small room to greet them.

The happiness in Preston's eyes was the first thing she saw when they entered the room. He went to her and kissed her forehead then slid his arm around her waist for support.

Jaden looked up at Dane Reid; it struck her as odd that she didn't recognize him. He didn't even look like the man she remembered. His eyes were a shiny deep brown, and the scruffy mustache and beard were gone to reveal smooth dark skin. The long, salt and pepper hair had been replaced by a rigid square cut that would fit beneath the molded hat of an officer.

It was too late for visitors, but they were here on behalf of hers and Preston's future. She had managed to get a lemon cake in and out of the oven around taking a shower. She dressed conservatively in a simple blue skirt that had a printed cotton shirt that matched. She tied her hair back with a cream-colored scarf, put on a light coating of makeup and stepped into a pair of sandals. She felt awkward having this meeting with Dane Reid considering their last meeting was such a disaster; however, she chose to let go of the negativity and focus her energy on the wonderful things that had been a result of it. She had found a soul mate in the young man standing next to her and they were blessed with love; the child growing inside of her was a constant reminder of the joy that had come to her life. Her love for Preston was bigger than any awkwardness she may feel.

"I don't exactly know what to say, Colonel." She held her hand out to him. "Hello."

Dane took her hand noticing how small it truly was and how young she looked.

"Jaden, I owe you an embarrassing and shamed apology. Please, I ask you to forgive my previous behavior. I have no excuse other than being a drunk and arrogant jackass." He released her hand and gave her a slight smile.

The Colonel's demeanor put Jaden's heart at ease and she returned his smile. When she looked at Preston, she could see that he was happy.

"You're forgiven, Colonel. I have a lemon cake that's still warm from the oven. Please do sit down. Would you like iced tea or coffee?" She went to the kitchen, and Preston followed her.

"Iced tea sounds good," he answered.

Dane pulled out the chair at the small breakfast table and sat down. Because of his sobriety, he and Preston had been able to converse with one another about life, the unpleasant facts that were a matter of public record and the separate direction their lives were headed. It was the reason they had come to a meeting in this small, but cozy house. He watched Preston retrieve three glasses from the cabinet then fill two of them with ice; he poured those with tea and the other with milk. Dane looked around at the small, well-kept dwelling while he listened to Preston tell her the milk was getting low. She asked him to add it to the list on the refrigerator. The young woman's voice was close, and it drew the Colonel's attention back to the kitchen area where she placed a short stack of small plates, napkins and utensils on the table. Preston asked if there were anything else, she could think of while he was writing. She paused a moment to think then told him to add cornmeal, eggs, bananas, clothes soap and toilet paper. Dane watched in a captivated silence as the two interacted in a way that displayed nothing but respect and consideration for one another. He realized these two had already mastered something he and Preston's mother had never managed to find.

Dane took notice of the simple and elegant way the girl presented herself, and he remembered why he had approached her in the first place. She had impressed him with her intellect and clever wit.

Preston brought the glasses to the table while Jaden followed him and placed the beautifully glazed cake in the center of it. Dane suddenly made the connection between the refreshing smell that hung in the air and Jaden's culinary skill, and with it came a clearer perspective of this evening and the circumstances that were unfolding between these young people. They had embraced each other physically; however, it had not been a self-seeking and exploitive act, but rather one committed out of compassion and loneliness. Clearly, Preston was a better man than him. It was a humbling feeling that spread through Dane's chest, and one of pride. It pleased him that Preston had cared enough to intercede on behalf of a drunken father and a stranger. He realized Preston was wise enough to recognize the exemplary qualities this young woman possessed. She was smart and funny, but she was also thoughtful and kind. Her domestic skills were quite proficient, and she seemed to enjoy sharing them with his son, but she was also willing to forgive those who had trespassed against her.

The three of them sat together and talked for almost two hours. Preston told Jaden what he had asked of his father. Dane watched her closely without staring. He had no doubt about it; she was in love with Preston. He wasn't sure what events in her life had brought her to this place of vulnerability in relation to trust, while at the same time, she was so confident about everything else. He concluded it was because of people like him who had preyed upon her loneliness. It was obvious that she was hardened to counting on herself, just like Preston.

Considering that it was Tuesday night, Dane proposed they meet at the courthouse in Dallas the following morning. Since Jaden worked in the city, it made sense for him and Preston to accommodate her schedule rather than she misses half a work day driving to Westville. The Colonel referred to the busy city office being less likely to scrutinize the difference in age.

Preston had learned about the legal requirements that were necessary for them to marry. He told Jaden she would need her social security card and her birth certificate for the Circuit Clerk's office. He told them the waiting period was 72 hours, but he didn't know who could do the ceremony on a Saturday. He commented that he didn't really know Shadow Groves' pastor where Charlie went to church.

Jaden suggested a justice of the peace.

Preston thought of Sheriff Cotton, but he didn't mention it because he was sure his friend would not approve of their plans.

They departed with the Colonel agreeing that the marriage would be the best thing for them whether he was of issue to it or not.

The drive back to the houseboat was quiet, but surprisingly surreal. Preston said goodnight and retreated to his room upstairs. He organized his things somewhat, so moving would be a simple task. He had no sooner stretched out on the single bed when he heard the stairs creak then a knock came to his door. It was weird. He didn't really know this version of the man that was his father. It was sad because he thought they could really build a friendship if they had a chance. It was something that he couldn't change at this point in their relationship. The truth in it made him even more determined to make sure his own child knew its father.

Preston cut on the small lamp then opened the door.

"Yes Sir?"

Dane held out a small silk bag.

"These were your mother's and mine. I don't know if you would want to use them. Hell, they may be cursed after we did such a pitiful job respecting commitment." He shoved the bag in Preston hand. "But I'm certain you and Jaden have the power to change that, Preston. You decide what's best. I'll say good night."

Dane turned and descended into the darkness. Preston closed the door and sat down on the bunk. He untied the bag and poured three sparkling gold bands out into his hand. They all matched because of the same overlapping circular pattern repeated around them. A magnificent oval-shaped diamond was mounted on the narrow band; it caught the light in a dazzling prism of color. Preston smiled at his father's thoughtfulness. He put the rings back in the pouch then laid it on the small night table and turned out the light.

Preston found Dane waiting for him in the kitchen the following morning. He had converted into the stalwart Colonel overnight which made the fact he had been re-activated in to military service even more real to Preston. He had patchy memories of this man in uniform, but he did not remember all the distinguishing metals and stripes that were required by his rank and earned in duty. Despite everything that was between them, he was proud of his father's dedication to his country. The image of him in full dress would stay with him always because he was not a boy any more. The uniform and the fact that he was wearing it again proved that Colonel Dane Reid's service was valuable and needed. Preston understood the Colonel was relinquishing his hold on him as a boy.

The paperwork at the courthouse went without a snag. Jaden took the marriage license and put it in her bag. She ignored the haughty glance the lady at the counter gave her for preying upon a boy.

When they were free of scrutiny and in the sunlight again, Jaden stopped on the sidewalk outside of the courthouse and looked at them.

"Thank you, Colonel... for trusting us, and for not judging me."

Dane smiled as he put on his hat and situated it to just the right spot.

"Jaden, I'm asking you to take good care of him. You are both very lucky to have each other. I told Preston last night, I am certain the two of you will love each other and make each day count."

She smiled as she looked up at Preston.

"I will Colonel; I plan on doing exactly that."

Preston leaned over and softly kissed her lips. He was thinking about the next hurdle he had to deal with today, and that was telling Charlie, Owen and the Sheriff about their plans.

"I have a lot to do at work today. I'll call you this afternoon."

Jaden nodded her head as her eyes sparkled at him.

Preston kissed her again then said in an anxious voice.

"Oh, I almost forgot. I need you to keep something else for us." Preston dug in his pocket and pulled out a small bag. He grinned at her as he dug in it for a moment then he dropped to one knee and took her hand. The diamond ring glistened in the morning sun as he slid it on her finger. It caught on her knuckle then agreed to go on with a slight push. Preston kissed it.

"It was my mother's, Jaden. Dad wanted us to have them." Preston glanced over to his father and turned her hand, so he could see it.

The Colonel smiled and gave an approving nod of his head.

"It's beautiful... and right where it should be," he said with conviction.

Jaden swallowed the lump in her throat.

"My word... you fellas are determined to make me cry before I get to work." She brushed her fingers over her cheek. "Thank you both so much. I will always cherish and respect it. I promise."

Preston stood and pulled her against his chest as he stuck the velvet bag in her hand. He pressed his lips to her temple as he spoke.

"These are the bands, Honey. I'll see you tonight. I love you."

Preston and Dane rode in silence, each consumed with their own thoughts. Classes started at 8:00 that morning, but Preston had not had time to call Charlie and let him know what was happening. He had called the day before, but his buddy had been out on the land running fence.

The Colonel's voice interrupted his thoughts.

"I think I know someone who will do the ceremony for us, Preston. He's a retired Chaplain; he married me and your mother. I'll ask... if you want me to."

"Yes Sir, I would appreciate that. I need to tell Charlie. If you don't mind, I'd like him to stand up with me."

"No, I don't mind. I think that's appropriate; he's going to be here for you. But Preston, I want you to know that you can call me. I want to hear from you. It's true, I may not be able to drop everything at that moment and come if it's an emergency, but I swear to you... I'll find someone who can. Do you understand what I mean?"

"Yes Sir, I think so." Preston wasn't going to go there. He would just have to cross that bridge if life forced him to.

"I want you to know that you are my beneficiary... should something happen to me. I've already transferred my savings into your account, because I won't need it where I'm going. And there's this," Dane handed him a large envelope that lay on the seat between them.

Preston took it with a frown; it was insignificant to him until now. He opened it without comment and thumbed through the documents. It was the title to the houseboat and the original deeds to the two different pieces of acreage bordering the river. They each had an updated version attached to them that added him as the joint tenant in common with full rights of survivorship. He started to ask what this meant, but Dane beat him to it with an explanation.

"I've signed them over to you, Preston. Baxter Hollingsworth is ready to file them for us as soon as you sign them. I've already paid him for his services. His firm has handled the Breaux family business for as long as they've been established. I know when your mother passed it was the old man, Litton Hollingsworth, who contacted me about her estate. He told me he and an investment company were over-seeing the business of her estate until you were old enough to make some decisions concerning it. I'm not sure what that means exactly; her family was very secretive about everything. Anyway, he said that your mother left his father instructions, you were to be contacted upon coming of age, and since he handles the estate now and you will be a married adult, he needs to speak with you. He told me when the time comes for him to retire, he will hand it down to his predecessor or the attorney of your choice, or sooner... should you deem another time more appropriate.

"It would be my suggestion that you and Jaden move to the houseboat for a while; it would enable you to cut expenses for now. I know it's not safe for a toddler, but it could still give you a year and a half... maybe two, before you need to make other arrangements. The land is yours to do with as you please. And by the way, the cemetery where your mother and her family rest are part of a 9000-acre tract of land; the deed to it is in your name as well. I wasn't aware of this fact until I spoke to him yesterday. It came up due to the relevance to the others he was taking care of for me. Baxter Hollingsworth told me it is part of your mother's estate. I knew she had some property, but since she wouldn't take anything from me, I assumed she had sold it to sustain the two of you. Umm, believe it or not... it encompasses the old growth from the edge of the cemetery all the way up the river beyond Wolf Bluff."

Preston didn't know what to say other than the truth.

"That's the 'big-woods'! Sir, are you serious? I... gosh..." mumbled Preston. He looked at his father for a moment and could tell Dane was telling him the truth. "I... I'm shocked," admitted Preston. "Everybody has always thought that land belonged to some rich-cat that owned the Traxler Paper Mill."

"As I understand it, Litton Hollingsworth leased it to them at your mother's request right after her parents were killed. I don't know any more details, but I'm certain it was more than enough to sustain the two of you after we split up. I can only assume the firm has been managing those funds all these years. You'll have to talk to Hollingsworth to find out any details."

Preston was stunned and had no idea what to think of all of this. He didn't want to get into a conversation about it because he could see Dane was sensitive to this news. He understood why Dane had kept these private things about his mother to himself; they were memories of a time and place in his life that were painful. The bigger truth being that until these last few months, Dane had seen him as a troublesome kid.

A reflection of when he was a boy surfaced in his mind. *He remembered the Spring day his mother and him had a picnic in the edge of the woods on the bluff that overlooked the big house. She spread a blanket in the green grass and they shared fresh strawberries, cheese sandwiches and homemade butter cookies. After lunch, he played in the dirt with some wooden cars while she sat behind an easel and painted the house with the river bending around the property.* He had questions about his mother and her family but asking them would only bring his father pain. Preston believed Dane had confessed the troublesome deeds that haunted him over all others. Besides, Preston sensed his father had as many questions about his mother and her family as he did. It didn't matter now, there was no one left to answer them even if they were asked.

Dane had taken the highway on the way home from Dallas and they merged into traffic before Dane spoke again.

"What do you remember about her? Did she ever tell you about your people, and how they came to this country from France?"

"She told me about them, but it always made her sad. It used to scare me... sometimes she would cry so hard her nose would bleed. I stopped asking questions about the house... or Grandpa Preston. I have her family photo album. I took her picture out and framed it, so I could see her and remember her every day. I'm ashamed to say that I haven't looked at the album in a long time."

"I want you to read the documents in that envelope Preston. We'll talk about the things you should know after the fact. I don't know a lot about the Breaux history, but I'll try to answer your questions about the estate... and me and your mom."

Preston couldn't help himself; he wanted to know everything Dane could tell him about them, and he told him so.

Dane saw an opportunity in the sequestered drive and told Preston how he had met Caroline at her college graduation, and about their brief courtship. He told Preston they had been seeing each other a little over a month when he had got his new orders to come to Washington. And, because they had begun a physical relationship with each other, he persuaded her to marry him before he left to protect her reputation. He told him about the simple ceremony on the balcony and how incredibly beautiful Caroline was in her mother's wedding dress.

"She was only 19 years old when her parents died in a car accident. I understand her grandfather stayed by her side until he passed a few years later. When we met, she was alone in the world and rattling around in that huge house all by herself. I'm sure you've heard the same story I heard when I was young... about the old house on the bluff being haunted." Dane shook his head. "That house was an indulgent project, built by a man that had more money than sense. Like I told you yesterday, for some reason your mother had Hollingsworth put the house on a separate deed. I've thought about it a lot through the years, if it was an issue of trust then she wouldn't have put me on the deed to start with. Still, she didn't file it." Dane stared at the road in front of him a few moments, and then his thoughts slipped passed his lips as they came to his mind. "I can't believe the chancery clerk filed it, usually all parties have to sign a document in front of them before they can notarize and file it. The Breaux family was eccentric... financially and even more, when it came to privacy. Everybody knew it. I figured I lucked-out, and they filed it because of the fact. Either way, I betrayed her by filing it, and I stabbed her in the back when I sold it. I put the money from the sale of the house in an account at Worthy and Massena; it's been there drawing interest all this time." Since he revealed this truth, Dane was motivated to disclose another piece of family history. He told Preston about the elaborate possessions in the house and where they were stored for safekeeping. After all, this was another responsibility the young man was inheriting concerning his mother's estate. "I had the bank add you to the account, Preston. You'll need to go by and show them your driver's license and sign the account card, so your signature will be on file. The storage bill is being paid by withdrawal out of the interest earned on the account; the documentation is there with the deeds as well.

"I know this is a lot to dump on you, Preston. I'm sorry things have unfolded like this, but I don't have a choice. Hollingsworth will help you figure out anything you have a question about, and I'm willing to help you any way I can before I leave.

"I went by to see her yesterday after I got out of the hospital," commented Dane. He glanced over at Preston and shrugged his shoulders. "Apparently, sobriety makes me want to be accountable for all my mistakes. I... I needed to tell her what an arrogant shit I was, and that I was truly sorry for all the hurtful things I did to her... to us." Dane sighed. "I don't know... maybe she heard me."

When Dane turned on to River Road, Preston realized that they had talked the entire way home.

"Are you scared?" asked Dane.

"Yes Sir, I am."

They turned into the gravel drive and Dane stopped the truck. He turned to Preston.

"That's good, Preston. I'm not going to tell you not to be because fear can keep you sharp and, in some cases, alive. Any man that tells you fear, and courage can't live in the same place is a damn liar. You can't have one without the other. Remember that, Preston. It'll see you through."

"Yes Sir, I will. Dad, are you scared? I mean, what they need you to do must be really important... even dangerous," surveyed Preston.

"Yes, I am. Our government is fixing to grab the horns of a bull that's so huge... if it shits... it'll bury this country and a disgraceful amount of our young men in the process. Preston, if that should happen, I'll do my damnedest to keep you out of the mix. I don't want you to lose sight of what's important like I did."

"No Sir, I can't ask that of you. I'll do what I should do; Jaden would expect me to. Can I ask where you are going?"

Preston watched this man look out over the river. He didn't know this side of the man next to him; still, he had been raised to be cautious, and he recognized it when he saw it in others. He sensed he was looking in to the face of a soldier who knew the odds were impossible.

"It's a big red bull that's formed an alliance with North Vietnam." He shook his head then changed the subject. "You better get going. Do I need to write something to get you into class? I could call and tell them we had a legal appointment this morning?"

"No Sir, there's no point. I'll be withdrawing and enrolling in the general education program if the Sheriff will allow me to work full-time. I'll tell them I was with you." Preston got out of his father's truck and went to the Jeep, so he could catch the rest of his classes that day, but most of all he needed to talk to Charlie.

He signed in at the office then went to Algebra. He handed the instructor an excuse from the office. Preston ignored the curious eyes and focused on his best friend, who moved his books from the seat next to him, so he could sit. They didn't speak because lunch break was only 30 minutes away for them.

Charlie stared at Preston as he processed what his buddy had told him.

"Say something, Charlie," stated Preston.

"Of course, I'll stand up with you, Preston. You know I will… I like Jaden. And I know that I'm not losing my best friend. It's nothing like that Buddy."

"Then what is it? You've got the same expression Dane did a little while ago.

Charlie sighed as he shook his head then lifted his face up to the sun and closed his eyes.

"Don't you feel it?" stated Charlie in a soft tone of voice.

"Feel what?" questioned Preston.

"Change… it's coming again, and we get to watch it this time. You even get to make the decisions concerning your life and that of your own little family this time. Man, Preston… I'm excited for you!"

Preston smiled at his prophetic friend and the way he had just assured him that he would be by his side to witness his and Jaden's journey into parenthood. He agreed with Charlie in his own way.

"That's the thrust of life, isn't it? Evolve, grow stronger and wiser, so we can teach our kids how to survive?"

Charlie opened his eyes and looked at his friend then held out the small bag of potato chips in his hand.

"A baby," mumbled Charlie. He grinned at his buddy. It was a new and different kind of joy inside of him at being a witness to his buddy's happiness. Charlie was proud because no one deserved it more than Preston. "So where is the wedding going to be?"

Preston stuck his fingers in the bag and snagged more than a fair share of the chips.

"I was thinking about that little pier down by the river with the gazebo, but I'm not sure yet. When you're a heathen, there aren't many options." He crammed the wad of thin fried potatoes into his mouth and began chewing.

Charlie's smile disappeared.

"You're not a heathen, Preston, and neither is Jaden." A minute of silence hung between them. "Do you want to come out tonight and tell Owen and Estelle, or do you want me to?"

Preston appreciated the fact that Charlie was always able to tune into his feelings and the way he looked at the world.

"I feel like I need to tell them. They've been good to me and I appreciate it. I feel like I owe it to them."

Charlie pointed out an advantage of him doing it as soon as possible.

"Estelle is making chicken and dumplings tonight... bring Jaden to supper."

"Are you sure, Charlie?"

"Absolutely." The bell sounded, and Charlie stood. "Remember, it's ready at 6:30 p.m., oh... and bring the Colonel too."

Charlie slipped up behind Estelle and hung his chin over her shoulder. She held the spoon up to him and he opened his mouth and stuck his tongue out. She dragged the chocolate covered utensil down his tongue as she laughed at his silliness.

"Mmm, that's good." Charlie turned and leaned against the counter.

Estelle knew him well and something was on her little brother's mind that required a woman's point of view.

"What's on your mind brother?"

Charlie's attention met Estelle's then moved downward to where her belly was growing rounder with each day.

"Have you felt her move yet, Sis?" His older brother had referred to the baby as a girl since Estelle told him they were expecting, and naturally Charlie had become accustomed to doing the same.

"I have... your brother tries, but he hasn't managed it yet. I told him to be patient... it won't be long, and he'll be asking me to turn over in the bed, so he can get some sleep." Her face was glowing.

"I'm sorry I put you on-the-spot tonight. I stuck my foot in my mouth before I realized it was Wednesday. I appreciate the way you always make Preston welcome. Can I help with anything?" He had called her from school and told her that he had invited Preston and his father. She seemed truly interested in meeting the man.

"I have everything ready. We're going to buffet off the sideboard. I've got the cake iced." She turned her attention to him. He was listening to her, but he was preoccupied. "Is Preston all right, Charlie? You've got me worried."

He turned to her and shoved his hands in his pockets.

"I need to tell you something, 'Stelle. He wants to tell y'all, but I feel you'll be so shocked... that I need to say something first. He's the best friend I ever had and well, we aren't kids anymore."

The look on his face was strange. Estelle knew it was still awkward for him to talk about some things with her. She decided to help him.

"It's different for children who grow up in the country Charlie, especially on a farm or working ranch. There's no time to halter life while we break it to you gently why things are. I understand that you're a man now. Just tell me, I doubt you can shock me."

Charlie unloaded on his sister, and she listened without saying a word.

"That must have been the girl I saw at the rodeo. I noticed her beautiful auburn hair and the way she seemed to be physically attached to Preston. I thought I saw stars in her eyes when she looked at him. At the time, I would never have guessed they were from such different worlds. Y'all never talked about her around us, I suppose this is the reason why?"

Charlie nodded his head.

"He loves her, and she's crazy about him. He's happy, Sis. What do you think? Should I tell Owen before they get here?" asked Charlie.

Estelle's face was unreadable as she shook her head.

"No. He'll just have to accept it. He's going to feel like this is his fault no matter what you say or do."

Charlie's spine stiffened at her words.

"Why? Preston made his own choices, and he's more than willing to assume the responsibility for them."

Estelle pointed out that which he had not thought of.

"Obviously so, but he was in our trust at the time," she exclaimed factually.

Charlie spoke up.

"He never lied to either of you about seeing her. He always did what he said he would do and what was asked of him. Maybe this isn't a good idea. I'll call Jaden."

Estelle spoke to him in a scolding tone of voice.

"No, you won't! It's too late for that. It's too late for a lot of things. I can't believe you couldn't see that he was getting in over his head, Charlie. This is a child's life we're talking about."

The condescending way she made her point struck Charlie with a hurtful blow to his own self-esteem.

"So, you're saying that Preston betrayed both of you because he fell in love with someone who loves him back? And I betrayed you and Owen because I didn't tell you he's happier than I've ever seen him. It's your opinion that a child is a blessing... as long as it's born to parents like you and Owen?"

Estelle shook her head as she continued her protest.

"No, I didn't say that. Charlie, he hid the fact that they were seeing each other, and you helped him. That means there is something to hide. You said she's a nurse. That means she's older than him. The age of consent in this state is 17. She knew better. It's bad enough that he's been victimized by his father his whole life... now she's done it too. That's not love."

Charlie's emotions got the best of him when Estelle trivialized his friends' feelings. He couldn't believe that she was being so imperious, or that she felt righteous in her prejudice. He had more than his share of pent up feelings concerning the things he had been forced to face in the past. He had buried them for many reasons, but Estelle's judgmental arrogance hit a nerve. Charlie's emotions erupted, and his sister-in-law had no chance to get out of the way.

"Estelle, I used to lie in bed at night and listen to my mama whimper and try to control her sorrow, while that lusting bastard forced her to do whatever he wanted. I can remember him grunting and swearing in his pleasure... using her like she was meant for nothing more than his personal slave for satisfaction. He never treated her with respect, or like she was a human being with feelings. I would lay there and wonder how a boy my age could kill such a scathe of a man and set my mama free." Charlie stood up straighter now that he had openly admitted this; there was no need to sugar-coat the truth at this point.

"Preston's my friend because he understands me. He lets me say anything I need to get off my chest, and not one time has he ever judged me for it. I won't do that to him either. He understood Jaden just like he understood me. She's never known a home... a mama, or a crummy excuse of a father. She got used by people she was supposed to be able to trust... just like my mama was used. She ran away when she was 14 because no one would help her. She lived in a laundry mat for seven years doing other people's laundry and sleeping in the supply closet and still managed to put herself through school to make something of her life.

"Preston idolizes the two of you. He formed his opinion about how to treat and cherish a woman by watching the way Owen treats you. When he met Jaden that's what she saw... a good man like my brother. She wanted him to love her. When your body has been disrespected in a wicked and brutal way, and then a gentle, loving breath of hope stirs your heart... who wouldn't reach out to it? They have found hope with each other, Estelle. That's what they are to one another.

"I apologize to you for inviting them and causing you to be exposed to the side of life that is not a rose garden. Like me, you were blessed to have some good people care about you when the world turned mean.

"Jaden and Preston are just as deserving as we were and yet, all they have is each other. They are braving the world by themselves. Preston wants to tell you and Owen that his life is changing, and that he appreciates everything you've done for him. It's a matter of respect to him, and I think he's brave for wanting to tell you in person.

"I'm standing next to him on Saturday... no matter what. I have to as a tribute to my mama." Charlie pushed his hair back away from his brow as his attention went to the cake Estelle had made. He realized his friends would not have anything like the celebration his brother and Estelle enjoyed at their wedding.

"I asked him earlier today where the wedding was going to be. He told me he didn't know yet, because when you were a heathen, there weren't a lot of options. I thought that was the craziest thing I had ever heard because I know what's in his heart. I understand what he meant now. They accept the bad with the good in each other. I've wished so many times that I would find someone to love me like she loves him, but I know now that I'm kidding myself. Preston's better than me, Estelle. It's a fact; I'm not good enough for anyone to love... and I never will be. I haven't assumed responsibility for the choice I made, and I sure don't deserve to live in this magical place. The truth is... by all that's right and decent; I'm the biggest heathen of all." Charlie looked his sister in the eye as he told her the guarded truth. "I'm the one who murdered L.B. Thomas, Estelle... not Mr. Silver." Charlie turned and left the room before he lost his emotional battle in front of her. His bedroom door slammed due to the suppressed emotions that her brash words had unleashed inside of him.

Estelle's stood there with her arms crossed. She was disconnected from the ache inflicted by her fingernails digging into her flesh as her discernment grasped what Charlie had just said. Shame swelled in her chest. She had been a snob, taking her blessings of this house, her husband and the conception of her baby for granted while passing judgment on another for their lack of.

"Oh, Father God, please forgive me, Lord." Estelle covered her mouth with one hand as her other went to her swollen middle. She could hardly breathe as the claws of guilt and remorse tore at her heart. She was so consumed with regret that she had not noticed the headlights of Owens truck pull into the driveway, nor did she hear the back door open and close.

"Estelle, Honey... what's wrong?" Owen's chest brushed her shoulder as he stopped beside her. "Is it the baby? Come sit down." He pulled out a chair at the breakfast table then pushed her into it.

Estelle's knees buckled in response to her emotions and her husband's concern. She looked at him unable to speak. She realized that her husband and his work partners had conspired to keep this terrible truth between them, to protect Charlie. He had not told her because she would become part of the conspiracy.

Owen sat a glass of water down in front of her. His voice emanated with fear as he asked her for guidance.

"Honey, please talk to me. Do I need to call the doctor?"

"I'm all right... and the baby's fine." She swiped at her tear-soaked cheeks as she reached out and tugged on his hand. He knelt beside her. "Listen to me, Owen. I must tell you what's happening, and we'll have to talk about details later. I... I've hurt Charlie... bad. I didn't mean to." Tears seeped from her eyes again and she swallowed several times as she explained in a hurry. "Preston and his father will be here in a few minutes, and he's also bringing a young lady with him for us to meet. They're getting married this Saturday. His father will be leaving afterwards... he's been re-activated. The marriage will make him an adult and give his child a legal birthright when it's born in April. The situation is not ideal to me and you, but to them and the lives they've endured, they feel very blessed to have found love and understanding in each other.

"I want to offer them the gazebo in the backyard for the ceremony. He needs and wants your approval, Honey. They're so brave, but they'll need help... everyone does at some point. I want us to continue to be there for him. He's part of our family now. And, I want..." she paused because her choice of words sounded haughty. "No... I need Charlie to forgive me."

Estelle gripped her husband's hand as they opened the front door to greet their company. Charlie came out of his room freshly showered and groomed, and the foyer filled with introductions. Preston's eyes glistened with love as he introduced Jaden Sullivan. She was snuggled beneath his arm and gazed up at him with pride before she held her hand out to greet them.

Owen's manners kicked in before Estelle's did. Estelle had only seen the young woman from a distance and now that Jaden was standing in front of her, she was struck dumb for a moment.

"Ms. Estelle, are you okay?" Preston's soft voice and warm hand on her arm prompted Estelle into action. She pulled her eyes away from the young woman and looked at him.

"Oh... yes, Preston. I'm sorry." Estelle stepped up to Jaden, and the small girl met her gaze with uncertainty. Estelle couldn't help herself; instead of shaking her hand, she wrapped her arms around the young woman and hugged her tight. When she met Jaden's eyes again Estelle greeted her in earnest. "My goodness, Sweetheart... we could be sisters. Welcome Jaden... to our home, our lives, and our family!"

Jaden's face changed from fearful to radiant as she responded to Estelle.

"Thank you, Ms. Kagel. Sisters... my goodness, what a wonderful thing that would have been," exclaimed the girl.

CHAPTER 14

Estelle sprayed Jaden's soft, spiraling curls so the summer breeze would not ruin their handy work. The bride bent her knees, so Celia could secure the ring of yellow rosebuds and baby's breath around her crown. Estelle's fingers combed through the long streamers of white ribbon so that they hung evenly down Jaden's back. Ava smiled as she held up the camera and snapped a picture. The ladies took special care in preparing Jaden for this significant event in her life; it was like attending to a princess. They stepped back as the young bride turned to them with a smile so bright, the sun couldn't even match it. Jaden was incredibly beautiful and radiant with happiness. Ava snapped another picture of her friend before she and Celia left the room to ensure the reception tables were ready.

Jaden had found the ivory-colored dress at the second-hand store next to the hospital on Wednesday afternoon and bought it. That night at dinner, she had asked Estelle if she would look at it and give her an opinion of whether it was appropriate. When Estelle saw the dress, she envisioned her looking exactly this way.

The soft, woven silk stretched across her bosom to reveal the classic collar bones and long neck of a maiden, and the body of a temptress. The antique lace was attached around the neckline in small, gathered swags; they draped around and hugged the top of her arms just enough to hold the dress in place over the feminine endowment of her breasts. The bodice clung to and defined Jaden's body to her thighs, where the lace swags were repeated. The design added distinction to the full skirt which fell in soft delicate folds to the floor and extended three feet behind her. Jaden wore a thin satin ribbon that had been crafted to fasten like a piece of jewelry around her neck. The simple necklace featured a small satin bow with a yellow rosebud decorating the center. Jaden and Estelle had met with the florist on Thursday morning to order the bouquet and discuss the other items they would need for the ceremony. When the florist saw the dress, she suggested the halo of roses and the necklace. She made them to compliment the bouquet, the pear-shaped glass drops Jaden would wear on her earlobes, and Preston's mother's ring.

Estelle gazed at the beautiful young woman in front of her, she smiled as she spoke.

"You are so beautiful, Sweetheart. Preston is such a lucky young man."

Before she could say anything else, Jaden shook her head and choked with emotion.

"No, Ms. Estelle... I'm the one that is favored. I've survived some horrible, unspeakable things during my life, but I can't help but feel that something... greater than this world has always watched over me. When I was a girl, I really thought I was cursed; a child no one wanted and threw away. I... I promised myself that I would never bring a child into this cruel and uncaring world." Jaden swallowed the emotion she felt then shook her head as not to doubt this wonderful day that had come to her. "But Preston... he's like..." she paused to choose just the right words "... forgiveness, happiness and hope all rolled up and tied with love. I can't take it all in... I can't even breathe when I look at him sometimes."

Estelle held her arms out and Jaden came to her.

"I don't know how to be this happy, Ms. Estelle. I'm scared to be this happy."

Estelle thought of her little brother. Charlie was as precious to her as Owen, and he was still avoiding her. She didn't know if he would ever forgive her. Estelle shared her heart as she hugged her tight.

"Honey, you deserve to be loved and happy... both of you do, and this is just the beginning. Cherish every moment. He's like another little brother to me and that makes us... sisters." Estelle pushed away from her and patted her stomach. "We're going to waddle together and get chubby together and raise these babies together. We're going to share all of life together."

Charlie played a soft love song on the guitar and sang. He was accompanied by one little sparrow which perched on the railing as though he had a special invitation for the ceremony. Scherry and Mollie, once again, shed their boots and were transformed into little ladies as they dropped rose petals on the grass in front of Jaden. She carried a single long stem, yellow rose with a satin bow as the older Spanish gentleman, Pedro Enriquez walked her out of the house and down the back steps. The ranch family, Colonel Reid, Sheriff Cotton and Mr. Cox, and the Enriquez family gathered around the gazebo over-looking Silver Pond to witness the marriage of these young people. Even the elderly neighbors, Spencer and Alicia Gillis, who the children loved like their own grandparents had wanted to be a part of Preston's new life and helped prepare for the wedding.

Estelle watched Preston as Jaden came closer into his view. His cheeks drained of color for a moment then became flushed. Charlie finished the song then took the guitar off and handed it to Eli. He came to stand across from the lovely, young Spanish woman. They waited for Preston to take Jaden's hand from Mr. Enriquez and approach the Chaplain beneath the gazebo, and then they followed. Charlie took his place next to his friend just as he said he would do.

The couple could not keep their eyes off each other as the Bible was opened and scriptures were read binding them to each other forever. It seemed even the earth and all its gifts of life were reverent at this special place in time. When they verbally promised to love, honor and cherish each other, Estelle saw a tear slip down Preston's face. The marriage was sanctified, and they were pronounced husband and wife. Everyone cheered and clapped as Preston kissed her and Jaden held on to her husband for a long moment; it was as though neither of them could believe it was true.

The Colonel shook Preston's hand and patted his shoulder with an approving smile, and then he gently kissed the back of Jaden's hand. Estelle could see that the Colonel was very capable of being a dashing and charming man when the need arose; however, she was baffled by the man. Was his abrupt change in behavior due to being sober? Was his patriotism and the love of his country, greater than the love for his son? He seemed distant from his son, even now, and Preston seemed to take it in stride. 'What choice did he have?' thought Estelle. She watched Preston kiss Jaden again, and her perspective gained even more clarity concerning the things Charlie had wanted her to see. Jaden was Preston's life now; they had seen the best in each other from the moment they had met. If she believed in destiny, they had to be the proof of it.

Ava Enriquez had brought a professional friend of hers along and he busied himself with recording the day with his camera.

The large white tent which they sometimes used at the church was in the side yard. The three-tier, ivory-colored wedding cake was simple, and at the same time, spectacular stacked on a large white pedestal dish. The baked delicacy was traditional vanilla in flavor, a poured icing left it smooth and glistening. The array of fresh, white angel trumpets and yellow roses were arranged to spill out in all directions from beneath the pedestal dish, making the cake an elegant and breathtaking centerpiece of the reception. The roses were from Celia's garden, and the angel trumpets were from Alicia Gillis' side yard. Ms. Gillis had joined Celia and Estelle on Friday morning to help make the cake, and all sorts of mouth-watering treats for the reception. The Gillis' had grown very fond of Charlie and Preston during their endeavors of helping her husband cut and bail hay and keep up with his small herd of cows. Spencer Gillis also had a gully that was damned up and full of fat, hungry bass; it was his secret fishing hole. The boys had gone with him a lot in the last three years because he was getting feeble and his wife didn't want him to navigate the jagged and steep terrain alone.

Scherry and Mollie flittered around in their white Sunday dresses with flowers in their hair and handing out rice bags.

The afternoon was warm, but the breeze off the pond made it romantic and surprisingly bearable.

Cotton greeted them with a hug. He told Preston how beautiful his bride was and that he was very happy for them. He had been shocked when Preston stood in front of him on Wednesday afternoon and told him he was going to be a father that he was marrying Jaden on Saturday. When he told Cotton of his plans, there seemed to be nothing they hadn't considered. Besides, Cotton knew he had no right to throw stones. He also knew they were going to need every person they could get in their corner. He concluded that since Dane was leaving, they could live not only in love, but in peace.

Estelle was so glad they had consented to have the wedding at their house. This was where they should be, with the ones who loved them. She asked God to forgive her one more time for being so judgmental. She could see His presence in their lives and their hearts.

She remembered the day when a few of the people in the congregation wanted to shun a poor migrant worker and his family. Pastor Storey's wisdom was humbling; his words were impressed on her heart. 'We are fishers of men.

God wants us to catch them and leave it to Him to do the cleaning.'

Preston stood in front of his father on the sidewalk and looked him in the eye. It was an emotional moment for him because he didn't know if he would ever see this man again. The Colonel offered Preston his hand as he congratulated him one more time. Preston ignored his father's rigid demeanor and wrapped his arms around the man who had caused him so much pain. The Colonel stood there a second then his arms folded around the young man and tightened as he spoke.

"You are a fine man, Preston. I know your mother would be very proud... and so am I. No man could ask for better than you, Son."

Hearing his father's words made Preston realize that it was the first time this man had ever addressed him as such and something stirred deep inside of him. A moment passed then the Colonel's body became rigid once again as he pushed Preston away and looked at him.

"Thank you, Sir. Please be careful... I love you, Dad." Preston turned and left whatever was between them there.

He took the hand of his bride, both still wore their wedding attire. They smiled at each other knowing this day was the beginning of the rest of their life together. Preston let out a holler of joy and hooked his bride around her waist with his arm. He lifted her off her feet and made a dash for the car. They laughed happily while enduring the shower of rice that pelted them from every direction. They waved as they drove away; the streamers flapped in the wind while the tin cans bounced on the pavement behind them.

Estelle crossed her arms and watched them as they disappeared around the bend in the road, and even though out of sight, she could hear Preston still honking in celebration of his new life with Jaden.

The Enriquez's insisted they stay and help with the clean-up. Estelle and Celia were versed in understanding the language and accents of their culture. They learned the Enriquez family had taken Jaden in off the street when she was only 14 years old. Their daughter, Ava, who was in medical school at the time, had made it her calling to educate the child and help her get a leg up on life. They were good people and visited with the family long after the dishes were done, and the yard was put to right.

Owen and Estelle were cuddled together in the wicker love seat on the back porch watching the sun sink behind the tree line on the other side of the pond. The spring on the back-screen door yawned and Owen looked up to see Charlie standing there with his hands in his pockets. He had been withdrawn the last two days and Owen still wasn't sure what all had transpired between his brother and his wife. Estelle had been too busy to explain. He figured it was on purpose because she didn't want to talk about his brother behind his back.

Owen held his hand out to Charlie and his younger brother smacked it with his palm like he had taught him to do when he was small.

Charlie spoke to them with humility.

"The wedding was wonderful. I still can't believe y'all did that for them. I know Preston told you 'thank you' about a hundred times, but... I haven't. Thank y'all for doing something so incredible for him, especially you, 'Stelle. I know it had to be your idea. I know you did it for Preston... and for me."

She sat up and reached for his hand. Charlie let her take it because he was too ashamed to make the first move in the way of an apology. She stood and wrapped her arms around her brother then laid her head on his chest. Owen witnessed his little brother shyly fold his arms around her.

"I asked God to forgive me for being so brash to you the other night and for being judgmental. I was wrong,

Charlie, and I hurt you. I'm asking you to forgive me. You're always challenging me to discover something new about myself by just being who you are, sometimes I'm surprised and sometimes... I'm ashamed. I love you. Please... don't stop being my friend and my brother because I'm pig-headed."

Charlie laughed suddenly, and his arms squeezed her tighter.

Estelle stood on tiptoes as she stretched up to kiss his cheek.

"I'm sorry too, Sis. I really am. Thank you for loving them like you did. I've never seen him so happy." He visually connected with his sister-in-law. "Do you think there's someone out there... that might love me that much?"

"Oh yes, Charlie! Yes! You are an incredible young man and you have so much to offer that special person. There's a girl out there that will need your heart and these arms to make her life complete. You are worth loving, Charlie. This family loves you... all of us, but you belong to me and Owen, and that's just the way it is. When you fall in love; she'll belong to us too. We consider Preston a part of our family, and so is Jaden." She smiled up at him and patted his cheek.

Charlie searched her face for a moment then he smiled and kissed her forehead as his arms squeezed her one more time. He shifted his tall frame, so he could grin at his brother.

"I'm keeping a close eye on you, Cuz," exclaimed Owen playfully. He deliberately borrowed one of the slang expressions his brother and Preston used to communicate.

Estelle shook her head at their constant teasing each other.

Charlie released her then dropped to the ground from the edge of the porch and started toward the fence gate.

"I'm going to see to Ransom. You have anything else I need to do?"

Owen folded his arms back around his wife as she snuggled against his side. He called out to his little brother.

"Check your clipboard!"

Charlie stuck his hand up and kept walking.

Owen pressed his lips to his wife's sweet-scented hair and inhaled a satisfied breath.

"So... can you tell me what happened now?" Owen asked her softly.

Estelle lifted her chin to her husband, and he kissed her lips several times. She turned around to face him in the loveseat then stretched out across Owen's lap where he could caress her belly. She told him about the altercation and he listened. That afternoon, Owen openly and deliberately relived the night his friends helped rescue his family.

Estelle came to understand why her silence was so valuable.

"What good is 'to serve and protect' if you can't get anyone to help you?" stated Estelle. "Thank God we have Cotton."

Owen's fingertips brushed lightly over her cheek.

"I don't like asking you to conceal a lie, Darlin'," he mumbled. His hand went back to the round bulge at her middle.

"Owen, I don't feel that way. I understand why the three of you did what you did. I'll protect him and Cole... you know that. But Charlie is bothered by this; he feels like he harbors a wicked secret. I think he even feels like he's the wicked part. That's just wrong. I'm not sure that it won't manifest itself one day. He's ardent about reading his Bible, maybe you can point out some scriptures that reveal the cause of righteous anger." Estelle jumped in surprise as she felt a little jab from within.

Owen's eyes sparkled with excitement.

"Was that my young'un?"

She nodded as her hand guided his to the exact spot. She moved it a small fraction to the right and pressed in as the baby pushed back with enthusiastic jabs. Estelle's grin mirrored her husband's as she spoke.

"She's getting stronger every day; it amazes me every time I feel her move."

Owen's eyes made love to her while his palm absorbed the feel of the life they had created to together.

Cotton held the bouquet of weathered roses in his hand as he stared at the white marble angel that watched over the small plot where Caroline's body lay. He had been preoccupied of late concerning the truth she took to her grave. There was nothing he could do about it even if his suspicions were fact. He refused to doubt the depth of her heart.

Emmett closed his eyes and inhaled the warm, scent of the surrounding foliage. The summer was ending, and the sun made everything in nature give off a warm, earthy scent. He loved coming here; it was the most peaceful place on earth. He opened his eyes and looked out across the field at the thick blanket of bright yellow and purple wild flowers; they were one of the earth's colorful contributions to fall.

His attention settled on the large, dilapidated mansion guarded by the huge live oaks. The place was sad and yet still romantic, magical and beautiful just like Caroline. It was a place that made him smile and at the same time, he wanted to cry. He had wondered a thousand times what today would be like if Caroline had asked him to help her, that afternoon he had taken his daughter, Julianna, to visit her for a piano lesson. What would have happened if he had not been called to service? His eyes caressed the house as he slipped into that melancholy place in his mind where he relived his time with her.

He had wanted them to fight for her freedom together, but she lived in fear of her husband's wrath. He dreamed of what might have been if he had only looked beyond his jealousy and understood what was happening to her.

He thought of her round belly beneath the pale cotton blouse and the way her hand caressed it. The way things were left between them that day consumed him of late. He wondered how things would be if he had dared to ask that one important question about her child. Instead, he had taken his love for her to the war, hoping the circumstances of their lives would change with time. When he returned from service, he was stunned to find out Whisper Bluff had been sold, and strangers occupied Caroline's unique home. He was concerned and could not accept it as reality until he found out what had happened. He located her in the adjacent county, living a frugal existence compared to the way she was raised. He took Julianna with him to visit, because his daughter spoke of her often, and Caroline had instilled a love for the piano in his daughter.

Caroline was still elegant and beautiful, but she was thin and ghostly pale. His heart still pounded at the sight of her and there was something familiar in her eyes, even when she declined his invitation to dinner. She told him that she was still married but thanked him for his concern and thoughtfulness. He had not seen her son that day, but she spoke of him with love and adoration. During the week that followed, he attempted to re-establish a friendship with her on two more occasions. She was polite, but refused to allow him access to her life, or to her son. He realized the woman who filled his heart possessed a broken spirit. There seemed to be nothing he could do for her and nothing she would ask of him. His heart was heavy, but he had no choice but to respect her wishes and not contact her again.

He still didn't understand why Caroline had let go of the magnificent house in which she was raised. And, because of the numerous strangers that had resided at Whisper Bluff in the last 16 years, he had long questioned the validity of what he had seen and experienced during those momentous three days he had spent there with her. There was a time when he yearned to investigate the secret things which she had shown him; however, her death had changed the yearning into an ache deep in his soul.

Emmett had been lost in his own thoughts to the point of not hearing the old truck come to a stop beneath the oak trees on the other side of the graveyard fence.

The brittle voice startled him.

"I have always known that the person who kept those flowers on her grave was the son-of-a-bitch that ruined my life. After everything you've done, I shouldn't be surprised, but I am."

Cotton turned suddenly to find Colonel Dane Reid standing there. His chin was stiff, and his stature seemed menacing; the windows to his soul were shadowed by the brim of his service hat. Cotton didn't know what to say. It was awkward no matter what the man thought; keeping flowers on a grave for 11 years was an act done out of love. He stood his ground out of respect to the woman and the love she had bestowed upon him so long ago.

"Have you told Preston?" questioned Dane. "Is that why your opinion means so damn much to him?"

Cotton stared at him, curious as to what the Colonel meant by that statement.

"What are you talking about, Colonel?"

Dane came a few steps closer; his hands remained fastened behind him.

"That you're his real father?" His tone of voice was as wooden as the man's rigid stance.

Cotton was again caught off guard, not only by the question, but by Dane's fist. It came into view in the corner of Emmett's eye just before it bashed in to his temple and there was no time to get out of its way. His neck twisted in painful recoil and Cotton bent over as he waited for his vision to come back to his left eye. He realized now that his suspicions had merit, especially since Dane was still carrying this measure of hostility over the betrayal after all these years. Cotton's instincts told him to confess to nothing at this point.

A few moments passed before he straightened up and looked at the hard, unforgiving man in front of him.

"What makes you think I am Preston's father, Dane?"

"If you weren't making love to her... if you didn't take her in my bed... feel free to hit me back. I have it coming." He stood there for a couple of minutes waiting for his answer, and Cotton's silence gave it to him.

Dane yelled at him.

"DAMN YOU EMMETT! DAMN YOU TO HELL!!" The stiff posture of the man in front of Cotton became even more rigid as he stood there glaring at him. "She was the best thing I ever had in my life!" He snarled through gritted teeth. "I sensed you when I walked through the back door that day. I touched her, and she withdrew from me. She wouldn't even look me in the eyes. I knew there was someone else. I could have her body, but she had given her heart... her soul to another. When the boy came before time, I had my proof. But I didn't know who had done the deed, and she would never admit to infidelity. I wanted to kill you. I wanted to hate her... because she loved that child and the man who had fathered it so goddamn much. I couldn't hate her... so I punished her."

Cotton stared at him.

"What did you do to her, Dane? Cut her off emotionally? You did that the day you married her, and you've punished Preston every day of his life! And, for what? You've blamed him for sins he knows nothing about and certainly had no part in committing. You're a pitiful excuse of a father... and a man."

Dane's malice overwhelmed his judgment and he spit out the truth of his vindictive deed before he thought better of it.

"I did what I had to do!" snapped Dane. "Since I didn't have a clue who had been inside my wife, and since he lay between us in my own goddamn bed, I took away the bed and the only thing that sustained her." He stared at Cotton with vengeful eyes. "I figured if she wasn't in that house to relive you every day and commune with all the damn ghost of her family, it would leave her feeling abandoned... just like she had made me feel! It worked too! But she despised me for it. When she died, I lost her a second time."

287

Emmett was struck dumb for a moment by the things Dane said. The larger picture of their lives, and how they had been woven together by the consequences of choice was made clear for the first time since the day Caroline had walked out of his life. She had not revealed her reasons for selling her home when he asked about it. Rumor suggested she couldn't afford to keep the house. He never believed it, not with the things he knew about her family's wealth and the secrets hidden within the house. He realized now, the price to keep her home wasn't a matter of money, but something more valuable. It would have cost her self-respect. After all the years of speculation and unrealized dreams, he was sickened by the truth. Emmett's heart felt emotions overflowed with zeal.

"You're the reason her family's home... Preston's heritage... was sold?!" Cotton looked at the sad and mistreated mansion that had been the setting for the most beautiful memories of his life. "You pitiful, tormented fool!" Cotton's words echoed with disdain.

"Shut the hell up! You don't know anything about me! And I'm not the fool here!" growled the Colonel. "I don't understand you. If you loved her so damn much why didn't you fight for her? Why didn't you fight for the boy? It wasn't enough that I had to live with her ridiculous and juvenile adulations of her family; no... I had to compete with the ghost of a man that had stolen my wife. Goddamnit Emmett! She shut me out of her heart and grieved over you. I couldn't even cum inside my own wife without her closing her eyes. She never looked at me with anything other than contempt, and she never touched me again after you bedded her!" Dane shouted at Cotton again. "YOU'RE A PATHETIC COWARD!"

Cotton's anger surfaced all at once and he busted Dane in the mouth with a powerful upper cut that was intended to relocate the man's top lip into his sinus cavity. Dane bent over as his eyes watered from the searing sting, blood gushed from his nose to the ground. He was the one to search for his senses while Cotton took it upon himself to clarify a few things.

"You don't have any right to call me pathetic! I dare you spew your self-righteous bullshit at me, you egotistical, womanizing bastard! You treated her like she was a possession you could take out of a display case at your convenience." Cotton's mind chose that moment to reflect on the night he saw them through the bedroom window. At the time, jealousy ruled his heart and all he could see was Caroline on her knees in willful submission, offering her body to satisfy her husband's gusto for sex. The following day she met him in the clock tower closet. She was upset, even a blind man could see that she was scared. He knew something was terribly wrong, and the way she left so abruptly instilled many other questions which had no answers. Today his memory gained clarity as he revisited that heartbreaking and confusing night in his mind. Caroline's left hand clutched the edge of the mattress while the other held on to the bed-post for stability. She had no choice because of the controlling grip Dane had on the back of her neck as he rammed himself into her over and over. They were angry and punishing thrust, inflicted by a jealous and savage man. He looked at things as they really were, and he understood her fear. Dane's treatment of Caroline was meant to chastise her for needing more than he could or was willing to give her. Cotton relived the following day when he had seen her alone; it was their last intimate moments together as lovers. The shadow under her eye and the bruises on her neck and arms rekindled his remorse then heaped shame on top of it. Caroline couldn't have refused Dane no matter how much she wanted to or tried because he wouldn't have allowed it.

Emmett could not contain his temper.

"You forced yourself on her, didn't you? In your selfish, twisted mind you believed you owned her. You raped her body and her sweet spirit? You used fear to make her stay with you!" accused Emmett boldly. "You mean and hateful son-of-a-bitch! You make me sick!"

Cotton's fist tightened into a weapon; he slugged the man again because he had viciously tried to take Caroline's self-respect. Emmett was so enraged that he disregarded the stiff joints that had succumbed to the service injuries of years past. It was time somebody kicked the shit out of Colonel Dane Reid, and he was the right man for the job.

Dane's brain exploded into a cascade of stars. He was unable to keep the starch in his legs and folded to his knees. He shook his head to clarify his thoughts. He wasn't expecting this kind of belligerence from a man who valued the star on his chest and was so dedicated to keeping the peace. When Dane opened his eyes, and saw Cotton advancing on him again, he lunged forward and grabbed him around the waist. He took the sheriff to the ground, but Cotton wrapped his legs around Dane's body while his tree trunk of an arm fastened around his neck. The sheriff's fist slugged Dane in the head over and over without mercy. It felt like a baseball bat struck him, and each time it made contact was with the precision of Babe Ruth. They physically struggled in the dirt as Cotton kept the upper hand. Dane was angry, but he had trod in this ocean of disappointment and hostility for years using alcohol as the water, and he was tired. The Colonel realized that Cotton's disciplined and mild-mannered personality had led him to suppress his feelings, and today the sheriff had been given provocation to unleash them with a vengeance.

"You're the one that better being looking over his shoulder for the hounds of hell!" declared Cotton through gritted teeth.

Dane's head felt like it would burst if he took another blow and for the first time in his life, he called on humility to help him. He stopped struggling and held his hands up in surrender.

"Goddammit, Emmett... enough! You're right... I admit it! I'm a lecherous bastard! I get it!" shouted Dane.

The Colonel's verbal concession curbed Cotton's anger so that he held reign over his trembling fist, only now did he realize that it was throbbing with pain. His labored breath seethed out of him due to the exertion he had expended on something that was pointless. He thought of Preston being his and Caroline's son. The fact that he had a living, breathing piece of her in his life rekindled his faith in the love they had shared. He thought of what Preston would think if he were to see the two of them fighting and rolling in the dirt as though they were wild, unruly children. He swallowed the fury because hope had taken root and was growing at a rampant pace. Still, there was a part of him that wasn't willing to give in until he spoke his mind.

"If she had ever told me that Preston might be my son, I sure as blazes would have intervened and found a way to take him and her away from your spiteful, arrogant ass.

"How many women did you have while you gallivanted all over the globe with your big-shot, tough-nuts ticket to anywhere? Huh? I bet you don't have any idea how many women you've used... just like you used her. I can't believe you had the gall to accuse her of infidelity when you've probably screwed half the women in Washington."

"Shut up! You son-of-a-bitch!" yelled Dane angrily.

"HELL NO! I won't shut up! You started this and you're going to hear the truth. You say you felt my presence in her? Well guess what, she felt all those women in your body too. She was devoted to your marriage, and she tried to be a good wife to you. She even went to Washington for your birthday that year. She told me she had wanted to surprise you because you were tied up in meetings and didn't have time to celebrate your own birthday. She told me you invited her, and because she was tired of being scared to venture out beyond her home, she challenged herself to go. She paid the maid to let her in your suite, and in doing so, she bought herself a front row seat. She saw you with her own eyes and her own heart!" stated Cotton.

Dane yanked himself free of Cotton's hold and stood up. He leaned over because the blood still spilled from his nose, but his eyes drilled a hole into Cotton's awareness.

Emmett's shirt sleeve had absorbed most of it. He ignored the pain and stiffness in his body and followed Dane to his feet, determined to never find himself at a disadvantage with this man again.

Dane shook his head and pressed the sleeve of his jacket to his nose as he stared at Cotton; his narrowing eyes conveyed doubt. The Colonel proved that he didn't believe a word of what he had been told.

"You're a damn liar! She wouldn't ever get on a plane and go to Washington by herself. She would barely come out of that blasted house!"

Cotton pointed an accusing finger at the Colonel. He was a lot of things, some good and some bad, but he was not a liar.

"Yes, she did... and she saw for herself who you really were. She told me that she was so shocked at what she saw... and she left in such a hurry, that she knocked a vase of flowers off the foyer table on her way to the door."

Dane remembered that day. The vase hit the floor like a gunshot blast and he practically threw the two women he had bought himself for his birthday onto the floor out of reflex. Dane's heart grew cold in his chest; he didn't want to believe that Caroline had seen him in such a lewd and compromising situation.

"I don't believe you, Emmett." His voice echoed with denial.

"Believe what you want. It doesn't change the fact that she saw you! She witnessed for herself how much you honored her love and your marriage." Emmett pushed the point just because Dane was so arrogant about Caroline turning to someone else for the love and understanding that he had denied her. He did it because Dane's self-righteousness was a joke and it pissed him off. "She saw one woman riding your lap, and the other was sitting on your face while they entertained each other... in living, perverted color!" elaborated Cotton rudely. "I'd dare say they were your birthday present to yourself... taking in to account the self-indulgent and conceited fool you are."

Dane swung at him again, but Cotton side stepped him and shoved the man off kilter. The Colonel's sobriety enabled him to recover quickly. Cotton continued to tell him the truth even if it did come out as ridicule and condemnation. He did it because he felt Dane deserved it.

"She came home and filed for divorce. The papers were ready, and she had already signed them long before our paths crossed that night. You blame me because you couldn't hold her or make love to her without feeling someone else? It was your own ill-disciplined and selfish behavior that caused her to close the door to her heart. You've got no one to blame but yourself." Cotton swore again then snatched a handkerchief out of his back pocket and held it in front of Dane's bloody face as he continued. "You were gone from her heart, Dane... long before I dared to love her. I know it was so because she was a good woman. When I touched her, I didn't feel your presence... and I didn't see you in her eyes either. I touched her thinking of nothing else but her. Did you ever once hold her because it felt like heaven to do so? No... of course not. A man like you can't believe in Heaven, can you? You can't see past your own ego!"

Dane spit a couple of times then snatched the offering away from Cotton's hand and pressed it to his face as he stood up straight.

"You really expect me to believe she never told you that Preston was your son?"

Cotton shook his head as he held up three fingers.

"She was in my arms and my life for three days!!" he confessed painfully. "You came home on Tuesday and it was over for us. I wanted to approach you man to man, but she told me she couldn't let me do that. I saw the bruises you left on her. I even tried to talk her into seeing the doctor and filing assault charges against you, but she wouldn't do it. I could tell she was scared and wasn't telling me something. When I pressed her on the matter, she said we were a mistake and that I had to let her go. It didn't make sense; I knew she had the divorce papers ready for you. But I loved her, and I wanted her to be happy. Like I said, she was a good woman." Cotton studied Dane's face. These last few minutes had changed both their perspectives on life. He couldn't speak for Dane, but he was wiser now; the years had sharpened his instincts and gave him an edge on human nature which was incisive as a razor's edge. There were things she had told him during their time together that found order in his reason.

"I remember her telling me that after the marriage... before you left her for duty, you warned her about her faithfulness as a wife. She said you told her that your job was to eliminate specific targets for our government, and you could find out anything... about anyone... at any time." Cotton stared at the Colonel knowing the man was capable of horrible things. Suddenly, he realized that Caroline had not turned away from him out of fear for herself, but out of fear of what Dane would do to him. She had withdrawn her love to protect his life. Cotton's heartbeat sped up because he knew in his soul it was true. "You threatened her, didn't you? You told her when you found out who she had fallen in love with he'd be a dead man, didn't you? She panicked and tried to protect me with her absence... and her silence. She knew you would have someone watch her from then on!"

"Yes, of course I did! It worked, didn't it? I wouldn't have harmed her, I loved her. But if I had known who you were, I would have killed your ass. And yes, she knew I hired a detective to watch over her and the boy." Dane turned the handkerchief and pressed it back to his nose. "What in the hell did you expect me to do, Emmett? She was my wife... not your girlfriend!"

Cotton thought Dane Reid had to be the most despicable man he had ever known.

"I disagree. You forfeited your rights as a husband when you started screwing other women after you married her. Your attitude tells me that it was her job to keep herself for you; however, you had no intention of being faithful." Cotton thought about the years he had been denied with the woman he loved and their child. He released a frustrated sigh.

"Caroline and I knew each other as kids. We crossed paths on one lonely, vulnerable night. Yes, I fell in love with her, and by God, it was the most incredible experience of my life. I love her to this day," admitted Cotton with pride.

"I saw her in town one morning after she had broken things off with me. She was walking along the boardwalk at the Independence Day Celebration. I spoke because we were face to face before either of us realized it. I was about to be deployed, and somehow... she knew it. She was glowing like a ray of sunshine... just beaming with happiness. She caressed her middle and told me she was excited about the baby. I didn't even know she was expecting until that day. Y'all were still together and even though it hurt, I was glad to see that she was happy and doing well. She could have told me then, but she never said a word about the child being mine. I accepted things were as they should be.

"My concern for Preston was because he was a part of her... not me, and because he had a mean, drunk asshole for a father!"

Cotton watched as Dane's eyes traded off between the house in the distance and the pale tombstone. The man looked as though he was trapped in a private hell that went deeper than the ill-treatment of a wife and a son. Clearly, something in Dane's life had made him the bitter, hard man that he was. And, his heart was surely scarred for carrying out the callous deeds ordered by the government. 'How else could he be so cruel to the people who had dared to love him?' concluded Cotton.

Suddenly, Cotton wondered if Dane had made personal contact with any of Caroline's 'juvenile adulations' he had mentioned a few minutes ago; if so, it could be a contributing factor as to why he had sold the house.

Dane faced him.

"I have to go soon; are you done here? I'd like a minute with her. Alone."

Cotton watched as Dane shoved the handkerchief in his pocket then took out a piece of paper and a napkin that contained a piece of charcoal. He respectfully walked around the grave then knelt beside the tombstone. Cotton watched as the man pressed the paper over her name and began scrubbing the dark medium over the details of the stone. The afternoon wind was not making it an easy task.

Cotton couldn't stand by and not understand the man's need to take a piece of her with him this time, especially since he had relinquished the idea that he had a son.

Emmett stepped over to the opposite side of the tombstone then knelt, so he could hold the paper in place for him. They didn't say anything else as together they witnessed the shadowed memory of the woman, they both loved, but so very differently, appear before their eyes. It was a reverent moment for Cotton; he could only guess what Dane was thinking.

They stood together a few minutes before Dane spoke again.

"It's your place to look out for him now, Emmett. He's an extraordinary young man. Honestly, I know of none better." Dane looked at him. "The day I met her I fell hard. But I had nothing to offer her, and I was no one to be given the chance to pursue the likes of her."

Cotton didn't like him, and other than being a brave soldier, he had very few admirable qualities, the most important being that he did care deeply for Preston. Still, he had come home to provide and see to the child, even though Emmett thought he had done a poor job of it. It was then that Emmett's heart contradicted his head and reminded him of what a fine young man Preston had turned out to be without any input from him. He concluded that the Colonel had done something right.

"I've asked Preston before about your kin. He said he didn't know any of them and you never spoke of anyone. Is he all you have in the world, Dane?"

Dane turned and picked his hat up off the ground. He stood there a moment brushing the dirt off it. When he spoke, his spine stiffened to match his uniform and his voice was apathetic.

"I grew up in the seedy part of Houston. I come from nothing Emmett. My mother was a waitress in a bar and she would take up with any man that would buy her a carton of cigarettes, a six pack and a new dress. I don't know anything about my old man because she never knew who he was. When I was young, I remember playing with some wooden blocks on the back dash of her car until I fell asleep. The confine of that car was where I was supposed to stay until she finished her shift. When I got older, I learned to dodge and survive the fist of whoever she was screwing from month to month. It was Labor Day when that changed for me. I had been 14 years old the whole of two weeks. She was setting a record for herself because she had been with Dino Taggart for four months. Being a holiday, they had a few of his friends and some of his family over to celebrate. They were all about half drunk and she said something to piss him off, and before I knew it, he had her on the ground by the throat and was squeezing the life out of her. Everyone was terrified of him, but she was my mother. I jumped on him and it was with enough force to break his hold and give her the chance to get away. He grabbed me and punched me in the face; it broke my nose and split my head open when I landed on the edge of the brick patio. He told her to take her goddamn brat and get out of his house. My mother..." Dane paused and stared at the emblem on his hat for a few moments, "... my mother begged him not to make her leave. He told her to choose. She told me to get lost and don't come back. I had no choice but to obey her... one last time. I swallowed my fear, and I deliberately let it churn in my gut... growing hatred over all the other shitty things she had done to me through the years. I didn't know where I was going, hell... I didn't have anywhere to go, but it didn't matter. I was through with her and her string of bastards smacking me around all the time. I had walked a few miles down the road when Dino's sister, Josie, came along and picked me up. She took me to their uncle who had been a medic in the service. His training was old-school and disciplined. He gave me a stiff belt of bourbon for the pain before he cleaned and stitched my head. She asked if he had any of his son's old clothes stored, thinking maybe she could find me something to wear. He brought out a box and told me to take all of it.

"She took me home with her that night. She was this side of 30 and had a steady job, her own place, and she was easy on the eye. She told me to go get cleaned up while she sorted through the used clothes for that worth keeping. I came out with a towel wrapped around me and my dirty clothes. She was standing in the washroom in her slip. She handed me a pair of pajama bottoms then threw my stuff in the washer with the other things. I was scared, but I was determined not to show it, so I dropped the towel and put on the bottoms. She was impressed with my courage, and my erection. She gave me my first blow that afternoon while I sat on the dryer, and by nightfall... I knew how to fuck a woman in four positions. When morning came, the only room we hadn't screwed in was the bedroom... so we gave that one a go too. She asked if I wanted to stay with her for a while. She was nice to me and a good cook, and like I said, she was easy on the eyes. She had her share of bums take advantage of her through the years and she was tired of it; she wanted a quiet life. A couple of months went by, and then she got a job at the chemical plant and I moved to Westville with her.

"I stayed with her under the pretense of a younger sibling. We lied whenever it was necessary to keep everyone at bay. I went to school and got a part-time job to earn money for the things I needed. I kept up the chores around the house and Uncle Poe's... the landlord. He was old, and his hands were so crippled he could barely hold his dick to take a piss... much less grip the handle of a lawnmower. I raised hell occasionally with some older guys that hung out on the river front. I made it a point not to get into trouble, and I never brought anyone home with me. I couldn't take the chance that they would find out I was screwing 'my older sister's' brains out every night and enjoying the hell out of it. Josie Taggart was the longest relationship I've ever had. Hell, truth is... it's the only relationship I ever had that was completely truthful, and that includes my mother and my wife. How pitiful is that?

"I stayed with her... and we took care of each other's needs for four years. When I was old enough to join the service that's exactly what I did. She cried when I told her that I was leaving, and she told me I was the only man that had ever treated her descent. It gave me food for thought, and I started sending the landlord rent money because I wanted to do something good for her. She wrote to me on a steady basis when I was in basic training, but then it suddenly stopped.

"When I came back on furlough after basic, Gamel Poe walked across the street to greet me. He told me that Josie had been shot and killed in a domestic dispute at our older brother's house in Houston. He told me that law enforcement had questioned him about her and told him what had happened.

"Her brother, Dino, was celebrating his birthday. It was his lousy luck that my mother was still with him. At some point during the evening, he missed her and went looking for her. He found her in another room with her legs wrapped around some guy while he held her against the wall and shoved his dick into her. Dino shot the man in the back with a .45 at close range. The bullet killed the guy, and my mother then went through the wall and caught Josie in the back; it lodged in her heart. She never knew what hit her or who pulled the trigger. The old man let me know that law enforcement had no record of them having a younger sibling. I didn't go into detail about mine and Josie's personal relationship. Still, I told him the truth about my mother and Dino, and how Josie had taken me in when not another soul in the world gave two shits about me. He knew no one would make up such a twisted lie, and he accepted me as I was. He asked if I wanted to keep the residence or move our things. I kept it. It was the only home I had ever known. I sent him money for rent, the electricity bill, and to have the lawns mowed every week. When I had a furlough, I had somewhere to go and someone there who accepted me. When Uncle Poe died, he left both houses to me in his will because he didn't have anybody else. He said he was proud of me because I had made something of myself despite my unfortunate and floundering youth."

Cotton watched as Dane idly rotated his hat in his hands while silence fell on him. When he spoke again,

Cotton listened closely because, whether he liked it or not, he was invested in this man.

"When I met Caroline... she took my breath away. She was like looking at a delicate and rare flower that could only bloom once. I... I wanted her to love me so bad. I knew combat tactics, strategies... and how to fuck, but nothing about the delicate nature of a woman's heart, or how to finesse it. Compared to her life, my world had always been crude and on the edge of subsisting... morally and economically. She was alone and cautious, but I could tell that she liked having my interest and the assertiveness in which I pursued her. The only way I knew how to keep her in my life was to seduce her, compromise her, and then convince her to marry me should she already have my child inside of her.

"Other than Josie and Uncle Poe, I've never told another soul about my past, Emmett. The way Poe and I saw things... it died when Josie was murdered. I'm telling you these things because I may not return, and in case Preston ever asks. You're a man of principle and sound reason; I know you will tell him what you think is best.

"I've kept a lot of things to myself, Emmett... important things that I never told Caroline. The thought of her giving herself to someone else was a kick in the gut. I had hoped it wasn't true, and that you didn't exist. When no one came forth on her behalf or the boy's, I believed that I would die with the pretense I had fathered the child. You're right; I drove her away because I was a selfish and jealous bastard." Dane shook his head as he looked at the tombstone again. "I can't undo the hurt I caused her. I swear to God... I wish I could. But it's time for me to let it go. It's why I should tell you the truth about the things I have hidden.

"They told me in '41 that I was sterile... malaria; I contracted it when I was in Asia." Dane stood there a moment. Hearing it spoken out loud made him consider all the women he had been with through the years. There were too many to even try to count. He had not even known the name of some of them, and he was certain he had forgotten a few. Dane realized no one had ever made an accusation of paternity against him, and it was time for him to accept that he had not fathered Caroline's child either. "I've wished a million times that it wasn't true... that he was my boy. I thought for sure she would contact the boy's father." Dane shook his head. "Preston was the only man in her life after we split.

"I found the key to the safe deposit box, Emmett. I discovered the divorce papers she had drawn up, and the new deeds to the house and the land. I saw that she had signed the divorce papers, and it made me furious... so much so that I used it and forged her name on the house deed. I filed the deed with the Chancery Clerk's office to make it legal. A few weeks later, I was contacted with a cash offer for the house. It got me to thinking that without her home she would have to turn to me for refuge. I forged her signature again then I destroyed the divorce papers. I sold her home out from under her without a second thought. The outcome was inevitable; she was through with me. I can see now, I pushed her in to a decision based on bitterness... just like my mother had done to me. It was a shitty thing to do but committing unscrupulous acts against other people was what I had been taught to do... by my mother and my country. I never tried to separate my scruples from my personal life until it was too late.

"It's because of where I came from that I came back and tried to do right by him. I was 14 years old when I found myself alone in this harsh world... and he was only six."

Cotton heard Dane's voice become strangled. The man stood there a few moments. His words quivered with the truth as he continued.

"There's irony in his finding and falling in love with Jaden. Our boy... is a good man, Emmett. I owed him the respect of an adult... so that he could follow his heart and his own convictions. He wanted the woman he loves and his child to know without a doubt that he loved them, and that he was there for them. I respect him more than any man I know.

"I was a stingy, possessive man when it came to Caroline. I didn't know how to show my love for her. I knew I didn't deserve her, but I feared losing her. I was a terrible husband, and I was a lousy father." Dane's attention met Cotton's as regret echoed in his voice. "I swear... I do love him. He's going to need you more than ever. He is your son, Emmett."

Cotton's eyes searched the Colonel's face for any hint of deceit but found none.

"It's true. Damn it, he even walks like you." Dane rubbed the plain beside his nose. "He's got a brick-bat for a fist like you too. Hell, he even wants to be you one day."

Cotton swallowed hard as the emotion began to swell inside of him.

"He knows I've left him the boat and all the property that's in my name. The cemetery and all the original acreage her family farmed was on a separate deed from the house; he needs to talk to the attorney about all of it. Baxter Hollingsworth is expecting to hear from him. There's over 4000 acres in the tract along the river. I understand it's under lease and the taxes are being paid by the bank. It's how she had things set up in her will. I've already told him, but you should know that I've put him on my bank accounts. I was a bastard for selling the house, but I never spent a dime of it. It's been accumulating interest all these years. I've notified all the parties concerned that he's my benefactor, everything is legal. I also transferred my personal savings into his and Jaden's account; it'll be available to him in a few days." Dane paused a moment. His eyes clung to her headstone; they were full of sadness. "Just so you know... I told him what I did concerning the house. And, I did tell him that I accused his mother of being unfaithful, but that I never had any proof." Dane shook his head as a tender silence fell on them.

Cotton recognized the look on his face. The man was hoping if he stared at the marble angel long enough, he could will it to life with Caroline's spirit. He realized that this was an anointed moment for the living and he needed to do the right thing too.

"Dane, I never knew it was possible to love a woman like I loved her. I can't stand here and tell you that I regret it. But you were right... she was your wife, and I apologize to you for all the hurt."

Dane rubbed his eyes on his sleeve then pulled the bloody handkerchief from his pocket and pressed it to his nose another moment.

"It's my fault she died, Emmett... may God forgive me. She was still my wife. I continued to carry health insurance on her and she needed it, but she detested me so much she wouldn't ask for anything. Good God, how she must have hated me. She would rather die destitute than allow me to help." Dane released a haggard breath. It was as though the wicked deeds he had committed were slowly releasing him with each confession.

Cotton thought about that because he knew Caroline had money available to her. It was one more thing that he questioned knowing he would never know the answer. Still, he understood Dane's position; confession was good for the soul. And whether they liked it or not, he and Dane were bound to each other because of Caroline, and because of Preston. Dane wouldn't admit it, but Cotton knew the Colonel trusted him, and he knew this could be the last time he ever saw this man alive.

"I don't suspect I'll ever see him again considering what's brewing. I told him... and I'll tell you; I'll do my best to keep him out of the conflict, but another damn war is coming. If he should go, I will find him a safe place in which to serve. I doubt it would be under my command."

Cotton's attention clung to Dane knowing he was bound by the law of confidentiality; still, he had overheard the Lieutenant talking to the Chancellor. He knew what Colonel Reid did for the government, he and his team were responsible for the covert disposal of specified targets that were detrimental in the decisions of a strategy for the enemy. He knew in his gut that Dane was being straight up about all that he had told him, even the personal things about his youth. No child should be subjected to such treatment. The scars on this man's heart and soul were deep and painful. No one had ever loved him so that he could learn how to love. Emmett couldn't help but see Dane Reid in a different light. Despite the question of paternity, he had tried to offer Preston what he never had... a father. The man had done the best he could, and like himself, he had dared to dream of Caroline Janee Breaux. 'May God have mercy on them', prayed Emmett silently.

Dane asked him.

"So... will you tell him?"

Cotton shook his head.

"What good would it do at this point? He loves you, Dane. I swear to you, I will do everything in my power to look out for them, and for the baby. I wish you God's speed and protection on the assignment. I hope you get the chance to come back and be part of his family. You are his family, Dane... whether you care to see it that way, or not. You and I share a bond... because we both love Caroline, and we love Preston. There is no need to upset his world. The fact that you and I know the mistakes we've made and can make peace about it is good enough for me."

Dane's next words surprised Cotton.

"I've thought about it, Emmett." The Colonel looked him in the eye as he spoke. "Don't tell him about me and where I come from... unless you come clean with all of it. You are a decent God-fearing man, and he should know that he comes from something better than what I am."

Dane's expression and the defeated tone in his voice struck a nerve with Cotton. Like himself, this man had made mistakes which had eroded his personal life. Still, here he stood with hat in hand charging him with the responsibility to finish life while sharing it with the son he had been denied. It was a priceless gift, and Cotton was not going to allow the Colonel to forget about or brush off the personal sacrifice he had made on Preston's behalf.

"You are Colonel Dane Reid, War Council Member to the President of the United States of America. You walked away from the duty long enough to help a little boy become a fine man. You hold your head up, Dane. Everybody makes mistakes, and today you and I have admitted ours and taken steps towards forgiveness. That's what's important." Cotton looked down at Caroline's grave. "It seems appropriate for all of this to be sorted out while standing here next to her." He offered the hand of truce to the Colonel because it was the right thing to do, and Dane took it.

"Remember, God's grace is sufficient for *all* of us who ask. You keep someone you trust at your back, Colonel," exclaimed Cotton soulfully. He released the man's hand then turned and walked away from Dane Reid, the Colonel and Caroline's husband, but not from Preston's father. There were so many feelings swirling inside of him; he thought he would fly apart all at once, especially when he heard Dane call out to him that Preston loved him too.

Cotton shook his head at the thought of that young man being his son. A smile inched over his face. He couldn't help it. He had a daughter-in-law and a grandbaby on the way.

In the whole of his life he had made love to two women, loved them deeply, and he had managed to get both pregnant. He realized Preston had to be his son. He wondered if the young man could accept all of this, and then he thought of Julianna and how much his older sister would love him.

CHAPTER 15

Cotton parked in his usual spot in the fenced lot at the Sheriff's Office. He looked down at his uniform covered with Dane's blood then in the rearview mirror at his swollen eye caused by the lump on the side of his head. He couldn't even bend his right hand. He was ashamed of the way he had behaved but could see now it was a blessing.

He put his hat on as he walked to the garage. He contemplated taking the stairs knowing it would be easier to make it to his office unseen if he did; however, his knees were throbbing nearly as bad as his hand, so he bypassed them for the elevator. He managed to make his way into the building without being bombarded with a dozen questions. He wore his sunglasses and kept them on once he was in the building, so he wouldn't have to explain something he could not talk about. He stepped off the elevator and Lennis' eyes passed over him and then came back to focus on his face. He opened his mouth to ask, but Cotton turned right into the kitchen to deliver the foil package full of Preston's wedding cake to June Lee. She did a double take when he sat it down and gave her a verbal message from the boy that she was so fond of and kept walking.

Cotton closed his door and turned his chair around then fell into it like a bale of hay that had just been kicked off the trailer. He closed his eyes as his pounding skull ached with truth and physical pain. He didn't know which hurt the worst. He wished Caroline had told him she was pregnant with his child. He chastised himself because he hadn't mustered up the courage to ask her. Had she really grieved over their separation as Dane said? Had the memories of them lived as deep in her heart as they did his? Cotton's thoughts were like a puzzle of scrambled facts due to this afternoon's confrontation with Colonel Reid. The privacy of his office provided a few minutes of uninterrupted thought, and one fact surfaced, which held precedence over all others. Emmett realized Dane had not told Caroline that he was sterile. Clearly, he had lied to her, so she would marry him, under the false pretense, he may have already made her pregnant. If she had known Dane was sterile, then she would have known the child could not have been his. Of course, that was at the root of all this deceit. She had not known who fathered her child because Dane had come home and gave her no choice but to accept him into her body. Cotton recalled the last time she was in his arms; she was terrified of Dane. His discernment took over and began to organize his thoughts. He could see that Caroline had cut off all contact with him because it was the only way she could protect her lover and her child. Cotton's jaws clinched instinctively at the truth of it all. It made his head hurt even worse; however, his spirit stilled at the blessing which was hidden amid the lies and pain.

Cotton knew his door had opened because the radios in dispatch grew louder. He turned slightly and saw June Lee close it behind her. She walked around his desk and stopped next to his chair then placed a towel covered ice-pack on the side of his head in front of his ear.

"This swelling is pretty nasty, Sheriff. I brought you one of those aspirin packs and a glass of lemonade. It's here on your desk. Can I do anything else for you?" Her voice was whisper soft with compassion.

Cotton moved the ice pack to the swollen knuckles on his right hand as he spoke.

"Thanks June. Will you marry me?" he mumbled.

She chuckled with amusement.

"What would people say... you marryin' a woman so much older than you?"

"Nothing... until you came up pregnant," he sighed.

June Lee started laughing. She picked up his wrist and removed the ice, so she could get a look at his hand.

"You're that sure of yourself, Sheriff? Hmm, it could be convenient... since I'm here almost as much as you."

Cotton turned his chair towards her then pulled his sunglasses off and tossed them to the mound of paper work on his desk. He picked up the glass of lemonade. June Lee put the ice back on his hand then opened the medication for him. He swallowed it as he looked at the fluffy, older woman and remembered how Caroline had cried the day he told her about this woman being mistreated by her husband. June Lee's caring blue eyes were like having a part of the sky hovering above him. The wicked scar on her throat was a reminder that she had murdered the man who once tried to hang her. During her testimony, she told the judge that it was a good thing her ass was as wide as a barn, or Moby might not have dropped her like he did.

Cotton released a weary sigh before he spoke again.

"You're incarcerated, June Lee. How could I be here more than you?"

She reached over and patted his furry chin as she answered.

"Stop approving my weekend furloughs and you won't be. That hand looks bad. If you can't open and close your fingers, then you've got some broken bones. I'll bring you another ice pack, but you need to have it looked at by a doctor." She smiled then headed for the door. "Want the light out? It'll help that headache, and folks won't knock if they see a dark window."

"Yes, please. Thank you, Honey," mumbled Cotton.

"You're welcome, Pumpkin," chuckled June Lee.

Cotton felt a distinct ease come to his head when the surrounding atmosphere was thrust into darkness. He turned his chair back around and propped his feet up. He drifted off into a relaxed state... not sleep, but not bothered by the world beyond his office door. He relaxed and took the time to be still and quiet.

The next time Cotton stirred was because his feet had gone to sleep while propped up on the shelf. He moved, and the damp ice pack fell from his head onto his shirt. He looked at the clock on the wall. It was hard to believe that no one was bothering him. He thought of his confrontation with Dane, and the sad, desolate mansion popped into his mind. The small house in which he lived had been paid for five years ago, and more than once had he thought about selling it and moving into the boarding house. Julie had graduated and moved to Fort Worth to build a life of her own. Still, he wanted her to have a place to call home, and he had made memories there that he couldn't let go. He could pass her room, even now, and hear her talking to her toys as she served them make believe tea. He would never forget her ambitious first steps across the living room floor. It was like she had waited for him to get off his shift that night, so she could make her debut walk for just him, while holding her little arms out in greeting. These memories were precious. The bad ones, like the day he found Vicki in their bed with another man, had been erased when he donated the bed to the thrift store and bought a new one. The memories he had made in the new one with Caroline were something he re-lived daily. And, since Preston had come into his life, it seemed his mind stayed in the past more than the present.

Emmett thought of the money he had inherited. His father had sold the home place when he fell ill because he knew his son's weakness for sentiment. His parents had blessed their granddaughter with college tuition and made Emmett deposit the rest.

Cotton's mind went back to the abandoned house on the bluff. He reached for the phone and dialed Lowell

310

Bennett's number. He was the Tax Assessor for Liberty County and had been for the last 24 years.

"Lowell, this is Emmett. Have you got a minute? I need some advice." Lowell was an old friend and sharp as a tack about the county's business. "It's about the Breaux Estate... Whisper Bluff, who owns it now?" Cotton listened as Lowell told him all he needed to know. "No! Are you serious? Is it just the house for sale?"

Lowell told him the deed encompassed the main house, the stone structure, and the surrounding 30 acres down to the river with an easement for the driveway. He told Emmett that he hadn't looked at the land deed for the surrounding property in a long time because the taxes were paid by the bank. He told Emmett the Breaux Estate had always been managed by The Hollingsworth Firm, and that he believed the trust passed to Caroline Breaux's son, when he came of age. He asked Emmett if the rumors of Preston getting married and the Colonel being re-activated to the War Council for the president were true.

"Yes, Preston married this afternoon; it was a beautiful ceremony. Colonel Reid is on a plane to Washington as we speak. So, Lowell... is there any way under the sun that I can pay the levy on the house before it goes to auction?" Cotton's mind began to embrace the thought of owning and protecting Whisper Bluff, and all its secrets. He wanted to give Preston's heritage back to him. He wanted to do it for Caroline. "How does a silent auction work?" Cotton thought about the secret room in the attic and wondered if anyone had discovered it in all these years. If not, and he could secure the property then he would have the means to make the needed repairs to the house and grounds. Cotton began to get excited, and the questions poured out of him faster than Lowell could answer them. "That's good... I think. Can I bid on the property, considering I'm an elected official? And is there an appraisal made available to the public? How do I know where to start with a bid? I don't want any favors, Lowell. I just want this property really bad, and I don't want to screw it up because I don't know what I'm doing." Cotton scribbled down some facts as Lowell told him how the silent auction worked. He told Cotton that the property was in a poor state, and the only one that had expressed an interest was an outside investment company that was planning to tear it down. Cotton changed his mind when he heard that. He told Lowell he couldn't allow that to happen and he had to secure the property. He asked Lowell if he could help him without getting into trouble. Lowell told him that since no one else had bid, he doubted there would be a problem. He suggested that Emmett get a private attorney to place the bid for him. Cotton hung up with Lowell promising to bring him the necessary paperwork on Monday morning.

Cotton leaned back in his chair. He thought about how bad the condition of the manor house must be after being long neglected. He knew there had been more than a dozen families in it in the last 15 years, and none of them stayed very long. The Sheriff's Department had answered a lot of calls out there through the years, usually because the residents were scared there was an intruder due to noises they had heard in the house. Cotton remembered the day they had been called out there with the fire department several years back. The new tenants had been getting the yard in shape for spring and were burning leaves, down limbs and grass from mowing. The wind shifted from the river causing the fire to get out of hand to the point of threatening the house. They were surprised when the sprinkler system cut on and extinguished the fire. The fire chief inspected the system and told them that the sprinkler system had not been functional in years, and they had to be mistaken. Cotton had looked around the perimeter of the house while the residents argued with the chief. He looked through the window of the solarium and saw that the pool was empty of water. Memories of a private nature flooded his mind and his heart and caused searing chills to sting his arms and the back of his neck. He fought the urge to ask permission to enter the house because he could think of no good reason to make the request other than curiosity.

After speaking to Lowell, Cotton was excited, and he wanted to drive over and look around. He wondered if Dane was gone. He looked at the fluorescent hands on his watch; it was 7:00 p.m. He thought about Preston and Jaden and wondered if they had made it to Wichita Falls yet, or if they had stopped along the way to celebrate their union. He smiled every time he thought about the young man; he couldn't seem to stop himself. He thought he better smile all he could unless he planned on spilling his guts to Preston when the young man asked why he had a stupid look on his face.

The green button on his phone blinked, Cotton punched it then spoke as though it were a person.

"Yeah, what's up?"

Truitt's voice seemed cautious as it echoed in the small room.

"Sheriff, are you, all right? Do you need something else to drink? June Lee said you had a migraine and that you needed an hour. Preston is on line one, do you want me to take a message?"

A jolt of worry leaped in Emmett's chest knowing Preston should be the last person to be calling him.

"No, I'll get it. Thanks Truitt." Cotton punched line one. "Hey Preston, are you and Jaden okay?"

Preston's enthusiastic voice gave him cause to exhale.

"Hey Sheriff, we're great. Listen... I'm sorry to bother you, but I didn't get to talk to you before you left. I wanted to tell you thanks for coming to the wedding. I opened the card you put in my pocket. You shouldn't have done that Sheriff; I don't know what else to say. I appreciate everything you've done for me, Sir. And, there are things that I want to tell you. It's just... you're so real with me and the way you treat me. You've always tried to help me, and you've given me the opportunity to do something constructive with myself. Well, I guess what I'm trying to say is... I know you care about me. It makes me feel like I'm your boy sometimes... instead of the Colonel's. I don't know; I guess... I just wanted to talk to you. I wanted to say, hey, and thanks. I promise we won't waste one cent of your gift, Sir."

A pleased smile shifted Cotton's swollen face, but he was so happy he didn't notice the discomfort.

"Preston, you're very special to me son and well... I want you and Jaden to be happy. She's beautiful. You two look like you were made for each other."

"We are, Sir. Everything is going to be great!" A moment of silence fell on them.

"Sheriff, can I ask you something?"

"Sure... you know you can ask me anything." Cotton took a deep breath. He knew that Preston was wise for his years, and if Dane had confessed all that he claimed then Preston surely had unanswered questions.

"June Lee told me once that you had a daughter. What's her name? Will you tell me about her sometime?"

"Her name is Julianna. She used to live with me, but she moved to Fort Worth a couple of years ago after she graduated college. She's got it in her mind that she has got to make it on her own. I'm proud of her, but I miss her. Let's see... she's 25, and she's an attorney. Well, a public defender; she decided it was a good place to start and gain experience. Her old man thinks paying customers are a better idea, but she's smart and she knows what's best for her. She works hard and comes up empty sometimes, but she's got grit and that's what makes the difference in this world. Maybe you and Jaden can go to dinner with us next week. We try to pencil each other in every two weeks to jaw over life and its possibilities."

"I'd like to meet her, Sheriff. Umm, I've been thinking, I know I've got to be 21 years old to enter the academy and be on enforcement staff within an agency. Do I need to be 21 to work in dispatch? I was thinking that... if I could learn all I can from that aspect of the job then it may give me a leg up on the academy. Is it at all possible to hire on, at some point in the future, and work with you, Sir?"

Cotton smiled.

"I'll train you to dispatch now, Preston, and you definitely have a position with me when you get out of school. That is, if I'm still here. I'm elected, so I can't promise you that the citizens will keep me working. If not, I'll write you a letter of recommendation and I'll get you in under someone who has a solid grip on life. Don't worry." Suddenly, Cotton wondered how it was that Preston could stay on the phone with him and have a new bride waiting. "Preston, are y'all in Wichita Falls already? Am I keeping you from… something?"

His son laughed softly.

"We decided not to go. Jaden wanted to spend our first night as husband and wife at home… in our own bed. Well actually, I'm at the store up the road getting her some corn chips and chocolate ice cream to dip them in. She is getting a surprise ready for me. I'm supposed to give her half an hour." He laughed again.

"Yeah, I've been there, Buddy. This time with her… watching the baby grow, loving each other and making plans for tomorrow… that is what memories are made of. They're the kind of memories that go so deep in your soul they'll be in your thoughts whether you're conscious or not. Don't take one second with her for granted, Preston," encouraged Cotton. "We haven't had the chance to talk about personal things with each other and that's something I would like to do one day soon, but just so you know… I was 17 when Julianna was born. I understand more than you may think. It was hard, but it was worth it. I feel honored that you called me at such a special time. I hope to see both of you real soon."

"Yes Sir, you will. Sheriff… Dane left me the deeds to all the property, even the boat. He's not coming back, is he?"

"I can't answer that based on anything other than my gut, Preston."

"Yes Sir, I know. That's why I'm asking you."

Cotton realized that this boy trusted him as much as he did Owen. He was honored; there was no other way to describe how he felt.

"No, Preston... I don't think so, not breathing anyway. He's a soldier; obviously, he's been asked to do something that is very dangerous and valuable to the future of this country. Honor him, Son... in all his faults. It takes a hard and brave man to command others and obey orders... and a gentle one to know the cost and value of the sacrifice."

Preston told Cotton what was really on his mind.

"There are so many sides to him that he's showed me in the last three days; they're things that I like and respect. I feel cheated out of really having the chance to know him and I can't help it."

"You were, Preston. I know what you mean; I talked to him this afternoon. I spoke with a different person too." Cotton wanted to tell him they needed to meet and take this conversation a step further, but it was not the right time to do such a thing.

"I guess I better go before Jaden starts feeling the same way. I appreciate you, Sheriff... take care, and thanks again for the money. We're starting a savings account for the baby with it."

"You are welcome, Preston... be sure and hug Jaden for me." Cotton hung up and leaned back in his chair then propped his feet up. He hadn't felt this satisfied in a long time.

Preston opened the door to a still house that smelled of all sorts of aromatic scents. The candle on the table was lit, and the radio played softly. He put the ice cream in the freezer and laid the corn chips on the table then leaned over and blew the candle out before he ventured down the hallway.

He saw a glow from the bathroom and pushed the door open to find a collection of glowing candle jars sitting in the floor and around the edge of the tub. He smiled at his naked, pregnant wife lying in the cloud of bubbles, her chin rested on her delicate shoulder while a soft snore echoed from her nose.

Preston squatted down next to her and took it all in for a moment. His manhood had honored her ever since he saw her walk through the gathering of family then came to stand next to him. She had looked like an angel without wings in the flowing dress and the wind caressing her long hair. He was thankful for the tight black jeans she had bought him to go with the borrowed coat from Owen.

He stood and pulled off his boots then tossed his clothing over the small chair in the corner. He stepped into the tub, careful of her legs as he went to his knees. Jaden opened her eyes and looked up at him. Her attention caressed his body a moment; it made him even more solid. She sat up and pressed her face to his abdomen as her arms went around him.

"I love you so much, Preston. I never dreamed my life could be so wonderful," she whispered.

"You haven't seen anything yet, Baby," he mumbled as he pushed her back against the tub. His mouth consumed hers with a possessive and anticipated kiss.

CHAPTER 16

The early morning sky was a breathtaking canvas of blue, orange and purple hues artistically painted by the Almighty. It was a gift to those who would rise before the sun came up and look up towards the heavens to watch His magnificence unfold. Preston and Jaden had been fortunate enough to receive this gift. They had been married four weeks today, and it was Preston's birthday.

They had been invited to supper with Sheriff Cotton the previous night and had the unexpected pleasure of meeting his ex-wife, Vicki, her husband, Autry Cantrell, and Cotton's daughter, Julianna. Preston was amazed at how all of them got along so well; he didn't miss the friendly way Jaden had interacted with Julianna. His wife had no close friends other than Ava and Estelle, and he could tell she enjoyed visiting with another female closer to her own age. During the evening's conversation, Jaden had mentioned that she and Estelle were going to Dallas to the new shopping center in the developing outskirt of New Hope. Vicki Cantrell told her about the Mommy and Baby Shop that an old friend of hers had opened near the center. Jaden listened to the directions and smiled when she comprehended where the shop could be found. It wasn't far from where she had lived, and she made a mental note to tell Estelle about it should she be interested in visiting the establishment.

Estelle had suggested they come to the ranch for breakfast on Saturday morning; that way she and Jaden could head to New Hope and leave Preston to get into an assortment of things with the rest of the men. They would return that afternoon and grill hamburgers for Preston's birthday.

Preston and Charlie cast their way around the bank of Cloud Lake while Eli, Travis and his friend, Joel, dove off the pier enjoying the last swim of the season. Scherry stood on the end of the pier wanting to jump in, but still had not mustered the courage to take a leap of faith into the deep artesian water. She finally found it when Travis promised to be waiting to catch her.

Cole lay stretched out on a blanket under the small stand of oaks listening to Mollie read her homework assignment to him. His little girl's love for reading caused her to devour every book she opened. This was discovered the day he had dropped the five-year-old off at the veterinarian clinic with her Uncle Lucien, while he went to a public meeting with the Board of Supervisors about their plans to build a new county road.

Lucien found himself answering questions about muscles and the anatomies of certain animals. She would appear at the door of his laboratory and ask her question, and after receiving the answer, she would retreat. After an hour of such behavior, Lucien followed her to his office. He discovered she had a collection of his textbooks pulled down into the floor with her. He told Cole what had happened and asked if he could talk to a friend of his who was an English Professor concerning how to best encourage and develop this amazing gift. The child could read and sound out anything, but she was too young to understand everything she read without a lot of it being explained. The Professor met with them and was amazed at Mollie's ability as well. She agreed to teach Mollie how to comprehend and speed read. One of her favorite books was the reptile dictionary in Lucien's collection. The family teased each other concerning their own knowledge of the world around them. Everyone in the family had learned something new and interesting from listening to the child read a lesson then discuss the material.

By mid-morning, Estelle and Jaden had visited the outdoor shop and found Preston the shotgun she had seen him looking at in the sale paper and several necessities to accompany his hunting gear. They scanned the sale tables at the linen store and each of them came away with a set of sheets. Estelle purchased several fall tablecloths, and Jaden found some new curtains for the houseboat. She and Preston had moved into it the last weekend in September because it made no sense to own something and keep a check on it while paying rent to live somewhere else. Jaden had to drive further to work, but she had applied at Westville Memorial, and was furthering her career there starting October 15th.

They dropped their packages in the trunk then got in Jaden's car and headed to their next destination.

"Oh Estelle, there's a Markie's Grill. Do you like shrimp?" questioned Jaden.

"Yes, I love it. I can't say that it always loves me, but I'd rather eat it and let my fingers and feet swell rather than not," she laughed.

"They have the best angel hair pasta with shrimp and garlic cream sauce. It'll make you slap your mama... figuratively speaking of course. The orders are rather large; we can order an extra side salad and split one if you like. That way we aren't stuffed for Preston's birthday supper tonight."

Estelle nodded her head.

"That sounds yummy." The mention of lunch made her think of Preston's birthday supper that evening. "I made and seasoned the burgers this morning while Owen fried the bacon. I left them covered in the refrigerator. I told Owen to start the grill around 4:00 if we weren't back yet... that we wouldn't be too long. Everything else is done. I'm so glad Preston has you Jaden. He looks so happy!"

"I hope so Estelle. I know he makes me happy! I wanted to make his birthday special for him. I hope you don't mind that I ordered the cake. He told me that he's never had a bakery cake before and..."

"Oh Honey... no, of course not! I think it's sweet that you do things for him that he's not had a chance to experience."

Jaden giggled, but she didn't say anything about what was funny.

Estelle was not a complete prude.

"I take it he was a fast learner at a lot of things."

Jaden's smile softened as she thought about Preston waking her up that morning. She pulled into the parking space and cut off the motor. She turned to Estelle as she spoke from her heart.

"He's not the only one. I've never been around a horse. There's no comparison between petting one and riding one. He said I would love it and he was right; I did." Jaden's eyes sparkled with love. "He's the most wonderful person I've ever met, Estelle. I don't know if it's wrong to be so consumed with a person... wanting to make them happy, but it's all I think about. I can't seem to help it."

"I know what you mean, Sweetie. I feel the exact same way about Owen. After my mother died so tragically, I didn't think I could go on with the burden of guilt I was carrying. When they offered me the job at the ranch, I never dreamed it would end up like this for me. The peace and the happiness I have found... combined with the opportunity to love and be loved by such a man is nothing but a blessing from God." She sighed with a smile that said it all.

"Estelle, this peace that you talk about; it's something that God gives you?" surveyed Jaden.

Estelle looked at her.

"I ask Him for it. I talk to God like I talk to you. I know it can be overwhelming... trying to understand the Bible and believing that God created all things. The idea that He would give His child to an innocent young girl to be born of flesh and bone was intended to include mankind as his children. His son brought the message of faith and hope. The Son of God willfully stood in condemnation, humiliation and was judged as a fraud. His sacrifice is incomprehensible to mankind but was made so we could have a one-on-one relationship with His Father. This is the very reason why I can talk to God in such a personal way. The sacrifice of earthly flesh... the son He loved so much... was symbolic as the price paid so you and I could choose to believe," explained Estelle considerately. "I look back over my life and see how He was guiding me, even to this very day that I could be here with you." Estelle clasped Jaden's hand. "I feel like I have a sister in you." Estelle smiled at her. "God didn't only send you to Preston, He sent you to me too."

"Do you ask God for things you want and need?" surveyed Jaden.

"Yes, I suppose I do."

"Have you ever been disappointed?" questioned Jaden sincerely.

"Oh yes... quite often. Children don't always know what's best for them, being a child of God is a parent-child relationship. Sometimes, the answer is 'no'. I accept that He knows what's best for me, and I try not to question. It's a matter of faith, and it's not always easy."

Jaden shook her head.

"It sounds like God gets treated like a Genie in a bottle," mumbled Jaden. She threw her hand over her mouth suddenly as her eyes closed. A moment passed. "Oh, Estelle... I apologize. I shouldn't have said that. I didn't mean it as a judgmental statement."

Estelle laughed softly and squeezed her hand.

"Jaden, Honey, you are so refreshing. You're right. I'm sure I have approached prayer that way before; all I can say is... I believe and trust Him because I've felt the power in His presence. He's like a parent who holds you in invisible arms. It's because I choose to believe, that I find strength when I'm weak and courage when I'm scared. My mother dying in the house fire was tragic, and yet, I found hope in living at the ranch and joy overcame my sorrow. If a person can... or will take their attention off themselves and look around at life, they will see that He's all around us. He's in the regeneration of earth and her seasons, and He's in the love between a husband and wife. He's in the first living cell of a child, and the love between friends. It's our place as believers to extend His love beyond ourselves, caring enough to share a part of our joy with someone who needs to be uplifted. You see... these things reflect Christ."

Jaden's attention met Estelle's as she thought about what her friend said.

"That's what you and Owen did for Preston, and because you loved him... you loved me too," reasoned Jaden softly.

Estelle's smile widened as she nodded her head.

"You two are very easy to love, Honey. I don't know why some people seem to have things come so easy for them, or why some people are so bent that they thrive off hurting others. It's certainly not a godly thing. But Jaden, your heart has so much to give. You became a nurse against tremendous adversity. You are the perfect example of grace. Why is that? Why aren't you bitter?"

Jaden shrugged her shoulders.

"The Enriquez's were like angels for me. Meeting them and feeling their concern for me, made me see that there were people who loved just because it was who they were. Their faith in me and their kindness gave me hope. I knew I wanted to be like them. I wanted to become a person who was productive and self-sufficient, while at the same time compassionate and kindhearted. I just couldn't give up." Jaden blinked several times as the truth of what she said was clarified inside of her. She recognized the similarities in the simple message Charlie, and now Estelle, had shared with her. It was about loving others as Christ loves us.

Estelle sensed Jaden's heart and mind were beginning to merge.

"God used them to help me... just like he used Ms. Celia and the family to help you... just like you helped Preston and me. I'm supposed to become strong in my faith, so I can be used to help someone else. It's all about loving other's... so they can learn to love someone else." Jaden thought of Pastor Storey. "By the way, I met Pastor Storey at the grocery Thursday. I could get really attached to him, Estelle. He's wonderful."

Estelle and Jaden continued to talk as they got out and locked the doors. They were lost in the discussion about love, life and hope and the blessing of their babies to come. They didn't notice the white Ford pickup that had followed them from the pro shop and had pulled in the gas station at the corner of the shopping center.

Russell Butler had spotted the auburn beauty from the other side of the store. The sight of her brought back the humiliation he had endured from his buddies that night at the rodeo. They had taken pleasure in mocking him for getting jaw-jacked by a kid then puking his beer from the sucker-punch to the gut. The sight of her nudged at the humiliation he had felt, and it made him angry all over again. He remembered how she felt beneath him. She had twisted his feelings around her little finger and then dumped him once he had laid claim to her body as his. His mind began to contemplate how he could give her high school boyfriend a taste of the real world and satisfy his personal grievance with her at the same time.

Russell parked a couple of spaces down from Jaden's car then got out of the truck. He tugged on his cap and made sure his sunglasses were secure before taking the gas can out of the bed behind the driver's seat. He kept a vigilant, but discreet watch on the store front where they had gone as he walked over to the blue and white Impala. He opened the gas cap and added the contents of his can to the tank. He scanned the parking lot to see if anyone noticed him while doing so. No one seemed to care, and a satisfied grin crawled over his teeth.

Jaden grinned at Estelle as she rolled her eyes and pushed her plate away from her. Her friend picked up the glass of sweet tea and took another drink.

"That was wonderful. We're going to have to find this recipe, so we can make this at home, Jaden. Owen loves pasta. He would roll away from the table after getting his fill of that."

Jaden put her fork down and watched as Estelle's hand caressed the busy little bump in her middle.

"The baby liked it too?"

Estelle turned in her chair.

"Yes. But my bladder isn't tolerant of my love of iced tea. I'm sorry; I've got to go to the little girl's room again, Honey."

"Go ahead. I'll be right behind you." Jaden made eye contact with the waitress. She came over with the ticket. Jaden complimented the meal and her service then handed her enough for the bill and an appreciative gratuity to back it up.

They had not moved the car yet because everything was in walking distance and the exercise was good for them. Jaden visited the restroom too, and then they browsed through the candle shop they had passed on the stroll to the restaurant.

Estelle was fascinated by the eclectic selection of merchandise from candles to wind chimes. They were drawn to the lighted display of fragile and exquisite glass figurines. Estelle thought of Mollie's birthday being the next in line. She took advantage of the outing and the fact that the holidays would be upon them soon and chose several of the glass horses for different members of the family. She would let Charlie have first pick for Mollie's birthday. He was no different from the rest of them and doted on the small wisp of a girl; her love for the horses, riding, learning, and living each day with zeal was contagious.

Jaden was drawn to the wind chimes. She chose the set that was made of copper pipe because its deep mellow tones reminded her of the sounds of the river. She had been pleasantly surprised by the tranquility that living on the boat offered. She found the cove to be romantic and peaceful and observing the wildlife only added to the miracle that was her life with Preston. They had splurged and bought a new king-size mattress for the main cabin. Preston and Charlie had done a fine job enlarging the storage frame that held the mattress, and her husband had painted it a dark pine green to compliment the dark hardwood floor and the new comforter. The new sheets were an extra set for the new bed, so she would not have to launder the only set and put them back on in the same day. There were no bad memories as she feared; the Colonel's apology and the time they had spent with him before he left had taken care of those. The few possessions she owned had blended in nicely with the things that were already there.

Jaden's eyes surveyed the silver crosses in the display case below the register while she waited her turn for the clerk to ring up her selections. She saw one that resembled the P on her necklace. She reached up and unfastened it from around her neck as she asked the other attendant if she could see it for a comparison.

Jaden smiled and handed the cashier the money for her purchases. She was putting her change away when the other lady behind the counter came back with the thin delicate cross attached to her necklace and laying over Preston's initial as a protector. Her smile widened.

They got back to the car and Estelle handed her a bag.

"What's this?" Jaden pulled out the leather-bound Bible. She opened the lid of the box. A pleased smile graced her face.

Estelle told her.

"A month ago, I would have worried about coming across as being self-righteous, but not anymore. I think you and Preston should have one of your very own. That piece of paper in the front is something that Pastor Storey gave me years ago. He called them the meat in the bread of life. I thought you could start there... like I did."

Jaden pressed the gift next to her heart as she smiled at Estelle.

"Thank you so much. I can't wait to share our day with Preston."

At 3:45 p.m., they put the last of their bounty in the trunk and set out for the hour drive home. They put the top down and their jackets on along with their sunglasses. Estelle tied a colorful scarf around her head and Jaden tugged down on the cowboy hat Charlie had given her and fastened it beneath her chin. They rolled the short distance through the parking lot and pulled into the gas station. They giggled at the silly way they looked but smiled and made no effort to rectify the fact. Estelle went inside to use the facilities before they got on the road while Jaden used the pay phone and called the ranch to let Owen know they were at the filling station and about to start on their way home.

Jaden turned on Highway 6, it was the route they promised Owen they would take because of the good condition of the road. They were 20 minutes into the drive home when they came to a mishap at the crossroads where a hay trailer had turned over and spilled its cargo in the middle of the intersection. There was no way to go around the small catastrophe and the sun was close to shadowing the tree line. They decided it would be better to detour to avoid an anxious delay and cause a worrisome gap in time from when Jaden had last spoken to Owen.

Jaden made a U-turn and started back up the highway like several of the others who waited behind them.

She turned on to Woodswamp Road knowing it would cut 15 minutes off going back to the main highway and around to the next junction. It was a two-lane road that was built up high because of the mile-long stretch of swampy backwater from the Liberty River, known as Greasy Creek. They rolled along with the wind swirling around them. Jaden admired the incredible sunset and compared it to the one she had seen greet the day early that morning with Preston. Her mind stayed in that beautiful memory a few seconds for there was a mystical silence on this stretch of road due to the dense woods on either side. The road was scenic because the huge, majestic Cypress trees in the bottom lands. It was a good road and well-tended by the county, but at times the critters that crossed it could be creepy.

"Oh my… this is beautiful," exclaimed Estelle. "Please don't have a flat… or break down. I may panic on you," she chuckled.

Jaden saw the caution sign for entering the narrow bridge through the orange glow of the setting sun; her eyes cut to her rear-view mirror when she noticed a pair of headlights make the same turn in the distance.

Jaden slowed down, and the car dipped slightly with the pavement as they crossed onto the reinforced cement of the long bridge. The car sputtered once in the center of the overpass.

"Oh Lord, I'm sorry," breathed Estelle. "I didn't mean to speak that into reality." She looked at Jaden as the car began to jerk its way across the last stretch of the bridge then without further warning, the engine died.

Jaden pressed the clutch but did not touch the brake, so she could guide the vehicle out of the way of oncoming traffic. They coasted to a stop some 30 yards past the bank of the creek. Jaden pulled off onto the gravel between the guardrail and the pavement; the embankment on the other side of the railing was steep and lined with huge rocks to prevent erosion.

"Are we out of gas?" questioned Estelle then she answered herself. "No, of course not… we checked it before we left. I'm sorry." Estelle realized she needed to keep a level head; after all, she had just told Jaden the source of her strength.

Jaden frowned.

"It sounds like... and acts like... we got some bad gas." She turned on her flashers. "Start praying, Estelle." Jaden laughed. "God knows I'm not a mechanic."

Jaden got out and Estelle followed her because there was no room between the car and the rail to open the door. Jaden raised the hood and checked the obvious things she had seen Preston do that morning before they left. He was conscientious of the car's functions and made sure that she could depend on it. The battery was connected, the hoses were all new and so were the spark plugs and connectors; she could not find a problem with them. She checked the oil next and found it was right on the mark. The car did not register as running hot, so she didn't bother the radiator, and the distributor cap was snug. She could see no reason for the sputtering or for the motor to just shut off like it did. She sat down and tried to crank the motor again. It whined a few seconds then coughed sending a puff of white smoke out of the tailpipe. That was when the lights from the vehicle entered the bridge on the other end.

"Oh, thank goodness," sang Estelle. "Let's catch a ride to the next phone and call the fellas."

Jaden didn't want to stay here, but she didn't trust people either. She would rather wait it out until Preston came for her.

"That's not a good idea, Estelle! We would be better off walking back to the main road where they are sure to look. I'm not too trusting of strangers," stated Jaden.

"We have to do something, Jaden. We detoured... remember?"

Jaden reminded herself, it was natural for Estelle to be a little panicky, even in the tragedy of her mother's death she had been protected by people who were concerned for her. Her friend was not acquainted with being vulnerable. Jaden got out and walked to the front of the car. She rebelliously checked everything again while Estelle waved her arms for help. Jaden knew it wouldn't be long before Preston and Owen would be looking for them. She addressed Estelle's God respectfully and asked that He please let her see the precious husband He had given her again.

Jaden saw the white truck pass by slowly in the corner of her eye then she heard the gravel crunch beneath the tires as it pulled off to the side of the road. Estelle's friendly voice greeted the driver then told them of their dilemma. Jaden heard the masculine voice tell Estelle that it would be a pleasure to look and he bet he knew exactly what the problem was. Jaden rubbed the chills from her arms as she turned in response to something oddly familiar.

"Well now... fancy meeting you here." Russell Butler smiled down at Jaden. His menacing eyes and crooked half smile assured her that she had been foolish to come back into his neck of the woods. "Hey Jaden, how's the new man?"

Jaden watched him walk past Estelle as though she was insignificant to his cause. He stopped and looked down at the motor beneath the open hood of the car, and his sinister smile widened.

"What did you do to the car, Russell?" snapped Jaden suddenly.

"Nothing you didn't have coming," he retorted in a smug tone. Russell Butler made fun of their situation by acting as though he were her friend. "Aren't you going to introduce me to this pretty lady, Honey?"

"No, I'm not!" responded Jaden curtly. "She's a decent woman who shouldn't be subjected to a devious slug like you."

Russell's eyes passed over Estelle's body without discretion.

"Well, it didn't look that way to me when she was jumping up and down in the road waving her arms. She's even more voluptuous than you are, Honey. I guess I'll just have to introduce myself." Russell turned toward Estelle, and she instinctively crossed her arms over her chest and backed away from him.

Jaden leaped in front of him.

"We've already called home, Russell. Our husbands will be looking for us in a few minutes. You've paid me back by sabotaging my car; please... just leave us alone."

Estelle clinched her teeth in fear. She had been self-righteous in assuming she were the wiser of the two of them. Because of that she had acted foolishly by welcoming this person into their midst. Estelle suddenly had to accept that Jaden had survived from being respectful of all her worldly lessons.

Estelle's bones leaped inside her skin when Russell back-handed Jaden across the face; the impact was hard enough to spin her around so that her eyes met her friend. Estelle took a step towards her as she reached out to help, but Jaden shook her head in warning and Estelle froze in place.

Russell's temper grew with fury. Jaden's arrogance concerning the boy she was screwing, and the so-called better life she had found with him had churned deep inside like a hurricane all afternoon. He had no restraint left, so he punched her in the face when she turned back to him just because payback felt good.

Jaden fell across the motor and cut her hand on a metal bracket as she caught herself. Her eyes watered, but she stood up and faced him again knowing that she had to keep Estelle out of harm's way.

"Okay, I get it. You're still mad at me for moving on without you," specified Jaden. "I'm sorry, Russell, but you hurt me, and I got scared, so I left." She pressed the back of her hand to her bleeding lip. "Obviously, it wasn't such a bad idea. How long have you been following us anyway, and what do you want?"

"You're a stupid bitch, I've been on you since this morning!" He bragged outwardly like there was someone who would hear him and be impressed by his manipulative and devious accomplishment. "The hay truck was a nice surprise. Your husband doesn't know about that little disaster, does he? What did you do... marry that stupid boy?"

Jaden's resolve enabled her to remain calm. She knew Russell was here to hurt her. Hurting her was what he did when he wasn't angry; she could only guess what his intensions were at this point.

"Why can't you let it go, Russell?" she asked him in earnest. "Why can't we just get on with our lives without you feeling I owe you something, or that I did you wrong? I'm married now. I don't mean to put you down; I'm just tired of being used. I'm tired of the violence, mentally and physically. That's not my life anymore. Can't you understand that?"

His fist grabbed her denim jacket, and he snatched her up close; the worn garment tore under the force of his malicious temper.

"You think I don't know about your so-called husband. I asked around about him. It's a damn joke, Jaden. He's a snot-nosed kid that you wrapped your whoring legs around and showed him what it feels like to be a man. That's what you're best at!" He loomed over her in an intimidating way.

"I can't argue with you about that, Russell. It's true. I am a whore, because every man I've ever trusted has used me like one... all of you, except for Preston. He may be a boy to you, but he's a hundred times more of a man than you'll ever be."

Russell held on to her as his other fist slugged her in the chest. His keys were in his hand, and one of them stabbed him between the small bones of his hand causing him to drop them as he yanked his fist back.

Jaden's blouse ripped at the shoulder as her back landed hard on the gravel. She rolled to her side and grabbed her chest while trying to catch her breath. Hot tears flooded her eyes and her head pounded from hitting the ground so abruptly. Her survival instincts were still sharp, but she couldn't see a way out of this situation. It seemed she was destined to end up in the angry hands of a violent person. Why had God interceded on her behalf and given her all these wonderful treasures of a happy life, only to have Russell detour her and take them away from her? Jaden pushed herself up to her elbow as her breath came back to her lungs. It occurred to her in the middle of her distress that maybe she had been on a course that crossed Russell's all along and Preston had been the detour. He was a blessed gift in her life, so she could feel the essence of true love before her demise.

She was scared, but moreover, she was worried about Estelle. Her friend had nothing to do with any of this and she knew Russell didn't care. Jaden knew in her soul this would not turn out in her favor, but she had to find a way for Estelle to escape. Jaden could think of only one way to give her friend a chance to escape, so she asked God to forgive her promiscuous behavior one last time. She tried not to think of Preston or their commitment as she used her body to manipulate this dangerous man. Men had used her body for their own gain her entire life; however, today she would offer it to protect her friend and her sister.

"You're right, Russell. Preston's sweet, and he thinks he's my hero. It was nice for a while, but I'm bored with it. I'll go with you." She pushed herself up to her hands and knees. Her hand touched his keys, and she gripped them in her fist. She stumbled as she stood because her balance was wobbly. The cowboy hat dangled around her neck; she snatched it off breaking the draw string in the process.

Estelle's pale expression was horrified; still, she reached out to steady her friend. Jaden let the keys slide into the hat from her palm as she pushed it at her friend. She looked at Estelle and mouthed the word, 'go'. She pushed Estelle away from her because she was certain Russell was watching. She pushed her hair back away from her face then turned to him and brushed herself off. He was watching her all right, like a wolf waiting to pounce. She took a step towards him but felt her nose drain of a hot, wet liquid. Jaden pulled the tail of her shirt out of her skirt-waist to wipe the blood from her nose. She slammed the hood of her car then sat down on the fender.

"I have to admit you're pretty crafty... so what did you do to my car?"

Russell smiled with pride as he alienated Estelle by turning to Jaden.

"It was easy..." he boasted, "... water and gas don't mix."

Jaden looked up at Russell aware that Estelle eased her way towards the truck.

"Well, I'm not much to look at right now. I guess I'm going to have to learn to stop ticking you off." She smiled at him while her heart rebelliously slammed against her ribs. "Have you ever tasted fresh blood, Russell? It's kind of a turn on."

He stepped up between her knees and pulled her against him as he looked down at her. Jaden reached up and covered his ears with her hands to try to distract him further from what was happening behind his back. He leaned over and invaded her mouth with his tongue; it was an angry and punishing kiss.

Estelle reached the door of the truck but hesitated and turned back to Jaden. She didn't want to leave her friend, but a voice deep within reminded her that if she had listened to Jaden in the first place, they could be looking at different circumstances. Estelle made herself do as Jaden had told her and slid beneath the stirring wheel of Russell's truck and gently pulled the door closed. She slapped at the lock with one hand while the other jabbed the key at the dash in search of the ignition. Her attention was drawn to the side mirror as the wicked man grabbed a fist full of Jaden's hair and yanked back on it while forcing his kiss on her. Estelle began to cry when she saw him shove Jaden backwards onto the hood of the car then pushed her knees apart. Estelle's shaky hand finally united the key with the ignition; her bottom lip quivered as she turned it. The motor whined, so she gave it some gas. The starter of the old truck cried out painfully as Estelle kept trying to get it to turn over. It was as though the truck knew better than to obey anyone other than the bully that drove it.

Russell turned at the sound of the motor trying to turn over and realized what was happening. He yanked Jaden off the car and threw her to the ground like a mean-spirited child that was tired of playing with his favorite toy. He dashed for the truck and grabbed the handle pulling on it in a fierce and violent show of temper while cussing and threatening Estelle with bodily harm.

Jaden scrambled to her feet and followed him determined to stop him from preventing Estelle's escape. She tightened her arms around his neck and hung on while Russell scuffled around trying to rid her from his back. Instinct made him shift his weight then lunged forward, the sudden change sent Jaden's small body flying over his head and crashing to the ground. He delivered a scalding slap to her cheek and Jaden returned the gesture. Her defiant spunk inflamed his temper. Russell wrestled with her a few moments as Jaden fought him like a wildcat that refused to be stuffed in a sack. When his hand landed on her throat and clamped down shutting off her airway, she knew she had been defeated.

Russell shook her as he roared in her face.

"You're a lying, viperous slut, Jaden. I hate you! You and your boyfriend are gonna pay for making a fool out of me!"

Jaden heard the engine in Russell's truck screech to life; however, Russell heard it too. He reacted and tightened the hold on her throat then picked her up and slammed her against the driver's window. The force behind his temper caused Jaden's skull to shatter the glass. He dropped her then reached in and snatched the door open. Estelle began to fight him as he jerked her out of the truck. Jaden's breath had been forced from her lungs when she hit the window and her body felt as though it was stuck in quicksand. She recognized Estelle's trembling voice pleading with their attacker to have a change of heart, but she screamed out in fright. Jaden lifted her head just in time to see Russell punch Estelle in the face and her body crumple in his arms. He picked her up and walked over to the guard rail then tossed her limp body over the embankment, thoughtlessly discarding her as he would a bag of trash. Jaden cried out in a labored gasp. Russell turned away from his heartless deed and looked at her. Her mind transformed him into the evil demon he really was.

Tears rushed her eyes as she faced the consequences of her own stupidity. She knew she was injured and there would be no way to get away from him. She put her hands over her ears as the deafening sound of the woods buzzed so loud, she thought her head would explode.

His feet stopped in front of her just before he inflicted another unexpected jolt to Jaden's body and her understanding.

Russel's arm caught her around the waist and snatched her from the ground. He carried her over to the railing. Jaden expected him to send her over the embankment to join Estelle, but he didn't. He went to his knees as he dumped her on the ground then rolled her to her back. He began tearing at her clothing and her body with animalistic hands and hateful, stabbing fingers. Jaden thought about the innocent life inside of her and she found a burst of resistance deep within. She fought back but was clumsy in her efforts because of her injuries. Russell got tired of it and shoved her hands behind her as he forced her legs apart with the weight of his body. He growled vile and cruel things to her as he shoved his clothing out of the way.

Jaden sucked in a shuttering breath as the first enraged and sadistic thrust of his body ripped her flesh. She knew instinctively that the innocent, little heartbeat of her and Preston's baby would not survive his vicious attack. She cried but gagged on regret as her swollen throat would not allow her to swallow and breathe at the same time. She called out to Preston, but Russell covered her mouth with a smothering stab of his tongue while his hurtful erection gored her womb with a spiteful and wicked vengeance.

Jaden's mind became fixed on the wailing of the insects in the woods as he punished her with his hatred. She used the pounding in her brain as an escape from

Russell's lustful grunting and depraved promises of further torment. She stopped sobbing because sorrow had consumed her to the point that she had no more tears. She lay helpless on the side of the road with her hands confined behind her back while he destroyed any shred of happiness or decency, she had managed to find these last few months. It was painful to breathe. It was painful to think of the innocence that was destroyed because they dared to love and trust a person such as herself.

Jaden saw her sweet husband's smiling face in her mind. The love she felt for him filled her heart and banished the sorrow because love was stronger than hatred. Her talk with Estelle gained precedence in her understanding and her spirit. She began to think of all the things she had been able to experience in this short time with Preston, and the family that loved him. Everything in her life began to find order in her heart. The truth was revealed to her as to the essence of what life was all about. Everything had been about love, sharing and giving of one's self, and one's faith. She remembered the words Estelle whispered over their food at lunch, 'His grace is sufficient'. Jaden's heart urged her to talk to the Heavenly Father.

She stared into the stars above her as she spoke to Him.

"God, are you there? Is it true? Can you really love me like a father? I want to be your child. I've never had a father." She felt a tingling warmth rush over her and there was a stillness in it yet, her heart quickened. The wailing echo from the woods changed into a song; it was one of peace, like a lullaby. Estelle's words came back to her again, 'His presence holds you like invisible arms of a parent'. Jaden's spirit was consumed with assurance. She knew there was something beyond this place where she lay. She knew something beyond physical degradation was happening to her. The essence of peace was so strong it had the power to fill her heart and soothe her spirit. She allowed herself to receive another embrace of love that was even more precious than Preston's. Faith had the power to turn this moment in time into the most important moment in her life. With each memory of Preston and these people that had come into her life; she began to see and feel, and to comprehend the very essence of unconditional love. She realized she had been able to return it to them on a small scale, but because she had not been able to let go of the life she had known, it had caused her to not trust the God no one could see. She whispered to the stillness beyond, knowing that something other than loneliness and sadness, something beyond the emotional bondage and disappointments of this earthly life waited for her.

"I don't know you like Estelle does... but I feel you. I believe you're real and that you've been with me many times before now. I'm sorry for my mistakes and my weaknesses. I need you to forgive me... and love me like the father I never had... and love my baby too. Please God... don't leave me. Please God, don't leave Preston either... even though I found you through loving him, he doesn't understand who you are yet."

Russell rose to his knees and pushed his hair back off his sweaty brow. He fastened his jeans while he stared at her through wary eyes. She had been mumbling since he climbed on top of her. He reasoned that he must have hit her harder than he intended. It was dusk. He had been lucky so far; there had been no interruptions until now. He had seen the headlights reflecting off the pavement beneath her car, the tires changed sounds as it rolled on to the bridge. Russell grabbed her wrist and jerked her hand up so that he could see what he was doing. He quickly worked the diamond ring and its mate off her finger and shoved them in his pocket and then stood up and pulled her to her feet. He turned his back to the on-coming vehicle and leaned on the hood of her car then wrapped his arms around her. He forced her body against him and her head to his shoulder. It was a twisted attempt to protect his self, pretending they were a loving couple caught in an intimate and private rendezvous.

Jaden's frame of mind was jolted by the sudden movement. A hot fluid drained from her body and she looked down to see the blood that stained her legs in the oncoming glow of light.

Russell's fingers dug into her arm as he warned her.

"Watch yourself, Jaden, or I'll toss your ass to the bottom of the swamp to join your friend."

She looked at the blood on the gravel and realized that it was her blood, and the blood that had run through her baby's tiny veins. It was on the front of Russell's jeans too. Jaden knew in her spirit that God had heard her. A breath of righteous anger caressed her skin and energized her body, and she began to try to wrestle her arm away from him.

Russell was surprised by her sudden revolt. He got spooked by the headlights and who may be coming upon them to catch him in his despicable deeds. He could not manage her any longer or how strong she had suddenly become. It was as though he had just raped the lady of justice and her blindfold fell away when she stood up. He decided she had gotten what was coming to her, so he released her with a mighty shove of hatred and dashed for his truck.

Jaden's body appeared in front of the log truck with no help from her feet. The grill of the truck struck her as its brakes locked up and squealed across the pavement. Her body took flight and landed in the center of the road; the headlights of the truck defined the spot where she lay unmoved. Russell barely missed her as he spun out in the gravel and nearly lost control in his haste to escape.

"My God in Heaven... did you see that, Henry?" The driver of the truck looked at his friend and found eyes bigger than his own.

Henry asked in a shaky voice.

"Was that angels that laid her down? One had a sword! Did you see him, Calvin; he had a sword! It was on fire?!"

Jaden looked up at the two men who spoke to her, yet her eyes became fixed on the surreal and glowing being which stood next to them looking down at her through eyes of compassion. She could hear them even though her mind was in a state greater than this world. She couldn't feel anything in her body as the caring eyes that gazed down at her brimmed with tears. He kneeled and touched her cheek. She thought of Estelle.

"Is Estelle dead?" she asked.

He shook his head.

"Have you come for me?"

He clasped her hand in his and peace filled her.

"Will you stay with me for a while?"

He smiled and nodded his head.

The man who drove the truck came into focus. Jaden told him that her sister had been thrown over the rail to the water's edge. The driver told his companion to go find her.

Jaden's eyes went back to the celestial being that held her hand. He looked up to the heavens as another appeared from the darkness of the night like a falling star. The winged soldier wore a golden breast plate and sheathed a fiery sword with majestic precision. His wings folded behind him and his radiance softened to a golden hue as he knelt at her side. He removed his helmet, revealing the halo of light that adorned his head. His vivid blue eyes smiled at her.

"My Father in Heaven... He... heard me?" whispered Jaden.

The winged warrior nodded his head then reached over and rested a soothing palm on her brow.

Jaden closed her eyes.

CHAPTER 17

Owen had cooked the burgers, so they would be ready when Estelle and Jaden arrived. The meal had been ready for almost two hours, so Celia went ahead and fed the children. The men had become tired of speculating and Preston called Cotton to see if he could find out if there had been any accidents between here and their designated route on Highway 6. When they didn't hear back from him within the hour, Owen and Preston decided they would check the route themselves. Charlie was on their heels as they made their way down the back steps at the main house to Owen's truck. When they saw headlights turn through the gate, a flood of relief slowed their heartbeats. That was until they realized the car that rounded the corner of the drive was the sheriff's patrol car.

Cole and Rueben had made their way down the steps by the time Cotton stopped. He didn't take the time to get out, but his window was rolled down. His voice conveyed inner turmoil when he spoke.

"Owen... Preston, ride with me. Cole we're on our way to East Dallas Memorial. There's no time to explain."

Charlie didn't ask permission; he climbed in behind his family. The Sheriff punched the gas before Charlie secured the door.

"I can't give you specifics, because I would have to speculate. Sheriff Savoy said it was bad. All I know is that their car broke down and someone stopped to help. It was a predator. Savoy said that one of the women had been strangled and was pushed in front of a log truck, and the perpetrator got away. She was thrown some 30 feet when the truck struck her. The loggers found her companion at the bottom of the levy. Apparently, she was dropped over the embankment railing and bounced some 50 feet over the rocks before she hit soft earth. The identification they retrieved from the car verified that it is them, but he said they were..." Cotton's throat constricted at the mental images of what he was saying and how these men, his friend and his son, must feel.

"What Cotton? You've got to tell us everything that you know. We have to be prepared," stated Owen.

"The fact that they both have red hair made it impossible to determine... who was who."

Owen's voice had lost all calm.

"What does that mean Emmett?! How is that possible?!"

"They were unconscious. It was dark, and they were too battered to recognize specific features from the personal photos they found with them. Listen, I know you're scared, but they are both alive! That's what's important! They had just arrived at emergency when I spoke with Savoy."

Charlie looked over at Preston. His friend sat in silence staring out the window of the car watching the darkness as it, once again, closed in on his life.

Preston approached his beautiful wife in disbelief. He stopped next to her and could not figure out why they did not see her as he did. His hand slid into hers and he caressed the raw flesh of her cheek with his lips as tears rolled down his face. He kissed her lips several times. Her breath was warm, but faint. Her eyelids began to flutter then she turned her head slightly and opened her eyes to look at him. A sweet smile tugged at the corners of her mouth. There was thankfulness in her eyes and love in her weary voice.

"Preston, I've been waiting... for you. I asked God... to let me see you one more time."

Preston mentally resisted her words. He shook his head as he battled his sorrow to breathe.

Charlie stepped up behind him. He blinked several times at the shocking sight of the beautiful girl who had brought love and joy to his friend. Her face was raw, bruised and swollen. Her lips were maimed, and the clotted blood from her nose stained her cheek. A monitor was attached to her heart, and a tube was taped to her ribs, small measures of bloody fluid emptied from her lungs and slid into the hose every few seconds.

The room, even though busy, was very quiet. Her chin quivered as she began to speak to Preston. Her voice was whisper soft, but because of the truth she spoke it was like nothing else in the world existed for those few moments.

"Baby, I know this hurts you. I'm so... sorry. I promised... I would never hurt you. I promised," she paused and tried to swallow then began again. "I promised I would never leave you." The monitor began to leap, and a warning sounded off as fresh emotion pushed what little breath she had out of her lungs.

The doctor came to her bedside and pressed his stethoscope to her chest, but she pushed it away from her body with a shaky hand. She had told him not to interfere because her husband loved her, and this was his last time he would see her on this earth. Her breath became more labored as she told Preston what was important to her.

"Preston, it's because... you dared to love me that I was saved... today. It's your birthday... but, I'm the one...

reborn. I love you so very much. Thank you... for loving me."

Preston was speechless, and he trembled with emotion as he cuddled next to her ear. Her trembling, weak hand sank into his hair while her eyes connected with Charlie's.

"Seek Him, Preston. Charlie... will help you. Your son and I will be waiting. Love again, Preston... you have so much to give. I love you... my cowboy... my husband."

Preston kissed her lips then he snuggled close to her face as he cried. Charlie and Cotton watched her caress his cheek with her own then her smile wilted, and she closed her eyes. Her small hand slipped from his head to her chest.

Owen clenched his jaw teeth as the emotion welled up inside of him. His eyes watered while the doctor explained that they could not find the baby's heartbeat, and that it was detrimental they focus their efforts on his wife's recovery from the trauma. He told Owen there was no reason why they could not get pregnant again in a few months and that he was truly blessed. The physician handed him the clipboard with the necessary documents attached.

Owen stared at the consent forms that would give the doctor permission to do whatever was necessary for the well-being of his wife. The doctor's words had left his heart weighted with sorrow, and grief churned deep inside of him. He and Estelle had dreamed big together concerning this child and their responsibility as parents. He had already picked out a name for a little girl and had day-dreamed on how her angelic voice would sound calling him 'Daddy'. He held Estelle's hand, uncertain how she would react to losing the baby after suffering the painful death of her mother; even more, he worried that she would blame him for consenting to end this wonderful dream. He believed that God was the Great Physician and was hesitant to make such a decision without Estelle's input. He had prayed all afternoon, and even now, he stood with a humble heart as he asked the Lord what he should do.

Suddenly Preston's sorrow spilled over into the room, and the doctor's practical words gained lucidity in Owen's understanding.

"NO! Jaden no! Don't go. Jaden, please don't go!" Preston scooped her up in his arms trying to hold on to the woman he loved and needed so desperately. She was at the center of his life and his happiness. And, even though he had not made a personal allegiance of trusting Charlie's God to oversee his life, he was not too proud to beg the Almighty for mercy on behalf of Jaden's. "Please, God, please... don't take her. She's so wonderful... so special. Please God, don't take the only wonderful thing I've ever known. Please!" Preston held her tighter against his chest, his strong will refused to accept that she had already passed from this world. He was so grief stricken he could not see or feel the anointing in her words, or the blessing she had just given him. He could only see that he was being abandoned again and loneliness was back to torment him, along with a heart wrenching sorrow he wished would kill him.

Preston looked at her peaceful face and finally saw what the man had done to her. He couldn't believe this was happening. His hand went to her belly where his child had thrived; he sobbed so hard it shook the small bed where she lay. He kissed her lips over and over as he gently rocked her.

"I love you... and I love my babies," he whimpered quietly.

He sucked in a deep breath and pushed her bangs back as he searched her face; it was as though he was waiting for her to open her eyes and smile at him.

Charlie absorbed his friend's sorrow and found it difficult to watch a person relinquish their hold on the one they love to the grasp of death, especially when a part of their soul is dying with them.

The attending physician cut off the mocking sound of the heart monitor and the truth of his loss became too real. Preston laid her back against the pillow then clutched her hand as his spine straightened. The doctor cut off the other machines that had attempted to keep her alive while the nurse rolled the bedside tray out of the way. Preston released his hold on her and took a step back. His hand went to his chest and rubbed the plane over his heart as he sucked in a couple of deep breaths then his fingers raked through his hair as he shook his head. It was final. His wife was gone, and he was on his own for sure this time.

Preston was overwrought by the cruelty of life as he knew it. The storm of emotions that rose in him was too much to contain. He spun around sending an angry and powerful fist through the window. The wire mesh inside the glass grabbed his wrist and held on. Preston's anguish was so great that his strength was amplified, and he yanked his hand back through the jagged and gnarly edges, not caring that they sliced at his flesh.

"Preston, don't Son!" Cotton rushed to Preston's assistance, but he was distraught with grief and could not listen to reason. Cotton wrapped his arms around the young man in a bear-hug then confined him against the wall. He didn't know what to say or how to help, so he spoke from his heart.

"I love you, Preston. You're not alone Son, I swear... you're not alone." He held on tight to the heartbroken young man because he understood the sinkhole of despair that could swallow a person if someone who cared did not intercede. "I won't leave you, Preston. I swear no matter what... I won't let you down."

Finally, Preston's arms grabbed a hold on him.

"I need her, Sheriff. How do I live now? How do I live without her... without my heart? I got nobody now."

"Yes, you do, Preston. I promise... we'll figure it out together."

Cotton swallowed the gagging chunk of possessiveness that was stuck in his throat as his son cried in his arms. He wasn't aware of just how much blood Preston was losing until the young man's knees buckled forcing Cotton to go to the floor with him.

Charlie dragged his sleeve over his eyes as he looked at his friend and then to the small, broken woman that was illuminated by the florescent light over the bed. Her words of hope had attached themselves to his heart. Charlie knew that she was trying to share something momentous with Preston; she wanted him to know that she had met Christ on this day. Chills ran over Charlie's arms and scalp at the thought. He realized that Preston's birthday would never be the same for any of them. He knew this day would never be a day of celebration for Preston again, not until his friend discovered for himself that which Jaden had found. Charlie felt an awesome responsibility stir inside of him because Jaden had left him with the charge to help Preston find the truth. His attention traded off between his new friend's lifeless body and the distraught sorrow of his kindred brother. Charlie asked the Almighty to show him how to help Preston look past his sorrow to gain understanding after experiencing something so tragic and immobilizing to his heart and his spirit.

Charlie and Eli were mesmerized by the magnificent southern palace that stood at the end of the tree covered lane beyond the cemetery. The rumors Charlie had heard at school concerning Whisper Bluff were accurate. It was huge, and it looked spooky, but it was also stately and fascinatingly beautiful. Charlie thought back to the first time Preston had come over for supper. He and Owen unintentionally entertained Estelle and him most of the evening as they poked fun at each other's sense of humor. When the time came that Preston had to leave, Owen made sure that his buddy knew he was welcome in their home any time. That night while they helped Estelle clean up the kitchen, his brother asked him how much he knew about Preston. That was when he first learned that Preston came from a long line of French entrepreneurs, the last being his mother who had died when he was a boy. Preston had never talked about this place, and because he ignored the instigators at school and their ghostly stories about the house, Charlie had always done the same thing. He knew where Preston lived even though the Colonel's reputation prevented Owen from allowing him to visit the houseboat. His friend didn't hang out there anymore than he had to, so it had never been an issue for either of them. He supposed that was the reason why he had never really thought about his buddy's heritage. But this place was incredible, and he couldn't help but wonder what had transpired in the past that had affected Preston's right to call this place home.

Eli's voice interrupted Charlie's thoughts. He commented that his friends at school tell lies about an old ghost that lives in the house. Charlie shrugged it off and changed the subject to the task at hand. They accessed the small and isolated plot of ground where Preston's kin were buried and agreed on an organized plan of action to refurbish the aged and overrun cemetery. Charlie unloaded the lawn mower from the back of Owen's truck while Eli gathered the yard tools and gas can. Charlie was curious as to why Preston had never mentioned this place, especially since his entire family was buried there. It was an undeniable fact that Preston was connected to this place and the house. The ivory colored angel glowed as it caught a ray of sunshine, the name and date below it was as Sheriff Cotton had said. That was the spot where Preston's mother rested, and he wanted Jaden to be next to her.

Charlie knew Eli's young heart hurt for Preston, and he wanted to do something to help. He had asked if he could help him with this important task, and now that they had assessed all that was needed, Charlie was glad that Eli had offered. The younger boy mowed the healthy grass in and around the small graveyard while Charlie cleaned the headstones and added a bouquet of new flowers to each one. He raked and tidied up the grounds and existing graves while Eli finished up on the other side of the overgrown fence.

The wrought iron boundary was something they would tackle together. Clearly, someone cared about the place because the wild foliage which hindered the structure was dead and dry from being cut off at the roots. Considering it was Sheriff Cotton who asked this of him, and then produced a box from the trunk of his car that contained 24 cans of white enamel spray paint and a wire brush, Charlie accepted the challenge without needing or expecting an explanation. He knew Sheriff Cotton cared about Preston and that was good enough for Charlie.

Eli untangled and gathered the dead vines from the fence, and Charlie came behind him with a wire brush and knocked off the loose paint and trash from the spindles, so the paint would adhere to the iron.

Charlie was proud he had been asked to oversee this important and special task of bringing the small cemetery back to a respectful nature. He had discovered five generations of Preston's grandparents and an aunt were buried here with his mother. He also found eight separate graves on the far side of the cemetery with headstones that bore the name, 'Silver'. He was curious, but now was not the time to study on such a thing, so he didn't mention them to Eli either. Their attention and energy had to stay focused on the needs of their friend. The first was getting the cemetery ready because the funeral home would be there that afternoon to dig the grave.

Eli dumped the last wheelbarrow of weeds on the trash pile at the edge of the woods, and then he came back to where Charlie worked. He stopped a few feet away and picked up the cardboard box that held the paint cans then gathered several more empties which Charlie had discarded and added them to the carton. Eli admired their handy work while conscious of the sadness that moved inside of him because of this tragedy which had changed Preston's life. He had felt this way one other time in his life and, because he still missed Travis' mom, he knew a little about the sorrow and hurt that had come to his older friend.

Charlie nudged Eli's shoulder as he stopped next to him and looked at their accomplishments. The headstones were each distinctive, clean and ready for visitors. His eyes clung to the grassy spot next to Preston's mom he had marked with the paint. He realized Preston was right, this was Jaden's family. He suddenly imagined Jaden Michelle Reid, walking through the gates of heaven carrying a small baby in her arms and being greeted by her mother-in-law, and all the rest of Preston's family. A warm peacefulness spread through Charlie's chest at the thought, until Preston's tormented expression reminded him that she and Estelle had been victimized by a stranger and left for dead.

Charlie wanted to show his appreciation to Eli for his help, so he stopped at the drive-in to treat him to a milkshake, burger and some fries. He was worried about Preston and he guessed Eli could tell because the younger boy suggested they eat while they drove back to the ranch. The police radio was on the seat between them. Charlie turned the truck radio down when he heard the transmission come across the airway that the Dallas County Sheriff's Department had received an anonymous report that could be connected to the perpetrator in the assault on Woodswamp Road. He and Eli listened carefully, but there were no details that Charlie could recognize. They heard Sheriff Cotton acknowledge the information.

Charlie drove carefully; his driver's license was only two weeks old, and he wasn't taking any chances with Eli. They stopped in front of the stable office at the ranch. He thanked his buddy again for the help and went to the office to speak to Cole and Rueben. He called Owen while he was there to check on Estelle. They talked a few minutes then he handed the phone off to Rueben and left. Cole called to him as Charlie opened the door of the truck. He turned to see the mountain of a man jog toward him.

"Charles, it's not my intention to make you feel like you can't wipe your own nose, but... I just want you to know that I'm here if you need me. What's happened is so unbelievably heartbreaking and unfair. I know you've been in the thick of things with Preston... and Owen." He exhaled as he looked Charlie in the eye then he reached over and laid his large hand on his shoulder. "I'm a little worried about you... knowing how sensitive you are to pain of this nature. If you need me, Charles, or you think there is anything I can do to help... please tell me."

Charlie released a pent-up sigh that he didn't know he was holding on to. This man had always been tuned into him and Charlie was glad that he cared so much about him. He was almost eye level with the man now and possessed a confidence in their relationship that enabled him to speak freely about what troubled him.

"Sir... I was standing next to her and Preston in the emergency room. She knew she was dying, but she wasn't scared. I saw peace in her eyes. The only thing that troubled her was leaving Preston without the spiritual assurance she had found." He shared her message of faith to Preston with the older man, and what she had asked of him just before she passed. Mr. Silver's eyes were the windows to an understanding soul. "Don't worry about me, Sir, I have my family. Other than the Colonel, Preston doesn't have a soul when it comes to blood kin. I've got to be solid for my friend... just like you were for me and Owen. Still, he may need to talk to you, Sir, with all due respect... you may be the only one that can understand his loss enough to help him."

Cole squeezed his shoulder lovingly as he nodded his head.

"We love him. He is a member of this family, Charles, and he always will be. He's going to need you; it's going to get harder for him before it gets better. It's probably going to get hard for you to deal with him too, but don't give up on him."

Charlie nodded his head as he smiled at Cole.

"No Sir, I'll never give up on the people I love."

Ava agreed with Preston that a simple graveside service would be exactly the way Jaden would see things.

The young man managed to make the necessary decisions, choosing a hand-rubbed walnut casket with silver hardware and a blanket of beautiful white lilies and yellow roses. The only decision he had asked for help in deciding was the time for the service.

He expressed a desire to go ahead and choose a headstone for her while he was there. He had been drawn to a specific photograph in the collage of advertisements on the wall while they waited for the funeral home representative. It was the reason why he chose the oblong pedestal of polished gray marble; the front was carved like a scroll, so the name could be added. Ava thought it an odd choice, then Preston reached across the desk and picked up the brochure of artistic hand-carved statues which had not been made available to him. He turned several pages then stopped and pointed to the one that spoke to him. Tears rushed Ava's eyes at the sight of the celestial statue that was the color of alabaster. The angel was sitting with her legs folded to one side and holding a small baby in her arms. She wore a halo of rose buds; her wings were tucked close to her body and her long hair flowed over her shoulder in a cascade of whimsical stone swirls. Her gown was carved in soft folds around her legs so that her toes peeked out from under the hem, and her mouth was open as though she were singing to the sleeping infant. She was accompanied by a small rabbit at her knee and a sparrow was perched on her shoulder. It was the most breathtaking and elegant thing Ava had ever seen. She had to fight to hold on to her composure as Preston told the representative that he didn't care how much it cost. The representative assured him that the statue could be placed on the marble pedestal and it would be a lovely memorial to his beloved wife. Preston finalized the arrangements by adding his initials next to the printed information that would be carved on the face of the pedestal's scroll then he took out his checkbook from his shirt pocket. Because the hand he depended on was bandaged, Preston wrote out the bank draft that would bury the love of his life with a shaky left hand. Ava witnessed the older man squat down next to him to hold the small pad steady. Preston signed it then pushed it towards the older gentleman. The sheriff tore out the draft and left it on the desk then encouraged Preston to come outside with him for some fresh air. Ava had taken an immediate liking to Sheriff Cotton, who seemed to love this young man like his own.

Ava thought of Nevell, her new husband. He was a soldier and had come home on furlough to marry her. Jaden and Preston had celebrated the day with them along with the rest of her family. She ran her hand over her middle where he had left their baby growing inside her body. She had only found out on Friday that it was true. She had not had a chance to share the news with Jaden. She wouldn't get to now. Ava was having trouble accepting the fact that her best friend was gone. The outrageous cruelty that was inflicted on Jaden haunted Ava's spirit; however, watching Preston's courage, knowing his sorrow was even greater than her own, touched her to the core of her soul. The chivalry he expended on Jaden's behalf the day they had met was the same valor he displayed in her death. Ava knew the young man was hanging on to his composure by a thread, but she also knew that his heart and his will were strong. She believed the impact Jaden had on their lives was anointed and part of a greater plan. She prayed that time would heal Preston and that he would find the joy in his time with Jaden. Ava understood the hurt that had taken root inside of him, and in honor of her friend, she was going to make sure her life stayed connected to Preston's.

Charlie went by the house to shower and change into fresh clothes. He took his black dress pants and a white, long sleeve shirt from his closet then thought of the black dress coat Preston had worn in the wedding. He retrieved the garment from the hall closet, secured the back door and headed for the truck. He noticed when he backed out that he needed fuel and stopped at the station on Highway 11 to fill up the tank. He bought a root beer and a bag of corn chips to munch on the way to Preston's.

His thoughts bounced around a few minutes before landing on his sister-in-law and the conversation he had with his brother. Owen had been with her every minute, but Estelle had not gained full consciousness due to being medicated. He wanted to be there for Owen, but his brother was supersensitive to Preston's loss and didn't want him to be alone. Owen had admitted that he was worried about Estelle's reaction when she found out about Jaden.

Charlie thought about Preston's numb response concerning the injuries that had caused her death. Ava Enriquez had spoken to the coroner and, out of professional courtesy, was given the specifics of what caused her death. He was by Preston's side when she shared them with his friend. Jaden's injuries had been extensive. It was determined that she had died from heart failure due to a collapsed lung, but the fractured skull and hemorrhaging on her brain would have left her in a coma with a slower prognosis of death. It was a miracle that she had hung on long enough to see Preston. Their baby had died during the brutal, sexual assault inflicted by the man that had not yet been identified. The news had sent Preston into a devastated silence.

He had learned at an early age that there were many faces of death, and part of life was learning and trying to understand the shadowed countenance as it challenged the living. It is a fact that death goes hand in hand with life; however, this part of life was complicated and often traumatizing to a person. He did not remember his real father, and he tried every day to not think about L.B. Thomas. The cruel man's death had been justified, but it had left scars on a young boy's body and life that had not gone away with age. It was the same for Owen; he had witnessed the tragic accident that killed their father, just as Estelle had been helpless to save her mother from the flames that engulfed their house.

Charlie thought of Grandpa Hawk and the celebration which took place when he passed away. Pastor Storey's words at the service had been a new lesson for him and he would always remember them.

'Hallelujah! Benjamin Elijah Hawk welcomed and embraced death. He lived his life in preparation for Heaven. He sowed good seeds that yielded strong, spiritual fruit then left the baggage of this world behind and danced his way through the pearly gates in celebration of his journey which was complete'.

That was the day Charlie fully understood that Grandpa Hawk's life was a living testament. He understood the reality of free-will which makes it possible for mankind to prepare in this world to enter the next. He understood and willfully embraced his faith in Father God and was committed to living life to reflect it. He understood that a person could live with such devotion to the Maker, their friends and loved ones, that in death, those left behind could celebrate a journey that ended at the gates of Heaven. He had never known Papa Silver, but he remembered Grandpa Hawk saying that Jacob was waiting for him on the bank of the Jordan River and they were going fishing.

Charlie realized Jaden's death was another of life's lessons for him. His eyes were opened to the harsh and ungodly act of premeditated murder driven by hatred. This face of death denied the living of all understanding, snubbed justice and threatened peace. This face of death was so painful and senseless that sometimes a loved one never recovered. The emptiness and the hollowness of loss were like a mortal injury. Charlie understood that this is what had happened to his friend. He thought about the hole in his own life that was created by Jaden's death. He had cared for her because she brought so much joy to Preston's life, and a treasured friendship to his. He missed her deeply and he would never forget her. He couldn't even begin to imagine the depth of pain his friend was suffering. He didn't know how Preston would choose to approach life after this. He wasn't sure how to help him, but he was determined to try.

Charlie had stayed by his friend's side since late Saturday night. Preston had ended up with 62 stitches in his hand and wrist. He had been medicated upon leaving the hospital, but once at home he had refused to take anything else. That night, they sat outside on the boat deck until the wee hours of the morning. They exchanged very little conversation, but when they did, it was about Jaden and something they had done together. He hoped Preston did not feel smothered, but when he had asked if he wanted to be alone, his friend had asked him not to leave.

Sheriff Cotton was never too far away from him either. Preston had not wanted to leave the boat, but Cotton had tactfully pointed out that Jaden's husband was the only one who should decide the burial arrangements for her. Ava had offered to meet Preston and the sheriff at the funeral home on Monday morning, should there be any details in which they needed help. It was the opportunity Charlie needed to attend to the cemetery.

Sheriff Hillard Savoy was grasping at straws in the investigation. He did not have the opportunity to speak with Jaden before she passed away, and the doctors had kept Estelle medicated, feeling it was in her best interest until she was stronger.

The circumstances surrounding the attack were sketchy. The drivers of the log truck could only attest to the moment she had appeared in the road in front of them. They had given a description of the vehicle the perpetrator was driving, but it was dark, and they were not certain of the make and model. They told Savoy they had been so shocked when the angels came out of the darkness that they didn't see much else. The only leads the Sheriff's Department had concerning the crime was that the driver of the vehicle which had fled the scene was their perpetrator, and hopefully Estelle Kagel could identify him. The physician in charge of Estelle Kagel's health had told Sheriff Savoy that she had been so traumatized by the ordeal; she should be allowed to recall the details on her own. Clearly, the circumstances were working against them in solving this horrific crime.

Sheriff Cotton instructed Floyd Cox to tow Jaden's car to the county garage for safekeeping, and to see if he could determine why the car had left the women stranded on the roadside. He had gone over it with the skill of an ace mechanic, and after draining the gas tank, discovered almost a pint of water in it. He assured Cotton and Sheriff Savoy that this amount of water was more than condensation; someone had purposely put it there.

CHAPTER 18

A cab was pulling out of Preston's driveway as Charlie slowed down to turn in at the houseboat. He was relieved to see Sheriff Cotton's patrol car under the large oak; it meant that Preston had not been alone while he was at the cemetery. Charlie parked next to the sheriff's car then gathered the clothing and got out. He started across the yard towards the boardwalk when Colonel Reid and Sheriff Cotton walked out onto the deck of the houseboat. They stopped next to each other facing the slough. He heard the Colonel ask Sheriff Cotton if he had told Preston yet. The sheriff replied, no. He told the Colonel he had thought about it and he did not want to risk their friendship by complicating it with the mistakes neither of them could change. The Colonel insisted that Preston had a right to know the truth.

Charlie didn't understand what he had heard; however, a strange feeling came over him. He sensed that if they knew he was near, the verbal exchange would not have taken place. Whatever was at the heart of their words was obviously important to both men, and none of his business. He had come too close not to be noticed, so

Charlie tossed the hanging clothes over his shoulder and called out a greeting. He entered through the gate hoping the expression on his face was close to natural.

"Colonel, Sir, I'm glad you are here." Charlie stuck his hand out as he approached the man. The Colonel caught his hand in a tight angry grip. Charlie turned to Sheriff Cotton as he told him.

"It's finished, Sheriff. Can you think of anything else that needs to be done? I brought the black coat he wore from the wedding... just in case." Sheriff Cotton had been to the barber shop since he saw him earlier that morning. His hair was cut short and groomed back away from his forehead, and his face had been shaven leaving his beard neatly trimmed to frame his mouth. It was the first time Charlie had ever seen this much of his face. He tried not to stare, but he couldn't help but notice a resemblance between this man and his best friend. Preston's square jaws were distinctive, and after meeting Jaden, he had begun to grow his mustache and beard to frame his mouth.

Sheriff Cotton shook Charlie's hand and smiled. Charlie noticed that their eyebrows were identical in shape, just like the quirky growth of their hairline over their right eye.

"You're a true-blue friend, Charlie. He's very lucky to have you."

Charlie's observing eyes went to the dimple in the sheriff's cheek that had always been concealed by his beard. He forced his mind to process what the sheriff had said amid being so distracted.

"Umm, no Sir, he was lucky to have Jaden... even for the short season. She was awesome." He swallowed because his throat was suddenly dry. "Is he okay? Can I go in?"

Cotton nodded his head.

"Sure Charlie. He laid down when we got back from the funeral home."

"He hasn't slept. I stayed up all night with him Saturday and yesterday. We went to bed around 3:00 a.m. this morning. I woke up a few hours later and went to check on him; I found him sitting out here. He drank a glass of milk with me, but he would not let me fix him anything to eat."

Charlie excused himself politely then turned to leave them, but Cotton spoke to him again before he got to the door. He stopped and faced the man out of respect.

"Charlie, do you know if Preston has had a confrontation with anyone since he met Jaden?"

Charlie's brows shifted, and his eyes lit up in response to the memory of Preston shutting-down the tall guy at the rodeo.

"Yes Sir, there was a confrontation at the rodeo back in July. I saw this tall, wiry guy talking to Jaden. He was holding her arm... like he was angry and not going to allow her to walk away. When she snatched herself free of him, he grabbed her and started pushing her through the crowd towards the side door of the equestrian center. I was mounted on Ransom on the other side of the arena, or I wouldn't have seen what was happening. I went and got Preston. The guy was so tall, and he had a yellow feather sticking in the band of the black hat he was wearing; it was easy to spot him again in the crowd. He was moving fast and practically dragging her through the maze of parked cars, but Ransom made it easy to catch up to them. Preston called out to her and the guy shoved her to the ground as he turned to face us. Preston slid off Ransom and in two steps he punched the guy in the gut so hard he threw up as he went to his knees. He tried to swing at Preston, but Cuz jacked him in the jaw. We left him lying there holding his gut and rolling around on the ground because Jaden had got up running. When Preston caught up to her, she was a mess... crying and shaking all over. She was embarrassed that he had come to her defense again." Charlie stopped suddenly and cut his eyes to the Colonel. "No disrespect intended, Sir."

Colonel Reid shook his head as he responded.

"None taken, Charlie... finish what you were saying."

"Well, she said they had dated a couple of months last year... until he hurt her. She said he broke her collar bone and some of her fingers... so she dumped him. She said he wouldn't leave her alone, and she had to move to get any peace." Charlie took a step towards them as he rubbed his brow and thought about that night. "Umm, seems like his name was... Russ. No wait, it was Russell. I remember her saying he worked for an off-shore company... umm, Trans-Bexx Drilling. Dang, what was his last name?" mumbled Charlie as he searched his memory. "Butler! That's his name, Sheriff... Russell Butler."

Cotton looked at Dane then started walking towards the gate. He cuffed Charlie on the shoulder in appreciation as he passed by him.

"I need to use the radio. Thanks, Charlie."

Charlie watched Cotton undertake the boardwalk in a fast pace to his patrol car.

"Did Butler do this, Sheriff?" asked Charlie.

Cotton looked back at him as he answered.

"I don't know yet... stay with Preston, Charlie."

Charlie was stunned at this development; however, it made perfect sense that Russell Butler would be the villain that had committed such a wicked deed. He turned back to the Colonel. The hard and chiseled man leaned against the railing as he touched his lighter to the end of a fresh cigarette. He took a long drag on it then blew the smoke up into the atmosphere before he told Charlie what he wanted to know.

"He can't tell you the truth because they haven't located Butler yet. They had an anonymous tip this afternoon. The guy that called said Butler was trying to sell a diamond ring and wedding band because he needed money to get out of town. It was odd that the caller would connect that fact to the girl that was killed on Wood Swamp Road. It was a red flag. When asked about it the dumb-ass panicked and hung up. It never crossed his mind that they would obtain his information from the phone company. Law enforcement showed up on his doorstep and he spilled his guts. He was pissed-off and called in because his so-called buddy, Russell Butler, broke his nose when he refused to part with any cash. Apparently, Butler let it slip during his unwarranted solicitation of funds that he had witnessed an accident at that location and he'd get blamed for it." The Colonel's tone of voice made the hair on Charlie's arms shift beneath the sleeves of his shirt. "You just verified for law enforcement that Butler had a volatile connection to the victim, prior to the attack and her death. He's the guilty bastard, Charlie. But don't worry... his hours are numbered. Preston's gonna have justice, I owe it to him."

The Colonel took another long drag of the cigarette then flicked the glowing remains into the still water of the cove.

"I'm out of cigarettes, and I need to check in with my boss. I'm going to run to the store to use the phone... tell Preston I took the truck and I'll be back in a few minutes. You need anything?"

Charlie shook his head for he was too overwhelmed by this truth to speak.

Colonel Reid turned the carton of milk up and gulped down the last swig as he held the receiver of the pay phone to his ear. He scanned the darkness out of habit while he waited for the person, he had contacted earlier that day to answer.

"Kingston Five," answered the voice on the other end of the connection.

"Rook... Kingston Five, copy this.

"Go ahead Rook," responded the voice, somewhat mechanically.

"White male... brown hair... 190 pounds... six feet and four inches. Name... Butler, Russell. Repeat... Butler, Russell, Trans-Bexx Drilling... white Chevrolet truck... License R H B 788. Repeat... License... Ready Hell Bound 788. Dallas resident... locate him. Notify me when it's done. No, there's a reliable witness. I'll judge him. He'll make reparation for what he's done; he won't have a choice."

The Colonel hung up and stood there a moment as his gut twisted into a punishing, tight fist of pain that begged him for alcohol. Dane exhaled and looked out over the river. He had to stay in control. The way he saw it, this was the most important job of his life. This was something he could do for Preston that no one else could, especially Cotton. He knew how to do this, and he was good at it.

Estelle opened her eyes but squinted at the brightness of the overhead light and closed them again. She tried to remember what time Owen had come to bed; she couldn't remember kissing him goodnight either. She couldn't remember what day it was, or why she would still be in bed with the sun bright as noon.

She tossed the cover back and swung her legs off the bed. The sudden pain in her head and her belly stopped her, along with the gentle touch of the man she loved. She opened her eyes.

Owen squatted down in front of her.

"Hey Darlin', where ya going?" He smiled and pushed her hair back away from her bandaged brow.

Estelle looked at him a moment then at her surroundings. A frown distorted her face then she looked down at her middle. She blinked several times then it all came rushing back.

"Owen... our baby?!" Tears filled her eyes as she touched her empty belly. "I lost the baby?"

Owen couldn't stop the emotion that seeped from the corners of his eyes.

"The doctor said we can try again in a few months, Honey. I still have you, Estelle. I still have you... and that's what matters most," he told her softly. He sat down next to her and pulled her into his arms.

Estelle laid her head on his shoulder and wept. Her sorrow had an unmerciful grip on his heart and was disparaging to his spirit. He silently asked God to help him know what to do because he didn't think she could deal with the rest of it.

"I... remember!" she mumbled then looked at him with fearfulness in her eyes. "Owen, that wicked and brutal man did this to us. He deliberately put water in the gas tank, so we would break down. He was proud of his self... and even boasted about it. He was pure evil." Estelle crossed her arms as though a sudden chill attacked her body. "Jaden was so brave. I wish I could be like her. She's a little thing, but she fights like a feral barn cat."

Estelle looked at her hand and all the things that were attached to her.

"What day is it? Where is she? I want to go home. I need to see Jaden. I need to see for myself that she's all right. She saved my life, Owen. She protected me." Estelle pushed at his arms, so he would get up and help her make this happen. "Come on... help me! I need to go home."

Owen sat there; the expression on his face was pained.

Estelle was bothered by the fact that he made no effort to do as she asked.

"Owen, what's wrong with you?"

He stood up and began to fuss over her cover while his mind sorted through all the things that he needed to tell her and where he should start. He chose the easiest answer first.

"It's Monday afternoon, Honey. You've been through a lot. Please, just lay back... you need to rest."

Estelle did just the opposite and stood on wobbly but determined legs.

"No, I can't! I need to see Jaden. You don't understand what happened between us. She's been curious to know about the Bible and how to live a spiritual life. She confided in me about her life... the things she didn't understand. I shared our faith with her, Owen. I spoke to her about trusting the Lord. We shared things. We shared things other people wouldn't understand. We... we became sisters in Christ. I know we did."

She placed her palms on the front of her husband's shirt to gain his full attention because he had not looked her in the eye since she mentioned Jaden's name.

"What are you not telling me, Owen? He hurt her, didn't he?"

Owen shook his head.

"Estelle... Honey..." Owen paused, his throat constricted at the sorrowful truth that he held inside of him.

"Please... just tell me," she insisted.

Owen didn't know anything else to do but tell her the truth. She knew something was wrong; she would have sensed it from anyone who had been here with her. He was glad it was him. Owen's voice was gentle but straight forward as he looked her in the eye and gave her the news.

"He left both of you for dead, Honey. Jaden's gone. She died two days ago lying next to you in the emergency room. Her funeral is tomorrow afternoon. I'm so full of sorrow, and yet... I'm full of thankfulness that I still have you with me." He observed his wife as she went silent and all the color drained from her face. Her knees buckled, and he held her in strong-weak arms as she sat back down on the bed. "I'll call the nurse for a sedative," he stated softly then reached for the call button.

Estelle put her hand over it as she shook her head. When her eyes met his again, there was something different in them. He saw sorrow, but there was also resolution. It was in her voice as well.

"Ask them to discharge me. I can't stay here any longer. I need to be with Preston. I... I love that girl." Her face distorted as comprehension of what he had told her tried to take over her will. She covered her mouth a moment to compose herself then she began again. "Please don't make me stay here while they lay her to rest. Please don't make me feel like I let her down a second time. She needs me to see to Preston. I know that is what she would want me to do. I need to do that for her. I've got to be there! Help me do this for her, Owen. Please!"

Owen knew this woman too well to think that he could deny her this. She had befriended Preston and then Jaden with her whole heart because she loved his little brother the same way. Estelle didn't know how to love any other way.

"Alright Honey, I'll go see if the doctor's in the hospital. You rest for me. I'll be back as fast as I can." He thoughtfully lifted her feet on to the bed as she lay back then he covered her. He kissed her brow, and she gripped the sleeve of his shirt for a moment. He didn't want to leave her, but he had promised to do this for her. He had almost reached the door when she asked him.

"Is he in jail, Owen?"

"No, Honey. They don't have any idea who they are looking for. There were no witnesses, and there was only time for Preston to talk to her a few short minutes before she passed. He's devastated, Honey... and I still have my heart to put my arms around. I'm scared for him. I don't know how he's going to deal with this. Charlie's so worried about him, he hasn't left Preston's side."

Estelle stared aimlessly at the door her husband had closed as he left. Her heart felt like a stone inside her chest. She sucked in a broken breath as her mind showed her Jaden's smiling face. She remembered how they laughed together, and how the sun shone down on them while the wind swirled around their bodies as they rolled down the highway that afternoon. She recalled some of the plans they had talked about and how wonderful it was going to be to raise their babies together. Estelle held on to the bed rail as she slowly rotated to her back and closed her eyes. She began to pray but couldn't get past the images of the enraged man choking Jaden and shaking her with fury. Estelle covered her face with both hands as she tried to talk to God and started over for the third time. Finally, she shook her head and told Him she was sorry, but she just couldn't manage it at that moment. Her pain consumed her then filled the room.

The sun came up on Tuesday morning; the birds sang a joyful song while a gentle wind blew the clouds to the east. The trees swayed against a vibrant prism of color as the sun caressed everything it touched with tenderness. The beauty and magic of this day suggested that Mother Earth did not notice Preston's world had become an empty, miserable place.

Arrangements were made for the Gillis' housekeeper to care for the girls; however, the boys would not be left out of this day. Cole had talked with Travis and was honest about what had happened to Jaden without offering unnecessary details. Travis had asked a couple of questions, but Cole sensed that the boy understood more than he gave him credit. The important thing was that both boys knew Preston had lost something very precious.

Cole looked in the rearview mirror at the silent young man whose turbulent life had once again been turned upside down by someone else's temper and lack of self-control. Preston didn't look well. He was pale and had dark circles under his swollen and bloodshot eyes. Charlie had told him that Preston had not slept since Friday night and neither he nor Sheriff Cotton had been able to get him to eat anything. Preston kept his thoughts to himself; those that loved him felt helpless in the face of this painful tragedy. What had happened had impacted all of them, yet they had each other. Cole prayed Preston would allow them to be there for him.

Charlie had ridden in the backseat of Cole's sedan next to his friend, while Travis and Eli sat in the front with Cole. Charlie felt a spark of hope when he saw Pastor Storey's car drive slowly into the graveled clearing and park beneath the trees. His mind went back to Sunday afternoon when he had answered Preston's door and found the aging shepherd standing there with his Bible in his hand. His greeting was friendly and his concern for Preston sincere, admitting that he was apprehensive about how his visit would be received.

He had introduced the aging shepherd to his best friend then fixed them a glass of tea before he excused himself outside to wait on the deck so Pastor Storey and Preston could have some privacy. He prayed his friend would not be upset by the visit from someone who didn't really know him or Jaden. Preston had never attended church with him in all the times he had asked. He knew Preston was self-conscious because of his father's reputation; sometimes people labeled him with it and treated him as such. He had always accepted Preston's decision not to accompany him to service. His friend was used to being cautious as not to invite ridicule and bring unfair judgment on himself.

That afternoon he had shoved nervous hands to the bottom of his pockets to wait; it had been a long time since he had felt a surge of perpetual hope clash into a hesitation of this magnitude. But to his surprise, Pastor Storey opened the door and asked him if he would join them in prayer and getting to know one another. Pastor Storey was wise and recognized that Preston was just as nervous to reach out to him as he was to extend his belated love and concern after Jaden's tragic death. He would never forget the strength in Preston's grip when he sat down next to his friend. Pastor Storey prayed for him, and then he thanked the Almighty for the precious gift of friendship and love they had all received from Jaden Reid. His friend listened with his heart as Pastor Storey spoke to him. He confessed to Preston that he had humbled himself on his knees before God to gain the strength he needed to be able to come to him. He apologized to Preston for not being brave enough to confront his father with courage and love on his behalf.

Pastor Storey had surprised them when he told Preston he had a personal encounter with Jaden Reid the previous Thursday. He explained how she had gone out of her way to care for him in his hour of need. He told Preston she had shared her deepest fear with him, as well as her most treasured gift, which was her husband's love. He told

Preston he had peace in his spirit concerning Jaden and he had dreamed of her the previous night. Pastor Storey shared that in the dream Jaden was gently rocking side to side while she softly sang to the infant in her arms. When she looked up at him, she smiled then sang to him as well. The old shepherd sang the song to them in a tender melodic voice, 'Jesus loves His little children'.

He had almost lost his composure when Preston broke down in tears and told Pastor Storey that Jaden was carrying their child when she died. He had not expected to hear Preston tell the old shepherd about Jaden's last words to him. He had wondered if his friend had truly heard her through his distress and sorrow. Even though her words were impressed on Preston's heart and mind, he did not understand what it meant, and he asked for clarification.

Pastor Storey smiled and nodded his head as he expounded on his convictions in relation to Preston's question. He explained that Jaden had responded to the spiritual truth which had taken root in her heart and reached out to the Almighty asking to be recognized as His child. She had displayed her faith in something greater than herself, and in doing so, she gained her place in Heaven.

Charlie knew without a doubt the Maker was at work in all this pain, for calm had begun to ease his heartache. He gripped Preston's shoulder as the wise man of God held his friend in loving arms and prayed for him. He remembered the way Preston held Pastor Storey as he cried so hard, he trembled. Preston had asked Pastor Storey if he would come today and share what he had told him. The old shepherd was here out of respect to Jaden and the promise he had made Preston.

The Enriquez's arrived. Rueben and Celia pulled in behind them with Mr. and Mrs. Gillis in the truck. The Colonel had left with Cotton early that morning and was arriving with those who came to pay their respects and support Preston, even Dr. Jordan and Joel had come to join them.

When the long, white station wagon appeared at the brick columns then slowly rolled through them, Preston leaned forward and put his face in his hands. He didn't make a sound, but Cole could see him shaking. He told the boys to go wait with Celia and Rueben for a few minutes. Charlie retrieved his guitar out of the trunk and followed the younger boys because he wanted Mr. Silver to have a few minutes with Preston. He wanted his friend to have the privacy he needed to feel everything he was feeling.

Cole got out and opened the back door then squatted down next to Preston. He recalled the day he had buried Lana as he reached in his coat pocket and took out the small blue handkerchief and put it in the young man's hand.

"Preston, I don't have any words that will make this hurt... or this tremendous burden you're carrying any easier. I don't want to belittle your pain by comparing it to my own. I just want you to know that you married one of the most precious little ladies I've ever known, and so did I. You should grieve for her, Preston, and honor her by treasuring the love you two shared. What you found with Jaden is a true miracle! Y'all found each other because you cared more about someone else than yourself, most people don't... or won't... give of themselves for the good of another. They squander their life in search of worldly things to make them happy and wonder why they are so miserable. Son, look at me for a minute... this is important."

The young man respectfully did as he asked. Cole's discernment and kindness emanated from him as he gave something meaningful and very personal to help this heartbroken young man.

"When I lost Lana, I thought no one could understand what I was feeling unless they had been dropped into the middle of the ocean of sorrow in which I was sinking. I felt like I was going to drown and the biggest part of my spirit... the part that belonged to her... wished I could. I was smothering in anger, regret and disappointment. Breathing was painful and remembering all that 'was' hurt even worse. When I considered all that had been stolen from my life... existing seemed to be all that was left. When I compared that to the plans we had made, I felt cheated and empty. I looked at my little boy, who was grieving too, and a tiny and helpless baby girl; I was all they had, and I was terrified. I didn't feel like I had anything good inside of me... and certainly nothing that my children needed.

"I was sitting in the stable office one afternoon... going through the motions of my life; I had a couple of weeks of existence behind me. It was late in the afternoon and I almost had another day finished. I went to the drink box and got an orange soda. They weren't my favorite, but everything I did reflected her absence in my life and Lana craved them like a hummingbird did a flower. She was disciplined about such things, but occasionally she would give in to the weakness of wanting one. She would drink it so fast; I would tease her about needing the nectar like a hummingbird. My wife was diabetic; the illness is what took her from me.

"Anyway, I turned the bottle up and took a drink. I was careless and went through the movements too fast and the soda bubbled up and ran over on me and the desk. I reached for some napkins off the side table and when I turned back, a hummingbird flew in through the door. The tiny thing was like a ricocheting bullet, darting around the office. Suddenly, the little bird circled my head several times; it got so close the tip of her wing tickled my cheek. I watched as it flittered back and forth across the desk for a few seconds then it hovered over the spilled soda and started to drink. The wings hummed a magical sound as it fearlessly floated some 18 inches in front of me and drank the orange soda. I remember thinking how awesome it was to see something so beautiful and delicate... something that's usually too fast for the human eye to behold. And suddenly, I realized the moment was so much more than that Preston. I realized the little bird was an angel. A messenger of hope and a reminder she was still with me in a multitude of ways if I would only take the time to see with my heart rather than only feel. That afternoon... in the magic of those few minutes, I felt her all around me.

"Preston, you're going to find out in the most unexpected of times, she'll reach out to you. You'll begin to listen and look around your life each day for a glimpse of her. You'll feel her... and you'll know she's with you. She will never pass from your heart. I speak the truth to you, Son. She'll speak to you in the simplest of ways. You'll know it's her, and you'll be receptive because her love lives inside of you.

"I love you, Preston. Our family loves you, and we claim you and Jaden as our own. You're raw to life right now and it may be hard to be alone... if so, move into the house with us until you're stronger."

The young man swiped at his face with the handkerchief as he stared down at his lap. He sucked in a deep breath then shook his head. When he looked up his red and swollen eyes targeted the small tent that had been erected in the small cemetery.

"Thank you, Mr. Silver, for caring so much that you would share something so personal with me. You're right; I'm feeling all those things you spoke of. Truth is... I'm so restless I can hardly sit still. I don't feel like I belong anywhere right now. Like you said, I'm raw to life... too much to be around the younger ones. I can't risk that... I know you understand what I mean. You and the family mean so much to me. You've made me, and Jaden feel a part of your lives; I don't want that to change. I know you're worried about me, but I'd better stay at the houseboat; it's what's best for your family."

Cole squeezed his shoulder as he had to accept the young man's decision. He stood so Preston could get out of the car. Cole closed the door, and they walked across the graveled lot to where the other men had gathered, next to the white iron fence. Everyone was reverent as they watched and waited for the hearse to back up to the cemetery gate.

The Colonel took Preston into his arms and hugged him tight. The man's presence was a comfort to him no matter what anyone else thought. Preston had already noticed that Dane's arms were no longer rigid when it came to him. He spoke to Preston in a low voice, but his words were powerful.

"You can do this, Preston. I swear you and Jaden will have justice." It was the way the Colonel looked at him that assured Preston his father was going to see to it.

Another vehicle pulled in and stopped; the urgency in which it did so drew attention. Owen got out and went around to the passenger side, then opened the door and cradled his wife up in his arms. He kicked the door closed and started walking toward them.

Cotton touched Preston's arm to gain his attention. Preston looked at him then followed his attention out to the shade trees. The moment was as though the earth stopped and every single person was respectful to what they witnessed.

Preston leaped over the iron fence that protected the small cemetery and practically ran to Owen and his wife. Estelle held an arm out to him, anxious to connect with the only living part of Jaden that was left. When Preston reached them, he took her away from her husband and cradled her in his arms. She fastened her arms around his neck as Preston held her. Estelle had suffered with his wife. She had been spared, but not without a price. Still, she had come to be with him during physical pain and personal loss, and Owen loved him enough to bring her for both their sakes. A bond was secured between them on this day; it was an unspoken covenant that would last until their own death.

Emotional weakness sent Preston to his knees, but he didn't let go of her. Owen knelt with them; he understood that Jaden's love connected them and always would.

Estelle cried as she told him the truth she held in her heart.

"Preston, she tried to save me. She fought him with the heart of a lion." She lost her breath during her tears. "I'm so sorry. I didn't realize we were in danger until it was too late. But she knew, she had a wisdom that I didn't understand. I'm sorry. Please, forgive me. I was so scared; I didn't know how to help her."

"Shhh, Ms. 'Stelle... don't get upset. It's not your fault." Preston went to his haunches for extra support. He held her tight while hoping that the pain inside of him would ease. "I'm so sorry about your baby." His voice cracked. He reached out and grabbed the back of Owen's neck. Owen leaned over and wrapped his arms around them. What else could the three of them do, but share the emptiness together?

Finally, they both helped Estelle stand, and each took an arm as they walked to the graveside.

Cole, Rueben, Mr. Gillis, Cotton, Mr. Enriquez, Floyd Cox, Charlie and Dane carried the beautiful, walnut chest that held Jaden's body to the grave site. A blanket of white lilies, yellow roses and daisies was draped over her, each one held a special meaning to Preston and those closest to her. Rueben spoke to the Almighty in reverence, and then Charlie played his guitar and struggled vocally to sing about grace and how amazing it was to one's soul. It was his way of honoring his friend; the heartfelt delivery was a testament to his own faith.

Pastor Storey stepped out of the gathering of people and took a stand at the head of the casket, he read from the Word of God, choosing a passage from the first book of Corinthians, Chapter 13. He shared the Almighty's message of love then he read the formal information that was a fact about Jaden Michelle Reid, and the family left behind to mourn her. It didn't take long because legally, there wasn't anyone but Preston. Pastor Storey's words became tender and very personal.

"I went to the grocery store last Thursday morning. It was routine, the same time and the same day of the week. A creature of habit, I had the same things on my list... some of them were still in the cupboard from the previous week. I haven't felt too chipper the last couple of months and I started not to go. When you get my age, every ache and pain want attention. But I enjoy getting out and talking with people and I knew I would miss seeing everyone if I didn't go. I did something completely out of character... something rebellious and dangerous for my lifestyle. I love Sugar Smacks and, even though I'm diabetic, I added them to my list. I felt a twinge of guilt, so I added bananas too. I don't really care for them, but the doctor said my potassium is low, and since they're so nutritious I should eat them, anyway.

"When I entered the store, I waved at Oscar in the booth and gave Margaret a hug. I got my cart and began gathering my few things. I was there a little while visiting and shopping, and I turned onto the dry goods isle to get my reckless cereal. There was a young woman standing there reading the label on a box. I remember thinking that her hair was a beautiful auburn red. I didn't know her, but I smiled a good morning and asked if she were well. She returned a smile that was so bright, it was like a window from heaven had opened and the light of fellowship caressed her face and mine too. I tell you folks... it warmed my spirit.

"She wished me a heavenly day. Those were her exact words, 'Good morning. I'm fantastic. It's a heavenly day, and I hope it is for you too.' I agreed that it was beautiful outside. She said it was more than that to her, that it didn't matter where she is or what the weather is like, because God gave her the most wonderful new life a few months ago. Being a minister, I assumed she meant that she had been reborn in Christ. I asked her what church she attended; after all, it is my duty to expand His kingdom. I reached for my Sugar Smacks from the top shelf as she answered me. 'I've never been to church,' she said. I was so surprised that my eyes went back to her, and I clumsily fumbled the box. It tumbled off the top shelf and the corner edge struck me on the forehead. Blood began to roll from my old, thick skull and I felt a chill come over me.

"This young woman cleared a spot for me on the bottom shelf by pushing the Cheerios off into the floor. Her confident personality bid me to sit. She had a tissue on my head and began asking me questions. I thought she was assessing me to see if I had been knocked silly, but within the span of ten minutes, my head was treated and bandaged. She discovered that my potassium was low, and she had persuaded me to eat a banana and drink a glass of water. When organization came back to my system; she and Oscar helped me stand.

"She sent Oscar to gather the rest of my list while she held me steady and pushed my cart to the front. She paid for my groceries then put me in her car and drove me home. When I pointed to the parsonage, she looked at me with surprise. She said, 'Are you... Pastor Storey? Estelle and Owen's, Pastor Storey? I'm so excited. We haven't met yet... I'm Jaden Reid, Preston's wife.' She parked then came around and helped me out of the car.

"I knew then who she was. I had prayed with Estelle about her concerns for this young couple. She had told me how very brave they were because of their love for each other. She was protective of them and concerned rumors would discourage them from ever wanting to become a part of our church family.

"This young woman helped me inside to a chair then poured me a cup of juice. While I'm basking in the kindness of a stranger, I'm amazed that this compassionate, assertive and dynamic young woman had never been to church, and even more, that she didn't consider herself to be a soldier for Christ. She headed for the door and I thanked her for her care. She gave me another one of those magnetic smiles before she left.

"I sat there a moment feeling burdened; our meeting kept tugging at my heart. I decided a bowl of soup would be good for lunch and while it warmed, I would direct my mind and efforts toward something constructive and wash the dishes from breakfast. I started to get up when my back door opened. Yep, it was Jaden Reid again. She stepped through it with her arms loaded down with my groceries and began putting them away. She asked me if a bowl of soup was okay... that I really needed to eat something else. I assured her the soup was a great idea.

"Folks, without my asking for a thing, she washed my dishes while warming the soup and even grilled me a cheese sandwich to go with it. Clearly, God was moving all around this young woman on my behalf and she didn't even know it.

"I asked her to tell me how it was that she had come to have a new life. We sat and visited together over a bowl of tomato soup while she was open with me about her life. She was happy and joyful because she had been blessed with the love of a gentle and thoughtful man like Preston. Because of him and the people who loved him, she had gained a deeper understanding of true happiness and joy. She wanted me to know that Preston's love and acceptance was her treasure in life, and together they were excited to discover and learn about all the seasons and blessings that awaited them. She said each day with him was a new lesson in faith and believing in unconditional love. She explained that no matter the circumstances, she had made it a point to always find something good in each day, but when she was young, the deprivation and cruelty in her world never allowed her to dream of love. She never knew there was something greater than her own will to survive.

"I was curious, so I asked about her parents. She told me she didn't know anything about her father and that she had spent her life confused about her mother. She spoke of the most heart-wrenching treatment that no child and no young girl should ever have to endure. I listened to a girl who, along with her mother, had been beaten and neglected by the man with whom they lived. This man told her repeatedly that she was a burden and a curse on her mother. When she was five, instead of a birthday celebration, her mother took her out of the only home she knew and abandoned her at an inner-city church. She was told to stay put and then watched her mother walk away and leave her; she was too confused to follow and too terrified to stay. She was completely alone... not given to anyone with an explanation of why she was there other than a piece of paper pinned on her coat with a name and date of birth. She was sick, hungry, cold... and heartbroken. This church was only a building, for it too had been abandoned. She stayed in that desolate corner of the building not getting more than a few feet away from that pew for several days before a police officer found her on a random walk through the building.

"I had a personal revelation when I learned that she was safer living on the street than she was in foster care. The system that was supposed to protect her was a series of fearful placements with strangers. She was forced to survive by her own rules and persistence... and without trust. I learned it was during this period of her life when someone saw that special quality of tenacity she possessed. They gave her a chance, a job and without her knowing... they gave her hope. That spark of hope took root inside of the girl and guided her to grow into an educated and compassionate woman, and it inspired her to become a nurse. What a fantastic story of triumph and victory. I was convicted, even at my age, to dedicate myself to find something good in each day.

"This child was lost in a foster care system where she endured unfathomable cruelty and servitude. I listened, and I saw a young woman who, because of slavery, had learned to serve. Because of injury, she had learned and studied to be a healer. Because of fear, she had learned to have courage. Because of the impossible, she had learned to find hope. Because of overwhelming poverty and loneliness, she had learned to see the value of a slice of bread and a bowl of soup, and she had learned how to share kindness. She received grace from the Enriquez family and because of them, she learned to trust again.

"She told me the need to be loved was her biggest flaw because it weakened her judgment, but still she was thankful... because that weakness had led her to find the strength in Preston's love. She wouldn't have discovered he had needed her as much as she had needed him. They offered kindness and compassion on behalf of each other's need. That selflessness established a friendship which grew into a serious commitment and deep exchange of love during the time they shared together. They were married on September 6 of this year.

"I asked her that afternoon, if there was anything, I could do to show my appreciation for her kindness. She told me she had not entered a church building since she had been found by the police so many years ago. She asked if I would take her into the sanctuary. I was surprised at her simple request, and humbled. I sensed it was a momentous thing or she wouldn't have asked, and I wanted to share it with her. She stopped at the door of the sanctuary and without knowing it, she caught my hand. Only then did I understand how scared she was because her small fingers were trembling. I realized that amidst all her triumphs, a part of her was still that abandoned little girl who believed she was something flawed and unworthy. Fear had gripped her little heart so tight that she had lived all those years in this bondage of a lie.

"She took her time and looked at each stained-glass window that told the story of Christ. She asked me if she was a curse. I told her there was no way... that God had created her in His image and she was very precious to Him. I told her that she was His child and He was her Creator... her Heavenly Father. I witnessed that brave, young woman confront, what I believe, was her greatest fear. I remained next to her and as the minutes passed, she let go of my hand. She stood there looking up at the cross as she confessed her shame in fearing the Maker. She admitted she had harbored bad feelings in her heart toward her mother too, and that she remembered how terrified her mother was of the man that used to hit them. Jaden demonstrated her ability to find the goodness in life and people; when she told me that she could see that her mother had left her in the safest place she thought possible to protect her child when she couldn't protect herself. I was moved by this admission and her wisdom. She stood there looking at that cross as she told me that God had stayed with her when the police came and took her out of the church building that day, and He was still with her.

"I asked if I could pray for her and even then, she asked me if I would include Preston, because everything one of them did now affected the other. She smiled and told me again how much she loved him."

The old shepherd's words grew thick with feeling.

"I can't remember ever praying for someone while feeling the entire time... that I was the one receiving the blessing... and the one being honored."

Pastor Storey began to cry as he continued.

"I visited with Preston on Sunday after the morning service. I was scared to go to him. The truth is... I was ashamed to go to him, because I had never made the effort. I knew his life was difficult. I didn't know how to help, or if I even could. My heart was broken over Jaden. God convicted me about the truth of my fear, and I... I imagined her holding my hand as I fearfully faced her husband.

"I stand here before you folks today to tell you what a special young woman Jaden Reid was, but also to tell you... rather, confess to you, this young woman ministered to me in the only way she knew how. She offered me compassion in a mighty way and she displayed the heart of Christ. I needed it because I was on the verge of apathy. A wise woman, Mother Teresa, spent her life teaching others about human kindness. Jaden Reid practiced this in her daily life, and I was a grateful recipient. The message is so simple and yet, so powerful, 'Through small acts of kindness... done with great love... we can change the world'. I grieve the loss of my new friend. I needed her too. I stand before you today humbled that Preston loves me enough to forgive me, and he's allowed me to share this with all of you. I stand here to tell you that... the Lord used a box of Sugar Smacks as the open door to..." Pastor Storey reached out and laid his hand on the walnut chest, "... bring this precious and brave young woman, Jaden Reid, into my ritualistic life. Her kindness and joy challenge me to look at the world through another's eyes. I tell you, God has a rejuvenated soldier in Christ. My living dangerously... with joy and courage... has only just begun.

"I don't know why her young life was taken. But I know because of the Enriquez's... because of her husband, Preston and all his family, she finally felt loved and accepted for who she was. I know that in all her pain, fear and disappointments, she finally understood God had always been with her, and that He is good. I know, during this tragedy and our loss, Jaden Reid now sits at the Almighty's table of grace."

The old shepherd pressed his hand over his heart as he held the other towards the heavens then proclaimed to all of those gathered.

"I want to be like Jaden Reid. I want to be a soldier of love. I want to share life with my neighbor. I want to be joyfully thankful for the love in my life so that I treat every day I have left as a heavenly day and glorify the Father in it."

Preston agreed to go home with Charlie, Estelle and Owen. He was emotionally and physically drained but being near Estelle seemed to calm him. They waited until the grave was covered and the mounds of flowers were placed so they could visit the grave after it was prepared. Celia and Ava fussed over the placement of flowers for a little while. The grave seemed bare without a stone, and the monument Preston had ordered would not be delivered and set for two months.

They all watched as Preston knelt next his wife once again; his bandaged hand rested on the dirt that covered her. He just couldn't seem to pull himself away from her. Finally, Estelle went to him. Her arms slid around his neck from behind and she caressed his cheek with hers. Her body was weak and so was her voice.

"Preston let's go home and rest for a little while. I know you must be as tired as I am. We'll come back later and watch the sun set with her. I'll come every day, I promise."

Preston couldn't help but respond to her and he stood.

Estelle hugged his arm as she rested her head against him.

He looked down at her; his voice was thick with feeling as he spoke.

"When you're up to it... I need you to tell me what happened. I need to know who did this... and why."

Estelle lifted her chin and her eyes met Preston's sad ones. She realized that she needed to talk to Cotton as well.

"Are you sure? I don't want you hurt anymore, Honey. I don't know what happened after he hit me."

Preston gazed at her.

"I have to find out all I can. I know she wouldn't want me to stay the way I am now..." he sucked in a shaky breath as he shook his head. "I can't see tomorrow, 'Stele and I don't want to... not without her."

Estelle reached up and wiped the tears from his cheeks with the tissue in her hand. She nodded her head.

"I do understand, Honey. I know how hard it's going to be, but I'll help you, Preston."

Cotton let go of a pent-up breath when Estelle started toward them with Preston at her side.

CHAPTER 19

The Colonel thought about Preston while the cab moved through the quiet streets. The shadows cast by the late afternoon sun flickered in and out of the vehicle's interior seemingly taunting him with hidden truths he should have been man enough to admit. He had said goodbye to the boy once again; this time had proven to be more difficult than the last. He had left him in the gentle and loving arms of a beautiful wife the last time. He would have to trust that these friends Preston had made, would help him find his place in the world. Dane reminded himself that any of them were a damn sight better than he had ever been as a friend or a parent.

He had one more chore to carry out before he could board the plane that awaited him. He paid the cab driver and got out at the river front where another car waited. The Colonel got in and closed the door; he looked over at the familiar, but now middle-aged, soldier who had always complied with what he was ordered to do. The Colonel's voice was curt and his manner rigid as he addressed the Captain concerning the business at hand.

"Was he difficult to locate?"

"No Sir, I picked him up coming out of his apartment. He was packed, and he had these in his pocket, Sir."

Captain Peck handed him a small plastic bag which held the rings he had given Caroline so many years ago. Dane's blood began to boil.

"He's banged up pretty bad, and he's talking sort of crazy, Sir."

The Colonel detected a hint of mercy coming from the Captain.

"What's your point, Captain?!"

"He's in bad shape... that's all."

Colonel Reid got defensive.

"He beat her... violated her... murdered her unborn child then threw her in front of a moving vehicle. He may as well have cut her throat; it would have been more merciful. What are they going to charge him with? How will they prove it? She can't testify... she's dead! The other victim can only give a sketchy account at best, and that would only be for assault... not murder. The other two witnesses are imbeciles... babbling about angels. He did this deed, Captain, he must be held accountable. I swore to my son he would be held accountable." Dane felt something inside his chest stir at his words.

The Captain stared at him a moment.

"Did they happen to mention swords?"

Dane's brow wrinkled.

"They... who?"

Captain Peck responded with conviction firm in his voice.

"The witnesses. Did they mention swords?"

"Yes. Why?"

The Captain shook his head as he spoke.

"Butler said that a man in a white robe and a golden chest plate was standing in the road in front of the truck. He said that he was to the point of running him over when the man grew a pair of shimmering wings then drew a sword of fire from out of nowhere and struck the driver's side of his truck. He said it hit so hard it flung him off the road."

The Colonel stared at the Captain for a moment; he sensed the man was spooked. It happened to all soldiers eventually, especially the ones who've seen battle up close and experienced things that challenged the boundaries of logic. He knew of it firsthand from the aspect of war and life. There were many unexplainable things which he had experienced and sensed while living with his wife at Whisper Bluff... things that had no logical or practical explanation. He recalled them with clarity of thought but deliberately suppressed them due to guilt over his ill-treatment of Preston's mother.

The Colonel voiced his opinion concerning the Captain's thoughts.

"It's disturbing what a guilty conscience can do to a person... the things it can make them see. Alcohol can do the same thing to a man. I know that's the damn truth."

Captain Peck shook his head in defiance.

"I found his truck. It was wrapped around a tree down in the swamp about three miles from where your daughter-in-law was ambushed. It was deep in the swamp. He had to have been hauling-ass when he left the road."

"And?" questioned the Colonel as to why the Captain felt the need to go look for it or tell him that he had done so.

"And... I was curious about his credibility."

"His credibility?!"

The Captain sighed.

"Colonel, all I'm saying is... you should see things for yourself, Sir."

Dane met the Captain's gaze knowing that of all the soldiers he had ever served with and trusted through the years, this man was truly 'the best of the best'. He could not and would not ignore that fact.

The Colonel put his hat on the dash then took the large flashlight Captain Peck offered him. There was a thunderhead in the distance; the electricity in the clouds could be felt in their skin. He got out of the car but paused as an eerie sensation slithered down his spine. He had been in the presence of negative and sinister energy most of his life and recognized it without fear. He was accustomed to standing face to face with it while emanated by another human being and was very capable of emitting a version of his own when necessary. He was even guilty of emitting a corrosive version of it that had been self-destructive to his own life, and the few who had dared to love him. But this energy was something else. He found it daunting, yet powerful, and for reasons beyond his understanding, he felt intimidated. The Colonel looked in both directions of the road and could not establish a vanishing point to the east, nor the west. A goading chill nudged him forward, and he followed Captain Peck into the dense foliage while his newfound sobriety embraced the fact, he had a 44 Caliber pistol beneath his coat. They cut on the spotlights then stepped off the road into darkness and an underworld of spores, offensive odors, and things that flew, crawl, hiss and bite. The Colonel followed the Captain downward into the hole the truck had cut into the underbelly of the wooded swamp. The ground was like walking on a sponge and the smell was rancid from the fungus that grew everywhere. The Captain stopped; however, the Colonel walked past him with the light fixed on what they had come to see.

Captain Peck waited while the Colonel examined the condition of the truck. The hum of life was deafening, and he could feel eyes everywhere beyond the sturdy beam of light. He saw Colonel Reid rub a large palm over his short, boxed haircut to disturb the insects that were determined to feed. The long, clean gash into the metal hood and fender of the truck in front of the steering wheel was exactly as the Captain remembered from his earlier inspection; it was exactly how Butler had described it.

The Colonel's rigid personality did not falter as he tried to rationalize the bizarre things that were in front of his eyes.

"Any of these limbs could have done this Captain considering the force in which it entered the woods. It's what... 25... 30 yards off the road?" He turned the light he held upward and inspected the trees where some limbs had been ripped from the trunks due to the point of entry where the truck had left the embankment.

The Captain didn't respond but walked over to the truck. He rocked the hood open and concentrated his light to reveal that the engine block held the same clean slash. It was like something hot had severed the metal.

"Colonel, you know I respect you and like yourself, I've been in service a long time. We've both seen enough of war and the unexplained during it, to admit that there are things at work... that are not of this world. We both believe in Hell, wouldn't you agree?"

Colonel Reid looked at him. He could not dispute that he had seen things that could only be from such a place. His expression and silence told the Captain that he didn't disagree.

"Is it such a stretch to believe that God in Heaven is real and that there are soldiers of righteousness that do His bidding? I know that you've been ordered to do some terrible things... God knows, I've done them with you. And I understand your heart is involved with the crimes this man has committed against your family. Sir, this man is a firebrand on humanity. He has lived his life committing selfish and wicked deeds against others for personal gain. I believe this man's soul has been marked by something greater than this world. Colonel... Sir... with all due respect, do you really want to interfere?"

The Captain's words were combustible to the Colonel's already smoldering temperament, and he reacted as such.

"What would you have me do, Captain, let him go... turn the other cheek?! I can't do that! I won't do that!" Dane paused and turned away from the Captain, the air in his lungs suddenly felt like a heavy fog and he couldn't breathe. He had no choice but to look at the hard truth about himself since sobriety had been forced upon him. It was intuitive now and functioned as a twin to the conscience that had been born while he was hospitalized.

He was stunned when he received word from Sheriff Cotton that Jaden had been killed and he needed to speak with him as soon as possible. He contacted Emmett while his assistant made the arrangements for him to fly out of Washington. When he arrived in Westville two days ago, he went to the funeral home before going to the houseboat. He did not recognize the bluish girl that lay motionless on the cold metal table. He was appalled at her distorted and maimed features. They could not be masked for family viewing no matter how creative the talent. While standing there, the image of Jaden's gorgeous and happy face, smiling at Preston on their wedding day, leaped to the forefront of his mind. It had stayed with him when he left, and it was still with him now. After hearing Pastor Storey's tribute to her and a Divine power, he believed the mental image of her was an ambassadress. He believed her memory was imposed on him by a growing sense of right and wrong to remind him of how badly he had mistreated her... and Caroline... and so many other women. It had not occurred to him until a few hours ago that his ill-treatment of women was something he had in common with Russell Butler and, although there were differences, he despised himself for this. The very thought of it irritated the rancid sore of self-loathing that was already rotting away inside of him.

Dane sighed. He believed the Captain was right; Butler had been marked by a higher power. Because he believed this to be true, he feared that his rotten deeds in life had already withered his soul into decay so that any benevolence by a higher power was impossible, leaving him marked and condemned as well. The things he knew of life were many and more times than not unfair, but the things he knew of love and forgiveness had been because of Preston. That young man was the best thing in his life. Dane swallowed the sentiment that attempted to strangle him.

"Captain, we buried that girl earlier today. She was a special person, and she deserves to have someone make a sacrifice on her behalf. I'm a lost cause no matter what; I owe this to her... and to my son." Thunder rumbled in the distance. The Colonel turned abruptly and headed back to the vehicle knowing this wasn't a wise place to be during a down pour.

Captain Peck had never seen the Colonel show any sign of remorse before today; he supposed it was possible for it to snow in July after all. He shoved the hood of the truck closed then scanned the terrain with his light as he followed his superior out of the swamp. He undertook the embankment with powerful legs and was climbing the last few feet up to the road when he saw the Colonel open the trunk of the sedan. Captain Peck sucked in a deep breath and pushed himself to the pavement ready to intercede on behalf of his Colonel, and the peculiar frame of mind in which he seemed trapped. But to his surprise, Colonel Reid just stood there staring at the man that had committed this horrible deed.

The kitchen at Owen and Estelle's house had an ample supply of food that had been brought by thoughtful friends and church family. Estelle wasn't hungry, but she sat down at the kitchen table next to Preston and allowed Owen and Charlie to take care of them. She ate what her husband put in front of her, so Preston would be encouraged to eat something as well. When they finished, she sipped a cup of coffee and relived the horrible afternoon as best as she could recall. She answered their questions while Cotton taped it for Sheriff Savoy.

Preston was distraught when he realized it was Russell Butler that had done this to Jaden and destroyed their life together. He told Cotton the attack was deliberate payback. Bitterness ruled the young man's voice as his blue eyes turned stormy with loathing. Cotton became worried, especially when Estelle confirmed the accusations. She told them Butler bragged about following them since that morning and that he had smiled when he boasted about putting the water in the gas tank.

The day had been difficult and emotionally exhausting for Preston and Estelle. Owen insisted his wife take one of the muscle relaxers the doctor had prescribed before she got ready for bed. Preston refused to take any medication to help him rest. He was wound up tight and functioning on pure misery.

Charlie suggested his buddy take a hot shower and get out of the dress pants and shirt, so he would be more comfortable. Preston agreed. Charlie retrieved an armload of wood for a fire while his friend showered. Preston commented on the fire as he collapsed on the couch in his boxers. He put on a pair of socks then tugged a clean tee shirt over his head. Charlie pointed to the large mugs of apple cider sitting on the sofa table. The aromatic elixir was just one of Preston's favorite things when it came to Estelle's culinary skills. He picked up a mug and held it under his nose for a moment, so the sweet steam would caress his face. He blew it for a second then paused and sniffed the mug. He cut his eyes to his buddy and asked if there was alcohol in it. Charlie smiled slightly and nodded his head. He told Preston there was two tablespoons of bourbon, two aspirins, a squeeze of lemon and a peppermint melting in the bottom of both mugs. He picked the other one up and stirred it with the cinnamon stick before he took a sip. He commented that it was Dr. Saucier's recipe for a winter nap and he was tired. Preston didn't comment further as he stirred the mug then turned it up for a big gulp. It didn't take long for him to finish the hot drink. He stretched out on the couch and pulled the quilt over his bare legs.

Charlie added several more slabs of dried oak to the fire then poked it a few times before he put the screen in place. He knew Preston found the warmth of the fireplace soothing and the couch in front of it comfortable. He sat down on the coffee table then turned to face his friend as he finished his mug of cider. He listened and was glad Preston was willing and able to vent his anger and disgust for Russell Butler to him. Charlie didn't caution his friend about the hostility he felt because he understood where Preston was emotionally. It took over an hour for his friend to unwind. When Preston's eyes closed, his breath became smooth and relaxed, Charlie stood and covered his friend's still body with the quilt then eased out of the room.

He went to the kitchen, poured himself a glass of milk and retrieved a bowl from the cabinet. It was obvious the sheriff was worried about Preston because he had not eaten much of anything. When he asked about Preston, Charlie assured him that his buddy was asleep. He helped himself to another bowl of chicken and dumplings; they were barely warm, but he didn't care. When Cotton commented on how good they smelled Charlie sat the bowl in front of the sheriff, along with the plate of cornbread and a fork. He poured another glass of milk and fixed another bowl of dumplings. He sat down at the table with Sheriff Cotton and they talked while they ate. Owen was doing laundry going back and forth to the washroom, but together they managed to finish off the rest of the pecan pie.

It was after 8:00 p.m. when the phone rang. Charlie jumped to his feet and reached for the receiver before a second ring woke Estelle and Preston. Owen had just brewed a fresh pot of coffee and had suggested that Cotton stay in the guest room for the night. Cotton agreed because Deputy Ingram, the Sheriff's second in command, was working a 24-hour shift so Cotton could attend the funeral and be available to Preston.

Charlie's voice drew their attention.

"I'm not sure, Sir. Preston's asleep. Sheriff Cotton is here... do you want to -" Charlie words stopped short and Cotton's attention shifted to him. "Yes Sir. I understand... hold on a minute." Charlie laid the phone down and went to see if Preston wanted to talk to his father. He came back in a few minutes and hung the phone up.

"What's up, Charlie?" asked Owen.

"I'm not sure. It's the Colonel... he wanted to talk to Preston. It sounded important; he said it couldn't wait."

"I don't like the sound of that," mumbled Cotton.

"I thought he had to fly out this afternoon," commented Owen.

Cotton shrugged his shoulders.

"I did too. That's what he led me to believe, anyway."

Owen stood and disappeared down the short hallway that led to his and Estelle's bedroom. He quietly opened the door and saw she was still asleep. He thought the room was cold, so he ventured in and added a blanket to her cover.

A few minutes had passed when Charlie looked up to see Preston standing in the doorway of the kitchen. He was dressed in a pair of old jeans and a denim shirt, putting on his jacket.

Owen didn't ask if he wanted a cup of coffee; he poured him one and sat it down on the table. There was a fall chill in the air and it had begun to penetrate the inside of the house.

Preston sat down and added a spoon of sugar and a little cream to the cup. His bandaged hand made it impossible to maneuver things in the usual way, so he picked up the cup from the opposite side across from the handle and took several healthy swallows. He could not hide the fact that his hand was trembling even if he had tried. He sat the cup down and rubbed his warm palm over his face. He looked over at Charlie as the four of them experienced a strange silence. Preston broke it with a sigh before he spoke.

"I'm going to meet Dane. He said it was important. He wouldn't say what it was about... only that I had a decision to make." He sat there a minute.

Sheriff Cotton asked him.

"Do you want me to go with you, Preston?"

The young man sat there staring into his cup. When he spoke, it was a man that answered.

"Yes Sir, but... I need to get used to being alone and I may as well start now." Preston drank a few more swallows of his coffee. He stood and went to the sink where he rinsed out the cup then placed it in the drain rack. He got to the backdoor and stopped; his voice was as shaky as his hands. "I'm meeting him at the west end of the bridge over Greasy Creek."

Cotton stood up hastily as a frown dented his forehead.

"Preston don't go… nothing good can come of this. He's up to something. There's no reason for you to go there."

They knew Preston was edgy and stressed, it was not a surprise when he turned abruptly and lashed out at the sheriff.

"No reason, Sheriff? My wife was beaten and raped… then left there to die. My baby was murdered there… and Owen's little girl too." Preston's throat constricted with emotion as the brutal, truth finally crossed his lips. He trembled due to the inner turmoil as he looked at the older man in front of him. He didn't know what else to do with himself other than what Dane had asked him to do. He turned back to the door. "I… I apologize for biting your head off. I have to go." Preston quietly closed the back door as he left.

"Dammit!" growled Cotton. He grabbed his hat and started for the door. When he touched the doorknob, he pulled his hand back as though it were hot. He sighed and turned back to them. He didn't know what to do. He didn't want to damage his relationship with Preston, but even more, he didn't want the young man to get into trouble because of Dane's rough-and-ready perspective of the world. Cotton rubbed the tense muscles in the back of his neck.

Owen didn't have a problem with being the voice of reason.

"Do you want me to call Sheriff Savoy, Cotton? It is his jurisdiction." He stood to face Cotton as he spoke. "I think you should go after him… take Charlie with you. He can drive you in the truck, so you won't be obvious. He can talk sense to Preston when no one else can."

"I'll get my jacket, Sheriff." Charlie was back in only a few seconds.

Owen stepped in front of his little brother; their eyes were level with each other now and they exchanged an unspoken understanding.

"You be careful and think smart in this, Charlie. We've had enough tragedy."

"I will, Owen, don't worry Estelle with it. I promise, we'll bring him back safe."

Charlie and Cotton shared a tense silence while they moved through the darkness. The lightning streaked across the sky and the wind blew in sporadic gusts, yet it hadn't started to rain. The wind made it difficult to hold the truck on the road; Charlie thought Preston must really be having a hard time in the Jeep with only one good hand. If the situation and the weather wasn't cause enough to be antsy, the Sheriff's worry added to the smothering anticipation inside the truck. Charlie cracked the window a little. He couldn't stop thinking about what he had overheard between Cotton and the Colonel the other day. The fact they were on their way to intrude on the meeting between Preston and the Colonel gave Charlie cause to wonder about the connection between his friend and these two men. He knew it was something in which he should not speculate, but it was difficult not to.

"Sheriff, you want me to go in from Highway 6?" asked Charlie. There were a pair of tail lights a mile or so in front of them, but he couldn't tell whether they were Preston's.

"If those tail lights disappear before we get over the next hill... I say that would be Preston. Let's stick close to him, Charlie. I hope my fears are wrong, but Dane can be a dangerous man whether he's drunk or sober."

"What do you think is going on, Sheriff?" asked Charlie pointedly.

"I'm not sure. I just think it's strange that this Russell Butler asked everybody he knew for money on Sunday and no one would help him. Now he's fallen off the face of the earth.

"Sheriff Savoy has questioned some residents at the complex where he lives after getting the tip. The superintendent opened the door to Butler's apartment because he's late on the rent. Savoy said they found bloody clothes in the floor of the bathroom. He didn't have a warrant, so he couldn't remove anything. That was before I talked to you, Charlie, and you gave us a solid connection between him and Jaden. Savoy said one of the complex residents called him from the laundromat. They claimed they saw a man in black pants and a pullover come out of his apartment Sunday night around 10:00 p.m. Savoy got a search warrant. When he tried the door, it was locked. When they got back into the place, the clothes were gone."

Preston slowed down as he neared the bridge, lightning flashed behind the clouds to brighten everything around him. The yellow crime scene tape tied to the guard rail blew out across the road; it had been left behind in case law enforcement needed to come back to the scene. Preston's eyes clung to it a moment before he acknowledged the black sedan parked a little further up on the shoulder of the bridge.

Preston stopped a short distance behind the car. He didn't have to wait as the light inside the sedan cut on when the driver's side door opened. The brass buttons on the dark overcoat reflected in his headlights as the man put on his hat then tugged it down on his brow. Preston couldn't see his face, but he knew by the collage of metals and ribbons on his chest that it was Dane. He thought he saw movement in the backseat before the light went out. Preston didn't know why he was here, but he was certain Dane was sober, or he wouldn't have come to meet him.

Preston cut off the motor. The door of the Jeep moaned when he opened it to get out. Dane stopped to wait on him between the two vehicles. A creepy darkness closed in on them from the outskirts of the swamp. The vivid, white moon overhead was spooky and bright. He could tell his father's expression was strained. Dane spoke to him in a factual manner; however, his tone of voice was full of feeling and so were his eyes.

"Preston, I know I was supposed to be gone, but it seems I've developed a conscience in my sobriety. I came back because I... I couldn't let you go through this without me... without knowing how much I care. And, I came back with the intension of rendering justice on the guilty. It's what I do for this country, Preston. The war council renders the judgment on specific targets that threaten the safety of this nation, and I locate and carry out the sentence. I can never escape from the things I've done in the name of patriotism. The alcohol helped for a while but had adverse consequences that neither you... nor your mother deserved. I'm bound for Hell, Preston. I..." the Colonel paused as he swallowed a couple of times, "... I offer my services to you because you're the person I care for most in this world. You are the only one who has the right to judge him for his crime. The offense was committed against you too because Jaden was a part of you. I understand the significance in the love and trust you shared with her, Preston. It was truly a special thing that was stolen from you. So... I need you to tell me what to do in this matter."

Preston looked at him.

"What matter, Sir? I don't understand."

Dane reached in his coat pocket and retrieved the small clear pouch which contained the rings that first belonged to Preston's mother and then his wife. He put it in his son's hand.

"The matter of his sentence; it's your choice, Preston. He murdered half of you. It's your right as her husband. I'll turn him over to the authorities, or I'll execute him... here and now... at the same spot he committed this injustice against Jaden and against you. I've been appointed to do this for my country and I've already sold my soul in the name of patriotism. I was a shitty father, but I'm skilled at this. I want to offer myself to you because... I... care so much about you... and about your pain."

Preston witnessed his father reach inside the overcoat, beneath all the ornamentation and distinguished honors which proved he was a brave and dedicated soldier. The Colonel's hand surface baring a nickel-plated pistol from the holster that hung beneath his arm. He turned abruptly and walked away as though he were on a mission. Alarm shot through Preston's veins as he looked at the rings in his hand then back to his father. He shoved the pouch in his jean's pocket as he was motivated to follow.

Dane opened the back door behind the driver's seat and the light came on again.

Preston's attention shifted from his father, recalling that he had seen someone move in the backseat. Russell Butler lifted his head and looked at them. A burning surge of hatred stung Preston's scalp and stiffened his spine. He shoved past Dane as his temper exploded. He grabbed Butler by the hair and the throat and yanked him out of the car then slammed him to the ground. Butler's hands were taped behind his back, but Preston didn't care. The fiendish man had shown Jaden no mercy, and he deserved no favor.

The tall lanky man instinctively began to kick and cuss in his defense, all the while, Preston's fists pounded away releasing all the anger and hurt this man had inflicted upon him. He wanted, no, he needed Russell Butler to experience the agony and terror he had inflicted upon Jaden.

Dane did not interfere with Preston's rage. He reasoned the young man was justified in his anger. If beating the hell out of this piece of shit would help ease Preston's pain, he was glad to oblige him. Besides, he had left the Captain out of this since it was personal, and they had conflicting opinions about Russell Butler's judgment and sentence. Still, it had been Captain Peck's idea to allow Preston to decide the man's punishment since he had been the one to suffer the offense. Dane knew the Captain had suggested it because Preston lived in the civilian world of rule and law, and he believed the young man to be more grounded in decency than his father. Because the Captain was a soldier, he had faith Preston would do the right thing; after all, in a soldier's world, honor came before dedication and principle.

Preston slammed Butler's head against the pavement for the fourth time.

"Why?! Why did you kill her?! You hateful, wicked, murdering bastard... you're the one that's hell-bound!" yelled Preston.

The Colonel's feet came closer and the silver pistol in his hand flashed in the corner of Preston's eye. The young man was motivated by a sorrowful vengeance and responded to the inclinations of his distraught frame of mind. He grabbed the handgun so fast the Colonel's index finger discharged the first round out of reflex. It struck the pavement next to Russell Butler's head with a spark then settled somewhere in the darkness, no longer a threat.

Preston shoved Dane out of the way as he leaped to his feet and pointed the gun at the man that had stolen his life.

The Colonel respected the steel in Preston's spine and the vinegar of courage in his veins; under different circumstances he would be proud of the young man's grit. But he had underestimated Preston's ability to hate, and it had caused him to lose control of this situation. The circumstances had turned dangerous for Preston and Dane responded as a father.

"Preston, wait! It can't be this way! You can't have this deed against you! Don't you understand? It's too late for me, I've got to be the one to do it! Please Son, give me the gun and let me finish it. Please!"

Preston held the gun with both hands and still it shook like a stray puppy needing a kind word.

Dane didn't know he had a worst nightmare until that moment. He didn't understand the depth of love he felt for this young man until he was faced with the truth that he was responsible for this cataclysmic mistake. He realized that he had opened the door to Hell and shoved Preston in front of it. He could not allow this to happen, not to Preston, not to the only son he'd ever know.

Dane's words seemed to fall on deaf ears as Preston backed away from Russell Butler and began giving the man orders.

"Get your ass up, Butler! I MEAN IT, GET UP!!!" commanded Preston. His fury echoed through the night. The atmosphere responded to the chaos that was unfolding with another streak of lightning, the heavens rumbled, and the earth trembled beneath the power of distant thunder.

Dane couldn't decide if Butler was scared stiff, saw an opportunity, or was just incredibly stupid as he did what he was told.

After they went around the barricade which closed-off Woodswamp Road, Cotton had Charlie turn off the truck's headlights. The hair on Charlie's arms shifted beneath the sleeves of his jacket. There was a mystifying moon in the sky overhead and a chilling feel in the night that had nothing to do with the temperature. The thunderstorm seemed to be all around them ever since they left the ranch, but never on top of them, like the moon. They had not seen one drop of rain, even though the wind blew in lively, forceful gusts. Cotton pointed when a streak of lightning illuminated the atmosphere and revealed there were people standing in the road ahead of them.

Charlie stopped in the road a short distance from the Jeep. He was out of the truck before Cotton got his door open. He heard Preston's irate voice in the darkness, but he couldn't make out what was happening. He broke into a run out of concern.

He passed the Jeep then froze in his steps. Preston was in the middle of the road holding a pistol that was pointed at Russell Butler; the man's hands were fastened behind his back as though he were facing his execution. Charlie was suddenly angry at the Colonel for providing the means and opportunity for Preston do such a thing in his frame of mind. The Colonel's voice of reason echoed through the darkness and took hold of Charlie's understanding. He was talking to Preston like a loving, concerned father; it was obvious the Colonel's plan had backfired.

Russell Butler interrupted the Colonel.

"I saw her in town. I didn't mean to hurt her... or the other woman. I was stoned out of my mind that day," proclaimed Russell Butler as though that were a justifiable excuse.

Preston took a step towards him.

"She's dead!" he yelled in the guy's face as though Butler was dense, and the two simple words would give him clarity of the heinous deed he had committed.

Charlie eased along the wall of the bridge behind Preston and stopped when he was even with his friend. Preston had not seen him; Charlie knew that could or could not be in his favor.

Suddenly, Russell Butler's demented insolence shocked all of them. It was like a trigger had gone off inside of him and Preston's temper had squeezed it.

"She was mine before you came along you stupid, horny little son-of-a-bitch! You should have left her alone. It's your own damn fault that she's dead. I warned her in the beginning where she belonged; she should have listened. I bet you were a cherry! She taught you how to fuck and you couldn't get enough! I know for a fact she was damn good at it... most whores are. Now you know... you don't take another man's cunt without reaping the fury!"

Preston smacked Butler in the jaw with the barrel of the handgun. The tall guy went to his knees, but Preston's weight sent Butler to his back as rage ambushed him and caused him to shove the gun into the guy's mouth.

Charlie reacted and dived at his friend rolling Preston off Butler before something terrible happened. He found himself in a contest of wills as Preston sprung to his feet.

Charlie followed and blocked him from advancing on Butler. His large hands pushed against Preston's chest to keep him from ruining his life.

"Preston... it's me, Charlie! Stop! Look at me!" The friendship they shared had its times of play and they had wrestled each other a lot as they grew into men. Charlie was taller, and he was strong, but Preston was older and his muscle more defined and experienced. Charlie had to take the chance that he could gain some leverage over his friend.

"Charlie, get out of the way. Didn't you hear him... what he said about her? I can't let it go! Don't you see? I can't let it go!"

"I'm not telling you to let it go," proclaimed Charlie through gritted teeth.

Cotton had stopped when he realized Preston had the gun. But when Preston hit Butler, he advanced on the struggle to try to stop something awful from happening. But now he didn't know what to do. He stopped next to Dane as he spoke.

"My God Dane, what have you done?"

Dane looked at him with a fear in his eyes.

"This wasn't what I intended, Emmett. You go right... I'll go left."

Charlie felt the weakness in Preston's body trying to take over. He took advantage of it and fastened his long arms around his friend confining him at his waist. Charlie clamped down on his own wrist with a vice-like grip, making it difficult for Preston to take a targeted aim with the firearm. It was a risky move at best, but at that moment, he was grasping at anything that could detour his friend from committing the sinful act his over-wrought judgment would have him do.

"You don't understand... you can't!" exclaimed Preston emotionally.

"Yes, I do, Buddy! Look at me... I do understand, Preston!" Charlie hesitated a moment, but he felt he had no choice but to tell Preston the shameful truth hidden in his heart. His words were only meant for his friend, but they held an authenticity that could not be denied. "I killed my step-father, Preston. I shot him down for what he did to my mama... and to me. I looked him in the eye and I pulled the trigger. I was afraid of what he would do to us if I didn't kill him first. I hated him so much! But I didn't realize what it would do to me after the fact. I swear it haunts me every day. Do you hear me... it haunts me every day?"

Preston's eyes went back and forth between Butler and his friend for a few seconds. Finally, his attention clung to Charlie's, so he would know for sure that his friend had told him the truth.

"You're lying to keep me from shooting him," he mumbled.

Charlie shook his head.

"I wish I was, Bud. You are meant to be a lawman, Preston. You can't do this. You've got to let the courts take care of him. Jaden was so proud of being married to you. She was proud of your keen instincts, your ability to rationalize things, and your heart for others. She was proud of the plans you had for your life and that you included her as an important and equal part of them. This is not what she would want. This is not how she wanted your future to be."

"Well, I'm not going to have that future with her, am I?!" snapped Preston in a pained voice.

"No, you're not," conceded Charlie. "But you can stay on course and claim the parts that are within your reach. That's what she would expect you to do... and you know it. You were meant for more than this. How will you honor her with your life if you go to jail?"

Preston's grief weakened his body and melted his resistance. He let his hand drop to his side in surrender as he rested his forehead on his buddy's shoulder.

"I don't know what to do without her, Charlie."

Dane appeared out of the darkness and took the pistol out of his hand. He instinctively wiped it off and put it back in his holster out of sight.

Butler was back on his feet. He let go of a cynical laugh and callously goaded Preston with disrespect.

"Dammit boy... you're a whiney, little puss! What... no titty to suck anymore?"

The Colonel spun around in contempt and slugged him in the mouth.

"Shut the hell up, Butler! I'm not done with you yet!!"

CHAPTER 20

Blue lights burst into the darkness on the other end of the bridge and in only seconds headlights pushed away the night to reveal all of them. Charlie urged his friend to back as far away from Russell Butler as possible.

Sheriff Savoy and two other cars came to a stop on the bridge. Cotton went to meet him while trying to decide on the best approach to explain all of this. Russell Butler began spewing a declaration of his rights.

Savoy stopped in front of Cotton. He tried to remain respectful to their friendship.

"What in the devil is going on here, Emmett?"

"Hill, this whole ordeal has been unbelievably hard. Please, just listen to me a minute. Your perpetrator, Butler, is over there with his hands taped behind him. Jaden Reid's father-in-law is Colonel Dane Reid. I don't have time to explain him in depth, but he's Special Forces and a member of the war council to a couple of Presidents, the one sitting as a matter of fact. He's used to cleaning up certain things for the government, and he tracked down your man. This hit home, and it got personal for him and for the girl's husband. We buried her today, Hill, and

Preston is distraught with grief. Please, don't let this ruin his life. He has plans for himself. I'm asking you, from one lawman to another, not to allow this twisted jackass to ruin his life any more than he's already done."

Everyone present could hear Russell Butler declaring that his rights had been violated.

"Emmett, I can't control what he tells his attorney, the judge, or the media. You know that." Sheriff Savoy shook his head. "This is one hell of a mess. You got any suggestions? Let's hear it."

"I do, Sheriff." Colonel Reid spoke up from a few feet away. "If I may?"

Sheriff Savoy faced him.

"I guess I don't have much of a choice... do I, Colonel? Well, let's hear it since you've contributed to this shit-cluster in the first place."

Dane reached beneath his coat and retrieved his sidearm then handed it to Sheriff Savoy knowing he had erased any trace of Preston's fingerprints from it.

"You'll find my prints, Sheriff. I detained Butler. He's a bit worn... most of his injuries he got from his truck being wrapped around a tree about three miles down the road. It seems no one noticed it Saturday night during the havoc he created on this end. Somehow, he made it back to town unnoticed. I got him last night at his apartment... right from under your man's nose... as a matter of fact."

Dane held his wrist out to the sheriff.

"I take responsibility for the assault and obstruction of justice concerning Russell Butler... your perpetrator."

The aging sheriff looked at Dane through wise, discerning eyes.

"You really think that will solve this screwed-up mess?!" Sheriff Savoy's gruff tone relayed his frustration concerning the situation the Colonel had created in his jurisdiction.

"Yes Sir, I do. I'll stand with whatever charges you deem appropriate," assured Colonel Reid. "The evidence I removed from his apartment is in a bag on the front seat of the sedan."

Sheriff Savoy huffed in frustration.

"Processing you will be a waste of time and you know it. The powers that be will have you out of here so fast you won't even get ink on your fingers."

Cotton spoke up in a hopeful voice.

"So, what's the problem, Hill? Take him... you would be doing your job. Why should Preston's future be scarred because of grief?" Emmett's frustration surfaced. "Dammit, Hill! Butler's a snake; I want to crush his head under the heel of my boot too!"

When Dane spoke next, his calloused side emerged to shock Savoy and Cotton.

"Come on Sheriff... the man's got a death-wish, and he's still alive. He's a vein waiting for a needle and you know it. Question is... how many others will he destroy before our justice system gets to that conclusion? If you want something sound so the charges will stick... then give me my sidearm back for a moment. I'll blow his goddamn brains out with you as a witness. You can charge me with murder and in less than five seconds, justice will be served all the way around. I'm certain Sheriff Cotton will be glad to testify for you."

Sheriff Savoy stared at Colonel Reid as he contemplated this man that stood in front of him and who he really was. Savoy considered himself to be as wise as he was old. He had served his country as a soldier and an elected peacekeeper. He had witnessed a lot of eye-opening things and met many types of people through the years. He knew there were certain kinds of people who worked for our government. These people were patriots, but due to the callousness of life during their formative years they felt like misfits and were drawn to the armed forces to find acceptance and a dignified place in the world. Uncle Sam welcomed them with hot meals, a uniform and gear, vaccinations, and an identification number. They were given a purpose in life, and the physical and mental training to back it up. It was a fact that the objectives these men and women were ordered to complete were unscrupulous and ruthless; their conscience would have to be loyal to a greater cause than themselves. These soldiers would be considered hard and brittle by nature and would, no doubt, offend others living within in a normal and constructive environment. This was the first time he had found himself at odds against one of them. Colonel Reid gave him chills; however, he couldn't help but respect him because someone had to do the things that was required and expected of this man. Hillard Savoy knew he was backed into a corner; still, he had a solid grasp on the decision which faced him. He would always be a soldier at heart and because of this fact, he would do this and stand behind his decision even if it cost him his career. He pulled out his cuffs and secured the Colonel's wrists then walked him to the back door of his car. He instructed his deputies to take Mr. Butler into custody.

Preston reacted out of confusion and started towards the man that had raised him.

"Dane! Wait!"

Cotton cut Preston off as the young man approached them.

"Sheriff, what's happening? Why are they taking him?"

"Preston, it's just a formality because of the things Butler is saying. He's protecting you and Sheriff Savoy. He knows what he's doing. He'll be fine. He owes you this, Son. Trust me... he knows what he's doing," assured Cotton.

Savoy's deputies put their hands on their service revolvers as they approached Russell Butler from both sides. He didn't resist them, but he didn't cease his verbal assault of how he was being mistreated either. They each took hold of an arm. The young deputy asked the older what to do about the tape around his wrist. The older deputy took out his cuffs and tried to secure Butler, but found the tape encumbered the prisoner's wrists up to his muscular forearms. The older and seasoned deputy concentrated the beam from his flashlight on the man's hands. He held him and instructed Butler to go to his knees. They laid the prisoner belly down on the pavement. The older deputy put his knee in Butler's back and relinquished his hold on him while he took out a small knife. He opened the blade and handed it to the younger officer, then re-established contact. The older deputy kept a knee and one hand on the prisoner while he held the flashlight for the rookie.

The position and the robotic way the older deputy spoke to his prisoner enhanced the reality of incarceration in Butler's mind. They couldn't have known that desperation was taking over his rebellious temperament. Jail was not where he wanted to be, and Butler began to panic.

The younger deputy began to slice through the tape while instructing the prisoner to be still. He sawed at the top layer of thick silver tape for a minute; the aggravation in it escaped in the way of a huffing breath as he started on the second layer. He didn't notice that Butler had become silent due to the annoying chore at hand. When the tape finally gave, Butler's defenses were wound like a coiled snake; he took advantage of the situation and struck the rookie with menacing precision. He wrenched his body in an unexpected and distorted jerk, slamming his elbow into the young officer's temple while grabbing for his sidearm. The older deputy was knocked off kilter by the force of the younger officer's body falling against him. He scrambled to recover, only to be struck in the hand and then the chest as the prisoner opened fire. The young deputy lunged at Butler; he took a round in his torso and another in his calf while he was airborne. This violent crime was committed by a dangerous and impulsive man and unfolded within a matter of seconds.

Sheriff Savoy had drawn his revolver; it wasn't clear from where the shots originated until Russell Butler jumped to his feet and his deputies did not. Sheriff Savoy pointed his sidearm at him and ordered Butler to drop the weapon.

Russell Butler ignored Sheriff Savoy's command, turned and set a course for Preston. He lifted the handgun and pointed it at the younger man that had made a fool out of him.

Cotton bent over to retrieve the small snub nose pistol that was strapped to his ankle; all the while, Butler disregarded Sheriff Savoy's commands to desist.

Dane yelled out in urgent warning from the confines of the vehicle for Savoy to shoot him.

Butler fired another round as Cotton stepped in front of Preston and pointed the pistol at him. Preston caught the older man in his arms as Cotton's body stopped the bullet that was meant for him; the impact took them to the ground.

Butler turned and pointed the pistol at Sheriff Savoy. The old sheriff dropped to the ground and fired just as Butler pulled the trigger again. Butler kept walking towards Sheriff Savoy. He laughed at the fear he saw in the face of the old lawman.

A single shot echoed through the night; it was distinct and unlike any of the others. It sent Russell Butler to the cement ground, and his death.

Savoy scanned the darkness with his sidearm pointed; no one knew from where the shot had come.

A male voice called out to the Colonel from the darkness requesting permission to join them. The Colonel yelled back instructing him to do it and stop talking about it.

Charlie watched as Sheriff Savoy held his pistol on the shadow that appeared from the darkness; he ordered the man to identify himself.

The man called back to him as he knelt by the wounded deputies and began to assess their injuries.

"Captain Bradley Peck, Sir, United States Marines."

Captain Peck found the young deputy was blessed to be alive; the bullets passed straight through his flesh, but he was bleeding profusely. The Captain quickly packed and dressed the wounds to control the bleeding then he rose and moved to the other officer. The older deputy sat up. The Captain believed the man's efforts, after being shot in the chest, to be a combination of will and adrenalin. The Captain's trained hands moved over the senior deputy's chest assessing his injuries while the old gentleman coughed convulsively trying to catch his breath. The deputy fumbled for the flashlight that lay beside him on the pavement. The Captain concluded the man was a miracle.

Captain Peck picked up the flashlight and held it for the sake of certainty. He felt a chunk of metal missing from the shaft of the light even though it still shown bright. The Captain shook his head at the power that was in this place knowing it had to be Divine.

"My heavens... would you look at that?" mumbled the older man. The expression on his wise face was sheer enlightenment to the fact he still possessed breath. His fingers ran over his badge that held the bullet. "Thank you, sweet Father in Heaven," mumbled the man. He looked at Captain Peck and smiled. "I thought I was a goner. I am ready... but He knows my Mary needs me. She doesn't have anyone else."

The Captain gripped his shoulder with understanding then placed the old man's hand on the distorted handle of the flashlight as he spoke.

"If you don't believe in angels, Deputy... now is a good time to start."

The older deputy turned his attention to the bleeding rookie who was his responsibility.

The Captain moved on to where Cotton lay in the boy's arms. He knelt next to Cotton and laid his rifle on the ground then opened the backpack he carried and produced another medical kit. He addressed Sheriff Savoy while he worked.

"Sheriff, you have my Colonel in your cruiser... do you really think that's necessary at this point?" He turned his attention and spoke to Charlie who was next to him, and an extra pair of hands.

Charlie moved quickly and went to retrieve another light from the sheriff's car. Savoy released the Colonel then got on the radio.

Dane dropped to his knees next to Emmett. He reached over and gripped the back of Preston's neck then pressed his forehead next to the young man's in a show of thankfulness and support. The feeling that passed between them was short lived due to the urgency at hand. Dane looked down at the man who had sacrificed his own well-being to save Preston. He spoke to the Marine as his priorities realigned in his mind.

"Tell me what to do Captain; I'll thank you for disobeying orders later."

Savoy joined them with two more flashlights and held them where the Captain instructed. He checked Cotton's back to see if the bullet had passed through and discovered it was still in his side.

The disinfectant didn't stir Cotton; however, when the Captain began to probe the hole in Emmett's side with his gloved finger, he opened his eyes. He was perspiring badly and was disoriented from the searing pain in his middle. He flinched twice. He spoke as his eyelids fluttered.

"Dane..." Cotton's voice was weak.

Dane pressed the gauze firm on the pressure point where the Captain instructed as he answered Cotton.

"I'm here, Emmett. You're losing blood too fast. Hold on while we slow it down. We're fixing to transport you in a few minutes. Hold on... that's an order." They could hear a helicopter in the distance and the spotlight that was attached to it was scanning the terrain below as it moved.

Emmett closed his eyes.

"Ouch!" he growled. "Dammit, you're not hoeing cotton! I'm not one of your grunts, Dane... so don't tell me what to do." Emmett fussed, but his voice grew weaker by the second. He sucked in a deep breath at the sudden blinding and stinging agony that gripped his nervous system; it caused him to tremble all over.

A couple of stressful minutes hung between all of them then the Captain held the plastic field tool up with the bullet in it and shook his head. He looked at Charlie with a pleased smile and then dropped it in the bag Charlie held open for him. The Captain finished attending to the wound so that Cotton could be ready for proper medical assistance. When the blunt of his distress subsided, Cotton asked about what was most important to him.

"Dane... is our boy all right?"

"Yes Emmett, look up."

Emmett opened his eyes again and found Preston looking down at him. Emmett held his hand up and Preston gripped it.

"What about Butler?" he mumbled.

"It was his judgment day after all," answered Preston.

Emmett held on to Preston's hand as he closed his eyes to rest.

Preston walked to the ambulance with Sheriff Cotton. Units from three counties and three branches of service had responded to Savoy's distress call that went out over the airways of three officers down. Ned had slid to a stop in his patrol car; he was the first to make it to the scene. Owen had called him after he had called Sheriff Savoy.

Because officers had been shot in the line of duty, the state police would take jurisdiction of the investigation. Dane and Savoy had talked and came to an understanding. The Colonel had apprehended Russell Butler and requested Sheriff Savoy to meet him at the scene of the crime to pick him up and retrieve Butler's vehicle from the woods. However, the Colonel was still willing to bear the responsibility when it came time to place blame.

The paramedic asked Preston for the third time to come to the emergency room, so they could treat his hand. They closed the door to the ambulance and Preston backed out of the way to the side of the road, so they could back up and be on their way. He stuck his good hand in his pocket; the other was throbbing due to the confrontational rage he inflicted on Butler.

Preston looked down at the soiled bandages. He didn't know if the blood was his or Butler's. There was something fearful inside of him that did not want to go back to the place where he had held Jaden while her life had slipped away from him. He didn't think he could go back there. A few moments of indecision hung in his reason. The sheriff had risked his life to protect him. He wanted to be there for Sheriff Cotton because the man had always been there for him.

His breath became shallow and the surrounding turmoil faded into the distant corners of his mind as his vision went past his hand to the gravel where he stood. The yellow tape was trapped beneath his boot, but it was insignificant compared to what was beneath it. Preston blinked at the soiled spot on the ground. He squatted down because he suddenly felt dizzy. His palms held his forehead as he stared at the spot. He reached down and touched it with his fingertips; his heartbeat sputtered in his chest as his eyes watered. He blinked several times; when his vision cleared, he recognized something shiny in the glow of the headlights from the surrounding vehicles. Preston's finger pushed several small rocks away from the object. He swiped at the ground a couple of times then picked up one end of the braided strands of leather. He gently shook it free of the sandy earth then held up this personal message that could only be meant for him. Preston's body was enthralled by calm as his eyes clung to the silver initial of his first name. He touched the silver cross that was attached to it. Mr. Silver's words resonated in his mind, 'In the most unexpected of times, she'll reach out to you'.

Preston blinked, and hot tears spilled onto his cheeks. He knew Jaden was with him and he spoke to her.

"I know you're there... I feel you, Baby. I can feel you. I miss you... and it hurts... so bad." Preston was overcome with emotion for a few moments then he made her a promise. "I swear to you Baby, I'm gonna become the man you deserved, Jaden... because I love you... and because you loved me."

Charlie hung up the phone after letting Owen know where he was and what had happened. He headed back to Preston who sat on the gurney in silent thought. The doctor had repaired some sutures in his hand and warned him about possible nerve damage if he didn't take care and allow it to heal without further trauma. The nurse had taken over the job of bandaging it while the doctor went to the next patient.

Dane entered the busy room and came to join them. They were anxious for information concerning Cotton.

"He's in surgery. They said it would be a couple of hours. They've run into a snag. It seems he left a large amount of his blood on the ground and they're out of B negative. They have family on the way to donate." The Colonel rubbed the back of his neck as he waited a few seconds for the nurse to finish and move on to another patient. He needed to tell Preston some things that were important to him before he left.

"I'm very sorry, Preston. I shouldn't have called you... none of this would have happened if I had just..."

Preston butted in as he moved his numbed fingers back and forth.

"Sir, you are who you are, and you did what you thought was right." Preston lifted his head and looked at the man in front of him. He knew now that even though a man was flawed, and his heart calloused with the scars of his mistakes, it did not mean he couldn't be trusted, or that he could not love. "You're my father and you care about me." His perspective came flowing out. "You, me and Charlie, we knew what kind of scum Butler was... now everybody else knows too." Preston's eyes touched Charlie's for a second then he looked around the room to make sure he had complete privacy before he spoke again. "Sir, I need you to promise me something before you leave."

"Of course, Preston, what do you need?" questioned the Colonel.

"You heard what Charlie said to me tonight... concerning his step-father. Would you keep it to yourself? It was settled some years back... and it needs to stay that way."

The Colonel put on his hat as he looked at Preston then Charlie.

"Absolutely, it makes me feel better knowing you have such a friend as Charlie. I know he's a man you can count on."

"Yes Sir... I do too." Preston gazed at his father and one side of his mouth turned up. "I wish we could have been friends, a long time ago. I'll miss you."

Dane nodded his head.

"Me too, Preston. It was my fault. I wish I hadn't allowed alcohol to rule my judgment like I did. I am very sorry, and I regret it... and the way I've treated you. I sure don't deserve your forgiveness... but I want it."

"You've always had it, Sir," stated Preston in a quiet voice.

Silence hung between them a few seconds.

"I wish I didn't have to leave you like this," admitted Dane. "I've re-learned that being sober allows a person to feel everything around him... even the pain of others."

"It's okay to be human, Sir." Preston's voice was sincere as he looked Dane in the eye. "Dad, I understand where you're coming from... where you've been... and where you're going. Really, I understand now. When my mother died, you went against the grain of who you are and came for me. You stayed and made a home for me because I had no one else... and because you loved her. You could have dumped me, but you didn't. It was hard; we did the best we could. The way I see it, because of Jaden, we made it through. She told me she didn't regret or resent the hardships in her life because they were the soil that grew understanding. You have a job to do, Sir... go do it without worrying about me. Honestly, I have no regrets about us. Stay safe and watch your back. Who knows, I may run into you somewhere in a couple of years."

"I swear I hope not Preston." The Colonel and Preston stared at each other a long moment. "Preston, I want you to know that I..." the Colonel paused as he idly turned his hat in his hand.

"I love you, Dad." The strong young man held out his bandaged hand to his father.

The Colonel looked at it then ignored the rigid gesture and wrapped his arms around him. The young man grabbed a firm hold on him and Dane's arms constricted as tender warmth spread through his chest. In the whole of his life, he had never felt anything that came close to the acceptance and esteem this young man gave him.

"I love you too, Son," affirmed Dane in a raspy tone of voice.

Preston and Charlie watched the Colonel walk away from them, knowing they would probably never see him again. They also knew that Colonel Dane Reid's life had been changed by Jaden as much as anyone's.

The doctor walked past them, and Preston addressed him with respect. He stopped long enough for Preston to ask him where he could go to donate blood.

Charlie and Preston sat in the surgery waiting room along with two dozen Sheriff Departments' staff from Liberty and Dallas County. Sheriff Savoy and some state police had arrived a few minutes ago; they lingered in the hallway until they had a word on Cotton and the rookie who was also in surgery with his shoulder and leg wounds.

The outcome of the evening, being what it was, gave Sheriff Savoy and Colonel Reid the leeway to disclose the basic truth of the evening's confrontation. The Colonel's handgun had been stored away before Savoy and his men arrived, and Butler's civil rights had expired when his lifeless body dropped to the pavement. Colonel Reid had located and detained the perpetrator and Savoy had gone to meet him and take the prisoner into custody. The details of the Dallas officers being shot were explained by the older deputy and Savoy gave an account on Cotton's behalf. Captain Peck told the state police that the Colonel had gone to meet his son and let him see for himself that Butler had been apprehended. He told them that he followed because his duty is to protect his Colonel. If there was speculation surrounding the night's events, no one was talking about it.

Preston was in a drug-induced calm, but he was very much aware of where he was and why. Charlie saw the beautiful young woman when she entered the congested waiting room. She stood there looking around for a moment. Ned spoke to her as he stood. Charlie watched her go to him and they hugged each other like they were family. She and Ned spoke for a few minutes then Ned smiled and looked around at the other's waiting. Charlie witnessed some of them stand and approach the two of them. Obviously, she was bearing good news. It was then that the young woman turned and looked straight at Preston. She was crying now and headed their way.

Charlie elbowed Preston as she approached; his manners sent him to his feet. Preston raised his head. Charlie glanced back to him, so his friend would know they had a visitor.

The young woman smiled at Charlie as she swiped at her cheeks, but she stopped in front of Preston and went to her knees. Preston's eyes finally met hers.

"Preston, I've been out of town with work. Mom told me what happened this morning when I called. I'm so sorry. I got back as soon as I could get a flight." She wrapped her arms around him. Charlie sat back down as Preston rested his forehead on her shoulder and spoke to her.

"The man that killed her shot your dad tonight. He was trying to protect me. I'm sorry, Julie."

Preston's demeanor was older and wiser now. Charlie reasoned that they had crossed over into adulthood together. He realized that they could never again sit around the firelight as the boys they once were but would do so as the men they were becoming.

"Oh Preston, I'm so thankful that he did! Dad loves you. He talks about you all the time. There's no reason for you to apologize." She touched his face with her palms as she looked at him. "You look so tired. I'm here to stay with him, why don't you go home?"

Preston shook his head.

"I can't, Julie. I need to see him first, I need to know if he is going to be okay. The doctor told me that he needs blood. I'm B negative, but they wouldn't let me give because of my hand."

Charlie noticed the way the young woman's expression changed as she looked at Preston. Her eyes were full of thankfulness and love. She smiled then she nodded her head in agreement.

"Don't worry... he's in recovery and he's doing well. He sent me to check on you. He told me to make you go home." She looked at Charlie and held out her hand. "Hey Charlie, I'm Julianna Cotton. I'm glad to meet you."

Charlie shook her hand while wondering if this young woman may be Preston's sister. He sensed she was thinking the same thing. He chided himself for the thought because the two people that had unknowingly raised his suspicions concerning the matter were obviously going to leave things as they were. He surely had no business butting into something so private, especially when what he had overheard was so vague. He reasoned that if Cotton had something to say to Preston, it should be between them alone.

"Yes Ma'am, it's nice to meet you too," responded Charlie in a polite and quiet voice.

Julianna gripped Preston's uninjured hand as she spoke.

"If you're going to stay then you may as well come with me."

423

Cotton heard the noise from the hallway in his altered consciousness; it took a moment for him to process the pain he felt and why. He opened his eyes and blinked a couple of times then focused on the beautiful face of his daughter and a worried frown on the face of his son. The monitor assured them that Cotton's heart was beating with a sturdy pace.

"My word, this is a sight for sore eyes," he mumbled then the corner of his mouth turned up slightly.

Julianna teased her father as she fussed over his bedding.

"I tried to make him go home, Daddy, but he needed to see you for peace of mind. I told him I was sure they had a mule at the ranch that would be more pleasant to visit than you, but he insisted." She leaned over and pecked her father's brow with a kiss.

"Heehaw," mumbled Cotton. His eyelids fluttered a few seconds then closed.

Preston stood next to the man who had changed his life and had risked everything for him. He reached over and laid his palm on the sheriff's brow. Cotton opened his eyes and turned his face to Preston then smiled. His voice was weak when he spoke, but his words were strong.

"Dane loves you... but so do I. You've been through a lot son and you need to rest. Do it for me," mumbled Cotton. "Charlie?"

"Yes Sir, Sheriff... I'm here." Charlie stepped up to the foot of his bed.

"Take care of him for me, 'til I'm stronger."

"Yes Sir, I will," assured Charlie softly.

Cotton reached for Preston's hand and gave it a caring squeeze.

"All right, I'll go... but I'll see you tomorrow." Preston leaned over and hugged him. He had to tell the sheriff what was inside of him. "Thank you for going with me tonight,

Sheriff. You're always there when I need you. I wanted to be here for you. You mean so much to me and I love you too, Sir."

Cotton's eyes were closed, but his smile assured Preston and the others he had heard him.

Preston closed the door of Sheriff Cotton's hospital room. Julianna looked back to her father and found him staring at it; his eyes were tearful. She put the bed rail down and climbed up beside him then pressed her cheek next to his forehead.

"Daddy, he's your son... isn't he?" she questioned softly. She waited a moment for her father to answer. She knew it was a private thing she was asking him.

"Yes. I believe so, Honey."

"He is Dad. He's B negative too. He tried to donate for you, but they wouldn't take it because of his hand injury." She sat up, so she could consider her father's eyes. "How long have you known this? Does he know?"

Cotton shook his head.

"I started looking out for him because he was living in a dangerous situation and because... I loved his mother so deeply. His birthday gave me cause to wonder. My suspicions about him became clearer the day they got married. Dane and I had a come to Jesus meeting when he found me putting flowers on Caroline's grave.

"I fell in love with her while he was in service. He treated her like a possession... not a wife. She went to visit him for his birthday and because he wasn't expecting her, she caught him in the act of adultery. It hurt her beyond repair. Their marriage was over; he just didn't know it yet. She filed for divorce when she got home. When he came home, he sensed it was over and he tried to force her to love him, but it was too late. The irony is... it seems he was sterile when he married her. He never told her, and rightly so... she didn't know who had fathered her child, so she wouldn't tell me. He knew all along that the boy wasn't his and he punished her until she died... then he blamed Preston. He's a good son and a good man... despite the destructive people in his life." Cotton shook his head again; a few seconds of silence slipped by as he thought about that time in his life. "He doesn't know. It's best this way, I guess. It's what's supposed to be."

"Daddy, I like the idea of having a brother. Besides, he has a right to know. You should tell him."

Her father's words were becoming feeble from all he had endured, and this wasn't the time to be dragging a confession out of him, no matter how excited she was at the truth in it.

"I just found him, Julie. I'd rather be his friend than risk losing him over his feeling betrayed. He's been through so much pain in his life. Don't tell him, I trust the Almighty to let me know when the time is right."

Julianna considered what her father said and, as happy as she was about Preston being her brother, she had to respect his wishes. Suddenly, Julianna's perspective came full circle concerning what her father had told her. She nuzzled her father's cheek then softly kissed it.

"Daddy, Ms. Caroline... my piano teacher... is Preston's mother? She was carrying my little brother when I met her and spent time with her?"

"Yes, Honey. Caroline said you were her best student. I wish I could tell him about her too... and about us," whispered Cotton as he drifted back to sleep.

Julianna held her father as her mind went back to the day, she met Caroline Breaux-Reid and memories of that time in her life began to surface. She thought of the antebellum castle under the huge quiet oak trees and remembered how she anxiously awaited her piano lessons each week. She remembered Caroline's mesmerizing alto voice as she sang and played the piano, and the way they laughed together as they danced to the old phonograph upstairs in the music room. Julianna's thoughts focused on the memories she had of the beautiful and elegant woman. She remembered the way Ms. Caroline taught her to hold her arms out and twirl around in place as motivation to change a bad mood. And, she remembered pressing her ear and her hand to Ms. Caroline's round belly, so she could feel her baby move. Julianna smiled with understanding because those momentous days had been her first contact with her little brother.

CHAPTER 21

Cotton watched through sore red eyes as the nurse pushed the medication into the port in his arm. He had tried to deal with the pain in his side, but it was quickly spreading throughout his entire body to the point of being unbearable. They kept telling him to rest, but his blood pressure would spike every time the medication wore off and he had developed a fever. He thought he remembered the doctor telling Julie that infection had set in and they were going to put him on a stronger antibiotic. His mind was cloudy, so it could have been a dream. His daughter's face was etched with worry again and she hovered over him seeing to his needs, so it must have been a memory. He knew better than anyone how memories can have roots so deep that there seems to be no distinction between them and reality, especially when you face life alone.

The nurse stepped away from his bedside and Cotton closed his eyes. He felt a warm, feminine essence fill the spot just before he was blessed with her touch. He basked in her nearness as her cool and delicate fingers gently combed through his hair. He opened his eyes to see her beautiful pale skin, full pink lips and shining blue eyes smile down at him like an angel. The medication slid through his veins bringing with it a warm, floating sensation. He watched as tears pooled in her eyes; their deep blue turned purple beneath the fluorescent light. He blinked unable to believe that Caroline was standing next to him. A tear ran down her cheek as she spoke.

"Emmett, I'm with you, don't give in to the weakness; you have to focus your energy on living. I was afraid to tell you when I had the chance... because of the way things were for us... because of the uncertainty that ached in my heart. I knew the minute he was put in my arms that he was your son. I loved you then and I love you now. I've always been here waiting for you, but your work is not finished. Preston needs his father. You must take care of him. He's meant for wonderful things, Emmett, but he's not strong enough now to make it... not without you." She traced his lips with the tips of her fingers; a warm current passed through his body in response. *"I should have told you of the possibility, but I feared Dane's vengeance. Forgive me. You fill my heart so completely. When the time comes to tell him about us... tell him he brought love, joy and peace to my life. Emmett, it's in this realm of consciousness that I can be with you, but you can't stay. You must go back; Preston is not strong enough to make it without you... not yet. I love you, Emmett. I love you so very much."*

"No wait! Don't go, Caroline... wait! Please wait!" Emmett sat straight up in the bed as he cried out and reached for her, but as always, she was just beyond his grasp. He rolled to his hip in hast and dropped his feet off the bed. Emmett cried out again, but it was different this time as his body shuttered with pain. He lost his breath and his head started to spin.

Julianna's mind was snatched out of sleep only a couple of seconds before she leaped off the small couch and rushed to her father's side. She grabbed his shoulders to push him back into the bed, but he was stronger than she realized. His eyes were bloodshot, and he was crying as he pleaded with someone that was very real to him.

"Daddy, stop! You can't get up... you're going to hurt yourself." She managed to slap the call button while she wrestled with the man she loved most in the world. Tears brimmed in her eyes and she began to cry with him at the passionate way he pleaded with whoever was in his mind's eye. It was as though he was delirious and trapped in a dream state.

The door burst open and two nurses rushed in to help her comfort him. The doctor was not far behind them. It was God's grace that he was, because her father was attacked by a seizure and his body jerked in response to the spastic chaos taking place in his brain. They urged her out of the way as more staff came to assist them in her father's care. Julianna stood at the edge of the room and watched as the small hospital bed shook beneath his body. She threw her hands over her mouth to try to control her emotions as fear crippled her heart.

The fevered turmoil in Emmett's body wreaked havoc on his system, his mind and heart were affected as well. But there was something strong inside of Emmett that had begun to grow more than eighteen years ago. It had the strength to battle all that was wrong inside of him; it had the strength to hang on, so his body could heal.

Julie watched as the staff worked diligently to stabilize her father. When the seizure finally let go of him, the doctor and staff began to assess and treat his immediate needs. She waited in a panicked state wondering what was happening to him after he seemed to have come through surgery so well.

The internist stopped next to Julie as the nursing staff began to load some equipment that was attached to her father onto the edge of his bed. She questioned the doctor as to what was happening.

"Dr. Lawrence, what are they doing? What's happening to my father?"

"Miss Cotton, I'm moving him to the Intensive Care Unit. His fever is high, which means he's fighting a serious infection, and his heart rhythm is erratic. I've consulted with a cardiologist; Dr. Newsom is one of the best in Dallas.

We need to run some specialized tests. It's possible that his body has become septic. He needs more concentrated care at this point. There's a waiting room on the 5th floor; it has everything you'll need for a prolonged stay. I'm afraid you'll only be able to see him for 15 minutes every two hours. Let me get him stabilized and comfortable, then I'll get some tests started. I'll come back and talk to you in a little while when I know more about his condition."

Julianna nodded her head as she watched them roll her father's bed out of the room. There was a short delay at the doorway because of another patient being brought to the floor. She hurried to organize her things from the floor and the couch, so she could follow them. She opened the small closet and removed her father's bag and quickly shoved his things inside of it. When she turned to the small sink to collect his razor and toothbrush, she saw Preston. He was standing in the hallway next to her father's bed and holding his hand with a fearful dent in his forehead. It was in that moment and from that perspective that she saw her father's profile in him, the same brow and jaw line, and the dimple in his cheek. He wasn't quite as tall as her father, but he was young and more than likely had some growth completion left in him before his body was through. His attention traded off between her and the man that meant so much to them. When they were free of the doorway and started up the hallway with him, Julianna's fear surfaced. She threw her arms around Preston and she began to cry. He held her in strong arms as she told him through her tears what was happening.

Preston acted quickly and helped her gather their belongings, so they could ride up to the ICU with him. They caught up to Cotton as they loaded him on the elevator and the staff made room for them.

Julianna leaned over and kissed his cheek then nuzzled his ear. She remembered the fear she felt when her mother divorced him. She felt like that scared little girl and her daddy was being taken away from her all over again.

"I love you so much, Daddy! Promise me you won't forget that I'm here waiting for you! Promise me, Daddy!"

The heart monitor sounded off with a shrill and warning series of pings.

"He's crashing!" announced Dr. Lawrence in an urgent voice. The medical personnel had already leaped to action at the alarming sound of trouble.

Preston's arms folded around Julianna and pulled her out of the way of the medical staff as they surrounded the bed with the purpose of saving the brave man that had saved him.

Cotton's heart skipped several beats as his scared little girl shared the pain in her heart. Somewhere in his feverish mind... while suspended in the glimmers of past and present... Emmett heard her.

He shook his head as his little girl's tearful voice echoed through the phone into his ear.

"I love you so much, Daddy. Promise me you won't forget that I'm here waiting for you! Promise me, Daddy!"

"Julie, Baby... daddy's not going to forget you. I promise, Sweetheart. I could never forget my baby girl! It's just not possible." Emmett placed his forearm against the wall and rubbed his brow on his shirt sleeve. His disappointment and frustration weighed heavy in his chest. He opened his eyes and blinked several times as he swallowed the rising emotion in his throat. His little girl felt just as betrayed as he did, and yet there was nothing he could do to better the circumstances for either one of them.

"I don't understand why everything has to be their way all the time, Daddy. I had my suitcase packed so I could come home this weekend. I want to come home, Daddy! You're a deputy... can't you make her leave me with you... put her in jail, or something!" suggested his eight-year-old daughter.

Cotton wished it were that simple. If it were, this mess would have been over two years ago when he caught Vicki in bed with another man.

"Julie, you know I can't do that. Honey, we've talked about this. Your mother and I are not married anymore. And…"

The eight-year-old butted in to reveal just how much she did understand.

"I know that, but the judge said you get to keep half of me and that means I get to be with you as much as I have to stay with mama, but it always gets messed up. It's my turn to be with my daddy. It's not fair!"

He smiled because she was right.

"I know that Sweetheart, but the weather has turned bad, and your mother said y'all are stuck in Arkansas. I'm just as disappointed as you are. I promise you, Honey. We'll have the next two weekends together." Cotton swallowed again. "Put your mama on the phone and I'll make sure she understands that."

"I can't, they've left already," answered the child.

"What do you mean… they've left? Where did they go?"

"They went to some concert tonight. I heard Autry tell her to dress warm because it was cold outside."

Cotton's jaw teeth clinched together as he realized that Vicki had lied to him again, so she and Autry could have their way. Clearly, he and Julie could be damned if it interfered with their personal agenda.

"Julie, I'm sorry. I don't appreciate your mother doing things like this to us, and I am going to speak to her about it. I shouldn't say this Honey, and I ask that you not talk about it to either of them, but you will reach the age when you can decide where you want to live."

"Really, Daddy… how old do I have to be?" she questioned.

"I'm not exactly sure, 12… I think. I'll find out this week and we'll talk next weekend. I'll have to work Saturday, which means you will have to visit with Nanna and Pop until I get off."

"That's all right, Daddy. I stay with the maid at Autry's most of the time, anyway. I like helping Nanna with her sewing. You will come for lunch won't you. I can make

434

tuna salad now... boil the eggs and everything! Oh! Can we eat at the diner on Saturday night?"

Cotton chuckled. She liked the chicken and dumplings at the diner as much as he did.

"Of course, guess what I had for supper tonight?"

"Chicken and dumplings! Are you calling me from the diner?" she asked.

"Yep, it's getting late though. I was dreading going home to an empty house since... well, you know." A moment of silence hung between them. "Anyway, I miss you, Honey. I'm already looking forward to tasting that tuna salad. I'll plan to pick you up next Friday night. I love you and I'll talk to you tomorrow."

Emmett smiled as his little girl told him goodbye. He hung up the phone breaking contact with the only person in the world, other than his parents, that offered him unconditional love.

He walked over to the corner booth by the window and sat down. The place was empty for a Friday night considering the Mustang's basketball season was in full swing. He did some paperwork while he ate his meal, and half an hour later, he found himself drinking a cup of coffee and enjoying some cherry cobbler with his boss, Sheriff Cyrus Vance. He was divorced too, but had a lady friend, Emma Jolly, that doted on him. She was 36 years old, and everyone knew they were sweethearts. Sheriff Vance had just turned 50 and all his staff assumed that his quiet mood of late was because of it. He had not expected the man, who was a friend of both him and his father, to sit down across from him and ask if he could talk. He shared with Emmett that he was burdened because he had fathered a child with Emma. He hadn't been blessed with children in his previous marriage of ten years, and here he was past middle age, but still wanting everything he wanted in his younger years. He wanted to get married, to be a good father and a devoted husband, but he considered himself an old man.

Emmett watched his boss back out of the parking spot in front of the diner. The sheriff held up his hand as an *appreciative smile claimed his expression. Cotton responded the same way.*

He picked up his cup and drank a swallow of coffee. Emmett realized his boss had talked himself into doing the right thing while using him for a sounding board. The inspiration his boss displayed had inadvertently changed his gloomy outlook concerning the spoiled weekend with his daughter. He respected the disappointment that was inside him; otherwise, he wouldn't have found out that Vicki and Autry were doing a number on him about the weather. He was tired of their manipulation. Julianna was old enough to tell Judge Adler what was really happening. His mind was made up, and he was going to take them back to court.

His thoughts were interrupted by the waitress as she offered him some fresh coffee. He declined the offer then asked for his ticket. She smiled and told him that the sheriff had taken care of his meal. Emmett retrieved a stick of the cinnamon gum from the front pocket of his shirt then opened it and shoved it into his mouth. He took the brass money clip out of his trouser pocket and laid a bill on the table then picked up his cup and finished the last sip of coffee.

Being the last weekend in January, the night was crisp and cold. He had worked double shifts through the holidays, so some other men could be off with their families. He was off the schedule until Monday morning at 6:00 a.m. and he was determined not to pester his parents all weekend. He had been looking forward to spending time with Julianna; however, the unexpected trip to Arkansas at the first of the week had messed up everything. His time off was precious and Vicki knew this. It was a blatant reminder that she no longer possessed any consideration for his feelings, and Autry was where her interest was focused. The bitterness he felt made his heart as cold as the biting winter night. The diner was homey and a lot warmer than the small, empty house he once shared with his family.

Emmett's attention was snagged by the pale movements in the shadows across the street. It was 8:30 p.m., and he knew the Circuit Clerk, Evander Tillman had dismissed his staff and was locking up for the weekend. That year was not an election year, but their senator had died unexpectedly in a boating accident and a special election was being held to select his replacement. The Circuit Clerk's staff was working overtime trying to get the precinct boxes ready to be delivered throughout the county. Mr. Tillman always made it a point to enlist the help of the Sheriff's Department with the distribution and pickup of the ballot boxes. He wanted it known that he took every precaution possible so that the citizens of Liberty county would have their voices protected and heard.

He recognized Caroline Breaux-Reid immediately when she emerged out of the darkness into the soft light of the street lamps and crossed the courthouse lawn. The French-Indian beauty would catch any man's eye. He remembered that in her youth her long black curls had always cascaded down her back, but as a married woman she wore it up. Her skin was flawless and pale because of her French blood, and he knew for a fact that her eyes were so blue they appeared to be a deep purple beneath the right light. They had gone to school together and because of their jobs, he saw her all the time. But rumors seemed to be all he knew of her. She was shy, and there had always been something about her which gave him pause. The way she looked at him was like she had something on her mind but could not speak. Whatever she had been thinking had remained unspoken to this day. They passed each other in the hallways of the courthouse on a regular basis and they always spoke to one another. Still, due to personal commitments of past and present, they had never had the chance to establish a real friendship. He remembered her as a quiet and invisible girl. He believed she had been raised to be stealthy and cautious like the rest of her family because of their assets and securities. Everyone was surprised when she married a local serviceman who as a youth had a vague and questionable reputation in the county. The marriage seemed troubled from the start because she was not glowing with happiness like most brides. It was understandable that she would be even more unapproachable as a married woman than she was in her younger years. But sometimes, he caught himself wondering about what was on her mind that she could not say.

He watched her and remembered the mysteriously beautiful girl from his youth as she stepped off the sidewalk behind the courthouse and got in the 42 Coupe. When she got out and raised the hood, he realized the automobile had let her down. She tried to crank it one more time after he witnessed her try more tricks to revive the motor than most men would have attempted. He decided she needed assistance, and he didn't care if her hard-nuts husband found out that he had helped her. It was his job to serve the public. He stood and went to the coat rack to get his jacket, calling out a goodnight to Mr. Vickers and his wife, Annie, the owners of the diner.

Cotton turned towards the door just in time to see her slam the hood, and then she disappeared across the courthouse lawn into the darkness from where she had come. He went to his patrol car and cranked it then turned on the heater. He backed out and circled around the square then headed down Main Street.

The evening was cold, and she had set a brisk pace for herself. He caught up to her three blocks down, at the end of Main Street. She had crossed the pavement at the intersection and was headed toward the river-walk. He stopped in the street and rolled his window down then called to her.

"Good evening, Caroline! I was having supper at the diner and noticed that your car wouldn't start. I'd be happy to look at it... if you want me too."

She had stopped in her tracks when he slowed down and called to her, but now she stared at him in that strange way that was familiar, even though he had not seen it in years. When she spoke, she couldn't seem to find the right words and blundered through her response making no sense for which she began to apologize.

A car came to the stop sign behind him, so Emmett pulled over to the sidewalk where she stood and got out. The car turned at the corner and slowly rolled past them. She remained silent as Westville's Mayor, Yancy East, rolled his window down and asked if there was a problem. Deputy Cotton told him that Mrs. Reid's car wouldn't start, and she was going to leave it parked on the square. He told the Mayor that a mechanic would see to the car in the light of day. His explanation satisfied Mayor East, who made it part of his duty to drive around the town every night before going to bed. The deputy had given him the lengthy explanation, because after seeing the two of them talking in the darkness, he knew Yancy East would see her car and assume the worst of them.

Emmett watched the Mayor's car disappear around the next corner and when he turned back to her, she was staring at him. He smiled as he approached her.

"You're looking well, Caroline. I haven't seen you in the hallway lately; Evan has kept his staff busy the last few weeks."

She gazed up at him and he couldn't help noticing the starry glimmers reflecting in her eyes beneath the street lights.

"Umm, no, Emmett… it won't start. I mean, good evening… and no, it won't start… and yes, we are working long hours. How are you?"

Her eyes were mesmerizing as always, but tonight they looked dreamy in the shadows of the night.

"I'm fine. I will look at the car tomorrow; if you would rather. I could take you home. It's too late for a young woman to be out walking alone." He pointed out politely.

"I appreciate the fact that you even noticed me, Emmett. And, I appreciate that you have come to my rescue even though our Mayor tends to have a wagging tongue."

Emmett chuckled lightly and nodded his head in agreement.

"Yes, he does. But you are a lady in distress; although, if I hadn't interrupted your walk, you would probably be home by now." His smile turned into a grin.

439

"Besides, I couldn't care less what Yancy East may say about me. I've already been the talk of the town, but you don't deserve it. I will respect your wishes if you prefer that I not bother you anymore this evening."

She surveyed his face for a moment then her countenance changed right in front of his eyes; her right eyebrow shifted upward as she smiled back at him. It surprised him when she consented to the ride home with a simple nod of her head then bravely stepped off the curb and headed for the passenger side of his car.

Emmett followed her and politely opened the door. He went around to the driver's side and opened his but paused and unfastened his service belt which he put it in the trunk of the car. He joined her then turned the heater up a notch, so her feet could warm. It was a small town and whether you were friends or not, everybody knew everybody. He was aware that her husband, Colonel Dane Reid, had been away for almost ten months due to his job being in Washington and she had been left to make do on her own. After watching her try to fix the car, he deduced she had learned how to become self-reliant.

Her place was a couple of miles out of town on Riverfront Road. It was once the most beautiful home in the county and her family was the wealthiest.

Emmett initiated a conversation.

"I heard a rumor that it was going to snow tonight... it's supposed to blow in from the north. I was told by my ex-wife that it was already snowing in Arkansas; however, I spoke to my daughter a little while ago and it's cold and clear. I suspect the rumor of snow was spread by someone wishing for it."

Caroline responded in a way that resembled the comfort of old friends.

"I heard the same forecast from Evan earlier. I think everyone feels cheated because we kept hearing of it during Christmas but never saw any."

Emmett thought her voice sounded hopeful as she spoke about the possibility. He asked her a question concerning work.

"So, do you know what day we'll be distributing the ballot boxes?"

"I believe we'll be ready by Thursday. That'll give the precincts time to test them and should we need to replace any, we'll have plenty of time to do so before the election."

They talked in an easy comfort as he drove. Emmett realized that the shyness he assumed was her way, was really a preconceived notion on his part. He was caught off guard by her spontaneity when she mentioned the rumors concerning his wife leaving him because he didn't want to be a father anymore. She looked him in the eye and asked if he would tell her the real reason they had divorced.

His answer fell by the wayside as he slowed down and turned between the brick columns that designated the entrance to her property. She asked that he follow it around to the backdoor then explained because the house was so large; she had the front part shut off for the winter. Cotton was intrigued by the house; he had always thought of it as a sleeping lady, mysteriously tucked underneath the shadows of the pilgrim oak trees. He asked her if she got scared living out here alone.

Caroline shook her head and confessed she didn't feel alone. She told him the rich history of her family had left their spirits alive inside the house. She told him she had a lot of interests and it was easy to keep busy.

They sat in the patrol car for a while with the heater on and talked about her family. He admitted to her that he had always been fascinated by the house and the curious stories of her family. He told her he had heard a story at school about the ghost of her great grandfather and how he sat on the front porch every year at Halloween and handed out candy. He confessed he had been so intrigued and curious about the story when he was a boy that he pestered his father to bring him to see if it were true.

At that moment, the clouds shifted, and moonlight filled the front seat of the patrol car. She smiled at him and he watched her eyes glisten with energy. The unusual violet color he remembered from years ago was revived beneath the secrecy of her thick, feathery lashes. When she spoke, her words were playful, but at the same time they cast a new spell of mystery.

"Yes, I remember. It was the first time I saw you in uniform. You were eight years old then... only the star on your chest said 'Sheriff' and you were sporting a huge mustache that was curled up on both ends, oh... and two six-shooters." She laughed softly.

"You remember that night... and my costume?" he mumbled.

"Yes. That was my first year in school. I was the ballerina that was on the balcony above you. It was past my bedtime... but the adults were having a masquerade party for my mother's co-workers. My father was a child at heart and he tucked me in that night, so I could stay in character a little longer. I snuck across the hallway into their room then out to the balcony to watch the older kids from town come and go. So... did you see Grandfather?"

Emmett grinned as he recalled the sparkling little girl with the flowing tutu and rhinestone crown. She was standing on the edge of the large square pillar that held the cathedral-like columns of the porch; it was the perfect perch to watch the activity below. It made sense, she would only be doing something that dangerous if she were daring and unsupervised.

"Yes, I did." Emmett chuckled. "He was dressed like an Indian chief and was sitting by a campfire in front of a life-size teepee in the yard. He gave me a bag of goodies and offered my dad a puff off his peace pipe. I was surprised when my father accepted it then took a drag and blew the smoke rings into the darkness. He told me to shake the chief's hand, so I would get over the ghost story and give him some peace."

Caroline started to giggle, and Emmett laughed with her. It was as though they were the closest of friends. He sensed that a part of her really felt that way.

"I'm amazed that your grandfather Vincent managed to settle and flourish in a place so wild by himself. Obviously, he was a daring and courageous man. Hmm, that must be where the little ballerina standing on the porch railing got her courage." He turned to her and crossed his arms then encouraged her response with a smile.

"He was courageous, but he didn't actually settle this land by himself. He had help."

Emmett was enjoying this unexpected and unique pleasure of visiting with the mysterious beauty and he wasn't ready to be liberated of her company.

"I can feel the history... and almost taste the flavor which surrounds this place. Tell me about Vincent Breaux, Caroline; I would love to be more familiar with who you are... and the people who are responsible for it."

The subject of her family and home was dear to her heart, and he became mesmerized as she openly shared the stories of her heritage in passionate and intimate detail.

"My great, great grandfather, Vincent Leflore Breaux, bought this land sight unseen in 1849. The family owned a textile mill on the outskirts of Paris. He grew up working in it and later managing it. He was educated as a solicitor, so he could handle the family business, but he wanted to do something else with his life. When his father died, and he gained control of the company's future, he sold it and came to Texas. He was fascinated and seduced by the stories of the wild West and the Alamo. He wanted to see the rich land that spread as far as the eye could see or the mind imagine. He wanted to explore it for himself."

She pointed to the long building made of stone that was situated further down the bluff. Cotton's eyes clung to its ghostly appearance beneath the shadows and the moon.

"The stone house down there was the first dwelling he built. He cleared and settled the land then planted crops of tobacco, cotton and corn. He opened a law office and started a ferry service which transported people back and forth across the river, as well as, up and down the Liberty. The country was growing and changing, and the demand for the ferry service was overwhelming. He commissioned a special paddleboat to be built like a barge. It's massive size and openness would enable wagons and goods to be easily loaded and off-loaded. The business revolutionized trade and commerce in this area, and within a few years he was operating a dozen boats that were freighting goods and passengers up and down the river. He even capitalized making one of them a social enterprise for dinner cruises and theatre events. He was a man with vision and he had enough money to invest in his ideas, so he could make more. Because of his contacts in the homeland, he began to import all sorts of goods which were unobtainable here in the states.

"He built the old theatre downtown and the first five buildings at the university. My grandfather donated them to the county in 1920 with the agreement that the county would use them as a public learning institution. The administration building, library, auditorium and the science buildings were the original school, all the other buildings were added after it opened. He was a businessman and was full of ideas, but he wanted to learn how to work and manage the land, so it would flourish.

"Vincent originally left Paris with a wife, but she died during the trip. He arrived in his new country with a broken heart and dedicated his efforts to making a place for himself. He quickly found out that this new world was rudimentary and primitive in comparison to the refined lifestyle to which he had been raised. He hung on to the important things that made a good man, but he quickly learned he had to evolve and adjust daily to survive.

"He hired a lot of workers in those beginning years, but he knew he had to have a man that he could trust to help him in this wild new country. He needed someone who was honest, knew the customs and wasn't afraid of Lucifer himself. He spoke to the federal judge for the territory about his needs. The judge told him of a man whom he had sworn in as a federal marshal to hunt down the bad ones. The judge told him the man had a death wish because of grief and he was fearless. He explained the man was once a blacksmith by trade and had been the local minister until some outlaws rode through the territory. They shot him in the chest then burned the church down because he would not shoe their horses on Sunday. They took his wife when they rode out; her father hired some town's men to go after her. They found her body a few days later, her hands and feet were bound, and she was hanging by the neck in a tree. She was seven months pregnant when they took her; they don't know what happened to the baby. Vincent Breaux sought out and secured the aid of this man, his name was Truman Silver.

"Grandfather told Mr. Silver who he was and what he aimed to do. The things that caught Silver's attention most was that Grandfather was a decent man, a widower, a dreamer, and he aimed to have law and order on his land. The only thing Truman Silver asked for in exchange for his dedication was some private quarters and a protected piece of ground in which to bury his wife's body. Grandfather built a blacksmith shed and lodge on the north side of the bluff just beyond the new barn; it became Mr. Silver's new home. He and grandfather chose the shaded spot at the edge of the cottonwoods for a cemetery. He helped Silver collect his wife's body from the brick crypt that was borrowed from a family member who was not in need of it yet. They buried her in a Christian service and Mr. Silver covered her grave with white roses. I understand that in those days a white rose was symbolic for eternal love. Grandfather told me that even after Mr. Silver re-married some years later, he still visited her grave every day. Vincent's and Truman's friendships were established the day they met and remained solid until my grandfather's death... even after, I think. Truman Silver is buried in the cemetery as well. His body rests between his first wife, Brooke, and his second wife, Eden. The Silvers, who live in the Shadow Grove Community are descendants of Truman's and Eden's.

Caroline shifted in her seat and pulled her legs up beneath her skirt. She flashed him an apologetic smile as she commented.

"Listen to me babble about my family. You must be fighting exhaustion after working a 12-hour shift then escorting me home."

Emmett shook his head as he responded with zeal.

"No, don't stop. I'm captivated by your family... and your willingness to share them with me, Caroline. Please, continue... tell me some more about Vincent Breaux. You said his wife died during their passage to the states. I assume... like Truman, he re-married?"

Caroline's smile changed into one of pleasure and she began again.

"This country presented him with many surprises. One day a small group of wagons came through following the river north. They were drifters... undesirables who left trouble behind where ever they went. They asked if they could camp down by the river for a few days. Vincent offered them work in exchange for their hunting and camping on his land. They agreed to saw and chop two trees that had fallen next to the tobacco field into firewood. They had an Indian girl with them; she had chains on her ankles and waited on them as a slave. She was washing dishes down by the river one morning after breakfast when my grandfather and Silver approached her. They were curious as to why she was shackled. She told them she had been stolen from her people the year before by a shaman. He had forced himself on her because he wanted a child, but after many months of her belly not accepting his seed, he stole another and sold her to the drifters as a slave.

"Vincent did not take this information very well. He told her he would speak to the man about her freedom. That afternoon he and Silver rode to the work site where they were supposed to be chopping and loading the firewood and found the Indian girl doing the work. It infuriated him, so they went to their camp. They rode in and found them drunk and asleep, lying about the fire with full bellies. There was a roasted calf over the fire; they had eaten until they were *stuffed. Vincent put out the fire with the water he had seen her bring up that morning after she washed the dishes. The crackling steam woke some of them and they jumped up defensively and demanded to know what he was doing putting out their fire. Vincent told them that slaughtering one of his beef was not hunting, and it was not in the agreement that they lie around drunk and worthless while he provided for them. He demanded they pack their belongings and get off his land. He told them he would take the Indian girl as payment for the beef they had stolen. Vincent came to this country an excellent marksman; it was a sport in France, but here it was survival. They pressed him on the matter and Grandfather shot one of them while Silver cut down two more that drew on them. I was told that the two men who were not dead by the end of the confrontation agreed to leave with no argument. They dumped the dead men in the river because they did not want to expend the energy to dig graves for them. They took the roasted meat with them and left the Indian girl behind as payment.*

"The next morning Grandfather went to their camp to make sure they were gone, and he found the Indian girl still sawing and chopping the wood next to the tobacco field. He asked her what she was doing, and she told him that she was finishing the work in hope that he would allow her to camp and hunt. She told him she could do any job a man could do, and she would work for him in exchange for somewhere safe to stay. He asked her why she did not go back to her people. She told him when her father found out that she had been used he would be shamed. She said it was best that he believed her to be dead. He asked her name, and she told him it was Little-Star.

"Grandfather told her she could stay, but he wanted her to make camp closer to the stone house, so no one would bother her. He asked her if she would put a garden in next to the stone house and see to the animals that he depended on for food. She was to keep his clothing and house clean and his things orderly while he worked. She agreed and followed him to the stone house. He had her pick her camp spot then one of the black men that worked for Grandfather,

took some board lumber that was left over from the construction of the barn and built her a dwelling. It was very small... only big enough to hold a rope bed, a table and chair. He put an old pipe stove in it for her but had to show her how to use it for warmth. The next day, he awoke to the smell of bacon and coffee. She had figured out the larger stove in the stone house worked the same way as her small one. She fed him and Silver a breakfast of fresh eggs, salt pork, and sweet churned butter with hotcakes and maple syrup. They went to work leaving her to care for the farm yard, Vincent's house and the domestic needs that came with it.

"He had watched her from the back porch as she went to the river wrapped in the blanket from her bed. She would bathe in the edge of the river in the moonlight then wash her tanned dress and leave it hanging on a limb near the fire outside her dwelling. After the first week, he offered her something else to wear. She asked if her native dress bothered him. He assured her that was not the case. Vincent gave her two silver dollars and explained that she was doing a fine job keeping the house and grounds for him and she had earned the money. He told her his wife had died on the journey to this land and most of the things in the trunk at the foot of his bed had never been worn. He explained to her there was fabric and a sewing box in it as well, and she was more than welcome to have whatever she could find useful. She told him she didn't feel right going into his things while he wasn't there. Grandfather admired her honesty, and he brought the trunk into the main room by the hearth for her. He opened it and handed her the sewing kit. She held up the scissors then gave him a strange look. He laughed at her expression then showed her how they worked by cutting a piece of ribbon in half. He started to leave, and she asked him why there was a big trough in the back room off the kitchen. He explained that he had taken a fall from a horse that injured his left leg and it ached by nightfall. He told her he heated water and poured it in the trough then soaked his leg in it for a while before he used the water to bathe. He told her it helped him sleep.

"Little-Star took the seeds he gave her, and his garden flourished at her hands and tender care, as did his animals. She took the fabric and the two dresses that were in the trunk and by taking one apart, she learned how to make her own clothing. The people in town came to know her as his housekeeper. That fall he bought her a comb, hair brush and a mirror to celebrate the harvest.

"They became accustomed to each other's personality and disposition, and their friendship grew naturally. She would even have his bath water ready for him and he would enjoy it while she finished preparing supper, which she had begun taking with him. Grandfather paid everyone who worked for him, but some black people had families and they formed a little community on the outskirts of the property. She became friends with all of them and they shared their talents with each other. They taught her how to preserve vegetables in jars. And, she showed them how to tan fur and how to make a paste out of grating dried fruits, seeds and nuts then kneading it with lard. It's kind of like a course peanut butter with all sorts of goodies in it.

"Anyway, Grandfather Vincent fell in love with the Indian girl who, by then, he called Star. He asked Star if she would be his wife. He assured her he knew what he was doing, and that she was no more used than he was being a widower. They were married by the circuit judge two months after Christmas. She was sharing his bath and his bed by then and even though they didn't know it, Vincent's son was already growing inside of her.

"It was May when she heard horses outside; she looked out and recognized her father. Vincent went out with her to greet him. Her father was glad to see her and that she was alive and well, but he was angry that her belly was swollen with a child. He was against them being together. He did not like the fact that she looked like a white woman. She told him that the white women didn't like the fact that she looked like an Indian. She told her father she loved him, but she loved Vincent too. She told him Vincent treated her with kindness and he looked at her with as much fascination as he did the stars in the sky. She told him she understood why he felt the way he did, and she had already accepted that she would be dead to him. She asked him to go home knowing that she was happy and remember that she would always love him as her father. She told him she would teach his grandson about him.

"My grandmother loved her family, and she loved her life that she built with Vincent. She enjoyed wearing beautiful dresses and having her hair groomed in ringlets and pulled up in beautiful combs, but she loved working with her hands more. She continued to practice her sewing and working the land. Zane Leflore Breaux was born during the next harvest. Vincent saw it as a gift from the Almighty and a symbol for a fruitful life.

"Late one afternoon... almost a year later, her father rode in sick and longing to see her. Vincent took him in as family and when he was well and stronger; he stayed and took up residence in the small dwelling that used to be Star's. The big house was constructed in 1854 to shelter their growing family. It was a smaller version of the family estate in Paris and Grandfather Vincent's way of paying tribute to his heritage. He wanted to provide Star and his son with the same comfort he had been given. Whisper Bluff flourished because Vincent befriended and trusted Truman Silver, and because he dared to love Star. She brought love, hope and contentment to his life, while Silver's presence and companionship gave him peace of mind.

"Their son, Zane, was my Grandpa Preston's father. Preston Renee Breaux was his full name. He was the funniest and sweetest man I've ever known. My father, Lee Renee, was born to him and his wife, Ophelia. When my parents were killed in the car accident, Grandpa Preston barely left my side. I'm the only living daughter in four generations. I've always loved him and his name. I thought... if given the opportunity to carry on our family with a son, I would name him Preston.

"Grandpa told me that Star's father was a Paiute chief... and their shaman's magic had led them to her. When they went back leaving her in the white man's world, the shaman was angry and put a curse on our family. His hatred for the white man condemned the soul of Vincent Breaux, and that of every child born in the bloodline after him, to be trapped in this house for eternity. The shaman believed that Vincent deliberately flaunted his wealth and seduced Star into his bed, so she would turn her back on her own people. It was the punishment because of Vincent's greed in taking what did not belong to him. I guess they didn't believe in true love."

Emmett was enthralled by her verbal chronicles of the Breaux family and something she said stuck in his head, so he asked her about it.

"You said you were the only 'living' female heir in the Breaux family... in which generation was there another?"

"My Grandpa Preston and his wife, Ophelia adopted a baby girl who Truman rescued down by the river's edge. He heard it crying and found her tied up in a flour sack next to the remains of where she had been delivered. Grandpa told me they thought she was a biracial child, and that was why she had been abandoned. He said she was a pretty, little thing with gray eyes and smooth black hair. My father was only a few months old when Truman brought her to the house. Grandma O told me she was screaming and writhing about in Truman's arms. I was told that Grandpa Preston gave her a warm bath in the kitchen sink while Grandma nursed my father at the table. He diapered her and wrapped her in a warm blanket, and when Ophelia was finished with daddy, she put the baby to her breast. Grandpa said the baby latched on like a little pig... grunts and all. He said that after she nursed, she opened her eyes and smiled at them and it was that moment they knew she was meant to be their little girl. They named her Star Leflore Breaux. I understand she lived until she was six years old then she took a fever and never recovered. She's in the cemetery too. It was easy to see that they loved her very much, and they missed her. I guess that's why I was so special to them." Caroline smiled as her sparkling eyes met Emmett's. "I like to believe I have characteristics of each of the Breaux men. I love this house and I love this land. It doesn't boast of crops *and fat cattle anymore... since I'm alone. Timber is easier for me to manage and it keeps the land productive."*

Emmett gazed at her with his eyes wide open. She emanated with life and it was so strong he could feel its pulse from where he sat. It energized her veins and made her heart to pound.

CHAPTER 22

Caroline smiled and shook her head as she suddenly realized she had been talking for almost an hour. She apologized, but Emmett told her he was fascinated and asked her about her Grandfather Preston.

Emmett listened with an entertained ear while he watched her with an inquisitive eye; the story of her family revealed her passion for life and love. He learned the actual truth; her ancestors had been highly respected in the upper circles of France. Vincent Leflore Breaux had migrated to this country from Paris. He brought with him the ambitious idea of forging his education, the money he had acquired from the sale of the textile mill and his wanderlust, into a successful plantation and a solicitor's office in the wild frontier of Texas. He bought this land because he was smart enough to know he could use the river as the vehicle for a working plantation to ship their tobacco, cotton and grain to the manufacturer. He made his own contacts through the law firm and he met a man who had an idea to engineer a floating shipping system, and the investment paid off.

Emmett was curious about the small stone house on the bluff being where her great grandfather was born. It looked sturdy even though the years had not been kind to it. It needed some work being it was the first dwelling built on the place and hardly dramatic compared to the main house. Considering both structures were close to a hundred years old, they were treasures by any means in his opinion.

She told him of how the main house was erected from supplies which had been purchased and shipped here by boat from all over Europe. She gave him an account of their dreams, disappointments and the hardships. He asked if the curse covered the stone house as well or just the main house. He could tell that she was surprised by that question. She smiled and told him that Vincent used the stone house for his office, even after the main house was built, and he spent a lot of time there. She told him that her grandfather Vincent's spirit preferred the stone house, and then she smiled.

Emmett thought about that for a moment and concluded if the shaman's curse had been attached to the main house then Vincent would not be able to visit the stone house. He decided she was pulling his leg because it was a way to keep her family alive in her memory. He didn't mind in the least. He knew the value of this time with her, listening to the history that she shared with him. He was educated to the strengths, weaknesses and secrets of the Breaux family and this magical, historical fortress from years past, known as Whisper Bluff. He realized she was the last one of this strong and unique family.

She changed the subject on him.

"So, Emmett," she looked at him with a twinkle in her eyes. He liked the way his name sounded when she said it. He found it as gentle and comforting as a soft wind that blew through the trees.

"Will you tell me about your divorce, or shall I change the subject to something else?" she surveyed in the same soothing voice.

"I'll tell you... I don't have any secrets. I say that with the hope that people around here will be courteous concerning my daughter and her feelings on the subject. She's having a hard time with being taken out of her home *and away from me, and her grandparents. I have worked my tail off through the holidays, so I could have this weekend off with her. We were going to the movies and skating. It's the first full weekend I've had off since we split up."*

Caroline tilted her head to one side as she gazed at him.

"Were... going to the movies and skating? What happened?"

She seemed to be interested in his life, so Emmett told her the truth as he saw it.

"Her stepfather had a family emergency in Little Rock on Tuesday and they had to fly up there. His sister was hospitalized due to a car wreck. She was released yesterday, but the weather turned bad and they couldn't get a flight out this morning, so they're staying over until Sunday. I called to talk to Julie earlier because she was so disappointed. I asked to speak to Vicki, but it seems they've gone to an outdoor concert this evening."

Caroline's eyes drifted past him for a moment then she looked down at her skirt and traced a pleat with her finger as she told him.

"It hurts to be treated like an idiot by the person that promised to love you. It's a scary truth when you realize just how fine the line between love and hate can be.

"If you would extend your trust to include me, Emmett... I want to know what she did to you that ended your marriage."

Emmett was honest with her about his life and his feelings concerning it.

"I love my daughter, Caroline... with all my heart. I thought I could convince her mother to leave her with me, but she dug her heels in against it. The fact that I came home at lunch one day and found her in our bed with her brother's law partner, Autry Cantrell, slapped me in the face concerning our marriage vows. Honestly, I had no idea it was taking place. I got so mad I tossed him out the front door in the raw and with a bloody nose. I did it before I thought about Julianna being caught in the middle. My

temper didn't change things, and spite drove her settlement demands to the point of unreasonable.

"Her brother, James used to be my best friend. He was her attorney. He knew all along they were seeing each other, but he let me find out like a fool. I felt like he held the knife to my back while Vicki and Autry pushed me into it."

She asked him what explanation Vicki had given him for doing such a thing.

Emmett bared his soul to her because she had shared personal things with him concerning her family, and because he felt comfortable doing so.

"She told me she knew there had to be more to life than what we had found and that she had fallen in love with Cantrell. He was good in bed... but with a lot more perks other than desire. According to her, Cantrell is a man with more ambition... more time... and more money." Emmett couldn't seem to reign in the bitterness that tainted his heart and his words. "She said that Autry's life was more exciting, and he was home every night with her. She told me she was tired of trying to live off the embarrassing and ridiculous salary of a want-to-be sheriff, and Autry Cantrell could give Julianna all the things that I can't."

Emmett felt the ache in his heart all over again as he spoke those devastating words. He could not look at her at that moment because of it. But when she spoke his name and captured his hand inside of hers, he couldn't help himself. He was deeply moved when his attention met Caroline's. Her eyes glistened with emotion as she squeezed his hand in hers. It was like his pain had become her heartache as well.

"That's just cruel, Emmett. I'm so sorry for your loss. I know how it feels to be abandoned."

He listened to her while she expressed her feelings on the matter.

"It's not the time apart specifically, I mean... for two people who are devoted to one another, separation should make their relationship even richer. It's a matter of how much of themselves they've invested in each other while together that endures. And that's another thing..." she was anything but reserved as she conveyed her opinion, "... serving and protecting the citizens of this county is an honorable thing. You make personal sacrifices to do it! She should be proud of you and help you with her support. Anyway, thank you Emmett... for your consideration in seeing me home safely."

Emmett wondered why they had never had the opportunity to talk with each other before tonight, especially since they frequently crossed each other's path at work. His mind toyed with the idea of 'what if?'. He imagined how different things could be if Caroline had been the one in that game of spin the bottle. A twinge of guilt attacked his chest, and he immediately reigned in his thoughts. He loved and needed Julianna; she was his reality now. He looked at Caroline and knew she meant what she said; she was sorry Vicki had treated him so badly.

"I would think that you understand Vicki's perspective as well... loving a man that is never home."

The expression on her face was strained as she shook her head. When she spoke, her voice held some bitterness.

"I don't need a man for his money. All I ever wanted was a man to see the good in me, and to love me with his whole heart while appreciating that I offered him the same devotion." She shook her head again. "There is no comparison between me and Vicki Russell, other than both of us had a crush on you in school. She was older and more outgoing; it wasn't a surprise that she found a way to get your attention." Her words and her tone of voice were adamant.

"What?!" Emmett's face cracked with a surprised smile.

Caroline confronted him with an unexpected question.

"Is it funny that the little mouse girl had a crush on you? That is what everyone called me behind my back, isn't it... mouse girl?"

Emmett jumped on the answer because he was pleased, and he had not meant to offend her in any way.

"No! Oh Caroline, I'm flattered! There's nothing funny about it. It's just... I never knew. You never said anything to

457

me... or did anything that would make me think you would have liked to get to know each other better. I waved to you when I passed you on my motorcycle and I smiled in the hallway, but you were so shy that you never responded to me."

She pulled her hand away from his subtle-like; it was as though she were self-conscious over the fact that they were still touching each other.

"That's not completely true, Emmett. I ran into you in the hallway of the art building that day... remember?"

He smiled at the memory and nodded his head.

"I remember that I plowed you down like a bulldozer. I was afraid that I had hurt you. It was the first time you ever made eye contact with me. I remember your eyes that day; they were so blue I thought they were purple... then you touched that scratch on my arm. I felt the same electricity then that I did a few seconds ago." He smiled at her. "I walked away from you thinking you were a gypsy girl and you had magical powers."

Her lovely face created another smile that was even more amazing than the last.

"Really? I like that, Emmett. Would you believe I used to play dress-up with my grandmother before she passed away? We would tie scarves around our heads and decorate our wrists and ankles with jewelry then we would dance and laugh while she played the tambourine." Caroline's eyes danced as she shared the fond memory with him.

"I've always remembered the boy sheriff and his big mustache. I used to look for you at school or when we were out about town. When I got older... I used to walk past your house on the way to school hoping I would see you. I wished that one day you would ask me if I wanted a ride to school on your motorcycle. I dreamed of doing something crazy with excitement... something completely reckless and carefree with you. When Vicki started showing up on the back of your bike, I was crushed. I had to know once and for all if you had ever noticed me.

"Would you believe it took me a month to trace your daily routine? I knew you cut through the art building on the *way to third period. I had been waiting on you in that spot all morning. I even got a detention for cutting my second period class that day, but it was so important to me that I be in that spot at the right time." She crossed her arms and shrugged her shoulders as silence fell on them a moment. "When I looked at you that day; I saw Vicki in your eyes. I realized that I had to let go of the dreams I had about the handsome boy with the golden blonde hair."*

Emmett was stunned to hear that she had special feelings for him at one time and he never knew it. He looked at her but didn't know what to say. He felt sad, and he wasn't sure why.

"I wish I had known that, Caroline. So... do you still see her there?"

She turned her body in the seat slightly then pushed her bangs back off her brow as she looked at him. Moonlight filtered into the car as the wind continued to rearrange the clouds above them. They gazed at each other knowing their paths in life had finally aligned and honesty should be sovereign.

She nodded her head as she answered.

"Yes. But it's all right. It's the fact that you love her anyway that makes you such a good man."

"Caroline," Emmett swallowed the lump that was suddenly stuck in his throat. "You give me too much credit. The truth is, the love you see... it's for the little girl we made together. I try to respect Vicki because she is Julie's mother, but it's hard after the way things have turned out. We were stupid kids who discovered the thrill of physical pleasure together and mistook it for love... at least I did. I had her pregnant by the end of the summer; it's why she didn't come back her senior year. I remember how scared I was, but at the same time, I was excited and happy at the possibilities ahead of us. There was no turning back for me. I wanted the baby, and the responsibility of taking care of and providing for them. But she wanted to go away and have the baby... then put her up for adoption. She wouldn't even hear of me assuming the responsibility as a single father because it would have made her look like a bad person. Her parents

didn't want to take on the responsibility of raising another child. I wanted to get married and be a family, and our parents saw it as the only choice. I can see now... we sort of ganged up on her. She didn't want to be a family or spend the rest of her life with a mistake she made when she was 17. I should have known that I was setting us up to fail at the marriage, but I loved and wanted my daughter. I think of her and what a blessing she is to my life. I realize... I can't afford to have any regrets."

They sat together in a comfortable silence for a couple of minutes.

"Maybe I could meet her someday, Emmett," suggested Caroline.

He smiled and nodded his head.

"I would like for her to know you, Caroline, a genuine southern lady with a spunk I didn't know she possessed."

They began to reminisce over school days and the things they had in common. He learned she used to watch him lift weights in the gym with members of the football team. And, he discovered she was the one responsible for the stick of spearmint gum he found in his locker every day after lunch for the last two years of school. He wondered why he had never thought of it as a kindness someone showed him because they had cared. It would have been so easy to watch and see who was doing it, but he never took the time to do so. He wanted to kick himself now.

"Emmett?" Her soft voice drew his attention back into the moment.

"I'm sorry, what did you say?"

"You look sad suddenly... have I offended you? I spend so much time alone; I suppose I've grown calloused concerning the outside world. These days, I'm out of practice using delicate words when conversing with people."

Emmett sat up a little straighter as he answered her.

"Everything about you is delicate, Caroline! And you did not offend me. Honestly, I'm peeved at myself for being so dense and self-consumed that I never saw your gesture of kindness as the gift it truly was." He shook his head. "You know they may have called you mouse girl behind your *back, but it wasn't for the reason you think. The other girls did it because you were so pretty, and they thought you were untouchable. You may have come across as withdrawn, but you were still confident in who you were. You never tried to be something else. They were curious about you and people tend to ridicule the things that they don't understand. I'm ashamed and I could kick my own rear for not watching my locker to find out who was leaving the gum."*

Caroline held her skirt in place as she shifted her legs beneath it then leaned her head back against the window.

"You would have been embarrassed if your friends had found out I was stalking you. They would have started making fun of you too."

Emmett's hand grabbed the place over his heart as he made a face.

"Ouch, that hurt," he mumbled.

"I'm sorry, but kids can be mean, and you know I'm right." She reached over and patted the side of his face with her palm as she laughed at his silliness.

Emmett reached up and caught her hand then placed a kiss to her fingers.

"I'm sorry too. I'm sorry I didn't take the time to really look at... and see the world around me. Thank you for the 400 pieces of gum you shared with me those years we were in school together, and for having a crush on me... just knowing it makes me feel good. And whether you believe me or not, I'm glad it was you." He shrugged his shoulders. "It seems we have changed places. I will dream about you... and envy Colonel Reid for being smart enough to get your attention."

Her expression became solemn and her tone of voice came out rather stiff when she spoke.

"He may have got my attention, Emmett, but it wasn't the love story I dreamed about. I guess nothing in adult life compares to the romantic dreams of a girl."

"He's been gone a long time this time, hasn't he?" questioned Emmett.

"Yes. Ten months, three weeks, six days and..." she looked at her watch, "... eleven hours. He's probably in a third world country... somewhere off the beaten path. I'm sure he knows where to find the whores in every city on earth by now. I've stopped living my life in consideration of him. Honestly Emmett, I don't care if he ever comes back. I'm lost to him and he's too self-consumed to know it. It doesn't matter, and I'm not upset about it any longer. Things are what they are, and he is who he is."

Emmett was shocked, and he wanted to know what she was talking about, so he asked her.

"Caroline, what happened?"

"Do you really feel like you neglected Vicki in your marriage, Emmett?" Her question was blunt and to the point.

"I tried not to... I didn't think I had, but now I'm not so sure."

"Why? What's made you doubt yourself?"

The way she looked at him motivated him to look at things as they really are. He still held her hand even though he didn't have a reason other than her skin felt like hot velvet and the energy in it made him feel alive.

"The 400 pieces of gum someone gave me in kindness... that I took for granted," confessed Emmett truthfully. "So, what's the difference in you giving up on Dane and Vicki giving up on me?"

Caroline looked down at her hand where his thumb timidly caressed her knuckles.

"Did you ever have sex with another woman when you were married to her?"

"No, I was a husband, and I was happy. If I hadn't been, I would have tried to talk to her and figure out how to fix what was wrong. Obviously, she bypassed the talking part and solved the problem of being married to an underachiever by replacing him. I must have been the one who was self-consumed, because I had no idea, she was so miserable."

"I've witnessed the man you've become, Emmett. You serve and care about others beyond your own needs... beyond your own safety. You're a good and decent man,

Emmett. You're a noble man... in my eyes and so many others. I think Vicki told you all those hurtful things, so she would feel better about herself and her infidelity," exclaimed Caroline. She paused a moment wondering whether she should be more to the point about the things she had revealed about her marriage.

"Dane had a birthday back in August. He told me he would be home for it. I've heard that before and part of me didn't believe him. I didn't want to get my hopes up only to be let down again. We have never been together on his birthday and, despite my doubt, I wanted to make it a special day for him. The day neared, and I followed through with preparations to make his favorite supper and German chocolate cake would mark the occasion. I was taking the cake out of the oven when the phone rang. I knew it was him. I knew there was some detrimental matter of national security that was interfering with his coming home.

"He said he was sorry, but he had to be in meetings with the Secretary of Defense the next morning and the council had him on standby awaiting the next mission. He apologized then asked if I wanted to come to Washington for a late dinner with him. It was the first time he had ever been considerate enough to invite me into his world. I know now, that he asked me certain I would say 'no', and that was exactly what I did. He asked, so my refusal to come to him would justify his indulgent choices and remove what little guilt he felt in making them." She forced a quick smile as her eyes met Emmett's. "I've figured out all of this, after the fact. I'm not a naive girl anymore, Emmett; I've graduated to a cynical woman."

Emmett turned his hand over, so he could close his palm around her small hand. It was a warm, beautiful and fascinatingly delicate thing he held. She raked her nails back and forth over his palm sending a stimulating current of warmth throughout his system.

"What happened?" asked Emmett.

"I hung up and, well... Papa Zane dared me to go find out what kind of man I had really married. He even called me a coward. He has a confrontational side to his otherwise malleable personality... especially when he thinks I'm lying to myself." Caroline stopped suddenly as she realized what she had divulged. She wanted nothing but honesty to be the foundation of her friendship with Emmett. She had lived with the fact that her girlish dreams concerning him were not going to come true, but she so wanted to be his friend. She rolled her eyes and released a delicate sigh as she offered a reasonable explanation for her statement. "They're all trapped in the house with me, remember? We have differences of opinions all the time."

Emmett's large, sky blue eyes gazed at her as though he were waiting for the punch line. She wanted him to believe in her, but she dared not say anything else or he may think her to be mentally eccentric. She giggled and flashed him a playful smile then continued with her explanation while trying not to focus on the way his warm, strong fingers felt next to her skin.

"I dared myself to go because it nagged at me. I don't want to be a cowardly recluse... afraid to venture out into the world. Dane's arrogance in predicting my every move stiffened my determination. I cannot abide his using my weaknesses against me. I was scared, but I needed to prove that I am strong enough to take care of myself beyond this place.

"When I arrived at his suite, I paid housekeeping to unlock the door. Dane was supposed to be in meetings and I was going to order room service and surprise him. I heard music playing in the bedroom but didn't distinguish a feminine voice until I was almost through the doorway.

"I was stunned when I saw him naked and sprawled across the bed... one woman riding his lap and the other was on her knees straddling his face. Those women..." Caroline shook her head as though she did not want the memory to settle in her mind's eye, "... they were even touching each other. I was shocked and disgusted. I knew if he saw me, he would somehow turn the twisted situation around making it my fault. I wasn't prepared for something like that, or to defend myself in the face of it. All I could think of was getting back to my small world on Whisper Bluff, so I ran. *My shoulder bag knocked a vase of flowers off the foyer table on my way to the door, it crashed to the floor, but I just kept on running." She brushed her free hand over her cheek. "After witnessing what he's capable of... the respect he has for me as a wife and his commitment as a husband, I'm through with him, and the marriage. I can't trust him anymore, and I will never... ever give my body to him again."*

Silence filled the inside of the car as Emmett pictured the shocking event of which she had spoken. He could hear the disappointment and disdain in her voice. He was certain, Dane Reid was a fool.

Emmett considered what he knew of her in relation to the things she had shared with him this evening. His instincts and wisdom gave him a broader understanding of who she was. She had been a quiet, studious and unique girl, and she had become a beautiful and fascinating woman. Her family had a lot of money; however, she did not behave or conduct her life as though she was privileged. He remembered reading in the paper about her parents being killed in a car crash the week after her sophomore year at the University. It was a difficult time for her, but with her grandfather, Preston Breaux, by her side, she assumed responsibility of the family's business while she continued her education. The newspapers called her 'queen of the empire' her family had built. When her grandfather died a year later, it was rumored that loneliness made her vulnerable, and she was drawn to a rebel boy that had found redemption in the military.

Colonel Dane Reid came home on leave in May 1939, just before she graduated college. When he started pursuing her, all other suitors stopped, and by Independence Day, her freedom was gone. Dane had stepped in and taken over her life. In his absence, she chose to work in the Circuit Clerk's office. Emmett suspected she did so to be around people and feel some fraction of normal.

Emmett had learned to ignore the loneliness that rumbled inside of him; his divorce had been final, and his wife had been legally sleeping with another man for almost two years. He had not dated. What free time he had was devoted to Julianna even though he knew the day would come when she would leave him through the natural course of life. Still, he realized that he had a connection with this woman. He would have to be dead to not feel the loneliness that emanated from her. He was very aware of how sensitive he was to it, and her.

"It's almost 11:00 p.m., Caroline. I've enjoyed your company so much that I've overstayed my welcome. I'll walk you to the door... you must be spent by now." He released her hand and shut off the engine then got out before she could respond. He went around the car to open her door, but she got out without waiting for his assistance. She crossed her arms because it was even colder than when he had retrieved her from the darkness of the sidewalk.

He looked at her and smiled.

"I swear, Caroline... I feel like I have a new-old friend in you and I'm very excited. I hope you don't mind."

"Mind?! I'm so happy; my feet aren't touching the ground." She blew into her cupped hands as she gave him the most magnificent smile, and then to his surprise, she wrapped her arms around his waist and hugged him.

Emmett's arms responded without conscious thought being part of it and he squeezed her close. When he felt his body respond to her delicate essence, he turned and pulled her beneath his arm and started the walk to her door. He wished a dozen times between the car and the backdoor that she was his.

They stopped in the small cove of the back porch which was cloaked by shadows. He waited as she opened the glass door that led to a small room protected from the weather. She stepped inside then turned to him and stuck her hand out. He took her hand as she thanked him again for his assistance. He was pleased she hesitated in releasing it, and even more when she turned her hand over and stroked the smooth skin between his fingers. He studied her beautiful face while noticing how her long, dark lashes concealed her dreamy eyes. He was captivated by the way she looked up at him and the way the gas light from the yard reflected in them. They were entrancing with the color of midnight and yet, glowing with hope. It was as though she tapped into a well of hidden courage when she asked him if he wanted to come in for a coffee and to see the house.

He gazed at her while wishing that it would be a revived ploy to get him inside and that she would want to establish a new beginning with him. They had visited for almost two hours while sitting in the car. It seemed like he was in a dream state after being in her world. He realized he was staring at her while she waited for an answer.

"Caroline, I'm standing here wishing that destiny would give us another chance. But... you're still married."

She held up her hand and for the first time that night he realized that she wore no wedding rings.

"No, Emmett... he divorced me back in August. I've already seen an attorney; the papers are ready, and I've signed them. Whether he will, is something that I can't control. I'll have to cross that bridge when I come to it." Suddenly she pressed her cheek against his chest over his heart.

Emmett sensed that the soul of this place had been passed to her. The house and grounds, the dignified obscurity of her family, the composed intelligence and gentle grace along with her independent pride; they were shadows and reflections of her heritage. He felt her heartbeat and that of Whisper Bluff, pulsating against his chest and in his arms; it was strong and steady as it spread throughout his body. This magical place was bred into her and he wanted desperately to be part of them. She was a beautiful woman, and his instincts told him that she wanted and needed a new breath of life to touch her soul every bit as much as he did. He sensed the curiosity she had for him in their younger years still lived inside of her and she wanted to know if he could find her desirable.

467

He realized they were cut from the same cloth, not economically, but in ideals and in expectations of what made up a satisfying life. Their views were simple.

"You said you had all weekend now that Julianna wasn't coming. I'm braver now. Will you come inside? Will you stay with me, Emmett?"

Emmett asked himself if he was going to step into her magical world and see if he could persuade the mysterious gypsy girl to cherish him, or was he going home and be content in his cold existence of work and loneliness?

He caressed her brow with his chin and her arms tightened around him; her body fit against him as though she were a snug, soft garment he had put on for extra warmth. He inhaled a deep breath. It drew her face to the curve beneath his jaw and she nuzzled his throat in the most intimate of ways. Chills rushed over Emmett's entire body.

"You smell so good... and you feel even better," he whispered. "Caroline, she's the only woman I've ever been with; I'm not a great lover. You're so amazingly beautiful... like the first rosebud in the spring."

She lifted her chin and her eyes searched his face for a moment. Her lips were only a few inches away from him and her moist, steamy breath warmed his skin when she spoke.

"You're bothered that you may not be able to please me, Emmett?" Caroline shook her head as the glimmer in her eye dared him to kiss her.

Emmett pulled her even closer. He took a few steps inside the porch area and their bodies moved as one. The door closed softly behind him as he pressed his lips against hers.

The seconds slipped by and the longer they shared the same space, the stronger and more courageous they became. It was as though kindred spirits took over their dreams and guided their hearts.

Emmett's motivation grew as her nails seduced his spine. He kissed her face absorbing the petal soft skin with his lips. He went back to her lips, and she kissed him back *while a passionate yearning emanated from her. His hand caressed her throat; it was like they picked a bouquet of warm moist kisses together. Her lips parted, and the tip of her tongue invited him to taste her kiss in a more personal way. He stepped into her body and the kiss; their hot breaths caused a fog in the frigid night air. His decision was made, he wanted to love her and even more, he wanted her to love him back. Their lips forged with so much feeling motivating them. The physical contact between each other was like stirring a hearth of hot coals. Emmett's hands took liberties and caressed her body beneath her coat. She was a delicate woman; he could feel her small waist and slim hips as he traced the curves of her body. Her breath faltered as his hand caressed her breast, but her knee eased between his legs and her hip bone greeted his manly body. Their kiss deepened and the warmth they generated together was proof that they could be physically compatible. He brought the kiss back to their lips, so they could supply their lungs with air, but they did not sever the closeness they had discovered in each other.*

Emmett indulged on her lips as he asked her.

"Caroline, are you sure it's over with him? I mean... I know you can't speak for him, but I want to know. Is your heart done with him?"

When she gazed into his eyes Emmett knew it was so; still, he needed to hear it once more.

"Yes. I married him with the same promise of devotion that you made to someone and I have lived it. My body hasn't known another man." She shook her head as she held his attention and finished saying what was on her mind. "I can't say that about my heart. It belonged to a young girl, but it was full of you first, and... he has not been able to claim all of it." She kissed him softly on the mouth as her words sank into Emmett's understanding. "I've always known how to keep a promise, Emmett. And I learned the hard way how to separate myself from people I can't trust. I've always trusted you... always," she told him.

They looked at each other, both needing someone to care about them and both wanting it to be the other.

"We're not kids anymore; we don't have to make promises this time. Please... just let me touch you. I... want-" her words were cut short by his kiss.

Emmett's possessiveness surfaced, and he pressed her against the wall. He didn't need a promise. He was brave enough to leave a profound impression on her heart and her body if she was willing. The way her nails raked up and down his spine beneath his jacket inflicted a passionate chaos on his body, and by the way her hip massaged him, he was certain it was her intention. She pulled her lips away from his and looked at him; she told him she wanted to feel what Vicki had so foolishly thrown away. She stretched up to kiss him and Emmett's hands lifted her so that his lips could taste her throat. She unbuttoned her blouse and encouraged his kiss to the swell of her breasts. He explored what was offered, but it wasn't enough for him. Thanks to Vicki, he had never learned to be a teaser when it came to sex. He gently bit at her sensitive flesh through her undergarment. She responded to the feel of his hunger and tugged her blouse out of the waist of her skirt then boldly bared herself down to her pale skin. She looked at him and declared she would freeze if he didn't warm her immediately.

His mouth tugged on her excited velvety flesh and she stretched so that her hand could clutch at the front of his uniform trousers. The definition of him assured her that he could nurture and satisfy the lonely, ache in her body. She assured him of her trust and offered to be open and honest about everything that may happen between them. They shared a powerful yearning that neither of them feared. It was a fact, each of them had been wronged and mocked by the lover to which they had committed themselves. They wanted to offer each other the physical version of what they had been denied by their partner.

Caroline shivered as Emmett's mouth tugged hungrily at the tip of her breast, tasting one and then the other, all the while his body pressed into the valley between her legs searching for companionship. She pulled her skirt up and his hands slid into the legs of her lacy panties. She heard a gentle moan roll deep in his chest as both his hands claimed her bottom and began to knead her flesh. His kiss came to her lips for a brief kiss then he consumed her mouth with a level of desire that thrilled every cell of her body. Her heart began to pound with newborn feelings because physical exchange such as this was unexplored territory for her. The way Emmett touched her was gentle yet possessive; his touch was strong but guided by tenderness, and it was incessant and consuming. This was something she had never felt with Dane.

Emmett pushed at her panties and shifted his body so that she could lower her legs and step out of them. When she was free of the garment, he lifted her and confined her against the wall of the small shadowed porch. His hand caressed her private body and his kiss moved over her body and her throat until she could stand it no longer. She pleaded for more.

The sounds of boats on the river echoed in the distance and the night wind blew the leaves against the glass as they held each other in an intimate and yearning embrace. She fumbled at the front of his trousers as her fingers trembled with desire, need and rebellion. His palm left her body long enough to help her. When his engorged body greeted her hand, she shivered all over. She gripped him like he had always belonged to her and they were reunited at last.

His warm and craving touch explored her private body with great care while he nibbled on her lips. She gasped as he teased her with delving quick thrusts of his finger; he massaged her until she got dizzy from breathing in a large amount of air too fast.

"Look at me, Caroline." His voice was a masculine hum in his chest.

She leaned her head back against the wall and their eyes connected. He stopped the assault on her body; still, her hand caressed him. He skillfully aligned her body with his own and to his pleasure; she guided his body into the moist crevasse between her thighs. He kissed her plump lips as his manly body greeted her private with a tender exploration. Her hips began a timid rhythm that was stimulating and inviting. She couldn't help it; the feel of him called to the desolate ache of an unfulfilled woman. When she could stand the ache no longer, she tilted his head back and covered his mouth with a hunger that was reckless and honest.

Her private body was luscious, ready and waiting. Their eyes held, and they kissed as he slowly pushed into her. The narrow tunnel of her body stretched around him; the feeling brought a jumbled version of truth to his mind. She was a lady, there was no doubting that, and she was every bit as lonely as he. But the truth that he discovered was simple, she had been a married woman for three years and Dane had not been in her enough to even suggest that she had a husband. Emmett felt a crazed thrill of delight speed through his veins; he followed desire all the way to the core of her body then began to share himself with her. She gasped at the feel of him and quickly lost her pristine control. She began to cast a spell over him that would never let him go.

Emmett couldn't believe this was happening to him again. He wasn't a kid this time, and this wasn't Vicki. He agreed with her, there was no comparison between Caroline and his ex-wife. The way she kissed him was needful and sensuous; it felt as though she was drinking his kiss, and it was amazing. It was almost as amazing as the way her body held on to him while they moved in harmony to the fast drumming of their heartbeats. His eyes went to her lips as she parted them, so she could pull in more air for her muscles. She instinctively shifted her knees upward and Emmett got another fraction of her. Tears sprung to her eyes as her grip tightened on his shoulders and her hips worked him even faster. He witnessed her pupils dilate as the passionate storm raged inside her body. Her eyes shimmered with feeling while her pale skin glowed in the shadows. He was entranced by them, by the gentleness in her touch and the hunger in her body. Her inner muscles began to quiver, and when they constricted with rigors of climax, she cried out and shook her head. Tears pooled in her eyes then spilled down her cheeks. She gasped for a breath as she looked at him. He sensed fear, and he asked if she wanted him to stop, but she tightened her hold on him and kept pushing. Emmett felt the sting of satisfaction building in his loins. He dipped deeper into her body and leaned forward; it was the only way he knew he could keep his knees from buckling from the mounting need for satisfaction. Her inner body seized around him, and the physical delight he received from it overflowed into her belly; the passionate sighs of lovers escaped into the darkness. They moved together in a spirited waltz of deliverance leaving the feeling of satisfaction to wash over their bodies whenever it caught up to them.

Caroline chased her breath as stillness claimed her body. Emmett kissed her face then her lips as he told her how incredible she felt and how he would always think of her as his beautiful, gypsy lover. She smiled suddenly; clearly his words had made her happy. The way she looked at him, kissed him, and touched him was full of discovery and fascination. He knew now that her husband was a taker, and she had never been given the opportunity to feel what a woman deserved to feel while making love.

Emmett smiled back at her as he kissed her over and over. Her hands began to tremble with weakness and he wooed her into stillness.

"Shhh... Honey, breathe deep and give your body a few minutes to calm down. I've got you, and there's no hurry." Emmett kissed her brow as he pulled her wayward coat over her exposed skin; he snuggled closer and guided her head to his shoulder. He held her in his arms while needing the wall for support until she could find her way back to the moment. Her arms slid around his neck and she squeezed him close.

"Good heavens, Emmett... what did you do to me?" she whispered.

"I gave you what you needed, and what a woman deserves from her lover, Sweetheart."

CHAPTER 23

Emmett held her tight. He understood and respected the treasure in his arms. She was a delicate, southern woman who was as passionate about life as a small sparrow building its nest for a tiny egg. And she had the ability to make him feel like he was the only man alive who understood her. She was one of the unique wonders in life that most men never get the chance to appraise.

"Ready to try to stand?" he whispered.

She nodded her head.

He held her steady as he disengaged his body from hers then released her left leg. When she found her footing, he lowered her other knee. She leaned against the wall as her heartbeat and her bloodstream found a slower rhythm. He took a few seconds to put his clothing to right, and then he fixed her skirt and picked her panties up from the bricks beneath their feet and shoved them in his pocket.

"Emmett," her hand reached out for him and he captured it inside of his. She looked him in the eyes when she spoke. "I've never felt that before... you touched more than just my body. Is that what it's supposed to be like between real lovers?"

His heart trembled at her words. His fingers sank into the silky hair behind her ears and he kissed her a few times. Emmett's spirit was stirred by her essence; they were tied to each other now, but it was deeper and more powerful than the physical delight they had just exchanged.

"Yes, gypsy girl, that's how it's supposed to be between real lovers."

"Every time?" she whispered.

"If you care enough about each other... then yes, it should be every time. Although... exhaustion can get the best of you before you know it. We have arms and lips, and we can hold and kiss each other until we're rested." He laughed softly as he pointed out the best part of it, "Then we can start over again."

She threw her arms around his neck and hugged him.

"Why couldn't we have found each other first?"

Emmett hugged her while wondering the same thing. He was wiser, and he knew the value of this woman in his arms; however, he also knew the danger and the consequences of sin. The loneliness that reverberated through his daily life was like swallowing a daily dose of pain. He had found out a long time ago that in 'trying to live a godly life', there was no measure of success for a perfect life. He had come to understand the emphasis should be on 'trying' rather than 'godly' so that any measure of success was obtainable with respect to faith, effort and forgiveness.

"I don't know, Honey, but the thing that matters most is that we've found each other now."

Caroline nodded her head, and she reached up and smoothed his mustache with her fingers.

"I want to be your lover, Emmett. Will you come inside... and stay with me?"

"Yes, I want to stay with you." They both knew what was on each other's mind, that those words held a deeper meaning for some people than it did others. "I really should take the patrol car home and come back in my truck... just in case you have someone drop by."

She knew he was thinking with wisdom on his side. He was protecting her should someone see it here while safeguarding his livelihood. It was a matter of respect to her and his job.

Emmett reached inside her coat to help her put herself back together. They got tickled when they realized her blouse and bra were trapped at her right elbow inside the sleeve of her coat. Emmett reached behind her and fastened the lacey garment then she buttoned her blouse leaving it hanging loose about her hips inside her coat.

"Can I come with you, Emmett?" She caught his hand and pulled it up to her lips.

"Of course, you can." Emmett wrapped an arm around her and pulled her next to his body then kissed her forehead. "You must be freezing, Honey."

She slid her arms around his waist and snuggled as close to him as possible.

"I'm going to persuade you to warm me up again in just a little while," she stated confidently.

They hurried back to the car. He opened her door, and she sat down and pulled her legs inside in one smooth flow of motion. She was a rare find, and he was entranced by her. Emmett leaned over into the car and his eyes passed over her body as he spoke.

"Maybe I should just drive the car off in the river and you and I can go back to the house."

She responded to his playful suggestion, there was a glow about her face now that was not there a half hour ago.

"All right, that works for me. We'll have to put our heads together and come up with an explanation for Sheriff Vance. Oh, and I'll have to reimburse the county for the loss since it happened on my property. But good golly... you're worth it, Emmett!" She grinned at him and started to get out, but he pressed his lips to hers and gently pushed her back into the car. They couldn't seem to get enough of each other; finally, he pulled his lips away from hers.

"Come on... let's get moving so we can get back to more important things." He closed the door and walked around the vehicle to the driver's side.

She held his hand as they drove to his house. They didn't meet another vehicle on the way because it was late, and the small town was asleep. He turned into the driveway and parked the county vehicle under the shed.

"I need to change clothes… come inside with me for a few minutes?"

She nodded her head and picked up a small purse that was on the dash of the car. Emmett got out and hurried to open her door for her. They snuggled together and managed to kiss while they walked the rest of the way to the back door. It was crazy, but they had been energized with a passionate excitement and they felt like foolish kids.

Emmett held the door open, so she could enter the small house then he followed her. He secured the door then turned to her; they looked at each other for a moment. He was pleased when she pushed her coat off her shoulders and started unbuttoning her blouse. Emmett's attention took in the whole of her body as he approached her. He caught her around the waist and lifted her into his arms. Caroline wrapped herself around him and they sank into a passionate kiss. Emmett started walking towards the short hallway that led to his room. He entered the quaint dark room, but instead of putting her to her feet he just held her. It was important to take the time to look at her, kiss her face and lips, and absorb her warmth and goodness in this place that had been overrun by loneliness.

"Caroline, Honey… you are the most beautiful and fascinating woman I've ever known. I don't want to take one single second for granted while you're with me."

She loved the way his simple endearments rolled off his tongue so naturally when he spoke to her. And she appreciated the fact that he listened to her when she spoke. He made her feel as though what she had to say was important to him. She respected his wisdom of human nature and the fact that he considered time to be a gift.

"I've been enlightened in the last few years as to how protected I was and how naïve I really am. I have limited knowledge about the things that should be between a man and woman, Emmett. I watched my parents and grandparents share their love for years. It was often in the smallest of ways, like preparing an extra cup of tea when they made one for themselves, sharing a sandwich, and holding hands while they read the newspaper. I remember how they used to pause from the supper dishes long enough to dance to their favorite song on the radio... and how they would squeeze into the bluff swing together, so the other didn't have to wait for a turn. I thought all married couples behaved that way with each other and I expected to have the same kind of relationship too. I thought that the very act of marriage, the fact that you promised to love and cherish was defined by caring for the other more than one's self. I was a lonely and foolish girl. I traded one kind of loneliness for another... and my self-respect with it." She nuzzled his face for a moment then kissed his lips.

"Caroline, I have always looked at your family and Whisper Bluff from a distance. I believed them to be obscure... based on the stories of others. My father took me there one Halloween, so he could prove something to me. He wanted me to understand that, while your family was unique and different from ours, you were still individuals just as we were." Emmett laughed softly as he studied her face. "He even smoked the peace-pipe with your grandfather knowing my mother was going to smell it on him when he got home." He kissed her nose. "My point is... they taught you the truth by example, the essence of love is trust. You're not at fault for believing in the truth. We've both had our disappointments when it comes to trusting someone. I don't know what tomorrow holds in relation to life. And I don't have all the answers to why things are, but I do know how to be trustworthy. That's what I'll give you, Honey. Look around, you don't need anything else I possess."

She raked her fingers through his hair as she smiled.

"I disagree, Emmett. I need you. I want to experience and re-discover everything with you. I want to see life through your eyes, and I want to feel your energy... your essence all around me, and inside of me."

She stripped him of his clothing like she was his personal servant then Emmett watched her undress. Her French heritage dominated her skin color, but Indian blood was ablaze in her veins. Her square hips tilted slightly forward, and her ribs tailored down to meet her small waist. She was curvy in all the right places and her manner, delicate as a wild flower. The black silk between her legs was smooth even though his seed soiled her body. The loose ringlets around her face shimmered in the light from the hallway to match the glimmer in her eyes. She was breathtaking, but it was her ample, round breasts and their dark tips that he found so incredible and captivating. The way they responded to his hands, his breath and his lips was magical. She joined him in the shower and they explored each other with soapy hands and hungry lips. The friction between their palms and their slippery skin infused their senses with the growing desire in their bodies. They wanted to explore the sexual lightning that had struck them earlier in a more intimate way, so they hurried the shower.

Emmett took her to bed this time and made it his purpose to leave no part of her body untouched. She was somewhat shy when he parted her knees to admire her beauty; he caressed her into a relaxed state then he kissed her knowing his heart was ready to make an investment in what was happening between them. Her response was that of enchantment. He was positive that Dane had not taken the time to thrill her in such a way. He had questions about the man, but it wasn't the time for conversation. He focused his energy and his tongue on pleasuring that specific place where she was designed to be most sensitive, and in doing so, he awakened the sultry temptress inside of her. Her knees melted against the mattress and she rose to her elbows and watched him, captivated that her body could experience so much delight and madness at the same time. She inhaled a deep breath as her hips began to move in answer to the call of the desire that ebbed through her body.

"Emmett, that feels so beautifully erotic. Please, I want to feel you deep inside of me again. Can I... be on top? I've never done that."

Emmett gathered her in his arms and she wrapped herself around him as he took to the mattress on his knees. He cuddled her close and kissed her lips as he sat down in the middle of the bed and told her to take what she wanted and needed from him. His palms glided over the smooth skin of her back as her intimate body moved against him. She rose to her knees, so he could suckle but was quickly swept away by the thrill of it. Her movements were desperate and inexperienced. His palms kneaded her bottom as she writhed against him, but her sigh hinted at uncertainty. He lifted her up a little so that their bodies would be in line for something great.

Emmett groaned in response to the rush of feeling that washed over him as his body plunged into her belly. A beautiful language floated on her sigh and her body trembled all over for a few seconds as did his own. She needed no further guidance or encouragement. She reestablished the fact they were physically compatible, and she did it in her own time and her own passionate way.

He buried his face between her sensuous breasts while she transferred the fiery adrenaline in her blood stream to him. His arms and legs began to tingle in weakness as the center of his torso demanded more blood and energy. Emmett leaned back on his elbows for support. She caught a hold of the headboard as her hips gained momentum. He gripped the bedding in his fist and hung on as she rode him like a stallion she had just stolen and had no intention of giving back. He opened his eyes and was hypnotized by the whiskey colored tips of her breasts moving in front of him. He pressed his face against her as she pushed him deep into her body. She moaned at the loving gesture then slowed her quest, so she could offer them to him. Emmett kissed the excited flesh on the right side of her body before he drew it into his mouth and began to suckle. Every nerve in his body was firing off, and he needed to push with her something fierce, but moreover he wanted her to be in control and take whatever she wanted from him. He tried to relax and enjoy the gypsy that was stealing his will and his heart.

Her body rocked him in a rhythmic dance that was in unison with the percussion of their heartbeats. The torrid depth of her body started to ripple with physical adulation.

"Oh... Emmett!" She inhaled a large amount of air as she went over the edge into another dimension of feeling that enthralled her entire body. Her hips lost their rhythm as the precarious sensations of hot and cold echoed through their muscles, and uncertainty found her again. Her words were few but conveyed a slight fear all the same. "Emmett, help me!!"

That was all he needed to hear. He held her behind the knees as he rescued her with quick and assertive thrust. She held the headboard and spoke to him in the beautiful language of her heritage. He couldn't interpret it with his mind, but he could with his body. He pushed them into an explosion of gratifying delight while she breathed a poem of enchantment into the room. Finally, she collapsed on top of his chest and Emmett fastened his solid arms around her and closed his eyes as he chased his breath. He drifted off to sleep thinking about the incredible woman that lay in his arms, and how much he wanted to keep her.

He awoke some time later with her lying in the same place on top of him. His hands surveyed her body and found her bottom was cold. He shifted them to one side, and she stirred. He kissed her brow and told her he was covering them up. The spot where he had lain was warm and cozy; he laid her there then pulled the cover over them. She lifted her face to him and he smiled at her. Her hand caressed his chest then his spine as she kissed his lips. She laid her head on his arm as her hand slid back and forth over his backside a moment until it came to rest on his hip. She kissed his chin before she snuggled back against him. Emmett sensed the contentment in her and for some reason, he felt empowered. Her voice sent a passionate rumble through his chest.

"I'm falling in love with you all over again, Emmett," she admitted in a faint breath.

"You definitely have my attention, Caroline... my beautiful, sensuous little gypsy girl. I wish we could have done this to each other years ago, Honey. I swear I do."

He awoke next when she suddenly left his arms to go to the bathroom. He lay there a moment, but it registered in his mind that he had seen something on the pillow. He lifted his head again and found blood stains on the pillowcase. He rolled off the bed and went to see about her. She was sitting on the lid of the commode with a damp cloth pressed to her nose and her head tilted back. The sink was full of clotted blood and he got worried. The bun that held her hair was gone, and her wayward curls cascaded down her back. His hands sank into the silky hair behind her ears and he pressed his lips to her forehead.

"Baby, what can I do to help?" Emmett knelt in front of her; his hands went to her knees and his palms caressed the fronts of her thighs. His eyes passed over her body where there were drops of blood on her luscious breasts, too.

"I'm okay. I get a nose bleed every so often, they don't last long. I guess you got me so lightheaded my feet haven't touched the ground yet." She pulled the cloth away and refolded it while waiting to see if it was over.

Emmett turned her chin and inspected her small straight nose with the five tiny freckles decorating it.

"It seems to have stopped, are you dizzy, Honey?"

"No, I feel fine. But I am hungry," she admitted.

"You didn't have supper, did you?"

She smiled and shook her head.

"You know how Evander is when there's an election coming up, he has tunnel vision. The others stopped for some peanut butter and crackers, but I don't really care for the store-bought kind, so I kept working."

Emmett took the cloth from her hand then leaned over to the sink and rinsed it out. Her fingers combed through his short blond hair as he bathed the blood from her body. Emmett kissed her shoulders and her throat; she was so beautiful he just had to. He tossed the cloth in the sink as he surveyed her face.

She parted her knees and wrapped her legs around him then snuggled her breasts against his chest. She told him what was on her mind.

"Who needs food when they have a lover like you to satisfy them?"

Emmett's palms followed the lines of her body as she nuzzled his mustache then his throat. Her nails raked over his spine in a light teasing manner and his skin burst with chills as his erection took form for her again. He ignored it because she was weak, and it was important to him that he take care of her while he could.

"You do, Honey. You're very special to me, Caroline." Emmett sighed because he had begun to dream of her and that scared him. Her marriage was a joke, and she knew it. The man she was tied to was not only a fool, but a dangerous one as well. Whether Emmett was of issue to it or not, she didn't need Dane Reid in her life. "You need someone to care for you, and... I want to be that person." They eased into a passionate slow kiss for a few moments. "How about I fix you something to eat here, or if you would rather... I can take you someplace where nobody knows us and wouldn't care that we're together?"

She lifted her face and looked at him.

"Is there such a place? You know everybody, Emmett." They gazed at each other for a moment, and then she suggested. "I bought a smoked ham and some cheddar at Newsom's yesterday; they're just sitting on the shelf in the refrigerator at home. And, I bought some fresh eggs from Mr. Sellers day before yesterday... double yolks. Let's see, I also have some fresh spinach and mushrooms too. You should know... I make a mean omelet."

Emmett gazed at her trying to get a sense of her true feelings. He needed to know if she was all right.

"Caroline... Sweetheart, I'm worried... that's a lot of blood for a nose bleed. Are you sure you are all right? It's important to me... you're important to me. What's happened between us... is important to me as well." He paused a second because he hadn't meant to go here so soon, but everything involving them had been like a brushfire. He wanted to choose his words carefully. "What's happening between us... it's not something that I can forget or take for granted. Earlier, when I said I wanted to stay with you, I was hoping we might be able to make some changes in our lives. I'm hoping for some positive changes that would accommodate a relationship that we share openly. What do you think? Is that something you might want too?"

A tear slipped down her cheek and her bottom lip quivered.

"Yes Emmett, it is something that I've wanted very much... for a long time. I had let go of those dreams... because you were with Vicki."

"I understand, and legally... you're with Dane. Yeah, we have lousy timing, but we can change that, Sweetheart. He's got to be served with the divorce documents, so he knows where you stand. What grounds did you file it under?"

She answered him with the same sincerity in which he had asked the question.

"No fault. The attorney said I had to prove he was unfaithful. I have only my word as to what I saw, and he'll only deny it.

"Emmett, you need to know that he's a hard and angry man. I'm a possession to him... a trophy, and nothing more. I don't know why I didn't see it before things got so involved." She bit her bottom lip as she shook her head. "He'll never sign the papers. It will be a blow to his ego that I've dared to have them drawn up; he'll have to save face. I've been alone for so long, and I had lost all care for myself and what he would do to me. Filing for divorce was the only way I could think of to take a stand for myself and my feelings.

"When you stopped to help me tonight, hope sprung to life in my heart. I haven't felt it in so long I was thrown off kilter. It was the hope of a girl and every bit as exciting. When you asked if you could see me home; it was like you asked me to ride on your motorcycle. I couldn't refuse. I'm sorry." She shook her head as she looked at him with troubled eyes.

"So... you're saying that you're basically trapped and stealing time is probably all we'll ever have together?"

She nodded her head.

"I'm scared to hope for more," she whispered.

Their eyes held one another's; the room was so quiet Emmett could hear her heart beat.

"He may be a hard man, but you should know that I can be a determined man, Honey... especially when something is worth fighting for, and you are worth it." He pressed his lips against hers and stood taking her with him. When he pulled his lips away, he smiled. "Let's get you some nourishment... that omelet sounds mighty good to me. And just so you know... I can make a biscuit that puts my mama to shame."

Emmett backed his truck into the car house where she usually parked the coupe while she waited on him in the early morning light. It was a precaution, so his tag wouldn't be on display. His mind was racing with all sorts of thoughts. He wasn't an idiot or a gambler; he was aware that Dane could show up at any given time. But like he had told her, she was worth a fight. He was lonely, but there was more than that going on between them. He'd been alone and living on the edge of miserable for two years. There had been several women who had wanted to spend time with him since he and Vicki divorced, but the thought of introducing them to Julianna had not appealed to him, so he didn't pursue a relationship with any of them. He couldn't ignore that Caroline's and his paths had crossed again. The innocent concern he had shown her had been rewarded with the hidden truths of yesteryear, and he refused to believe it was by accident. If Dane should come home to catch them together, then so be it. The way he saw things, it would be the first step in her gaining her freedom. Besides, she had told him that when she called the number that was her designated way to contact him; she had been told he was out of the country for the next six weeks.

Emmett reached beneath the seat and retrieved the holster that held his personal sidearm before he got out. Her eyes touched it as he approached her and when he got closer, she wrapped her arms around him and hugged him. She tilted her face up to him and her eyes flashed with excitement. They engaged each other with a delicious, warm kiss. His heart felt like an eagle had swooped down and picked it up and was soaring over the horizon with it. When her hands squeezed at his backside, he knew she was dreaming up some ideas of her own for him.

Emmett followed her through the two different entry rooms as they ventured into the magnificent place where she had grown up. The first room was a plain space where a person could collect their thoughts, shake off the weather and, in his and Caroline's case, instill new hope in each other. The next room offered a small water closet off to the left, shelving which included coat hooks for a hat or umbrella, and a settee so one could sit and remove their shoes.

Emmett entered the kitchen and his eyes jumped around the unique and interesting room trying to take in everything all at once. It was huge by anyone's standards.

"Caroline, this kitchen is fantastic!" exclaimed Emmett.

She spun around and smiled at him as she slipped out of her coat and tossed it over the back of a chair where she had a work station set up.

"Shall I tell you about it?"

"Yes, it's incredible!" Emmett's hand passed over the smooth wooden counter that had obviously seen a lot of work through the last 90 years.

"Grandpa Preston and my father had the updated fixtures installed when they added plumbing and electricity throughout the entire house; the butane stove was added then too. I was just a little girl, but I remember the workmen being here and my grandmother Star urging them to be careful not to scratch the floors."

Emmett's eyes widened at her words.

"You got to spend some time with your Grandmother Star? My word that was a blessing! How old was she when she died?" he questioned curiously.

Caroline tilted her head and looked up at him with the sweetest smile.

"I was 15 years old when she died. She was 103 years old. She died on February 16... on my birthday. Her mind was just as sharp the day she died as when she was a young woman. She told me to remember our history, and it was my duty to add to it. She told me not to cry for her, and then she asked me to take care of Grandfather Vincent." Caroline paused then held her arms out and spun around, when she stopped, she was smiling. "She used to do that when our talks crossed over into sadness," she explained.

Emmett was mesmerized by her presence.

"So... everything else is the original designs, apart from the paint and the wall-coverings." She captured his hand in hers and pulled him further into the kitchen, stopping when they reached the refrigerator. She opened it and began taking out the things they would need for breakfast, adding the loaf of French bread to it because she thought a buttery slice of toast would complement the omelet. Emmett offered to help. She pointed to the equipment that hung over the island and told him they needed the medium sized copper fry pan, the whisk and spatula. Emmett retrieved the items while she took a red bowl from the bottom shelf behind her. She selected two plates from the collective array of beautiful dishes then pulled a cutting board out from a hideaway spot beneath the island. She opened a huge drawer that was loaded with cutlery and chose two knives. She handed one to Emmett and asked if he would carve the ham. Emmett agreed, and she offered him a soft kiss which he accepted without hesitation. He began his task while they talked; however, his eyes scanned the room in-between watching the exciting and beautiful woman next to him and carving the meat in front of him.

Caroline sliced the bread and coated it with fresh butter, then she made a pot of coffee and sat it on the huge industrial size stove. She retrieved a match and lit the burner and the oven. Emmett thought it a magnificent piece of equipment. The cooking area and grates were black iron, but the doors were coated with red porcelain and the handles were all copper. There was a large wide oven on the bottom beneath the burners and another on the left side with a griddle on top of it. A storage shelf ran across the top of the solid back.

"Would you like me to dice the ham, Honey, or leave it in slices?" he asked as he worked.

"Cut it to your preference, Emmett. Do you like mushrooms?"

"Yes. I like everything except rye bread. I have never been able to acquire a taste for it... and I don't care for sauerkraut either." He made a face and shook his head.

Caroline giggled.

"I don't like gouda. I love cheese, but that one smells like a stinky arm pit to me," she told him playfully. "I have some black olives... okay if I add them?"

"Yep, that sounds good." Emmett diced the ham into small pieces while Caroline prepared the other ingredients. The sweet hickory smell of the meat made his mouth water. He held a bite up to her lips, she took it then he tasted a small piece too. When the coffee lid began to rattle from the steam of caffeine, Emmett turned it down on low then helped himself to the coffee cups to which she pointed. He fixed hers with a dash of cream and a spoon of honey, freely moving around the kitchen with her guidance. He sat her cup down next to her, then leaned over her shoulder and kissed her cheek. He pressed his body against her and his hands massaged her waist then made their way to the firm round flesh of her chest. Her body responded to him so naturally it filled him with longing. He exhaled and pulled her back against him then wrapped her in his embrace and just held her tight.

"You are amazing, Caroline... and so fine." He pressed his face into her hair.

She leaned her head back, so she could make eye contact with him.

"I love the way you treat me... and the way you touch me," she whispered. "Kiss me, Emmett."

He did as she asked and took his time in doing so. When he pressed his lips to her forehead, she released a satisfied sigh that made him feel good.

She picked up the coffee and took a sip while they stood there and absorbed the feel of one another.

Emmett asked what else he could do to help her, and she had him break six eggs while she finished grating the cheese.

He asked her to tell him about the way the kitchen was designed. She explained that the size was because her grandfather liked to entertain, but the work stations and shelving were built to accommodate Grandmother Star. She had begun making baked goods for the general store in town, and the business had grown into quite a production. Emmett listened as his understanding connected with the reason why the walls were lined with shelves. They were mounted and held in place with ornate black wrought iron braces, one over another. The counters were custom built tables running along the walls in eight-foot sections with repeated shelving underneath for storage and an occasional drawer for utensils. They were installed this way so the ladies who helped her grandmother, could work within their own space without crowding each other. The legs and skirting of the work tables were painted cream, and the tops were slabs of black walnut, which were smooth from years of work and treatment. The counter heights were different in places regarding the task, and the ample shelving above them was for cooling baked goods out of the way of the next batch.

Emmett was mindful of his surroundings, taking in one space after another as she spoke of her heritage. He learned the surface of the center work island, which was an impressive 12 feet in length and six feet wide, was a solid slab of wood from an Appalachian Hemlock. Vincent Breaux had accepted the magnificent slab of timber in trade for a 100-pound bundle of cured, sweet tobacco. The distinctive sink was the length of a small fishing boat, it was made of hammered copper by the skilled hands of Truman Silver. The massive copper trough was built to accommodate Star's wishes, with three divider walls making it possible to catch water in four individual sinks. The sink depended on eight sturdy legs to bear the girth. Two faucets serviced the unit, one on each end catered to two compartments; the original pump had been left when they added running water to the house. Emmett's attention shifted to the beautiful floor; the chunky square bricks that covered it gave the large room a homey vibe. He learned they were made of red earth which was found along the edge of the Liberty River; specifically, where the bend cut around the massive cliffs on the northeastern end of the farm. The land in that region had an unusual concentration of pyrite which peppered the handmade blocks with golden flecks of ore. When Emmett commented on their dark, blood-red color, Caroline explained that her mother had them sealed with a protective coating which had enriched their color. The wall covering had been chosen to complement them; the smooth paper was decorated with brown, red and cream stripes in varied thicknesses; a small gold sparkle in the red strip matched the floor. A collection of ornate hand painted roosters and chickens hung along the walls in a collage of square and diamond shaped gold Lemay frames, giving a cohesive flare to the room.

Emmett was fascinated and asked her about all the dishes which filled all the shelves.

"Every bride in the family has chosen two sets of dishes... china and every day," explained Caroline. "The china is in the first pantry on display, and these in here are the ones used daily. The red ones are my mother's," she explained.

"Which ones are yours, Honey?" asked Emmett as he looked around the room.

Caroline shook her head.

"I never chose any," she answered.

Emmett heard that sadness in her voice again. He could guess why it was there due to what she had told him, but he sensed that there was much more that she had not said. He was curious, and he wanted her to tell him because she needed a confidant.

"Why didn't you choose a pattern, Sweetheart?"

She handed Emmett the whisk then picked up the small waste can from under the island table and disposed of the egg shells. She shrugged her shoulders as she shook her head.

"It... it just didn't feel right," she responded in a soft voice. She picked up the cutting board with all the ingredients piled up on it then added the small bowl of butter.

Emmett whipped the eggs, and she added a little cream to them while he did so. She said no more about it, so he didn't press her. Instead, he changed the subject.

"Julianna told me earlier this evening she learned how to make tuna salad. They have a full-time housekeeper, I understand the lady takes up a lot of time with her."

"That's nice of her." Caroline gazed up at him for a moment. "That hurts you, doesn't it?"

"Which part... the fact that my daughter spends more time with the housekeeper than her mother, or the fact that her mother is so selfish she would rather spite me and allow it, than do what's best for our child?"

Caroline stretched up to his lips and kissed him.

"I'm sorry, Emmett."

He surveyed her face a moment then he took advantage of her closeness and pushed her arms around his neck then kissed her deeply.

"Thank you for that. I can't change it right now. Maybe when she's older, she can be a bigger part of my life. One can only hope. Let's concentrate on each other. Today... this very minute... belongs to us. So, show me some skills, Beautiful. I am getting hungry too."

Emmett grabbed the potholder and moved the coffee so she could place the skillet on the burner.

He peeked at the toast then turned the oven off while Caroline melted some butter in the skillet. She dropped some mushrooms, olives and ham in the sizzling pan and scrambled them around to get them hot. The ham was smoked and ready to eat. She dropped some fresh chopped spinach on top and turned the heat down for a few minutes.

"Have mercy that smells good!" declared Emmett.

"It does... my stomach is growling. Did you hear it?" A soft and relaxed laugh bubbled up her throat.

Emmett stepped up next to her because he needed to be close to this wonderful creature.

"Just hang on a minute and mine will roar."

He watched her turn the heat back up and spread the ingredients out evenly then she poured the egg over it in a circular motion. She picked the skillet up off the heat and tilted it back and forth until the egg began to bubble and firm in the center. She sprinkled the cheese over the top of it, then folded the right side over the left and scooted it to the center with the spatula. She turned it and pressed it together.

He held the plate for her and she placed the golden pie in the center. He sat the plate on top of the oven to keep it warm and retrieved the toast while Caroline started the next pie.

Emmett took it upon himself to put things in the kitchen back in order. He went to the sink finding a small enamel dishpan sitting in the bottom underneath the faucet. It made sense to catch only what was needed, so he ran it half full and added some soap. Caroline told him not to worry with the dishes, but he had them gathered, washed and rinsed by the time she had the other omelet ready.

He moved everything to the nook overlooking the backyard and the river. Caroline followed him with their coffee cups and the pot. She sat them down, then disappeared into the pantry and came back with a small jar of red jam. She handed it to him to open. Emmett looked at the label and grinned then he put a sturdy grip on the small jar.

"Wild plum is one of my favorites, Honey."

"I love it too." She sat down and warmed their cups with fresh coffee from the pot. She was surprised when Emmett gripped her hand and bowed his head. He thanked the Almighty for the food and the person that prepared it then he asked for protection for his daughter, health and blessings for his parents, and protection, health and blessings for her. He asked nothing for himself only thanked the Almighty for His love and His grace.

Caroline was so moved that she felt her lashes get heavy with uncensored tears. She had never heard Dane pray... ever. She had never heard him say thank you either. When she made a choked sound, Emmett said amen. Without another word spoken, he slid her chair closer to his and pulled her hand up to his lips.

"Shhh, things are too wonderful to cry." He kissed her brow with tenderness then her lips.

"I know; it's been so long since I felt like someone cared for me."

"Well, Honey... you're gonna have to get used to it." He prepared her coffee as he had previously while she spread jam on their toast. They ate until they were stuffed. Emmett even finished her last few bites as he told her how delicious the food tasted.

They worked at the sink side by side to clean up the rest of the breakfast dishes. She asked him what he wanted to do next. He questioned her about his choices.

"I can show you around the house. We can go for a walk. We can soak in the tub then take a nap. We can play records and dance in the ballroom, or we can go for a swim in the solarium. When I was younger, and my mind stayed filled with romantic notions of you, Emmett, I used to imagine us together enthralled in each other's arms in every room of this house. I didn't know a lot about making love, but it was like a game to see how many rooms in which we could kiss and touch each other until we gave into desire. Of course, I was your wife in those dreams and..." her words stopped as she rinsed the last plate and stood it in the drain rack.

"And what, Honey?" surveyed Emmett.

"And we weren't committing adultery." She released a heavy sigh as she shook her head. "I was so lonely, Emmett. I had no idea what I was getting into."

He turned to her.

"Caroline, I choose to be here with you. I'm prepared to accept the consequences... whatever they may be."

She faced him suddenly.

"I don't mean with you, Emmett. I mean, in letting myself get trapped in a marriage like this."

Emmett reminded her she had another option.

"You don't have to stay in it, Caroline. I'll help you. We can confront him together, or I'll talk to him alone. In thinking about it… that would probably be the better idea."

She searched his face.

"You're so confident! I wish I could be. Nobody knows him like I do, and I realized some time ago that I don't really know anything about him. I thought we would learn everything about each other with time, but it was another foolish thing that I assumed about being married." Her hand went to her brow as she shook her head. "I was so incredibly stupid.

"Emmett, I didn't give myself to you in search of an ally that could help me get away from him. I will never leave my home. I just wanted to know what it was like to spend some time with that fearless and valiant blue-eyed boy with the blonde curls that lived on the edge of town. I knew why Vicki fell in love with you, but I'll never understand why she walked away. Now, I know for sure that she's just selfish."

Emmett hooked her around the waist with his arm and pulled her close, so he could press his lips against hers. He began to move his feet and body in a slow swaying motion.

Caroline exhaled and molded herself against him. Her nails caressed his palm a few moments before she gripped his hand. He pressed his lips to her ear and his words were inspired with the same sultry energy she felt emanating from his body. She was familiar with it now and she knew that his thoughts were of a personal nature. She liked getting personal with him.

"Dance with me, gypsy girl! We don't have a care in the world while we're in each other's arms." He brushed a kiss over her lips and Caroline returned a more intimate kiss as their bodies began a slow dance. They held each other tight as they swayed back and forth around the empty *space in front of the sink while their heartbeats supplied the music.*

Emmett gazed into her eyes and his feet took her into a gliding spin toward the doorway. He let go of her hand and turned her into a low dip. Caroline giggled and turned off the light switch. It thrust them into the shadowed hallway. Emmett spun them around and around into the vestibule. It was a huge and open space with a 30-foot ceiling to accommodate the curving staircase. She had told him the front drapes were closed in the parlor and library to keep out the cold, but it wasn't so. The morning sun filtered in through the massive windows in concentrated streams of light, adding a theatrical glow to the spirited nuance which surrounded them. The light held them while they held one another and twirled around the room. Emmett spun her through the double doorway into the parlor and they grinned at each other as they swirled around and around with each other. Their feet felt as though they were not even touching the floor, and Emmett stole a kiss from her lips every couple of minutes.

He changed directions on her and pressed his hips against her belly to back her across the entryway. She felt his manly body, and he leaned over and covered her mouth, so his tongue could dance with hers for a few seconds. His hand went to the small of her back where he pressed her even closer against his manly body. He moaned and pulled his mouth from hers then whirled them past the huge majestic mirror that stood from the floor to the tops of the doorways. They waltzed into the library. Caroline noticed these drapes were open as well, but she was not disturbed. She focused her eyes on the wonderful man in front of her as she recalled Grandpa Preston's words, 'that young man will be someone of caliber and integrity one day, Caroline'.

Emmett guided them around the tables and chairs then past the walls of books. He pressed his lips to her forehead as they exited through another door and whirled down the hallway again towards the staircase. Their feet were every bit as compatible as their bodies, and they celebrated the rhythmic unity as they waltzed through the parlor and library two more times.

Caroline threw her head back and her joyous laughter echoed through the house like music. Some of her hair escaped from the comb that held it and she reached up and pulled it out. Emmett witnessed the long black curls fall to her waist; they brushed the back of his hand before their celebrative swirling caused it to wrap around her waist. The sparkle in her eyes and the smile on her full lips, along with the pinkish tint of her cheeks and the plump bulges of her breasts pressing against the neck of her blouse was completely arousing to him. He suddenly couldn't wait to see her bare body again.

He slowed them down, and they fell back into the gentle sway as his kiss consumed her mouth. The back of his fingers grazed her throat then went to the neckline of her blouse. He manipulated enough of the buttons so that he could kiss the satiny tunnel between her breasts. Caroline's hand surveyed the front of his body. He covered her hand with his and rubbed himself against her palm as he kissed her again. She kicked out of her shoes and unfastened his belt, then his pant waist. Emmett didn't even try to restrain the urgency in which he craved her. They undressed each other while kissing and touching until they stood in the large foyer naked and wanting due to the careless abandonment in it. They panted for air from the exertion of their waltz, and now their needs were motivated by desire and had become something primitive and carnal once again.

"Caroline..." his hands were all over her body and his eyes shimmered with desire.

She pressed her fingers to his mouth to silence him then guided him over to the settee that sat opposite the mirror in the foyer. She climbed on to it and settled on her knees, then caressed his manly length with her cheek. Emmett's hands trembled as his palms traced the smooth skin on her shoulders. When she took his body into her kiss, he inhaled a deep breath then reached past her for support from the wall.

"*Gypsy girl, you're making me crazy,*" he breathed. He stroked her silky hair with his free hand as her palms possessed his backside and urged him to move with her.

Emmett knew he was fully invested in her... mind, body and spirit. He couldn't control the way she made his heart feel, and if he could, he didn't want to.

His grip closed around his erection and he exhaled as a quaking weakness tried to overcome him. She looked at him and rose to her knees then pulled her hair around over her shoulder. He looked deep into her eyes.

"*You're so beautiful and exciting, Gypsy. I swear I've fallen in love with you, Sweetheart.*"

Her large violet eyes clung to him as the soft pads of her fingertips teased the smooth head of his erection.

"*I've always dreamed of you, Emmett; I never really could let go of the image of us in my mind. Would you do something special for me?*"

"*I would do anything to please you.*" The passion he was feeling gave a rasp tone to his voice. He was lost to her and could do nothing else.

She told him what she wanted then turned her back to him. Emmett's knees found a sturdy spot on the sofa behind her then he pressed his chest against the petal soft skin of her back. She held on to the arm and back of the elaborate settee then leaned over and parted her knees. His palms claimed her warm, excited breasts, and he tugged at the berries of velvety flesh a moment while she greeted his body. Emmett dipped into the hot, moist slit between her legs then pushed into her gentle-like with the intention of taking his time. He tried not to think about the man that held her prisoner in a sham of a marriage; even though, he sensed that his time with her was as privileged as his body.

They moved together in a rhythmic sunlight dance while witnessing their union in the mirror across from the sofa. He understood her request now. Their bodies were painting a visual portrait, and the canvas was their memory. This portrait defined them as lovers, and they wanted it that way; they wanted to remember everything about each other and their time together. They had no idea how to discipline *their response to something that was so magical and erotic, especially when there was no way to control the measure of desire they generated together. This union became a sensuous and lascivious exchange of physical rapture. The reflection of two bare lovers was a captivating thing to witness. What a magnificent bond two people could create together in the design of their bodies while chasing away the loneliness in their hearts. This raw, but enchanted insight which passed between them was based on mutual acceptance and revered for the delicate and sturdy characteristics of their hearts.*

Caroline pushed his hand to her sensitive spot and arched her back. Emmett's palm honored the moist, softness like she had given him a priceless gift, and he took care in massaging her private body both ways. The flight of ecstasy that had taken off inside of her caused him to be swept away as well. His seed spewed into her with a fierceness that felt so good it hurt. He drove himself deep into her belly as many times as it took for the maddening fever to let go of him.

A bone melting weakness attacked his knees. Emmett held her against his body as he turned and sat down; her legs accommodated the position and folded back on each side of him. He knew by the way her inner body engaged him that she had not been released of the craving for fulfillment. He was tired, but highly sensitive to her needs. Emmett held her beautiful body closer and continued to stimulate that hypersensitive spot while her zealous hips exploited his manly body and pricked the wanton ache inside her belly into a satisfying climax. He laid his head back against the sofa and reveled in the feel of her while a gratified contentment washed over him. Clearly, she had gained assurance in herself and him as a partner and was able to take what she needed from him. The seed of promise had taken root and was growing with a discerning authenticity. Their spirits were weaving a heartfelt bond. It was becoming stronger and tighter with each minute they shared, each personal truth they revealed, each touch, each kiss, and each breath they expended on behalf of the other.

Somewhere in his exalted frame of mind, he heard her beautiful tongue celebrate the wave of delight that suddenly rushed through her body. He made a mental note that she was going to have to teach him how to speak French.

Caroline gathered her thick curls in her hand then leaned back against him and pressed her cheek next to his. Emmett's arm tightened around her ribs beneath her breasts while his other hand continued to caress the softness between her thighs. Her palms glided over the muscles and bone that held her while their hearts pounded between them. They sat together in the peacefulness of the house and listened to each other breathe while they gazed at their reflection in the mirror. Emmett's lips explored the bare skin of her shoulder as he spoke.

"You said earlier that you dreamed of doing something crazy with excitement... something completely reckless and carefree with me. So, how was that?" he mumbled against her ear.

"It was perfect," she sighed. "What's next?"

He laughed softly.

"You are perfect, Caroline, and the most wonderful surprise I have ever had in my life." His hand shifted from her private body to caress the flat plain of her belly. "You're so beautiful... you always have been."

"Thank you, Emmett, and you are so much better than fantasy." She smiled at him as the mirror revealed the glimmers of happiness in her eyes. It felt as though they were the only two people in the world.

"Would you make love to me in every room of this house?" she murmured.

Her question pleased him very much.

"Absolutely, Sweetheart, but it will take longer than the weekend to accomplish such an important task and do it justice."

She sighed with contentment, and Emmett smiled. He knew where it came from because he was feeling the same way.

"That's exactly what I was hoping you would say, Emmett."

A compatible silence fell on them for a few minutes then she told him what she was thinking.

"When I was a girl, I never imagined making love would feel this way, or that it could be this consuming. I didn't know that it could be shared and exchanged in such a tender, yet maddening way. I've never felt anything so satisfying and wonderful. I love... making love with you, Emmett. Does that make me a horrible person?" She caressed his chin lovingly with her cheek and then changed the subject before Emmett could answer her. "I'm finally exhausted. Let's curl up together and take a nap. When we wake up, we can take a hot, soapy bath. You can make us some of your famous biscuits while I slice some cheese and fry some ham to go with them. Afterwards, we can bundle up and go for a long walk. How does that sound?"

"It sounds perfect, Honey." Emmett's words were lazy because he too was tired; still, his mind toyed with what she had said a moment ago. He learned years ago that people look at life in black and white. Because people are the business of law enforcement, he had come to understand the black and white of life are in fact, the good and bad things that happened to people. They are the lessons in life that mold us in to the people we become. When he looked at Caroline, he saw only beauty, not only in her appearance, but in her heart. Goodness emanated from her spirit. Because she deserved nothing less in a mate, he was inspired to be a better man. He did not believe that what they had done together made either of them a bad person, but there would be consequences ahead of them. Good or bad, black or white, he was standing next to her and holding on tight to her hand.

"Gypsy, there is nothing bad about you... not a single thing," whispered Emmett.

They slowly untangled themselves from each other and the couch. She looked up at him as she held both her hands out. Emmett smiled at her as he intertwined his fingers with hers then pressed his lips to her brow; they were incapable of wasting one second of their time together.

CHAPTER 24

Emmett inhaled a sweet scent and the corners of his mouth turned up because Caroline's body was draped over one side of him beneath his arm. He stretched his legs out into the warm softness of the huge bed then shifted his torso closer against her bareness. They had closed the drapes, so the large room would be shadowed, and they could rest in the nuance of solitude. He listened to her relaxed breath as he lay there in a living fantasy and just took it all into his senses. He didn't know what time it was, and he reminded himself that it wasn't important. That was when he heard a door close beyond the privacy of the master bedroom. His first thought was that there was an intruder, and then it occurred to him that Dane Reid had decided to make an appearance in Caroline's life. He considered the crummy timing and became convinced that it had to be him.

Emmett gently eased his body out from beneath hers then tucked the pillow in his place and covered her up. He looked down at himself and realized that he didn't have anything available to put on, and he hated the thought of taking something from Dane's closet. He walked quietly to the double doors and looked out into the hallway. The house was still, and the glow of sunlight no longer filled the hallway. There was a light on in the kitchen; it was enough to define his path to where they had left their clothes in the floor of the foyer. Emmett stepped into the hallway and closed the bedroom door behind him. It occurred to him that he and Caroline had not left a light on after breakfast, and he was certain she had not left his side to revisit the room to do so.

Emmett moved quickly without making a sound. He found their things folded and hung neatly over the banister of the staircase. He wasted no time dressing in his shorts and pants. He by-passed his shoes while shoving his arms into his shirt sleeves then buttoned it as he walked over to the door that led into the kitchen. He looked around the door facing into the kitchen as he heard a cup clink against a saucer. It was a soft sound, yet distinguishable. He could see the orange sun through the window above the café curtains of the breakfast nook. Suddenly, it occurred to him that he had left his sidearm lying on the shelf by the refrigerator. Emmett realized the sun had relocated to the back of the house and he instinctively glanced over his shoulder to see the front drapes in the library were closed, which was why the inside of the house was dark. He had been with Caroline every minute since they arrived and was positive that if she had left the bed to do such a thing, he would have known. Still, this was the only logical solution for the drapes and their clothing being tidy.

The repeated clink of the coffee cup drew his attention back to the immediate moment, and he knew he had no choice but to face her husband. Emmett reasoned that it was best to do so while it was just the two of them, man to man. He turned up his sleeves and drew in a deep breath to stiffen his spine, then entered the kitchen prepared for whatever may come.

Emmett stopped in his tracks when he saw the aged gentleman sitting at the table reading a newspaper. His long, white hair flowed over his shoulder and he stroked a thick mustache with his fingers as he turned the page. He picked up the cup and took a sip, but his attention went to *something beyond the confines of the house. He sat the cup down and stood, then sidestepped the chair next to him so he could look out the window. The gentleman wore a white buttoned-down shirt with a banded collar and full gathered sleeves; a tailored, blue-striped vest was fastened neatly over it. The dark gray trousers fit his legs and were covered below his knees by the shaft of his black boots. The afternoon sun seemed to cut straight through him and Emmett shifted his body to one side to rid his eyes of the glare. His attention clung to the specter as the old gentleman shoved his hands in his pants pockets and turned to him as though he sensed his presence.*

Emmett had a flashback of the stories he had heard as a child about the old ghost that haunted the mansion of Whisper Bluff. He blinked to make sure he was seeing clearly, and in that fraction of a second, the man was gone. Emmett walked further into the L shaped room and stopped by the table as he looked in the cove where the stove, refrigerator and work station were housed.

He picked up the cup and found it warm as he saw the steam puffing from the kettle on the stove. Emmett recalled the joke Caroline had made about her grandfather calling her a coward. He did not feel threatened; however, he experienced a twinge of guilt move over his chest at the thought of his and Caroline's zealous unions being on display. He presumed that since she spoke of him the night before; he had just come face-to-face with Zane Breaux. He thought about that as a possibility, and reasoned that Caroline had an angel who loved her more than a guardian, but also as a granddaughter. Emmett smiled at the thought. He helped himself to a mug from the shelf then went to the canister on the counter for a tea bag. He began to prepare the mug while he respectfully greeted the older gentleman.

"Hello Mr. Breaux, my name is Emmett Cotton, Sir. I grew up around the corner from your family... on Riverwood Lane to be specific. Caroline and I went to school together when we were kids. In a way, I guess you could say we work with each other. I'm a deputy for the Sheriff's Department, that's why my sidearm is on the shelf." Emmett

didn't have any idea what to expect by initiating a conversation, but considering how he felt about Caroline, he continued to speak because it seemed to be the right thing to do. "I was aware of your granddaughter when we were in school, but she was shy... and I was two grades ahead of her. Our lives went in opposite directions and... we both made bad choices. It's one of those things in life that you wish you could do over... at least, I wish I could. Anyway Sir, her car wouldn't start last night. It was my intention to see her safely home. She knew my wife had left me a couple of years back, and well... I sort of knew that her marriage was troubled. It's not hard to surmise that she's been unhappy considering she's always alone. Honestly Sir, I've never thought too much of the man she married, but I didn't know her heart was as injured and lonely as mine. I admit that I've always admired her from a distance, but it was always a respectful distance, Sir. I never intended to intrude on or covet another man's wife. I apologize to you for wanting her attention so badly. I never expected our paths would ever cross like this, Sir. She's so wonderful. I want to be with her, Mr. Breaux. I want to take care of her and make her happy. I didn't know I could fall for someone so fast." Emmett paused as he thought about that, "Um... wait, that's not exactly true, Sir. I knew it was possible that's exactly how my daughter came to be. It's just... I'm alone now. When Caroline told me, her heart doesn't belong to him and that her marriage was over; I let my guard down. I began to hope we could find happiness together. I believe she needs me, Sir, and I know that I need her. She has a brilliant mind. She's gentle and kind. And... she's the finest thing I've ever known or touched. I wish things were different. I swear... I wish I was her husband. Anyway Sir... I feel better knowing you're here with her." Emmett turned around to the table; the cup sat in the same place and the sun was lower in the sky. He noticed that the newspaper that was on the breakfast table was now sitting on the work island directly in front of him. He took a step towards it and saw that it had a crossword puzzle that had been started. He read the *words that were filled in: foresight, enmity, temperance, Phragmite, antagonist, maiden, and perish.*

"Mr. Breaux, Sir... is it safe for me to assume that you're trying to tell me something?" asked Emmett out loud.

He was startled when the kettle whistled abruptly to release the building steam. Emmett spun around to remove it from the burner before it could awaken Caroline, only then did he realize that there was no flame underneath the pot. His hand went to the knob to turn the gas off and it was already secure in a safe position. Emmett frowned, then his instincts as a lawman took over and he turned back to the newspaper. He spoke as he began to reason out the words.

"All right Sir, my attention is all yours. Let's see, foresight... I assume that would be our meeting and your wisdom? Kick me, Sir, if I get off track." He waited a moment then continued. "I know enmity means, hostility. Temperance... is self-control. Phragmite? Hmm, I'll have to think on that one." Emmett reached for his mug and bumped the delicate handle with his chunk of a thumb. It sloshed out on the newspaper and began to soak in. Emmett stared at the damp spot as he thought about the word. The tea marred an advertisement which was promoting night classes at the university; they were geared around the opportunity for adults to re-educate themselves in a new field of study in night school. The text from the other side began to show through the damp spot and to the eye the first four letters of the word 're-educate' stood out. "R-e-e-d... that's it! A Phragmite is a reed." Emmett was silent a moment, then he spoke with enlightenment. "But you mean Dane Reid." His eyes moved to the next word because he was getting a bad feeling. "Antagonist. I don't really know him, but I understand that's he's a horse's ass. Yes Sir, he would definitely see me as the antagonist concerning Caroline." Emmett knew that was an understatement. "Maiden, which from your perspective would be your granddaughter, and his wife." Chills ran down Emmett's arms as he spoke the next word. "Perish? Sir, are you trying to tell me that he's going to hurt her... that he would kill her should he find out about me?"

507

Emmett's bones leaped underneath his skin when the fragile cup and saucer suddenly leaped off the breakfast table and crashed to the brick floor.

Caroline's voice came to him from the doorway.

"Is that the dispatcher you're talking to? Do you have to go, Emmett?"

"No, Honey... I was umm, reading the crossword puzzle actually." He watched her enter the room, but she stopped suddenly and inhaled a deep breath. Emmett realized that the sweet scent of tobacco floated in the kitchen. Her eyes became fixed on him and Emmett just knew that she was kindred to the man he had just met.

"Are you scared?" She questioned in a soft voice.

"Should I be, Honey?"

She shrugged her shoulders then pushed the shiny cascade of curls away from her cheek.

"Dane finds it difficult to stay here very long. He's a man that yields to authority, but he must believe in it before he can respect it. He also wears it like a second skin. He senses their energy, but he does not believe in angels. It's easy enough for him to believe in hell, and yet... the concept of heaven evades him." She walked over to the corner and retrieved the dust pan and broom that leaned against the wall. The floor length satin robe she wore was tied at her waist; it was a rich burgundy and the full skirt flowed around her legs like an expensive evening gown as she moved. Emmett watched her as she cleaned up the broken porcelain. When she headed his way, he pulled the trash can out for her. She disposed of it then took the time to consider his eyes as she questioned him. "Are you ready to run... now that you know?"

Emmett smiled and caressed her cheek with his thumb.

"Now that I know what, that your grandfather is here with you?"

She nodded her head.

Emmett admitted what was in his heart before he told her what was on his mind.

"I've heard stories about this house my entire life, Caroline. But last night I learned the history of this house and your family. I wouldn't presume to understand why or how things work when it comes to the spirit realm; however, I can't be a believer in the Almighty and not accept that it is real. I believe in and trust my judgment... and I trust my instincts even more. I know what I saw; honestly, I'm glad that he's here with you." Emmett smiled. *"I believed us to be alone. I apologized to him for expressing my... need of you without discretion. Respectfully, he is your grandfather. I assume he would be Zane? He's the one you made a specific reference to last night."*

Her response was somewhat absent as she spoke to him.

"They respect my privacy, Emmett; besides, all of them knew how I felt about you when I was a girl."

Caroline's brows shifted as she studied him. He could see that she was relieved somewhat, but he sensed she was bothered by something else. What could bother her beyond this reality, he wouldn't attempt a guess.

"Who did you see? He spoke to you?" she surveyed.

"He was an older gentleman with white hair and a mustache. He was having a cup of tea at the table and doing the crossword puzzle. And yes, he spoke to me... his way... I guess you could say."

Caroline crossed her arms over her body as a chill gripped her.

"I'm sorry, Emmett. I don't doubt you... it's just, they are all here in spirit. Based on your account, you met Grandfather Vincent. I've only seen him three times in my life and it was always when something life-altering was about to happen. I first met him when Grandmother Star was dying; he stayed next to her side and held her hand for three days. Grandpa Preston told me that only the bloodline was under the binding of the shaman. Vincent and Star knew it was the last time they would see each other because he was trapped here.

"The next time I saw him, he was here to greet my father after his death. The car accident was so sudden that

daddy grieved over being separated from my mother without being able to say goodbye.

"And he came to me when Grandpa Preston was about to pass; he held my hand as his grandson's breath slipped out of his body. I cried so hard that I felt I had lost my own. Grandfather Vincent let go of my hand and when I called out for him not to leave me, Grandpa Preston tapped me on the shoulder and held his arms out to me. He hugged me, and he began to chuckle then we started to dance. He's the one who taught me how to waltz. He was sure-footed, and he used to twirl me around so fast it was like we floated around the ballroom. The fact that you did that for me this morning meant the world to me, Emmett. I'll never forget it." Caroline reached up and caressed his cheek with her palm then she pressed her soft lips to his. *"I've never had to fear anything as long as I am within the walls of this house, because they protect me. But if he's here... then... he has come for me because I am all that's left. What did he say Emmett, how will death come to me?"*

Emmett shook his head as an urgent need to protect her rose-up inside of him. He had encountered her grandfather while thinking he was about to confront Dane concerning his feelings for Caroline. He was certain that her grandfather had known this, and it was as though he understood. Emmett hugged her close and kissed her face over and over while his heart ached. Was it true? Was their love going to have to remain clandestine so that she would be safe? He felt he had to tell her what her grandfather had showed him.

"I love you, Caroline, and don't you ever forget that Sweetheart," breathed Emmett. *"But this time... he came to warn me."*

"Warn you... about what, Emmett? You have to tell me."

"Yes, I know I do." Emmett kissed her tenderly then he pulled her hand up to his lips and pressed another into her soft, warm palm.

Emmett lifted her and sat her on the worktable. He began to tell her of the specifics that her grandfather had revealed to him and prepared her a cup of tea while he did so. She studied the puzzle as she listened. He stirred the ingredients he had added to the hot tea and finished the facts. Emmett offered the steaming cup to her, and she whispered 'thank you' as her small elegant hand accepted it. He studied her face while she took several sips.

"I can't believe I'm the one explaining something like this to you... of all people," stated Emmett with a smile. He picked up his mug and took a healthy gulp.

"He trusts you, or he wouldn't have made a contact with you." She shook her head as she looked at him. "I can't even fathom having to stay married to him because of his temper. Isn't that why I should be able to divorce him?" She ran her hand over her brow as she sighed. "How do I stay away from you now when every cell in my body craves to touch you and my belly trembles with the need to feel you inside of me?" She began to cry. Emmett wrapped his arms around her. He wasn't expecting her to lash out like she did.

"I was stupid, Grandfather! I admit it!" shouted Caroline. "I was lonely, and I trusted Dane. You saw how he was... how he just took control of my body... my life and my self-respect. The only thing he hasn't taken from me is the control of this house. Is there no way out for me?"

Emmett cupped her face in his hands and kissed her as he spoke.

"Shhh... he's worried about you and so am I. I'll find a way to make it right for us, Honey. I promise, Caroline... I'll find a way."

Emmett figured some fresh air would do them good even if it was cold outside. Because the afternoon sun would not wait on them, they bypassed the bath, and went for the walk she had mentioned earlier that morning. He put on his socks and boots, and she produced a thick, pullover sweater, gloves and a wool scarf for him to put on beneath his coat. Emmett smiled as he watched her dress in a small, but masculine pair of thermal underwear and a long sleeve button down top that matched. She put on a black wool skirt for warmth then layered a green and black checked dress over it that buttoned down the front to her ankles. Emmett touched the fabric and found it to be thick and supple. He teased her about being so gorgeous while at the same time farm-girl practical. She put on two pair of warm socks then pushed her feet into cowboy boots. Emmett grinned at her. She covered her clothing with a thick coat then pulled a wool hat down on her head. She giggled and held her arms out as she turned around in place a couple of times. He had already learned that her doing so meant she was happy.

They gathered a sturdy blanket and a thermos of hot chocolate then ventured into the woods on the bluff to visit her favorite tree swing. It was a dandy — the seat was made of a piece of split hardwood. They squeezed into it, side by side and swung for almost an hour. They talked about their childhood and got tickled at some goofy things their peers did in those years. They realized just how much they had in common even though they had lived separate lives. They hiked to the tiptop of the bluff where they settled on a fallen log to drink the steaming chocolate. Emmett carved their initials in the log then cut a heart around it. They were adults, but they approached the afternoon as though they were still kids in high school. They did it because they didn't do it when they were young and should have. They took the long path through the woods and came back to the house place along the river path. They visited the stone house and got trapped in a seizure of kissing and touching. Emmett asked her if she wanted to watch the huge riverboat paddle by just before dusk or go back to the house and make love again. Caroline told him she wanted to do both, but they had to start with the paddle boat.

The pier was still sturdy, and Emmett sat down and crossed his legs then guided her bottom into his lap. He wrapped his arms and the blanket around her then pressed his lips to her brow.

"Honey, would you mind telling me about how you and Dane came to be together?"

Caroline made a visual connection with him for a moment then smiled and caressed the back of his hands before she joined her fingers with his. She guided them beneath the blanket over her breasts then she began to share with him the things he wanted know.

"He was on furlough when I met him. He showed up at my graduation and the party after with one of the other graduates. She was a philosophy major, and I didn't really know her. He flirted with me and every time I turned around it seemed I tripped over him. He was nice and intellectually sharp, and the way he presented himself exuded confidence and integrity, and the uniform was proof of his patriotism.

"He dropped by the house the next night. I did not invite him inside, but we walked around the yard and he went to the cemetery with me to put fresh flowers out. He kissed me that night... it was my first. I was limited in my knowledge of romance. I had my daydreams as a girl. It was the first time that I was alone in the world without a 'living soul'. His attention seemed to be full of purpose, only I just didn't know what kind. He came by every night for the next week, so we could walk; his kiss and his advancements grew a little bolder with each visit.

"He noticed the brick barbecue pit on the patio and offered to bring beef steaks on Friday night and cook for me. I agreed. Friday night I prepared the table on the patio with everything we needed to complete the meal. He cooked a good steak, and we talked while we ate. He asked me if I would show him around the house." Caroline shook her head as she seemed stuck in her memories. "We never made it upstairs. The minute he walked into the master bedroom, his masculine and authoritarian demeanor took over. In only a matter of minutes I was naked, and he was inside of me. It bothered me mostly because it happened in the bed that once belonged to my parents. I was naïve about sex, Emmett, but I knew it would come into play, eventually. It's just... I was not expecting it to happen that way. He took control of my body without my having a say. I mean, I didn't even consider my virginity until the moment he took it from me. I felt like a stupid girl who had foolishly thrown away her dignity. It was my fault... I didn't tell him not to touch me. Anyway, he stayed the night and by morning he had established his claim to me physically and mentally. It took me a while to realize that my emotional tie to him was because of the physical exchange and because... I was so tired of being alone. I had never slept in their bed until that evening. In that one night, he moved into my life and my home, and I became the woman of this house.

"We were together for one month. He went everywhere I went and questioned me about every contact I had with the outside world. As a girl, I watched my grandparents... and my mom and dad interact with each other in the most loving of ways. I look back and realize that I wanted to be in love.

"Like I said, I was young and stupid. I thought his appetite for my body was the way all lovers felt... just like I believed that his possessiveness was love. I didn't know then that a man like him would never be satisfied with the devotion of a faithful wife or her body. He thought he could own me and control every aspect of my life. And, without understanding the danger in it, that's exactly what I allowed him to do.

"He suggested we marry before he had to leave because my reputation was at stake. He pointed out that as much as he had been inside of me, the odds of my having a child in my belly were rich. It took a few days to get everything together for a ceremony. We married, and he left the next day. I got my period two days later. He was gone for a few weeks then he came back for several days. It went on that way through the fall. He hasn't stayed here for more than a week since that first month we were together. His first long assignment came in December; he was gone for three months. The next time it was six months... then eight. The next time I saw him was when I went to Washington for his birthday... you know the rest."

"You didn't hear from him at Christmas?" asked Emmett.

"No, but I didn't last year either." Caroline shrugged her shoulders then caressed his chin with her brow as she pulled Emmett's arms and the blanket tighter around her *body and snuggled deeper into his lap. "I understand now that he has a ferocious appetite for sex and he must be in control of every second. After you, I realize that I was a vessel that he used to satisfy his needs, and an empty one at that. I'm not naïve anymore; those women I saw him with... they are just two of many." She was quiet for a long moment before she spoke again and when she did, a spell of devotion fell upon Emmett's soul.*

"This one day with you has restored my faith in all the things a young girl believed possible concerning love and the dreams of the heart. I love you, Emmett."

He pressed his lips to her temple and closed his eyes as he told her what was in his heart.

"I love you too, Caroline Breaux."

They watched the surface of the river mirror the gray sky and every few minutes, a swirl of north wind etched ripples on the surface. The air was freezing cold and tiny snowflakes had begun to fall on them in the last few minutes. They cherished the time together and patiently waited to see the piece of history her family had donated to the community. Caroline's gloved hands bumped together as she clapped her hands. Her eyes sparkled like an excited child when the festive white lights that adorned the floating dinosaur came into sight around the river bend. They could hear the faint echo of music coming from the Spirit of Liberty while the monster paddle wheel propelled it up river. They watched the historic vessel until it disappeared around the next bend. The wind had begun to blow in sporadic, breathtaking bursts. They clamped their jaw teeth together to keep them from chattering. Emmett gathered their things, then they snuggled beneath the blanket together and headed back to the house.

They climbed the back steps cautiously because the snow had accumulated enough to freeze and make them slippery. They gained a better footing once they were on the limestone. Caroline pointed to the back balcony as she told him about her wedding day.

"I was married up there Emmett. Dane had a Chaplain he knew in service perform the ceremony. He was from Cato

and they became friends because of the fact. I'm not aware of how well he knew Dane, but he was a nice man. He brought his wife, and she stood with me while Dane's second in command was his best man. I didn't have any family to invite, and it was such short notice, there didn't seem to be any point in making a fuss. But I did get to wear my mother's wedding dress... and the chaplain's wife took a few pictures for me."

Emmett stopped and looked up at the balcony and the huge patio beneath it. He imagined her in all the satin and lace finery of a bride, only the man dressed in black standing next to her was him.

"Mine was a 'no frills' too." He looked down at her, then touched her chin with his fingers and tilted it up so he could kiss her on the lips. He smiled. "I'm certain you were the most beautiful and elegant bride any man could hope for... no matter what the circumstances." He kissed her again then looked back up to the balcony and nodded his head. "It is a fine place for a wedding, Caroline. And, I would like very much to plan a wedding of our own design. I think it should be a grand celebration. Umm, to borrow one of my father's expressions, 'let's have a shin-dig of a party'." Emmett grinned at her; there was a playful sparkle in his eyes. "What would you like if you could have your heart's desire?"

Caroline's face bloomed with a warm smile and her cheeks took on a pinkish tint even though the weather was frigid.

"Hmm, I would like lights in the trees!" Her hand went up, and she waved it about to encompass several of the enormous oaks which surrounded the house and grounds.

Emmett visualized her dreamy words and then pointed to the gladiolas around the edge of the patio as he spoke.

"Absolutely Honey, I like that idea... let's not forget those over there."

"Oh, and the crepe myrtles... we can't forget those either." Caroline looked up at him and Emmett smiled at her then kissed her lips several more times. She hugged him tight and released a joyful giggle, then continued to share her imagination with him because she knew the bond between their hearts had the power to give life to their dreams. "I would like the ceremony to be in the ballroom. And I would like to have all kinds of wonderful food available on a hot buffet in the main dining room. Our wedding cake will be French vanilla and covered with hundreds of white roses made of glistening sugar. And I would like the diamond-shaped, rock candy clusters, like Grandmother Star used to make, to accent the trim. We can put it on a huge round table in the parlor with a white linen table cloth and candles all around it... like a centerpiece for the celebration!"

Emmett added his thoughts to the design.

"I love French vanilla! We should make it large enough to feed the entire county!"

Caroline nodded her head as she spoke.

"We can have all the doorways wide open... huge baskets of flowers everywhere... white tables and chairs on the patio and throughout the gardens. Everyone could eat and drink at their leisure... stroll about and enjoy the ambiance of the house and gardens. Oh, we can have a string orchestra playing on the balcony! I would love for beautiful music to float through the evening like a gentle wind, so the guests could dance whenever and where ever they pleased."

Emmett felt completely invested in this verbal painting of their dream wedding and he added an exciting twist to the fantasy.

"And at the stroke of midnight, we could have a spectacular firework show burst into the sky down by the river."

The smile on Caroline's face became even brighter. She added another suggestion to make the fantasy perfect.

"Each of our guests should receive a bottle of champagne to take home with them as a keepsake of the fine 'shin-dig' Emmett and Caroline Cotton hosted one fine evening in October. That is... if we had any guests."

"My goodness, Sweetheart, we've created a fine celebration. We'll invite everyone we know... and even some we don't," stated Emmett profoundly. "They will come out of curiosity... so they can see the house. We can hang lanterns in the trees starting at the front gate all the way to the house to welcome them. Heck! We'll just run the invitation in the newspaper, so everyone will feel welcome to celebrate our wonderful life together. I want the entire town to know... love has brought Whisper Bluff back to life again!"

Caroline studied his face as Emmett dreamed out loud; his suggestions went straight to her heart. The design of such a glorious day would live inside her forever.

Emmett's arm squeezed her closer and his warm breath against her cheek stirred her back to the reality of this moment.

"Brrr, come on it's getting colder. I imagine you're near frozen by now." His height and the firm hold he had on Caroline's body propelled her across the patio and into the house with little effort from her numb legs and feet.

Emmett secured the outer doors behind him then turned to the small mud room. Caroline had already shed her snowy coat. Emmett unwound the scarf from his neck then discarded his coat and hung them on the hook next to Caroline's. He sat down on the bench to remove his messy boots but got distracted when Caroline pulled up the hem of her dress and peeled off the long underwear. She kicked out of the cowboy boots leaving her socks in place then tossed the thermal leggings into the wicker basket in the corner. She had not put on any panties beneath the manly garment and his eyes caressed the dark silky hair at the junction of her thighs. The sight of her feminine beauty caused his blood to turn hot. Their eyes connected and the expression on her face changed. Her deep purple eyes glistened with mischievousness as she dropped her skirt and started towards him. He watched her with idle hands as she bent over and picked up a pair of suede slippers from the floor, which he had not noticed until now.

"Umm, someone left these for you." Caroline sat them on the bench as she stopped in front of him. A happy laugh *bubbled within her and Emmett found it as sensuous as her body. She leaned over, and he met her lips, starved for a deep luscious kiss. Emmett inhaled her scent and reveled in her feminine sex appeal while his palms kneaded her bottom with a possessive squeeze.*

She whispered as she nibbled his lips.

"They were my father's, Emmett. He must like you very much... to share something so personal with you."

Emmett gazed into her eyes knowing that this incredible place had welcomed him because Caroline cared for him. He looked beyond the mystical aspect of the gift to recognize the honor which had been bestowed upon him. He picked up the slippers as he told her.

"My goodness, I'm flattered, Sweetheart. I wish there was some way I could express how honored he has made me feel in your home."

Caroline pressed her lips to his brow then mumbled softly against his skin.

"All you need to do is put them on... my love."

Emmett began removing his boots as Caroline pushed the kitchen door open and left it ajar for him. The aroma of fresh coffee teased Emmett's nose and made his mouth water. He placed his boots under the bench where he sat then stuck his feet into the slippers; they provided instant warmth to his frigid toes. He expressed his appreciation to Caroline's father in a low and respectful voice.

"This is a very nice thing you did for me, Mr. Breaux. Thank you very much. Oh, and Sir... I know the value in your home is so much more than real estate. I will cherish my time here... and I will protect her with my life."

"Shall I fix your coffee the same as you took it this morning?"

Emmett looked up to find Caroline leaning against the doorway of the kitchen with her arms crossed and wearing a brilliant smile. Her long lashes were clumped together from the dampness of the snow and her nose and cheeks were red. Her essence was alluring and the way she carried herself was regal and elegant. She was so stunning that he had to remind himself she had just told him that she loved him. It was a reality check for him suddenly, looking at her standing there in this magical place. He stood up and approached her; she didn't budge as their eyes stayed focused on one another.

"Just so you know, Caroline, I absolutely love this place... your family... and I love you too. I... don't have words to tell you how much."

She stretched up on her tiptoes and pressed a warm, soft kiss to his lips before she spoke.

"Words aren't always necessary, Emmett." She kissed him deeply. "Just so you know... I absolutely love you too." She giggled her joy as she caught his hand and pulled him inside then closed the door. "We have hot apple turnovers and fresh coffee," she announced with new energy.

"What... apple turnovers? How did you -" Emmett's words stopped in mid-sentence when she handed him the mug of coffee then slid the plate of apple pastries between them. There was a glimmer in her eyes that thrilled his senses. Everything about her thrilled him.

"Through the years, I've learned to not question some things," she commented, "Rather... I just acknowledge the miracle in it and say thank you. It seems you understand that concept too, Deputy. By the way, what is your given name, Emmett? A person's name is something that is very important to my family."

Emmett's expression changed to one of hesitation.

Caroline leaned over and gripped his fingers with hers as she coaxed him to tell her.

"Come on... it can't be that bad, Emmett."

"I'm named after my father. He was Gabriel Emmett Cotton, but daddy didn't want Gramps to call me junior, so he and mama switched the order. My given name is Emmett Gabriel. Mama calls me Gabe most of the time. She says I'm so much like my dad I stink. I never asked, but I assumed that meant I inherited his articulate personality traits." Emmett took a sip of his coffee as he grinned at her.

"Gabriel?" Caroline's eyes flashed with a draft of feeling.

"What's this look, Honey? What just came to your mind?" surveyed Emmett.

"You defend the weak and you possess a righteous heart, and I've always been drawn to you. You spoke to my Grandfather Vincent as though he were standing next to you. And my family's... unbelievable situation... is believable to you. Emmett Gabriel Cotton, you are special, and I believe it is anointed that you are to be in my life."

She held the pastry up to his mouth and Emmett took a bite.

"I can tell you that my father loved to bake. My mother used to tell him when she needed to send a thoughtful gesture or a thank you for something, and he would bake a pound cake... sometimes cookies and muffins. But pastries were for special occasions, and like I said earlier, Gabe... you are wearing my father's favorite slippers." She shoved the last few crumbs of the pie into her mouth and reached for another. "You can make of it what you want to."

"I wish I could have spent time with all of them." He bit into another pastry and discovered the fruit inside was accompanied by sweet cream cheese. "Mmm, Mr. Lee..." he addressed her father respectfully, "... that is so delicious. And thank you again, Sir, for the loan of the slippers."

Caroline's eyes twinkled at him as she smiled.

"I'll show you the rest of the house when we're finished. I have something I would like you to see. I need your advice concerning an unusual and important matter."

CHAPTER 25

Emmett held his coffee cup in one hand and Caroline's small hand in his other as they stopped in front of a row of French doors that lined the inner wall of the parlor. She released his hand and stepped up to the doors. Her eyes glistened with excitement as she glanced over her shoulder at him then bedazzled him with a flirtatious smile. The air of mystery which surrounded her, and this house was real, and so were the kindled sensations that sped down the back of Emmett's neck. This young woman had a powerful effect on him and he was suddenly anxious to see what was on the other side of the doors. She turned the doorknobs and, in one sweeping motion, pushed them open and bravely disappeared across the threshold into pitch blackness.

A few seconds passed as Emmett waited for her to come back to him, but the anxiousness he felt changed to apprehension. He couldn't stand the feeling any longer, so he sat his cup down and followed Caroline into the unknown. He could tell by the reverberating silence and the drop-in temperature that he was inside an abyss of space. He glanced over his shoulder and was comforted by the sight of the doorway that was still open behind him. In an instant, the entire room was brought to life because of the three spectacular and impressive chandeliers that hung overhead. They dangled from the ceiling which was even higher than the one in the foyer. Each magnificent fixture was adorned with hundreds of tear-shaped crystals and light bulbs that reflected the light and cast a glimmering effect all around the room. The dark walnut floor was the same as the rest of the house, but it was dulled by a coat of dust. The walls were covered with a burgundy and gold striped fabric and accompanied by colossal mirrors that were ten feet in height just like the one in the foyer across from the settee. The edge of these mirrors was decorated with gold filigree in a whimsical pattern of swirling leaves, and they added depth to the already massive room. A small stage was at one end and a hearth big enough for him to stand in was on the other end. There was a triple set of French doors on the outside wall that opened onto the garden and porch area that bordered the driveway. The small tables and chairs situated along the walls were for guests. It was an impressive room by anyone's standards.

Emmett felt Caroline's hand slide into his palm and he gripped it out of instinct then turned and looked down at her. He shook his head in amazement as he spoke.

"I don't know what to say, Honey. I think 'Lady Caroline' fits you better than, 'Gypsy'."

Caroline pushed his hand behind her back as she stepped up next to him and shook her head.

"No Emmett, I like it when you call me Gypsy; it's the way I feel." She stretched up to him and Emmett met her lips for several soft kisses. She pulled away from him and held up her other hand. "I want to dance in here with you before the real world interferes with this wonderful joy you've brought to me... and my life."

Emmett's smile disappeared as he realized that she believed their union, perhaps even his devotion, was not something she could count on to change her life.

"Caroline, come here." He wrapped his arms around her and her arms slid around his waist in response. Emmett *kissed her forehead, then her brow while his heart drummed against his ribs. He wanted her in his life with a heartache that was as strong as the one he held for his daughter. "He's going to let you go, Sweetheart. He's got to, because I don't want to spend another day without being by your side. I need you, Honey... and I need you to need me."*

"I do! Oh Emmett... don't you understand?! I've always needed you!"

They held each other in a tight embrace because this moment was what they had to give to each other. When she lifted her head, and looked in his eyes, Emmett caught her hand and his feet started to move. The sunrise of a smile that graced her face was proof she was happy and in love. Emmett turned her then stepped into her personal space, so the dance would change directions. He was mindful of the symbolism in the gesture in relation to life and their places in it. At that moment, Emmett took on a new mindset; he was going to have a place in Caroline Breaux's future. He smiled at her, and somewhere beyond where imagination and reality met, the music of a string orchestra joined them. He spun her around and around the enchanted room while the magic of Whisper Bluff kept the rest of the world at bay.

Caroline took him up the curved staircase which led them into another grand room. She told Emmett they called this area the gallery landing. It was easy to see why because it housed two grand pianos - one which was obviously a collector's piece and the other was a modern Steinway. There were multiple groupings of furniture that were situated for visiting and listening to the piano. The walls were adorned with paintings of the Breaux family, landscapes of the house and river, both past and present.

The double French doors at each end of the room opened on to the front and back balconies. She told him the view of the river was spectacular from the back balcony. They didn't go out there because it was too dark to see anything, and their feet were finally thawed and comfortable.

Emmett asked Caroline if she played the piano. She nodded her head then commented that Zane's wife, Camille, was the true artist. She told him her father had bought the Steinway for her mother, Carol, as a wedding present.

"My mother taught me how to play. Grandpa Preston liked to 'jitter' on them. He was a clown. He definitely missed his calling for the comedic stage."

"Jitter?" exclaimed Emmett.

"That's what he called it. Grandma O used to tell him he played like a 'saloon dandy'. They were so funny together."

Emmett fished for details to appease his curiosity.

"Grandma O was short for?"

"Ophelia," specified Caroline as she laughed. "I can't tell you how many puns grandpa used to hand her at bedtime. 'Come on O, I need to feel ya.' She was good-natured about it, but now that I'm an adult I understand why they used to disappear during the day. I think she had him under her spell and he used humor in stating the obvious."

"Caroline, would you play something for me?" requested Emmett.

"Of course, what would you like to hear?"

"I would like to hear something beautiful... like you. Play me your favorite piece."

Emmett listened to Caroline play, 'Rustles of Spring', by a Norwegian composer, while he strolled along the walls of walnut and gold framed paintings and acquainted himself with each of her grandparents. He stopped at Vincent's portrait because of the respect he felt for the stately gentleman. He realized he had truly met this man, and he wished he could sit down and share a cup of tea with him as a grandson-in-law. His mind went back to the thing he and Caroline tried to put aside while they were together. He understood what Vincent was trying to tell him. Emmett knew he was going to have to keep his and Caroline's relationship strictly between them until she and Dane were *legally divorced. He spoke to the painting with the same level of respect as he had used in the kitchen that morning. He asked Vincent if he and the other grandfathers, along with her dad, could please protect her from Dane should he become a threat.*

He moved around the room and was conscientious of the composition in which the paintings were displayed. A descriptive painting of the Breaux heir hung on the left and one of his life-mate hung on the right, and in the center, a larger painting of them as a couple. Emmett noticed that a painting of their child hung between his mother and the painting of him as an adult heir. Emmett studied the faces of the women who stood with these men, so he would know something specific about each one of them. He admired their taste, for each woman was unique and extraordinary in her own individual way, and yet, each one loved a pioneer who was a descendant and next generation of the Breaux family.

Star was an Indian maiden, an entrepreneur and the mother of Zane Breaux. Camille was a concert pianist, a teacher and the mother of Preston Breaux. Ophelia was a writer of western novels, a horticulturist and the mother of Lee Renee Breaux. Carol Ann was a doctor and the mother of Caroline Janee Breaux. And Caroline was a business major and a brilliant artist; it was her name signed at the bottom of all the paintings. The painting of Colonel Dane Reid was dignified; the date proved it was done right after they married. Emmett stared at the portrait Caroline had done of herself; the date at the bottom revealed that it had been completed this past September. It captured the sadness in her heart, and the dark faceless shadow which stood behind her was how she felt about her absent and despicable husband.

"You're not going to hurt her anymore, Dane," mumbled Emmett. He stood there a moment as he thought about this man which he despised. His attention shifted to the image of the woman he loved. Emmett reached out and traced the graceful neckline of the painting with the tip of his fingers. He shuttered as a current of energy attacked the back of his neck then sped down his arm to his hand.

Suddenly, he knew that he was not alone. Emmett spoke out loud in hope that one of Caroline's grandfathers was listening. "Mr. Breaux, Sir... you were right; he'll have to kill me before I let him hurt her again. And if Colonel Reid should manage to do so... I pray the Almighty will bless her in it, and he'll be held accountable to the full extent of the law."

The room seemed to echo with the last note Caroline had played. Emmett turned and found her studying him. She stood and walked around the piano towards him. He thought her expression was somewhat tense; still, her eyes smiled at him. She told him that she had a collection of things stored in a secret place in the room that was hers as a girl. He asked her to show him anything and everything concerning her life and that of her family's, because it was important that he learn all he could about the people he cared about and loved. She held out her hand to him and Emmett took a firm hold on it.

She led him through the drapes that hung on the other side of the room into a wide hallway. Emmett pulled her beneath his arm; they ventured into this part of the house side-by-side. She pointed to several doorways specifying which ones belonged to her family. He absorbed her memories while he took in his surroundings. They were simple rooms, but elegantly enhanced by the craftsmanship. The walnut floors had been installed in a staggered pattern to frame the placement of the bed. The plaster ebbed across the walls in soft waves of petrified-movement; the beautiful mahogany furnishings and silk drapes completed a classic look.

She turned to him when they stopped at the last door on the left.

"This was my room when I was growing up," she told him in a quiet voice, "My parents shared the one across the hallway until Grandma O passed away then Grandpa Preston insisted, they move into the master suite downstairs.

Emmett followed her into an intriguing and unique room which was designed to stimulate the imagination of a young girl. He studied his surroundings; the aura was like he had stepped into a time capsule with her and the feeling of yesteryear clung to everything. The two outside walls were windows that spanned the height of ceiling to floor and gave the room the feel of being a tree house. She told him the view of the grounds and the river was spectacular and enhanced by the vast arms of the oak which shaded the east end of the house. They approached the windows even though it was dark outside, she pointed to the limb where several of the birds and squirrels used to visit her. Emmett noticed the outer corner was structurally sound because the house was built out of timbers. The corner was also a creative statement, built by an excellent carpenter who gave it a dual purpose as a corner display case. It was fact most young girls collected dolls, but in keeping with the unique woman that stood next to him, the shelves held a collection of angels. There were all kinds, and they were made from all sorts of things.

He turned when Caroline left his side. She climbed onto the large ornate bed on her knees and faced the headboard. The magnificent piece was carved from walnut and designed so that a dozen fat little cherubs held up the four shelves which were full of books and meaningful whatnots. Her possessions surrounded the large two-paneled mirror that was the focal point of the headboard. The illusion of secrecy that suddenly surrounded her drew him closer. Emmett witnessed her hands go to the plump cherubs at the top and bottom centers of the mirror and she pressed in on them at the same time. There was a quiet squeak, then the seam in the glass separated, and Caroline opened them like a cabinet. The compartment was a secret place because no one would know they functioned in this manner simply by looking at them.

Emmett's curiosity was aroused by what she revealed. He wasn't exactly sure what he was looking at, so he moved to the edge of the bed to get a better understanding of the collage of information stored in this mirrored safe. There were school pictures of him, and memorabilia of his football games and school activities. There was an old program from the Who's Who pageant his junior year and his football picture sporting the #66 on his jersey. There was a visual tribute to his high school graduation. And, a program from the law enforcement academy with his graduating class listed; his name was circled and a small picture of him was pinned next to it. She had accumulated clippings of other events in the community that he was a part of and candid photographs of him on his motorcycle. There was the newspaper picture of him and his father winning the big bass contest when he was 14; the photograph was next to the public service announcement when he hired on with the Sheriff's Department. There was even a napkin from his parents' 25th wedding anniversary party, the announcement of Julianna's birth, and the picture and story of his accommodation for bravery when he rescued a woman from her car that had gone into the river. The collage of information spanned the last 18 years of his life. It was true, she had dreamed on him all these years.

"I swear... I don't know what to say Caroline," he whispered, "I feel like such a fool."

"Oh no! You feel as though I've trespassed! Oh, Emmett! I'm sorry... that wasn't my intent!" She apologized to him in a soft, fearful voice.

He looked at her in surprise and somehow his hand found hers and pulled it up to his lips.

"No Gypsy, not at all! It's just... I wish you had asked me for that ride on my motorcycle. I could kick myself for not waiting to see who was putting the gum in my locker." He kissed her fingers again then looked back at the history of his life. He noticed she had given special attention to some newspaper clippings by mounting them on a large lacey card which looked like a valentine. He joined her on the bed so that he could get a closer look and she made room for him next to her. He read the public record's listing when Vicki had filed for divorce, which was next to another clipping that announced her and Dane's marriage. She had attached them side-by-side and taped a cut-out picture of a sobbing angel between them. It was symbolic because she had said 'I do' two days before Vicki filed for divorce. This discovery moved him deeply. It merged with the serious part of him that was the foundation in which everything he was had been built. Emmett swallowed the lump in his throat.

"Emmett," her soft voice drew his attention. When he looked at her, Caroline had unbuttoned her dress and the shirt beneath it. She pushed the garment over her shoulders then caressed the front of his trousers with a possessive hand as she spoke to him.

"Will you make love to me here... where I dreamed, so many dreams of you... and of us?"

Emmett felt his body push against his clothing longing for her warm and inspired touch. The sight of her elegant breasts and the way she offered herself to him made his heart slam against his ribs. He turned to her and began pulling his sweater and shirt over his head. Her kiss greeted his private body before he could get his arms out of the sleeves. He pushed his clothing out of the way then collapsed to the bedding, and her passionate assault followed. Emmett's fingers sank into her silky hair as sensations of pleasure rushed his entire body.

"My sweet passionate gypsy girl..." he breathed as he reached for her. "Come here to me, Honey." She rose and mounted him just as he had taught her the night before; their nerves trembled with excitement as his long, virile body filled her belly. Emmett wrapped his arm around her waist as he cupped her full breast in his free hand and drew the budding tip into his kiss. He suckled as her hips began to push against him; their union was slow and full of purpose. The singe of desire in his bloodstream made him feverish. He looked up at her because he needed to connect with the windows of her soul.

Emmett sat on the side of the bed as his passion numbed limbs regained feeling. Caroline turned his clothing right side out then pushed them over his head. He gazed at her through eyes which had gained a new understanding while his heartbeat pushed a consuming devotion through his veins. She kissed his lips over and over as her fingers combed through his hair to bring order back to it. She was glowing with happiness and he knew his face mirrored hers. She was incredible in every way, and every time she touched him and loved him, his possessiveness concerning her was rooted deeper in his heart.

He shoved his arms into the sleeves of his sweater then stood and attended to the rest of his clothing. He looked up when he heard her quiet footsteps pad across the floor and disappear into the closet. He took a step to follow when she spoke his name. She looked around the door facing at him then motioned for him to follow. He did so and walked into the biggest closet he had ever seen. The room was in keeping with the rest of the house, and like all the other heirlooms that documented and filled her life, her childhood clothing still hung in one section while her adult things were in another. Ceiling to floor shelving held an assortment of shoes, handbags and hats. An antique, freestanding jewelry case had been placed there for convenience and a huge floor length mirror was mounted on the wall in the middle of the assortment of apparel.

Emmett watched her as she placed her foot on a small board in the right corner of the closet beneath the hanging rod of small dresses. She leaned forward, and he heard a muffled popping sound that came from somewhere beyond where they stood. Caroline faced him and smiled. Emmett gripped her hips and instinctively pulled her close to his body. She brushed a kiss over his lips as she reached past him and turned the brass candle fixture on the wall a half turn, then back again. She kissed him several more times as her hands slid into his; their palms clutched each other's tight. She turned towards the mirror and took a step, and Emmett followed her. The sight of them together in front of the floor length mirror gave him a vision of the future he wanted so much. He tugged on her hands and she stopped and looked back at him. He kissed her again because they were under the spell of love that destiny had cast upon them. He turned her so that their reflection was as one, then he told her what he was thinking.

"Look at us, Caroline. Remember this moment and keep it in your heart. When you can, try to paint us as though we were a legitimate couple like your parents... and your grandparents. Do it because I love you. It's true, Caroline. You are so deep in my heart, I will never be the same man I was two days ago. Paint it because we finally found each other and became the lovers we were meant to be. Our paths did not cross by accident. I will love you and cherish you with everything that I am... for the rest of my days."

Emmett stood behind her and assumed the same position in which Vincent and Star had been captured in the portrait that hung on the wall in the gallery landing. His reflection smiled at her as his possessive arm slid beneath hers. His hand tightened lovingly beneath her breast and he pressed her against his body while his other hand came to rest against the flat plane of her belly.

"I know you won't be able to hang our portrait... as things are now, but you can hide it with the rest of our hopes and memories. I promise you, Gypsy, one day... it will hang with all the others... where it belongs." They paused at the opportunity to design a memory which would instill hope and courage for the new life they wanted to build together. Caroline's hands slid over the back of his and they stood there together gazing at the reflective image of the couple who looked so perfect together. A few moments passed then Emmett nuzzled her brow and pressed a kiss to her temple.

"Thank you for being so in tune to me... and my family, Emmett. I will always remember this moment... being with you in this room, and us standing just this way together," she whispered. "I will create a portrait of the lovers who are in my mind's eye... and live in my heart. And I promise I will spend the other half of my life still loving you."

Finally, she stepped out of his arms and pushed on the right edge of the mirror's frame. It swiveled open and became a magical gateway. He held her hand in a tight grip and followed her up the narrow staircase. Caroline stopped at another door and turned the knob, it opened in silence.

Emmett had no sooner stepped into the darkness than a light popped on to reveal a vault of gold and silver keepsakes. There were candlesticks, serving dishes, tea sets and a silver punch bowl that would take three people to carry. There, among the finery, was an old door which was a make shift desk. Chimneys of books, which looked ancient, were stacked in the floor surrounding it, and a pile of maps and survey documents pertaining to the Breaux estate were spread across the surface. Emmett's attention went to the shelves of expensive cigars that were still sealed and then was drawn to a narrow table which held an assortment of artistically carved wooden boxes. He reached over and opened one and was stunned by the matching trio of sparkling diamond jewelry housed within the velvet belly. He opened several other chests to find more exquisite feminine treasures crafted in silver and gold and holding rubies, emeralds and pearls. There were pistols that dated back into history even further than Vincent Breaux, and a tall wooden cabinet with glass doors that displayed an assortment of rifles. Emmett was sure that all of them would be considered rare and valuable, not to mention irreplaceable.

Caroline spoke his name, and he turned to her. She was standing in front of a massive armoire which was made of handsome tiger oak. The huge cabinet stood with its back next to a massive cliff of masonry brick. And, based on the way the bricks met the roofline, the wall provided support for several of the many fireplaces in the house.

Emmett joined Caroline, because her small, outstretched hand beckoned to him. He stopped next to her and his large palm squeezed her slim fingers. Her attention was fixed on the cabinet, so he took a closer look as well. The wardrobe's design was masculine, and the handles were gold to match the filigreed initials VLB which adorned each door. The B was centered, and the other letters wrapped around it to make an artistic statement of wealth and power. Caroline let go of his hand then took hold of the handles and tugged the doors open to reveal the details of its design. There was hanging space on each side and a row of meager drawers, one on top of the other in the center; the two shelves across the bottom held an assortment of footwear. The clothing inside was expensive and smelled of cedar. The wardrobe was beautiful; however, he frowned when she pushed on the small drawer in the center then stepped to the right side of the closet and slowly pulled the piece towards her. The entire cabinet swung open at her command. She reached for Emmett's hand again, so he could inspect what was in front of him.

Emmett blinked several times to make sure he was really seeing what his eyes conveyed to his brain. The wooden case was a dummy to hide the stash of slim gold bricks amassed in the wall behind it. Caroline handed him one of them and Emmett found Vincent's initials stamped into it. He listened carefully as she spoke because he knew this was the other reason why her family was so secretive.

"I told you about Truman Silver being a blacksmith and that he moved here to help grandfather keep up with the needs of the plantation. Truman maintained the justice needed to civilize Whisper Bluff, but he also made the mints for these bricks. The other cabinet..." she pointed to another wall that stretched beyond the timber trusses behind them, "... is the same as this one, and the smaller two contain silver."

Emmett stared at the other cabinets against the far wall as he held the gold brick and concentrated on what she needed to tell him.

"My grandfather didn't think much of paper money. When a crop was sold... payments for ferry travel and freight deliveries collected, he would accumulate the coin. Of course, Grandfather took paper when they began to circulate it, but he traded the paper for bullion at the larger banks. He knew the war was coming and the paper would be worthless. When the war was done, he continued to do so. He was a very wealthy man when he arrived in this country, Emmett. His business ventures were never at risk to his sustaining himself, or the farm... making money and doing a day's work was just who he was. He was very good at it... especially in the land of opportunity. He made some investments, but his son, Zane, invested in the railroad, Ford Motor Company, and some other companies. I was a business major; I like numbers, Emmett. But the success of these companies and the profit from our investments was overwhelming. I suggested to my father and Grandpa Preston that we should consider the idea of allowing someone else to manage our portfolio. I have always been surrounded by smart men, but Grandpa Preston was getting on in years and my father held a greater fascination for pastries and cakes than he did finance. Grandfather Zane agreed it was a wise and savvy idea. They charged me with finding a dependable man to help us. Our family established a business relationship with Litton Hollingsworth over 40 years ago and he has always been trustworthy. I consulted with him concerning our financial needs and he recommended Wescott Financial. We formed Leflore-Breaux Holding Company, the CEO of Wescott Financial, Emil Wescott, Jr., takes care of the account personally as stipulated in the agreement between him and his father, and our family. He places an allowance in a personal account for me at Worthy and Massena on a quarterly basis; I draw on it to sustain myself and this house. I have complete autonomy over all our holdings since Grandpa Preston died, but I will not be making any changes."

Caroline took a step closer to him and her expression became more serious and so did the tone of voice.

"I am much more astute in business than I am when it comes to people, Emmett. I'm sure living a guarded and protected life hindered my ability to read people; however, I'm a fast learner. I've already shared with you the details of my relationship with Dane. I... I was a girl when I met him. I wasn't aware until this past August, the measure of his lack of respect for me, and what a rogue he was at heart. What trust and regard I held for him is gone, and I refuse to leave my family's worth for Dane to squander on foolishness and whores. He thinks my paycheck from the Circuit Clerk job and the allowance he sends me is how I maintain. He doesn't know anything about my real financial state. I deposit his wages in the joint account he opened when we married, but I have never touched a penny of it and I never will. I'm fully aware of the mistake I made in my choice of husbands in relation to personal happiness and companionship. I used to get scared when I think of what a fool I was." She shook her head and her left brow shifted a fraction towards her hairline. "At this point in time... it just makes me mad." Caroline was quiet a moment as she looked at the gold brick in his hand.

"I'm not a girl anymore, Emmett. I'm a woman who has swallowed her fear and her pride. Mr. Wescott has advised me in protecting the family's investments... including the house. I want out of this ridiculous marriage, and I know I must make sure my family's property is safe. Because our holding company is protected by incorporation, Mr. Wescott suggested that I separate the house and the surrounding grounds, from the timberland that is part of the company. I had Mr. Hollingsworth draw up the divorce papers, and I asked that he draft new deeds which annexed the timber lands from the house and the 30 acres on which it sits. It took a while because I had to have the property surveyed for new land descriptions. Hollingsworth dropped the documents by my office the day before Christmas Eve. I read through the divorce papers on my lunch break. I found them to be correct and in order with my request, so I signed them. I liked the feeling of freedom that came with it, so I rebelliously signed the deeds as well." She shrugged her shoulders as she continued to speak. "I was foolish... but doing so made me feel like I was in control of my life. I didn't get around to reading them until later that evening. I was tired, so Grandfather Zane helped me while I warmed some soup. The description and the attached map were correct and easy to understand on the land deed, so it wasn't a big deal that I had already signed it. Like I said, Litton Hollingsworth has handled the family's business for four decades and Grandfather Zane has always trusted him. Never the less when we read through the deed for the house, we discovered they had added Dane as 'a joint tenant in common with full rights of survivorship'. It is a standard practice for most married couples, but as you know we are not most couples. I should have noticed the other line with his name beneath mine, but I didn't. I was at one job... tending to another while my focus was on neither. Grandfather Zane was angry, not so much at me, but rather over the fact we were drafting new deeds to protect our holdings from Dane in the first place. The fact of the matter is that Hollingsworth and I gave Grandfather cause to doubt. He didn't really say it, but I could see it in his face. I'm so glad he was helping me, if not, the mistake could have gone unnoticed. I was a fool and trusted Dane with my body and my heart. But, it's unforgivable to allow him to gain entrance to all that my family has built, because I was feeling sorry for myself and didn't follow through with my responsibilities. There was a lesson to be learned from it. Trust being a factor, or not... I won't ever sign another document unless I read it from beginning to the end. Anyway, I filed the land deed, but Hollingsworth is in the process of drafting another house deed to correct the mistake. His son, Baxter, is coming in as a partner and they are making some legal changes in the firm's operational format. He said it would take a couple of weeks to complete my request and he would make the correction himself. I haven't heard from him yet."

Emmett witnessed her expression change again. She placed her hands on his chest then rose to her tiptoes and brushed a kiss over his lips. His arm circled her waist, and he kissed her back. Her mouth formed a soft smile, and she studied his face as she spoke.

"Things have changed for me too, Emmett. I love you and I want to make some changes in my life... for us. I need to know that you and I are on the same page... so to speak. I want you to know that all the papers that are important to me are in a safe deposit box at Worthy and Massena. I'll give you a key for safekeeping and add you as a grantor to access; you will need to know that my password is 'Star Leflore'. I need to designate a beneficiary for this house in my will, or it will go to him should something happen to me. I'd like for it to be you, Emmett, if you would allow it. This..." she waved her hand at the stash of gold bricks, "I guess you could say, was Grandfather's idea of insurance. But none of my people went through a divorce so I have no idea what to expect. Do I need to get it out of here? If so, I'm not sure how to go about doing it in a hasty manner without bringing in someone to help me. The last thing I need is Dane to find out." Caroline shook her head as she tossed her hair over her shoulder. "What do you think I should do, Emmett?"

Emmett was floored with this development and by the fact she was so vehement in offering her complete trust to him. He sensed, she had borne this burden alone for so long that she was grabbing the opportunity to make him a legal part of her life whether marriage was ever a part of it or not.

"Please Emmett, it's important to me that you know about this place… just in case. I wouldn't ask if I didn't trust you… if I didn't believe you truly love me and had my best interest at heart."

Emmett placed the gold brick back where it belonged. He kissed her brow several times before his lips moved to hers. Caroline sank into a deep kiss with him as the breath of love swirled around them. Emmett held her close and rested his cheek on her head as she clung to him.

"I will help you, Caroline. I'll do whatever you need me to do, Honey. I adore you. Still, I need your family to know that you've trusted me with this information and responsibility."

Caroline looked up at him suddenly and smiled.

"They already know, Emmett. Grandpa Preston walked with you as you studied the gallery a little while ago, and Daddy sat next to me while I played the piano. He told me to bring you here."

Emmett remembered the tingles he felt on the back of his neck. This place was unbelievable, yet he believed in what was happening to him with every cell of his body. He could not hear Caroline's family of angels, but he felt them… just as sure as he felt the Almighty in his spirit.

Caroline smacked his lips as she giggled with delight.

"There's a kiss to seal the deal, Sheriff."

"Umm, sorry ma'am… but I'm not the sheriff," he pointed out playfully.

"You are when it comes to this matter," she proclaimed.

Their eyes clung to one another a moment then Emmett nodded his head. He knew what she meant; she was relieved that someone other than herself knew this place existed. She trusted him with this treasure just like she did the secrets of her family, her heart and the favors of her body.

"So, how long has it been here? What, at least 50 years I would think?"

"Umm, closer to 70 years," she specified.

Emmett couldn't even begin to speculate about the worth in what she was showing him.

"How many bars are there... do you know?"

"Each vault is stacked four bricks thick. Truman designed it into the support system of the house when they built it. The wall and the chimneys are tied together and have iron support braces within the masonry work and the timber joints. Let's see... there are 200 bricks that meet the eye, stacked four thick... 800 bricks at five pounds each. That would be 4000 pounds at 16 ounces... the current market is at $34 an ounce." Caroline spoke softly as she siphoned the figure in her head. "We're looking at... two and .176 in gold... which would be... umm, $4,352,000. for both cabinets. I have no idea what the market is on silver this week. There are twice as many bricks in silver; however, it doesn't weigh as much as gold and its value is usually about 25% that of gold. I would estimate the silver to be worth a million... give or take a hundred thousand."

Emmett released a deep breath as he shook his head in amazement. He studied on the matter for a moment and then was honest with his opinion.

"The circumstances being what they are at present, it would be hard to start a covert project without an idea of the Colonel's schedule. It's been safe here all this time, and the truth is... this place has a security system that a bank can't offer you. I think I would leave it be for now. You and I have other pressing legalities to get in order now." He smiled as he solicited another intimate kiss from her. "I have to admit... I am glad you're a woman of means so that you are not at the mercy of anyone else to take care of you."

Caroline's fingernails caressed his spine as she pointed out the facts.

"Yes. But there are some things that money can't buy, Gabe." Her hands got very personal as she shared her lips.

Emmett reminded her of something she had suggested earlier in the day.

"We never did get that hot and soapy bath."

Caroline pressed her body against him in that special way that made him solid as a slab of oak. He craved her and the way she clung to him. He thought of the painting he had admired only a short while ago. It was a colorful version of the sturdy stone house down by the river with a vine of wisteria stretching out over the roof and clinging to it for strength. That was the way she made him feel... strong, willing and devoted.

"I can do better than that, Emmett," she cooed softly.

The image of the wisteria suddenly gained a new perspective in Emmett's mind. He liked having her on top of him too.

"What ya got in mind, Gypsy?" mumbled Emmett.

CHAPTER 26

The heated pool was nestled within the potted tropical garden of the solarium. It was the one extravagance in her life and the expense of maintaining such a large house that she could not make herself give up.

Emmett sat on the bottom step and enjoyed the warm water as it swished against his naked body. His eyes and his thoughts drifted on a sea of possibilities while he watched her float. The soft glowing rays from the winter moon above them caressed her pale skin and gave her gorgeous body a mystical aura as the water suspended her beauty against the black ceramic tiles. The feminine mounds of her breasts peeked out of the water as the brisk night air tightened their dark tips. Her small waist, flat belly and the dark silk between her legs were mesmerizing. These visions were enhanced by the night shadows that had engulfed his reality; they would forever be branded into his mind as the erotic fantasy that it was.

She dipped under the water and he watched her while under a spell of fascination. She moved with ease, like a creature that considered the water to be home. She touched his ankles first then he watched in anticipation while the bubbles escaped from her nose as she surfaced between his knees. Her eyes were open, and an all-knowing smile was on her face. She caressed his masculine body with her cheek a few seconds before she surfaced for air. His body came to life at the intimate contact. She held on to his legs and asked if she could have her way with him. He smiled and told her she could do whatever she wanted to him. She coaxed him from the steps into the water and he spread his arms across the side of the pool for stability as she instructed. He floated while her lips teased his compliant body. It was an erotic feeling, being submerged and having her excite him in such a way. He was amazed at her ability to thrive beneath the surface.

His fingers played in her long, floating hair, but it became impossible to maintain his focus as his manly body began to throb. He reached for her and she surfaced then wrapped her body around his. He couldn't take his eyes off her and noticed that her long lashes were clumped together with drops of water. He let go of the side of the pool and kicked his feet; they floated back to the pool steps. He stretched out, and she didn't waste a moment situating her body across his lap. She was anxious to dominate his yearning, knowing she would be enslaved by it before she was done. She was insatiable in the way she gave herself to him and at the same time, vulnerable. Emmett understood that it was honesty she offered to him - an intimate look at her many faces. She was the strong, self-confident woman she strived to be, but she was also the vulnerable girl who was oppressed by a domineering man who was more a jailer than a husband. She was a prisoner of their marriage and the lies in which he kept her were the bars. Emmett's commitment to her was profound. He believed her when she said she cherished him. And, the fact she trusted him in the face of so many uncertainties, was exalting to his essence as a man, a peace officer, and her lover.

"Vous vous sentez si bon pour moi, Emmett. Je t'adore, mon amour."

Her delicate sigh was absorbed by his senses and he asked her what she said in a passionate breath of his own.

Her hips continued to move against him with great purpose as she pressed her lips against his ear.

"You feel so good to me, Emmett. I adore you my love." Her hot breath, mixed with the beautiful expression of love, sent fiery tingles of feeling over his skin, and then she kissed him. Her lips and her tongue were luscious and sweet like candy. The sensuous friction she kindled in his body was something his senses and his heart praised. She severed the kiss and drew in a deep breath as she prepared to take them to another depth of feeling.

Emmett's lips tasted her delicious body again. She was a beautiful and passionate woman who had discovered and understood the joy of sex with a partner who cared for her more than himself. He was honored to be the one trusted to guide her into the discovery, but at the same time, he could not ignore the growing possessiveness and sense of responsibility that loving her instilled in him. He wanted them to discover the rest of life together as a legal couple.

The soft swishing movement of the water was seductive by itself; still, his kiss indulged on the tips of her breasts with a greedy appetite. He was addicted to the feel of them in his mouth for they were extremely cooperative with his tongue. Her hands tightened on his shoulders as the muscles inside her body harmonized with the melody in her hips. He brushed his lips over her throat beneath her chin, so she would know he was kindred to her in every way.

She joined him in a deep searing kiss while her inner body shuddered, and the fist of desire gripped him tight. Emmett drew in a deep breath knowing she was going to take him to euphoria once more. He was suspended in the rapture of pleasure so much he couldn't think to breathe until his brain tingled. She began to celebrate fulfillment by sending him into her body with consuming, deep thrust; the entire time, she gazed at him. His attention stayed with her because he had promised her that he would never close his eyes while they made love. When the moment of deliverance came for them, he watched as tears pooled in the velvety blue prisms of her eyes. She smiled softly while her breasts danced wildly in front of him and her inner body demanded all he could give in an urgent state of carnal bliss.

They sat wrapped around each other waiting for calm to come over their bodies, but the only thing that found them was a chill. She shuttered then mentioned the huge, soft bed down the hall. Emmett mustered the strength and carefully stepped from the pool holding her steadfast while her inner body held him. She wrapped her legs around him to insure they stayed that way.

Caroline snagged the towel from the back of the lounger as they passed it. She scrubbed Emmett's short hair with it then dried their upper bodies as best she could. She twisted the towel around her long hair; all the while, her lover kissed the berries of flesh in front of his face. The way she craved him and the way he encouraged her to do so, made her feel detrimental to his happiness.

Emmett walked through the shadowed hallway; the water dripped off their legs as he carried her into the master bedroom. He stopped long enough to give the door a gentle shove with his foot. She nuzzled his cheek, urging his mouth to leave her breast and come to her lips. The covers on the impressive bed were as they had left them from earlier that day. Her tongue danced with his as he climbed on to the mattress. He pushed her body deep into the bedding with his weight. Her kiss deepened as her hands glided over his backside. They clung to one another seeking the warmth their bodies created while revering each glorious opportunity to let go of who they were and dare to become something wonderful together.

Emmett awoke to the sound of the wind outside. He looked down at her in the shadows. She was pressed close against his chest and her knee was between his thighs. He had to touch her. His hand caressed her arm then the small of her back and followed her smooth spine. She released a soft sigh then lifted her head. She smiled lazily and asked him if he was all right. His hand caressed her smooth body a few moments as she gazed into his eyes.

"I love you, Emmett," she breathed against his lips.

The bed was the epitome of comfort, and her body was heaven on earth. He rolled over and pushed her into the mattress beneath them. Her hands claimed his manly body and within seconds, she had him long, thick and pulsing with the desire to feel her again. She opened-up to him because it was second nature to her now, and he slowly pushed into her until she was full of him. Her legs folded around him and the inside of her body engaged him in that special way that was unique to her need of him. His body answered her and trembled all over knowing he would never tire of this magnificent addiction they shared for each other.

Her words were like a poem floating on the edge of midnight. She told him they were in the private chambers of the master's bedroom and she had taken a new master. She spoke from her heart about the way her body needed and coveted him. She praised the way he touched her as though she were valuable to him. She told him that every time they came together, he took a part of her spirit and left her with a soulful memory that no length of time could dull or erase. She vowed she would always love him and that their time together would echo through her and this house forever.

The large floor clock in the parlor chimed; its alto notes echoed throughout the mansion like a soft love song. Passion gripped her belly and her legs opened wide for him. His backside started to tingle, and his bloodstream churned because of the twister of desire that was wreaking havoc in his loins. He pumped himself into her in fervent, covetous lunges and told her of his heart's desire to spend his life with her. The clock echoed around them and through them as she whispered that it was midnight and magic had found them. Her body began to quake, and their eyes met. She asked him to promise he would keep her in his heart forever. A vow of love and devotion crossed Emmett's lips as he swore his heart would belong to her for all of time. The lightning of desire struck them, and his name was torn from her lungs and echoed in the large room as her hands clutched at his backside beneath the covers. Her thighs lay flat against the mattress and his palms cradled her bottom while he gratified the intimate depth of her body with a pulsating delight. When her hips began to gyrate beneath him, a current of living passion electrified them. The clock struck midnight's final note as they rode the wave of sexual fulfillment together. It felt as though they had become one person... like they had absorbed one another. The sensuous fever they forged beneath the covers had bound their hearts as much as it did their bodies.

The way she clung to him conveyed fear. Emmett knew there was something different about their union this time. He pressed her hand to his chest over his heart as he kissed her lips over and over. She pleaded with him to keep her in his heart and he assured her that he could do nothing else. Certainty ruled his spirit in this matter and she sensed it; silence fell on them as assurance took over. He loved watching the way her eyes changed into midnight reflections of blue and violet while they celebrated this spiritual connection with each other. He did not know how many times he had celebrated their love inside of her... the seductress... the desolate and lonely woman... the insubordinate wife... and the shy girl. They were all the same person, reflections of the woman in whom he had fallen deeply in love. He knew when he left here that he would be leaving his heart with her; however, he did not know that he was leaving his son behind to grow inside her body as well.

At morning's light, they soaked in a steamy, sudsy bath. She put on a romantic gown and robe while Emmett dressed in a pair of her father's silk pajamas. They made a huge breakfast of scrambled eggs, waffles, syrup and smoked ham. During the day, they didn't dress, but lounged in comfort. She played the piano while Emmett surveyed the collection of books which lay on the sofa tables. He discovered a treasure of family albums which were full of photographs and memorabilia. Emmett turned the pages stopping every few minutes to ask her a question.

Caroline's attention shifted from the sheet music in front of her to the man who possessed her heart. She closed the piano and joined Emmett on the sofa, so they could explore the history of her family together. A couple of hours passed before they were distracted by the scent of warm vanilla wafting through the house. They stored the albums back to their rightful place then went downstairs to investigate.

Emmett sliced the hot delicacy while Caroline poured them a glass of cold milk. He wore a youthful grin as he tossed a morsel of the buttermilk pound cake into the air and caught it in his mouth. He rolled his eyes and made a ridiculous moaning sound as he chewed. He was becoming accustomed to the surprises in this house and believing in the unbelievable was easy for him now. Thanks to the albums of documented history, her father's face was clear in Emmett's mind, so he spoke to Lee Renee Breaux as though he were standing next to him. He tossed another bite into the air and chuckled as he asked Caroline's father if he had made his daughter a cake too. Caroline crossed her eyes and made a face at the space next to her, then released a silly laugh as she conveyed her father's appreciation of Emmett's appetite. Emmett did not take for granted Caroline's willingness to communicate with her father in his presence.

They enjoyed the cake immensely then placed it on the glass pedestal and covered it with the matching dome. Emmett's arm gently hooked Caroline around the waist and twirled her around the kitchen floor. They danced their way into the hallway then further into the foyer; the tall windows welcomed them with the afternoon sun into the vastness of the house. Emmett noticed the old phonograph in the parlor and became intrigued by it. He gave it a quick inspection then with a little ingenuity and muscle, he worked a little magic of his own and brought the machine back to life. Emmett moved the music machine just inside the doorway of the ballroom and they danced to every antique record available in the Breaux collection. They spent the rest of the afternoon talking and exploring the other rooms of the house in fulfillment of the dreams she imagined as a girl. They kissed and absorbed each other as playful lovers. He enjoyed every second with her; however, they gravitated back to the master suite when the desire to share their bodies elevated into need.

They prepared a supper of chunky fried potatoes, fresh spinach salad and broiled beef steaks. After they ate and cleaned up the kitchen, Emmett expressed the desire to take another moonlight swim with her. She taught him how to do a half twist off the diving board. Caroline laughed and gave him two thumbs up for his effort even though he squeezed his nose between his thumb and fingers as he made the dive.

The house was still, and the silence gave Emmett comfort equal to that of an old friend. She lay stretched out on top of him in a sated bliss with her hands tucked beneath his flanks. Emmett listened to the peacefulness in her breath while he thought about them as a couple. His mind revisited all the things they had exchanged with one another. He could not imagine a future without her by his side. His grasp on life and human nature was fine tuned. She was joyful to be in his arms or holding his hand as they moved through the rooms of the manor, but he had not been in the presence of a girl. The fact that they had bypassed half a dozen other beds, so they could lay in this one was proof. He knew the value of a woman like Caroline had nothing to do with gold or silver. He had invested himself in her happiness and watched in fascination as her desire evolved into that of a mate. The innate bond they shared went far beyond physical harmony; their spirits were drawn to one another, and the alliance was powerful. Emmett thought of the river at the bottom of the bluff. He saw himself and Caroline as he did the river; they were eloquent and compelled by gravity.

Emmett's embrace tightened around the reality that lay in his arms. She inhaled a deep, contented breath and released it, then lifted her head and smiled at him as she slid her hands beneath her chin. Their eyes clung to one another's as they talked; all the while, Emmett's fingers played in the silky curls of her hair. They discussed work and found humor in the fact that they had been together ever since the mayor had stopped to investigate them Friday night. Her eyes changed color as she became serious, confessing to him that she felt awkward going to Sunday services since she married Dane. Emmett's palm glided over the curve of her smooth shoulder as he admitted he felt the same way since he and Vicki's divorce had been so public. They agreed that it would be wonderful to have their lives in order and attend church services together as a respectable couple. Silence engulfed them once again because the subject of church enhanced the fact that they were willfully committing adultery. Caroline didn't want to sacrifice their closeness, so she expressed her curiosity about his family by asking him to tell her about his grandparents.

Emmett felt gravity pull him even closer to her because she asked. He smiled and brushed a kiss over her lips then told her how blessed he was to have known his grandparents. He told her he had spent more time with Paw Cotton than he did with Pap Mazor. He clarified that his mother's father had passed away when he was 15 years old. He said that one of the things he remembered most about Pap was his ability to grow anything he stuck in the ground. He told her that when he confronted his parents about Vicki being pregnant his mother cried, but his father told her she couldn't be upset because the apple didn't fall far from the tree. Emmett explained that his parents had conceived him the first time they had been together. Considering his mother had nine siblings, his father had playfully blamed it on Mazor genealogy. Emmett laughed as he defended his heritage by enlightening Caroline to the fact his grandfather, Ephraim Mazor, was from a long line of Mennonites. He told her curiosity had sent him to the library to look up the meaning of the name and discovered it was of Hebrew origin. Emmett chuckled again as his eyes held a mischievous glimmer. He told her, Ephraim meant 'fertile' and Mazor meant 'bandage'. He pointed out that the last name contradicted the first, seeing how Pap had fathered ten children. They laughed together for a moment, until Emmett's mind got trapped in a mental examination of the consequences, he and Caroline could face from having unprotected sex. Clearly, he had been reckless in not protecting them from a pregnancy which she was certainly aware. He tried to reign in his thoughts, but he wanted to know the schedule of her body and if it were a possibility. He was about to ask, when it occurred to him that if she were pregnant, Dane would know it was not his child due to his absence. The arrogant man would need to save face and demand she releases him from the marriage because of her infidelity. This could be the way to secure their future. That notion settled in Emmett's mind and warmed his heart.

She asked him if he could tell her about the most dangerous call he had ever answered with the Sheriff's Department.

Emmett kept his speculations to himself and redirected his thoughts, so he could answer her question. He told her about a middle-aged woman and her children who lived a thorny existence because of the alcoholic husband and father. He revealed the man was ill-tempered and tended to overindulge when he drank, which always led to mean and cruel treatment of his family. He confided in her that he had recently been dispatched to the home during Christmas in response to the call for help placed by the children. The father had tried to hang their mother in the barn but had dropped her because she was a thick woman and he was too clumsy to hold her long enough for her to choke to death.

Caroline was crushed at the details and her tears made Emmett aware of just how tender her heart truly was. He assured her that the department was checking in on them every day, and so were family services.

During the wee hours of Monday morning they lay together in the bed that used to be her parents', the same one that on occasion, she shared with the man whose last name was legally attached to the end her given one. He held her in his arms with her back pressed against his chest. They talked and listened to the quiet while his heart pounded with a love that almost smothered him.

He remembered how the kids at school used to call her mouse-girl. He wished he had been brave and told her how pretty she was. It was then that a shadowed perspective of who he was and what he was doing came to his mind, and he saw himself as Autry Cantrell. The truth being, he was the one that was sinfully trespassing, swaying the heart of and stealing a physical part of another man's wife.

He could tell she had grown sad because he felt the same way. She asked him if they were both free would he... could he move in and stay with her forever. It sounded like the dream of a girl who needed a prince charming. He saw her as a beautiful lonely maiden that lived in an empty castle all alone. He told her the truth, that he was free to do such a thing, but that she wasn't. She rolled over and looked at him. He knew that wasn't the answer she wanted. He kissed her and swore that he wanted nothing more than to die trying to make her happy. He told her he loved her, and he was willing to take whatever time she could give him until she was ready to serve Dane with the divorce papers.

The moment became emotional, and she began to cry, unable to stop herself; still, the declaration of his love brought a smile to her face. At that moment, he realized just how little it took to make her happy. He was certain Dane Reid was a damn fool. He had everything in this woman and she was exceptional in every way.

They branded each other's bodies in loving and willful abandonment, trying to banish any doubt from tarnishing the image they had created of their future. It had to be this way because her married life had been spent in giving, but never receiving. Every touch and each breath between them *were intimate, they simply wanted to feel each other and remember, so it would give them hope for the days to come.*

When 5:15 a.m. found them, she walked him to the car. She made no excuses and asked for no promises. She kissed him goodbye, and she clung to him in such a way that he ached to be the man she would greet that evening and every night to come. It was a vision that would stay with him, along with the love they had forged. Forever was one of the few promises he made to her and it was going to be the easiest one to keep.

She looked up into his eyes and he accepted the responsibility and the burden for what he had done. He had fallen in love with another man's wife... a French beauty, named Caroline Janee Breaux.

Emmett went home and put the pajamas she had given him in his drawer then shaved because he would not use her husband's razor. He reported to work feeling and knowing that he was a different man. He found himself patrolling the area close to Whisper Bluff at 7:30 a.m. because she did not have a way to work. She was on foot and had just passed through the square brick columns that marked the entrance to Whisper Bluff when he rolled up beside her and stopped. When her eyes met his, he witnessed them warm with feeling. She got in and told him good morning again, then smiled when he threaded his fingers with hers and pressed the back of her hand to his lips. He drove into town with her small hand tight inside of his. He turned into the alley between the funeral home and its chapel. He did so because no one was there at this hour and he needed to protect her reputation. She told him thank you for thinking of her. Their attentions clung to one another for a moment then she leaned over, and Emmett met her lips. They couldn't part without taking another piece of each other.

That morning, he asked Floyd Cox, the head mechanic at the county barn, to look at her car. Mr. Cox installed a new set of cables along with the new battery and the vehicle was good to go. Emmett called her office to tell her of the repairs and she answered the phone. He told her that her car was functioning and sitting where she had left it. She thanked him then asked if he was having a good day. He told her his mind and his heart would be consumed with her for the rest of his life. She told him that she felt the same way. He asked her if she would come spend the night with him and offered to pick her up. His heart began to pound against his ribs when she agreed.

Once they were behind the closed doors of his house, they made love as fast as they could dispose of their clothing. It was passionate, and desire drove them to urgency. Afterwards, Caroline put on one of Emmett's shirts, then began to flutter about making them something to eat and doing the load of laundry he had neglected over the weekend because he was with her. She made herself at home in his small dwelling.

Emmett made Caroline a pan of biscuits as she requested and left it on the counter for her to put in the oven when she saw fit. He washed the few dishes in the sink then cut up a small bowl of salad greens while she made a skillet of pounded steak and gravy and a pot of mashed potatoes. They talked about everything under the sun while they worked together to accomplish the meal. They sat down together, and Caroline gripped Emmett's hand and bowed her head with a smile as he gave thanks to the Maker. His humility and respect were two of the many things she loved about the man next to her. They ate as they teased each other and shared quirky things about themselves they wanted each other to know. When the kitchen was restored, they took a hot bath in the old claw foot tub. She seduced him during the process and Emmett worshipped her body with gentle hands and tender lips as he surrendered to her. He put on a slow grooving album and they danced in their bare feet in the middle of the living room floor. When the record was over, she asked him if she could see Julie's room.

He stood in the doorway and watched her look at some of his daughter's drawings; she touched several of her dolls and toy animals. Caroline investigated Julie's painted pictures and her face lit up at the watercolor of her and her daddy fishing. She turned to him and exclaimed how sorry she was that he was separated from his little girl. She came to his arms, and he welcomed her in them. He took her to bed, and she gave him everything she could in the name of the love they shared. He hugged her naked body close to him as she sighed with contentment. He went to sleep with her in his arms and on his mind.

Emmett patrolled the county on Tuesday and went through the procedures of his job while thinking of her. It was an empty feeling not knowing when he would see or touch her again. The memories they made were so magical that they seemed like a dream in the normal course of a day. Because of the callous nature of his job, it didn't take loneliness long to insinuate doubt into his mind. He had hoped to call her and ask her to meet him for lunch at his house, but Sheriff Vance needed assistance with a domestic violence call out at the Pickett farm. It was the family that he had told Caroline about. The wife alleged that her husband had come home drunk from a hunting trip and was using their goats for target practice. They arrived on the scene just as Mr. Pickett let loose on several of the chickens that were scrambling across the yard to safety. The fowl darted to safety behind the tin that closed in the bottom of the house and porch, but Mr. Pickett fired all the same and sprayed buckshot across the porch catching the youngest son in the arm. Moby Pickett was arrested on an assortment of charges starting with assault and public drunk. Sheriff Vance despised the man's disregard for his family and added child abuse and child endangerment to the list. But Moby Pickett's disrespect didn't stop there, and he ended up having to stand accountable for resisting arrest as well.

That afternoon, Emmett took Mr. Pickett to the courtroom for an emergency hearing concerning the child's well-being, and Moby's reckless behavior. Caroline had been asked to assist the judge because his secretary was out with the flu. She typed up the no contact order issued by the judge and he signed it, then she walked it across the street to the Chancery Clerk's office for filing. Sheriff Vance took Mr. Pickett to lockdown and asked Emmett to wait for the order for Family Services.

They saw each other in the corridor of the courthouse. He noticed she disappeared into the hallway that housed the closet stairway to the clock tower. He waited a few minutes as several people went about their way then he followed her. The alliance between them proved to be as strong as ever when she leaped into his arms. He kissed her until they were breathless. Her hands assured him that she knew the body beneath the uniform. A moment of desperation gripped her heart, and she told him she loved him so much that it hurt and pleaded for him to hold her. He cradled her up into his arms as he leaned against the wall. Her arms were like fleshy chains around his heart as they held each other in the small musty closet. She kissed him like she would never have enough of him. When she reached out for reality again, he put a key to his house in her hand. He told her he wanted her to file for divorce - Dane didn't need her, but he did. She stared at the key with large eyes. He pointed out that no one interrupted them the night before, and his place was safe and not at risk should Dane decide to come home at some point.

She surprised him with her next statement.

"I'm going to send Dane the documents, Emmett. I'll go by the bank tomorrow on my lunch hour and get them; I'll send them by registered mail before I come back to work. When he gets them, he'll either tear them up, or burn them… either way he'll come home so he can do it in front of me to prove a point."

The desire for her to be free of Dane was raging inside his heart. It was difficult for him to be in a space they did not occupy together.

"Come back to my house tonight, Honey. I need you, Caroline."

She gazed into his eyes seeing the glow of love burning within him. It warmed her into her bones to know she was right about his character, even as a young girl. She agreed to come to him then asked if spaghetti and meat sauce would be alright for supper? They kissed a few more minutes. She gave him the document he needed as she promised to have supper ready by the time, he got home at 6:30 p.m. They departed from the closet with anxious hearts and bodies in anticipation of what they could do to each other with another night in his domain.

Emmett arrived home to an empty house and was very disappointed. He tried to call her and got a busy signal. He waited on her and paced the floor, but at 8:30 p.m. he decided to drive over to make sure she was all right. He followed his instincts and parked his old truck on the road then walked to the gates and up the driveway. His heart sank when he discovered a government issued car was parked at the back of the house. He couldn't leave without knowing if she was all right. He was cautious as he maneuvered the overgrown bushes that obstructed the huge windows. The drapes were all closed tight just as he thought they would be; however, there was a glow coming from the windows at the far end of the house he knew was the master bedroom. The drapes had been closed when he left Monday morning, but they were open now, and he could see that the light from the bathroom cast a soft definition over the room.

Emmett stood in the shadows of the huge gladiolas with his heart in his throat, not wanting to believe his eyes. Caroline was on her knees on the bed where they had shared their bodies so passionately. Training and experience had finetuned his skill of observation, but disappointment clouded his ability to think. His eyes clung to her trying to assess this unexpected development. Her fist gripped the bedding and the other hand held on to the foot-board while she accepted her husband's zealous and commanding thrusts into her body. Her hair was a tousled mess and he could not see her face, but he could hear Dane's salacious expressiveness from where he stood.

Emmett swallowed the sour taste of betrayal and reminded himself that he had no right to expect anything from another man's wife. He had been the one to covet and take what did not belong to him. He turned and walked away; his body was numb, and his heart was torn in half at this revelation. He was trapped in the confusion of what was and what might have been. He wondered if he had been a fool to believe that she could really love him. He thought of the living haze of a man he had encountered in the kitchen and he second guessed himself. Did his imagination produce the apparition that he had always heard lived there? Doubt had a powerful hold on Emmett so that he didn't know what to believe. He only knew that he had experienced something life changing with Caroline Breaux and he would never be the same man.

The next day, Emmett had been given the responsibility of seeing the prisoners to and from the courthouse for their hearings. He couldn't help but hope that he would run into her, or at least get a chance to look in her eyes. He believed that if he could just look at her, he would know whether he had been a fool or not.

The day progressed with no sight of her. He had just completed the last escort of the day when he caught a glimpse of her as he came through the end door to bring the docket paperwork to the Circuit Clerk's office. She was waiting for the elevator and he deliberately caught up to her, so he could give her the paperwork. He spoke as he held out the file folders to her. She wouldn't look at him, but she did accept the paperwork with a courteous demeanor. The elevator door opened, and she stepped inside. Since it was empty, Emmett followed her. He did not speak or approach her because the elevator was monitored due to prisoner transport. He noticed that she hit the third-floor button which bypassed her office and went to the hallway where the witness holding rooms were located for court. The hallway also led to the clock tower. The doors opened, and she mumbled a thank you when he held the door for her to exit; still, she did not look at him. She stepped off and turned toward the holding rooms. Emmett exited the elevator and went in the opposite direction. He walked around the corner and straight to the doorway of the clock tower. He climbed the steps to the first landing next to the window sill, then stopped and leaned against the wall and looked out over the town. A couple of minutes passed before he heard the door open then close. He was prepared to confront her about what he had seen and turned when her footsteps grew close, but when he saw her his anger left him. He knew something was very wrong. When she lifted her face, her eyes were brimming with tears. He held his arms out to her, and she walked straight into them. He was starved to touch her, and he picked her up to hold her this time. They kissed as though they could only exist in the warmth of each other's essence. He sat her on the window sill, so he could look at her. He slid his fingers into the hair behind her ears and she flinched from the contact. Emmett turned her head and pushed her hair out of the way. He suddenly realized that she was wearing it down today instead of the dignified bun. He saw the passion mark in the curve of her neck first and then the scratch marks behind her ear. A further inspection revealed two large lumps on the back of her head just above her neck. The way she nervously tugged at the sleeves of her sweater was like a child hiding something. He pushed her sleeves up and found some ugly purple handprints on her forearms. He unbuttoned her sweater and swore softly at the scratches on her chest above her right breast. He made her turn, so he could see the rest of her body. She was hesitant because of where they were, but Emmett's gentle voice swayed her to give in to him. His temper began to burn when he found bruises on both her shoulder blades and her right rib cage. He fixed her clothes back then turned her face up, so he could look in her eyes. The afternoon sun from the window revealed the shadow of a bruise beneath the makeup of her left cheek. Her words from the other night crashed into his brain, 'I will never, ever give my body to Dane Reid again'.

"My God, Caroline, he forced himself on you, didn't he?"

Huge tears rolled down her cheeks as her eyes dropped to the badge on his shirt; her fingers caressed it as she sniffed.

"He does not think of it in that way, Emmett. I am his wife; there is no refusing one's duty after taking an oath... or vows. I tried to stand my ground and deny him, based on the mistake I made in marrying him. It made him angry, and he called me a liar. He wanted to know who had been inside of me." She swallowed several times as she shook her head. "I couldn't bring myself to stand there and deny it. It... it just seemed wrong to deny what I feel for you."

Emmett recalled the image of them together. He looked closer at her hands and the way she gripped the bed. He realized that he had witnessed her fearful submission, and he had walked away leaving her to endure the disgrace.

She kissed him slowly, deeply, and thoroughly. He knew in his soul that it was goodbye; he felt it.

"I never got to give him the papers. My rebellious spirit infuriated him so that he lost what humanity he possessed. He grabbed my blouse and slapped me. He demanded I tell him who I had been..." she paused unable to repeat Dane's words.

"What? Caroline, you must tell me everything," urged Emmett in a soulful voice.

"He demanded I tell him who I have been... fucking... behind his back." She sniffed as she shook her head. "He... he knows there is someone else. He... said he could feel you inside of me. I've never seen him so angry... and I didn't know what he was capable of until then. I... I'm sorry, Emmett." She began to cry. "I was scared... and... I denied that you were real. I had no choice. You don't understand what he does for a living. He makes problems disappear. I love you, Emmett... but... you have to let me go."

"No! I can convince him to walk away, Caroline. I know I can! Better yet, we can let the law work for you. You should file charges against him, so it will be a matter of public record. I can take you to see Dr. Adams... he'll document these bruises. Dane wouldn't dare harm you if Sheriff Vance and I confront him with assault charges. You

can stay with me until he's gone." Emmett's voice was suddenly hopeful. "That's the answer, Caroline. It's the law... it will work for us!"

She shook her head as her face distorted in fear and frustration. She swiped at her cheeks then she snapped at him.

"NO, IT WON'T! You... of all people... can't risk confronting him, Emmett. He'll know you care for me." She scrubbed her face with her palms as her shoulders shook with emotion. "No, this is the only way I can be sure... it's the only way I can control what happens next. I can't see you again, Emmett! It has to be this way." She broke down and her emotions got the best of her. She covered her face as she sobbed.

Emmett grew angry at himself for doubting her; it was so clear to him just how much she loved him. She made him promise to remember her... and them... in the passionate sense in which they were bound together. This time when they kissed, it was full of sorrow. He couldn't explain it, but it hurt far worse than saying goodbye to Vicki.

"I may have been a girl, but I knew I was right about how good we could be together. I swear I will never forget you, Emmett. Never! I will live the rest of my days with you deep in my heart." She wrapped her arms around him and Emmett tilted her chin so that he could taste her kiss again. She was trembling, and he realized just how scared she was of the man to whom she was married. He felt desperate to hang on to her. She kissed him back, and he sensed there was something dire she had not told him. She hugged him so tight; he had not known that she was so strong.

"I have to go. I love you. I always have... and I always will." Caroline pushed at his chest as she quickly took to her feet. She dipped under his arm then started down the stairs.

Emmett caught her shoulders and wrapped his arms around her. She clutched his arms with her hands as she cried in silence for a few moments. He pleaded with her to see things his way.

"Come live with me, Caroline. He can't hurt you if you're with me. I can protect you from him."

Her voice was on the verge of desperation.

"Please Emmett... you have got to understand and do as I ask. I'm a possession to him... but you're not. He cannot find out about you. You must stay away. Promise me! You have to stay away from me!" She snatched herself out of his arms and boldly opened the door to the hallway knowing that someone could pass at any time and see them. She knew that in doing so, he would not follow her.

Emmett watched her as she walked away from him and did not look back.

The next day she was the talk of the building. According to the grapevine, her husband had shown up a couple of days before on a two-month furlough. Colonel Reid had called her boss that morning and voiced her resignation, effective immediately so she would be at home with him until he left.

Emmett fought the urge to confront the man who held her prisoner; he knew he could not do so without risking her safety. He had called the house several times without success; however, the last time he called, he discovered the phone had been disconnected. He looked for her every day around town hoping to catch sight of her. He even drove past the mansion several times a day, but it was like she had fallen off the face of the earth.

*E*mmett was surprised when he got called into military service. Sheriff Vance had tried to intervene because he needed him and because he was an only son, but the needs of his country were more important. He was scheduled to leave July 11, 1942.

Emmett took Julie to the Independence Day celebration at the river walk. Because it was summer, and she was out of school, Vicki had seen fit to allow Julie to stay with him until his departure.

The day was sunny and the sky a vivid blue. It was hot but bearable because of a gentle breeze stirring upward from the river. He strolled along the riverfront looking at some of the goods for sale while keeping an eye on Julie as she waited in line at a concession stand. He stopped abruptly when he found himself face to face with Caroline. She was alone and standing in front of him wearing pink slacks, white tennis shoes and a flowery printed top. Her sweet, angelic voice drew his attention away from the round bump in her middle which protruded out through the fullness of the blouse. His eyes absorbed the sight of her. Despite all his efforts to contact her, this was the first time he had seen her or spoke to her, since the day they left each other in the clock tower's storage room. She looked thin and her collar bones were more prevalent than what he knew of her, but her swollen belly conveyed that she was very pregnant. She was gorgeous and absolutely beaming with happiness.

"Hello Emmett, it's so wonderful to see you. How are you?"

"Caroline! I... I'm all right, considering." His eyes traded off between her swollen belly and her beautiful face. "You're expecting? I haven't heard from you... I didn't know!"

She nodded her head as her hands caressed her middle.

"Yes. I'm very excited about the baby. I've always wanted to be a mother. It's a boy! Well, Grandpa Preston says it is, anyway.

"I read in the paper that you're leaving for service duty next week, Emmett. I ventured out today... in hope that I would run into you. I wanted to tell you that I have been praying for you... and that I will continue to do so. Please, be careful Emmett... and... and come back to us safe." Her hand rested on her tummy as she looked at him. "I wanted to tell you that... you are taking my heart with you."

Emmett was consumed with the sight of her. He had to fight the yearning inside himself to touch her. There was no way to ignore the inspiration in which they had made love, or the fact that they had not used any caution in doing so. He wanted to ask her if the child was his, but how could he. He waited for her to tell him it was a fact, but she didn't.

She had been cut off from him for almost six months now. Since she was genuinely excited about the child, he had no choice but to assume that it belonged to her husband and things were as they should be with her life. He knew that a child would be something which would fill her days.

"How is Julianna?" she asked him.

"She's doing very well. Umm, actually... she's here living with me until I leave." At that moment, the blonde headed little girl with huge blue eyes walked up holding a cotton candy and gripped his hand.

"Hello, my name is Julianna Cotton. You are very pretty. When is your baby expected?"

"Well, hello Julianna. My name is Caroline." She reached out to his daughter and Emmett watched them shake hands. "He's due in the fall... the doctor says October. Are you having fun with your dad today?"

"Yes Ma'am, I always have fun with daddy. How do you know him?" Julianna held up the fluffy pink cloud of sugar that was wrapped around the paper cone. "Won't you have a bite?" The child's manner was considerate and was laced with a sweetness that was just like her father.

Caroline pinched off a piece of the candy and stuck it in her mouth.

"Mmm, that's yummy."

Julianna held the fluffy candy up in front of her father, and he tasted it as Caroline answered his daughter.

"Your dad and I went to school together, and I used to work at the courthouse."

Emmett stood there and took in the sight of these two very special people in his life conversing with one another. He listened to them talk about school and the fact that Caroline lived in the big house overlooking the river, but he was consumed with the fact that there was a child inside of her. Before he realized it, Caroline had offered to teach Julianna piano lessons and her first lesson was to be that afternoon, if it was all right with her father.

"Oh daddy, can I... please! I've always wanted to take piano and I've always been curious about the big house under the trees."

Emmett studied Caroline with an indecisive expression on his face.

"I don't know, Sweetie. Ms. Caroline has to see to her home and her husband."

"Actually, Emmett... he's out of the country for a few months. I can see Julianna two afternoons a week, or when she's with your parents. She can call me when she's going to be here in Westville and I'll pick her up for a lesson... if you wouldn't mind. Why don't you let me get her started this afternoon? As a matter of fact, the two of you should come and stay for supper! We're having homemade pizza, which you and Julie can help me make. I'll make a fresh spinach salad with all the goodies then we'll have fresh apple turnovers and ice cream for dessert. Oh... and bring your suits so you can go for a swim after supper. I sense Julianna will be a very good student." She gazed at him with honesty in her eyes. "Please Emmett, I would love to see you and spend some time with you before you have to leave us. I'll cherish every second with you and Julie."

Julianna turned to him with a regenerated excitement as she pleaded with him to allow her to start piano lessons.

"Oh daddy, I promise I'll practice every single day and I won't have to be reminded about it. I can write you every day and tell you about my progress. Maybe I can even help Ms. Caroline with the baby when it gets here! We'll be such good friends, I can feel it."

The annoying electrical sounds grated against his conscious and Emmett was confused over what was causing it.

"Daddy, shall I tell you about my week. We have a new attorney that started the other day. He's very handsome; something tells me we are going to be good friends, I can feel it.

"Preston's here with me. I've gotten so used to him; I think we're going to have to adopt him." Julianna leaned over her father's bed and kissed his forehead several times and his eyelids began to flutter. "Preston, come here... look at his eyes. Listen to his breath; don't you think his breathing has changed?" Julianna's voice was energized by hopefulness.

Preston stood anxiously and stepped over to the bed. He touched her father's chest with his hand then leaned over and spoke in his ear.

"Sheriff, hey there... me and Julie are here with you. We're waiting for you to come back to us. We miss you, Sir, and we need you. Can you hear me, Sheriff? I love you, Sir. Open your eyes and talk to me."

Emmett heard the familiar voice echoing in his mind and it stirred something deep inside the world of confusion in which he was suddenly trapped. His common sense told him that he had to open his eyes, or he would stay submerged in a world of wanting what he could not have. He sucked in a deep breath and tried to push his eyelids open tapping into his will and his courage to uncover the stirring that was taking place inside of him. He had to know who was speaking to him and why he needed to listen so closely to what they had to say.

"Who are you? Where are you?" mumbled Cotton.

"It's Preston, Sheriff. I'm standing beside you. Open your eyes and look at me."

Cotton opened his eyes and blinked several times as the dark-headed young man came into view. He had blue eyes like Caroline and his hair was the same color as hers, but his distinctive brow and square jaw line was like looking in the mirror. Suddenly, Emmett remembered who this young man was, and his heart began to beat with a new motivation.

"You look good, Son." Cotton smiled and reached up and touched the boy's face. "Where's... your sister?"

Preston grinned then caught the sheriff's hand as he chuckled.

"She's right there. See? I always wanted a sister, but y'all better talk about it before you adopt me. I've been known to eat my weight in groceries."

This was the first time in eight days they had gotten a coherent word from him, much less a smile. His fever had finally broken the day before and his blood pressure had leveled out.

He turned his head to look at his daughter.

"Hey Darlin'... you look good too."

Julianna leaned over and kissed his forehead several times.

"Oh Dad, I was so scared we were going to lose you. I've been crazy with worry."

Cotton's weakness was evident; however, his words conveyed determination and hope.

"No sweetheart, I'm not going anywhere. I was just resting for a spell."

Julianna retrieved the damp bath cloth next to the bed and bathed her father's face.

"That feels good... thank you, Honey."

"Are you thirsty, Sheriff?" Preston held the water container close to him then turned the straw so that he could drink.

Cotton took several long slurps from the straw as he gazed at the young man that he loved as much as he loved Julianna. Cotton bent his elbow, so he could hold his hand up to the young man. Preston clutched it with a strong grip and pressed the man's hand against his chest.

Cotton swallowed then released the straw.

"How's your hand?" he asked.

Preston sat the cup down then held the bandaged hand up; one side of his mouth curled slightly as he answered the sheriff.

"It's healing." His attention went back to the man that had risked everything for him. "Julie and I need you, Sir. You have to concentrate on healing too."

Cotton smiled again.

"I'm better now," he told them.

"I bet you're hungry," stated Preston. "Can I get you something to eat? Anything... just name it!"

Cotton wiggled his feet beneath the cover because his body had been lying in the same spot far too long.

"As a matter of fact, I would like to have a hot apple turnover and a cup of coffee... oh, and some cotton candy."

Julianna giggled and ran her fingers through her father's hair. But Preston just gazed at him, thankful that he did not have to face the world without this man he had come to love.

Recipes from the
SILVER-HAWK
KITCHEN

Rooster's Crow Jalapeno Cornbread

4 cups fresh ground cornmeal
4 fresh eggs (beaten)
1 tsp. baking powder
1 tsp. baking soda
1 tsp. sea salt
½ tsp. fresh ground black pepper
¼ tsp. garlic powder (optional)
4 Tbsp. self-rising flour
½ cup chopped fresh jalapenos (include seeds for a louder crow)
½ cup chopped fresh green onions
1 cup grated sharp cheddar cheese
2 cups milk or buttermilk
6 Tbsp. bacon renderings
1 - 15" cast iron skillet

Heat oven to 375 degrees, place 6 Tbsp bacon rendering in 12" cast iron skillet and heat in oven for 5 minutes. (Roll skillet so that renderings are dispersed over skillet surface.)

In large mixing bowl, combine dry ingredients and blend well. Add eggs, jalapenos, green onion, milk and stir. Add 3 Tbsp of hot bacon renderings to mixture and stir until well mixed. Add cheese and stir well. Pour cornbread mix into hot skillet with remaining bacon renderings left in bottom. Renderings will season skillet, add flavor and prevent sticking. Bake 25 - 30 minutes at 375 degrees. Check center before removing from oven, let sit on trivet 5 minutes before turning onto plate. Slice and serve accordingly.

Note: Some fresh ground meals are denser than others. You can add more milk if needed but wait until cheese is added to decide. Mixture should be thick so that you smooth it in skillet before baking.

Grandma Hawk's Hambone Turnip Greens

1 large hambone (sugar cured if possible)
2 quarts water
5 to 6 pounds of fresh turnip greens/washed (roots not included in weight)
1 large yellow onion
2 pounds of turnip roots/washed (small whole or large quartered)
2 tsp. sea salt
1 tsp. fresh ground black pepper
2 Tbs. bacon renderings
1 large stew pot

In stew pot, add your water and hambone, bring to boil. Add washed greens until pot is full, cover and let boil down a few minutes, then repeat process until all greens are in pot. Dice onion and add to pot with salt, pepper and bacon renderings. Stir every 10 minutes until greens are reduced (add water only if needed), reduce heat and let simmer on low for 1 & ½ hours checking as needed. Remove hambone leaving meat from bone in greens. Add a little water if needed and turnip roots (can peel if prefer) and cover, let cook for 1 hour stirring every 15 - 20 minutes (check turnips with fork for tenderness). Makes 12-15 servings.

W.C.'s Bacon Cheese Potatoes

8 large red potatoes (washed)
½ cup crispy bacon pieces
½ cup diced green onions
¾ cup cheddar cheese (grated)
½ cup sour cream
½ cup mayonnaise
1 tsp. salt
1 tsp. ground black pepper

In large boiler pot, quarter potatoes with skin and cover with water. Bring to boil and cook until pierce with fork. Drain water. Smash potatoes with fork then add bacon, green onions, cheddar cheese, sour cream and mayo, salt and pepper. Stir. Serve hot. Makes 10 servings.

Cream Cheese Deviled Eggs

15 large eggs boiled
1 - 4 oz. cream cheese (room temperature)
3 tsp. yellow mustard
½ cup mayo
¼ tsp. salt (more if desired/taste before adding)
¼ tsp. ground black pepper
A pinch of garlic powder
A pinch of onion powder
Paprika
1 tsp. baking soda

Place eggs in pot and cover with water, add 1 teaspoon of baking soda to water and bring to boil (baking soda will cause water to boil over if left on high heat/soda will help eggs peel better). Allow eggs to boil 4 - 6 minutes. Remove from heat pour off hot water and cover with cold water. Crack eggs and let them sit in cold water 10 minutes.
Peel eggs in cold water. Slice eggs in half and drop center yolks into bowl. You should have 30 egg halves. Mash yolks with fork, cut cream cheese into small squares and add to yolks. Add mayo and mustard, salt and pepper, garlic and onion powder. Blend with electric mixer for smooth consistency.

Spoon yolk mixture into egg-halves, or for a more decorative egg, place yolk mixture into a pastry bag accompanied by a large star tip, and squeeze into egg halves. Sprinkle top of eggs with black pepper or paprika. Makes 30 servings. Refrigerate until time to serve.

Cinnamon-Apple Cobbler

8 large Granny Smith apples (cored and peeled)
1 ½ sticks of salted butter (melted)
½ cup sugar
¾ cup brown sugar
1 tsp. cinnamon
1 tsp. corn starch
½ cup pecans
Crust:
¾ cup plain flour
¼ cup ice water
1 Tbsp. shortening
Pinch of salt

You will need a 10 x 13 pan or glass dish for cobbler. Wash apples, core and slice then place in large bowl. Melt 1 stick of butter and pour over apples and toss. In a small bowl mix white sugar, brown sugar and cinnamon (take out 1 Tablespoon of cinnamon sugar and set aside), mix remaining cinnamon sugar and corn starch, pour over apples and toss with fork.

Dough - In small bowl mix flour and salt with fork then cut shortening into flour with fork. Pour ¼ cup ice water in flour and mix with fork, adding water as needed to form firm ball. Cut dough in half and roll out thin on flour dusted surface, cut into 2" x 10" strips, repeat until dough is finished.

Melt ½ stick of butter (less 1 Tbsp.) and pour in baking dish then pour apples and cinnamon/sugar in dish and spread evenly, lay dough strips across the top in a striped pattern in both directions. Brush dough with butter then sprinkle with 1 Tablespoon of (saved) cinnamon sugar. Bake 35-45 minutes on 350-375 degrees (make adjustment depending on your oven). Makes 12 servings.

From the Author:

Thank you for taking the literary adventure to Westville, Texas, and becoming a part of the lives of Coleman Silver and Rueben Hawk, and all the extended family who share life and love with them. It is my hope that you have become emotionally invested in the Silver-Hawk community so much that you consider yourself part of the extended family. I invite you to come back and visit Liberty County and its residents in the next installment of 'The Flames of Silver-Hawk Series/Book II, **Sparks**'.

A wise friend and brother once told me, "It would be difficult for a reader to understand mercy and redemption without revealing the sin". Please consider the content of this story is of a real nature in relation to the daily choices between good and evil.

I leave you with a glimpse of Westville's future. I send you my best wishes until we meet again.

Melonye Wolf

The Flames of Silver-Hawk Series/Book II, **Sparks (Excerpt)**

The patrol car rolled at a steady speed as the two deputies talked between each other. Jay Abbott sat with his wrists and ankles unlocked, but they were not visibly free of the restraints should his jailers turn to make a visual inspection of him. The holster and keys were back in place underneath Ned's seat; however, the older deputy's pistol was behind Jay's back.

Jay resisted the grin that tickled the corners of his mouth while waiting for them to exit the town limits and enter the rural part of the county. They slowed down and crossed the railroad tracks then turned onto Highway 5 and headed north to Hunt County where the District Circuit Court Judge was seated today.

The deputies talked about the Westville Mustangs winning the state championship on Friday after Thanksgiving Day. Jay learned that they had played the El Paso Devils at the El Paso Stadium this past Friday night and it was a hell of a game.

Jay thought Ned to be a fair man, but careless. Today, this weakness was in Jay's favor. Ned looked in the rearview mirror to make a visual connection with his prisoner, and in doing so, he spoke to him in a way that was of a friendly nature. It was Ned's second major mistake of the morning.

"You've got a good Son-in-Law in that one, Jay. Joel's a good boy. He'll be a good provider for your daughter… a good husband too."

Jay's eyes became fixed on Ned's as a new fury revitalized his bad disposition. He had no idea who Joel was, or that he had a Son-in-Law. He counted on Lissy being like her mother and spreading her legs for a man that could give her something more than a physical rush in return. He needed the old deputy to give him more information. He gave it a shot because he had nothing to lose.

"So, I hear. I guess his rich daddy is gonna make everything just peachy for them," he commented.

Ned's docile personality was reliable, and he responded with the information Jay needed.

"Dr. Jordan's not like that, Jay. They're good, hard-working people. His boy's starting medical school in the spring."

Jay got angry all over again at the thought of his sneaky, lying bitch of a daughter marrying money and leaving him, with no thought to all he had done for her these 17 years. He had already eased the shackles from his ankles when they turned on to the highway, and now he slid his wrist out of the restraints as well.

"Is that a fact?" spit Jay in an icy tone of voice. "I don't know about that, Ned. I don't think he'll be around come spring."

Ned frowned as they came to the four-way stop. The old deputy checked the road before his foot pressed the gas pedal then his eyes met Jay's again in the rearview mirror.

"Oh? Why is that... are they moving?" questioned Ned.

"I guess you could say that," stated Jay. His words were bitter with disdain as he explained. "He stole something that belongs to me... and I'm gonna kill his thieving ass and send him straight to hell, that's why."

The windshield exploded as the firearm discharged in a loud, blaze of fury from the back seat. The speed in which the police cruiser was traveling sent small chunks of glass pelting the interior of the vehicle. The startling chaos hindered Ned's ability to drive. He tried to stay in control of the automobile and not shit in his pants.

Jay yelled at him to keep the vehicle on the road or he would shoot the rookie in the back of the head next time rather than the face.

Ned looked over at Deputy Reid and found the front of his uniform covered with blood. He was hunched over, and the hot barrel of the revolver was pressed to the base of his skull. The young Deputy was bleeding profusely as the discharged round had split his jaw open from his earlobe to near the corner of his mouth. The extent of the injury was unknown. Something clicked in Ned's mind, and his eyes leaped back to the firearm. He recognized the carved diamond pattern on the walnut handle to be the same custom work as his personal service revolver. The wheels on the passenger side of the cruiser leaped off the asphalt into the grass on the side of the highway. Ned jerked the wheel again and his distracted attention went back to the pavement in front of them.

Jay warned him a second time and told him he would splatter the 'pretty boys' brains across the hood of the car if he ran off the road again. The horrified look on the old man's face was amusing to Jay, and he boasted about his accomplishment.

"You never dreamed something like this could ever happen in your safe, little world... did you, Ned?!"

Jay shifted the pistol from the back of Deputy Reid's head and squeezed the trigger. The passenger window burst, and the young Deputy's body jerked from the sound and the impact being so close to his person. Jay shoved the barrel to the back of his head again and commanded him to put his hands on the dash and leave them there. Deputy Reid did as he was instructed. Jay leaned over and pulled the shotgun from its stand and tossed it out the window, then he confiscated Deputy Reid's sidearm and tossed it as well.

Jay Abbott was pleased with himself, but he had to take control of the situation once and for all. He looked around to acknowledge where they were, and after seeing the silos on the right side of the highway he made his decision. He told Ned to turn off the highway onto the gravel pit road.

Ned followed his instructions like an experienced chauffeur and turned left on Gravel Pit Road. Jay took notice that no cars were in route in either direction to see them do so. The young deputy had not said a word, and hopefully Ned was smart enough not to patronize the man with the gun.

Jay directed Ned to drive past the huge mounds of gravel and follow the narrow road which weaved further into the woods, then stop at the edge of the gully. The gun in Jay's hand was pressed firm to the back of Deputy Reid's head as he ordered Ned to get out and open his door, keeping his hands where he could see them. Ned did so without hesitation then backed away with his arms held out to his sides. Jay got out taking the shackles he had worn with him. He tossed them to the ground in front of Ned's feet then took several steps away from him. He ordered Deputy Reid to get out and walk around to the back of the car and face the trunk.

Deputy Reid followed Jay Abbott's command while his mind raced to figure out how to gain the upper hand on this situation.

Abbott told Ned to shackle the rookie.

Deputy Ingram dared to speak as he undertook the task.

"Preston, I'm sorry. This is my fault... don't be a hero. Please. I'll pay the price."

"Shut the hell up, Ned!" yelled Jay. He kicked Ned in the ribs and the older man went to the ground on his knees. Preston started to turn around and Jay hit him on the back of his head causing him to fall against the trunk. He wanted to see if he could rile the tight-assed young deputy. "Let the boy make up his own damn mind about who he wants to be... and how he wants to leave this world."

The tough, young deputy stood back up. He held the shackles in a tight fist and turned to face Jay Abbott, fixing cold, callous eyes on him. His face was a fright with the way his jaw bone showed through the bloody and gapping slash. Jay Abbott saw the rookie's courage as arrogant condemnation. He didn't respect much in this world, but he was impressed by the young deputy's grit.

Jay yelled at Ned to get up and open the trunk. He took a step towards the young officer and pointed the gun at his chest as he told him.

"It's a shame my little, snotty-bitch of a daughter wasn't screwing your ass, at least she would'a had a man with some nuts."

Deputy Reid spoke to Jay Abbott for the first time since he had been incarcerated.

"Yes Sir, I agree with you, Mr. Abbott. I learned a long time ago that the world isn't cruel; it's the people in it that prey on others. I'll tell you this, if you had done to my wife… what you did to Joel's, your ass would be cold, stiff and six feet under right now. And you damn sure wouldn't have a chance to pull this shit!"

The rookie's words struck a nerve with Jay and his temper flared, causing him to relocate the barrel of the pistol to Deputy Reid's forehead. He was so mad he couldn't stop his hand from trembling.

"I'll show you cold and stiff, you tuff-nuts bastard," gritted Jay through clenched teeth.

The old deputy's words attempted to help him gain some perspective.

"No Jay, don't do this!" Ned boldly stepped between them to protect Preston and talk reason to the man who was threatening their lives. After all, this entire conflict was his fault. He had made a grave error in judgment which had enabled Jay to gain control of his sidearm. He couldn't allow Preston to pay for his mistake any more than he already had. "You can still have your life back, Jay… it's not too late."

Jay's eyes left the rookie as his mind flirted with Ned's words of hope. He took a step back to put distance between himself and Ned, so he could think about his options. Suddenly, Preston shoved Ned out of the way and lunged forward tackling Jay Abbott in the chest with his shoulder. The prisoner fell backwards and hit the ground, and the young deputy's body went with him. The unexpected siege dislodged the pistol from Jay's grip and it landed a few feet away. Jay rolled to his belly and clambered through the sandy dirt to regain the upper hand over his future. Preston struggled against the shackles to stop him. He kept a level head and threw his body on top of Jay Abbott. They rolled in the dirt as they wrestled to gain control over the firearm, each of them was determined to be the victor. The young rookie was strong and agile, and Jay's muscles were trembling with fearful adrenalin. When Jay realized that his finger was on the trigger, he squeezed it twice hoping to scare the young rookie enough to gain his freedom.

Stillness hung between them for a few seconds until Jay got spooked by the accusing weight of Deputy Reid's body. Jay panicked and shoved Preston off him, kicking his way free of the young deputy's legs. He saw movement in the corner of his eye and leaped to his feet as he pointed the pistol at Ned.

Ned was so stunned he couldn't believe his eyes. He disregarded the danger he was in and stopped next to the young man who lay sprawled out in the dirt. He dropped to his knees and touched Preston's neck then he laid his hand on his chest. Ned shook his head as he spoke to Jay in a shaky voice.

"My God in Heaven, Jay… what have you done?"

Jay's feet felt weighted as he backed away from the deed he had just committed. He stared at the young man lying so still and final on his back, his arms and legs chained to his body while blood merged with the dirt on his shirt. In all his fits of anger, and with legitimate reasons for them, he had never killed a man. Jay realized that he had goaded this young man into a confrontation. He felt a surge of bile rise-up in his throat, but he swallowed it. Ned was wrong; he could never have his life back.

Jay began to act, and he ordered Ned to put the kid's body in the trunk of the patrol car. He watched Ned pick up the young deputy, but fear got the best of him and he threw up the churning contents of his stomach. It was an involuntary reaction, and what decency may have been inside of him came up with it.

Jay wiped his mouth on his sleeve as he approached Ned from behind. He saw that Ned had unlocked the shackles, so he could fold the kid's arms over his chest then he touched the young deputy's bloody shield and hung his head.

"Get in there with him, Ned. You can do it breathing or not… it's too damn late for me to care."

Ned was sickened and wasn't ready to quit on this frightful situation he had carelessly authored. He gained his motivation from the invincible brotherhood between officers, and the dedication to his duty rejuvenated his tired body. He slammed the trunk shut and courageously turned to face Jay Abbott.

"HELL NO!! You're gonna finish what you started… you chicken-ass, son-of-a-bitch!" yelled Ned angrily. "You can beat up a little, wisp of a girl… and you can shoot a defenseless man in chains," roared Ned. "Why don't you grow a backbone and put that damn gun down, so we can settle this and find out who the better man really is?" Ned's fists went up in the air and he motioned for Jay to join him. "Come on J.D., let's see what you're really made of!"

"Ned, stop!" warned Jay. He backed away from Ned, but the old man kept coming at him as he challenged him. The gutsy, old deputy swung and caught Jay on the chin sending him stumbling to catch his balance.

"Ned… goddammit, I said stop!" Jay pointed the gun at him.

Ned could tell that Jay wasn't going to surrender the pistol.

"It didn't have to be this way, now you're gonna have to kill me too… you sorry piece-of-shit! I can't live with that boy's death on my hands." Ned was distraught, but his heart had become impassioned with a motivation that Jay Abbott would never understand.

Ned kept coming and Jay backed away while pointing the gun at the angry, old deputy. His fear had him going in a circle as the old man spit out his fury.

"You may get away today, but I swear… me and that boy will be the hounds of hell on your trail. You will never be free of us!" yelled Ned. "DO IT! COME ON… DO IT!" Ned swung his fists at Jay Abbott in a fit of anger. One of them slammed into Jay's jaw while his other caught a hold of the man's shirt with a death grip. "You give me that pistol, damn it! We'll have the court right now!"

Jay panicked as the old man's, seemingly decrepit, body boasted a strength and nimble aggressiveness he had not expected. They struggled for a couple of minutes, but the old lawman's determination ambushed his prisoner with a show of brute force. Ned twisted Jay's arm behind him. The younger man's muscles were quivering, and his strength was dwindling due to this traumatic and unexpected chain of events. Jay knew if he didn't do something drastic, it was only a matter of seconds before Ned got the best of him. Jay panicked and took a step back then twisted his body while taking a nothing-to-lose swing with the pistol. The barrel crashed into Ned's temple, next to his right eye, with such force a blood vessel burst and sprayed Jay in the face. The old man hit the ground like a tree that had been chopped down, and he did not move again.

"Dammit to hell, Ned!" Jay stood there in disbelief. He felt like everything he had once believed about himself and about life was a cruel joke. He was coming unhinged. Jay clutched the pistol as he pressed his fists to his head and began to pace back and forth, unable to accept the deeds he had committed while trying to manage his house. He stopped abruptly and stared at Ned. He cried out in frustration to the man lying on the ground.

"WHY NED?! Why, goddammit… did you have to push me?!" Salty tears scalded the sockets behind Jay's eyes as an immobilizing weakness attacked his legs. Weakness came over him and he squatted down before he collapsed. Ned's eyes stared off into nothingness; the life of only a few moments ago was gone from them. Jay pressed his sleeve to his burning eyes then dragged it over his face to rid it of Ned's blood.

Jay's mind searched for answers as he tried to make sense of it all. The birds sang, and the sun came and went several times while the wind pushed the clouds about the sky. Finally, Jay accepted that he had crossed over into hell, here on earth and beyond. There was no turning back. Ned was a decent man to him, and the boy was brave. He had murdered them without cause, and without really meaning to.

Jay thought he heard a growling noise behind him. He leaped to his feet and turned with the shaking gun pointed but found nothing there. He looked in all directions. When he heard it again, he turned to Ned's body.

"Stop it, Ned!" he yelled. "I didn't mean too… goddammit! You know it was an accident!" insisted Jay. He squatted down again then reached over to close Ned's eyes, but it took three attempts before he could do it. He heard the noise again and snatched his hand back then covered his ears while still clutching the pistol. He cried out in fear. "Stop hounding me, Ned! I have a right to protect what's mine! Dammit! He stole her from me! He had no right!"

Those words sank into Jay's interpretation of the truth like stones tossed into a pond. He thought of Lissy Gale, and his demented perception convinced him that all of this was her fault. If she had stayed where she belonged none of this would have happened. This perspective brought vengeance back to his reason, which enabled Jay to assimilate justice with his horrible deeds. His courage received a fresh boost of supremacy and his conscience a pardon. He decided on his next move, then drug the old man over to the car and wrestled his limp body onto the backseat. He took the time to yank Ned's boots off and shove his feet into them.

Jay opened the driver's side door and shifted the cruiser into neutral then pushed it off the edge of the deep, vine covered gully just beyond where they had stopped. He stood there and watched the cruiser be swallowed up by the green sea of kudzu to the point that only the back bumper and taillights could be seen.

The hatred inside Jay's chest burned up the tender splinters of sorrow that had momentarily overwhelmed him and pushed his mind to refocus. Jay became fixated on the thing that had driven him to such extreme measures. There was a villainous spirit that now occupied his body. Jay turned abruptly and took out in a run through the woods. He had to find some inconspicuous clothing and transportation first, and then he would find Lissy Gale. He wasn't her real father, so what? He had half his life invested in her and as far as he was concerned, she belonged to him.

About the author,

Melonye Wolf was born and raised a southern girl. She celebrates life through many interests and creative talents and hopes to accomplish many things in her life. The love of reading as a girl enhanced her imagination, and she began writing short stories during high school. Melonye is married and has two sons. She likes to cook and bake, paint, work in the wood shop, sew, make pottery, care for her pups and raise chickens. Melonye invites you to venture into her imaginative world of fiction and become part of the community who are happy and content residing in Dreamtown, USA.

Like **MELONYE WOLF** on Facebook and keep up with the Silver-Hawk family and residents of Liberty County, Texas. Watch for the release dates of volumes to come.

E-mail - flamesofsilverhawk@gmail.com